THE YEAR'S BEST DARK FANTASY & HORROR

2018 Edition

THE YEAR'S BEST DARK FANTASY & HORROR

2018 Edition

EDITED BY PAULA GURAN

PRIME BOOKS

CONTENTS

CONTENTS

INTRODUCTION:
SAME OLD STORIES

Paula Guran

Cassandra Khaw begins her story "Don't Turn Out the Lights" (see page 439):

> Stories are mongrels. It don't matter whether they were lightning-cut into stone or whispered over the crackle of a dying flame; no story in the world has pedigree. They've all been told and retold so many times that not God himself could tell you which one came first. Yes, every story in creation.

That sentiment has been expressed in various ways by others, and some have also added the rest of the truth about it. Anna Quindlen completed it well: "Except that each writer brings to the table, if she will let herself, something that no one else in the history of time has ever had."

And that is what makes the speculative fiction—dark or not—being written today especially exciting. Once, not all that long ago, readers found the vast majority of published fiction was written by white heterosexual men who were primarily from the United States or the United Kingdom. Sure, each individual "brought themselves" to it, but the worlds, characters, and stories they created tended to reflect Western European culture from a male viewpoint. It is a valid way to tell a story. It's just not the *only* way, and it shouldn't be the predominate way.

Things, thank goodness, have changed. Now, even with all our stories written in English, a book like this is chock full of tales told by all sorts of people from a multitude of backgrounds, races, sexualities, and ethnicities, with different views of the world and unique voices.

When you are looking for the "best" you don't have to go out of your way to find this diversity. It is easily found.

Well, maybe not yet as easily as it should be or ultimately will be, but the point I am making is that it has become impossible to deny the "best" is vibrantly diverse. And the best of the "pale male" writers are no longer so monocultural or confined by their own gender. There's no excuse to fill a book with the same old stories told in the same old ways.

This is the ninth volume in this series. I'm grateful for the chance, every year—despite the grousing I grumble, the blood, sweat, and maybe a few teardrops I shed—to be able to read so many fine tales crafted in so many ways, to choose from them, and present to you here. The fact the stories can be so different while still resonating with us in a common human way gives me some faith that we may yet be able to keep reality from being overtaken with darkness.

Book Lovers Day 2018
Paula Guran

THE CROW PALACE

Priya Sharma

Birds are tricksters. Being small necessitates all kinds of wiles to survive but Corvidae, in all their glory as the raven, rook, jay, magpie, jackdaw, and crow, have greater ambitions than that.

They have a plan.

I used to go into the garden with Dad and Pippa every morning, rain or shine, even on school days.

We lived in a house called The Beeches. Its three-acre garden had been parceled off and flogged to developers before I was born, so it became one of a cluster of houses on an unadopted cul de sac.

Mature rhododendrons that flowered purple and red in spring lined the drive. The house was sheltered from prying eyes by tall hedges and the eponymous beech trees. Dad refused to cut them back despite neighbors' pleas for more light and less leaf fall in the autumn. *Dense foliage is perfect for nesting*, he'd say.

Our garden was an avian haven. Elsa, who lived opposite, would bring over hanging feeders full of fat balls and teach us about the blue tits and cheeky sparrows who hung from them as they gorged. Stone nymphs held up bowls that Dad kept filled. Starlings splashed about in them. When they took flight they shed drops of water that shone like discarded diamonds. The green and gold on their wings caught the sun.

Pippa and I played while Dad dug over his vegetable patch at the weekends. The bloody-chested robin followed him, seeking the soft bodied and spineless in the freshly turned earth.

Dad had built a bird table, of all things, to celebrate our birth. It was a complex construction with different tiers. Our job was to lay out daily offerings of nuts and meal worms. At eight I could reach its lower levels but

Pippa, my twin, needed a footstool and for Dad to hold her steady so that she didn't fall.

Elsa taught me to recognize our visitors and all their peculiarities and folklore. Sometimes there were jackdaws, rooks, and ravens but it was monopolized by crows, which is why I dubbed it the crow palace. Though not the largest of the Corvidae, they were strong and stout. I watched them see off interlopers, such as squirrels, who hoped to dine.

After leaving our offerings we'd withdraw to the sun room to watch them gather.

"Birdies," Pippa would say and clap.

The patio doors bore the brunt of her excitement; fogged breath and palm prints. Snot, if she had a cold. She touched my arm when she wanted to get my attention, which came out as a clumsy thump.

"I can see."

Hearing my tone, Pippa inched away, looking chastised.

Dad closed in on the other side with a forced, jovial, "You're quiet, what's up?"

It was always the same. *How are you feeling? What can I get you? Are you hungry? Did you have a bad dream last night?*

"I'm fine." Not a child's answer. I sounded uptight. I didn't have the emotional vocabulary to say, *Go away. Your anxiety's stifling me.*

I put my forehead against the glass. In the far corner of the garden was the pond, which Dad had covered with safety mesh, unfortunately too late to stop Mum drowning herself in it. That's where I found her, a jay perched on her back. It looked like it had pushed her in. That day the crow palace had been covered with carrion crows; bruisers whose shiny eyes were full of plots.

I sit in a traffic queue, radio on, but all I hear is Elsa's voice.

"Julie, it's Elsa. From Fenby."

As if I could forget the woman who brought us birthday presents, collected us from school, and who told me about bras, periods, and contraception (albeit in the sketchiest terms) when Dad was too squeamish for the task.

"Julie, you need to come home. I don't know how to say this, so I'll just come out with it. Your dad's dead." She paused. "He collapsed in the garden this morning. I'll stay with Pippa until you get here."

"Thank you."

"You will come, won't you?"

"Yes."

Ten years and they jerk me back with one phone call.

The journey takes an hour longer than I expected. Oh, England, my sceptred and congested isle. I'm not sure if I'm glad of the delay or it's making my dread worse.

The lane is in dire need of resurfacing so I have to slow down to navigate the potholes. I turn into the drive. It's lined by overgrown bushes. I stop out of view of the house and walk the rest of the way. I'm not ready for Pip and Elsa yet.

The Beeches should be handsome. It's crying out for love. Someone should chip off the salmon-pink stucco and take it back to its original red brick. The garden wraps around it on three sides, widest at the rear. I head there first.

The crow palace is the altar of the childhood rituals that bound us. It looks like Dad's lavished more love on it than the house. New levels have been added and parts of it replaced.

I stoop to pick something up from the ground. I frown as I turn it over and read the label. It's an empty syringe wrapper. Evidence of the paramedics' labors. The grass, which needs mowing, is trampled down. I think I can see where Dad lay.

A crow lands on the palace at my eye level. It struts back and forth with a long, confident stride as it inspects me. Its back is all the colors of the night. It raises its head and opens its beak wide.

Caw caw caw.

It's only then that the patio doors open and Elsa runs out, arms outstretched.

Job done, the crow takes flight.

Elsa fusses and clucks over me, fetching sweet tea, "For shock."

"What happened to him?"

"They think it was a heart attack. The coroner's officer wants to speak to you. I've left the number by the phone."

"How can they be sure? Don't they need to do a post-mortem?"

"They think it's likely. He's had two in the last three years."

"I didn't know."

"He wouldn't let me phone you." I don't know if I'm annoyed that she didn't call or relieved that she doesn't say *Perhaps, if you'd bothered to call him he might have told you himself.* "Your dad was a terrible patient. They told him he should have an operation to clear his arteries but he refused."

Elsa opens one of the kitchen cupboards. "Look."

I take out some of the boxes, shake them, read the leaflets. There's twelve months of medication here. Dad never took any of it. Aspirin, statins, nitrates, ACE-inhibitors. Wonder drugs to unblock his stodgy arteries and keep his blood flowing through them.

I slam the door shut, making Elsa jump. It's the gesture of a petulant teenager. I can't help it. Dad's self-neglect is a good excuse to be angry at him for dying.

"We used to have terrible rows over it. I think it was his way of punishing himself." Elsa doesn't need to say *guilt over your mother*. She looks washed out. Her pale eyes, once arresting, look aged. "I don't think Pippa understands. Don't be hurt. She'll come out when she's ready."

Pippa had looked at me as I put my bag down in the hall and said, "Ju-lieee," prolonging the last syllable as she always did when she was excited. Then she slid from the room, leaving me alone with Elsa.

Elsa's the one who doesn't understand, despite how long she's known Pippa.

Pip's cerebral palsy has damaged the parts of her brain that control her speech. It's impaired her balance and muscle tone. It's robbed her of parts of her intellect but she's attuned to the world in other ways.

She understands what I feel. *She's* waiting for *me* to be ready, not the other way around.

Perhaps it's a twin thing.

Pippa stopped speaking for several years when she was a child. It was when she realized that she didn't sound like other children. That she couldn't find and shape the words as I did. Her development wasn't as arrested as everyone supposed. Dad, Elsa, and her teachers all underestimated her.

I could've tried to help her. I could have acted as an interpreter as I've always understood her, but I didn't. Instead, I watched her struggle.

And here she is, as if I've called out to her.

Pippa's small and twisted, muscle spasticity contorting her left side. That she's gray at the temples shocks me, despite the fact mine's the same but covered with dye. She's wearing leggings and a colorful sweatshirt; the sort of clothes Dad always bought for her. That she's unchanged yet older causes a pang in my chest, which I resent.

Pip looks at the world obliquely, as if scared to face it straight on. She stands in the doorway, weighing me up and then smiles, her pleasure at seeing me plain on her narrow face.

That's what makes me cry. For her. For myself. I've abandoned her again and again. As soon as I could walk, I walked away from her. As we grew older, my greatest unkindness towards her was my coldness. As a teenager, I never wanted to be seen with her. After our twenty-third birthday, I never came back.

"Julieee."

I put my arms around her. I've not asked Elsa if Pip was with Dad when he collapsed, if she sat beside him, if she saw the paramedics at work.

The onslaught of my tears and sudden embrace frighten her, and I'm the one who feels abandoned when Pip pulls away.

Ten years since my last visit to The Beeches. Ten years since Dad and I argued. I drove home after spending the weekend here for our birthday. Elsa had made a cake, a sugary creation piled up with candles that was more suitable for children.

Dad rang me when I got back to my flat in London.

"I'm disappointed, Julie."

"What?" I wasn't used to him speaking to me like that.

"You come down once in a blue moon and spend the whole time on the phone."

"I have to work." I was setting up my own recruitment agency. I was angry at Dad for not understanding that. I was angry that he thought I owed him an explanation. "I'm still getting thing off the ground."

"Yes, I know your work's more important than we are."

"It's how I make a living. You sound like you want me to fail."

"Don't be preposterous. All I'm saying is that it would be nice for you to be here when you're actually here."

"I drove all the way to be there. It's my birthday too."

"You act like coming home is a chore. Pippa's your sister. You have a responsibility towards her."

"Yes, I'm her *sister*, not her mother. Aren't I allowed a life of my own? I thought you'd be happier that you've only got *one* dependent now."

"Don't talk about Pip like that."

"Like what?"

"Like you're angry at her. It's not her fault that your mother killed herself."

"No? Whose was it then? Yours?"

Those were my final words to him. I don't know why I said them now.

The following morning's a quiet relief. I wake long before Pippa. The house is familiar. The cups are where they've always lived. The spoons in the same drawer, the coffee kept in a red enamel canister as it always had been when I lived here. It's like returning to another country after years away. Even though I recognize its geography, customs, and language, I'll never again be intrinsic to its rhythms.

My mobile rings.

"Ju, it's me." Christopher.

"Hi."

I'm never sure what to call him. *Boyfriend* sounds childish, *partner* business-like, and *lover* illicit.

"The new Moroccan place has opened. I wondered if you fancied coming with me tonight."

Not: Shall we go? There's him and me with all the freedom between us that I need.

"I can't. Take Cassie." There's no jealousy in that remark. Over the two years I've been seeing Chris, seeing other people too has worked well for us. It's precisely why I picked a man with form. A player won't want to cage me but Chris keeps coming back to me, just when I expect him to drift off with someone new.

"I stopped seeing her months ago. I told you."

I don't care. It makes no difference to me.

"My dad's dead," I say, just to try and change the subject.

"Oh God, Julie I'm so sorry. I'd just presumed he was already dead from the way you talked about him. What happened?"

"Heart attack."

"Where are you? I'll come and help."

"No need."

"I want to."

"And I don't want you to,"

"I'm not trying to crowd you, but may I call you? Just to see if you're okay."

"Sure. Of course." He can call. I may not answer.

I hang up.

"Julie."

Pippa sidles up to me. We're both still in our pajamas. It's an effort but I manage a smile for her.

"Do you want breakfast, Pippa? Cereal?"

I'm not sure what she eats now. It used to be raspberry jam spread thickly on toast. She tugs on my sleeve and pulls me up.

A trio of swallows hang from her bedroom ceiling. It was sent one Christmas, like all my presents to her for the last ten years, chosen for being flat packed and easy to post. Pippa reaches up and sets the birds in motion as she passes.

It's the bedroom of a child. No, it's the bedroom of an innocent. It needs repainting. The realization makes me wonder what I feel. Our future's a knife.

"Look," Pippa beams.

Her childhood collection has grown to dominate the room. It's housed in plastic craft drawers that are stacked on shelves to a height that Pippa can reach. Her models are lined up above the drawers, on higher shelves.

She used to make them in plasticine. They were crude lumps at first. Now she's graduated to clay. They must fire them at the day center. Her years of practice are in the suggestive details. A square tail. The shape of the head with a pinched beak.

They're crows, over and over again.

Pippa opens one of the drawers and picks out buttons, one at a time, and drops them into my open hand. Each one's unique, only their color in common. They're white plastic, mother of pearl, enamel, stained fabric, and horn. She laughs as they spill through my fingers. The rest of that block of drawers contains buttons, each separated by compartment for the rainbow.

"Pippa, are all these from the crow palace?"

"Yes, birdies." She mangles some of the syllables but she's definite.

She shows me more. Her collection is sorted by type of object, or by shape where Pippa was unsure. Coins and bottle tops. Odd earrings. Screws. Watch parts. The tiny bones of rodents, picked clean and bleached by time.

I used to have a collection of my own, the crows left us treasures on the crow palace in return for food. They came with presents every day. I threw mine out when I started high school.

I regret it now, as I sit here with Pippa.

"Here." She thrusts one of the drawers into my hands.

Something lonely rattles around inside. I tip it out. I hold it up between my forefinger and thumb. A ring designed as a feather that wraps around the finger. Despite the tarnish, its lovely—the hard line of the shaft, the movement of the hundreds of vanes and downy barbs.

It's impossible that it's here because I'm sure Mum was buried with it. I watched Dad lay out the things for the undertaker: a silk blue dress, tights, a pair of leather heels, a lipstick, and this ring. He put her wedding band and diamond engagement ring in a box and placed it in his bedside drawer. For you, when you get married, as if this was given.

The feather ring was kept to go with her into the grave. *We were on holiday when she realized she was expecting. She chose this from an antique shop in France the same day that she told me. I was thrilled. I think she'd want to wear this.*

I close my eyes. Had I imagined that? As I do, the ring finds its way onto the ring finger of my left hand, which goes cold. I can feel the blood in my wrist freezing. I yank it off before ice reaches my heart.

"Where did you get this?" My voice is shrill. "Pippa?"

"Crows," she says.

I force myself to go into Dad's room. It's stifling. Being north facing and a dull day, the poor quality light brings out the green undertones in the patterned gold wallpaper. The dark, heavy furniture makes the room crowded and drab.

Everything's an effort. There's something about being back here that's put me in a stupor. I'm procrastinating about everything.

Looking through Dad's things should hurt but it doesn't. It's like rifling through a stranger's personal effects for clues. He was an unknown entity to me because I didn't care enough to want to find out who he was. Shouldn't blood call out to blood? Mine didn't. I felt more for Pip, my dead mother, and for Elsa. Dad's love was smothering and distant all at once as if I was something to be feared and guarded closely.

I pile his clothes in bin bags to take to the charity shop. I pause when I find box files full of football programmes. I never knew he was a fan. It looks like he went regularly before we were born. It crosses my mind that they might be worth something, but then I chuck them on the pile to get rid of.

It's only when I'm clearing out the second wardrobe that I find something that piques my interest. There's a steel box at the back with his initials on it, under a pile of moth eaten scarves. It's locked. I spend the next hour gathering together every key I can find, searching drawers and cupboards for them. Nothing fits.

I carry the box downstairs and put it on the kitchen table. It's too late in the day to take it to a locksmith. I'll go tomorrow.

Who knew that death is so bureaucratic? I'm relieved there won't be a post-mortem but there's still the registering of Dad's death and meetings with the undertaker, bank and solicitors. Elsa's a brick, taking Pip to the day center or over to her place if I have things to arrange.

The future leaves me in a stupor of indecision. I stare out of the kitchen window at where the pond used to be. Now it's a rockery in the same kidney shape.

What sort of people would have a pond with young children in the house?

The pond was where I found Mum's body, looking boneless as it slumped over the stones at the water's edge. I was four. I thought she'd just fallen over. I ran out to help her get up. A jay sat on her back. The bird is the shyest of all Corvids, flamboyant by comparison to its family, in pink, brown, and striped blue. It normally confines itself to the shelter of the woods.

I paused as the wind blew up her skirt, revealing the back of her thighs. Her head was turned to one side. The jay hopped down to look at her face, then pecked at one of her open, staring eyes.

The jay turned as I approached and let out a screech, blood on its beak. Or maybe I was the one screaming. I'd put my hands over my ears.

A shriek comes from the sun-room, next door. I drop my coffee cup, imagining Pippa has conjured the same image. She'd followed me out that day and seen Mum too. By the time my cup smashes on the floor and sends hot coffee up my legs and the cabinets I realize something's actually wrong.

Pippa's pressed against the window, shouting and banging with her fists. "What is it?"

I grab her shoulders but she twists around to look outside again. From here we have an interrupted view of the back garden.

A magpie deposits something on the crow palace, then starts to make a racket. Its blue-black-white coloring reveals its affinities for the living and the dead.

Only then does the sudden whirring motion draw my gaze down to the lawn. The cat's bright pink collar contrasts with its gray fur. A second magpie is pinned by the cat's paw on its spread wing. Its other wing is a blur as it struggles. The magpie's mate flies down and the cat breaks its gaze with its prey and hisses.

I know it's the natural order of things but I'm sickened and trembling. I open the patio door and clap my hands as if such a banal gesture can end this life-and-death struggle. Pippa's more decisive, stumbling out and I hold her back for fear she'll be scratched.

Flat black shapes with ragged wings darken the sky. Ravens. One swoops, catching the cat's ear with its bill as fierce as pruning shears as it passes over. The cat contorts, blood on its fur, releasing the magpie which makes an attempt at broken flight.

The cat crouches, a growl in its throat. Its ears are flat to its head, its fur on end, doubling its size. The birds are coming down in black jets, from all directions. The cat raises a paw, claws unsheathed, to swipe at its assailants. The ravens take it by surprise with a group attack. One lands, talons clutching the nape of the cat's neck. It writhes and screams. The sound cuts through me. The birds are like streaks of rain. I can't see the cat anymore. It's been mobbed by darkness.

Pippa and I clutch one another. The cat's silent now. The ravens lift together into the sky and all that remains on the grass are steaks of blood and tufts of fur.

I remember later that the magpies left us a gift, a task which made them careless of their long collective memory of their past persecutions by gamekeepers and farmers.

The key they left on the crow palace shines as if calling to me. The metal's so cold that it hurts to hold it, as if it's just come out of a freezer.

I have the queasy feeling that I know what it's for. It slides into the padlock on the steel box with ease and I feel its teeth catch as I turn it.

Everything I know about Mum is distilled from scant memories. I'm shaking at the prospect of something concrete. I open the lid. Here's where Dad buried her significant remains.

It contains a random assortment. A lady's dress watch. A pair of pearl earrings. A silk patterned scarf. An empty perfume bottle. I open it and the stale fragrance brings Mum back to me on a drift of bluebells. I wipe my eyes. I'd forgotten she always wore that. There's a birthday card signed *With more than love, Karen.*

What is there that's more than love?

We weren't a photographed family. There aren't any happy snaps that feature Pip and me. This pile of photographs are of Mum and Dad when they were young, before we were born. I shuffle through them. Mum and Dad at the beach, on bicycles, another in formal dress. Their happiness grates. Why couldn't they saved some of it for us?

The last thing out of the box is a handkerchief. Whatever's knotted within clinks as I lift it out. It's a pair of eggs. They're unnaturally heavy, as if made of stone. And they're warm.

I can't resist the impulse to crack one of them open. Fluid runs over my fingers. I sniff it. Fresh egg white.

A baby's curled up within, foetal like, her tender soles and toes, her genitals displayed. She's perfect. I don't know what she's made of. Something between rubber and wax that's the color of putty.

I break open the second one. Another girl. This one's different. She has massive, dark eyes that are too wide set to be normal. There are sparse, matted feathers on her back. Faint scale cover her feet.

I carefully rewrap the pair, trying not to touch them, and put them back in the box.

My phone rings. Then stops. Starts again. There's nothing for it. I answer it. "Chris." I try not to sound irritated.

"How are you?"

"Busy. You know."

"No, I don't. Tell me."

"Stuff to sort out. Dad and for my sister."

"You have a sister? What's her name?"

"Phillipa. We call her Pippa."

"What's she like?"

Pippa? She likes birds, me, the color turquoise, chocolate, having a routine, crow gifts, sunshine. She gets frustrated when she can't make herself understood. Her eyes are hazel brown and she has eczema.

"She has cerebral palsy. My dad took care of her."

"Will I meet her at the funeral?"

I'm about to say *Of course she'll be at the funeral* but then I realize that Chris is assuming he's invited.

"Why do you want to come? You never met him."

"Not for him, for you. Tell me your address."

"I don't need you here."

I don't understand. It feels like an argument, full of unspoken baggage that I didn't even know we were carrying.

"Julie, what are we doing?"

His tone sets off an alarm bell in my head.

"You must know that I—" Don't say it. Don't say *I love you*. He falters, "You must know how much I care about you."

I feel sick. I thought we were alike. Just my luck to find a man who falls in love with the one woman who's not chasing him.

"I'm not talking about marriage or children."

Children. For all the carelessness of my affections there's never been a child.

"I told you at the start that I'm not like other people. You promised me that you understood completely."

"There's more to us than just sex."

I can't believe he's doing this.

"Don't you get it?" I should be angry but a column of coldness is solidifying inside me. "There is no more. I'm not broken, so you can't fix me. I don't love you because I can't love anyone."

"Julie, please . . . "

I hang up and bar his number.

There's never been so many people in the house. I don't like it. I wanted it to be just us, but Elsa went on so much that I relented. I wish I hadn't now. I forgot to pack a black dress so I had to buy one in a hurry. I took Pippa with me, there being nothing suitable in her wardrobe either. The shop assistant stared at her while she touched the expensive silks. The woman's tune changed when it was clear that I didn't have to look at the price tags.

I picked out a neat black dress myself and a black tunic, leggings and ankle boots for Pippa. On impulse, I took her to a salon to get her hair dyed and styled. She was more patient than I expected. She liked being somewhere new. My favorite part was Pippa's smile when the shampoo was massaged into her scalp.

It was a nice day.

Today isn't. When we went out to the funeral car, Elsa said, "Look at the two of you. Pippa, you look so grown up. And Julie, wonderful. Black suits you more than any other color. You should wear it more."

Grief fucks people up.

The mourners come in, folding up their umbrellas like wings, dripping rain on the parquet floor.

"Elsa, are any of the neighbors coming?"

"God, no. All the one's you'd know are dead or moved away."

I don't know the people here. Some used to work with Dad, apparently, others knew him from Pippa's day center or through Elsa. They all greet her like she's long lost family.

It's unnerving that they line up to speak to me, something more suited to a wedding than a funeral.

The first is a tall, broad man, dressed in a shiny tight suit and winkle pickers. Spiv's clothes but he's gentle, paternal even. He takes my hand and looks right into my eyes, searching for something.

"My name's Charlie."

"Thank you for coming."

"I'm so very pleased to meet you, my dear. You're as lovely as I thought you'd be. I understand you're a smart lady too." Then as if he's just recalled why we're here, "I'm sorry for your loss."

A pair of elderly ladies are next. They're twins. Both have the same bob, cut into a bowl shape at the front, hooked noses and dowager's humps that marks their identically crumbling spines.

"Do you have children?" says the first one, which isn't the opener I expected.

The second one tuts and pushes her sister along. They're followed by a couple who call themselves Arthur and Megan. A first I think they're brother and sister as they're so alike, but the way he hovers around her suggests their relationship is more than familial. Her arm's in plaster.

"How did you know Dad?"

"Through my father." The man waves his hand in a vague gesture that he seems to think explains everything.

Young men, a few years younger than I am, come next. They're all in designer suits. Each is striking in his own way. They stand close to me as they introduce themselves. One even kisses my hand. The last one interests me the most. He's not the tallest or best looking but I like his quiet confidence and lively face. There's a yearning in his voice when he says my name that tugs at me. To smile at him seems weak, so I nod.

"My name is Ash."

"Ash." The word coats my tongue with want.

A woman edges him along.

"I'm Rosalie."

She has the manner of entitlement that only certain hard, beautiful women have. Her fingernails are painted black. The lacquer's like glass. She looks me up and down as she passes.

I sip my drink as more people introduce themselves, then go off to decimate the buffet and the wine boxes. I try not to look at Ash's every movement. It's a lovely agony. I close my eyes, the tannin in the red wine shrinking the inside of my mouth.

"How is Julie settling back in here?" It's Charlie.

"Well, she's here for now." I don't like Elsa's tone. She must be drunk too. I open my eyes. Charlie's suit can't settle on a single shade of black.

"I'm sorry Elsa. You must be missing Michael."

I turn away a fraction, not wanting them to know I'm listening. From the periphery of my vision I see him embrace Elsa.

The young men congregate by the hearth. Rosalie's berating them for something. I catch her final words: "I don't see what's so special about her anyway."

I know she's talking about me because Ash looks over and keeps on looking even though he's caught me eavesdropping. "Don't you?" he replies with a smirk.

"I'm Stephanie." A woman gets in the way, just when I think he's going to walk over and join me. "You're Julie, yes?"

"Hello."

There's a long pause. I sigh inwardly. I'm going to have to try and make conversation with her. She's in her fifties. She's only wearing one earring and most of her hair's escaped from her bun.

"Where are you from?"

"From?" she says.

"Your accent . . . " Her pronunciation's off kilter, her phrasing odd.

"I've lived in lots of different places." She glances around the room. "I think Elsa would rather I hadn't come."

She reaches out and swipes a sandwich from a plate, gobbling it down in two mouthfuls. "These are delicious."

The volume of the chattering around us bothers me. I've drunk too much on an empty stomach.

"This place hasn't changed since your mother's funeral."

"You met her?"

"Tennis club."

Tennis. How little I knew about her.

"Such a gracious, joyous woman." Stephanie twitters on. "Want and need. How they undo us."

"Pardon?"

Stephanie blinks.

"There are so many crows in Fenby now. They've quite pushed out the cuckoos." She speaks in a comedy whisper, getting louder with each word. "Your mother guessed that they'd double-crossed her."

The chatter's dying. Everyone's watching us now.

"You know how it works, don't you? They laid one of their own in your mother's nest . . . "

Charlie comes over and puts an arm around her.

"Stephanie, what are you taking about? Julie doesn't want to hear this rubbish." He pulls a face at me. "It's time for you to go home."

"You can't push me around. I have a right to be here. We had a deal." She breaks away from him and seizes me in a hug.

"I'm sorry. For all of it," she whispers in my ear. "It's true. Look under the crow palace."

I want to ask her how she knows that's what we call the bird table but Ash comes and takes her arm.

"Aunt Steph, I'll see you home."

"I'm not your aunt."

"No, Ash, you should stay." Elsa joins us.

"It's fine." Ash kisses my cheek. My flesh ignites. "May I come and see you again? Tomorrow?"

"Yes." It's as easy at that.

"Until then." He steers Stephanie towards the door.

The noise starts up again in increments. Ash's departure has soured my mood.

Pippa can't settle. As the mourners gathered around Dad's grave she cringed and started to wail as if finally understanding that he's gone. Now she's wandering about, refusing to go to her room but flinching when any of our guests come near her. She stands, shifting her weight from foot to foot, in front of the twins who are perched in her favorite armchair.

"Oh for God's sake, just sit somewhere will you?" I snap.

Pippa's chin trembles. The room's silent again.

Elsa rushes over to her but Pippa shoves her away. Elsa grabs her wrist.

"Look at me, Pippa. It's just me. Just Elsa." She persists until Pippa stops shaking. "Better? See? Let's go outside for a little walk."

Pippa's face is screwed up but she lets Elsa take her out onto the patio.

I lock myself in the bathroom and cry, staying there until everyone leaves. I've no idea what I'm crying for.

I wish this humidity would break. It' sticky, despite yesterday's rain. I feel hungover. Lack of sleep doesn't help.

I wave goodbye to Elsa and Pippa as they go out. Elsa's keen to be helpful. *I'll drop Pippa off, I'll be going that way to the shops. Why don't you go and get some fresh air on the lawn? You'll feel better.*

I can't face sorting out the last of Dad's clothes. The thought of the hideous green-gold wallpaper in there makes me want to heave. Instead, I take boxes of papers out to a blanket I've laid out on the lawn. It's prevarication. I'm pretending that I'm doing something useful when I should be sorting out our future.

All the ridiculous talk of swapped babies and symbolic eggs seems stupid now that I'm out in the fresh air.

How can I love her so much yet can't bear to be near her sometimes? I fought everyone who tried to bully her at school. I became a terror, sniffing out weakness and reducing other children to tears. I started doing it just because I could. They hated me and in return and I felt nothing for them, not anger, not contempt. That's how damaged I am.

I'm afraid that everything people think of me is true, but I'm not afraid enough to change. I *am* selfish. I like my own silence and space. I hated Dad for saying, "You will look after Pippa won't you? The world's a terrible place."

Need. Nothing scares me more.

Then I look at Pippa, who is far more complete a human being than I am. She's no trouble, not really. I could work from here and go to London for meetings. All I need to run my business is a phone. It would only need a bit of will to make it work.

I pull papers from the box. It's an accumulation of crap. Receipts from electrical appliances, their warranties long outdated, bills, invitations and old business diaries.

It's so quiet. I lie back. There's not even the slightest breath of a breeze. I shield my eyes as I look up. The trees are full of Corvidae.

Birds don't roost at eleven in the morning, yet the rookeries are full. Sunlight reveals them as oil on water creatures with amethyst green on their foreheads and purple garnets on their cheeks.

Rooks, weather diviners with voices full of grit who sat on Odin's shoulders whispering of mind and memory in his ears.

How Elsa's lessons come back to me.

She taught me long ago to distinguish rooks from crows by their diamond shaped tails and the bushy feathers on their legs. I find these the strangest of all Corvidae, with their clumsy waddles and the warty, great patch around the base of their beaks. It's reptilian, Jurassic, even. A reminder that birds are flying dinosaurs, miniaturized and left to feed on insects and carrion.

I turn my head. Crows have gathered too, on the patio furniture, the bird baths, the roof and, of course, the crow palace. The washing line sags under their weight.

I daren't move for fear of scaring them. Perhaps *I'm* scared.

Ash walks through their silence. They're not unsettled by his presence. He's still wearing the same suit. His stride is long and unhurried.

He doesn't pay attention to social niceties. He falls to his knees. I lean up, but I'm not sure if it's in protest or welcome. It's as if he's summed me with a single glance when I'm not sure what I want myself. He presses his mouth against mine.

He pushes my hair out of the way so he can kiss the spot beneath my ear and then my throat. The directness of his desire is exhilarating, unlike Chris' tentative, questioning gestures.

He pulls open my dress. I unbutton his shirt. He pulls down my knickers with an intensity that borders on reverence.

His body on mine feels lighter than I expect, as if he's hollow boned.

When he's about to enter me he says, "Yes?"

I nod.

"Say it. I need to hear you say it. You have to agree."

"Yes, please, yes."

I'll die if he stops now. The friction of our flesh is delicious. It's as necessary as breathing.

When Ash shudders to a climax, he opens his mouth and *Caw, caw, caw* comes out.

I wake, fully dressed, lying on a heaped-up blanket beneath the crow palace. There's a dampness between my legs. I feel unsteady when I get up. The shadows have crept around to this side of the house. It must be late afternoon.

When I go in, Elsa's in the kitchen. She's cleaned up after yesterday.

"I'm sorry. I was going to do that . . . "

"It's okay." She doesn't turn to greet me.

"Where's Pippa?"

"Having a nap. We're all quite done in, aren't we?"

She turns to wipe down the worktops. She looks so at ease, here in Dad's kitchen.

"What happened to my mother?"

I have to take the damp cloth from her hand to make her stop and look at me.

"It's all on record."

"I want to hear what's not on record."

"Then why didn't you ask Michael while he was still alive?"

I've been expecting this but the anger and resentment in Elsa's voice still surprises me. I take a deep breath. Retaliation won't help my cause.

"Because he hated taking about her."

"Then it's not my place to tell you, is it?"

"Of course it's your place. You're the closest thing to a mother that either of us have ever had." I should've said it long ago, without strings. The tendons at Elsa's neck are taut. She's trying not to cry. I didn't just leave Dad and Pip. I left her too.

"You were born in this house. The midwife didn't come in time. Your father smoked cigarettes in the garden. Men didn't get involved in those days. I helped bring you both into the world. I love you both so much. Children fly away, it's expected. I just didn't realize it would take you so long to come back."

"I know you loved Dad too. Did he love you back?"

"He never loved me like he loved your mother." Poor Elsa. Always at hand when he needed her.

"You sacrificed a lot to be with him." Marriage. A family of her own.

"You've no idea." Her voice is thick with anger. "It's utterly changed me."

Then she bows her head. The right thing to do would be to comfort her. To hold her and let her weep on my shoulder. I don't though. It's a crucial moment when Elsa's emotions are wide open.

"The papers said Mum had postnatal depression and psychosis."

An illness that follows childbirth. A depression so deep that it produces bizarre beliefs.

"They were desperate for children. They would've done anything."

"Anything?"

"Fertility treatments weren't up to much back then."

"So what happened?"

"Well, you happened. A surprise, they told everyone. I remember holding you in my arms. It was such a precious moment."

"When did she get ill?"

"When it became clear that Pip wasn't doing so well. You were a thriving, healthy baby but Pippa was in and out of hospital because she was struggling to feed. She slept all the time. She never cried. You were smiling, then rolling over, then walking and she was falling further and further behind."

"And Mum couldn't cope?"

"The doctors became worried as she had all these strange ideas. And you were a real handful."

"Me?"

"I'm sorry, maybe I shouldn't say this."

"Tell me."

"You were just a little girl, trying to get their attention. You'd bite Pippa, steal her food. When you we big enough, you'd try and tip her from her high chair."

"And what exactly was it that Mum believed?"

"She insisted she'd been tricked by the birds. They'd helped her to conceive and then they went and swapped one of you for one of their own."

I wake in the hours when the night turns from black to gray to something pale and cold. My mind's full. It's been working while I sleep.

Mum's insistence that she'd been tricked by birds. That they'd helped her to conceive.

They laid one of their own in your mother's nest . . .

Cuckoo tactics. Mimic the host's eggs and push out one of their own. Equip your chick for warfare. Once hatched, the hooks on its legs will help it to heave its rivals from the nest.

Look under the crow palace.

I pull on jeans and a sweatshirt. Dad kept his tools in his shed. I pull the shovel from the rack, fork and a trowel for more delicate work.

It's chilly. I leave footprints on the damp lawn. It takes a while because I go slowly. First I take up turf around the crow palace. Then I dig around the base. The post goes deep into the rich, dark soil. My arms ache.

I lean on the post, then pull it back and forth, trying to loosen it. It topples with a crash. I expect the neighbors to come running out but nobody does.

I have to be more careful with the next part of my excavation. I use the trowel, working slowly until I feel it scrape something. Then I use my hands.

I uncover a hard, white dome. Soil's stuck in the zigzag sutures and packed into the fontanelle. The skull eyes me with black orbits full of dirt that crawl with worms.

I clean off the skeleton, bit by bit. Its arms are folded over the delicate ribcage. Such tiny hands and feet. It's small. She's smaller than a newborn, pushed out into the cold far too early.

Mum and Stephanie were right. Here is my real sister, not the creature called Pippa.

Oh my God, you poor baby girl. What did they do to you?

"Are you okay?" Elsa ushers me into the kitchen. It's eight in the morning. She has her own key.

I can't bring myself to ask whether Pippa, my crow sister, is awake. How was the exchange made? Was it monstrous Pippa that heaved my real sister from my mother's womb? Was she strangled with her own umbilical cord? And who buried my blood sister? Was it Mum and Dad? No wonder they were undone.

"What happened to you?"

Elsa opens a cupboard and pulls out a bag of seed mix, rips it open and tips out a handful. When she eats, some of it spills down her front. She doesn't bother to brush it off. When she offers me some I'm hit by a wave of nausea that sends me across the room on rubbery legs to vomit in the bin.

"You've got yourself in a right old state." Elsa holds back my hair.

I take a deep breath and wipe my nose.

"Elsa, there's a baby buried in the garden."

She goes very still.

"You knew about it, didn't you?" I sit down.

She pulls a chair alongside mine, its legs scraping on the tiles. She grasps my hands.

"I didn't want you to know about it yet. I wish that cuckoo-brained Stephanie hadn't come to the funeral. And Arthur and Megan hadn't interfered with that damn key. You found the eggs, didn't you?"

I think I'm going to faint so I put my head on the table until it passes. Elsa rubs my back and carries on talking. When I sit up, Elsa's smiling, her head tilted at an odd angle. A gesture I don't recognize. "I'm actually relieved. It's easier that you know now you're staying."

"Elsa, I can't stay here."

"It's best for everyone. You've others to consider now."

I press my fists to my closed eyes. I can't consider anything. My mind's full of tiny bones.

"Mum knew that Pippa wasn't hers, didn't she?" I'm thinking of the human-bird-baby in its shell.

"Pippa?" Elsa's eyes are yellow in this light. "No, she knew that it was you that wasn't hers. She had to watch you like a hawk around Pip."

I vomit again. Clumps of semi digested food gets caught in my hair. Elsa dabs at my mouth with a tea towel. Her colors are the jay's—brown, pink, and blue. Was it her, stood at Mum's back and pecking at her eye?

Pippa stands in the doorway looking from my face to Elsa's and back again. I've never seen Pip's gaze so direct.

Now I know why my heart's loveless. Pip's not the aberration, I am. I'm the daughter of crows, smuggled into the nest. Pippa is how she is because of my failed murder attempt. I affected her development when I tried to foist her from the womb.

It's all my fault.

Pippa edges around the room, giving the woman who raised her a wide berth. She tucks herself under my arm and puts a hand low down on my abdomen. She peers into my face, concerned, and says, "Birdies."

=◆=

RED BARK AND AMBERGRIS

—◆—

Kate Marshall

After she was taken, Sarai lived two years with a cloth bound over her eyes, learning scent and touch and taste, never once seeing the island that was her prison. When the day came for the blindfold to be removed, she thought at first her eyes must have failed. Home was a world of blue waters and red-bark trees, of jewel fruits and opal-bellied songbirds. Even the sand shone honey-gold and glittered where it clung to creases in the rock, tucked there by a warm south wind. Here on Felas, isle of the essence-eaters, there was only gray. Gray stone and gray water, gray robes and gray faces.

Jarad laughed when she asked what was wrong with her and turned her by her shoulders toward the sea. He stretched out one finger, the tattoo that marked his Mastery stark against his skin. "See that? The crimson at the peak of the ocean's curve. That is the isle of Verakis, seat of our beloved queen and her court of misers. They hoard gold and joy in equal measure, and do nothing of value with either. That's where all the color's gone, little seabird. There's nothing wrong with you, only with this place."

She squinted, but her eyes were weak. She couldn't see and couldn't 'sense that far. Still she stared. That far and farther, on and on past Verakis, over a gray sea and then a blue one, far beyond where the eye could reach, there waited red-bark trees and opal-bellied songbirds; there waited her sisters and her brothers, her mother and her father. "I want to go home," she said. "I will go home." Defiant. A fool, but what child wasn't?

A croaked laugh from Jarad brought her chin up. She looked to the structure behind her, the once-fortress, now-prison that dominated the island. Even blind, she had known it was the largest building she had ever encountered. With her sight returned, she could scarcely bear to look at it: half carved from the island's rook-black rock, the rest a lighter stone stacked high enough that not even the narrowest spit of shore on the island escaped its shadow.

"Don't tell me this is my home now. It isn't. I won't stay here."

This only made Jarad shake his head. "This rock is no one's home, girl. But only the best of the poison-tamers can leave it, and only to go to Verakis and live in a prettier cage. The rest of us—scent-makers, stone-tellers, all— we must get used to the gray, for we'll never go home."

"Then I will be a poison-tamer," she said. She would go south, and then farther south, however she could. Over the gray sea to the blue.

"Verakis is no home either," he said. "And you are no poison-tamer. It is not your talent. Take this." He pressed a sachet into her hand, tapped it. "What do you 'sense?"

"Vanilla," she said instantly, scent and 'sense telling her true. She could feel the faint tug of it below her ribs, almost imperceptible—a gentle essence, not a powerful one. "A Nariguan strain."

"And what do you smell?"

She lifted the sachet to her nose, inhaled. "Vanilla," she said again, not understanding the lesson.

"For me it is home. It is the cook-fires in the field at harvest, it is the lines in my father's face. Take this." He took the sachet from her, gave her another.

"Red bark," she said, and lifted it to her nose without prompting. Closed her eyes. She saw her mother's hands, stained from working the bark. Heard her auntie's laughter and the rumble of her father's voice. Felt the slanting sun on her skin as she ran, ran, over the dry earth of the forest toward the beach, toward the shore. "Home," she whispered.

"The scent has power to you because of your memories," Jarad said. "Poison strikes us all the same, but scent is individual. A scent-maker must know the moments of their client's life, must know what scents define them. And then they can summon any emotion, evoke any memory. That is where our power lies."

"Scents are for a rich man's fancy," she said, echoing the scorn she'd heard from the other essence-eaters on the island. "There's no power in them at all."

She held out the sachet. He shook his head.

"Keep it," he said. "Your true training begins tomorrow." He left her on the southern cliff above the colorless, crashing waves, the red-bark sachet clutched in her palm as she tried to pick out a spot of crimson against empty sky. If she could get that far, she could find a way to go farther. To get that far, she would need to be a poison-tamer; she would need to be the best. And so she would.

The wind snatched at the blindfold in her hand. She let it go. The wind flung it back toward the island and crushed it against the rocks.

The day Sarai was taken, she had left her chores and her scolding father behind and gone to wander the shores. She was careful to go to the south, where the leathery tortoise her mother's mother's mother had ridden on as a child spent his days staring out to sea; the north shore hosted the black-stained bows of the queen's ships, here to collect what was owed the thrice-slain undying queen, and Sarai had been warned away.

She had little notion of what being a queen meant. No one from Sarai's island had stepped foot on the queen's, nor had the thrice-slain queen ever laid eyes on the shadow-green treetops of Sarai's home. Sarai knew only that her kinfolk gathered abalone and resin and red bark once a year and were given a stamped iron disk in return, which they added to the pile at the center of the village. Twenty-seven iron disks, twenty-seven years under the queen's rule. They did not tell the sailors or the gray-cloaked official that they kept, too, the thirty-four copper ingots stamped with the hatch-mark lettering of the Principalities. The island lay at the lip of the kingdom. No navies defended them, no soldiers rattled lances on their shores. The queen and the Twelve Princes had bloodied blades before just to shift a thin black line a centimeter across a page; they would do it again. Then her kinfolk would bury the iron, they would dig up the copper; all would continue as it had before.

Sarai understood none of this. She understood that the sky was vast and the sea was blue, and her feet were made for wandering. She sang to the old tortoise and turned cartwheels in the sand. She skipped among the shallows and picked up ruby starfish, prodded the translucent tops of jellyfish with her fat finger. And then she turned toward the *tug*.

A little thing, it was. Like a fishhook just under her left rib, minnow-nibbled. Tug-tug-tug, and something else with it, a deep sense, a dark sense. When she focused on it, the world seemed impossibly large, and so did she.

She found it nestled in the sand. A rock, black and yellow, the size of her father's fists closed and pressed together. Ambergris. She'd seen it before; her mother wore a piece of it, the size of a child's finger, on a cord around her neck. Proof that her mother was lucky, for she had found it the day Sarai's father asked for her to be his wife. She'd walked away from him to think, and found it, and smiling walked back. She told him yes and broke the ambergris in half, one piece for her and one for him.

This was tradition, not generosity. Half of what you found, you gave to the first person you met, or else misfortune fell on you. But if you did, you'd have great luck. The best luck. And the sailors and the officials always traded so much for even a small piece—and this piece was not small at all.

This will be my luck, she thought, and ran to share it.

Felas had no guards; only the sea. Its doors were never locked. There was nowhere to go. This dull-edged, lifeless place was where every essence-eater lived from discovery to death—if they were allowed to live at all.

Under Jarad's tutelage, Sarai made scents for the other apprentices. There were sixteen of them always, the apprentices; no more and no less. Gem-singers and stone-tellers and steel-weavers. The wind-kenner girl who huddled in the bitter cold to catch the taste of harvests and battles hundreds of miles away. The sea-breaker boy with his feet ruined from standing in the waves and 'sensing storms before they rose, with his master, more broken still, her hand always on the nape of his neck as if she feared the waves would snatch him away from her. The quiet, hungry pair who took up the poison-tamer's path.

Every year, one or two or none of them achieved their Mastery, earned their ink-stain brand, began whittling away the years they had left making trinkets and weapons and wonders for a far-away queen. Every year, one or two or more of them failed.

They did not speak of the dead. One child's fall was another's chance, and there were always more sails on the horizon.

Sarai listened to the other apprentices' stories, choosing dragon's blood or sandalwood, rose or lilac, moss or bryony. It did not always come readily, the work, but she could lose herself in it, could lose hours and days to the service of a single scent, and when it was done, satisfaction suffused her. The day one of her scents drove a girl, weeping, to confess that she had planned to throw herself from the bluffs, Jarad smiled.

"This is your talent," he told her.

But scent-making was the province of the unambitious. To serve the senses, to serve pleasure and whimsy. She would not win her way over the ocean with perfume-stained fingertips. She needed power, and for the essence-eaters, power was in poison. None of them were kept from the path to poison-taming, none forced to it; the queen trusted ambition more than coercion.

The best of the essence-eaters served one purpose: to keep the queen alive. There were six always, two and two and two to stand beside her, fingertips touching skin every minute, tasting and testing the essences inside of her. Three essences in particular: tarsnake venom, gillem oil, maddarek. Three times poisoned, not yet dead, because the essence-eaters kept the poison tame and still.

As Sarai would learn to do, and leave this catacomb behind.

Alone, because Jarad would not teach her, Sarai learned the ways these poisons killed, how quickly—six hours, three days, twelve hours. Boils, blackened skin, convulsions, liquefying lungs. She carried vials of them against her skin, fed pellets to rats and frogs and lambs so she could 'sense the way they moved in the blood.

She learned to 'sense new poisons. Hundreds of them. Dozens she ingested herself, to feel the racking shivers, the scorching fevers, the roiling sickness, and to alter them, ease them, draw them out. Some of the poisons, anyone could survive. Some could be endured if the effects were stretched out over days instead of hours, months instead of days. To be one of the six, to be even one of the eighteen who lived in Verakis in case one of the six fell, there were one hundred and sixty-three essences to consume and survive.

Jarad taught her tinctures to heal old friendships, to ignite new ideas. He taught her how to soothe, how to inflame. How to, again and again, bring simple pleasure, hardly noted, for some unseen courtier.

She grew to hate him. It was not talent that held her back, she thought; it was that her teacher dealt in scent and pleasure, not in blood and poison. She attended her lessons with him in his workshop, weathered tables carved with the names of apprentices who'd come before, learning to balance the over-sweet of honeysuckle with the damp earthiness of moss, to turn the rank stink of musk into pure silk. And then she scuttled to listen to the poison-tamers' lessons, to learn how the beating of the heart sustains and destroys, keeping the subject alive while pumping poison through them. To learn how to stop the poison without stopping the heart.

The rocks below her room were littered with the fragile corpses of birds, her windowsill scattered with poison-painted seeds. She had survived sixty poisons. She was thirteen years old.

After Sarai had found the ambergris, she raced up the beach. Her mother would be at the north bay, because she of all of them spoke the queen's tongue the best. Sarai wanted the first piece of ambergris to go to her, so that they would all be doubly lucky, and so she dodged the village, running through the thick trees instead with birds flitting above her, crying out so raucously she could not hear her own panting breath.

She burst from the trees onto sand and thudded to a stop. There, in front of her, was a man. A dust-skinned man, colorless compared to her own complexion, dressed in weather-worn clothes that might have once been blue. He turned to her with an eyebrow raised. His face was crooked, a slash running through it; he had only eight fingers and one of those half-gone. A queen's man, here to collect the queen's taxes, here to spoil her luck.

"Hullo," he said in a voice like water churning gravel. "Who's this?"

She sighed and stamped and split her ambergris in two, and handed him a piece. He turned it in his hands.

"What is it?" he said.

"Whale puke," she said, because she was feeling petulant, and because she didn't speak his language well. But it wasn't right, calling such a marvelous thing by such crude words, so she tried again. "Can you feel?" she asked. "It's all the way deep and all the way dark. For hours and hours, and then breath again." She moved her hand like a whale beneath the water.

"What do you mean, feel?" he asked.

"*Feel,*" she insisted, and tapped two fingers to the spot beneath her ribs where the tug always came.

"Come here," he said. "Follow." An odd tone to his voice. Sad, maybe. She followed, because he was going down to the shore and there was her mother up ahead anyway, and her mother would be so pleased. So very pleased.

It was the last time she saw her mother at all.

Jarad knew what she was doing, sighed over her. "It isn't your talent," he said when she lay in bed in her gray stone room with her muscles agony-tight, her joints hot as a bellows-fed forge. "You'll kill yourself like this." He read to her of distant places, of the scents that were found there. He told her of methods of distillation. He drilled her on accepted pairings, challenged her to create daring ones.

A new child was brought to the island, blindfolded and weeping. She made him a sachet of cloves and cassia bark, the scents of his mother's palms. He crept into her bed at night and she held him while he dreamed. His skill was slight, the island small. "I want to go home," he said. Three months after he'd arrived, he did; she was called to pack the cavities of his body with funerary herbs for the journey.

She swallowed wine laced with karagal and vomited blood for six days. "You have no talent for this," Jarad said, and set a folded note beside her bed: her next assignment. On the seventh day, when she knew she would survive, she took the note and went to their workshop, where Jarad already sat absorbed in his own task. She was sixteen years old; she had survived one hundred and fifty-nine poisons.

"Four left," she said. Jarad said nothing. She set to work.

The scent was for a woman from the Principalities. Sarai imagined the wrists the woman would dab the oil against, deep brown and delicate. Imagined her long neck, the pulse-points at the curve of her smooth jaw. Imagined her sprinkling oil-scented water on her blue-black hair, so that when her lover leaned close he would catch its scent and think—

Think what? Scent was individual. It sparked emotion, teased out memory. No scent spoke the same language to two people. It would mutter nonsense to one, sing sorrow to the next, laugh joyfully to a third. Sarai saw with satisfaction that Jarad had included in his instructions two tightly-scripted paragraphs—one for the woman, one for her lover. Where they were born, where they had wandered. Where they first kissed, where their hearts had been broken.

Sarai had set foot on two shores, the golden and the gray, but her workshop was a scent-map of the world, and she had memorized it all. Wintergreen from the frost-glazed north, pebbles of balsam resin from the west, cinnamon and sandalwood, cloves and bergamot, amber and rose. She knew which flowers grew in the spring on sun-drenched hills, which clung to shadows; which towns made garlands of poppies and which of forget-me-nots during the festivals and feasts of marriage, and which woods they would burn for the bonfire when they danced.

They had met in the winter, this woman and her lover, and kissed in the spring. They had fought once beneath the boughs of an oud-wood tree, and even though such wood was the most precious in the workshop, she twined its scent through, subtly, so they would not know the scent but would feel it—the fight, and the forgiveness afterward.

And in among the notes that sang of his life and hers, she hid the scent of red-bark trees, which grew only on the golden shores. A scent they would not know; a scent to make them reach for unfamiliar things, so they would not be caught up forever in the past.

When she was done she touched it to her skin. It would tell her little; everyone's skin was different, and the scent was not for her. But it bloomed like a promise, if only a promise for another, and she nodded in tight-curled satisfaction.

Jarad caught her wrist in his bony fingers and inhaled. "This is your talent," he told her. "And this is what you love."

"Four left," she repeated, and staggered on weak legs to bed.

Sarai would have stayed below decks the morning after she was taken, crying into the rough blankets of her new narrow bunk, but the scarred sailor who'd recognized her for what she was came to collect her.

"You'll want to watch," he said. "You'll want to see your home. Memorize it. You won't see it again, and you'll start to forget." He spoke like he knew, and so she went with him back up to the deck. The wind had caught their sails already; the island was slipping away fast, so fast. She leaned against the rope that ringed the deck, trying to see every detail one last time.

Was her mother there? Was she watching? There were figures on the rocks, the cliffs that ringed the entrance to the bay. Figures in white, the color of mourning. A dozen of them, three dozen—the whole village it seemed, climbing, standing, lifting something in their arms—baskets.

They lifted the lids of the baskets, and birds flew out. Not the opal-bellied singers of the forest but the delicate white birds of the shore. Dozens. Hundreds. Flying up, stretching wingtips toward the free open air, calling out in raucous condemnation. Flooding the sky. They wheeled and wailed, and the whole village called to her from the cliffs.

Come home to us, they called. *Come home.*

"They never even watched me go," the sailor said, but it was too old a wound for sorrow.

She watched until the island vanished; watched until the last bird vanished, too, and the sea turned dull and gray.

She was in bed again, recovering, in the small room above Jarad's workshop where she lived. They roomed alone, ate alone, wandered the gray halls alone; they were too uncertain of their fates for friendships.

The seizures this time had been short but brutal. She had very nearly not survived. Two left.

"What is my next assignment?" she asked, voice raw as reef-dragged flesh.

"No more assignments but one," Jarad said. "You've finished your training. You need only make your Mastery."

She scowled. How could she have thrown herself so thoroughly into the poison-tamer's arts, so thoroughly neglected her scent-maker's studies, and still reached Mastery in the latter before she survived her final poison?

"It's your talent," Jarad said, as if he knew what question she wanted to ask.

"It's useless," she said. "If I become a Master scent-maker, I'll be stuck here forever. I will never see the court."

"You don't want to see the court," Jarad said. "It's more comfortable but far more restricted. You would not go poling down the waterways or wander the museums. You would not attend the dances, except to prowl the edge and 'sense the drinks of fops, the soups of debauched heiresses. You would never leave your room except to 'sense. You would be poisoned a hundred times."

"I have already been poisoned a hundred times."

"You would never see your golden shores," Jarad said. "Never."

"What does it matter?" Sarai demanded. "Why do you care which cage I lock myself in?"

"Because I cannot abide loneliness," Jarad said, and rose. "Or the waste of true talent." He left her to her weakness.

Sarai did not ask for her Mastery. She did not even think of the task, or what Jarad might choose for her. She focused on poisons. She had two left, only two, but these were the worst of all. She would not be asked to consume tarsnake venom, gillem oil, or maddarek—even the very best poison-tamer could not survive their ravages, only delay them, and a 'tamer would be no use to the queen if they were too busy keeping themselves alive to see to her.

Still, the poisons were deadly enough. Varash powder killed slowly; the key was to burn through it quickly, three days and nights of horror instead of the three months it took for the poison to unweave the body. It was one thing to survive by lengthening and lessening the body's suffering; another to intensify it so extremely and yet maintain the focused will necessary to continue for three full days.

Bellman's Sigh was the nearest to the deadly three that could be ingested and still purged from the body. Only hours to kill, sometimes minutes if the heart or lungs were weak. It could not be survived alone, and in this the poison-tamer proved they could work in tandem with a partner, trading off seamlessly when they must rest, when they must sleep. A single second of failure would cause irreparable damage, such that even with the poison purged, the body would fail within the year.

It was customary for one's teacher to be the poison-tamer's partner, but Jarad would not do it for her, even if he had the skill. And so Sarai went to the 'tamers on the island one by one, accepting their refusals with bowed head and no argument.

There was one more. Nissa, who had stood at the queen's shoulder for twenty years before an assassin ended her career—not by poison but with a blade, slid toward the queen's spine and only Nissa close enough to stop it. She had seized it, turned it, sheathed it in her own thin frame. She lived, in pain. Spasms that came on without warning. Not often; quite rarely, in fact, but even an instant's inattention could cost the queen her life, and so she had sent Nissa away.

Nissa had been young the day the snake reared up and bit the girl who would be called the thrice-dead queen; on that day she began her work, but now she was old, and older still for grief. She was not like the rest of them, seized from fields and villages and distant cities. The court had been her home.

Sarai found her as she often did at the southern bluffs, wrapped head to toe in gray silk seven times as fine as any the others wore.

"I know why you're here," Nissa said. "Jarad told me you'd come. He told the others, too, and told them not to help you, but I will, if you wish it. If you'll risk it."

"It takes only two days," Sarai said. "You've lasted months without the spasms, before."

"And sometimes only hours," Nissa said.

"I'll risk it, happily," Sarai assured her.

"Did you see the ship that came yesterday?" Nissa asked.

Sarai hesitated, not because she didn't know how to answer but because she didn't know why the question had been asked. Ships came, ships left. They brought supplies, brought food since Felas grew none of its own; they took away the goods the essence-eaters crafted, scents and gems and weapons. Sometimes they took a student away, one who'd achieved the poison-tamer's Mastery. Or one who'd failed, who like the boy she'd comforted in the night would be sent home at last, with only Sarai's herbs to keep the scent of rot at bay.

"I saw it," she said at last.

"It brought news," Nissa said. "The Principalities are displeased with the queen's trade agreements. They tire of sending holds stuffed with gold and goods for a few small crates of red-bark and oud wood, abalone and ambergris. Not when they have so recently owned the source of such goods."

She was talking about Sarai's home. Sarai had never really thought about how valuable it was, that little island. The only place the red-bark grew. Host to stands of oud-wood trees. The home of the largest abalone with their prized shells. The island called by some Whale-Caller, since they came so often and left their ambergris upon the shore.

"What will they do?" I asked.

"They might war," Nissa said. "But it is more complex than that. They give the names of goods, but what they mean is—as long as only one of us can own it, one of us will be angry." She smiled thinly. "The queen means to burn it. When all is ashes, there's no need for war. Though it's more for spite than peace she wants it done, I'd guess."

"What?" As dull and startled as a seabird's cry.

"There are other sources for oud-wood and abalone and ambergris," Nissa said with a shrug. "Not as good, of course. And the red-bark would be lost, but what good is it for anything but rich ladies' perfumes?"

Sarai couldn't answer, couldn't think. Gone the golden sands, the red-bark trees, the opal-bellied birds. Gray instead—ash-gray, ash over everything, choking the lungs and coating the skin.

"I need to begin," Sarai said. "The poison, I need—It needs to be today, now."

"There's still the Varash," Nissa said. "And you will need to recover from that before the Bellman's Sigh."

"Three days. One to recover," Sarai said.

"You need more than that," Nissa said.

"I don't," Sarai insisted.

Nissa stared at her levelly. "And to what end? When you are Master, you will be presented to the queen. Do you mean to poison her, with her 'tamers at her side? Or put a knife in her? Have you ever used a knife to cut into a living thing?"

"Yes," Sarai said, thinking of the rats and birds and toads she'd vivisected, to watch the way they died as poison rotted them inside out or tightened their veins to threads.

"One that could resist you?" Nissa asked, and Sarai's mouth closed. "Have you ever concealed a weapon? Have you ever looked a man in the eye before you killed him? Hm. No, child, not a knife. But perhaps you'll find a way."

"If I can only meet her," Sarai said. The rest, she would fill in.

Nissa nodded. "I'll help you, I already told you that. But if you do intend to use the access you win to kill the queen, perhaps you could refrain from telling me. She is my sister, after all."

Sarai left Nissa on the bluffs. Nissa was only so casual because she did not believe Sarai could harm the queen. But no one had believed Sarai could come this far. She was not the best, but she was the most determined, and she would do what she must.

She returned to her chamber, where Jarad waited. "Nissa has agreed to help," she said.

"How fortunate for you," he said without expression, and indicated a slip of paper on the table at her bedside. "Should you change your mind about killing yourself, your Mastery awaits." He left. Sarai tossed the slip of paper onto the floor. She went to her shelf, where she had already placed the Varash pill. There was no point, on an island full of essence-eaters, in trying to kill one another with poison, and anyone careless enough to ingest it by accident was better off dead; she need only ask, and she had been supplied with it.

She swallowed it dry and sat to wait for the pain to begin.

She was aware, from time to time, of a cool cloth on her brow and a dry, soft voice, but when she woke on the third day, Jarad was gone. She was dressed in clean clothes, her skin was washed with citrus-scented water, and her hair had been brushed and braided. There was a vial on the table beside her bed, and a slip of paper. She took one in each hand. The left: the poison. The court. Perhaps a chance to save her home; perhaps a chance to return to it.

Perhaps a certain death.

This is not your talent, Jarad's voice whispered, but she shut her heart to it. She crumpled the paper in her palm, made to toss it away.

Then stopped. She would look, at least, and then she could say her choice was made eyes open.

The name at the top stilled her heartbeat for half a second. The queen. A scent for the thrice-slain queen. If she liked it, Sarai would have her Mastery; if she did not—well, scent-makers were not killed by their failures, or for them, so readily as the rest. She would have another chance, in a year, that was all. It was the safe path. The coward's path.

This is your talent.

She would not fail the scent-maker's test, she knew that. She had fierce hope and belief when it came to the poison, but she was not fool enough to call it certainty. But what good was certainty, when it was toward such a useless end? To craft luxuries, amusements? Scents to spice a kiss or a dance, to cover up the stench of wounds, to give stale air the illusion of fresh breezes.

To summon memory. To conjure distant places. To stir passion.

She had once made a girl burst into tears, suddenly wrenched back home by a single jasmine-muddled breath. She had started a love affair, and ended one. She knew the people here from days and years of trading stories like scraps of cloth, grown more faded and made more precious by every pair of hands that touched them. She could distill in a single scent the long thread of their lives or a single instant.

The righthand path: to make life brighter, but not for her. For her, always the gray.

The lefthand path: to chance death for freedom. Perhaps, to save her home. She shut her eyes. Opened them.

Come home to us, her mother said, and she went to find Nissa.

"You'll still need a way to kill him, even if you survive," Nissa said, when Sarai told her what she'd chosen. "There are ways to kill at a touch. Poisons that seep through the skin."

"The poison-tamers would 'sense any poison," Sarai said. Every poison had its distinct essence; she could feel them buzzing in the supply room down the hall, where they were kept, their malice clear. Just as she had felt the ambergris, just as she felt the wind-salt-earth of the red-bark she kept in a sachet above her bed. No harmful substance would be allowed within fifty steps of the queen.

"We are only speaking hypothetically, of course," Nissa said. "But theoretically, you have learned a great deal of poison, but you have also learned a great deal else. How to mask a scent, how to alter it. How to disguise one thing as another, how to balance something noxious into blandness, how to make the unremarkable exotic."

"You're speaking of scents, not poisons."

"I'm speaking of essence," Nissa said. "Have you never noticed how your scents alter the essence as well as the physical perception of a substance?"

Sarai stared at the waves. "Why would you tell me this? She is your sister."

"Sweet can be transformed into bitter. Love can be transformed into hate," Nissa said. "I had a home once, too. My sister turned it to ash."

"Was she always the way she is now?" Sarai asked. She had trouble imagining the queen as a real person. Sitting next to the queen's sister, seeing the lines of her face, she had to acknowledge it.

"Of course not. But one can only live stewing in the fear of death deferred for so long before one starts to rot," Nissa said.

"What was it like with her, before?" Sarai asked.

"Is that what you want to hear?"

Sarai considered. "No," she said at last. "Not exactly."

"Then what do you need to know?"

"Everything," Sarai said.

When Nissa was done, long after the sun set and stole the barest hint of color from the rock, she clicked her tongue against her teeth. "There's one more thing you need to know," she said. "You need to know if you can truly do it. Kill someone. Be killed in turn. They'll know it was you. You might be able to conceal the poison long enough for it to do its harm, but even if the queen dies they'll guess the source, and they'll kill you."

"At least I'll get to see the court," Sarai said. She imagined she could see the spot of crimson at the edge of the horizon. It was too dark, of course, but she had stared at it so many times it appeared like an after-image in her vision.

Nissa spat. "You will at that."

At dawn they would begin. Sarai could not sleep. She would suffer, she would survive. She would create the poison that could kill the queen, and when Sarai touched the queen's skin to prove herself by 'taming the poison in the queen's veins, she'd pass along a new poison. A masked poison. She thought she knew how to do it. Which poison to use, which essences to blend with it to make it 'sense harmless.

The queen would die, and Sarai would die.

But first, she had to live.

She stared at the vial. Bellman's Sigh. One 'tamer in twenty earned Mastery. Most gave up before it, accepted lesser tasks on the island, other Masteries. Or died.

A knock on the door signaled Jarad's entry.

"Come to argue me out of it?" she said.

He sighed. "No. I came to sit with you. One way or another, I lose you in a few days. I'd like a little time with you while I can have it."

She looked up at him, surprised. She was hardly his first student. Not even the first he'd lost.

"But you are my favorite," he said, as if he knew what she was thinking. "And you are the best."

"Not at poison-taming," she said.

"No," he agreed.

"You think I'll die."

"Yes."

"It would be worth it."

"It would help no one. Least of all your kin," he said, and when he said it she thought he hid himself within the echo of that last word. "Please, Sarai. It is not your talent," he said, and said no more.

It is not your talent.

She set her jaw. It was true; she could not let it be true.

She held the red-bark sachet to her nose. She saw golden sand, heard her mother calling her home. Saw ash and smelled charred wood.

You'll never go home.

She let the halves of her hope fall away from one another. Jarad was right. It was not her talent. She would fail. She could not go home.

She took up the slip of paper, on which was written the queen's name.

This is your talent.

She could not go home. But perhaps she could save it.

The day the someday queen had felt the tarsnake's bite, she was walking with her sister along a disused path, the scent of lemongrass twining around them. They did not see the man by the river until they were quite close, did not think he could be anything but a laborer until they were steps away. And the young girl who would someday be queen did not think, until the man turned and flung the snake, that anyone might fail to love her.

The someday queen's sister, ten minutes younger but already less loved, killed the snake with a rock. The palace guards killed the man. The queen's sister clutched her close and quelled the poison, and the soldiers carried her home. They wrapped her in linen cloth, and her sister lay beside her, hugging her long, bare arms around her body. The queen's sister smelled of spices and the loamy earth by the river. The not-yet queen's physicians packed her wound with compresses, sharp and medicinal, full of herbs the poisoned girl could not name. The queen's sister whispered stories to her, reminding her of the salt-tang scent of their summer home, of the flowers that grew on the hillsides there. Of every place she had felt safe.

The queen's sister did not sleep for days. That day and for twenty years after, she kept her sister alive with her craft and her devotion. And when the assassin's blade robbed her of her usefulness, the queen kissed her brow once and sent her away.

Other moments, other stories—the death of an advisor, the lilies in the blood-choked water of her first war. Nissa told Sarai them all; she had been at her sister's side every day, nearly every hour, keeping her alive and watching her wither. Sarai picked among them. Salt-tang, honeysuckle: the scents of bliss. The day that destroyed it: lemongrass and loam, linen and spice. The scent of the husband she loved and who betrayed her: bergamot and amber.

She built up joy, shattered it; brewed a tincture of love and the loss of it, of security turned to rank fear. And she made it beautiful.

She went to Jarad with the vial in hand three hours past dawn. She had not slept; neither had he. He looked at the vial pinched between his fingertips, looked at her. "What is this?" he asked.

"My Mastery," she said. "There is a ship down at the dock. Send it with them." She walked away, and pretended she had not seen that he began to weep with the violence of relief.

Sarai returned the Bellman's Sigh to the supply room and went to her room to wait.

A week later, she had her Mastery, a dark tattoo on the back of her hand, indelible. "The queen is pleased," Jarad said, a strange tone in his voice. "The queen is, by all accounts, entranced." He gave her a look that was fear as much as satisfaction. She smiled to try to ease his worry, but he only shook his head and left her.

It was another two weeks before Nissa came. "She isn't dead," she said without preamble.

"She was not meant to die," Sarai said. "It isn't my talent."

"She won't leave her room. She won't speak. She's fallen into a melancholy mood," Nissa said, voice almost sweet. "She mutters of deceit and death and shoves even the poison-tamers' hands away. Not that they let her, of course. They've plied her with poppy to make her sleep, and our brother sits the throne in her place. For now, they say, until she's well."

"A great misfortune," Sarai said, nodding.

"They suspected you," Nissa said, and Sarai tasted something bitter in the back of her throat. "But when they gave the scent to others, it did nothing. It smells lovely, that's all. Some don't care for it at all. One man said it reminded him of his brother."

Sarai smiled. "There was nothing of poison in that scent," she said. "Only memory." Distilled and woven to lift the spirit, to shatter it.

"You will never leave this place, now," Nissa said, but even then she was wrong. When Nissa left, Sarai took down the sachet from her wall and pressed it to her nose. Red-bark and ambergris, salt-tang and oud-wood. Memories leapt and sparked and danced. She was on the golden sands again, the red-gold cliffs. In among the green-shadow trees, bare feet flying.

Come home to us, her mother called, and, eyes shut to the endless gray, she did.

———◆———

SURVIVAL STRATEGIES

━◆━

Helen Marshall

Barron St. John must have been nearing his seventies by that point. The pictures I'd copied from magazine covers and newspapers charted his rise from a rake-thin tower of a man, nearly six-three, clad in a badly fitting white wool jacket with a thick crop of black hair cut like a bowl around his ears to his older self: hair grey but still as thick as it had ever been, fine laugh lines etching the curve of that grinning, maniac mouth. In his heyday people had taken him to calling him the King of Horror, a real scaremeister—that term always made me laugh—but the man I saw in those later pictures had the look of a grandfather, which I suppose he was, one who could spin a yarn, sure, but not the kid who'd posed with a shotgun for his university paper under the headline "Vote dammit!"

My university had given me a small grant for my research project into St. John's career. I had planned to stay in Hotel 31, the cheapest place Luca and I had agreed we could afford. He had wanted me in midtown so I could walk most places. He was a worrier, had never been to New York and the idea of me riding the subway right then made him uneasy.

"It'll be fine," I told him, "nothing will happen. It isn't like that anymore. It hasn't been since the '90s." We both knew that wasn't exactly true. The situation was different now, but scarier in other ways. There were journalists being stopped at the borders, asked invasive questions. Not everyone was allowed in. And Luca, for all his woolly sweetness and soft English manners, had a serious stubborn streak. He was protective, I knew, and didn't like the idea of me traveling on my own, not after I'd reacted so badly to the procedure, and certainly not "abroad" as he called it in that charmingly old-fashioned way of his.

But "abroad" was what I had wanted. Even if it wasn't home for me, which lay four-hundred miles north across the border in Toronto where my sister lived, New York still felt more familiar than the still-drizzly streets of London in the summer. Besides, I suppose there was a part of me that wanted to see how bad things had got.

And St. John was a new obsession of mine, one I'd taken up in my recovery. Luca had been reading his pulpy looking paperbacks for years but I'd never touched them. They were too scary, I'd thought, too low brow. I remembered the garish paperbacks though, the ones that showed off his last name in huge embossed letters. They'd been ubiquitous when I was a kid. Each had a plain black cover with a silhouette cutaway so you had to turn the page to get the full effect. Rosie was the first I ever saw, his debut, the starting point for his surprising upward trajectory. It featured a small New Hampshire town—eerily similar to the one where I'd grown up, what had once been a small farming community until the petroleum processing plants transformed it. The town was engulfed in a crackling lightning storm. *Gory and horrifying*, read the cover, *you can't put it down!!!*

St. John didn't live in New York, but his former editor did: Lily Argo.

I'd found her email address online. Like St. John she must have been in her seventies, but was still working freelance. There were no pictures. The best I could find was a black and white shot of her and St. John at the signing of his fourth book, *What Is Mine*, the last they worked on together. Lily Argo was an inch of two taller than St. John, glorious, an Allison Janney look-alike, which meant the two of them towered over the line of moist-lipped teenage girls who were clustered around the table. That was back in '79.

When I first approached one of my friends—an anthology editor named Dylan Bone (real name or not, I never knew)—about the possibility of an article on the publication of *Rosie*, he told me Argo had died. Dylan had even written up her obituary for *Locus*—but in retrospect he couldn't remember how he'd first found out. She'd been one of the few female editors at Doubleday back then, mostly due to her lucky discovery of St. John. When I mentioned I'd been in contact with her, that she'd agreed to meet me, Dylan had stared at me thoughtfully.

"Just be careful," he said.

"About what?"

He'd just waved his hand. "You know," he said before lurching off to the bar to fetch another round.

I didn't have any problems with the border guards. The customs line was tense, but I'd always had that feeling whenever I entered the States. Once I'd swallowed two painkillers before a flight back to London and the random swipe they'd done on my hands had registered a false positive for explosives or drugs. I'd been taken to a small backroom where a dark-haired woman in a uniform demanded to know why I had been in the country. I kept apologizing, I don't know why. She had to search me by hand and the process was brusque and businesslike. She asked me to remove my bra. Then someone else came in, a heavy-set man with a broad forehead. He didn't look at me. Neither of them did. Afterward they let me go but ever since I'd been stopped for "random" checks whenever I boarded a plane. This time though the guard took one look at me and waved me through. I must have looked harmless to him.

Hotel 31 was as old as the Overlook, mostly derelict with a walk-in elevator whose grill door you had to close yourself. The room was sparse, but by that point exhaustion had sunk into my skin. I called Luca to tell him I'd arrived and then collapsed under the thin covers.

All night I could hear animal sounds in the walls. The bodies of whatever moved beyond the peeling wallpaper hummed like batteries. Still, I slept. And in the morning I felt better than I had in weeks. Not mended, but stronger.

I was still in that dusky phase of grieving so that sometimes when I slept it felt I had fallen through a hole in the world. Each morning I woke up as a different person, discovered new wrinkles at the corner of my eyes, wires of thick, unrecognizable, gray hair. The doctor warned me of changes in my body, cramping, small clots of blood between my legs. I had expected my breasts to shrink but they'd only gotten larger. I read online the best thing to do was to bind them tightly with a snug towel and apply ice for ten minutes on, twenty minutes off. He hadn't told me how old I would feel after.

I had given myself three days to acclimatize to jetlag before I met up with Lily Argo.

In the mean time I'd arranged a visit to Doubleday, St. John's first publisher. In the last thirty years Doubleday had joined with Dell and Bantam which in turn joined up with Random House. Size, they had thought, was the best way to survive an uncertain economic climate.

Two weeks ago I'd contacted an editor at Random House in the hopes he might know if the company had kept some of the records from St. John's days. But after the bag search and the metal detectors, when I was buzzed into the offices, a blond receptionist told me my meeting had been postponed. She was young, slickly made up in that New York way with manicured fingers and perfect plucked eyebrows. I was wearing a dark blue cardigan which, seeing her, suddenly felt so English, so matronly I almost laughed.

So I waited in the reception for an hour, browsing the display copies of new books by Margaret Atwood and Chimamanda Ngozi Adichie. They too were slickly produced.

After a while I pulled out my beat-up copy of Strangers and Friends, a collection of short stories St. John had published in gentlemen's magazines like *Cavalier* and *Penthouse* over the years. The book had never been one of St. John's most popular but I'd been thumbing my way through it slowly for weeks. On the flight I had started a story called "The Survivalist" in which a doctor finds himself trapped alone in a bunker after a nuclear blast. He lives there for years, decades, devouring canned peaches and Spam until finally he comes to the end of his stashed supplies. He knows he doesn't have many options left. He can open up the door, risk contamination for a sight of the outside world—or he can continue to wait. The doctor stares at the door, wanting desperately to go out, but he can't bring himself to open it. The story ends as, driven half-mad with hunger, he begins to contemplate how long he could survive eating first the flesh of his legs, his thighs, how much he could withstand. He is a doctor after all, and he thinks it could be quite some time . . .

The story was gross, and it had all the macabre glee you would expect from a St. John chiller. But I didn't feel scared by it. No, what upset me most was its sense of futility. The doctor had given up on hope. He wasn't waiting for rescue. He didn't believe anyone else in the world was alive. He was simply . . . persisting. If he was the last man on earth he wanted to last as long as possible. It was grotesque. Why didn't he open the door? That's what Luca would said when I tried to explain the plot him. But then Luca was the kind of man who *would* have opened the door. He couldn't see another way of living.

Another hour passed. Eventually the receptionist waved me over. Her manicured nails glinted dully in the light. "I'm sorry, ma'am," she said, "but the records from those years haven't been maintained. I didn't even know we were the ones who published Barron St. John." She gave a little laugh.

I asked her what that meant for me.

"No one's free to meet you. We converted to digital years ago," she said, barely sparing me a glance. "Whatever we had we dumped back then. Besides, who reads that trash anyway?"

☙

After that I found myself at loose ends so I called up a friend of mine, Benny Perry.

Benny and I had gone to grad school together at the University of Toronto, both of us doing doctorates in medieval literature in those early days after the financial crash when we still thought the market would recover enough to give us jobs. I'd kept at it, spinning my work on the scribal culture that produced Chaucer's *Canterbury Tales* into a postdoc in Oxford and then riding that into a full-time position in Publishing Studies of all things at a former polytechnic university. It wasn't glamorous, not like Oxford had been, but I liked the students, I liked my colleagues and I liked the work itself: imagining how books moved through time and all the people who left their mark on them along the way.

Benny had taken another route. He'd always had talent with photography and after he dropped out of the program he'd moved to New York and taken a job with *House & Garden* before it closed. It'd paid well enough that he'd stuck with photography, jumping from one magazine to another until he had enough of a portfolio to go freelance. He'd taken one of those famous pictures of Trump, the one where his face seems to be receding into the folds of flesh around his neck. In the past couple of months I'd seen it on social media from time and reprinted in the papers.

"It's made things a bit hard for me," Benny told me as we sat sipping margaritas in The Lantern's Keep, a classy place near Times Square where the cocktails cost four times what they would at home. There had been a teary week before Luca and I made our decision when I'd given up alcohol, and even after we changed our minds I still hadn't felt like touching the stuff. This was the first drink I'd had in eight months.

"How do you mean?"

"Well it's brought me lots of attention, sure, but not the good kind, you know? Trump supporters *hate* that picture. Trump does too, which is why it gets recycled so often."

Benny's face looked strained and he fidgeted with his glass. He wasn't quite how I remembered him. Benny was always a big man, a cornfed Iowa type whose Baptist parents had taught him to shun dancing and drink. When I'd met him at orientation he'd been shy, a bit overwhelmed. But after those first awkward weeks he'd just thrown himself into everything. He had this irrepressible love of the new, and he'd taken to those things he'd missed out on most: booze, women—then men, dancing late into the night with this kind of unselfconscious clumsiness which made you want to join in.

He was much thinner now, that kind of thinness that didn't look healthy. "I'm worried about Emmanuel," he said, "worried about . . . well. Anyway. People can be absolute shits, can't they?"

I agreed that they could.

"But you're looking good," Benny said, and I caught his eyes skimming over my breasts. Even though it didn't mean anything coming from him I still blushed and pulled at the cardigan. "But not . . . I don't know, maybe not entirely good?" he was going on. "Hell. I don't know what I'm trying to say."

I took his hand gently and told him not to worry about it.

As The Lantern's Keep started to fill up eventually we wandered out into the street. It was hot and swampy, that kind of early August weather that makes you feel as if you've been wrapped in a damp blanket and beaten. We headed south toward the West Village by foot so I could see the sights. North was Central Park and Trump Towers, which were all basically off limits now. New York hadn't changed so much, not in terms of that strange and beautiful blend of architecture and anger, but there were bits that alarmed me. Like all the police cars all had stickers listing the reward for information on cop-killers with a number you could call.

While I told Benny about the project I was working on. It turned out he'd read St. John as a kid, which surprised me, given his background.

"What I remember about him was that my parents were reading him. They never read anything like that otherwise. Murder and cannibalism and demons and all that stuff. But *Faction of Fire*, you know, it was all about faith, wasn't it? In that book there was no getting around it: The Devil was real. And I suppose that's what my parents thought anyway. Good and evil weren't abstract concepts to them. There were good folk and there were bad folk. And it wasn't just that the bad folk made bad decisions. They were . . . *bad*. It was something more fundamental. Badness worked through them. It was something tangible, real. And St. John, well, his books were all about that, weren't they?"

Benny grinned at me and for a moment I could see his younger self peering out, that kid who'd never touched a drop of liquor in his life before I met him.

"How're your parents doing?" I asked him because that was the kind of thing we were supposed to ask one another now that we weren't kids anymore.

"Dad had a stroke two years ago," Benny said with a shrug. "I go back when I can to help her out. She's lonely, I know, but whenever I do go we just end up fighting."

I didn't ask him about Emmanuel, about whether his parents knew. I figured probably they did. There were enough profiles floating around about Benny's photos so you could only avoid knowing if you really tried.

"How are you and Luca doing?"

"Good."

"He didn't want to come with you?"

"Couldn't get away. You know how it is with these NGOs. Anytime he leaves he feels like he's letting people down."

"It's good what he's doing," Benny told me. "We need more people like him right now." After a moment he stretched and I heard the joints in his shoulders pop. "It must be hard writing horror stories now, you know? It seems like that's all we've got these days. I can't bear to watch the news anymore."

I didn't sleep well that night. When I'd glanced at the papers they were filled with stories about tensions escalating, something to do with the South China Sea islands and whether the US was being too aggressive. John Mc-Cain was trying to dial things back but you could tell he was getting tired of it. His eyes looked sharp and a little bit scared.

I'd had panic attacks all throughout the October leading up to the election. There'd been Brexit, of course, our own particular mess. At a conference last summer an American colleague had told me, "What we're seeing is radical politics. People stopped believing that they mattered to the system—but all that's different now. It's exciting, isn't it? Anything could happen." Trump had seemed funny back then, dangerous but still avoidable. They called it all a horror show but you could tell there was fascination underneath it all. How close could we come to disaster? But Hillary was ahead in the polls. Some of the Republicans were denouncing Trump, trying to put a little distance between themselves for when the eventual shellacking came on November eighth.

But it didn't come. For weeks after, all throughout the Christmas break, whenever I heard Trump's name it was as if there was a loud gong echoing in my head. My feed was filled with anguish, betrayal, heartbreak. But I had seen all that already. I felt immured, resilient—and besides I still didn't believe, not really, that it would happen. Then eventually the cold hard truth settled in when I watched the inauguration with Luca. As Trump walked to the podium

I burst out laughing, I don't know why, the sheer cognitive dissonance of the whole thing. I felt hysterical. My palms were sweating.

Afterward I learned St. John had written a novel about something similar, *Answering the King*, about a madman who cheats his way to becoming the President of the United States. Eventually it comes down to a fifteen-year-old girl tormented with visions of the past and the future to stop him. The question at the heart of it is: if you could go back in time to stop Hitler, would you? They had made a movie about it with Steve Buscemi. I don't remember who played the girl, only how wide her eyes were, how she captured that world-weariness so well for someone so young. She was a Cassandra. No one would listen to her.

That was the night when the whole thing with Luca happened. Normally we were very careful. I hadn't been in my job for very long and he'd just moved across the country to live with me. We had talked about having kids one day but . . . We weren't careful enough. Disaster crept in the way it always does.

I called Argo the next day. It was the first time I'd spoken to her and her voice was thin and cagey with a flat Ohio accent. It sounded as if it were coming away from much further away than the Upper East Side.
It felt strange to be listening to her voice and I thought about what Dylan Bone had told me. I'd read the obituary in fact, half as a joke and half because I knew Dylan didn't make mistakes very often. He'd cut his teeth in the eighties horror boom and still made most of his money by convincing writers like St. John and Clive Barker to give him new material. It might sound mercenary but it isn't, not really: Bone was a believer, a horror fanatic. He loved the stuff and even when the market dropped out of it in the nineties he had kept at it, putting out anthology after anthology with cheesy hand-drawn skeletons or zombified hands reaching out of the grave. Argo had been part of that, someone who'd *made* the genre in its heyday.

One the phone Argo was polite and she agreed to meet me for lunch the next day at a cafe. "It'll have to be close to my apartment," she told me, "I can't move very well now."

I told her I understood, and could meet her wherever she wanted.

"What's this about then? Really?" Her tone wasn't querulous, but wondering. "You know I wrote a chapter about working with St. John for some anthology twenty years ago, *Devilish Discussions* or something like that."

I hesitated because I didn't really have an answer. Yes, I knew the story about how she'd been sent St. John's first manuscript by mistake. It had been meant to go to her boss but he'd been on vacation. She'd liked it but her boss wouldn't touch it, and she didn't have enough support inside Doubleday to push it through, not then, a low-level assistant. But they'd kept in touch, writing letters when the mood took one or the other. Then when *Rosie* had come along it had been "a day of glory"—so she called it.

I gave her the answer I gave most of my colleagues. St. John had changed the genre, really changed it. For one brief moment horror hadn't been the red-haired stepchild of fiction. Horror had been *king*. And I wanted to know how that had happened. Part of my answer was true. I'd always been fascinated by the way books were made, the countless decisions that went into them. But if I were really honest it was simply because I'd become a fan, a real fan—maybe not Dylan Bone level—but my admiration for St. John was genuine.

It was more than that though. The real reason was one I couldn't quite put my finger on, but it had something to do with stories of chance— which St. John's certainly was. And that underneath every story is a pivotal moment when things changed. I wanted to know what that looked like. I needed to know if Argo had understood when that manuscript crossed her desk what it would mean, if she'd felt a chill when he opened the envelop. Like someone had walked on her grave.

That afternoon Benny took me out to the Cloisters for old time's sake, and it was beautiful, just like he'd promised it would be. The place was a mishmash of architecture taken from a series of medieval abbeys in France, Catalan, and the Occitan, simultaneously peaceful and surreal, liminal, a sliver of another world transplanted into New York.

"I thought you'd like it," Benny told me. We were staring at a tree that had been shaped to fit one of the alcoves in the garden. Its branches curved unnaturally like a menorah to fill the space. I couldn't help but wonder how it had been manipulated, what sort of subtle violence had pressurized the wood to assume the shape it had.

"I do," I told him, shivering despite the mid-day heat.

"So, tomorrow. The editor, what's her name again?" He snapped his fingers. "Argo, right? Lily Argo. You're going to interview her. What about St. John then? Any chance you'll get to speak to him?"

I didn't think so. St. John lived in New Hampshire and I had no idea what kind of relationship the two of them still had. If they kept in touch. If Argo would even like me.

"Of course she will. You're—well, you're the *makeles quene*, aren't you?" He smiled. "You are without blot."

"Someone back home said she was dead," I told him uneasily. I still didn't like that part of the story. Why would Dylan have thought that?

"Huh," Benny said. "It sounds like the beginning of a ghost story, doesn't it? Like she'll bestow her wisdom on you, settle her unfinished business, and vanish into the night."

"It sounds exactly like that."

"But maybe you're lucky, not seeing St. John."

I asked him what he meant.

"You know. He's bound to be pretty weird, isn't he? I mean he's been writing that stuff for more than forty years now. You can't keep that close to the darkness without some of it sticking to you."

It wasn't the first time I'd heard something like this before. I was used to getting it myself sometimes at the university. But the horror writers I'd met were among the most well-adjusted people I knew, certainly they were much calmer than the other writers I tended to deal with. Some people said it was because there wasn't much money in horror writing these days. But I thought it was something else: writers were good at channeling their anxieties into something productive. We all have those nasty thoughts, those worries that maybe we don't love our partners as much as we should, or maybe they don't love us. Fears that maybe something awful will happen tomorrow. The phone will ring and it will be the police. An accident somewhere. Or a fight escalated, a button pushed.

"When I studied the Middle Ages," I told him, "it always seemed like it must have been so difficult for those people. I mean, the Black Death wiped out forty percent of the population. Imagine whole villages lost, your family—everyone you've ever met—wiped out."

"I know," he said, "I just couldn't take living like that. I'd, I dunno. I'd go crazy, I guess."

I wondered if he really would go crazy. Or if he was going crazy right now, waiting for that call about Emmanuel. Waiting for Trump to finally get around to signing a new Executive Order. I had always liked Benny because he had a sense of outrage, a keen abhorrence of injustice. I knew he had marched in those early protests and knew that he wasn't marching anymore. He didn't want to draw attention to himself. Benny was strong but he was adaptable. He was finding ways to survive, to keep marking his art—but doing it so it didn't hurt Emmanuel.

Luca was the same way. Most nights he didn't come home until close to midnight. There was always more he felt he could be doing. For a while I'd felt really proud of him. And then when things got bad I'd just felt resentful, angry at him for spending so much time saving other people when what I really wanted was for him to save me.

In the gift shop I chose a postcard for him, a picture of the Flemish tapestry called *The Hunt for the Unicorn*. It showed five young men in aristocratic clothing with their spears and their dogs. If it weren't for the title you wouldn't have been able to tell what they were doing there. I wanted to choose one with the unicorn but all of them looked too violent or depressing. Something about the unicorn in captivity, collared, in a fence that can barely hold her, reminded me of *Answering the King*, and how the girl had been taken to prison after she shot the president. There had been a coda at the end of the novel, the little girl twenty years later, grown up, in solitary confinement. They had thought she had gone mad because she wouldn't stop hurting herself.

But St. John showed the real reason. The girl had had another vision, one worse than what she'd stopped all those years ago. But this time there was nothing she could do about it.

I couldn't get hold of Luca that night. He wasn't answering his email and when I tried him at home—and then at work—the phone just rang and rang. It wasn't that unusual. Sometimes there were emergencies, and Luca would become so totally absorbed in them he would forget everything else. There were emergencies like that, I knew, one every few days it seemed. So eventually I left a message saying I loved him. I tried the TV but got nothing but static. Eventually I settled down to read. It was another story from *Strangers and Friends* but this one was about a haunted house called "Question the Foundations." It was a twist on the trope: the houses weren't haunted by people so much as the people by houses. In St. John's world each person had a tiny space within them, an impression of the place where they had been born. And it remained there, like a scar, or a memory. And everyone else could see it too, who you were and where you came from. Except there was this young boy who didn't have a place like that. He had nothing. He had come from nowhere. And because he had nothing he scared people.

I put the book down, confused and unsure of myself. The story bothered me but I didn't know why. It was different from the others, softer, sadder. There was no real horror in the story. It had been about loneliness. How it felt to be hollow, an outsider. Rootless.

Maybe it was just those constellations of images, emptiness and violence. Luca had told me a story once about how his family used to keep chickens. He had lived in the middle of a wood. One day a fox break into the henhouse and tore open all the chickens. He'd found their bodies, or what was left of them, the next morning. Inside their bodies he had found strings of growing eggs, like pearls.

After he told me that I couldn't sleep and it was the same feeling now. I didn't have any regrets. Luca and I had talked, and he had left the decision to me. There had been no pressure, none from him anyway. But I'd been watching the news. And when the first bomb exploded in Paddington Station it had been like a warning sign. Not now. It wasn't safe. Things would settle down soon, they had to. And then we could try again.

I put the book down and touched my stomach gently, tentatively. Beneath my fingers all I could feel was my own thick flesh.

Three times I passed the cafe before I finally had the courage to meet Lily Argo. I could see her—at least I thought it was her—sitting in the courtyard with her walker folded up beside her. She had long white hair and a red-and-gray printed dress with long sleeves. I knew her because of how tall she was, even a little stooped over. She still had at least six inches on me.

"Ms. Argo?" I asked her and she nodded politely while I pulled up a seat.

"So you're the one who's come asking about Barron St. John."

"That's right." I tentatively launched into my pitch: an article on St. John's early publication history, documenting her involvement in acquiring and editing his first title. She stopped me with a wave of her hand.

"Sure, honey," she said with a wide, generous smile, "you don't need to go on like that. I'm happy to talk about those days though I confess they seem a while ago now. You know I got that manuscript by accident, don't you?"

I nodded and she seemed relieved.

"Good, so we're not starting from scratch. What you want is the story, I take it, of how Bear—that's what I always called him—and I got along in those early days? Where the horror came from?" I nodded again and took out my phone but she eyed it warily. "I'll tell it as best I can and you can make of it whatever you will—but no recordings, okay? You can listen and you can write down what you get from it but you only get to hear it once."

What was I supposed to say? Already I could feel a kind of strange buzz around her, the magnetic pull of her charisma. I had wanted her story and here she was, ready to give it to me.

"I was pretty young in those days," she began, "when I first started working for Doubleday. I'd grown up in Ohio which I never liked very much in part because it didn't seem like I was much use to my parents. I was a reader, even then, but they had wanted me to go to one of the nursing schools but I knew I'd never be happy with something like that, taking care of people all the time. So when I was seventeen I ran off to New York City.

"Publishing was still very much a gentleman's sport back then and if you were a woman you were either someone's secretary or you were publishing feminist pamphlets and burning your bra. I was the former." She paused and took a delicate sip from her Coke. Her lipstick remained unsmudged though it left a trace of red on her straw. "Most of us at the time wanted to be writers. I suppose I did as much as anyone, and so we'd spend our days editing and we'd spend our nights writing. What was funny was that we knew all the people we were sending our drivel to, we'd met them at luncheons or for afterhours drinks. I was embarrassed. I was a good editor and *because* I was a good editor I knew I wasn't a very good writer. I thought, how on earth will these men take me seriously if they see what I'm coming up with?

"So I did what most women did at the time, or anyone who wasn't Daphne du Maurier anyway, and I made up a name. Mine was Victor Wolf, which today seems so damned fake I don't know why no one thought anything of it. Or maybe they did but they just didn't care. Anyway I may have been writing garbage but eventually the garbage got better and I started getting some of it published. It was what they called Kooks and Spooks stuff, I suppose, sort of crime fiction but with some other bits thrown in, monsters sometimes, and ghosts. Possession—or Russian spies using hypnosis to control young American teenagers, that sort of thing. There was a real taste for that sort of thing back then. By the early seventies the papers were going crazy, telling us the irrationalism of our reading was helping the Commies and we had to get back to old-fashioned American literature. But *Rosemary's Baby* was an absolute hit, and then there was *The Exorcist* and people just wanted more of it.

"That was when Bear's first manuscript came across my desk. The two of us call it an accident but it wasn't that, not really. See, I was used to reading submissions for Donnie Rogers and when I finished Bear's first one I knew there was magic in it, raw, maybe, but magic nonetheless. And I knew Donnie was slated for laparoscopic gallbladder surgery. He was going to be off for at least a week recovering. That was when I tried to pitch the manuscript.

"Of course, I got laughed out of the offices. No one took me seriously and when Donnie came back he heard what I'd done and he bawled me out in front of the whole crew. Jesus, he took a strip off one side of me and then the other. After that I didn't dare try anything like that for a good long while.

"Still, Bear had appreciated the support. He was poor as a church mouse and he and Mya had a second little one on the way. He tried me with this and that a couple of times but it never really made it anywhere. I guess it was while he was sending me his stuff that I sent him one of mine. God, the nerve I had!" she chuckled and I couldn't help but chuckle along with her. "Well Bear wrote back and said it was pretty good, and I said it was better than pretty good, that *Playboy* had taken it. Bear had been trying to crack *Playboy* but hadn't managed it by that point.

"For six months Bear went silent after that and I guess I thought maybe I'd offended him. Men don't like being shown up, not then, not now. That's why there's all the craziness there is today. Women are afraid of violence, but men? Men are afraid of humiliation. Humiliation to them is like dying over and over and over again. And speaking of humiliation I had just about survived mine. Donnie Rogers had moved over to New American Libraries and I was covering for him while they looked for a replacement. That was when the next manuscript crossed my desk."

"That was *Rosie*?" I asked her.

"Indeed it was, though it was called Revenge of the Stars at the time which was a godawful title, I have to say."

"And this time it stuck?"

"Not right away it didn't. The ending was clunky. It had Rosie transforming into this giant radioactive slug thing and devouring the town that way. Pure St. John, you know. He always loved the EC Comics stuff. People want to say he's got literary chops, and sure he does, but a part of him is pure pulp and is perfectly content to stay that way, thank you very much."

"So what happened?" I wanted to know.

"Oh, that's the easy bit. Some good luck, I suppose. Ira Levin was big and Bear's book was enough like that for me to pull together an advance for him. Small, you know. The real success came later with the paperback sales and that wasn't me, not exactly. But I suppose if what you're after is who found Barron St. John then it's me as much as it was anyone."

She paused there to take another long drag of her Coke. While she'd been talking she seemed so animated, so full of vigor but as the seconds stretch on I could see how old she was now, how time had etched fine lines around her lips. Her wrists were thin and frail, the skin bunching and slack at the same time.

She moved then, pulled up a black leather handbag and began to dig around in it. Eventually she came up with a Christmas card. "Look at that," she said, her eyes sharp. The paper was old and creased in several places. When I opened it there I found a simple handwritten note. *To Lilian*, it said, *a real wolf in sheep's clothing. We owe you so much. Love, Bear and Mya St. John*

Lily was smiling slightly as she showed it to me, smiling and watching to see my reaction. I tried to smile back but there was a part of me that felt disappointed. Most of the story was what she had published in that chapter. Little of it really surprised me. It felt rehearsed, the way you keep old memories by telling yourself the story behind them again and again. Whatever I was looking for it wasn't there.

I was getting restless and it seemed like she was finished when she cocked her head to the side. "That's not what you wanted to hear, was it?"

I tried to tell her it was great, wonderful stuff. It would certainly make it into the article.

"Sure it will," she said, "but you didn't need any of it. Certainly you didn't need to fly over here from England just to get this story, did you? I could've told you that over the phone. You didn't need to come."

I shrugged.

"What you wanted was him, wasn't it? You wanted Bear."

"Maybe," I told her wearily. The heat was starting to get to me, making me a touch queasy.

"It isn't easy, you know," she said, "to try to tell your story when the best parts are about someone else." She sighed. "You know, I had to give up writing once I found St. John. It wasn't like it had been before. We were so busy all the time. St. John could write like a madman, he was *fast*. There was always another book. And then things got tricky with the contracts. You must know about this?"

I did. Everyone did. St. John had left Doubleday after a series of well-publicized contract disputes. Doubleday had been keeping most of the profits on the paperback sales and he felt he deserved a bigger cut. Doubleday wouldn't budge and eventually he left.

"There wasn't much I could do for him. They wouldn't give him a better deal and they wouldn't listen when I told them how serious he was about leaving. When he finally did switch publishers all those men at the top said it was *my* fault. I got parked for a while editing books on what types of music you can play to help your plants grow, that sort of kooky trash. After a year or so they fired me."

I fiddled with my own straw, unsure how to react to any of this.

"Bear didn't take me with him, see. I told him not to. I told him I had enough status in the company—but I was wrong. When you're on top you always think you're going to stay there forever, that there aren't sharks circling beneath. But I guess Barron knew about those sharks. The one thing he knew about was the sharks. He could be one himself when he needed to."

"You didn't want to go back to writing?"

"Nah, I felt I'd spent my chance by that point. I think I had one lucky break in me—and it went to St. John. There wasn't going to be another. I got by after that. I moved over to another house for a little while and convinced St. John to come do a book for us. But by that point things were different. He was a superstar and I felt spent. I had had enough of horror. It was the '80s. Despite everything it still felt as if the world was falling apart. There was the banking crisis, the AIDS epidemic. The people weren't reading the news though. They were reading Bear.

"I did write one more story though. I tried to sell it myself but no one would buy it. Victor Wolf had been forgotten. Bear liked it though. And he knew I was in danger of losing my mortgage. So he sent it out for me, under his name. When it sold to the *New Yorker*—his first real literary sale though God knows he deserved others and got them eventually—he gave me the profits." Her smile then was bitter. "I was grateful, you know. At the time he said it was only fair. I had made his name after all. I should get the use of it whenever I wanted.

"And I was grateful at the time. I kept my brownstone, paid it off eventually. When he sold the collection he gave me the whole advance. For a while I thought about going back to Ohio but I still couldn't admit to my parents I hadn't been able to last in New York. So instead I stayed."

She stared at me for a moment or two after that and I could feel the cool ripple of sadness passing over me like a shadow.

"Someone told me you died," I said, just to break the spell of her silence.

"Of the two of us, Barron was always the shark, you see?" she told me wryly, "No, I didn't die. I just learned something he never figured out: how to stay alive when you stop moving."

That evening I collected my things from Hotel 31.

Benny offered to drive me to the airport but I told him he didn't need to do that. I could get a taxi. The university had given me a budget for that. When he said okay it sounded like there was relief in his voice, and I wondered if that meant Emmanuel was home. Or maybe it was just that he didn't want to get so close to the airport. There were regular protests still going on. People were angry about the deportations but no one knew how to stop them.

"Did you get what you wanted from Lily Argo?" Benny asked me. "She wasn't just a ghost?" I told him I hadn't really known what I wanted but I was certain, despite everything, I had met Lily Argo. But probably I was going to scrap the story. My Head of Department would be pissed but that was how these things went. Sometimes you thought you had something and you didn't.

What she had told me felt too invasive to write about. What I had wanted, I realized, was not just her story but a glimpse of her secret self. I didn't have a right to it. And that's what had made me want it even more. Maybe we all have a secret self: some of us keep it chained in the basement of our minds while others like St. John learn how to feed it.

"Well," he said, "it was good to see you anyway. Give my love to Luca. You tell him to take proper care of you."

I promised I would.

While I waited for my flight to board I watched the news. We were all watching the news. We couldn't help it. Tense security officers patrolled the hallways with machine guns at the ready, just in case. There were fewer travelers those days, fewer coming in, fewer getting out. But I felt a kind of solidarity with the others as I eyes were glued to the screens. We were liminal people moving from one reality to another. We were going home.

So we watched the footage of explosions in Yemen. Pleas from refugees who had found themselves trapped in abandoned tenements, living in filth. It was only when I saw the story about the bomb that had gone off on a train along the Victorian Line that I remembered Luca still hadn't called me back.

I was watching them pulling survivors out of the rubble and the blood gelled to ice in my veins. I couldn't move. It had happened then. It had happened. Time seemed to slow. Luca mostly worked from Cambridge but the NGO had offices in London. He went there from time to time. When had I last heard from him? Who could I call to check? But by that point the attendant was calling me forward. I didn't move. She called me again and the people behind me began to murmur. I must have had a dazed expression on my face, a look they didn't like. The attendant called me a third time as an officer drew near. It was only then I was able to move. I showed them my passport and made my way down the ramp.

Inside the plane most of the seats were empty. The air was canned, stale tasting in my mouth. I wondered if I might have a panic attack but out on the runway I didn't dare check my phone again. The hostesses were murmuring to each other. I could tell they were twitchy. But I already a strange calm was taking hold of me—a sense of icy horror. There was something inevitable about what was happening. There was nothing I could do to stop it. Whatever had happened had happened.

And this feeling? It wasn't the same as all those St. John books I had read. There I could find purpose, structure—meaning in all the bad things that had happened. But outside there was only chaos. The unraveling of beautiful things into violence. It signified nothing.

As the plane taxied down the runway I settled back in my chair and tried to sleep.

———◆———

THE SWIMMING POOL PARTY

Robert Shearman

Once in a while a memory of Max will pop into her head, and she won't quite know what to do with it. Totally unbidden, and triggered by nothing in particular, and sometimes she won't mind, she'll let the memory play out like a little movie. That time, one Christmas, when they'd given Max his first bike—it had taken Tom ages to wrap it up, and once it was done it was just so obvious, the wrapping paper did nothing to disguise what was underneath at all; "We'll have to do it again," she'd said, "but this time we'll put lumps and bumps in," and Tom hadn't minded, they'd done it again, together, and in the end the present for Max under the tree looked like nothing on earth, and certainly nothing like a bicycle; that Christmas morning they told him to save that present for last though he was itching to open it, and he wasn't disappointed. Oh, she still remembers that exquisite look of joy and surprise on his face when he realized Santa had brought him the bike he wanted after all. Or—there was that memory of when they were on holiday, where was it, Cornwall? It was warm, anyway. And they were all sitting out in the beer garden, Max had a lemonade. There was a wasp. It landed on Max. They shooed it off, and the wasp went onto the table, and Tom upturned his empty pint glass and put it on top. And Max was crying, and she was suddenly so frightened—had he been stung? Where was he stung? Would he have an allergic reaction? But he wasn't stung at all— "The poor buzzie," he kept saying, "the poor buzzie." The poor buzzie was trapped, flying around its beery prison looking for some way out, bashing its body against the sides of the glass. Max was howling now, he said, "Please let the buzzie out, it's so scared," and Tom took the glass away, and the wasp didn't sting anyone, it flew off, and Max laughed, all tears forgotten, and went back to his lemonade.

Or, of course—there was that memory, the first memory. The doctor putting Max into her arms. And her realizing that it was really all over, the whole giving birth thing, and it hadn't been quite as difficult or painful as she'd feared. And Tom was grinning. And she'd spend so long privately worrying about this very moment—but when I'm actually there with it, with my own child, what happens if I don't like it? Don't want it? Can feel nothing for it? Max crying, and she crying herself with relief, that this tiny human being in her arms that had come from inside her and was a part of her was something she loved with all her heart, and she would love it forever, until the day she died.

Sometimes she's so moved by the memories that it takes her a little while to realize that nothing is wrong, nothing is lost—that it's Tom who's moved out, and Max is still there, and alive, and well, and probably playing computer games in his bedroom. And it would only take a moment to go and see him, and look at him, and give him a hug. And she might even do this. And she might not.

Max is in trouble at school again. It isn't his fault. (Oh, it is never his fault.) She shouldn't be too concerned, but would she mind coming in some time and having a little chat with the head of year? This Tuesday? Wonderful.

The head of year, a decidedly ugly woman called Mrs. Trent, invites her to sit down, and asks her if she'd like a cup of tea.

Max is being bullied. Yes, that little spate of bullying that had taken place in the spring term had been dealt with; this was a different spate of bullying altogether. Mrs. Trent is just wondering if something at home is the matter. She knows there's been problems, Max isn't very forthcoming, but . . . Would she like some sugar? Here, she'll pass the sugar. There you are.

"He still sees his father every other weekend," she says. "That's quite a lot. That's more than some kids get when their fathers live at home."

"How long has it been since you and your husband separated?" asks Mrs. Trent. She tells her. "And was it amicable?" Are they ever amicable, really?

"We just worry," says Mrs. Trent. "Because Max is a good boy. But we just think. That with the amount of bullying he gets. We just wonder. Is he in some way inviting it?"

Of course he's inviting it, she thinks. He's weak. He's weak, just like his father is. He's one of life's fuckups. You can see it written all over his face. Like his father, he's never going to be anyone, or achieve anything. It's like he's got a sign on his back saying "Kick Hard Here." What she says is, "What do you mean?"

Mrs. Trent gives a cautious smile. "Max doesn't seem to have any friends. Not a single friend at all. Does he have friends at home?"

She thinks, I want the bullies to go after him. I want them to hurt him. Maybe it'll knock some sense into him, make him grow up a bit. Is it wrong that I take the side of the bullies over my own child? Of course it is. This is the position he puts me in. He makes me into a bad mother. He makes me into a bad person. The little shit. She says, "He has friends. He has *me*."

Mrs. Trent doesn't seem very convinced by that. That cautious smile looks even more watery. She wonders if Mrs. Trent has children of her own. She guesses that she doesn't.

What they agree is, they'll both monitor Max more carefully from now on. In the classroom, and at home. Because maybe there's nothing to be worried about. But no one wants this to become a situation anyone *has* to worry about. It all feels rather inconclusive, and she supposes Mrs. Trent thinks the same, and she realizes that Mrs. Trent probably only called this meeting because it was part of her job, she doesn't really care what happens to her weak little son either. They shake hands.

Max is waiting for his mother on a bench in the corridor outside. He gets up when he sees her. "Well then," she says. She knows she'll have to come up with something better than that eventually. But right now it's the best that she's got.

"Are you cross with me?" he asks.

"No."

To prove she's not cross, on the way home she takes him to MacDonald's as a treat. She watches him as he joylessly dips French fries into a little tub of barbeque sauce, the sauce drips onto the table. "Any good?" she says, and he nods. Then she takes him home.

"Is there something you want to talk about?" she asks, and it's right before his bedtime, and she supposes she ought to have asked earlier, but she's asking him *now*, isn't she? He shrugs, and it's such an ugly little gesture. Then he drags his heels upstairs to his bedroom and closes the door. And she thinks: remember the bike. Remember the wasp. Remember when he came out of you, shiny and brand new.

She recognizes it as the exact same shrug Tom gives her a couple of days later when he comes to pick up Max for the weekend. She thinks she should tell him what had happened at school, about the teacher's concern their son has no one to play with; and there it is, that shrug, that's where Max has got it from. She should have known.

"I'm sure he's okay," says Tom.

"And that's it, is it? That you're sure he's okay?"

The shrug.

"What will you boys be getting up to this weekend?" She wonders if Tom is trying to grow a moustache or if he simply hasn't shaved. But there's no stubble on his chin, so he's shaving the chin, and that means he's deliberately not shaving under nose. Probably. She wonders whether it's to impress some other woman. Probably.

"I don't think we'll *do* anything," says Tom. "We'll just hang. We'll just chill. You know? Hey, superstar"—for Max has now appeared, and Tom has started calling him "superstar," and she guesses Tom's picked that up from a TV show—"Hey, you got your bag, you got your things? I was just telling your mum, we'll just hang and chill this weekend, okay?"

She bends down to give Max a hug. She doesn't really need to bend, he's nearly as tall as she is now, she hopes the bending to hug him makes the act look more endearing. "You be a good boy for your dad, yeah?" He grunts, he hugs back. She doesn't know why they're hugging, she supposes it's mostly for Tom's benefit.

"And, you know, don't worry," says Tom. "It's part of growing up. Being a boy. I know. I was a boy once!"

"Yes," she says to that.

"And you," he says suddenly, "You have a good weekend too. You're okay, you're doing okay?"

"I'm fine."

"Good," he says. "Good. Well. Bye, then." She never knows whether he's going to try for a hug himself or not. Three months ago he'd knocked on the door, he'd been in tears. His girlfriend had thrown him out, and she could have seen *that* coming, she was practically half his age. ("Two thirds!" he'd protested. "She's two thirds my age!") "I've made such a terrible mistake," he said, "you are the love of my life! I wish you could find some way to forgive me."

"But I do forgive you," she'd said, and she did, for the silly affair, at least, she did—"I do forgive you, which is why I'm not punching you in your fucking face." And she'd closed the door on him. He's never mentioned the incident since, and sometimes when he comes round to pick up Max he seems hurt and snippy, bristling with passive aggression, sometimes he just bounces about and makes jokes like they're cool sophisticated adults and it's easy and it's fun to ignore all the betrayal and all the waste. In the last three months he's never tried for a hug, but she knows it'll happen, one of these days it's coming.

And that's it, Max's gone, now starts her little fortnightly break. She gets Max on Saturday mornings, and he'll be back for Sunday evening, but otherwise she has practically the whole weekend to herself. She feels lighter already. And she feels guilty too. What will she do with her new won freedom? She doesn't know. She never knows. Maybe she'll do some shopping this afternoon, maybe she'll tidy Max's room. She goes into the kitchen and has some cold cuts from the fridge, there doesn't seem much point cooking when it's only for her.

A week or so later she asks Max, "Are things any better at school?" and Max manages a smile and says thank you, everything now is fine. That's just two days before he comes home with his face bruised and bleeding. Max insists it's nothing, but she sees red—she demands to speak to Mrs. Trent about the matter, but for some reason Mrs. Trent is now so much busier and cannot see any parents at all about anything, maybe phone ahead and see if she's available next week? And for three whole afternoons she pulls a sickie at work, and she sits in her car outside the playground, and watches the children when they are let out to play, and she doesn't get out of the car for fear that Max will see her, but she sees him—and she watches all the kids, and wonders which of them are hurting her son, and what she will do when she finds out. Will she climb the fence and go and protect her boy? Will she find the bully and track him down and beat him herself? What she won't do—what she doesn't need to do—she won't ask the bully why.

The invitation comes in the post. It's addressed to Max, but it's also addressed to her, in parenthesis—it says, "To Maxwell Williamson! (and also to Mrs. Williamson!!)"; either way, she doesn't feel bad about opening it first. "It's Nicky's Birthday!" the card says inside. "Come And Celebrate at Our Swimming Pool Party! (bring trunks)." And there's a little picture of a smiling fish, presumably because fish can swim, even if they rarely do so in chlorinated water. The envelope is scented, and that's an odd choice of stationery for a boy, she supposes the invitations were sent out by Nicky's mother.

She shows Max the invitation when he gets home. "Who's Nicky?" she asks.

"Just someone at school."

"Is he a friend of yours?"

"He's not even in my class."

"Do you want to go to his party?"

Shrug.

"You'd better go, mister." Lately she's been calling him "mister" whenever she wants to sounds stern—she doesn't know why, maybe she picked it up from a TV show. "The school says you need some friends, mister. You're going to that party."

The party is the coming Sunday. That's a weekend Max is supposed to spend with Tom; she phones Tom and asks him to reschedule. Tom whines about it, he says he's already got plans the following week. So she says it's up to him then—Tom can be the one to take their son to his best friend's birthday party if he wants, she's more than happy not to have to bother with it. Tom agrees to reschedule after all.

"Shall we get Nicky a birthday present? Shall we go shopping for a birthday present? What do you think Nicky might like?" Max says he has no idea. He's barely spoken to Nicky, he says, he doesn't know why Nicky's invited him, Nicky must have invited everyone. She supposes that is probably true—but she reminds herself Nicky's mother went to the effort of sending a postal invitation, and finding their address to do so, it can't be as random as all that. On the Saturday they go out to buy Nicky a present, all she knows is he must like the water, she buys him an inflatable Donald Duck for the pool—she also buys a card, which she'll get Max to sign—and she buys Max some new swimming trunks.

Sunday morning, and it's raining. Not the gentle sort either—it falls as mean sharp strips, no one would want to be out in this.

"What a shame," she says. Max brightens—does that mean he won't have to go to the party after all? She is having none of that. She tells him to get into the car, and he's sulking now, positively sulking, he's twelve years old and he should know better. He slams the car door and won't speak to her all the way there. She brings the birthday present and the birthday card, and she brings Max's swimming trunks too, just in case. The rain is thick and nasty as they drive, but as they reach the other side of town the weather starts to lift, and once they reach Nicky's house the clouds are gone and the sun is shining hot and warm, it's a beautiful summer's day.

"Come on," she says. "And for Christ's sake, smile a bit."

They ring the doorbell, and a little boy answers, neatly dressed, and beaming happily. "Nicky?" she asks, and he says—"Yes, yes!" He says to Max, "Maxwell, it is so very good of you to come." And he offers her his hand, "Mrs. Williamson, my mother will be thrilled that you're here. Please, come through, both of you. Everyone's out back in the garden!"

There must be about twenty children standing by the swimming pool, all of them boys, all of them in their bathing costumes. She thought there would be more of them, and she feels a weird thrill of pride for her son—now he's the twenty-first most wanted child at the party, and not, as she had feared, the hundredth. The water in the pool looks so blue and warm, it looks good enough to sleep in, good enough to drink. She says to Nicky, but why aren't you all swimming? And Nicky looks genuinely shocked and says, "We wouldn't start until Maxwell got here! That would be rude!"

The boys don't seem impatient or annoyed that Max has kept them waiting; they smile, a couple of them standing by the far end of the pool wave in greeting.

"Well," she says to Max. "Do you want to run along and play?" Max says, "I don't know these boys."

"What do you mean?"

"They're not at my school. I don't know any of them."

"Don't worry, Max," says Nicky. "These are my friends, and that means they're your friends too. I'll introduce you, and we're going to have such fun! Did you bring your trunks? You did? Let's go inside and get changed. I haven't got changed either yet; I waited for you." And he holds out his hand, and that seems such a peculiar thing—but Nicky is smiling so warmly, there is no malice in it, or sarcasm, or even just dutiful politeness—and when Max hesitates for a moment Nicky doesn't take offense, he smiles even more widely and gives his outstretched hand a little flutter of encouragement. And Max takes it. And they hurry indoors.

She feels suddenly awkward now, left all alone, alone except for the twenty little boys all staring at her. "Hello," she says, but they don't reply. She becomes aware that she is still holding a birthday card and a birthday present with Disney wrapping; she puts them down upon the poolside table.

And then, suddenly—"I'm sorry to have kept you waiting, what must you think of me!" Nicky's mother is not a prepossessing woman. She's short, and a little plump, and she doesn't wear any makeup; her hair is sort of brown and tied into an efficient bob. And yet it's curious—there's nothing drab about her, she looks comforting, she looks *mumsy*. And Max's mum feels a short stab of jealousy that anyone can look as *mumsy* as that, the kindly mother of children's books and fairy tales, the mother she'd hoped she'd be for Max. A stab of jealousy, just for a moment, then it's gone.

"Thank you for inviting us," she says to her.

"Max is so excited!"

"I hope you're excited too," says Nicky's mum, "Just a little bit! The invitation was for both of you! You will stay?"

"Oh. Because my car is outside . . . "

"Please. Have a glass of wine."

"And I'll have to drive back."

"Not for hours yet. Please. Everyone else stayed. Please."

"Oh, yes, Mrs. Williamson, you must stay! Everyone's welcome to my party!" Because Nicky is outside again, and he has brought Max with him.

Both boys are in swimming trunks. And it occurs to her that she hasn't seen Max's bare body, not in years. She'd always

huh?

supposed that he was rather a plain boy, the way he carries himself as he slouches about the house made her think he was running to fat. But that isn't fair. He's not fat. There's a bit of extra flesh, maybe, but it looks sweet and ripe. The skin isn't quite smooth—there are a few scab marks where Max has no doubt scratched away spots—and there's a little downy fur on his chest that can't yet decide whether it wants to be hair or not. But she's surprised by her son—he looks good, he looks attractive.

He is not as attractive as Nicky, standing beside him, and showing off muscles and tanned skin. But that's fine, that's not a slur on Max, she rather suspects that in the years to come no one will compete with Nicky.

"Please stay," Nicky says one more time.

"Yes, all right."

"You're staying?"

"Yes."

"Good."

"We got you a card and a present. They're on the table."

"Thank you. Well, Maxwell! Are you ready for the pool?"

"Yes," says Max.

"Oh, watch this," says Nicky's mother. "This is good, you'll like this."

The boys all take their positions around the perimeter of the pool. Nicky leads Max to the edge; he shows him where to stand, next to him. Max looks apprehensive, but Nicky touches him on the shoulder and smiles; Max looks reassured. Then, at the other side of the pool, one of the boys raises his arms high above his head, tilts his body, and dives in. And as he dives, the boy next to him raises his arms likewise, diving as well. It's like watching domino toppling, she thinks, as the actions of one boy precipitate the actions of the next—or, no, more like one of those old black and white Hollywood musicals, weren't there lots of movies like that once upon a time? Because it feels perfectly choreographed, each boy hitting the water a matter of seconds after the last one has jumped, and entering it so cleanly, there's barely a splash.

And she's frightened for Max now, as the Mexican wave of diving boys fans its way around the poolside to where he stands waiting. Don't fuck it up now, she thinks. Don't fuck it up. Three boys to go, two boys, Nicky himself. Max jumps. He doesn't dive, he jumps. His splash is loud and explosive and throws water over the side. He fucks it up.

"I'm sorry," she says. "Max's not much of a swimmer."

"Oh, but he's charming," says Nicky's mother. "And he'll learn." She taps at her arm lightly with a fingernail. "Come inside. Swimming for the children, and for the grownups there's wine and cigarettes and fresh fruit."

"Don't you think we should watch them?"

"Oh, we'll watch them. Indoors." That tap with the fingernail again, and then she turns and leaves. Max's mum follows her.

"Oh, this is a nice house," she says. "I like your house, it's nice, isn't it?" In truth, it's as unprepossessing as its owner—but it also feels homely, and warm, it feels safe. "Have you lived here long, Mrs. . . . ?" She remembers, ridiculously, she has no idea what this woman's name is. "Are you new to the area?"

"Have some wine," says Nicky's mother.

"Well, a glass of white, maybe."

"I'm sorry, I only have red." And she does sound sorry too. "But I think you'll like it, it's very good." She pours two glasses of red; she's right, it's smooth. "And a cigarette?"

"Oh, no, I've given up."

"So have I! Many times!" Laughter. And out from a plain wooden box on the table two cigarettes, and they are the whitest Max's mother has ever seen. She knows as she accepts a light that it's a mistake, she hasn't smoked in years—how long, not since Max was born, she gave up when she was pregnant! She used to enjoy smoking, that's something else Max has taken away from her. She prepares to cough. The cigarette is just as smooth as the wine. She recognizes the smell, where does she know that from? It smells like the scent on the birthday invitation.

And she stands there, drinking and puffing away, and on she babbles. "So, do you live here all alone, Mrs. . . . ? I mean, with Nicky, all alone. Is there a Mr. . . . ?"

"How is Maxwell getting on at school?"

"Oh. You know."

"Tell me."

"Good at some subjects. Bad at others! You know!"

"Yes."

She's somehow finished her glass. She's poured another one. "He's not an unkind boy," she says. "He never was. There's nothing wrong with him. I think. I just wish. I just wish he could be a bit more likeable."

"Likeable, yes."

"The way your son is likeable. Nicky, I mean, he's obviously very likeable."

"Nicky has always had a certain charm."

"You see, you're lucky! If it is luck. I don't know, maybe likeable is something you can work at. Maybe being better is just something you can make yourself be. I don't know. I just look at Max sometimes and think . . . You had such promise. Right at the beginning. Right when you were born. And then you just got worse and worse. What's that about? Like something went wrong, and I never noticed, and I didn't fix it in time, and now it's too late. But maybe it'll sort itself out! Kids. They grow up so fast, don't they?"

"They grow up just as quickly as it takes."

"Yes. Sorry. Of course. Yes. Do you think? Do you think we should check up on them?"

"Nicky's very responsible. But we'll check on them. Come upstairs. We can see better from there."

In the bedroom there is a sliding door that leads onto a thin little balcony. There are two chairs out there, and a table. On the table there are fresh cigarettes, fresh wine. There is a basket of strawberries. "Sit down," says Nicky's mother. "Make yourself at home." From the balcony they can both clearly see the pool, and hear the squeals of pleasure as the children splash about in it. Max sees his mother, waves up at her. He is smiling. It is good to see him smile.

"I like to watch them from above," says Nicky's mother. She has a pair of binoculars. Surely she doesn't need binoculars; the boys are only a few feet away? She peers at the children through them; she helps herself to strawberries as she does so.

It suddenly occurs to Max's mum: "Where are the other mothers?"

"There are no other mothers."

"But, I thought you said . . . "

"It's just me. And you." Nicky's mother takes the binoculars from her face and gives such a lovely smile. "And all my lovely children."

Max's mother thinks the smoke in her mouth tastes soft and warming, it tickles her nostrils as she puffs it out her nose, it tickles her tongue as she puffs through her mouth. Both ways are good, both are nice. "Try the binoculars," she is told, and so she does—she is startled at first by how close the boys in the pool now seem to her, she can see the very pores on their skin, she can see every sweet blemish. They're so close they're just flesh and hair, she can't tell them apart any more. "Try the strawberries too, they taste better with the binoculars," and that seems silly, but somehow it's true.

"I'm sorry," she finds herself saying. "For what I said. I'm sorry."

Maybe she was expecting some sort of reassurance. "Well," says Nicky's mother, "we're all sorry, aren't we?"

Nicky claps his hands, and all his fellows stop what they're doing. He's got a new game for them to play.

Nicky's mother says suddenly, "I mean, what about Jesus?"

She doesn't know what she means by that.

"Jesus turned out well, didn't he?" says Nicky's mother. "Or so some say. And he got off to a promising start. The stable was a bit uncomfortable, but the Nativity, and all the attention of the Nativity, kings coming to pay homage, angels, shepherds, stars leading the way. Well, maybe not so much the shepherds. But that's a great start for a little boy in a desert. And then what? The Bible doesn't tell us. It passes over his childhood in silence. Nothing for years. The next time we pick up the story, Jesus is a grown man, he's suddenly out there preaching, telling parables and healing the sick. At last! his parents would have thought. At last, he's finally making a name for himself. Because all that early promise seemed just squandered, you know? Get off your arse and do something with your life!"

For some reason, Max's mother finds all this very funny, and she laughs and laughs. Nicky's mother smiles at her curiously. Nicky's mother then says, "Do you think you're the first mother who couldn't love her child?"

"What?" And suddenly she feels so cold. "What?"

"The children are having such fun," says her new friend. "Look." Max's mother watches. "But what are they doing?"

"One of Nicky's favorites. And he's so good at it! They're playing the Drowning Game."

The rules to the Drowning Game are very simple. A boy dives under the water. He stays there for as long as possible. Whilst he does so, the other boys stand around the poolside in a circle and clap and chant.

"Shouldn't we help them?" she says.

"I think they're playing it very well without us, don't you think?" And so it seems. They watch in silence as one child stays beneath the water for four minutes, the next very nearly five. They pass the binoculars back and forth, they smoke and drink and eat strawberries.

"Ah," says Nicky's mother. "Let's now see whether your son is better than any of mine."

Max turns to look up at the balcony. He calls out to his mother, but she can't hear what he says above the chanting. She waves at him, she tries to get him to stop. He seems to misunderstand—he waves too, he grins, he gives her a thumbs up. He gets into the pool. He looks so frail and lonely now he's in there on his own. He takes a deep breath, then pops his head under.

"But of course Jesus had a childhood," says Nicky's mother. "Whether the Bible chooses to ignore it or not. And some of the stories got out."

She watches the surface of the water. There is not a ripple on it. And she can't help it, she steals a look at her watch.

"The stories aren't very nice ones. Maybe that's why the Bible didn't want them? Jesus killing children who so much as bump into him, blinding the parents who complain. I suppose you can't blame him. Having all those great powers, must be very confusing for an infant."

She checks her watch. A full ninety seconds has passed.

"This is my favorite story. Is it true or not? Who can tell? Jesus liked to play with his friends from school. One day he thought that the most fun would be to play on the moon. It was a crescent moon that evening and it was so close, he knew if he jumped high enough from the cliff he could reach it. And so he did. There he was, now he was the man in the moon, sitting back within that crescent as if it were a comfy chair. Come and join me, he called to his friends. Come and jump. Don't be frightened. Don't you trust me?"

Three minutes now. She tries to get out of her chair. She has to get down to the pool. She can't. Nicky's mother has got her arm. Nicky's mother has a story to tell.

"The children all fell to their deaths. Their little bodies smashed to pieces at the bottom of the cliff. Jesus was angry about that. He wanted his friends! If he didn't have friends, who could he play his games with? Who did he have left to impress? So he brought them all back from the dead, every last one of them." Five minutes. Max's beaten the high score now. He's beaten the target Nicky set. Surely they'll let him come to the surface now? Surely they'll stop their chanting, their cat calling, their hallelujahs and hosannas?

"Their bodies were broken, of course. And they couldn't speak any more. But what of that? He didn't need friends who could speak. His parents were angry. They knew he had to be stopped. The father spoke to him. Hey, superstar. We can't go around killing our friends and resurrecting them, can we? Then where would we all be? All right? Promise you won't do it again. But fathers are so weak, aren't they? They may love the child, but it's easy to love something when it's not been inside of you eating away for nine months. It's down to the mother, always, to discipline it. It's the mother who knows it, understands it, and can be disgusted by it."

Eight minutes. Even the children look worried now. They've stopped clapping. They've stopped their songs. All except Nicky, he sings his heart out, and how his eyes gleam.

"It's left to the mother. As always. She says, you let those children die right now. You put an end to this, or it's straight to bed with a smacked bottom. How Jesus sulks! He threatens her. He'll drown her. He'll curse her. She'll never die, she'll just suffer, she'll be made to walk the earth forever. But he does what he is told. The children collapse. Their hearts all burst at once, and their faces look so grateful, they fall to the ground and there they rot."

And now—yes—she sees Max's body. And for a moment she thinks it's just the corpse bobbing to the surface, and it'll be full and bloated—but no, no, up he comes, and he's laughing, he's splashing out of the water in triumph! Nine minutes twenty! Nine minutes twenty, and all the boys by the side of the pool are clapping him on the back, and none of them with greater gusto that Nicky, and Max looks so proud.

She wants to cry out she's proud of him too. She wants to cry out she loves him. She wants him to know he's her little champion.

"The point I'm making," says Nicky's mother. "Is there a point? The point I'm making. If your child is a somebody, or if your child is a nobody. If they have potential, or are a waste of space. If they're Jesus themselves. If they're Jesus. Then there's still only so much a mother can do with them. Were screwed either way." She gets to her feet. She claps her hands, just the once, and all her children fall silent, and look up to her. Max too, all the children wait to do whatever she says.

"Nicky," she says. "That's enough now. Time we all put our playthings away." Nicky's face clouds over. He looks like he'll throw a tantrum. His mouth twists, and he suddenly looks so ugly. But his mother is having none of it. She stands her ground. He gives in.

Once again, all the boys take their places around the perimeter of the swimming pool. Max takes his place too. Maybe he thinks they're all going to dive in like last time. Maybe he thinks it'll all be some Busby Berkeley number, and that he'll get it right this time. And maybe, given the chance, he would.

The first child doesn't dive. He merely steps into the water, and on contact he dissolves, the remains of his body look thick and granular in the water.

Nicky's mother watches with her binoculars as each of her children step into the pool and break apart like fine sand. She eats a strawberry. She licks her lips.

It does not take long before it's Max's turn. He looks up. He is smiling. He is happy.

"No," says his mother.

"No?" says the woman.

"Yes," she replies. It comes out in a whisper.

Max seems to take longer to dissolve, but maybe she's biased, maybe he's no more special than any of the other kids.

The swimming pool now seems thick and meaty, like gravy.

Nicky is the last to go in. He refuses to look at his mother, and as he drops down into oblivion with a petulant splash, he's still having his sulk.

Max's mother doesn't know what to say. She puts down her wine glass, she stubs out her cigarette.

The woman turns to her, gently taking her chin by her hand. Kisses her, just once, very softly, on the lips. And says:

"Listen to me. You are not the only mother who cannot love her child. It is all right. It is all right. And this can be your home now, for as long as you like. This can be your home, forever."

And the woman goes on, "This bedroom is yours. Enjoy." And leaves her, with a balcony to watch the setting sun from, and some wine to finish, and all of the cigarettes, and all of the delicious strawberries.

She lies in bed. She half expects the woman will come and join her. She half hopes she will. She doesn't. So, in the very dead of night, she gets up. She feels a little giddy. She cannot tell whether she is drunk or not, maybe she's in shock, maybe she's just very tired. She goes downstairs. She thinks the doors might be locked, but they aren't, she's free to leave at any time. She finds a discarded bottle of wine, she pours out the dregs, and rinses it clean from the tap. Then into the garden she goes. It is dark, and the swimming pool looks dark too, you'd think it was just water in there if you didn't know better. She stops down by the pool- side, right at the point where Max went in—it was here, wasn't it, or hereabouts? She holds the wine bottle under the surface, and lets the water run in. and the water runs over her hands too, and it feels like grit. The bottle is full. She'll take it home. It is the best she can do.

She sees, too, the birthday card and the birthday present, both unopened, still standing on the table where she left them. On a whim she takes the inflatable Donald Duck in its Disney wrapping paper. She doesn't bother with the birthday card.

She drives home, holding the bottle careful between her legs, being sure not to spill a drop.

She goes up to Max's bedroom. The bedroom is a mess, it's always a mess. Max hasn't even made the bed. She makes the bed for him, she smooths down the sheets and straightens the pillows. It looks nice. Then—she takes the bottle. She doesn't know what to do with it. In the light it looks like dirty water—mostly clear, but there are bits of grime floating about in it, you wouldn't dare drink it. She knows it isn't Max, but bits of it are probably Max, aren't they, most likely? She pours it slowly over the bed—the length of it, from the pillow on which Max's head would lie, down to where his feet would reach. The water just seems to rest on the surface, it doesn't soak through. She bends close to it. It smells sweet.

She doesn't know why on Earth she took the Donald Duck, and leaves it on his bedside table.

In the morning she checks on the damp patch on Max's bed, and she thinks that something is growing there.

She goes to the supermarket and she buys lots of bottles of red wine, and lots of packs of cigarettes. But no matter what grape she drinks, what brand she smokes, she finds nothing as smooth or as satisfying as what she tasted at Nicky's party.

She calls work to tell them she's sick. She calls school too. Tells them Max isn't well enough to come in for a while, and no one seems to care.

One morning she drinks too much wine and smokes too many cigarettes and pukes them all out, and, sadly, she realizes enough is enough, and she'll never find that happiness again, and puts the rest in the bin.

Is she too old to have another child? She might be. Online it suggests she is "on the turn." What does that mean? What a thing, to be on the turn. She wishes she hadn't thrown away all the wine and fags.

The smell from Max's bedroom is still sweet, but there's a meaty tang to it too.

And once in a while a memory of Max pops into her head, and she doesn't know what the fuck to do with it. That Christmas with his bike. And Tom took ages to wrap it up, and it did nothing to disguise what it was at all, the wheels, the handlebars, it was just so bloody obvious. She said to Tom, "I bloody told you not to leave it till last thing on Christmas Eve! Now what are we going to do?" She thinks she cried. Tom told her not to worry—it didn't matter—he'd wrap it up again. And it was fun, she wasn't expecting that, to be kneeling together under the Christmas tree, and be trying to bend the wrapping out of shape, put in all these little lumps and bumps so that no one could tell what was really hiding underneath. And in the morning—in the morning, Max got up early, it was Christmas day and he came into their room and he jumped on their bed, he couldn't wait any longer! What it was to be so excited by something, she had forgotten what it was like! She and Tom both groaned, but Tom said, let's just hang onto this because he'll grow up fast, it won't last forever—and how strange it was that Tom said something wise. They went downstairs to the Christmas tree. What on earth had Santa left him? What was that strange misshapen thing? Max wanted to open it right away, but no, they said, leave that one till last. Let that be the special one. And Max liked his other presents just fine, the board game, the anorak, the book of fairy tales from his grandma—but he couldn't wait to tear into that bicycle! Off came the wrapping paper, and he made a whooping noise as he tore into it, and Tom whooped too, and she joined in—there they were, all whooping! And there was the bike. A sudden flash like panic. What if all the build-up was for nothing? What if it was the wrong bike? What if he'd gone off bikes altogether? Kids could be so fickle. Max stared at the bike. Then he ran to it, and he hugged it, as if it were a new friend. As if it were his best friend in the world. And then he turned around, and he threw his arms around his father, thank you, thank you, he said—and he hugged his mum too. Thank you, it's perfect. And his face. The joy. The surprise. It was exquisite. And yet. And yet, as the memory pops into her head. As it plays there, like a movie, totally unbidden, and triggered by nothing in particular. She can't quite recall the face. She can't recall what it really looked like.

She has no idea what to feed the creature that is growing on Max's bed, so leaves it odds and sods from the fridge, and it takes what it wants and leaves the rest. It isn't really Max, she knows that—but there's Max in it. She's pretty sure she can identify bits of him, here and there.

⌒

Tom phones to ask whether he should pick up Max the usual time on Saturday. "I don't see why not," she says.

She answers the door to him. "Hello, hello!" he says. "How are you? You all right? Where's my superstar?" He's in a bouncy mood, that'll make it easier.

The moustache is full grown now, and when she kisses him, she feels it bristle, she can taste the sweat that's got caught in the hairs. "I've missed you," she says.

He looks properly poleaxed, he looks like he's having a stroke. She'd be laughing if this weren't so important. "I've missed you, too."

"Come on," she says, and she takes his hand, and pulls him in over the threshold, "Come on."

"Where's Max?"

"He's in his bedroom. Don't worry about him. Come on." They go upstairs. Tom hasn't been upstairs in nearly a year; he's never been allowed to stray further than the hallway and the downstairs toilet. Even now, he still isn't sure he's got permission to enter what used to be their bedroom. She smiles at him, pulls open the door.

"Wow," he says.

There are candles everywhere and there's soft lighting, and she's found something pretty to drape over the sheets, she thinks it might be a scarf or something, but it looks nice. There's a bottle of wine on the dressing table. "Do you want some?" she asks. "Get you in the mood?"

She can see he's already in the mood, he's been that way ever since the kiss on the doorstep. And she supposes she should be a little flattered by that, but really, does he have to be this easy? He makes one last attempt to sound responsible. "But what about Max? I mean, is he . . . ?"

"I told you," she says. "Don't you worry about him for now." She lies down upon the bed.

He pours himself some wine. He asks whether she wants. She doesn't, no, not any more.

She takes off her clothes, it doesn't take her long, she is ready. He takes his off too. Seeing his naked body for the first time in ages, she still feels a rush of the over-familiar. There's nothing new to be gleaned here. Well, she thinks, that's Max's genes right there.

He says, "I've missed you. Look. I wasn't prepared. I haven't brought any protection? Do you have any protection?"

"Oh, come on, Tom," she says. "You think I can still get pregnant at my age?"

"I don't know," he says.

"I'm still on the pill. Of course I'm still on the pill. Hurry up, and get inside me. I've missed you so much."

He's on top of her, he's excited, it doesn't take long.

He rolls off her. "Thank you," he says.

"That's perfectly all right."

"I love you."

They lie there for a bit. She wonders, if she says nothing at all, whether that will make him get up sooner. She starts to count the seconds go by in her head. It's the like the Drowning Game. How long till Tom gives up and breaks to the surface?

He gets up. He drains his glass of wine. She watches him, he's so sweaty and limp. "Listen," he says. "Listen." She raises her eyebrows, just to show that she's listening. "That was . . . I don't know what that was. But I should tell you. I'm with someone. It's early days, but I like her." So, the moustache was for a girl, what funny taste she must have. "And I don't know. I mean, is this just a thing? Or is this something?"

It's almost amusing. She says, "It's just a thing, Tom."

"Right. Because it doesn't have to be."

"No."

"I mean, I'd break up with her. If you'd like."

"No," she says. "That really won't be necessary."

"Right," he says. "Right." And he puts on his clothes.

She actually feels sorry for him. Up to the point where, now dressed, he stoops over her awkwardly, and tries to give her a kiss. She turns her head away.

"I'll go and find Max then," he says. "He's in his room? I'll go and find him." And he tries to give her a sort of smile, and then thinks better of it, and he leaves.

Now he's gone, at last he's gone. She can put up her hand to her belly, she can stroke it and nuzzle it, and she likes to think how soon—please God, soon—the belly might grow, it'll warp and distend. She gives her body a playful little shake, and she fancies she can hear new life sloshing around inside. And she listens out to hear what sort of scream will come from Max's bedroom.

oh my

THE LONG FADE INTO EVENING

Steve Rasnic Tem

Simon had nowhere to live until his cousin offered him a house in a run-down development on the outer edge of town. All he had to do was stay there to discourage vandalism. The development was almost empty, scheduled to be torn down.

"You're not suicidal are you?" Will asked as he handed him the key.

"Angela left me years ago. I haven't been successful in years. Why would I kill myself *now*?"

Will, pretending to shuffle papers, didn't look up. "I know it's been rough, and you're not getting any younger. It's just that a few of the families that are left have kids, teenagers. I'd hate for them to find . . . "

"Old fellows like me, we don't have the energy to kill ourselves. We usually just fade away."

Will stared at him. "I see. Do you need directions?"

"I lived in the neighborhood when I was a kid, in one of those old Victorians before they built this awful thing. Now here it's a wreck as well."

"I've read about that. There was some trouble wasn't there? Overcrowding, and some violence? Something about a fire?"

"What didn't burn they bulldozed. Everybody scattered, went their ways. Now here I am with nowhere else to go."

"I've arranged for someone to drop off a sleeping bag and supplies. I'm working on a bed."

"I'm deeply grateful," Simon replied. And he was. He'd just never understood who decided what goes, what stays, and where people got to live.

"By the way, we've had a problem with cats. Feral cats, running all over the place. Best not let one of them scratch you."

Simon examined the keys as if reconsidering. "I hate cats," he said.

On moving day he rushed to finish his final shift at the corner store and get his belongings—everything stuffed into a cardboard suitcase and a patched laundry bag—from behind the counter to the bus stop. Most of the shelves were empty. As ordered, he kept rearranging what remained from the "Going out of Business" sale for more appeal, while restlessly waiting for his replacement to arrive. Julie, always out on a date with no consideration for anyone. By now he'd lost everything of importance, but at least Simon held on to his manners.

A pack of twittering girls burst through the door and raced each other for the drink machine. He used to tell the teens to slow down but the way even the young ones would turn on you these days he no longer dared. Further evidence of how the new world was eating the old. "The girls are worse than the boys," someone he worked with once said. The sexism embarrassed him, but he worried it might be true. All he needed was a broken arm, or a deep scratch from a dirty fingernail.

He watched as they poked their phones, took pictures, and mixed different sodas at random into a single cup. Apparently they would share. They all appeared to have too many fingers, different colors on too many nails. The new world was raising them strange. Perhaps if he had a child of his own . . . but Angela always feared he would drop or lose it.

One caught him staring and flashed her tiny tit. The others screamed madly. He blushed and turned away, looking down at his things. He prayed the gigglers would be gone before he tried to haul it all to the bus stop. He hated when he had to pretend to ignore their catcalls.

His possible future caretakers ran out the door without paying. He was relieved not to have to ring them up. Julie came in after, smiling knowingly and smelling of booze. Simon gathered up his life and stumbled for the door.

The bus contained a few more broken types like him, an older woman in a nice dress, and a figure bundled in its oversized coat. Its head, wrapped in a scarf and topped with a watchman's cap, appeared too small for its torso. Its eyes were buried. The bus sped down the block passing the girls with their surplus of fingers, their writhing clump of shadow hungry and hideous on the greasy brick wall.

The bus struggled up the hill past bars spilling their last patrons, who hailed and cursed the driver who was too wise to stop. At the peak where the lanes grew wider he sped past abandoned storefronts, lots jammed with ancient equipment, the iron skeletons of dead buildings, the rows of silent warehouses with rusted doors flush to the road. There was the rare bus stop, the random passenger standing with one arm waving, but the driver never slowed. Simon believed this part of the city need never exist.

The route would not take Simon all the way to the development. The bus dropped him at a darkened stop to stand beside a crumbling, heavily graffitied bench. Some words were almost recognizable, but lay obscured beneath mindless exhortation. The ground rose steeply before him, and somewhere beyond that rise of shadow the aging development began. Smoky grayness drifted down from the low clouds and seeped out from the overgrown embankment. The hill's silhouette was deceptive, suggesting primeval forest more than cultivated landscape.

Instead of taking the road around, he pulled the flashlight from his laundry bag and sought a shorter path. He followed a trail of broken, grass-invaded sidewalk through the unkempt greenbelt and up the hill. He had to struggle through tall-weeded fields, ignoring unidentifiable animal sounds in the underbrush, the occasional glimmer of a red or yellow eye. Man-shaped spaces opened up in the dark vegetation a few feet away, but no one approached. He tried to remember what, if any, of these features had been here when he was a boy. It had been wilderness then, too, although even less controlled. He and his friends would venture there after sunset. He vaguely remembered the darkness, and the dreadful confusion of echo, but nothing else.

He was nerve-exhausted by the time he entered the murky blocks of identical one story ranch houses and sodden lanes of the development. The neighborhood of his youth had been a crowded slum but at least it had some grandeur in its height and architecture. A sea of bright holes identifying downtown shimmered in the distance behind him. Ahead were the squat rectangles of unlit homes, and houses with few lights on, and houses half-gone into ruin, a handful of dried-up gardens and trashed-out back yards, their wire fences plastered in random trash.

In an abandoned playground a shattered teeter-totter sprawled like a sacrifice across its steel pipe center. The swing framework still stood erect but rusted, its seats and slide gone without a trace. So where did the remaining children play, or were they too old for something so innocent? One was crying now, he thought, although it might have been one of those stray cats.

Simon had no way to determine which houses were actually empty, and which were occupied by people who just wanted to keep to themselves. Without knocking on doors, perhaps peeking through windows, which he wasn't about to do.

In the old days, in that other neighborhood of taller and less uniform homes, he heard a great many things: the voices of friends he hadn't seen in decades, music playing from a record player in a neighbor's upstairs window, misunderstood whispers from lovers hiding themselves in the shadowed strips near walls. All of that had been torn down and bull-dozed, the old neighborhood beheaded. It occurred to Simon he now had more memories than life. It was an uncomfortable way to travel.

Several houses had yellow police tape stretched across their front doors and around their near-identical porches. He assumed the police actions had something to do with drugs; in the news it always had something to do with drugs. That and gang activity. A lot of these poorer teens fell into gangs.

When Simon was young a bike ride to and from this neighborhood had been nothing. He'd fly down the steep curl of road and although the trip back up was a challenge he accomplished it without too much difficulty, feeling like a star athlete afterwards. Not anymore. He should have kept in better shape. Once here, he didn't expect to leave often. He supposed that was how older people became trapped.

He found the house Will was providing—low and dark and indistinguishable from the others. The newish lock looked inexpertly installed, the hasp mounted crookedly, and rattled as he fiddled with the key. Simon slipped inside and slapped the switch, lighting up the messy interior. He gasped involuntarily from the stench: human waste and aromas both sweet and sour underneath. He reminded himself that his cousin was allowing him to stay here for nothing.

Houses weren't built to last anymore, nor did it make sense to. Technological expectation changed so quickly it didn't pay to invest in building for the long term. People moved on, although not necessarily up.

When he first glimpsed the living room walls he imagined a crowd of onlookers, but the arrangement of shadows proved to be stains. Studs and nail head patterns were clearly visible beneath the thin paper.

Cleansers and chemicals and various old tools were stored in a closet with random junk. He couldn't tell how old any of it was, or how dangerous, but he did what he could, sweeping the foulness out the back door and dumping chemicals on the hardwood floors where they'd been deeply stained, windows open to the cold air to get rid of the smell. He just needed to get his situation clean enough so that he wouldn't mind sleeping on the floor. The revealed boards were scarred as if from games or ritual. Or maybe from cats. Cats can do a lot of damage if locked inside by themselves.

more messages he can't decode

On several walls sprays of relatively fresh graffiti obscured older layers of scribbling, and here and there certain words and symbols were emphasized by means of deep cuts. He could make no sense of it, although the patterns of marks created an emotional effect not unlike music, so he wondered if some of these marks referred to songs. Over the days to come he painted over the graffiti, but with no confidence it wouldn't return. *how?*

Long threads of dust floated through the rooms. The remnants of his old life were hardly more substantial than these. With most of the people he'd ever known gone, the fabric of day to day reality seemed thin. *reading instruction*

That old house where he'd grown up had probably been less than a hundred yards from here. It had a screened back porch where on late nights the adults filled their drink cups and the children consumed their allotted portions of sugar and ran mindlessly around the yard. This house and the ones around it had no back porch and he wondered when those had gone out of fashion. No doubt around the same time as gatherings with the neighbors.

fuel equivalence

He remembered games of hide and seek that lasted for hours and covered every lot in the neighborhood. He remembered childhood crushes on young girls whose names he no longer remembered. He remembered he would not take a bath when a certain babysitter was on duty, the one who always wanted to help. *childhood — fun + danger*

In one corner of the living room a sleeping bag, some toiletries, and food had been left for him. When he thought he'd cleaned sufficiently for a relatively untroubled night's sleep he crawled into the bag and succumbed almost immediately. *isn't it his stink?*

The morning came quickly. He had dreamed and sweated, and now the sleeping bag stank. He wondered who might have used it before. He crawled out and walked barefoot into the kitchen, splashed his face with water tinged a muddy rust color. He'd let it run until it cleared. He went to the back door and opened it for air and sun. *FIRST BREAK* *II MIDPOINT*

He was surprised not to see the sun, or even the sky. A few feet in front of him a tall brick wall with curtained casement windows blocked his view, awash in smoky gray shadow, part of a larger house that rose three stories. Looking straight up he glimpsed the old-fashioned soffits and Victorian roof. It looked somewhat like the house he'd grown up in, except larger. Turning his head he saw similar large houses out to both sides, an entire neighborhood of slummy Victorians in ill repair. He could also hear creaky music, children's voices, a cat's howl, the soft explosive echo of a

All of these details have been foreshadowed!!!

distant barking dog. But he couldn't make out any of the finer details of his surroundings, not even this close.

Simon went to get his flashlight for a more detailed look. But when he came back there was the sky, and the sun just over the treetops illuminating a vista of dull one story homes. The filth he'd scraped from the house the night before still lay piled around the bottom step. Sometime during the day he would have to bury it.

He took a breath. He hadn't been fully awake. It happened sometimes, even several minutes after walking around, a piece of dream still lodged in your brain changes the world. There were the sounds of children squealing like the damned in a nearby yard, but was that still part of the dream? The excited screams of children at play often fooled you into thinking there had been some grave tragedy.

Simon worked several hours in the bathroom and kitchen—scrubbing and throwing out the useless and the unsalvageable—not bad for an out of shape old man, he thought. He felt uncomfortably heated and propped open the back door. The outside temperature had dropped precipitously. He'd tried the thermostat but the furnace wouldn't come on. Another problem to ask Will about. Whatever sounds he heard—the whistle of a speeding car, the broken explosions as a plane pushed through the air overhead— were very far away. Whoever lived nearby was impressively quiet. "Safe as houses," as his mother used to say, but it never reassured. Some houses weren't safe at all.

Cooking smells drifted in from outside—some sort of richly spiced meat, perhaps a stew. Someone in the neighborhood knew how to cook.

He thought he heard a school bus pull up and children piling out, but the sounds faded quickly, swallowed by the increasing rush and push of the wind. It would be a breezy time for a walk, but he'd only have light for a couple more hours, and Simon wanted to see the neighborhood and some of its residents in the light of day.

The wind hitting the house made a constant groan. Simon wondered if the poorly built structure could bear it—he imagined minute fracturing exacerbating decay, perhaps even some sort of collapse. A sick apprehension heightened his need to get out.

Outside in his coat he walked toward the broken playground. He kept his eyes open for people, but after a few blocks there was nothing, not even any toys left outside or laundry on a line. He listened carefully for conversation or music—he was sure he'd heard some before—but all he heard now was the wind battering the shoddy roofs, and a whistling down the lanes between the structures.

There should have been teenagers out, even if the adults had the sense to stay inside. Teenagers were the adventurers and the hasty ones, those always said to be "at risk."

A sudden clamor from several houses over made him pick up the pace. But it was just a piece of roof blown off into a side yard. He wondered if his own roof was sound. He stared hard at the twisted bit of wreckage, the curly shadows trapped beneath. Then a mass of the curly shadows unfurled and escaped around the edge of the house on its too many legs. A cat with insulation tangled into its fur, he presumed, living in the house's attic. Poor thing. That's when it started to rain.

He liked the smell, like damp earth everywhere, moist dirt in the air he breathed, like a memory of his future, as if the rain had released something from the dirt of the aging neighborhood. The air grayed around him, fading everything it touched. Or was it his eyes failing? He hadn't been to an optometrist in years, afraid of what he might be told. Complete failure took a long time to occur, it seemed, but the process was relentless.

The rain was light, so he continued walking for several blocks around the complex. He saw no one, no signs that children had recently played, no signs that any of these houses were occupied at all. There were lights on in a few, but with the lack of residents he guessed they might simply be on for security. And yet he couldn't believe his cousin had lied to him—what would be the point?

"Hello! I say hello! Is anyone else here?" His voice bounced and echoed against the brick.

As if in reply a distant truck horn sounded like a large animal in distress. Simon was reminded that you couldn't always trust your senses to tell you the truth. He turned the corner and walked in a different direction, hoping for a new perspective. He peered over fences and gleaned a few new details—mud-encrusted junk, old foundations exposed between patches of unmown grass, an abandoned barbecue lying on its side like a felled animal. But nothing recent, nothing indicating current occupation.

He became gradually aware of the faint stench of invisible smoke, like the memory of an old barbecue, or when his grandmother used to lie about her smoking habit and snuck off behind the house for a drag or two before the cancer eventually took her.

He came to a wide circle in the lane with a bent and dead streetlight poised over it like some kind of giant predatory insect. When he was a boy the neighborhood kids used to gather beneath the streetlights and ride their bikes at night. He stooped down—there were warm cigarette butts beneath the crippled lamp post. He looked around, saw nothing, and the charcoal sky split open from the weight of water, beating him momentarily to the ground.

He looked up, saw the dark twisted shapes lingering nearby like a collection of corroded statues, their rude fingers pointing as they plotted their harassment. All around him the blurred outlines of the houses had added a story or two, with high roofs swaying precariously overhead. Cats encased in their wet and wiry fur took swipes at his face. Simon ran to find shelter, pushing himself against a greasy brick wall. He thought he recognized the house—someone's aunt had lived there when he was a child. But that was impossible. He looked up to find the window where she used to watch for her husband, and found slanted yellowed eyes staring at him through the rain—he thought maybe some feline's eyes, or child's. The pale face that suddenly appeared around the eyes was much like a skinny child's face, surrounded by a matted cloud of ashen hair. But he was greatly fatigued, and this was the only face he'd seen in a couple of days, and he found it increasingly difficult to see in this dimness. *This is what getting old is like*, he thought. *A long fade into evening.*

The rain began to ease and so Simon headed toward home. With each step the force of the rain lessened and the clouds of moisture dissipated, and no house was over a story again, the houses beaten down, until he reached his own house where everything was remarkably dry. Something escaped out of his back yard—a tangle of broken or too-many-segmented legs. A truck was parked out front and two squat men were unloading the bed his cousin promised.

There was a leak in the kitchen faucet, the water oozing like syrup. It had begun raining again, beating against the house like a thousand tiny fists. The house appeared to resent the abuse and issued some grumbling complaints of its own.

At least the bed made Simon feel more civilized. It wasn't particularly comfortable, though better than a sleeping bag on the floor. But now he could imagine uninvited guests hiding beneath. He wasn't a child anymore, of course, but he was feeling very little like an adult. He tried to sleep but could hear tiny tappings on the house's most distant windows, water still dripping from the rain or maybe the trapped beating of moths against the glass. Eventually succumbing, he dreamed of a small riot he'd witnessed as a child—teenagers throwing bricks, someone's mother screaming, faces washed in blood. The young sometimes simply couldn't take it anymore and had to strike out because of conditions. But sometimes when you were old you were too wrapped up in your memories to move as fast as you should—you got hurt lying in the way.

The next morning he found long strands of, presumably, animal hair coiled in the corners of the room and lying across his blanket. But he had been cleaning aggressively and couldn't imagine where these coarse strands had been hiding. As the sun rose the movement of shadow inside the house became unceasing: trees bending outside the windows, the travel of clouds across dark patches of sky, and the nearby houses rising up hazily and swaying in the wind. *uh oh!*

He crawled from out of the covers and staggered to the back door in trepidation, but there were no big houses in the back yard today. By the fence a cluster of weeds and something else unrepentantly tangled. He looked for eyes but could find none.

He thought he heard children playing in some remote yard, bossy and excited and dramatic and now and then hurt and crying over nothing and everything. But this might have been a memory. He didn't bother to look around. He suspected he wouldn't find anything.

Gazing up at the overhead electrical lines that traveled over the back yard Simon observed their poor state of repair. Tiny bits of black insulation lay scattered like dead bugs all over the grass. *brush low*

He took another stab that morning at cleaning. It shouldn't have been necessary, but dust seemed to come out of nowhere to spoil the rooms. The floorboards weren't tightly fitted—dust from the crawlspace underneath seeped through. Dust also came down from the ceiling, from the flaws at the corners and the holes where plants once hung. It came back as fast as he wiped it away. Dust also issued from the loose-fitting windows and from under the front door. Many of the yards in the development had gone back to bare ground and now the wind was redistributing them.

He stayed away from the windows, not even wanting to look. Sometimes outside there were old house facades that shouldn't have been there, and slanting shadows from tall houses torn down decades ago. He could see the way the light shifted inside as the outside world impossibly changed—and if he were to look out he'd have to doubt his own sanity.

dust from everywhere

fighting bricks

He still had seen no teenagers, no children of any kind, but he heard their feet scuffling outside, and the ragged sounds of their breath as they ran away. Where were their parents? Where were anyone's parents? No doubt hiding beneath their beds. At least the cats he'd seen had left him alone.

As if in answer his own bed creaked and something shifted in the light, but Simon refused to turn around. If he just kept his mind on cleaning he would be fine.

Early that afternoon the clouds lifted and light glared across the bedroom ceiling. He witnessed the vague lines in one corner of the heavily textured surface, the slightly depressed outline of a trapdoor into the attic.

It made sense, of course. Each of these houses would have some sort of attic. He could see a fuzz of lines along one side of this small hatch—cobwebs or insect legs or simply an accumulated string of dust hanging down. Perhaps if he removed some of the attic dust he wouldn't have such a dust problem below. And besides, there might be things put away up there and forgotten, treasures no one remembered.

He had no ladder, but he could slide the bed into the corner. From there it was a simple matter of standing and pushing the panel up and to the side, and then the strenuous but doable labor of leveraging himself up into the darkness.

He saw no treasure, but copious amounts of dust. Much of it had accumulated into furry mounds in the corners. He caught a glimpse of daylight, and shifting himself for a better view saw that a corner of the attic had been damaged, rotted out all the way to the outside air, ragged as if chewed.

Long, coarse hairs from the mounds glistened, moved. Then one of them shuddered, and a ragged gap in the middle opened wide.

Simon dropped back onto the bed, hastily fitting the panel back into place. Over the next hour he rummaged through the junk in the closet, finding a few strips of metal he could screw into the panel's edges and secure it to the ceiling. He slid his bed back into the middle of the room and lay there watching the fastened ceiling panel. At one point the metal strips might have wiggled, but that might have been his eyes and nerves fraying from staring too long. Outside the teens ran around the house—he could imagine bands of them looking for trouble, or was it the pets they'd left behind? He was too old and too nervous for this. Tomorrow he would hike out of here and visit his cousin. *Thank you and sorry and thanks but no thanks.* He wasn't sure if he'd tell him what he'd seen and heard. Old men had been locked away for less. He fell asleep pondering if there was anywhere else to go, and dreamed of being dragged screaming from his bed.

But he woke up still in his temporary house and on his temporary bed. The ceiling panel remained safely in place. What was different was the redness of the room, as if Simon were seeing it through a veil of blood. He shook his head and rubbed his eyes. The intense redness still permeated, brighter near the window. He slid off the bed and fumbled the curtains aside.

A glorious scarlet sunset had swallowed the world and retrieved the tall old grandfather and grandmother houses from his childhood. The residents were outside shouting their enthusiasm as they walked toward the center of the development where the air was brightest, as if the sun were descending at that moment into their neighborhood. He could see little more than their rapt and shiny faces, the rest looking thin and dark as lamp black. His eyesight was clearly fading. He knew he would see nothing of the new world now.

He wasn't sure what to do but couldn't bear the thought of remaining in this cramped little hovel with all that human activity going on outside. Why had they hid themselves away from him? One glimpse from their hiding places should have told them he had neither the inclination nor the ability to do them any harm. And with those things in the attic he felt safer outside. He jerked open the door and hurried out, determined to get a good look and become a part of whatever was to come.

A few of the neighboring ranch homes appeared unchanged, but as Simon followed the stragglers toward their brilliant destination he saw that the remainder had gradually warped into two stories or three or four, the walls stretched vertically thin to transparency, as if they were decaying upwards into these phantom rectangles with deteriorated regions allowing the night sky to show through. In some places a bright oblong of window appeared to float high in the air with a shouting person inside, with no discernible supporting structure around it.

He turned to the rioter next to him to share his amazement—it was an old man gone to crumbling cinders from his ribcage down.

Turning the corner he came face to face with the blackened crisp remains of youth gangs, shouting and punching those around them even as they had fingers and limbs flaking off. At the block's center a hollow building

displayed a boiling fire inside, dozens of those furry bodies exploding out
from its blazing core like flaming cannonballs fashioned of fur. ''

They had their dirty, dirty hands all over him, their sooty clothes
reeking of smoke and booze and the stench of new-fangled habits. He tried
to reason with them but discovered he no longer spoke their language.
There was nothing he could do, it seemed, and when they dragged him into
the flames he found he no longer wished to resist.

GRAVEROBBING NEGRESS SEEKS EMPLOYMENT

Eden Royce

I pried apart the corpse's lips, their slackness telling me she'd been dead more than two days, and worked the tip of my finger inside her mouth. It opened enough for me to wedge the funnel in, its tip clinking on her teeth. I tipped my porcelain-lined hip flask—metal was a no-no—to spill the tea into her mouth. She didn't have to swallow; enough would make its way down for the magic to work. I leaned back from the shallow hole she lay in, my aged joints protesting something fierce, then recapped the hip flask before hiding it away with the funnel inside my stocking. Wasn't nobody looking up these skirts.

Tonight was kind. The temperature along Charleston harbor had dropped, creating a soupy fog the moon couldn't quite cut through. Enough light to see my way home, but too little to give busybodies a clear view. My ear was always open to the rustle of feet or the clop of hooves approaching, except I wouldn't have to worry about avoiding carriages tonight—those horses' eyes weren't good in the dark no way. Even so, I looked around me as I crouched on the pile of fresh turned dirt next to her, waiting.

She stirred. A brief jolt like she'd been run through with a tease of lightning. When her eyes opened—the first thing they all did was open their eyes—they were just starting to turn milky. I took her hand and helped her rise from the pit she'd been thrown in.

"Come on, honey. Maybe in your next life, you'll learn to pick better men."

Her dress was ripped, exposing one small breast; her hem was stained stiff with blood and fluids. Did the best I could with arranging the little coils of her hair to cover the angry rope burns around her neck and the hole in her skull, 'cause tea don't fix everything. I wrapped my cape around her narrow shoulders and leaned her back against a tree while I filled in the hole. Then we started walking, her with an awkward bow-legged hobble and me not much better.

Chilled wind blew in, clearing the dense blanket of fog, and I hurried our steps. A hurricane lantern burned in the back window of one of the little shotgun houses off Maple Street and we headed toward it, avoiding the backyards because of the dogs yowling, torn between the need to protect their territory and their fear of the dead. I tapped on the closed screened door with a ragtime rhythm and after some scrabbling and heated whispers, it opened.

"Oh, thank you, Jesus." The woman inside, young-looking with old eyes, sagged against the uneven doorframe when she saw the pair of us. Her man stood behind, large and silent and watchful.

"You got a place for her to be?" I asked. The effect of the tea wouldn't last forever and having a dead body lying around wasn't good for no one, especially not Colored folk.

"Baby?" the woman asked.

The girl turned toward the voice. "I'm so sorry, Mama." The words came out thickened and slow, pushed past the decaying tongue. The girl's mama broke down, sobs wrenching from her throat as she pulled and tore at the scarf covering her head.

Her man came to her, took the woman and her daughter each by an arm and led them to a sturdy, homemade table. He set a kettle on the stove to boil, then slid my cape off the girl's shoulders, folded it, then returned it to me. As he pressed coins into my hand, he said, "Reb Fielding got a special little place for her to rest in the St. Matthew graveyard now that she home." His eyes skitted away from mine. "How long we got?"

I reared back to look at the sky. The moon hadn't reached its high point yet, still a ways to go before sunrise. "Till day clean. 'Round five or six hours."

"Thankee now."

I nodded and headed off home. Cold was creeping in on the evening, and I pulled my cape tighter. Time for my own cup of tea.

The sandy-haired Negro boy gave me the signal. Casual-like, I turned to notice the street cart where it sat with its hand painted sign—*P'nut Man & Hot Fried*—and made my way over.

"How much for a lil bag?"

"Half penny, Miz Prosper." He shook his head slightly as he said it and I knew there was news. "Got some hot fried that's good today, though."

"Please for some."

I watched as he dropped a scoopful of chicken gizzards coated with seasoned corn meal into the hot grease and set the lid back on the cast iron kettle. Sun was blessing the day with warm breeze, but the heat coming off the cart felt good in my bones. He sold a couple steaming bags of boiled peanuts to some longshoremen, who clomped away to put in their time loading and unloading the ships, leaving empty brown shells sucked dry of briny juice to litter the walkway. The boy fished my hot fried out, sprinkled them with salt, then placed the crispy bits in newspaper, folded real careful-like. I handed him five pennies and he started to refuse, but I pressed them into palm. He looked at me with damp eyes and closed his fingers around the money, the back of his hand marked with scattered grease burns in circles and lines, a dark Morse Code on his light brown skin.

"Keep that. If you get the chance, you look out for me, hear?"

"Yas'm. Thank you, ma'am."

I knew he already did, like most of the other Coloreds 'round here. If they didn't, I mighta been caught long ago. Even though most church-going Negroes claimed to be scared of me, saying what I did wasn't natural, I eased their minds by returning their kin to them so they could rest on blessed ground. Whispers about me had been going around the city for years, in the parlors and in the paper mills, on the farms and in the ironworks. If you can find your dead, then you better next find Miss Prosper.

Most of my work was from lynchings—Negroes dragged off to their ends for talking back, for having a business that started to cut into the white man's, or for having independence of mind. Sometimes an unwelcome suitor who after the fire of passion died, dug a shallow grave to hide his shame. Might think it gets easier over the years, but no.

Even though my customers welcomed their dead back, I could see their deeper thoughts—anybody messin' with life and death can't be right with God. Of course, I ain't evil, but what most minds can't get a grip on…they call the devil's work. I don't work for Old Scratch, though I expect I'll meet him one day if talk makes things true.

I turned my attention to the paper as I walked away, popping a steaming hot gizzard in my mouth. The chewy meat split as it bit into it, letting a stream of rich juice coat my tongue. Searching for the line that spoke directly to me, I found the young man had kept it just out of reach of the grease splashes.

Employ Available – Negress Preferred
A remover for a large number of fragile items is promptly needed. On
the main street of this city, a few doors down from the courthouse. The
terms may be known by applying therein.

The word *courthouse* was run through with two lines, striking it out. Next
to it, written in lead pencil was the word *blacksmith's*. After reading, I rolled
the rest of the chicken onto the marked paper, letting the grease cover up
the pencil marks. Then I finished my lunch and headed home to make the
Life Everlasting.

Big Mama taught me how to make the Life Everlasting when I was a
girl. It was from a recipe brought over here from Senegal, or somewheres.
Like their jollof rice became our red rice, the recipe changed from family to
family until nobody really knew which one was the first. I'd heard her and
my gran, both strong root ladies, talking about it when they was making
other teas to keep away fellas the ladies didn't want, to keep bosses sweet,
to win at the numbers . . . But I'd had to prove myself time and time again
before they would teach me this blend.

"Never use this 'less you have to, hear?" Big Mama told me before she
lay out all what went in the tea. "Little glug, Prosper . . . Only little glugs 'til
you's sure how much to take. And make it weak at first."

I still lay out the ingredients for the tea like she taught me that first day
so long ago. What was it? Ninety years or so now? I wondered what they
would think of me using their tea to move the dead. Shoot, maybe they
already knew what I used it for.

It was getting harder to find everything now, but I found I could make
small changes and have the tea work just fine. Long as I could get pepper
berry and sun gold root, it'd be okay. The redbush tea leaves and kola nuts
I grew myself.

I steeped everything in my clay pot, no metal could touch this blend,
then left it to cool. Once I strained it through two layers of muslin, it would
be ready. I stoked the flames in my fireplace to warm the room and keep my
hands from shaking. I had to fill the jars careful-like, not wanting to waste
a drop of my hard work.

A knock came on my door, gentle like it was scared, but firm like it had
run outta choice. If they stood at my door, they likely had.

I opened the door to see a wide eyed boy, not more than eight or ten, on the step. He was breathing hard, musta been running like a bat outta torment. His high water pants with no socks told me all I needed to know.

"Come on in here now, chile."

He was scared, and I couldn't blame him. No idea what kinda stories he heard about me. But I knew what I looked like, right 'round forty or fifty some odd years old—old enough to command like a wise woman but spry enough to do the job. When the cold got in these bones, though, I felt every one a my hundred years. I never was pretty, but that was a blessing my mother had given me. Pretty women caught too many eyes. And hands.

The boy edged inside, keeping his hand on the doorknob. His eyes darted around like flies on road kill.

"You want something to eat? Drink?" He shook his head roughly. "Didn't think so. Well, why you here? Crack ya teeth, son."

"They foun' my brother."

"Who chile is you?"

"Francis Station, ma'am."

I whistled long and low. Francis Station's son had been missing for years, since Mayor Bradley found out his daughter had been sniffing around him. I can't say he wasn't sniffin' too, but he shoulda known not to let nobody see them together. Heard some white man dragged him from behind one of them machines he used to work on at the paper mill and nobody seen him since.

"Where?" I asked.

"Out the marsh by Runnin' Jack place. 'Neath that sick-looking poplar tree. I made a mark like they said I was to."

I sat back in my chair. Dangerous. Jack ran numbers and liquor, but he wouldn't stand for nobody on his property. I don't know how the boy got out there and back, 'cause Jack tended to shoot first and never ask questions. They say not to trust crackers who live near Negroes. I had to hope I could get in and outta there quick and not let him catch me.

"All right, chile." The job in the paper had to wait. Had to hope they'd understand. "I'll go, but—"

The boy held out his hand, stopping my words. Two Stella coins lay in his palm. "Mama said she know it ain't safe, so she'll pay you first. And two more when you get him."

Sixteen dollars total. Christ rising. I took the coins and patted the boy on the shoulder. "You tell her I'mma go there tonight."

"Yes'm."

After he left, I sat there for about an hour, looking at the door until nightfall, the moon and stars lighting up my table. Then I filled my flask, tied the funnel to its neck, got my shovel, and left the house. The tea was still warm where it pressed against my inside thigh. I'd had a swig of it myself earlier and it erased the ache in my joints, gave me a bit more energy. The shovel I tied to the inside of my cape and it bounced silently against my generous bottom as I walked to where the marshland met the dirt.

Outta the corner of my eye, I could see Runnin' Jack's place edged up against the marsh, where fireflies dove in and around the reeds. Big ol' house, but not much to look at with its peeling paint and flaking wood. Barn didn't look much better. Splintered wheels and broken buggies dotted the backyard. All was quiet, save for the chorus of frog song, making me think this was just gonna be like any other cemetery visit.

Sorry to say it wasn't.

I managed to find the poplar tree, with its white chalk mark slash pretty easy. It was sick, likely from the rot in the soul of the person who buried the dead here. I loosened my shovel from inside my cape and said a swift prayer that this was gonna be a cakewalk.

A patch of grass lifted away in one straight piece. Underneath, a layer of earth was loose, releasing the smell of rich soil. I scraped it away. Against the black dirt, white bone shined. The boy must have stopped here and run to his mama because the rest of the dig was into harder dirt, like the earth had to make up for the soft dank pluff mud of the marsh just feet away. Glad I didn't have to come through that way. Charleston was famous for its pluff mud and even binyahs like me lost a shoe once or twice to its sucking hold.

I grunted as the shovel only broke through fingernail-sized bits of dirt at a time, making me use elbow grease I didn't have. Hot and sweaty, I stopped for a moment, easing my back upright, taking big glugs of the cool air off the marsh. It held the sweetness of life and death, swampy and ocean cool. I lost myself in it and didn't hear the footsteps approaching.

He tackled me from behind, holding my legs together, and sent me head first toward the base of the tree where it poked through the hard pack dirt. I kept from slamming my face into the gnarled roots of the poplar by twisting my body and taking the knock on my shoulder. The wind flew out of me and I rolled to my back, the shovel thudding to the ground. I heard Jack grab for it and toss it away. His weight felt like a stone where he had me pinned to the ground, pressing his man parts against me like we played night games. His face was weathered, pale skin drawn tight against his skull.

Salt-and-pepper whiskers and a beat-up fishing hat covered most of what else I tried to see. But those rabbit gray eyes held me sure as his body.

"What're you doing on my land?" He growled the question out and its scent reached me, swimming in tobacco and fish grease. His fumbled for something in his pants and my breath caught, but he just pulled out a revolving gun, the kind Army men tended to have. Satisfied I had seen it, he lay it against my belly.

There was something in his face that I knew. I couldn't place it, but it was there. The shape of his brow, the line of grizzled hair running along his cheek? I saw it, felt it in my spirit. Knew it as sure as I could breathe. Breeze blew up off the marsh, shifting the clouds and letting more of the moon's smile through to touch his pale face so close to mine. The answer called to me in a memory of blood.

"You a Negro," I whispered.

"And you're a witch. Facts neither one of us wants told." He cocked the gun. "Now where's that leave us, Miss Prosper?"

I eyed the oiled metal barrel, then frowned. "With you lettin' me sit up off this cold ground."

He thought about it, then sat back, freeing my legs. I shuffled to sit up, smoothing my long skirt down. He didn't help, just watched me with them rabbit fur gray eyes and tapped the gun on his knee.

"Why're you here?" he asked again.

"To do a job. You got a child buried out here, Mr. Jack and I—"

"You ain't taking nothing from my property."

"What? I'm talking about a child. His mama just want to bury him. That's all."

He shook his head.

"A boy someone lynched for looking sideways at a girl, that's all. A Negro boy. Or don't you care about your own people?"

His eyes stayed on mine and I shivered like ghosts was looking in my face. "I said you are not to take a thing off my property."

Frustrated, I thumped the ground with my fists. I had nothing, no weapon, and I felt foolish for never thinking to bring one. Never needed to before. "It's a dead, Jack, a dead! Why you wanna keep a dead here?"

He thought about my question, then he spat out a thick wad of wet tobacco. "Leave 'em be. No good comes of draggin' up the past."

As he sat on the cold ground looking down at me, I realized. Whispers said it was white men who had taken them children off over the years to

God only knew what kinda fate. And it never occurred to me that someone might use that fact to hide his own sins.

Real fear took me then and I shook with it. "It was you. All this time." When he didn't say anything, I yelled. "Wasn't it?"

"Whites kill coloreds all the time." Jack worked a finger into his ear, digging. Wiped it clean on his dungarees. "Everybody knows that. I just had to make sure I picked the right ones; ones they woulda gotten to eventually. All I had to do was keep to myself and dig fast."

I felt tears burn my eyes, run down my face in hot trails. "Why?" I choked on the word. The marsh grass *shooshed* in the still air.

He shrugged. "I can't help killin'. I need it . . . like breathing."

My heart flipped in my chest. I searched the ground for something, anything, to use to save my life. The tea running through my system would buy some time, but it wouldn't heal me from gunshot. A flicker caught my eye and I saw the cutting edge of the shovel for a moment as the clouds passed over. Nestled against the marsh reeds, out of reach.

Jack got to his feet, towering over where I sat on the ground next to the half dug hole. He'd probably finish digging it and slide me in next to the dead.

"It keeps me calm. Helps me sleep." Training the gun on me, he turned up first one shirt sleeve, then the other. "I plan to sleep well tonight."

"You sho is, Mister Jack." The voice came from behind him and as he spun around, the crack of a rifle followed.

His head flung back like he was about to offer up a prayer, but I knew that couldn't be as I could see the sky through his skull. He swayed, crashed to the ground. Slow-like, his body fell back, meeting up with the trunk of the poplar.

I swung my head to see Francis Station lowering her husband's rifle and my breath eased out of me. Her young boy, the one who had come to me earlier, stood behind her. They were both barefoot, feet covered in shiny brown pluff mud from the marsh up to the ankles.

"My boy told me you was coming tonight. I just . . . wanted to see."

I didn't ask why she thought she had to bring a gun, but I was grateful and I told her so. "Glad you came, honey. I 'preciate you."

We both dug, me with the shovel and her with the hoe that the boy had brought along. Soon, we uncovered what was left of a reed-thin young man, once handsome from the way his bones and what was left of his dark skin came together. I tried to cover most of the rot with my cape, but she stopped me.

"No, I wanna see him. His pa . . . ain't gone want to."

"Alrighty." No need to pull away the lips; they were mostly gone. I poured the tea through the exposed teeth, where it ran across and down into the space just before the jawbone hinged to the rest of the skull.

While we waited, she asked, "Can you make him whole? Just for a little while? It's been . . . "—she cleared her throat—"a long time."

"No, I can't," I said, grateful that tea can't fix everything. I didn't want *that* magic. "Spend this little time you have with him, then let him rest. That's always my advice."

She pressed her lips together, but nodded and I was sure she'd heed me. I turned to the rustling now coming from the makeshift grave. "Come on now. Time for you to get on home."

I parted with the Station family at the top of their road, promising to show up at the services if I was able. I guzzled the rest of the Life Everlasting I'd made on my way home, hoping it would ease my aches and bruises. As I shuffled along, I was starting to wonder if I was up to whatever the job for the blacksmith was. How was I supposed to remove any more fragile items when I felt like one myself?

I chafed my fingers, the brief warmth fighting off the creeping chill of the hushed night. And how many was a "large number," anyways? Ten? Twenty? Sure, I could brew up enough tea, but what about the cost to myself? Seeing my people broken up and beat down, tore and tattered made me weary. Forever after, I'd be wondering how many of 'em Jack killed, after giving in to that mad fever in his head. A few more empty streets brought me shuffling up to my doorstep. Never have I been so happy to see my little house, but it made my mind run on how many others was out there waiting to be found so they could catch they final little piece a home.

Once inside, I made myself a cup of Forty Winks tea to help me sleep. Something to calm my mind, help me stop thinking about this last job, what it meant to my peace and my future in this town. I breathed in the scent of magnolia bark and mulungu, and took a small sip. I shook myself at the taste—like perfume on dry roots—and said a silent prayer for God to guide my mind. All the while knowing I was gonna take that job, no matter how dangerous it was. I stayed up all night drinking that brew and staring out into the dark, because tea don't fix everything.

SUNFLOWER JUNCTION

Simon Avery

That winter I started buying old vinyl records from the junkie who lived downstairs from me. He was selling all of his possessions in order to keep the lights burning, some food in his belly and his habit alive. His name was Colin. I couldn't tell you how old he was but he must have been pushing sixty at least. He looked like he'd been drawn by Robert Crumb. Slow moving, heavy limbed, lugubrious. Long hair the color of cigarette ash, Brylcreemed into an unlikely, gravity-defying wave that washed away from his forehead. It put me in mind of a painting that I had to Google to place: *The Great Wave off Kanagawa*. Seriously. Every time I set eyes on him—that painting. His eyes were quick but utterly unfocused, as if he were charting the movement of an invisible cartoon mouse around the room. But they were a strange piercing blue, those eyes. Paul Newman blue.

We never talked about the smack. I didn't partake in the hard stuff. But that November his vinyl collection was my gateway drug of choice. It took me away from myself. I bought a high-end turntable, an amplifier and speakers that sat on an IKEA table in a room that was otherwise empty. I traveled light. But we didn't talk about that either.

It started with a mint Mono copy of Pink Floyd's *Saucerful of Secrets*. Colin offered it me while we sat outside on the garden wall one morning, watching the sea crash over the promenade across the street.

"How much?" I asked, inspecting the sleeve and then the vinyl itself, cigarette gripped between my teeth. It seemed like a question hardly worth asking.

"Forty," he said after some hemming and hawing.

"Quid?"

"Forty quid and it's yours. Take it or leave it."

I studied him for a moment, looking for treachery in his eyes, but he was in many ways, utterly guileless. For a junkie. I opened my wallet and then counted the cash into his hand. He gave me the record and said, "Don't play it too loud, I'm planning on an afternoon nap." Then he stood, saluted me and went back inside, leaving me with a record worth ten times what I'd paid.

After that I wasted my days in his front room, talking and playing records. I raided the remnants of my savings instead of looking for work, instead of starting again. I suppose I'd intended this to be a new life in a new town. But it was the same old life. We lived in a Victorian townhouse on the seafront in Hastings, a seaside town in Sussex on the south coast. The building had probably been quite grand in its heyday, but now it was just an assortment of elegantly high-ceilinged, yet shabby rooms with temperamental plumbing and electrics, its facade weathered and beaten by the sea air and the harsh winters. I hadn't intended to stay long, but I'd already been here for eight months by that November. It was cheap and I didn't need much. I knew how to survive at this pragmatic level. I'd stopped considering tomorrow. Or the next week, or month. It wasn't living. I realize that now. It was just existing. But it was fine.

One day Colin showed me a strip of four black and white photos that had been taken in one of those old passport photo booths. In the pictures was a young man with a beautiful girl, who was sat on his lap. They were laughing, happy, kissing. I was so dazzled by the girl that it took me a moment to clock that the young man was Colin. It was the impossible hair and those eyes.

"We were only together for four weeks," Colin said. He took the strip of photos back and stared at them. "I was sixteen. Just left school and I got job bricklaying. Good hard work but it was a bastard during the winter. She walked past me one day on the street, and I couldn't take my eyes off her. She was all rolling hips and heels. Then I saw her again that night in a pub, about a mile away from here. She must have clocked me staring. She came over and told me she liked my quiff. I could barely look her in the eye. I was so fucking terrified. No experience. But then we went back to her place and sat up and played records and talked all night. We didn't sleep together until the third date." Colin sighed, looked away out of the window, his eyes glassy. I didn't know what to say, so I waited.

"Her name was Sally," he said finally. "It was the best month of my life."

"What happened?"

He shrugged. "What always happens, I suppose. I got paranoid.

It happens when they're that pretty. They get all the attention. I started following her on the nights we didn't see each other. I got jealous, kept asking questions about where she'd been. You know how it is. The first of a lifetime of mistakes." Colin shrugged. "I never really bothered again. My heart wasn't in it."

It took me a moment to grasp what he meant by this. "What, you mean she was the *only* one?"

"The only one who mattered, yes. There were others but I quickly realized that there was no point trying after that. I mean, *look at her*," he said, showing me the photos again. "That wasn't going to happen to me twice, was it?"

I pondered what he'd said that night and tried to imagine such blind infatuation. I could all too easily understand that feeling of being over-whelmed by something precious, but to go almost fifty years without really attempting to make it work with someone else seemed not just sad, but foolish. He'd kept the memory of her in these pictures, preserved in aspic for all of these years. Sally would be drawing a pension by now. She'd prob-ably married, had kids, grandkids, worked, retired . . . A whole lifetime. She'd probably never thought of Colin once.

In the meantime Colin had at some point turned to writing. Aside from the prodigious amount of records and books and newspapers, there were stacks of manuscripts on either side of a battered old Remington typewriter. Every night, if he wasn't high, Colin would knuckle down to imagining those four weeks of his early adulthood in increasingly beatific terms. He had never intended for them to be published. They were just a way for him to access that beautiful part of his life again and again. A doorway into summer, grasping at that elusive feeling; like trying to wrap your arms around a ghost.

Then one day a CD in Colin's collection caught my eye. The cover was amateurish, just a photocopy of a blurry image of a pattern I found vaguely familiar. It was called *Sunflower Junction*.

"Who's this?" I asked. "Hugo Lawrence."

Colin studied the CD for a moment, turning it over in his hands until his fragmented senses placed it. "He was a local chap, I think. Only produced the one record so far as I know. This one's about a year old. I think I must have got it at one of the gigs he did." He shrugged, passed it back to me. "Take it," he said. "It's on the house. You'll probably enjoy that shit more than me."

That *was* the shit I'd become partial to. I listened to *Sunflower Junction* later, after we'd parted ways. Colin had a late-night rendezvous with a dealer at Bottle Alley, the half-mile long double deck promenade on Hastings' Seafront, and I had my own assignation with Ingrid, who lived on the third floor.

Ingrid was an alcoholic. She was a few years older than me. A lifetime of abuse had damaged her (I assumed) beyond repair. I thought she looked like one of those Hollywood starlets from the thirties or forties, but ten years on, after she'd been told she was too old for the screen. A faded glamour. Every now and then you caught it in the right light, or bad light. She often talked about suicide in a lazy, delirious way; the poetry of the hot bath, the pills and the bottle of Scotch, the razorblades drawn vertically down the wrists. Sometimes in bed she made me choke her until I could see she was about to lose consciousness, her eyes swimming with a febrile contentment and certainty that this, above all else would lift her away from the baseless fabric of the life she'd made for herself.

Afterwards we had nothing to say to each other. In fact unless we were fucking, we had no reason to spend any time in each other's company. We'd keep trying, but neither of us wanted to open that lid on our pasts, to share those wounds we clearly carried around like those guys with sandwich boards, proclaiming THE EARTH IS DOOMED. What was there to say about those people who'd carried us out onto the sea, only to leave us marooned on our own lonely islands somewhere? Nothing new. We weren't looking to be healed or coddled, or sympathised with. Not then, at least.

So we talked about anything but the past. And then we fucked and we turned over and went to sleep. Or I left the bed and came home, sat with all the lights on, daring exhaustion to claim me.

So it was after midnight when I finally put *Sunflower Junction* on, but I was instantly engulfed by it. The warm currents of languid guitar, the tight, jazzy upright bass and drums, the speckled sunlight of the Fender Rhodes piano and vibes, and then the punctuation of the restless trumpet or clarinet. It sounded like late period Doors, or Tim Buckley or early Van Morrison, like *Bitches Brew*-era Mils Davis. A stoned, summery, somnambulant trip. Every song had something to say to me. A midnight crawl through an empty Los Angeles on *Baby Blue Eyes*; a pastoral rumination in an English meadow at the height of Spring on "Forget Me Not"; a tight jazzy tour through a sweaty Parisian club and its backrooms on "Johnny Jump Up"; and then there was the centerpiece of the album: the long, almost improvisational jam of "Sunflower Junction," the words conjuring bizarre images, the music spiraling and turning into a mantra, an enchantment, a summoning; circling and retreating, repeating and shifting like a mathematical equation, each time changing one number, one word, one note in order to find its way into something even more heightened, more ecstatic . . .

I slept and dreamed of Emily. I tried to turn away from her but my subconscious had been denied her for another day. It wanted me to feel *something* again. And every time I turned away, she was there, as perfect as she'd ever been. Another woman preserved in aspic, but for different reasons.

The dream was on my pillow when I woke. It was a broken, ugly thing, like the head of a dead sunflower, the yellow petals blackened at the tips, curled in over the center. I picked at the sticky petals and caught fractured glimpses of the dream I'd had; quick flashes of memory, tugs of loss and longing that I'd trained myself not to feel. But curiosity got the better of me and I pressed my fingers deep into the puckered flesh of its folds, and felt her there, felt something I hadn't felt in a long time because it was the past, and the past was an empty room to me now.

I withdrew finally, and watched the grey light of day creep across it. Finally I found an old jam jar in the cupboard, gathered up the dream and placed it inside. I put it on a shelf a closet where I couldn't see it.

There wasn't much to discover about Hugo Lawrence on the internet, which surprised me. Most people make music not just to be heard but to be seen, to make money, to get laid, to be adored. I knew the drill. I used to be a music journalist a long time ago. But Hugo had no Facebook profile, no Twitter account, no social media presence anywhere. Even minor local musicians knew the internet was a tool to reach the audience they craved.

I finally located a blurry shot of Hugo on stage in a poky little club in Brighton, all hair and fire and sweat, and a review of the show that was enthusiastic despite the lukewarm reception of the audience of hardcore Folkies. Some of the extended jams lost them after ten minutes of stoned, uncommunicated reverie. They retired to the bar, but Hugo didn't seem to care. He played the rest of the gig with his back to the dwindling audience.

I played the CD again to be certain of its strange allure. A late night can sometimes romanticize music, people, moments. It's easy to get lost in yourself after the lights have gone off. But everything that had moved me or stirred me then did so again. I went back to Colin and asked about Hugo, but he didn't know much.

"What about the gig you saw him play?" I asked. "What did you make of him?"

Colin puffed out his cheeks. He seemed muted that morning. He hadn't opened the curtains yet, and the room had that familiar bittersweet, burnt vinegar smell of heroin. The air was thick and fetid with it. It left me feeling heavy limbed, eager to leave. Colin was generally pretty diligent in keeping that aspect of his life suppressed from anyone who visited him. I should have asked him how he felt. I know that now. I should have cared more.

"He wasn't really my cup of tea, to be honest," he said finally. "He played a lot of dive bars and clubs as far as I know. And he wasn't much of a performer. That much I recall."

"Is he still around?" I asked. I wanted to see him for myself. Whatever it was that everyone else couldn't see would be clear to me, I'd decided. Something of the journalist in me was aroused by the music, my curiosity about the man piqued.

Colin wrote an address down on a piece of paper. "Go and see Allan," he said. "He was with me that night, and he was the designated driver, so I assume he was relatively sober. He'll probably be able to help you more than I can."

His friend owned an old record shop down a narrow side street in the old part of Hastings. It was a Sunday. To be honest, like the song, everyday really is like Sunday in Hastings. No one around, broken down arcades with ancient games, dusty windows stuffed with yellowed newspaper, sudden moments of ancient architecture leaning out from the tacky tourist shops and chip shops and pubs. The sound of the sea had diminished by the time I reached the store. All that remained were the lonely cries of seagulls, drifting high above me on the uncertain air currents.

Allan's Record Xchange was closed today, but Colin had arranged for me to meet its proprietor there. I knocked on a window that was almost entirely coated with ancient posters for local bands until he opened the door and peered out to inspect me. Allan was an old dandy. Despite the decrepitude of his business, he still fussed about the racks in a stiff white shirt, a paisley cravat, a waistcoat and scuffed wingtips. His hair was fine and grey and long, pulled into a limp ponytail that danced around his head as he moved and talked. The shop was dark and dusty and crowded from floor to ceiling with records. Over the years his stock had overflowed into crates and boxes and across ancient shelves that bowed beneath the weight of all that old vinyl.

"This record, *Sunflower Junction*, is good," I said after we'd made small talk for a while. "It's not just me, is it? There's a sense of history to it, knowledge of what's gone before, and then he's taken it somewhere else." I wasn't sure what it was I was trying to convey but I was all too aware that this was as motivated as I'd felt for months. "There's an intelligence to it. It's raw but there's something happening beneath it all."

Allan paused from rifling through a pile of music papers behind the counter. "Well, yes, I suppose so," he said. "But it also could be seen as wildly derivative of all kinds of those jazz-folkies from the late sixties, early seventies. And it's awfully self-indulgent at times, but yes, it certainly had potential. *He* had potential."

There was something else, something fragile and elusive in the music that I couldn't decide how to articulate, an element that people seemed to have missed, but I let that go for the moment. "How was he that night?" I asked instead.

"Well there was no *performance*, you see," Allan said. "No attempt to connect with his audience. And it was a good turnout. A lot of people had presumably heard the same thing you have in the record and came out on the strength of it. I suppose it's something you can't put your finger on.

"But what worked on disc just didn't work live. Some people said he'd changed after the record was done. For most of the night he barely acknowledged the audience, and if that hadn't alienated them enough, he decided to turn the show into an extended jam session that lasted almost half an hour. The same song, over and over."

"Sunflower Junction," I said.

"Yes. It was as if he was trapped inside the song." Allan paused for a moment. "I thought he looked lost that night, utterly lost."

"Do you know anything about him?" I asked. "I looked online, but he's like a ghost."

"Indeed," Allan said. "I have friends who know him. Or *knew* him. I can hook you up with one of them. He hasn't really resurfaced since those gigs. Someone told me he was working on a new record but whether that's true or not, I honestly can't say. I heard he'd ended up homeless, crashing on friends' couches or even rough down on Bottle Alley. I don't know where he is now. Ah, here we are . . ."

Allan produced a yellowed music paper from one of the piles he'd been ferreting around in. He leafed through it and placed it on the counter when he'd located the appropriate page. "There it is," he said. "The one and only interview with Hugo Lawrence. Take it," he said. "It's on the house."

ALTERNATIVE BRIGHTON TIMES
At the Sunflower Junction with Hugo Lawrence.

Hugo Lawrence is a prodigious talent, touched with a chameleonic quality that allows him to slip from bucolic acoustic reveries to psychedelic jazz workouts and all points in between. After earning his spurs in the bars and clubs of London and Sussex, Lawrence's improvisational skills and virtuoso guitar playing have led to him being compared to Nick Drake or Tim Buckley. He's chosen to surround himself with a group of hugely accomplished musicians and *Sunflower Junction*, his first album, is released this week.

I talked with Lawrence before his recent Brighton show to find out where this fusion of folk and jazz comes from.

ABT: How did you get started?

HL: Well, I've had a few lives in music. I started out in punk bands, playing the Underground clubs in London. Sleeping on basement floors, waking up with scabies, that sort of thing. That was how I learned to play - just five shows a week, in and out, cash in the back pocket if you were lucky. Then I got tired of that and started getting into folk and jazz, just tracking down record stores and absorbing whatever the old guys in there would turn me onto. Then I got onto the folk circuit, collaborating and doing improvisational stuff, trying to push the envelope, take the music somewhere new. Just jamming, you know? Learning what your style is, what it is you want to say.

ABT: And what is it that you want to say?

HL: Oh man, well with this first record it started out as one thing, all these musical influences coming out and me trying to transpose myself across them. But then we started jamming one night after doing mushrooms and we got *Sunflower Junction* out of it. I'm glad someone was there to press the record button because I'm pretty sure we couldn't have got back to that place again. Lightning in a bottle s**t!

ABT: And what is *Sunflower Junction* to you?

HL: That's a difficult question to answer. The night that we played it for the first time, it seemed to already exist, and we just sort of summoned it into the room, fully formed. It's very personal to me. To all of us, I guess, but something changed for me that night. It was like an out of body experience, like I got close to something I can barely describe, even though I try every night we play it. *Sunflower Junction*, man . . . Mathematical biologists love sunflowers because of the seed spirals. And young sunflowers follow the sun, did you know that? It's called heliotropism. Imagine an endless field of sunflowers with the sun moving quickly from the east, across the sky and setting in the west. This place, I've seen it since I was young. I've glimpsed it. Like it was overlaid across our world, or hiding in its cracks and hollows. I've had a craving for it since I was a child. So I try to get close to that first night when we made *Sunflower Junction*. Every night. I haven't succeeded yet. But I keep trying.

I dreamed of Hugo later that night, even though all my subconscious had to go on was a blurry photo, the music and some hearsay. It was enough. I was following Emily through the silent backstreets of Hastings, but she was always just a little too far ahead of me to reach. She disappeared behind the door of Allan's Record Xchange. The old music posters were crumbling from the windows. There was a light inside that seemed too bright to be contained. I pushed open the door and stumbled into a field of sunflowers. The stems were dry and stiff, towering around me. The air was heavy with pollen, weighted down with immanence. The sun was passing overhead in some sort of time lapse, and the sunflower heads followed its path like passively curious aliens. There was a sound like static, and I kept catching the ghost of Emily's voice as it rose out of the folds of white noise. I chased it through the sunflowers. They dwarfed me. Their big dry heads seemed to slyly monitor my progress. Me and the sun. Hugo was there, twisting from stalk to stalk, a poorly printed black and white facsimile of a man with a guitar. When I reached the hospital bed, I stopped. The sun had gone. The bed was bare. The old sheets removed. Emily was no longer there. Hugo was on the bed. Then he was crawling off it like a demented spider, and then he lifted his head and opened his mouth. The sun was in there, and it spilled out its brilliance, all across me.

There were petals scattered across the bed, and the static remained, fizzing and angry. It was a sudden confusion of the senses. I couldn't decide if the dream had really ended. There were fragments of it everywhere. Ingrid wasn't in bed beside me. When I rose, there were sunflower petals fluttering in the air, and a carpet of them beneath my feet. They were parted to suggest a path to the bathroom.

The radio was tuned to a dead station at maximum volume. A vacant sound. Ingrid had opened up her wrists. Blood had sprayed across the bathroom tiles, had turned the water a shade of red so beautiful it was hypnotic. There were pills under my bare feet on the bathroom floor beside an empty bottle of cheap supermarket Scotch.

"Christ, Ingrid," I heard myself saying in a high pitched voice. "*Christ.*"

I vacillated between finding my phone and then attempting to rouse her and staunch the bleeding from her wrists with towels. She hadn't cut them properly. I was waiting for the remains of the dream to detach itself from me. Waiting to understand the world again. I must have called an ambulance, put on some clothes. I held her and stared emptily at the tiles until the paramedics arrived.

I went with Ingrid in the ambulance and then sat in the waiting room with a coffee that tasted like cigarette ash while they pumped her stomach, stitched up her wrists, arranged for a psychological assessment. I assumed they'd detain her this time under the Mental Health Act, and she'd be transferred to a secure psychiatric unit. At this point, it probably wouldn't make much difference. Some wounds are too deep. The razorblades were just her way of exerting control over a situation that had defeated her years ago. The burden of trying to live a life you no longer understood.

I sat with her in the ward later on. She woke after an hour and stared at me absently, and then unexpectedly she reached out for my hand. "Hey," I began and leaned forward, trying to smile, trying to be something reassuring for her, but then her face creased into tears, and she folded in on herself. I relinquished her hand and sat back while she wept silently.

It was almost light when I got home. I went upstairs and let myself into Ingrid's flat. I spent an hour cleaning the bathroom of blood and pills and sunflower seeds. The petals that had showered down from my dream had come to rest on every surface. I made the bed and found the dream I'd had. It was just the husk of a sunflower head, or a heart made of fractured triangles, I couldn't decide. When I pushed aside the soft folds with my fingertips I caught glimpses of the field of sunflowers, the hospital bed, the musician with his mouth filled with sun. I teased open the folds, touched the warm, inviting flesh. It invited me to tumble back inside it. Instead I found a jar in Ingrid's cupboard. I washed it out and placed the dream inside, along with as many of the petals as I could gather. I took it downstairs and placed it on the shelf in the closet and closed the door on it.

Toby King met me outside a pub across the street from Flamingo Park. It was raining. There were no tourists, no children, no calliope music. The rides were covered over, dripping wet. Seagulls wheeled above us. The sea crashed against the promenade, restless, violent, surging.

We sat beneath the pub's awning, nursing beers it was too early in the day to drink. Toby was in his fifties. He had a hard face and arms that looked like they were made from granite. He wore a pork pie hat without apology. He tapped the table with his calloused fingers, then the chair, his knees, anything. Allan had given me his number. He had footage on his iPhone of one of the shows he'd played when he was in Hugo Lawrence's band.

"I suppose I should get one of my kids to upload it to YouTube one of these days," he said.

It was a typically shaky hand-held video, but I honestly didn't care. At this point, it was like being granted the sight of the Flying Dutchman overhead. The band was mid-way through a delirious rendition of *Sunflower Junction*. Hugo's head was down, his hair falling over his face, swaying, his guitar clasped like a talisman, utterly abandoned to the moment. The band was building to something ragged and ecstatic. Finally, reaching some kind of euphoric high, Hugo raised his face. His eyes were wild; sweat was beading at the tips his hair. Just as it seemed there was nowhere else for the music to go, at his indication, the band circled back around and began to build again, like waves crashing repeatedly at the shore. As Hugo turned his back to the crowd, the video ended.

"Christ," I said.

"Intense, right?" King lit a cigarette and exhaled a plume of smoke as if he were post-coital. "It was like that every night. *Every fucking night*. Shit for the audience, but an absolute fucking trip for us."

"What was it?" I asked. "What was he trying to achieve with that song?" I think I already knew at that point, or I sensed it, like something settling into my bones. It felt like my life was infected with it already.

King shrugged. He took off his hat and rubbed at his bald head. "Fucked if I know, mate. I just turn up and play my instrument."

"Did you work on the album?"

"Yeah, yeah, man."

"Were you there that night you all came up with *Sunflower Junction?*"

King grinned. "Yeah, I was there. We were booked into the studio down the road for the evening, so Hugo brought some magic mushrooms and some weed and we started jamming while we waited for the 'shrooms to kick in. Hugo would start something, some idea he had and we'd join in, work at it until we hit a groove. By the time we were peaking on the mushrooms, we'd fallen into something good. We could *feel* it. None of us were thinking consciously about what we were playing, you know? Just instinct. And we were all in sync with each other. It was *fucking heavy*. I've never experienced anything like that night. None of us have."

"What about Hugo?"

King sniffed, looked at me from the corner of his eyes, sizing me up finally. He shook his head. "It fucked him, that night, you know? It was, I don't know, *transcendent* for him, for all of us, but it broke him too. He was ecstatic about it that night, and then the next day when we realized that it sounded good and we'd got it down on tape, you know? This fucking incredible piece of music that seemed to take you somewhere if you wanted to go."

He sighed. "But Hugo couldn't get back there. He told me he'd caught a glimpse of something, and I said 'Yeah, man, me too. The walls were fucking melting.' But he said 'No, none of that mushroom shit. Something else.'"

"Did he say what it was?"

King laughed. "Sunflowers? It's all in the lyrics, ain't it? This glimpse of something he's been seeing since he was a little kid. Somewhere better than here, than this shit.

"Either way, man, it fucked him up. But gradually, you know? We finished the record and then we toured it, and for a while he was the same old Hugo. Still intense, but you could drink with him, talk about women and shit. But it was *that* song. We played about twenty gigs and each night he'd get to that song and he'd want to us to get to *that place* again, just like that first night. But it was lightning in a bottle, man. You can't replicate that sort of shit, night after night.

"So we'd play that song and we'd go round and around, like it was some sort of mathematical problem."

"That pattern on the album cover," I said, realizing it then. "It's a Fibonacci spiral."

"If you say so, man. He sort of explained it to us once in the van on the way to a gig, but you know, I'm a bass player. It doesn't mean shit to me. I just try to keep time and not fall off the stage."

"So what happened after the gigs were over?"

King shrugged. "We stopped hearing from him. By the end of the tour, he wasn't really talking to any of us anyway. We took our cut of the door and went our separate ways."

"And, what, that's it?" I said. "You never heard from him again?"

King had finished his beer. I ordered him another. He said, "People come and go in this game, mate. Look, I heard from Jez, our drummer that Hugo had sold all of his gear. Couldn't afford the rent and got kicked out on his arse. He was sleeping rough for a while. Still got his guitars and some recording gear in storage. Heard he was trying to write some new material but the drugs were getting in the way. No cash flow so he was borrowing and not paying it back. Last I heard he was in a squat with Jez and a couple of girls. Still playing. Still not talking. Still trying to get from here *to there*. You know?"

"Do you have an address?" I asked. "For the squat."

"What are you anyway," he said, "the *fuzz* or something?"

I didn't know at that point why I wanted to find Hugo Lawrence. But I'd caught a glimpse of that uncertain geography, and I could see how it could flood your life, for better or worse. King made a couple of calls, and then, somewhat reluctantly, gave me the address.

I don't know what I expected to find. The squat was in a row of boarded up terraces, narrow little homes in a warren of backstreets. A shithole of an estate. Feral kids roaming in packs, dogs straining at leads like unexploded bombs, young men and women with permanently listless scowls on their faces.

I assumed it was where Hugo Lawrence had come to die or else to find a way out or in. To *break on through to the other side*. I clambered over a fence and found a smashed back window that I could crawl through.

The smell assaulted me as soon as I dropped through the window. The scent of honeysuckle and jasmine, phlox and tuberose. A dizzying and suffocating mass of flowers. But it was not just that. Nothing is ever just one thing. There was something broken and corrupted too. It was the kind of smell you wouldn't assume you could identify, but there it was: not just shit and piss and the fug of heroin, but the putrefaction of bodies, the slow, ugly decay of flesh. I stumbled through the kitchen, taking a breath and holding it, my mind gone blank, narrowing to a point of light.

There were three of them in what remained of the room, long dead on the floor, their bodies beginning to liquefy into the carpet. The smell of spoiled eggs and shit. But that was not the most significant part of the room. It really wasn't a *room* anymore. The floor was flooded with clover and cow parsley and tangled grass; there were bluebells growing between the corpses' fingers, in the places where their bodies had decomposed the most. Claiming them for the earth. Gypsophilia flooded from between one of the women's legs, across the room and up one of the remaining walls. It was scrawled with a set of numbers and mathematical symbols that I had neither the time nor the inclination to inspect. The geography of the house had been corrupted from within. It wasn't evident from the outside. The transformation was beautiful, rich beyond words. The heavy, blossom-laden branches of a hawthorn tree. A sea of weeping willows hanging over grassy banks, meadows and copses at the limit of my vision, all seemingly illuminated from within. A drowsy hum to the earth; a heavy stillness that fizzed in the blood. A guitar had been abandoned on a granite outcrop and claimed by lichen. A stream sprang from the rocks, singing quietly and rolling gently around the body of a young man. His long hair was crawling with lice and beetles. The leaves of a Rowan tree, tremulous with dew. Heather and foxgloves, little collapsed stone walls. Everything was flooded with small details, expanded beyond all comprehension. What remained of the room simply resembled old ruins in an ecstatically rendered landscape.

Hugo Lawrence wasn't among the bodies, so I went in pursuit of him. I fled through a field of poppies toward the promise of summer, or the remains of it. For a while I felt like part of something. I walked for an hour or more. My feet were soaked and my mind was tranquilized. There was immanence to the place. Something I could only call magic, because I had no other words for it.

What else can I tell you? I didn't find Hugo's Sunflower Junction. There was a place here for someone, but not for me. This was the ghost of someone else's imaginings. I lay for a while in the gorse on the side of a valley, breathless and weeping. I don't really know why. A vague sense of exile perhaps, or of the evanescence of things. I found another guitar on a rock, along with a small digital recorder. I waited for a while, but Hugo was long gone. I took the recorder and made my way back. I glanced behind me now and then, thinking I'd caught a glimpse of a sea of sunflowers somewhere, just beyond a rise, through the trees, across a river. But I was mistaken. It wasn't mine to find.

A week after Emily died I packed a bag with just the essentials. Toiletries, a few changes of clothes, my wallet, cards, phone, laptop. I didn't even take any pictures of her with me. There were some on the phone anyway. I paid the last of the rent, talked to the insurance people and solicitors, put the furniture and our belongings in storage. There was no one I needed to say goodbye to. No family and no more than a handful of friends whose lives had taken them away from me as we'd hit our forties. I stayed for the funeral, and then I left.

We'd married young. Emily was seventeen and I was twenty-two. Those relationships tend not to last, but ours did. A few bumps in the road but what we had was clearly too important to walk away from. So many things that seem important when you're young fall away from you as you get older. And all that remains is love. The short list of things that you wouldn't do for each other. I think so, anyway. Time has clouded my judgement.

Emily was three months pregnant when she was diagnosed with leukemia. The doctors told us that the baby would have to be aborted in order for Emily to begin chemotherapy. We made the decision for her to have the abortion after days of gentle and quietly dismayed discussion. But it made no difference. A complication occurred. Something to do with white blood cells; a doctor speaking to us in quiet, uninflected tones on a bright day in June. My memories of that time are scrambled, purposely left vague to stop me coming to harm. Emily spent three months in a hospital bed, gradually diminishing, day by day, getting further and further away from me, until she finally succumbed.

I remember the bed, stripped of its sheets afterwards. I remember it quite clearly. The awful absence of life.

I left the squat and made an anonymous call to the police from a heavily vandalized phone two streets away. When I got home, the house was almost unnaturally still. Usually I could hear Ingrid on the floor above me, laughing at some nonsense on the TV, or running a bath, or crying in her sleep. But she had been sectioned at a clinic ten miles away along the coast. I didn't know when she'd return. After an hour of circling Hugo's digital recorder which I'd left on the coffee table, I picked it up and took it downstairs to tell Colin what I'd found.

But Colin was dead. I found him on his threadbare sofa, his head slumped forward. The needle and the tourniquet had slid between the cushions. I checked for a pulse, hoping perhaps he was just wasted. But there was nothing. He was clutching the strip of photos of his sixteen-year-old self and a girl called Sally, the making and the ruination of his life.

I stood up and paced the room, a breathless emptiness clutching at me. Like the anticipation of just plunging off the edge of a precipice. Rage and sorrow, all at once. That all too familiar wound.

There were fresh pages in the typewriter on his desk. Another waltz into the past. Those four perfect weeks. I wondered if he'd pulled off Hugo's final magic trick, and part of him now belonged to a time when his life was right and good. An escape from a life that he considered inconsequential. These pages were his access point.

But this was no escape. This was the corpse of an old man who'd simply stopped living his life.

I called the police. They arrived and asked their questions, and then the body was removed. I realized that I couldn't stay here in Colin's rooms without him. That part of my life had been a gentle anesthetic but it was over now. Exhausted, I went back to my flat and fell asleep in my clothes. I dreamed but I couldn't recall it when I woke. It was there on my pillow anyway, but I didn't try to peer between its folds. It began to crumble in my hands when I put it in a jar with the others.

I never played whatever was on Hugo's digital recorder. It wasn't for me. It belonged to someone else's great escape. I ended up putting it into the jar that contained the final dream. I put lids on them and walked down to the promenade. The sea was rushing in. There was no one else around. I flung them as far as I could and let the waves take them. Then I walked away. They were just dreams. They had no weight, but I felt lighter for giving them away.

I packed my bags that afternoon. There wasn't much. Just that hold-all I'd used to escape almost a year ago. I left the turntable and Colin's records behind. I didn't really need them. No one did. It was just stuff.

I stopped to see Ingrid on the way out of town. I found her alone at a table in one of the common rooms of the hospital. She looked bereft in her dressing gown and slippers. Her ashtray was overflowing. She was staring out of the window. It had begun to snow - huge flakes, falling in slow motion in a lonely garden. I sat down beside her and we talked. I told her about Colin. I said I was leaving. I looked at the chipped paint on her bitten fingernails, at the bandages on her wrists. She'd tied her hair back; the nape of her neck looked bare and impossibly vulnerable. I saw flecks of grey in her eyes. All of these things, these little details; they discovered something in me then, coaxed light into places I'd left in shadow for what I assumed was my own good. She studied me. At first her eyes were vague with the medication but gradually her consideration hardened. Was I the man I seemed to be, or the man she hoped I could be? At some point I said Emily's name, and I told her this story. All of it. It took an hour, maybe more. At some point I realized that her hand was in mine.

And then we kept on talking.

WELCOME TO YOUR
AUTHENTIC INDIAN EXPERIENCE™

⟫━◈━⟪

Rebecca Roanhorse

*In the Great American Indian novel, when it is finally written, all of
the white people will be Indians and all of the Indians will be ghosts.*
—Sherman Alexie, "How to Write the Great American Indian Novel"

You maintain a menu of a half dozen Experiences on your digital blackboard, but Vision Quest is the one the Tourists choose the most. That certainly makes your workday easy. All a Vision Quest requires is a dash of
mystical shaman, a spirit animal (wolf usually, but birds of prey are on the
upswing this year), and the approximation of a peyote experience. Tourists
always come out of the Experience feeling spiritually transformed. (You've
never actually tried peyote, but you did smoke your share of weed during
that one year at Arizona State, and who's going to call you on the difference?) It's all 101 stuff, really, these Quests. But no other Indian working at
Sedona Sweats can do it better. Your sales numbers are tops.

Your wife Theresa doesn't approve of the gig. Oh, she likes you working,
especially after that dismal stretch of unemployment the year before last
when she almost left you, but she thinks the job itself is demeaning.

"Our last name's not Trueblood," she complains when you tell her
about your *nom de rêve*.

"Nobody wants to buy a Vision Quest from a Jesse Turnblatt," you
explain. "I need to sound more Indian."

"You are Indian," she says. "Turnblatt's Indian-sounding enough because you're already Indian."

"We're not the right kind of Indian," you counter. "I mean, we're
Catholic, for Christ's sake."

What Theresa doesn't understand is that Tourists don't want a real
Indian experience. They want what they see in the movies, and who can

blame them? Movie Indians are terrific! So you watch the same movies the Tourists do, until John Dunbar becomes your spirit animal and Stands with Fists your best girl. You memorize Johnny Depp's lines from *The Lone Ranger* and hang a picture of Iron Eyes Cody in your work locker. For a while you are really into Dustin Hoffman's *Little Big Man*.

It's *Little Big Man* that does you in.

For a week in June, you convince your boss to offer a Custer's Last Stand special, thinking there might be a Tourist or two who want to live out a Crazy Horse Experience. You even memorize some quotes attributed to the venerable Sioux chief that you find on the internet. You plan to make it real authentic.

But you don't get a single taker. Your numbers nosedive.

Management in Phoenix notices, and Boss drops it from the blackboard by Fourth of July weekend. He yells at you to stop screwing around, accuses you of trying to be an artiste or whatnot.

"Tourists don't come to Sedona Sweats to live out a goddamn battle," Boss says in the break room over lunch one day, "especially if the white guy loses. They come here to find themselves." Boss waves his hand in the air in an approximation of something vaguely prayer-like. "It's a spiritual experience we're offering. Top quality. The fucking best."

DarAnne, your Navajo co-worker with the pretty smile and the perfect teeth, snorts loudly. She takes a bite of her sandwich, mutton by the looks of it. Her jaw works, her sharp teeth flash white. She waits until she's finished chewing to say, "Nothing spiritual about Squaw Fantasy."

Squaw Fantasy is Boss's latest idea, his way to get the numbers up and impress Management. DarAnne and a few others have complained about the use of the ugly slur, the inclusion of a sexual fantasy as an Experience at all. But Boss is unmoved, especially when the first week's numbers roll in. Biggest seller yet.

Boss looks over at you. "What do you think?"

Boss is Pima, with a bushy mustache and a thick head of still-dark hair. You admire that about him. Virility. Boss makes being a man look easy. Makes everything look easy. Real authentic-like.

DarAnne tilts her head, long beaded earrings swinging, and waits. Her painted nails click impatiently against the Formica lunch table. You can smell the onion in her sandwich.

Your mouth is dry like the red rock desert you can see outside your window. If you say Squaw Fantasy is demeaning, Boss will mock you, call you a pussy, or worse. If you say you think it's okay, DarAnne and her crew will put you on the guys-who-are-assholes list and you'll deserve it.

You sip your bottled water, stalling. Decide that in the wake of the Crazy Horse debacle that Boss's approval means more than DarAnne's, and venture, "I mean, if the Tourists like it . . . "

Boss slaps the table, triumphant. DarAnne's face twists in disgust. "What does Theresa think of that, eh, Jesse?" she spits at you. "You tell her Boss is thinking of adding Savage Braves to the menu next? He's gonna have you in a loincloth and hair down to your ass, see how you like it."

Your face heats up, embarrassed. You push away from the table, too quickly, and the flimsy top teeters. You can hear Boss's shouts of protest as his vending machine lemonade tilts dangerously, and DarAnne's mocking laugh, but it all comes to your ears through a shroud of thick cotton. You mumble something about getting back to work. The sound of arguing trails you down the hall.

You change in the locker room and shuffle down to the pod marked with your name. You unlock the hatch and crawl in. Some people find the pods claustrophobic, but you like the cool metal container, the tight fit. It's comforting. The VR helmet fits snugly on your head, the breathing mask over your nose and mouth.

With a shiver of anticipation, you give the pod your Experience setting. Add the other necessary details to flesh things out. The screen prompts you to pick a Tourist connection from a waiting list, but you ignore it, blinking through the option screens until you get to the final confirmation. You brace for the mild nausea that always comes when you Relocate in and out of an Experience.

The first sensation is always smell. Sweetgrass and wood smoke and the rich loam of the northern plains. Even though it's fake, receptors firing under the coaxing of a machine, you relax into the scents. You grew up in the desert, among people who appreciate cedar and pinon and red earth, but there's still something home-like about this prairie place.

Or maybe you watch too much TV. You really aren't sure anymore.

You find yourself on a wide grassy plain, somewhere in the upper Midwest of a bygone era. Bison roam in the distance. A hawk soars overhead.

You are alone, you know this, but it doesn't stop you from looking around to make sure. This thing you are about to do. Well, you would be humiliated if anyone found out. Because you keep thinking about what DarAnne said.

Squaw Fantasy and Savage Braves. Because the thing is, being sexy doesn't disgust you the way it does DarAnne. You've never been one of those guys. The star athlete or the cool kid. It's tempting to think of all those Tourist women wanting you like that, even if it is just in an Experience.

You are now wearing a knee-length loincloth. A wave of black hair flows down your back. Your middle-aged paunch melts into rock-hard abs worthy of a romance novel cover model. You raise your chin and try out your best stoic look on a passing prairie dog. The little rodent chirps something back at you. You've heard prairie dogs can remember human faces, and you wonder what this one would say about you. Then you remember this is an Experience, so the prairie dog is no more real than the caricature of an Indian you have conjured up.

You wonder what Theresa would think if she saw you like this.

The world shivers. The pod screen blinks on. Someone wants your Experience.

A Tourist, asking for you. Completely normal. Expected. No need for that panicky hot breath rattling through your mask.

You scroll through the Tourist's requirements.

Experience Type: Vision Quest.
Tribe: Plains Indian (nation nonspecific).
Favorite animal: Wolf.

These things are all familiar. Things you are good at faking. Things you get paid to pretend.

You drop the Savage Brave fantasy garb for buckskin pants and beaded leather moccasins. You keep your chest bare and muscled but you drape a rough wool blanket across your shoulders for dignity. Your impressive abs are still visible.

The sun is setting and you turn to put the artificial dusk at your back, prepared to meet your Tourist. You run through your list of Indian names to bestow upon your Tourist once the Vision Quest is over. You like to keep the names fresh, never using the same one in case the Tourists ever compare notes. For a while you cheated and used one of those naming things on the internet where you enter your favorite flower and the street you grew up on and it gives you your Indian name, but there were too many Tourists that grew up on Elm or Park and you found yourself getting repetitive. You try to base the names on appearances now. Hair color, eye, some distinguishing feature. Tourists really seem to like it.

This Tourist is younger than you expected. Sedona Sweats caters to New Agers, the kind from Los Angeles or Scottsdale with impressive bank accounts. But the man coming up the hill, squinting into the setting sun, is in his late twenties. Medium height and build with pale spotty skin and brown hair. The guy looks normal enough, but there's something sad about him.

Maybe he's lost.

You imagine a lot of Tourists are lost.

Maybe he's someone who works a day job just like you, saving up money for this once-in-a-lifetime Indian Experience™. Maybe he's desperate, looking for purpose in his own shitty world and thinking Indians have all the answers. Maybe he just wants something that's authentic.

You like that. The idea that Tourists come to you to experience something real. DarAnne has it wrong. The Tourists aren't all bad. They're just needy.

You plant your feet in a wide welcoming stance and raise one hand. "How," you intone, as the man stops a few feet in front of you.

The man flushes, a bright pinkish tone. You can't tell if he's nervous or embarrassed. Maybe both? But he raises his hand, palm forward, and says, "How," right back.

"Have you come seeking wisdom, my son?" you ask in your best broken English accent. "Come. I will show you great wisdom." You sweep your arm across the prairie. "We look to brother wolf—"

The man rolls his eyes.

What?

You stutter to a pause. Are you doing something wrong? Is the accent no good? Too little? Too much?

You visualize the requirements checklist. You are positive he chose wolf. Positive. So you press on. "My brother wolf," you say again, this time sounding much more Indian, you are sure.

"I'm sorry," the man says, interrupting. "This wasn't what I wanted. I've made a mistake."

"But you picked it on the menu!" In the confusion of the moment, you drop your accent. Is it too late to go back and say it right?

The man's lips curl up in a grimace, like you have confirmed his worst suspicions. He shakes his head. "I was looking for something more authentic."

Something in your chest seizes up.

"I can fix it," you say.

"No, it's all right. I'll find someone else." He turns to go.

You can't afford another bad mark on your record. No more screw-ups or you're out. Boss made that clear enough. "At least give me a chance," you plead.

"It's okay," he says over his shoulder.

This is bad. Does this man not know what a good Indian you are? "Please!"

The man turns back to you, his face thoughtful.

You feel a surge of hope. This can be fixed, and you know exactly how. "I can give you a name. Something you can call yourself when you need to feel strong. It's authentic," you add enthusiastically. "From a real Indian." That much is true.

The man looks a little more open, and he doesn't say no. That's good enough.

You study the man's dusky hair, his pinkish skin. His long skinny legs. He reminds you a bit of the flamingos at the Albuquerque zoo, but you are pretty sure no one wants to be named after those strange creatures. It must be something good. Something...spiritual.

"Your name is Pale Crow," you offer. Birds are still on your mind.

At the look on the man's face, you reconsider. "No, no, it is White"— yes, that's better than pale—"Wolf. White Wolf."

"White Wolf?" There's a note of interest in his voice.

You nod sagely. You knew the man had picked wolf. Your eyes meet. Uncomfortably. White Wolf coughs into his hand. "I really should be getting back."

"But you paid for the whole experience. Are you sure?"

White Wolf is already walking away.

"But . . ."

You feel the exact moment he Relocates out of the Experience. A sensation like part of your soul is being stretched too thin. Then, a sort of whiplash, as you let go.

The Hey U.S.A. bar is the only Indian bar in Sedona. The basement level of a driftwood-paneled strip mall across the street from work. It's packed with the after-shift crowd, most of them pod jockeys like you, but also a few roadside jewelry hawkers and restaurant stiffs still smelling like frybread grease. You're lucky to find a spot at the far end next to the server's station. You slip onto the plastic-covered barstool and raise a hand to get the bartender's attention.

"So what do you really think?" asks a voice to your right. DarAnne is staring at you, her eyes accusing and her posture tense.

This is it. A second chance. Your opportunity to stay off the assholes list. You need to get this right. You try to think of something clever to say, something that would impress her but let you save face, too. But you're never been all that clever, so you stick to the truth.

"I think I really need this job," you admit.

DarAnne's shoulders relax.

"Scooch over," she says to the man on the other side of her, and he obligingly shifts off his stool to let her sit. "I knew it," she says. "Why didn't you stick up for me? Why are you so afraid of Boss?"

"I'm not afraid of Boss. I'm afraid of Theresa leaving me. And unemployment."

"You gotta get a backbone, Jesse, is all."

You realize the bartender is waiting, impatient. You drink the same thing every time you come here, a single Coors Light in a cold bottle. But the bartender never remembers you, or your order. You turn to offer to buy one for DarAnne, but she's already gone, back with her crew.

You drink your beer alone, wait a reasonable amount of time, and leave.

White Wolf is waiting for you under the streetlight at the corner.

The bright neon Indian Chief that squats atop Sedona Sweats hovers behind him in pinks and blues and yellows, his huge hand blinking up and down in greeting. White puffs of smoke signals flicker up, up and away beyond his far shoulder.

You don't recognize White Wolf at first. Most people change themselves a little within the construct of the Experience. Nothing wrong with being thinner, taller, a little better looking. But White Wolf looks exactly the same. Nondescript brown hair, pale skin, long legs.

"How." White Wolf raises his hand, unconsciously mimicking the big neon Chief. At least he has the decency to look embarrassed when he does it.

"You." You are so surprised that the accusation is the first thing out of your mouth. "How did you find me?"

"Trueblood, right? I asked around."

"And people told you?" This is very against the rules.

"I asked who the best Spirit Guide was. If I was going to buy a Vision Quest, who should I go to. Everyone said you."

You flush, feeling vindicated, but also annoyed that your co-workers had given your name out to a Tourist. "I tried to tell you," you say ungraciously.

"I should have listened." White Wolf smiles, a faint shifting of his mouth into something like contrition. An awkward pause ensues.

"We're really not supposed to fraternize," you finally say.

"I know, I just . . . I just wanted to apologize. For ruining the Experience like that."

"It's no big deal," you say, gracious this time. "You paid, right?"

"Yeah."

"It's just . . . " You know this is your ego talking, but you need to know. "Did I do something wrong?"

"No, it was me. You were great. It's just, I had a great grandmother who was Cherokee, and I think being there, seeing everything. Well, it really stirred something in me. Like, ancestral memory or something."

You've heard of ancestral memories, but you've also heard of people claiming Cherokee blood where there is none. Theresa calls them "pretendians," but you think that's unkind. Maybe White Wolf really is Cherokee. You don't know any Cherokees, so maybe they really do look like this guy. There's a half-Tlingit in payroll and he's pale.

"Well, I've got to get home," you say. "My wife, and all."

White Wolf nods. "Sure, sure. I just. Thank you."

"For what?"

But White Wolf's already walking away. "See you around."

A little déjà vu shudders your bones but you chalk it up to Tourists. Who understands them, anyway?

You go home to Theresa.

As soon as you slide into your pod the next day, your monitor lights up. There's already a Tourist on deck and waiting.

"Shit," you mutter, pulling up the menu and scrolling quickly through the requirements. Everything looks good, good, except ... a sliver of panic when you see that a specific tribe has been requested. Cherokee. You don't know anything about Cherokees. What they wore back then, their ceremonies. The only Cherokee you know is ...

White Wolf shimmers into your Experience.

In your haste, you have forgotten to put on your buckskin. Your Experience-self still wears Wranglers and Nikes. Boss would be pissed to see you this sloppy.

"Why are you back?" you ask.

"I thought maybe we could just talk."

"About what?"

White Wolf shrugs. "Doesn't matter. Whatever."

"I can't."

"Why not? This is my time. I'm paying."

You feel a little panicked. A Tourist has never broken protocol like this before. Part of why the Experience works is that everyone knows their role. But White Wolf don't seem to care about the rules.

"I can just keep coming back," he says. "I have money, you know."

"You'll get me in trouble."

"I won't. I just . . . " White Wolf hesitates. Something in him slumps. What you read as arrogance now looks like desperation. "I need a friend."

You know that feeling. The truth is, you could use a friend, too. Someone to talk to. What could the harm be? You'll just be two men, talking.

Not here, though. You still need to work. "How about the bar?"

"The place from last night?"

"I get off at 11:00 p.m."

When you get there around 11:30 p.m., the bar is busy but you recognize White Wolf immediately. A skinny white guy stands out at the Hey U.S.A. It's funny. Under this light, in this crowd, White Wolf could pass for Native of some kind. One of those 1/64th guys, at least. Maybe he really is a little Cherokee from way back when.

White Wolf waves you over to an empty booth. A Coors Light waits for you. You slide into the booth and wrap a hand around the cool damp skin of the bottle, pleasantly surprised.

"A lucky guess, did I get it right?"

You nod and take a sip. That first sip is always magic. Like how you imagine Golden, Colorado must feel like on a winter morning.

"So," White Wolf says, "tell me about yourself."

You look around the bar for familiar faces. Are you really going to do this? Tell a Tourist about your life? Your real life? A little voice in your head whispers that maybe this isn't so smart. Boss could find out and get mad. DarAnne could make fun of you. Besides, White Wolf will want a cool story, something real authentic, and all you have is an aging three-bedroom ranch and a student loan.

But he's looking at you, friendly interest, and nobody looks at you like that much anymore, not even Theresa. So you talk.

Not everything.

But some. Enough.

Enough that when the bartender calls last call you realize you've been talking for two hours.

When you stand up to go, White Wolf stands up, too. You shake hands, Indian-style, which makes you smile. You didn't expect it, but you've got a good, good feeling.

"So, same time tomorrow?" White Wolf asks.

You're tempted, but, "No, Theresa will kill me if I stay out this late two nights in a row." And then, "But how about Friday?"

"Friday it is." White Wolf touches your shoulder. "See you then, Jesse."

You feel a warm flutter of anticipation for Friday. "See you."

Friday you are there by 11:05 p.m. White Wolf laughs when he sees your face, and you grin back, only a little embarrassed. This time you pay for the drinks, and the two of you pick up right where you left off. It's so easy. White Wolf never seems to tire of your stories and it's been so long since you had a new friend to tell them to, that you can't seem to quit. It turns out White Wolf loves Kevin Costner, too, and you take turns quoting lines at each other until White Wolf stumps you with a Wind in His Hair quote.

"Are you sure that's in the movie?"

"It's Lakota!"

You won't admit it, but you're impressed with how good White Wolf's Lakota sounds.

White Wolf smiles. "Looks like I know something you don't."

You wave it away good-naturedly, but vow to watch the movie again.

Time flies and once again, after last call, you both stand outside under the Big Chief. You happily agree to meet again next Tuesday. And the following Friday. Until it becomes your new routine.

The month passes quickly. The next month, too.

"You seem too happy," Theresa says one night, sounding suspicious.

You grin and wrap your arms around your wife, pulling her close until her rose-scented shampoo fills your nose. "Just made a friend, is all. A guy from work." You decide to keep it vague. Hanging with White Wolf, who you've long stopped thinking of as just a Tourist, would be hard to explain.

"You're not stepping out on me, Jesse Turnblatt? Because I will—"

You cut her off with a kiss. "Are you jealous?"

"Should I be?"

"Never."

She sniffs, but lets you kiss her again, her soft body tight against yours.

"I love you," you murmur as your hands dip under her shirt.

"You better."

Tuesday morning and you can't breathe. Your nose is a deluge of snot and your joints ache. Theresa calls in sick for you and bundles you in bed with a bowl of stew. You're supposed to meet White Wolf for your usual drink, but you're much too sick. You consider sending Theresa with a note, but decided against it. It's only one night. White Wolf will understand.

But by Friday the coughing has become a deep rough bellow that shakes your whole chest. When Theresa calls in sick for you again, you make sure your cough is loud enough for Boss to hear it. Pray he doesn't dock you for the days you're missing. But what you're most worried about is standing up White Wolf again.

"Do you think you could go for me?" you ask Theresa.

"What, down to the bar? I don't drink."

"I'm not asking you to drink. Just to meet him, let him know I'm sick. He's probably thinking I forgot about him."

"Can't you call him?"

"I don't have his number."

"Fine, then. What's his name?"

You hesitate. Realize you don't know. The only name you know is the one you gave him. "White Wolf."

"Okay, then. Get some rest."

Theresa doesn't get back until almost 1 a.m. "Where were you?" you ask, alarmed. Is that a rosy flush in her cheeks, the scent of Cherry Coke on her breath?

"At the bar like you asked me to."

"What took so long?"

She huffs. "Did you want me to go or not?"

"Yes, but . . . well, did you see him?"

She nods, smiles a little smile that you've never seen on her before.

"What is it?" Something inside you shrinks.

"A nice man. Real nice. You didn't tell me he was Cherokee."

By Monday you're able to drag yourself back to work. There's a note taped to your locker to go see Boss. You find him in his office, looking through the reports that he sends to Management every week.

"I hired a new guy."

You swallow the excuses you've prepared to explain how sick you were, your promises to get your numbers up. They become a hard ball in your throat.

"Sorry, Jesse." Boss actually does look a little sorry. "This guy is good, a real rez guy. Last name's 'Wolf.' I mean, shit, you can't get more Indian than that. The Tourists are going to eat it up."

"The Tourists love me, too." You sound whiny, but you can't help it. There's a sinking feeling in your gut that tells you this is bad, bad, bad.

"You're good, Jesse. But nobody knows anything about Pueblo Indians, so all you've got is that TV shit. This guy, he's . . . " Boss snaps his fingers, trying to conjure the word.

"Authentic?" A whisper.

Boss points his finger like a gun. "Bingo. Look, if another pod opens up, I'll call you."

"You gave him my pod?"

Boss's head snaps up, wary. You must have yelled that. He reaches over to tap a button on his phone and call security.

"Wait!" you protest.

But the men in uniforms are already there to escort you out.

You can't go home to Teresa. You just can't. So you head to the Hey U.S.A. It's a different crowd than you're used to. An afternoon crowd. Heavy boozers and people without jobs. You laugh because you fit right in.

The guys next to you are doing shots. Tiny glasses of rheumy dark liquor lined up in a row. You haven't done shots since college but when one of the men offers you one, you take it. Choke on the cheap whiskey that burns down your throat. Two more and the edges of your panic start to blur soft and tolerable. You can't remember what time it is when you get up to leave, but the Big Chief is bright in the night sky.

You stumble through the door and run smack into DarAnne. She growls at you, and you try to stutter out an apology but a heavy hand comes down on your shoulder before you get the words out.

"This asshole bothering you?"

You recognize that voice. "White Wolf?" It's him. But he looks different to you. Something you can't quite place. Maybe it's the ribbon shirt he's wearing, or the bone choker around his neck. Is his skin a little tanner than it was last week?

"Do you know this guy?" DarAnne asks, and you think she's talking to you, but her head is turned towards White Wolf.

"Never seen him," White Wolf says as he stares you down, and under that confident glare you almost believe him. Almost forget that you've told this man things about you even Theresa doesn't know.

"It's me," you protest, but your voice comes out in a whiskey-slurred squeak that doesn't even sound like you.

"Fucking glonnies," DarAnne mutters as she pushes past you. "Always making a scene."

"I think you better go, buddy," White Wolf says. Not unkindly, if you were in fact strangers, if you weren't actually buddies. But you are, and you clutch at his shirtsleeve, shouting something about friendship and Theresa and then the world melts into a blur until you feel the hard slap of concrete against your shoulder and the taste of blood on your lip where you bit it and a solid kick to your gut until the whiskey comes up the way it went down and then the Big Chief is blinking at you, How, How, How, until the darkness comes to claim you and the lights all flicker out.

You wake up in the gutter. The fucking gutter. With your head aching and your mouth as dry and rotted as month-old roadkill. The sun is up, Arizona fire beating across your skin. Your clothes are filthy and your shoes are missing and there's a smear of blood down your chin and drying flakes in the creases of your neck. Your hands are chapped raw. And you can't remember why.

But then you do.

And the humiliation sits heavy on your bruised up shoulder, a dark shame that defies the desert sun. Your job. DarAnne ignoring you like that. White Wolf kicking your ass. And you out all night, drunk in a downtown gutter. It all feels like a terrible dream, like the worst kind. The ones you can't wake up from because it's real life.

Your car isn't where you left it, likely towed with the street sweepers, so you trudge your way home on sock feet. Three miles on asphalt streets until you see your highly-mortgaged three-bedroom ranch. And for once the place looks beautiful, like the day you bought it. Tears gather in your eyes as you push open the door.

"Theresa," you call. She's going to be pissed, and you're going to have to talk fast, explain the whole drinking thing (it was one time!) and getting fired (I'll find a new job, I promise), but right now all you want is to wrap her in your arms and let her rose-scent fill your nose like good medicine.

"Theresa," you call again, as you limp through the living room. Veer off to look in the bedroom, check behind the closed bathroom door. But what you see in the bathroom makes you pause. Things are missing. Her toothbrush, the pack of birth control, contact lens solution.

"Theresa!?" and this time you are close to panic as you hobble down the hall to the kitchen.

The smell hits you first. The scent of fresh coffee, bright and familiar.

When you see the person sitting calmly at the kitchen table, their back to you, you relax. But that's not Theresa.

He turns slightly, enough so you can catch his profile, and says, "Come on in, Jesse."

"What the fuck are you doing here?"

White Wolf winces, as if your words hurt him. "You better have a seat."

"What did you do to my wife?!"

"I didn't do anything to your wife." He picks up a small folded piece of paper, holds it out. You snatch it from his fingers and move so you can see his face. The note in your hand feels like wildfire, something with the potential to sear you to the bone. You want to rip it wide open, you want to flee before its revelations scar you. You ache to read it now, now, but you won't give him the satisfaction of your desperation.

"So now you remember me," you huff.

"I apologize for that. But you were making a scene and I couldn't have you upsetting DarAnne."

You want to ask how he knows DarAnne, how he was there with her in the first place. But you already know. Boss said the new guy's name was Wolf.

"You're a real son of a bitch, you know that?"

White Wolf looks away from you, that same pained look on his face. Like you're embarrassing yourself again. "Why don't you help yourself to some coffee," he says, gesturing to the coffee pot. Your coffee pot.

"I don't need your permission to get coffee in my own house," you shout.

"Okay," he says, leaning back. You can't help but notice how handsome he looks, his dark hair a little longer, the choker on his neck setting off the arch of his high cheekbones.

You take your time getting coffee—sugar, creamer which you would never usually take—before you drop into the seat across from him. Only then do you open the note, hands trembling, dread twisting hard in your gut.

"She's gone to her mother's," White Wolf explains as you read the same words on the page. "For her own safety. She wants you out by the time she gets back."

"What did you tell her?"

"Only the truth. That you got yourself fired, that you were on a bender, drunk in some alleyway downtown like a bad stereotype." He leans in. "You've been gone for two days."

You blink. It's true, but it's not true, too.

"Theresa wouldn't . . . " But she would, wouldn't she? She'd said it a million times, given you a million chances.

"She needs a real man, Jesse. Someone who can take care of her."

"And that's you?" You muster all the scorn you can when you say that, but it comes out more a question than a judgment. You remember how you gave him the benefit of the doubt on that whole Cherokee thing, how you thought "pretendian" was cruel.

He clears his throat. Stands.

"It's time for you to go," he says. "I promised Theresa you'd be gone, and I've got to get to work soon." Something about him seems to expand, to take up the space you once occupied. Until you feel small, superfluous.

"Did you ever think," he says, his voice thoughtful, his head tilted to study you like a strange foreign body, "that maybe this is my experience, and you're the tourist here?"

"This is my house," you protest, but you're not sure you believe it now. Your head hurts. The coffee in your hand is already cold. How long have you been sitting here? Your thoughts blur to histories, your words become nothing more than forgotten facts and half-truths. Your heart, a dusty repository for lost loves and desires, never realized.

"Not anymore," he says.

Nausea rolls over you. That same stretching sensation you get when you Relocate out of an Experience.

Whiplash, and then . . .

You let go.

MOON, AND MEMORY, AND MUCHNESS

<hr/>

Katherine Vaz

I begin at three o'clock in the morning. There's a glaze over tonight's rind of the moon. Sometimes—this being a club-dense part of the East Village—I jump out of my skin at the sound of breaking glass, a quarrel; I almost cry out for Alicia. I assemble the adorable, tiny pots of lemon curd and mango jam and the comfits that my customers steal. I use a butter-cutter pastry tool on the best butter for the pumpkin scones. A *New York Times* food editor asked for my secret ingredient in the crystallized-ginger muffins, but I demurred, not because it is exotic but because it's frightfully simple: I add coconut extract. My walk-in freezer is packed to its gills, but everything is precisely labeled. Grief can do this: There's a ferocious desire to control and align the world, as if that stops or reverses the time. Mini-quiches, miniature tortilla molds for lentil salad. I fix roulade sandwiches with Russian dressing, turkey, and Cotswold cheddar. Does a person ever conquer an eating disorder? Everything screams, Eat Me, Drink Me. As a young wife and mother, I blew up two sizes, melted down three, over and over. Now I survive on practically nothing, toast and rose-hip infusions. My Wonderland Tea Shop and its kitchen are downstairs, and I perch in small quarters above. After one day's prep, service, and clean-up, it's always time to start over again.

What is the "bargaining" stage of grief? Since I've never figured that out, I fear I'm trapped in whatever "it" is. If I hold my temper when a customer spills clotted cream on the floor, will Alicia reappear? If I smile as a woman changes her order from white tea to rooibos to the Zen Mix, will my child's ghost appear? If I throw out the news clippings about the two young madmen who tormented and murdered Alicia, will I get un-stuck in Time? (Is that even something I want?) My ex-husband, Bill, lives with a new wife and son (already a schoolboy!) in Phoenix, and we chat on occasion; we have lunch (I watch him eat while I can't finish my soup) when he returns for the parole hearings. I'm glad for him. He blamed me for Alicia, but I blame myself. At an arts-and-crafts emporium in Chelsea, while gathering holly and garlands for Christmas, I turned my back, and the earth swallowed her.

Above the shop, my rented rooms are so minute it's as if I live in the cutaway of a whelk shell. Painted on the face of the ticking tabletop clock is a girl on a swing, her Mary Janes frozen toward heaven. There's never wine on hand, because I'd drink it and then there'd be no wine anyway. Occasionally I resort to pills for sleep and glide in technicolor dreams, flowers talking, flamingoes playing a game with me as the baseball. I maintain, intact, the pint-sized tea table that Alicia loved arranging for Mr. Bun, her stuffed rabbit, and Mabel the mouse, and Jackie the toucan. At each setting are plastic wands filled with water, glitter, and tiny keys. Bill joined the little parties we threw for her animals, mint in sugar-water and vanilla wafers; he was a warm father and husband.

I used to teach poetry at a small college on Staten Island, but those eager faces, even the ones ravaged by wild partying, blazed their hopeful innocence in my direction, nearly burning me alive. Bill was an accountant. We lived modestly, us three, in Murray Hill. We sold our apartment and shared the profits after the two boys—rich, with a lawyer passionately loud about the burden of their privileges—were sentenced to only twelve years. Alicia died at age six. Eight years ago. It was yesterday.

Of course Kumiko Mori is the first employee to show up, clear-eyed, cheerful, with a red streak feathering her hair and her signature thick belt accenting a cinched waist her boyfriend likely spans with his hands. "Morning, Mrs. Dias."

I've told her to call me Dorrie. Or Doreen. Old-school, she resists. I should return to my maiden name, Lewis—I'm a custard of Welsh, English, and Finnish—but then I wouldn't have Alicia's final name anymore. Bill Dias is of Brazilian and Irish stock.

Kumiko picks up the sign-up sheet at the counter to see how many people want to try a tea ceremony. Zero. Her grandfather is at the ready, should we enlist enough takers. *Chanoyu*. Sweets served to balance tea's bitterness. Everything spotless, arranged with flowers. Tranquility, the meaningfulness of nothing-meaning-much: Who in modernity can bear submitting to a breakdown and examination of every action and minute?

I joke about how many entertainments vie for our attention nowadays, and tea ceremonies of painstaking slowness are a tough sell.

Kumiko grins and unwinds the eternity scarf from her neck. It's autumn; our décor is purple and gilt. She hangs her scarf and coat on the hook in the kitchen as she takes the teapots from the shelf, and she says, "I need to tell you something, Mrs. Dias."

Why does my heart skip a beat? All the servers eventually leave, but I hate giving her up. Her beauty, grace, and hard work. The faint promise of a ceremony of tea.

"Kumiko?"

But then in barrels Jason, sleepy, mild, a decent waitperson, good with card tricks at the tables while the tea brews. He wants to be an actor. The older man he lives with might be cheating on him. He's pleasant. Less so is Alex, dragging himself in, a lean practitioner of the faint sneer, eager to convey that he's primed for better things when he graduates from Columbia. His financial-world parents—he lives with them—encourage his refusal to abase himself with a mice-filled, starter studio apartment. I should fire him, but he keeps his disdain subdued, and it's hard to find help.

Kumiko unlocks the front door, and hordes on their way to work pour in for cinnamon rolls and croissants to go, and the mothers-at-ease trundle in their squalling children, babies wrinkled as piglets. I feed off the tumult of children, though Alicia was quiet. Why didn't she bellow and scream when those boys abducted her?

A girl in a fairy princess outfit tugs my apron and says, "I like apricots!"

I kneel to meet her eyes with mine, delighted. "Guess what? I made apricot tarts last night." All true! I treasure these unexpected little connections as victories.

The mother, a natural beauty in a ponytail, a child herself, says, "Wonderful."

Then laughs. Because *wonderful* and *wonder* belong in *wonderland*.

I never remember that Alicia would be fourteen now. I live for these girls who come with their mothers, a special treat. They're joyful in this make-believe realm I've made. Throwback to gracious times. Tea, gen-til-i-ty. Bite-sized salmon sandwiches. The pots warmed British-style, loose leaves if you have more time, an extra spoon for the pot. I'm not raking in a fortune, but I've kept my nose above water.

Kumiko carries a tray of Earl Grey. More customers sweep in. Morning rush. The walls offer murals of white and red roses, white rabbits. Fish-footmen. A queen, a chorus of humans as playing cards. A caterpillar on a mushroom, hookah in mouth; the college kids flock near that one.

I wave at Kumiko over the tables, the sea of speeding New Yorkers. She does a funny mock-dance of panic. Her red-and-white Wonderland apron is spotless. Crash! A child has dropped her fragile cup; an accident. Kumiko comforts her and sweeps it up. Alex checks his phone until he sees me glaring. Jason's sleeves are already stained with jam.

My child once found a songbird, egg-yolk yellow, with a head wound, during a walk with us in Central Park. She fed it with an eyedropper at home. Bill and I warned it wouldn't make it. She insisted that it would, or at least it wouldn't die alone. She was all of five, one year left to live. She named the birdie "Dodo." I'll never know why. Came the dawn that the bird flapped around her room, and Alicia opened the window and chanted, "Go now, go away. Fly! Go on," though she was in tears.

One night, as a prank, Alicia put crayons in Bill's and my bed. Her reason was that we seemed so drained she was afraid we were dreaming in black-and-white.

When I ask Kumiko, as breakfast cedes to the lunch crowd—more sandwiches, more tiered stands with savory items on top and petit fours below—what she needed to tell me, she says, "Mrs. Dias, I got that internship at Bellevue." Her smooth skin suddenly looks like satin balled up in a fist and then let go. "It's full-time."

No surprise, really. She wants to be a psychiatrist, and she deserves any portal that opens. Her future is unfurling before her. But as she gently gives two-weeks' notice, I drop into the chair behind the counter, because the purple room is spinning.

"Hey," she says. "Hey, Mrs. Dias. I'm so sorry."

I say I'm glad for her. And I am. I hiss at Alex to get off his phone and stop pretending he can't see the guests at Table Five waving their arms as if they're in a lifeboat. For a horrid moment, I imagine unlocking the drawer near the register, extracting my silver pistol, and scaring the dumb grin off his spoiled face.

"I'll come back with my grandpa if you get the sign-ups for a tea ceremony," Kumiko whispers, an arm around my slumped shoulder. Jason glances my way as he passes with a lethally large serving of éclairs. What is wrong with me?

There's work to be done, it never stops; I hug her, flooded with a vision of Kumiko in her late twenties, married, telling a depressed patient in a sea of tears that *there are endless reasons* to go on. Her office has bronze statues of naked bodies. On the wall is a picture colored by the son I figure she'll have, a smiling family with a cat, all bigger than their house.

Alex forgets the chutney requested by two grand dames at Table Three for their walnut bread. They declare, in ringing tones, that they did not ask for the jasmine teabags; they want the expensive Tienchi Flower, twelve dollars a cup.

Jason approaches them and says, "Shall I fix that?"

"Someone should!" trumpets one with so much plastic surgery that her nostrils are holes, her head a skull. She seems ready to start throwing the dishes.

"Where is the manager?" asks her friend, wearing an honest-to-God turban with a jewel on it, like the kind favored by fraud magicians who saw people in half.

Am I invisible? Alex stands helpless, a pleading expression trained on Jason for rescue. Much of my tearoom is staring.

"Shall I get their tea?" whispers Kumiko. "Or just kick their asses?"

She does make me smile.

Because she knows what to do without being constantly told, Kumiko sidles into the kitchen, unlocking the cupboard where I store the expensive stuff. I have some Yellow Gold Bud—it sounds like weed—painted edible gold: $120 an ounce.

Turban Lady launches into a tirade about the city falling apart; I gesture at Alex and Jason to attend to the rest of the room, to distract it, as I force myself to coo at the women that we'll put everything right. Did they know Tienchi Flower—a refined choice!—relieves pain and cure rashes?

They assault me with a barrage of nonsense: Is the water in my Wonderland Tea Shop drawn from the tap, or do I have a proper reverse-osmosis system? Did I bribe some inspector to grant me that "A" grade? Why do so many menu selections start with "M"—mountain mint, marvelous mango, mascarpone, macaroni, moon cakes, and much about melons? Molasses. They suggest I need a haircut. I venture they needn't be rude. Why is the Duchess on my mural so fatheaded? Why can't I say what I mean? Why is the clock on the wall five minutes fast? Are the macarons—another "M"—stale? Why are crumbs on their butter knives? Why is my expression blank; why am I trembling?

"Excellent, ladies, here's your tea," I murmur as Kumiko brings out a fragrant batch in the teapot painted with Dutch children skating on a pond. I want to gorge on a stack of pressed cheese sandwiches until my body threatens to resign.

After the imperial pair finishes and offers parting complaints and leaves nary a tip for Alex or Kumiko, I notice a mother and daughter tucked in the corner. The girl is black-haired like my Alicia, five or six; I wander closer to see that yes, her eyes are Alicia's green. She smiles, a tooth missing.

Alex interrupts my reverie with a rare apology; sorry he got that order topsy-turvy. His apron is off; he never stays a second past his shift. His lashes brush the lenses of his hip glasses.

I assure him it's not the end of the world, not by a long shot.

He's not accustomed to admitting a failing, to feeling bad. He's not used to making a slight mistake that someone pounds into the dirt with a sledgehammer.

Kumiko and Jason commandeer the room as I approach the corner table. The mother lights up and whispers at me companionably, conspiratorially, "Gosh, those ladies were something else. How do you stand it?"

"There are worse things," I say. The child is daintily eating the mozzarella—M!—flatbread, and her teacup, the artful scarlet-rose one, holds the Sweet Dreams & Citrus that shivers when she brings it to her lips.

What else may I do for them; are they having a good time; what else may I bring?

The mother is around my age, nearing forty, though she is much more in the forty-is-the-new-twenty category, olive-skinned, mahogany hair with yellow highlights. Her bracelets jangle out music. The girl has a rhinestone barrette shaped like a spider, and she tells me proudly that her name is Charlotte.

"Did you spin any webs for Wilbur?" I ask; my blood flows as if gates have lifted in my veins. The child beams at me. "Yes!"

We chat about the places where *Charlotte's Web* made us cry, and the mother adds that she even gets teary-eyed in public when she recalls certain parts.

I almost say my little girl loves books, too. I wrote and taught poetry, once.

"I'm Betty," says the mother, "but my friends call me Bird."

The creature my child saved, brought back to life. Yellow feathers now yellow streaks in hair. Betty praises the butter's sweetness and the apricot tarts, today's special. It's lovely to be here. Her clothing is pressed, high couture. Piercing her ears are diamonds. "Look at us, enjoying high tea," she says to Charlotte. Because it's around twelve o'clock.

I explain that high tea is so-called because the *tables* are high. People at a social gathering wander and graze on food and drink set up for easy access.

"High" doesn't signal the hour. Americans think of high noon. Gunslingers! Time to settle scores.

"That's amazing!" Betty proclaims. Her daughter nods. They've learned something, together. They probably dance at night, Mother making Baby giggle by offering to toss her into the stars. I'm dying to ask what Betty "does," other than care for this smart, pretty, alert child. My skills in chatting with customers need sharpening.

Charlotte swings her legs and gazes with a devotion at her mother so profound that I glance away, because it's not meant for me. Well-trained, a city girl, she thanks me for the tea, the cup, the mozzarella and desserts. Kumiko clears tables; Jason shines the coffee urn. My staff knows nothing about Alicia, nothing of my history. Charlotte near-shouts, "Could we have my birthday here, Momma? May I, please?" Her fingernails shine with dots of crimson polish still wet-looking.

Betty wholeheartedly agrees . . . Certainly! Charlotte's sixth birthday will be here next week, at the Wonderland Tea Shop! We live only two blocks away! Sorry she must hasten now, she tells me, but she has a deadline. Her aspect clarifies as familiar, from the papers and from my long-ago, long-slumbering days as a poet. It's Betty Lezardo, the novelist whose successes have been capped recently with a National Book Award.

A soaring career and the most darling child alive; a woman my age accomplished and kind.

When I inquire if she's Betty Lezardo, she shyly nods and asks for my name.

Dorrie. Doreen Dias.

A hand extended to press against mine. Betty/Bird says, "I have a question about your murals." She points—artist's eye—toward the Hatter and March Hare, the crazy duo at their table, in leg irons. That, she avers, is odd enough. "But where is the Dormouse?"

Almost no one catches that omission. That absence.

"The Hatter and Hare pinched the Dormouse several times, in the original story," I say. "Remember? It didn't do them any harm. They used it as a cushion. They poured hot tea on its nose, to torment it. I don't want to stick it anywhere near those two."

Betty finishes her tea. Basic green, superior for weight-watching and longevity.

For fear of upsetting the child, I omit mentioning the other detail about the Dormouse that gets glossed over: When Alice left the table, the two

madmen *were stuffing the poor tiny thing headfirst into the teapot.* Another
reason I had the muralist clap the madmen in leg irons. *Were they trying
to kill it? Or just escalate the torture?* The Dormouse appears at Alice's trial
in the famous book . . . so it survived, unless its appearance is obeying the
rubric of fantasy and it's come back from the dead. But the madmen, at the
very least, must have watched it struggle for air.

Betty and Charlotte's tea and edibles are on the house, in thanks for
wanting the birthday under my roof. My face is an unreadable mask over
agony when Charlotte throws her arms around my middle to say goodbye
and rests her head where I can hold it, that soft dark hair.

No reason to add that the two Princeton dropouts who drowned my
child for kicks stuffed her headfirst into a drainpipe near the Hudson. She
was not raped. The defense attorney cited this as cause for leniency. I hold
my breath sometimes, to own the exact feeling she suffered. But I can't
begin to fathom it. I'm not at the mercy of someone else.

The customers disappear, a breather before the late afternoon tide, and
then nothing; we close at six; then prep for tomorrow and me under an
afghan as I watch an umpteenth rerun of *Mad Men*, starving myself, alert
to street noises. I should take my pistol upstairs, but I hate having it near
Alicia's Mr. Bun, Mabel, and Jackie. Does Charlotte have a spider doll, a
pig? Is Betty's book award in a frame? The water runs hard in the kitchen;
Kumiko is scrubbing the grill pan. Baking soda and boiling water clean
the pots; no detergent to interfere with the delicate balance of tea. Jason is
belting out lines from *Cats* because he's in the chorus; Kumiko groans and
orders him to stop. She meets my eyes with sadness that she'll soon be gone.
I let myself feel touched she'll miss me.

Some drunken fool is yelling as time-wasters spill out of a bar. Two in the
morning. Scratchy blanket, gut like a drum. I awaken from my recurring
dream of carrying a sleeping Alicia, her head on my shoulder. Since her
death, she is sunk everywhere, and therefore everything is Alicia: flour,
lightning rod in the distance, Mrs. Marcy's lapdog drowsing as she drinks
chrysanthemum tea. Alicia is the blue of the caterpillar on my wall.

A prayer for her phantom to visit; a prayer I won't keel over of fright. A
rattling of my shop's door! I should sleep with the gun near, though I barely
know how to fire it.

The sound goes away. Probably they'd only invade my refrigerator.
Zucchini frittatas tomorrow; hibiscus herbal tea on special.

In the week of planning Charlotte Lezardo's party, I get to know her and her mother better; they stop by for tea daily. Charlotte favors a brooch with a fake-emerald lizard. Momma allows her a hint of rouge, "just for fun." Betty wrings her hands about writer's block, and I say, Oh, that must be awful. Terrible.

Betty has ordered new living room furniture. I picture their high-ceilinged home, with bookcases and a kitchen in candy shades. The fireplace has tiles from her love affair with Art Deco. Tempera-painted pictures by Charlotte. Of jellyfish and friends, Mom and Dad, the aurora borealis she discovered on a nature show, leaving her stunned.

Betty/Bird splurged on a Carolina Herrera dress to attend an upcoming literary event and got a matching floral number for her child. Her husband, Vincent, is a corporate lawyer on business in Chicago and promises to be back in time.

"Beautiful Momma!" cries Charlotte.

"What do you think, Dorrie?" Betty says, showing me a picture on her phone of her modeling the dress. She gleams with pleasure. Is she ever scared or afflicted or desperate?

"Not bad," I say.

Yesterday my landlord increased my rent. I tuck Charlotte's hair behind her ears as she sips from the cup with a winking man in the moon. Kumiko makes her celebrated corn fritters, her last days drawing near.

A glorious truth about tea is that it's like that quote from Heraclitus, about not being able to step into the same river twice. No sip from a pot is like a preceding mouthful. The steeping deepens; the color mellows. A second pot aiming to recapture the perfection of an earlier one is doomed. It's itself, with its own intensifications.

We shut the restaurant for Charlotte Lezardo's sixth birthday. I am blurry with insomnia, puffy from succumbing to such lunatic, midnight cravings that I wolfed profiteroles drowning in chocolate sauce, a shameful sight, chin dripping, fingers smeared. In addition to my rent going up, I've received notice of a tax increase.

About a dozen girls and six of the mothers—and one father—show up at four o'clock. Jason finishes tying balloons to the chairs. We've shoved a few tables together. Alex has the day off. Kumiko is cutting crusts off the tomato-and-basil sandwiches. Charlotte is a vegetarian because she does not want to harm animals. My Alicia was the same. I'll never forget the evening she wept enough to smash me to pieces when she looked at a pork chop and realized it was from a piggy.

"This is fantastic!" declares Betty/Bird, gripping Charlotte's hand and surveying the streamers twisting from the ceiling's light fixtures to the sconces.

"Mrs. Dias!" the birthday girl cries, flinging herself into my grasp. Grateful. She's in a sparkly peach-tinted belted dress, and Betty/Bird wears a chic white shift. Does she never spill? She moans about the price of the blow-out she treated herself to. We exchange girlish asides about how women lie to husbands about the cost of salons. I haven't much focused on my good years flying by without a real romance since my divorce. (One or two misfiring relationships, sex tales from the crypt, don't count.)

Another mother exclaims how terrific it is to discover this darling spot hiding in the Village. Everyone piles into seats, Charlotte in the place of honor. There's mint and orange tea, and Charlotte's Birthday Mix, rose and lemon. The grown-ups down mimosas as if they're on fire inside. Kumiko, Jason, and I cart out teapots, desserts, and finger food.

Jason offers to read tealeaves. There's squealing. Gifts stacked high are wrapped in neon papers with cascading, curled ribbons. I keep a tiara on hand for these events, and I crown Charlotte. She rewards me with her happiness.

Jason, reading her leaves, announces, "Well! This is incredible!"

"Tell me!" begs Charlotte.

"Mmm," muses Jason. "What'll you pay me?"

The birthday girl giggles. "Please?"

A dramatic pause. "Miss Charlotte. I believe I see—" and he scrutinizes the cup. "I hate to disappoint you. But since you're already *adorable,* you're stuck with growing up adorable. Since you're already smarter than I am, you'll get even smarter. Hmm . . . it's murky. I'm trying to read what you'll do with your life . . . "

"I'm going to be a writer like Momma," Charlotte offers, voice hushed.

"Don't tell her," he replies in a stage whisper, "but you're going to have so many fans, they'll mob you. Your picture's going to be everywhere! How does it feel, to be a star?"

Applause. Betty's the perfect vision of the proud mother. Charlotte reaches up to award him a kiss. She's not timid with strangers. Her mother should warn her about how that's good in one way but bad in another.

Jason moves on to a woman waggling her cup (violet sprigs) at him.

The dipped strawberries and cucumber sandwiches vanish. Betty calls for champagne! Out come the flutes, and the red velvet cake with vanilla frosting and piping of a web cascading off "Charlotte." Happy sixth birthday, love. The gifts are abundant, T-shirts and a lacey dress that elicits sighs, and from me, *Through the Looking-Glass*. She contemplates the book in a hush, solemnly rises, embraces me again, and says, "Best present ever." Betty converses with a friend, slapping the table with glee over a story I can't hear.

Charlotte continues, her face upturned toward me, "One day, I'm going to paint you a picture, Mrs. Dias."

I tell her I can't wait.

And I don't know what comes over me, my sorrow at peak agony; maybe my unrest is from cramming a surfeit of sickly-sweet junk down my gullet alone in the chilly hours after days of hunger. It might arise from something as simple as Kumiko and Jason having no clue about Alicia; what could they possible offer, were I to break down and inform them? They clearly haven't Googled me. Maybe I'll flat-out die if I mount those stairs to my bide-a-wee lodgings tonight where, under a waning moon with my memories, I'll tolerate another night of intoxicated dolts in shouting-distance putting their twelve-dollar drinks on their credit cards because, God knows, the hour of reckoning will never come. Maybe I've always been murderous about wanting to kill those guffawing bastards who took my Alicia. Or maybe I'm welling up with nothing, and everything, a formulating of an admission to the police: I thought my girl was gone, but she's come back to say hello, to tell me, using the tea party I prepared for a birthday numerically matching the last one she knew on earth, that she would have been sensible and strong, lovely and thriving, unafraid of the arts and other people, maybe, just maybe, like the mother I lost my chance to have been. She's come to my rescue. Or rather Charlotte has lightly muscled her into view.

A trance envelops me; a mist descends. The party's streamers sway. Kumiko gathers the ripped paper and puts the gifts in our Wonderland tote bags. She says softly, "Bellevue wants me to start tomorrow, Mrs. Dias. A few days early. What should I tell them?"

I smile and hand her an envelope with the bonus I've been saving, along with a set of blank books with ornate covers. She has mentioned wanting to take notes about patients by hand. Her head is bowed. Mine, too.

The guests file out, profuse in their thanks, and Jason is rushing because he has an audition . . . I tell him I'll clean up. Go on.

Kumiko cries at the door. I hug her and say, "There, there. Going now isn't much different from leaving in a couple of days, right?" The children want to know what's wrong, and I say nothing. Nothing; my friend is moving on. And I watch her disappear.

Betty is lingering over more champagne. As if it's finger-painting, frosting mars the table, floor, and chairs. Betty glances up as if she just noticed she's in my place. Empty now, except for her and Charlotte and me.

I'm behind the counter. While Charlotte heads to the ladies' room, Betty comes over, weaving slightly, to pay the bill. "That was memorable," she says. "So glad we found you." She adds she's not sure when they'll be back but hopes it's soon.

What possesses me? I'm calm. I take her money. The gratuity is twenty percent on the nose. I unlock the drawer that holds my silver pistol and take it out and put it on the counter, the business end pointing in her direction. Her eyes turn the size of saucers.

"I want to see your home," I say. I stick the gun in my large, floppy handbag. Exhaling in gusts, she says, "Dorrie? What are you doing?"

"I won't scare your girl," I say, nestling the pistol against the debris in my bag. "She won't see this, unless you refuse to do as I ask." I need to absorb the dwelling that might have been mine, what it looks like, feels like; I want to observe, via Charlotte's room, how Alicia might be enlivening her own space. The one upstairs is stuck in time.

Charlotte bounces back to us, haloed with the lavender from the bathroom's soap dispenser. There are three tote bags of presents.

"Good thing there're three of us!" I trill. "I'm free to help you carry the gifts to your house. It's a way to keep the party from ending." I keep one hand in my purse, as if I'm about to pull out my wallet. Betty's mouth stays open.

"Oh," says Charlotte. "That's nice." But she's watching her mother and says, "Momma?"

"Yes, my sweetheart," says Betty/Bird. A damp patch blooms on her white shift. She bends to kiss her daughter's head. "Let's go home."

Out we go, and I fumble with the outer lock, and as Betty glances around, I bring my purse around to face her, and she freezes. Charlotte is merry from the festivities.

I don't get out much. The air is crisp with fall, spiced and reddened and golden. People stride by, in a hurry. The sidewalk is cracked. "Slow down," I hiss at Betty.

After a tiny yelp, she starts shaking. She whispers, "I would have invited you. I don't understand. I would have invited you over."

"That's not true," I say.

Charlotte, carrying the lightest tote bag, stops to adjust it on her shoulder.

"Did you have a lovely birthday?" I ask her.

"The best ever, Mrs. Dias," she says. Her spider barrette catches a glint. "Thank you so much."

Betty, color drained, begins to hyperventilate and gasps at me, "I don't understand."

"Charlotte," I say, "didn't you promise me a picture? Why don't we get it, once we get home?" The child is slowing, staring at the grownups.

"But I haven't done one specially for you," she says.

"How about if you pick one you've already done, and I can have that?"

She weighs this and speaks with caution. "All right. Momma, what's wrong?"

My hand rides the pistol, cool, silver. The poor woman loses the starch in her knees and buckles. "Momma!" Charlotte shrieks.

"She's fine," I say, gripping her arm to help her along. "It's just a little too much champagne."

"That's right," croaks Betty. "We're almost home, honey."

They live close but at a remove from the racket of the bars. An Indian market offers its scents of turmeric, star anise, and cumin; the fruits on display shine like jewels. I'm a mite faint myself. A boy on a phone jostles Betty, and her cry is sharp and anguished. Charlotte becomes more puzzled. She pats her mother fondly on her back. Leaves scratch the asphalt, and the tips of midtown peer over the streets to watch. The fear in Betty's eyes has infected her whole being, saturating her. She's quivering. Charlotte puts an arm around her mother and seems to be humming, singing. I had to witness a child giving comfort, a mother and daughter bound together to defy terror, while at the same time I protect the girl from the worst of it.

Their doorman in his cap and jacket with golden frog-closures leaps forward to help with the packages. I blurt, "No, we're fine!"

"Mrs. Lezardo?" he says.

"We're okay, Ralph. Thank you." Betty looks ejected from a wind tunnel, and her daughter guides her ahead. My hand trembles on the gun.

Betty collapses into sniffling in the elevator as we shoot up to a top— but not *the* top—floor. There are mirrors and elegant brass trim, and the unscratched wood is polished. I adjust the angle where I stand to keep the pistol in my bag trained on her. Charlotte hasn't registered how steadily I've kept my hand out of view.

And then at their threshold—her reaction is worse than I expected—Betty shoves the key in her lock after the fourth try and cracks, disintegrates into a shambles, weeping. She genuflects from trembling and drops her tote bag. I scoop it up. Charlotte bleats, "Momma, are you sick? What's wrong? What can I do? What happened?" Her pleading eyes on me, she beseeches, "Help us. Help me."

My turn to shake, rendered speechless. Did some disturbed part of me long to see a cheap imitation of my Alicia's fear and worry in her last hour, so I could heal it? "Let's go inside and get her some water." I can't look at Charlotte; I'm propelled forward despite knowing I should bolt.

Disappointingly predictable: It is in fact my dream apartment. Large and open, lined with books, flooded with light. The large kitchen at the far end has bar stools so dinner company can chat over appetizers as Betty watches the water boil for pasta. Corked bottles of wine display various levels, half, or a few fingers remaining, or three-quarters, rich purple-reds. How do Betty and her husband Vincent not hear them screeching, Drink Me? Under one of those netted domes to deflect insects is a plate of cookies . . . Don't they shriek, Eat Me? In the adjacent dining area, the chairs are wrapped in beige cloth with ties behind them to resemble the backs on the dresses of bridesmaids. An office is visible off to the side, a laptop open. More rooms farther down a hallway. A spiral staircase to a loft.

Crayoned pictures on the living-area wall. I venture slightly out of Betty's range as I inspect them. A blue cat floats in a sea of red water. I fall in love. What's in Charlotte's childhood realm; what are her toys, dolls, books, paints? But I can't explore that and still keep Betty at bay. I can't maintain a gun trained on her from another room. She's slight, but fear might impart the strength she needs to disarm me, or worse.

"I would have invited you in!" Betty shouts, dropping onto the plush red sofa. She unleashes a fresh wave of sobs.

"Momma!" Charlotte screams, and then it happens, what I've wanted to see, what I half-sensed—and didn't—was my reason for doing this worst thing of my life: Charlotte hugs her tight, and Betty clutches her as if she'll die if she doesn't and swings her daughter to a tucked-away point, to protect her. "Go to your room, Char," she whispers.

"Not while you're sad. I love you, Momma! Don't cry! What's wrong? I love you!"

"I'm good," Betty whispers. "Baby, don't you worry. I've got you."

I take my hands out of my purse and it's my turn to crumble, into a Lucite chair with a stylish decal of a teenaged girl with standing-up cobalt hair. There was a lot of pure hate in what I did, I'm aware of that: Such a perfect existence you have, Betty; it's a replica of the reel I starred in, inside my brain in my youth. What do you look like when you might be in danger of loss?

But mostly: How else can I enact some message to my Alicia that she's the only one I wanted to comfort me in those days and weeks and months when I sobbed and shook and couldn't face the terror? *What might it look like, my child holding me when I'm afraid, sickened by the world's violence? She holds me and begs me not to be shattered because she's here, here to stop my grief. I've wanted her consolation.*

Does anyone fathom what it's like to be scared every second walking down the street, afraid a monster will lunge? No wonder I seldom go out.

They're crooning together, guarding one other, clinging.

There's one thing—it should have been obvious—I didn't count on. Brilliant child, attuned, she's calculating that the only thing different in their home is . . . this virtual stranger.

"Why are you here?" Charlotte asks me, sitting next to her mother and holding her hand. Betty raises her head.

"I came to carry your gifts, and to look at your pictures." I get to my feet and calculate the distance to the door. "I should be going."

The green eyes study me; the sequins on her peach-tinted party dress catch dying light. "Did you make Momma cry?"

If the windows could open, I would leap out of one.

"Mrs. Dias wanted to make sure we got safely where we belong, bunny rabbit. Isn't that nice?" says Betty/Bird. She's sitting straighter, wiping her eyes, turning a hollow stare at me. "Sometimes grown-ups get a little sad."

The exit is perhaps a ten-second sprint. I'm not sure what she's doing, other than a masterful job of reassuring a child.

"What made you sad?" asks Charlotte.

"Oh," she says, gathering her daughter's hands back once again in her own. "I was crying because . . . well." Betty bites her lip, drawing a spot of blood. Her aura of stellar cheer roils with darkening shades, and she peers at me with downright tenderness. No wonder her writing wins prizes: She reads deep; she kindles; she is aware of others.

I hear the words from her float into the air. "Mrs. Dias once had a little girl too, and some very bad things happened."

"What?" asks Charlotte, scarcely breathing; she turns her attention full at me.

I'm arrested, immobile, unable to inhale.

"Well, just some bad things," says her mother. "The little girl went to heaven. It's too bad we can't visit there, while we're here on earth. So this lady wanted to spend more time with someone who reminded her of—" and she stops. No need to finish.

It is my turn for water to stream from my eyes. I can't blink it away. Easy enough to Google my name and learn my nightmare. Betty did that. Like everyone who knows my story, she had no blooming idea how to bring it up or convey how she wished she could take away my pain: Surely the birthday party was her trying to share with me a fleeting memory of joy. And this is how I repaid her. Charlotte dashes to me, and I kneel, and the size of my baby when I lost her is in my embrace. Betty trembles on the sofa.

How long do I hold on?

Another shock awaits: as I rise to go, Charlotte patting my back as she did her mother's, a stirring, a rustling, happens above.

A girl about aged thirteen or fifteen appears at the railing cordoning off the loft. Her hair is tousled, as if from sleep. She's in those jeans ripped to shreds and a loose shirt, with a black bra strip drooping. "What's going on?" she asks.

"You're home from school early, Elsie." Betty's voice is subdued.

"Flu, I think." Elsie regards me and says, "Hello. Do you know my mother?"

My mouth opens, fish on the shoreline, last air, nothing coming out.

Elsie says, "Dad's at the airport, I think, Mom. He's on his way."

"I was just leaving," I manage, barely loud enough to be heard.

Charlotte tells her older sister that she had a great tea party thanks to me, and that I'm sad.

"No," I say to the birthday girl. "I'm happy I met you."

I run a hand through my hair. Elsie is the age my Alicia would be. Charlotte isn't my stand-in for Alicia; Elsie is. And it's like standing in the surf, when it drags its curling self back to the sea and a person feels she's sailing backward even though she's not moving. I've barreled through the worm-hole, speeded forward in the time machine, gone through the glass, lost my grip on make-believe: *This would be my baby now.*

They let me stumble away. I don't look back, not even at Elsie, rumpled and blossoming, self-possessed, appraising me from on high.

I ask Time to dash forward, and He obliges in spades; the months bunch up in heaps. The slightest crashes still startle me, either at work in Wonderland or in my upstairs rooms, with the compounded fear that the police have come to drag me off. This never happens: This is how thoroughly Betty and Charlotte—and Elsie—want to be shut of me. I should be glad for the immensity of Betty's forgiveness. No wonder her existence in the world-at-large is more vast and far-reaching than mine.

I've turned Alicia's shrine into a study, to write in. Mr. Bun sits on a shelf, watching over me. My spirit thanks Betty for reminding me that words matter. I touch the pictures Alicia did ages ago, so the colors enrich my blood. I eat and drink normally, or close enough. I speak less and less to Bill, my ex-husband. I'm happy alone. The stars over the city are pinpricks that soothe me. All the heavens do. When the moon shines in a curved rim at its bottom, it's called the Old Moon holding the Young Moon in its arms.

An editor who read a story of mine in a small magazine asked if I'd write about The Real Thing That Happened To Me. I replied that it's bad enough those boys will be free in a few years; why do I want to bolster their notoriety? I'd submit page after page of:

Alicia Renée Dias, Alicia Renée Dias, Alicia Renée Dias, Alicia Renée Dias, Alicia Renée Dias, Alicia Renée Dias, Alicia Renée Dias, Alicia Renée Dias, Alicia Renée Dias, Alicia Renée Dias, Alicia Renée Dias, Alicia Renée Dias, Alicia Renée Dias, Alicia Renée Dias

The accent marks can serve as a guide to letting it be sung.

I won't turn my child or criminals into cash. To atone for my own violence, I'll do something that stays known only to me. Aid to a victims' support network, I'm thinking.

The serving girl who replaced Kumiko is exasperating. I fired Alex. It's a revolving door. We lack enough sign-ups for a tea ceremony, though I hope for a reason to contact Kumiko. One day I'll marvel at bumping into her by chance and confess I need her as my psychiatrist.

The Dormouse remains missing.

Now and then, I picture Charlotte growing, attending school. Does Elsie get in some harmless teenaged trouble? Vincent, their father, loses hair. At the dinner table, he entertains his wife and daughters with anecdotes that leave them hysterical with laughter.

One day, on Facebook, I note a picture on a friend's page and gasp. It's Betty Lezardo. In another fashionable dress, at a literary event. I enlarge the photo, clicking until I can better countenance her face. There's no mistaking it, and it's my doing, I'm sure: A slight but definite sidelong glance distorts her eyes, as if fearing what's behind or not trusting what might be gaining on her. She clutches a glass of white wine with a burning marble of fluorescence in it, from the lights overhead. Her face screams forty-ish more than what I saw on her, like a time-lapse. She appears completely haunted.

Next to her is Elsie, in an LBD, a gateway garment to female adulthood. The skirt flares. Elsie Lezardo, the person who pried me out of fantasy and hurled me into the reality of forward history. Is she sixteen? Has that much time sped past? What are her crushes and career plans, her despairs so enormous she refuses to believe they'll subside with time? There's no Charlotte, because this is a grownup party.

Once, thinking of Alicia as she'd be—Elsie-sized now—I fell asleep in Central Park in Sheep Meadow, on a sloping lawn, and leaves like crisp scuttling crabs walked sideways over my face. I sat up with a start. I am alive, I thought.

I'll never behold Charlotte, Betty/Bird, or Elsie again in the flesh. If we happen upon each other by accident, I'll cross the street unless they do it first. When I awaken in the morning, I put on a kettle and answer it when it screams. And then I open my front door to Wonderland, and the strangers come in, good and ill, and I serve them the best of what I've made from my hours in the night.

ON HIGHWAY 18

Rebecca Campbell

Jen bought a 1982 Plymouth Horizon for four hundred dollars just before they graduated high school, so if she and Petra wanted to get into town for the Bino's—open twenty-four hours—to eat fries and pale, oily gravy, or drink the bitter black coffee of three a.m., it was Jen who drove. Petra rode shotgun, watching the highway unfold, and refold, and unfold again as it wound through clear-cuts. Sometimes they had a place to be, a pit party, or a dozen people meeting up at a doughnut shop on the highway. A lot of the time, though, it was just the two of them, driving four hours to an empty beach on the Pacific coast of the island, arriving in darkness so absolute they couldn't see the waves, only hear their roar at low tide, sitting under the starless, overcast sky until the sun rose.

Mostly they took Highway 18 into town, running from the island's coastal valley to its interior mountains. Everyone else did, too, as though at one end or the other something might happen, and if you missed it you would miss the only thing that had ever happened or would ever happen on the island.

Anyway, after Jen bought the Plymouth they often found themselves in town, driving through well-lit and desolate streets to the 7-Eleven, where they would buy Orange Crush and gummy sours. Their only company a few kids squatting in the parking lot under lights that turned their acne scars purple and glazed the concrete a brassy gold, all these kids with blue freezie-stained mouths.

Petra often thought about Highway 18, and about how it spilled from the empty stretches, unlit, into the parking lot, the kids, the Bino's. While Jen chatted with another long-haired boy, Petra walked through the cars to the highway and watched the trucks full of logs so enormous it was hard to believe they grew that way as they barreled through town like it wasn't a place, just an interruption on the long peregrinations lumber takes from hillsides to sawmills and freighters and then out across the Pacific.

The kids in the 7-Eleven parking lot knew everything that happened from one end of the highway to the other. They knew, for example, about the last girl who'd been found—the one in the ditch beside the Petro-Can.

"Be careful, man," he said, a kid Petra had known in tenth grade, "you know how ghosts like highways. Watch out for hitchhikers."

"Ghostly hitchhikers?" she asked, watching Jen and her Jesus-haired boy.

"Yeah, man! They're all over. I talked to a truck driver and he told me about this girl he picked up north of Port Alice, and she told him shit. I won't even fucking repeat it. She told him what's going to go down in like the year 2000. And when they got to the bus station in Nanaimo, he pulled over and she was gone. Like bam. Gone."

"Have you ever seen her?"

"Maybe? Like. I thought I did once, but I didn't pick her up. But if I get a chance again, I'll pick her up and ask her all sorts of shit about what's coming."

After she talked to the kid in the parking lot, Petra began to watch for hitch-hikers. She knew the types: northbound tree-planters; a man and his toddler Petra saw on Monday mornings; guys on their way in to work or back home again. There were kids from the university headed for the beaches on the west coast.

It wasn't until a few weeks after the 7-Eleven parking lot that she began to see—or think she saw—the other sort of hitchhiker. The first time, it was just a thin girl in ten o'clock summer twilight or the very early morning. This kind might only appear as a silhouette, a girl who disappeared as one glanced down to adjust the radio.

But then Petra saw her on a long straight, when they were driving behind a truck. She knew that in the cab of the truck, a man—she was sure, always, that it was a man—had seen the girl as well.

The truck stopped. As they passed, the girl had reached the passenger door and was illuminated by the interior light, and though Petra looked back to see her face, she saw only her dark hair and the driver's silhouette in the cab. The sight was so familiar, Petra wondered if it happened every time they drove that road, every time they saw a girl stick out her thumb to get a little further down the highway.

Her mouth was dry when she finally asked Jen, "Does it feel weird, to you?"

"What's weird?"

"That girl back there."

"It's not weird, it's *stupid*. Remember what happened to Nicki?"

And then the thin whine of stretched magnetic tape interrupted Jen as she was about to mention, say, the girl they found in the ditch by the Petro-Can, and talk about how they should all know better.

Of course Petra hitchhiked, too, everyone did, even if they never talked about it. The bus only ran twice daily. You didn't have a car. It was different on an island anyway, you all knew each other, though she was rarely picked up by anyone she knew, which meant her parents didn't have to hear about it. Things happen, of course, but when don't they? Girls are lost, then they're found again, and that's often worse than thinking they've disappeared somewhere, into the city maybe.

The last time she hitchhiked was at the end of a long day on the river in the July before she left town for university. She was supposed to get a ride with someone's cousin, but they wanted to stay so Petra started walking back to town. She still had fifteen km to go—and was at least ten from a payphone—when she decided to push her ratty, river-tangled hair behind her ears and stick her thumb out into the empty road.

A huge beige car emerged from one of the driveways in the subdivision past which she walked, just right there, like he'd been watching for her.

He unlocked the door and she asked, "Where are you headed?"

"Just returning some tapes to the video place on Festubert, that good enough?"

They chatted about one of the tapes he'd rented. *The Thing*. There was one part with a defibrillator, where the man's chest opened up and the doctor shoved his hands right up inside the body. But that monster—it bit his hands off and swallowed them and then turned into something new and then something else new. He laughed. He said it again, about the doctor's hands plunged inside the man up to his wrists and bitten *right off*.

Then, halfway into town he asked, "Are you working?" And Petra said no, she was going away to school in September, so she wasn't even sure if it was worth looking, though last summer she'd got a job at an ice cream place. That had been okay.

"Oh." He sounded disappointed. "I was looking for a girl."

"Yeah," Petra said. "Ha-ha."

Ten minutes later, they pulled into the parking lot of the Video Pantry.

She picked up his three VHS tapes and reached for the door. It locked under her hand.

She pulled on the handle.

"You want to go have coffee?"

"No, no thanks. Ha-ha," she said.

"Too bad."

She pulled on the handle again.

"I have to get home. Ha-ha. My dad—"

She pulled on the handle. She didn't see him move, but this time the door opened. She returned The Thing and the other tapes, then waved over her shoulder and fled along the sidewalk of the strip mall hoping she would not look up to see the beige Reliant and the man watching her. As she walked the rest of the way home, she thought not of the instant the door clicked shut, even though it was a sunny Saturday afternoon, and even though she was in a parking lot full of minivans and children.

She fixed him in her mind: the man with the scaly red skin along his white hairline, the heavy ring on his left pinky, the tuft of white hair poking through the placket of his golf shirt. His khaki slacks. The pine-scented beige-velvet interior of his car. The doors that lock and unlock and lock again.

Not that it was the first time someone had asked if she worked. It starts early. Fourteen on the sidewalk after the movie let out, waiting for Petra's mom. A car pulled up close and the driver—some guy with a scrubby moustache and the ubiquitous baseball cap.

"You girls want to party?"

Jen giggled, and Petra said something like, *Um. I don't know?* Her voice weak-sounding, the way it rose at the end. The guy pulled away without saying anything else.

"He was kind of cute," Jen said.

This was how it used to be. You are both sixteen. You will be an actress. You will be a world traveler. You will direct great films, or write epic novels. You will fuck a million beautiful men. Just for now, though, you're lying together on an air mattress in a backyard and listening to a mix tape you have listened to a thousand times already and which has been distorted by all those listenings and by the cheap cassette deck in the car, and by the heat of summer. For twenty years afterward you will keep the tape, and when you listen to it, and hear the familiar distortions that time and repetition make, it will break your heart a tiny little bit.

When you're sixteen, though, that doesn't matter, because you'll be out of here pretty soon, and mix tapes are easy to make and easy to lose.

Jen says, "This is the start of a montage. Like. The opening part."

And yes, Petra thinks. Because these are the sharp, poignant scenes that spark the story, and what begins with two sixteen-year-old girls pledging their eternal ambition and their absolute affection will, in fact, end somewhere else entirely.

This is true.

But this was how it ended up happening. In July there are parties in someone's woodlot or in a gravel pit where even on a hot night the air is cool and clammy. Some girl was playing Bon Jovi and someone else insisted, noisily, on Guns N' Roses. There are two guys. Chris with the startling dark eyes and the buffalo plaid, his chin angry with pimples, drinking Kokanee or Carling High Test. He's brought a friend, Eric, whose eyes are not so startling but who is otherwise identical, down to the High Test. Eric was obviously instructed to entertain Petra while Chris chats with Jen, and Petra is aware of this.

For these reasons she shotguns the gin she stole from her parents, and is surly, and thinks, *This is just so stupid*, but Eric sticks with her. Jen and Chris move farther away, and a little closer to one another, then farther again from where Petra sits on the hood with her attendant Eric talking about Guns N' Roses, who suck.

Jen says something Petra can't hear, but she knows what's happening because she's seen it before, when Jen was faced with any number of men, gas station attendants, and waiters, with the boys in their Consumer Education class, with Petra's own younger brother. His looks were always plaintive when Jen came to dinner, with her very blue eyes, and her very dark hair, and her translucent skin, the fine, long bones of her fingers, her narrow ankles, the pale stem of her wrist.

"So, what's going on with you?" Eric tries again.

"Just. Stuff. Summer stuff."

"Cool. Cool," he says, then, "Yeah." Then, "So you hear about that girl?"

"At the Petro-Can?"

"No. She was off the trail at Skutz Falls. Don't know how long she'd been there, but someone saw her on the highway a few days before. It's pretty stupid, you know, it's pretty stupid to go out there alone."

"I guess," she says.

"I heard her neck was—"

Petra listens for a few minutes longer than she can stand about what happened to the girl.

Abruptly she has to pee, so she explains to Eric, who is like, Um, okay, and she knows he's happy to interrupt their conversation. Petra walks through the long, spindly shadows the bonfire casts among the trees, and though the night is very dark around her, she keeps her back to the light and pushes through the bush. She can feel around her the night that engulfs them, the deep reaches of the island's interior, its valleys and mountain ranges. And she thinks, as she often does—because this scene is not singular, but often repeated that summer—about how far she would have to walk to reach the dark places of the island. How long, she wonders, would it take to become lost?

She'd walked the trail to Skutz Falls a dozen times. She'd gone on field trips there and camped with Jen, hanging out on beach towels by the river.

For a moment she hears—as though she was still in the beige-velvet Reliant—the sound of a door locking and unlocking, locking and unlocking.

When she got back, Petra was happy she couldn't find Eric anywhere. She crawled into the back seat of Jen's car and put her head down on a bunched-up sweatshirt that smelled of Cool Coconut Teen Spirit. She sank into the uncomfortable, paralyzed state that is necessary when one tries to sleep in the damp backseat of a Plymouth Horizon, but she did not sleep. Time passed quickly and slowly and quickly again, so when she closed her eyes, "Patience" was still playing on the tinny speakers of a car somewhere nearby, and when she opened them it was "Stairway to Heaven." Between closing and opening her eyes she had lived only a few, fretful moments.

The night was short, though, and when the sky lightened she got out of the car and walked past sleeping-bagged bodies in the beds of pickup trucks or curled as she had been in the back seats of cars—though not alone.

Jen must be somewhere among them, in the back of Chris's truck, or lying on a tarp on the other side of the fire. Petra decided, *That's enough, fuck it*, and wrote a note to leave on the dashboard. *Going home. I hope you had a really really really great time with Chris.* She followed the rutted driveway from the pit to the road where, under the first yellow stain of dawn, she saw a girl. It was Jen.

"Hey!" Petra shouted. "Jen! Wait for me!"

The girl didn't move, so she shouted again, and then a car left the pit, gravel popping like gunshots. Petra glanced upward without thinking to see the stars wink out as the sky turned from black to blue. When she looked down again, Jen was gone. The car stopped and someone's older brother asked if she wanted a ride back into town.

Petra tried to explain about the note, but by August Jen didn't have any time. She moved in with the Parkinsons to look after their three kids when Mr. Parkinson headed to Yellowknife for three weeks a month. After the kids came Chris, and after Chris there was Jen's mother, and after that it might be Petra, if she was lucky.

It didn't matter, she told herself, because sometime soon Jen would call. They'd escape together in the car, and if they saw a girl hitchhiking, Petra promised herself, they'd pick her up. She would make Jen do it, before it was too late.

Jen never called. Petra finally caved on the last weekend before she left for university, and Jen agreed, if reluctantly, because she had to work six days that week, and it was going to be Chris's birthday soon.

They drove for two hours to an empty beach with a spiral slide and a tire swing. They ate jelly worms and drank Orange Crush and drove home just before sunrise.

Petra saw the girl first. She was a slightly darker shade of gray than the predawn highway.

"Let's pick her up."

"What? No. Do you know her?"

"Just once? Okay?"

They reached her, their headlights sliding across her pale face—the dark hair, the skinny limbs in denim—and Jen, still bristling, pulled over onto the shoulder.

Petra opened the door and got out.

"Hey!" she called back. "You need a ride?"

So quiet on the shoulder that when she heard a crow overhead she glanced up. When she looked back, the girl was gone.

Inside the car, Jen rested her head on the steering wheel. "I need to sleep," she said. "Hurry up."

"She's not there."

They drove on in silence, Jen's knuckles white, her eyes fixed. When they reached Petra's house, Petra said, "You don't want to go for breakfast?" her voice plaintive in a way that surprised her.

"I have to work in, like, two hours."

"Do you think she looked like you?"

"No."

"I thought I saw you before, once, that night at the gravel pit. You were hitchhiking"

"Why do you keep—"

The last word cut short in a sob. Petra got out of the car. The last thing she said to Jen was, "Will you come visit me, maybe?"

"I don't know," Jen said.

"You could come visit," Petra said again, and even she could hear how plaintive her voice was and knew—without Jen saying anything—that the answer was *no* because who would pay for the ferry?

Petra didn't call and Jen didn't call and by the end of the week whatever had happened between them, it felt final. Petra was going to say something, but she'd wait and find a cool postcard from some bookstore on the mainland. She'd write a real letter. Or maybe next time she was home she'd phone, or they'd run into one another downtown. It was stupid not to call, but the longer she waited, the harder it was to break the silence.

When her parents drove her to the early ferry on her last day as an islander, it seemed to Petra that girl after girl stood on Highway 18. The fading moon cast long, uncertain shadows occupied by girls who reached out into the darkness to flag down a car that might take them away.

"Could we stop for her?" Petra asked, pointing at a distant figure.

"I don't see anyone," her mother said, and when Petra looked again the highway was empty.

In the end, this was how it happened.

Petra spent the summer after university lying on the bleached grass of her parents' yard with a yellow-paged paperback falling open on her stomach. When the silence got to her, she drove into town. She talked to the kids at the 7-Eleven, and shared a freezie that glowed an atomic pink. She was invited to a pit party, and saw the logs still leaving the clear-cut valleys. A girl had been found out behind the garbage dump.

At twilight on an empty stretch of highway, headed home, she saw the girl. As she pulled over, the evening felt so familiar it might be the reenactment of something that had already happened, or maybe a meeting she had arranged and forgotten. She glanced back into the darkened east, away from the fringe of green sunset—maybe to give the girl her opportunity for escape—but the girl was still there, making her way toward the car. Petra opened the door and said—as though they had rehearsed it—"Do you need a ride? Where are you going?"

She was careful not to take her eyes off Jen. In the twilight she looked no older than she had four years before, or five, or however long it had been.

Jennifer did not speak. The sunset fading, and the stars emerging, and Petra remembered again how dark night could be.

"I'm on Ypres," she said, "right on the corner near the school."

They drove in a musty kind of silence, Petra's eyes fixed on the empty road, darker and darker until the world outside her headlights vanished.

"What happened to the Plymouth?"

"It broke down after a year or two. The Parkinsons let me go, and Chris had a car, so you know. He drove me around."

Petra wanted to say how sad she was about the Plymouth. She wanted to talk about how she was really considering going back to school for library science or something. Or how she could get an internship or teach English overseas. There was something confessional about the night, something in the smooth passage of concrete beneath their lights and the sky overhead darkening.

It was full dark, proper dark, by the time Petra pulled into the little gravel drive off Ypres and finally said something true.

"I miss you."

The voice that responded was drowsy and flat, not much like Jen's at all, but what it said had the quality of a prophecy: "That is true, as far as it goes. One thing you need to remember: for you it was always going to be different. You will teach English in Korea. You will cry in front of a pho stand in Hanoi. On a beach in Crete you will fuck a boy whose name you can't pronounce. You will come back here the autumn you turn thirty and, when you are cleaning up your old room in your parents' house, before they sell, you will find a box that contains your old report cards, and the star-shaped notes we used to exchange in tenth grade, a card I gave you for your sixteenth birthday, and you will wonder where I am, and you'll go into town and ask around, but no one will know. They'll remember the last time they saw me, and think maybe I headed for the mainland after I broke up with Chris. My mother will have moved, and when you call her number—which was my number, and which you will remember to the last day of your life—a stranger will answer."

Somewhere, Petra heard the sound of a door locking.

"You won't know what to do, exactly, and people disappear all the time, and I seemed pretty smart. Not like those other girls, you'll think, though that won't be true, either. I am exactly like those other girls. All of them."

"Jen—"

But Jen was gone. At first it felt so silly that Petra looked in the footwell, and the backseat, and through the window.

She got out of the car and walked across the gravel to the cottage with its unpainted trim, and the asbestos shingles a dull green moss. Somewhere, the incessant barking of a dog.

As she was hesitating, the front door opened, and there was Jennifer. The dog barking inside the house, louder now.

Somewhere a man shouted, "Who is it?"

"It's—" Jen began.

Petra cut her off. "Let's go somewhere. Let's go to the Bino's. I'll buy you all the fries and gravy you can eat. I'll buy you the big order." She knew it was stupid to say out loud, but she went on, "We'll listen to mix tapes and we'll go to the beach in the middle of the night. We'll go now. I'll buy gummy worms. I'll buy freezies."

"What are you even doing here?"

"Please," she said, "just come out for a drive."

That was the last she saw of Jen, as the dog started barking again, and the door closed, and the light inside the cottage went out.

THE LITTLE MERMAID, IN PASSING

Angela Slatter

"Go on. It'll hurt for a while. For your whole life, really, but there's always a cost, isn't there? Go. Go on, up to the surface. Up, up, up, you silly flighty little thing. To the beach, when the sun hits you . . . well, you'll see soon enough. Off you go."

I watch as the girl hesitates, looks at the pretty amber bottle clutched tightly in her webbed fingers, face caught between gleeful longing and uncertainty. She opens her mouth to say something, ask a question she should have asked earlier, but all that issues is a wet puff of blood that dissolves in the water around her. Ah. My suturing needs work.

But it's a small thing, I tell her, part of the bargain. I don't say, but perhaps I should, that the price for something you want desperately, but should not have, is always red "Go on now, away with you."

And, voiceless, she goes.

The tail is magnificent, a glimmering limb of now-green, now-blue, now-stormy scales, reflecting the glow from the phosphorescent sea creatures that pass through this place, lighting the rocky cave entrance as they come and go. I'd have contracted for that if I could, if she'd not required it for her own ends. The hair, too, is lush and dark with bright points as if stars rest there; it won't look so wondrous out of the water, but she'll need it all the same. No matter; what I have is superb enough. I'm just being greedy, greedy as a mortal, coveting what I've not got whilst forgetting what I do have.

I watch until she's no more than a speck against the watery sky of my kingdom, nothing more than a black dot against the flickering light that drifts down from the above-world. It's so long since I've been there, since I've bothered to breathe the salty air instead of wetness. I'm not sure I'd even be able to use nose and lungs in place of gills anymore. Anything you don't value, don't use, don't exercise, will desert you.

Just a dot, now, just a mote, then gone. She's broken the surface. She'll head for the beach, if she's smart, before she opens the bottle and drinks the contents. If she's stupid she'll do it in the wrong order, and will likely drown. When the legs come through, they will hurt. She'll feel cleaved, she'll panic. When you panic, you drown.

Still, I did warn her.

Didn't I?

Sometimes I forget the script, the patter; I'm so very tired. I always warn them, but perhaps I omit some of the lines, through boredom or forgetfulness. Sometimes spite. Sometimes these girls are so . . . haughty. Demanding. Entitled. Mean. An almost unending list of sins, I suppose. Those who look down on me as if I am somehow less, as if refusing to live as they do, where they do, makes me questionable. Refusing to be one with the Mer Queen's safe, tidy little enclave.

They don't know—care?—that I was like them once; that, though changed by the things I do, I share their blood. My true history has been lost, I imagine, fallen through the cracks between years as those who knew me have disappeared or died, for we are immortal but not invulnerable and can be killed. Only one remains of my contemporaries and I doubt my name passes her lips too often.

I am made pale, yes, by my acts: bleached as whale bones on a strand. White as if the water has washed much of me away, but whatever I lost of myself was replaced by something stronger, a power and pragmatism that others have envied and feared, sought and bought. I have become a concentration of prices paid, of deals done, of treasures left behind. I am the place where folk come when they have nowhere else to go, when their wants and desires get the better of them.

Like that silly little girl. A granddaughter, no doubt. Or a great-grandchild, perhaps. I can see her bloodline in the cast of her face, the tilt of her head. An echo of my sister's cheekbones, the pout of the lips. The girl who is gone and will never be again, not as herself. She'll be something else, something new; something less. The joke is not lost on me.

I recall the object in my hands, clutched as tightly, as greedily as the girl did her amber bottle. Mine is a purple jar, fat as a glutton's belly, a silver lid firmly holding down the contents, which would otherwise float and flee, perhaps follow its former owner, try to reunite with that little fool. It swirls inside the colored glass, like a fog trying to blow itself out.

Her voice, so lovely, so perfect.

So lightly held.

So unvalued.

So easily bargained away.

Little fool.

All for a man, and not even one who lives beneath, not one of her own kind who swims the ocean. A man who moves by *legs* alone, who breathes air, whose near-dead face was apparently so beautiful its sight knocked the sense from the girl's head, put a cloud of idiot desire in her mind and set her heart's course askew. So that nothing else would inhabit her thoughts, so she'd be haunted by it until, at last, she went and begged.

I wonder how long it took? How many days, weeks, months of pleading and whining until her grandmother's patience wore out, heart wore through, until it was obvious to the old fish that the girl had one final decision to make, one chance left, one last hope. I can count on five fingers the number of maidens who've come to me and, in the end, not gone through with their plan. So few who hesitate, take a moment to think, realize that the price is always too great, that their lives are not over if they do not have this purported heart's desire, the absence of which has been tearing at them. So few who say "no" when I've named the price, who've bent their heads and backed away, swum off with nothing more than their gods-given gifts and my grudging respect.

So few, so rare.

But enough. I have matters to which to attend. A twitch of my own tail, I knife through the water, back to the deep cave from which I reign. Make my way to the place where my magic resides.

We have all suffered. We have all lost precious things. We have all been faced with the choice of losing ourselves to gain an idea of love.

My mother made her own such decision. Destined to marry one man to please her father, she went to the Sea Witch of old who then ruled this dark corner of the ocean, and she overthrew everything fate had intended for her. She got the man of her dreams and much good it did her: he was a wastrel, cared not a jot for her heart once she'd brought him the pearly crown, the coral sceptre. She thought, poor fool, that if she could have children, ensure their grasp on the throne with a dynasty, he'd love her again—which presumed he ever loved her in the first place.

But the price she'd paid in return for her heart's desire was her ability to bear children. She was as barren as a desert is dry. She tried everything she could, enlisted every sorceress and enchantress, but they had no power against such a sacrifice, no way to undo what had willingly been given away. And so back to the Sea Witch at last she went.

There was nothing she could do, the dark queen told her, tail slowly batting back and forth as she sat on the throne of bones and shells and coral and such. But something about the Sea Witch's smile told Mother that the old woman wasn't being entirely honest, so she pressed: she'd give anything. Anything.

Anything?

Anything!

I will name my price later, then. Are you prepared for that?

And my idiot mother nodded and agreed to a bargain, the cost of which she did not know.

The Sea Witch gave her two pearls, one milky-white and twisted, the other smooth and black, and instructions to take both but choose only one; swallow only one. She knew enough about my mother from their brief encounters to understand that she would not listen, would not honor their pact.

Mother gave birth to twins, myself and my sister, with little difference in our appearances except our hair—hers was noticeably darker, mine lighter—and we were loved equally. We shared a cradle made from a giant clam, strung with shells and things that shone; together we breathed the same water, learned all the things we might ever need in order to rule when our turns came, shared all our toys, clothes, eventually lovers. She was my sister and my other self, no two could be closer, more loving, more devoted.

Until . . .

Until one day Mother died, and that loss changed my sister. Where once possessions had been *ours*, they became *mine* and *yours*; she held all things tighter, lovers included. We fought as we never had, items were snatched from my hands, beaus seduced away, kept at her side by sheer dint of tantrums and bribes. And the kingdom we were meant to rule month about, the throne we were both meant sit upon? She gave it up at the end of her cycle only unwillingly.

Perhaps we'd have come through. Perhaps with time she'd have softened, loosened her grip. Perhaps she'd have come to her senses, apologized, and we'd have been as we were before.

But then the message came from the Sea Witch to say there was a debt owing and we must answer for it. That this was the one true inheritance left to us by our mother.

৬১

She's a beautiful thing that I've made, though patched and stitched. Sometimes I close my eyes, run my fingers over the skin just to feel smooth then coarse, the ridges where cuts have joined as if living flesh had healed. All those given-up bits and pieces, all those crimson-colored tithes, all tacked together into a whole of sorts.

All those things that silly little girls don't value until it's too late. All the things they sacrificed for one stupid reason. They all come for the same thing: for love. For something selfish and venal. *Make him love me. Give her to me.* Give me, give me, give me. Never once do they think what the other might want. That love, if it were true, if it were right, would find its own way. And, sometimes, they leave debts others must pay.

When the missive arrived, my sister and I talked long into the night, and it was as if the past months of discontent, of selfishness and spite had not been. The bitterness was gone, the competition. She was my other half once more, and I hers. We were one and we would go together to the Sea Witch. We would face her, for we knew from the old tales that if we did not she would come hunting, and her rage would be all the greater.

Alone we departed, leaving advisors and friends behind. We swam for days, into the darkest part of the ocean, but nothing harmed us—why would it? We were daughters of the seas, mer queens in our right. Who would dare? Yet we were afraid: afraid of what we might hear, might find, might have to pay. We swam until at last we came to the rocky overhang that hid the entrance to the cave of the Sea Witch. Clasping hands, we drifted into its maw, deeper and deeper until we found the place she called her own.

She sat on a massive throne of bones, skeletal limbs clasping each other in a tight embrace, cemented in place with coral. A tall woman, pale as the watery moon, she waited, watching as if our appearance was no surprise. Her tail was so long and thick that it curled three times around the base of her seat, and then some. Hair the color of a storm played about a face haughty and scaled, and her eyes were so black they seemed like nothing so much as holes. But they caught us and held us, drew us in. She nodded as if pleased, satisfied. "You came."

"You called," we replied.

"So I did."

And we waited a while for her to speak again. We'd agreed not to ask. Not to show weakness. Not to beg

"Your mother died owing me," she said, and we trembled. All the tales told of the terrible things that came when a debt was outstanding; by her death Mother had cheated the Sea Witch and left only my sister and I to answer for her. Then the old woman told us how we'd sprung from a broken bargain; how we belonged, now, to *her*. "But," she said, one finger raised to forestall any protest, "I am not an unreasonable woman. I only want what's necessary to balance the books. So, I give you a choice: one of you must be the forfeit."

We stared at her. We stared at each other.

"We will not—" I began, shaking at the thought that all our mother's love had meant nothing; that she had left us to this.

"Wait, sister," my other self interrupted, her fingers tightening around mine, grip solid, stable, assured. "What if . . . "

"What if . . . "

"She will never rest until this is settled. She will haunt us, blight our kingdom; our subjects will suffer. But we have ruled together. We have shared our throne. Let us share this punishment, bear this burden together. Let us take it in turns, sister, one shall rule while the other pays this tithe. Then we switch. If *this* Majesty," she tilted her head to the Sea Witch, "is willing, I will go first."

"No," I said. "I have just completed this cycle of my reign. You return alone. I will pay this first month. If *this* Majesty will allow?"

And the Sea Witch looked at me as if I were a fool, as if she knew my sister better than I, but she smiled and nodded. My sister held me for so long yet so short a time then swam away, out of the cave and up, up, up. I imagined her as a speck against the watery sky of the kingdom, nothing more than a black dot against the flickering light that drifted down from the above-world. She would return. The old woman knew nothing of the shared blood that ran in our veins, of the invisible cord between our hearts, of the thoughts that began in one mind and finished in the other.

I raised my chin, arrogant, even as I submitted to her will.

My sister did not return.

The Sea Witch was not kind, but she was never unnecessarily cruel. She did not say my sister's betrayal was only to be expected, did not say her word was as weak as sunlight on the bottom of the ocean, an unfaithful, feeble thing. For the longest time I dreamt my sister had met with some terrible fate on her way back home, without me to guard her. And the Sea

Witch tethered me so I could not flee, could not go looking for either my sister or her corpse; she would listen to none of my entreaties. After a while, however, after the first of the little mewling maids came to beg bargains in the name of love, sent by her Queen, I at last understood that my sister bore more of our mother's blood than I did.

My years of servitude became an apprenticeship of sorts. The Sea Witch taught me true, every spell, every magic, every enchantment under and over the waters, all the knowledge she had gathered in her very long life because she knew, even when she'd called us to her, that her time was coming to an end. She desired a daughter, a successor. In me she found a willing student. Betrayed, lost, I needed a place to belong and the Sea Witch, with her heart of salt and seawater, gave it to me.

When at last she wore out, I did as instructed. I removed her flesh, stored it in jars and bottles and tubs for use in spells, then took the bare bones and wound them into the body of the throne, adding to its height and breadth, as every new Sea Witch's had done for millennia. And it became mine.

I could have returned home, then, but to what end? I could have revealed my sister's treachery, claimed what she'd stolen from me, but I had been long gone from the kingdom and had begun to change in both appearance and temperament well before my mistress died. I would not have returned to any good purpose, and I'd have had to witness so many faces frozen in terror at the sight of what I'd become. Besides, I'd found a love for the power, the knowledge, the darkness to which I was heir, and the patience to play a long game.

I have never seen my sister again, but she sends me tribute. I know she still lives, for the girls keep coming even after all these centuries, and I ask them who rules. She sends me all those little girls and young women who want too much, who long for things they cannot have, whose yearning makes everything else in their lives appear insignificant. She has sent daughters and granddaughters, nieces and great-nieces. Fools all. Perhaps it's a test for those silly little things: if they're willing to trade with me, they get what they deserve.

But perhaps she simply fears if she didn't send them, I'd return home.

I think about the latest child, with her lovely hair and lovelier voice. I wonder how long before disappointment strikes, before realization hits, before she or someone who truly loves her comes to me, begging a solution. I'll give them the knife, the same one I always do, I'll tell them their choices and we shall see what we shall see. Whose blood she'll choose to spill, her own or his—I suspect her own. Not out of love, no, but shame; it's easier to die than live on under the weight of humiliation. Again, I can count on five fingers the girls who've come limping home, who are strong enough to bear the burden of consequences.

In the deepest darkest part of the cave, in a tiny alcove, on a bed of coral lies my own child, my own successor, the work of my own hands, the sum of those silly little girls. Over the years I've cobbled their pieces together to make one being, a daughter of stitched-together sorrow, made with all the things those girls discarded as unimportant: their very best gifts, the cores of their secret and best selves. An amalgam of sacrifice and loss and pain.

In all my years I've never seen a girl worthy to take my place, never saw in another face whatever the Sea Witch saw in mine. Whether that's good or bad I do not know, I only know that a broken bargain will make a witch do terrible things. Like this.

She's ragged and lovely, my daughter; at last I have her voice. When I put that inside her she'll lack just one final thing: life. And when I breathe that into her—when I give up the core of my very best self—she'll take my place.

Imagine: all that loss, all that sacrifice and grief, all those pieces of self, exiled from their very being. Imagine: all that rage. Imagine: my last breath, my last desire, my final instruction and knowledge of my home; my sister, the broken bargain.

Imagine her, my child, my girl, my successor.

She will be terrible.

And I will be free.

FALLOW

—◆—

Ashley Blooms

They find the bottle in the barn. There are a lot of things there, whole piles of things: tractor-part things, tire things, cutting things and bolting things, all tired things, slowly fading toward the same color of rusty brown. The inside of the barn smells of stale hay and beer. Misty picks the bottle that is the least broken and William holds it between two fingers and lets the water drain from its open mouth onto the packed-earth floor. The base of the bottle has a deep crack running through it that snakes along the length, almost all the way through. The crack raises up a little, just enough to tear their skin if they aren't careful.

They sit so their bodies form a triangle, William and his best friend Misty and her sister Penny. They sit in the corner of the barn, there among puddles of something that might be water. This way, no one can see them from the road. It's William's idea. The whole game is William's idea.

The bottle spins and spins and they kiss what they are given. Wooden beams. Metal pipes. Once, for William, a grasshopper. The bottle seems to find only the gaps between them, the space that separates their knees from other knees. It doesn't land on a Body, not the whole time they are playing, even though William moves them three times, convinced that it's the ground or the shadows or the moisture from the puddles that is warping the bottle's path, but nothing changes.

They decide there will be one last spin, and William reaches out, and William is sure this will be the spin that changes the game, when a car pulls into the driveway and a voice calls, "Penny! Misty!"

The girls are gone before William can ask them to stay. Only Misty pauses in the doorway to wave, and William waves back. He listens to their mother's voice, to the rustle of grocery bags, the slam of a trailer door. He waits until he can hear the water in the creek near his house. Then he spins the bottle one last time. The glass clinks and grinds over the dirt, kicking up breaths of dust so small that you have to squint to see them. The bottle stops with the mouth pointing at William's knee.

When the girls are gone, William sits by the barn door, which is always open, propped on two crumbling cinder blocks. He watches Earl, whose trailer sits behind William's, by a field that Earl tilled many years before. In all ten years of William's life, he has never seen a single thing grow in the field. There is a word for places where things don't grow. William's mother taught it to him. Fallow, she said, and said it again when William asked her to. He liked the way it sounded, a little like hollow, or holy. He said it to himself sometimes, at night, repeating it over and over just to feel the letters rolling on his tongue.

The fact that nothing has ever grown in the field doesn't discourage Earl, who is bent double over the plow, driving it into the soil. The dirt gives on either side of the blade, opening up, gutted. The earth exhales a damp smell. Creek water and must. Earl keeps going. William spins the bottle again and again and it lands, every time, with its mouth pointed at his knee. Earl plows and plants until the sun begins to set and then he curses and walks to his trailer. Without him, the quiet takes over the field, and the crickets are born out of the quiet, bringing noise.

Earl pauses at his trailer door, squinting to see William in the shadows of the barn. "You ain't supposed to be in there," he says.

"I know."

"Well." Earl looks toward the trailer he rents to William's mother. There's no car in the driveway and no lights in the windows. "Just be careful," he says. "There's broken glass and God knows what. You're liable to catch tetanus or some shit."

William nods and he waves to make Earl go away, Earl does, waving a broken chain in his hand, thick flakes of dust breaking from its links and falling through the sun-bitten air.

William buries the bottle in the fallow field. If anyone had asked him what he was doing, he wouldn't have known how to answer. He doesn't have the words to describe how the field reminds him of himself. The dark shape of it, the earth torn up and left to cool in the dark, a little steam rising. How it feels like maybe the field needs something only William has, and all William has is the bottle.

He waits until Earl shuts the screen door to his trailer, hemming out the darkness and the cool air that it carries. He waits until all he hears is his own breathing and the creek water running, until the two sounds are one sound, the same. Like all he has to do is walk to the creek and open his mouth and a whole stream full of minnows and rocks will come rushing down his throat, running over the bare bones of his ribs, collecting in his fishbowl belly where nothing could ever get out again. William can almost taste the water, sour and green and a little sweet.

William buries the bottle at the edge of the field. The solid door to Earl's trailer is still open, and the thought of Earl appearing now that he's had time to drink scares William a little. But burying the bottle only takes a minute. The soil is loose and dark and warm between William's fingers, and when he is finished, the earth is smooth, like the bottle isn't there at all, or like it has always been there.

William lives with his mother, who is beautiful, and younger than any other mother William has ever met. Her name is Shannon. She has white-blond hair and a scar in the crook of her arm and even that is beautiful—in the way that it raises up from the rest of her skin, in the way that it curves, in the way that it never changes.

She comes home that night even later than usual. She is smiling though, and she smells like peanuts and sugar. She tells William this is the best date she ever had. That he was tall and wonderful and worked in the mines. That he was in line to be a boss. That he called her "kitten" and took her dancing, like out of a movie, like a real cowboy.

"Have you ever been dancing?" she asks.

William shakes his head. He is sleepy and a little hungry, but more than anything, he is glad that she is home, glad for her noise, which fills up all the empty corners of the trailer. Even the stained yellow carpet seems prettier, golden, as she stands on it barefoot, reaching out her hand to him.

"Dance with me."

She is a little drunk. A little stumbling. She steps on William's toes and William laughs. He rests his head in the center of her breasts and closes his eyes and lets her twirl him in slow circles around and around the living room.

William wakes the next morning to the sound of voices. The sound of car tires. A honking horn. He walks barefoot onto the back porch. The air is heavy and mist clings to the tops of the trees. There are more cars outside than he has ever seen and more people, too, gathered around the fallow field. William is shirtless and he feels as though his teeth have been replaced by stones that he has spent the night grinding, grinding into dust.

Earl is at the center of the crowd, kneeling before something William has never seen before, but somehow recognizes. The object stands at the edge of the field where William planted the bottle and, for an instant, William can feel the bottle in his hand, a phantom weight, cool and steady. He makes a fist and the feeling is gone.

The crowd shifts to allow more people in. The thing in the field is taller than any of them, even Earl, who is the tallest man William knows. It has a head-shape sitting on its shoulder-shape, but it has no legs and no arms, either. It is as smooth as the shadow that William casts behind him in the middle of the day, but this shadow is made of bright green glass that shines when the sunlight breaks through the clouds and everybody makes church-sounds, low mmms and ahhs. Most of them are people William has seen before, at Sunday School and at basketball games and at Save-a-Lot on the first of the month. He knows them all, even remembers most of their names, but no one is looking at him. They are looking at what William made. Even though he couldn't have known what would happen, some part of him believes he had known that something good would come from the bottle, from him. Something beautiful. Something that would draw sixty people into a muddy yard on a weekday morning to stare open-mouthed at a statue grown from fallow ground, and William stares, too. William never wants to stop.

They gather in the yard between the trailers, William and Misty and Penny. The crowd has thinned and Earl is building a new fence around the fallow field. The sound of hammer and wood echo across the bottom so it sounds like the whole holler is being rebuilt.

Penny says, "I don't know why everybody's so crazy about it. It's creepy. Ain't it creepy?" She looks at William and Misty, who are looking at the field. Penny is starting high school in the fall and she's never talked so much. Now that she knows the sound of her own voice, she can't help but say things. Like the minute she stops talking it will be the last, and she has to make sure it's the right word, the right sound. She says, "And ain't nobody know where it comes from neither. I don't hear nobody asking about that. What if somebody planted it on purpose? What if it's some kind of poison? Mrs. Crawford said it could be a bomb. Or chemicals. It could be some toxic mineral grown up from the mines."

"I think it's kinda pretty," Misty says.

William says, "I think it kinda looks like me." Especially here, from a distance. All the indents are in the right places—his eyes and his mouth, his ribs and toes. It could be William if he were taller, a William made of glass.

"I don't see it," Penny says.

"Maybe from up closer," Misty says. Penny goes to find out, and calls for Misty to join her, but Misty says William's name instead and when William turns to look at her, he can't see anything. Misty's face has become the yard and the sky and everything in between. Her lips are on his lips, pressing, soft. William blinks when she pulls back.

Misty smiles. "Come on," she says, and takes off running through the grass.

"Where's your mother?" Misty asks.

Side by side, bent double so their faces are barely a foot away from the earth, they are looking for worms. Misty's backyard is the shadiest. The ground is always damp because the trailers have no gutters, so there is nothing to protect the earth from the rain. The ground grows soggy, the soil darkening. Misty's trailer is farther away from Earl's, too, which didn't matter once, but it matters now. Even here, they can still hear the voice of the crowd, can hear someone shout, "Step back!" as William reaches down and digs his fingers into the earth.

"Did you hear me?" Misty asks.

"Dunno," William says.

"You dunno where she is or you dunno if you heard me?"

"Dunno."

They find three more worms, all fat and wriggling, their segmented bodies writhing until they are dropped into a Dixie cup half filled with dirt.

Misty says, "My dad hasn't been home in three days."

"He working?"

Misty shrugs.

"Don't he always come back?"

"So far," she says.

William picks at the dirt under his fingernails. He watches Misty part the dirt with her hands. She is gentle with it. She runs her finger back and forth across the ground until, slowly, the backs of worms appear.

"What's Penny say?" William asks.

"What's Penny always say?"

"Something dumb?"

Misty smiles. "Something dumb."

They walk the worms to the creek. Outside Earl's trailer, the crowd has thickened. William wants to join them, to hear the things they are saying about the green statue, which has grown another few inches since it appeared two days ago. He wants to hear them talk about how beautiful it is and how strange, how they have never seen anything like it before in their lives, but it seems to scare Misty—the people all knotted together, some they know but plenty they don't, and the way that Earl drinks right there in front of everyone instead of waiting until he's inside his trailer like decent folk.

William and Misty go fishing instead. They sit side by side on the muddy ground, trading worms. They catch nothing but faded Pepsi cans and mosquito bites and when they retreat across their shared yard at dusk, the crowd is still there, still watching the fallow field.

Sometimes, late at night, William's mother crawls into bed with him. Her breath is hot against his neck. It feels like a fever does, only it's on the outside of his body instead of the inside. She makes their shapes fit—her knees behind his knees, his back against her front. No spaces. No gaps. Even her words gum together when she speaks. They stick in places that they shouldn't, the places where they are meant to come apart. She says things like:

"I'm sorry."

"You shouldn't never trust a man."

"He pushed me down. We was thirty miles from anywhere, what was I supposed to do?"

"It's like glass. Like your whole body's made of glass."

"I never wanted to marry him. I never even wanted to kiss him, but when has that ever stopped a man? They take things. That's all they know how to do. Take and take and take."

"Don't ever be like that, William. You promise me?"

"I don't know what I'm doing."

"I'll be your father, all right? I'll be the man."

"I'm sorry."

"You know he hit me? Your daddy? That's why he never comes around no more, because I told him I would kill him if he ever did, and I meant it."

"Promise me, William. Promise."

"I'm sorry."

〜

They play spin-the-bottle again. This time, it's only Misty and William. They sit in the barn where it's growing dark. They spin the bottle and it lands on William every time, even when he is the one spinning it. To play fair, he kisses the back of his hand, the curve of his knee, the space between his fingers. Misty kisses him, too, and each time, William presses harder into the kiss, and holds it for longer. He thinks of his mother and wonders if he is doing it right.

Outside, it begins to rain, and the thin crowd grows thinner. Fat drops of water slick down the sides of the green statue, which still stands alone. Umbrellas pop open, making a roof over the crowd, and the ground dries under them in pale brown circles that overlap and crisscross and disappear when the people shift from one side of the field to the other. After a while, Penny comes walking through the crowd looking for Misty, but Misty isn't anywhere that Penny is looking, and the bottle spins and spins.

Certain things don't grow. This, William knows for sure.

Every night for a week he goes out to field after his mother is asleep. He waits until the house is quiet and he can hear the cricket song through the thin walls and the thinner glass of his window. It is less quiet outside, where he isn't the only one awake. There are bullfrogs and whippoorwills under the deep white moon.

There, alone in the field, William buries his new shoes and a plate from the kitchen and a pair of mismatched earrings that he took from his mother's dresser. Nothing comes of these. When William tries to dig them back up, they are gone. He is more careful now, about what he offers to the field. He only wants to give something that will give him something in return.

The crowd that has been visiting the field every morning is growing restless. They've stopped taking pictures. They've stopped bringing their friends. Maybe they're wondering if the field was special after all, or if it was all a mistake. Misty's mother says the crowd will find something new to be excited about soon, and that scares William, the thought of things going back to the way they were. So maybe, if William buries the right object, then the right statue would grow, and Misty would love it, and his mother would love it, too. They would have dinner on the back porch, the three of them, together, and they would listen to the crickets trembling in the grass and they would say how beautiful the statues were. Their delicate bodies and glowing edges. Like angels, winged and glorious. Like God. And then William could tell them about burying the bottle, how it had been him all along.

William wants to show Misty something. He has been thinking about the right way to do it for a while now. It can't be raining outside and Penny can't be there and neither can their mothers, and it has to be before dinner, too. All these things are important. He thinks for days and every time he thinks about it, it makes the palms of his hands itch like they can already feel it, like the William from four days from now is telling him it is all right to do this.

William takes Misty to the barn again. He swept the floor the day before and the barn smells like damp hay and leaves. It isn't a bad smell.

"I want to show you something," he says. William lies down on the ground and tells Misty to lie down beside him.

"Why?"

"Because," he says. "That's how it works."

Misty pushes her hand into her back pocket and pulls out a handful of firecrackers. "Why can't we just light these?"

"This is better."

"You want me to go get a bottle?"

"No. Lay down." And, when she still doesn't listen, William says, "If you don't want to play, then go on home."

Then he closes his eyes and lets the sun turn his eyelids bright red. When Misty lays down, he tells her to close her eyes, too. He tells her about the tattoos on his mother's boyfriend's back. How the boyfriend plays with the hem of her shorts. How he comes up behind her and puts his mouth on her neck. William rolls onto his side and leans over Misty. He talks the whole time that he is pushing at the button on her shorts. He talks about black ink bleeding into blue ink, about wings on things that shouldn't have wings, about green light and bodies made of glass. William only stops talking once he rests his hand between Misty's legs. He moves his fingers back and forth to feel the skin beneath her underwear shift and give. They lie there, side by side on the dirt, waiting for something to happen.

William tears a soft piece of wood from the barn's door. He plants that, too.

In the morning, there is a new statue. This one is shorter than the glass man, though much wider. This statue is a handmade of gold—five fingers and an unlined palm. The fingers curl gently toward each other. The index and thumb almost meet, like there is something the hand means to take hold of, something that William can't see, or can't see yet.

༄

"It kinda looks like me," William says.

They are on the porch together, William and his mother. There is a small mirror balanced on the rail and Shannon is bent double in front of it. She has one eye closed as she puts on mascara. She is wearing a dress that ties around her neck. William can see the skin between her shoulders, the way it moves, bunching and releasing. She makes a low sound in her throat, a skeptical sound, like when William wakes up late for school and tells her that his stomach hurts, he has a fever, his tongue is a boulder that could weigh the world down, and he can't imagine going to school today. Not like this.

He says, "It does. Just look at the nose." He touches his own nose, flattens it into his cheeks. "And my head. The little lump on the side of it." He touches this, too.

"Which one are you talking about?" Shannon asks.

There are three statues now. William planted a scrap of Misty's shirt and it grew almost immediately, bronze and tangled, something that might be a heart or a pair of lungs, something internal, something that would be slick with blood if it were anywhere else but here, in the field.

"The green one," he says, and she says, "I don't see it," even though she isn't even looking at the statue, but at the curve of her own eye in the mirror.

Days pass and William and Misty play together like they always have, at the creek and in the woods. They find a thicket of blackberry bushes and dig out a hole beneath it. It is cooler under the thicket, dim with golden light crisscrossing their faces, and they can pluck berries from over their heads any time they want. They can eat until they're full, and they do, until the berries are gone and the thicket grows hot under the sun.

Some days it's like nothing has changed. Like there are no statues growing in the field and no crowd of people growing around the statues. Like there is no barn, either. Like William knows nothing about the color of Misty's skin under her shirt and how it's different from the rest of her, different from anything he's ever seen before.

The man who took William's mother dancing, the miner, is gone. This man is a mechanic. Blond, not brown. He wears a heavy gold cross around his neck.

William's mother says, "He's right in the next room."

"Come on, he's asleep," the man says.

"You don't know that. He could be listening."

"Then we'll be quiet."

"I don't—"

"Shhh. You'll wake him."

The man in the next room, the mechanic, laughs. And maybe if he didn't laugh, things would have been different, but he did, and they aren't, and William lays in bed and listens to the sound they make, this man and his mother, and he tries to imagine what it looks like from their side of the wall.

William goes to the barn and waits for her. When she doesn't come, William goes to the yard and waits for her there. Misty said she would meet him. She promised. William waits until his hands get cold, and then he walks home, feeling tired and hungry and something else. Something like anger, only smaller and meaner. Something with neat rows of teeth that fit behind his own so he feels both like himself and not himself.

William walks around the trailer, not wanting to go back inside, not wanting to sleep. Earl is sitting by the field in a lawn chair with a cooler and a bottle of beer.

William says, "Hello."

" 'lo." Earl looks at him with bloodshot eyes. "What you doing up?"

"Couldn't sleep."

"Me neither. Have a seat."

William sits on the grass next to Earl. They look at the field, where many things have grown, so many things that there is little room left for much else. Copper things and bronze things and hulking stone things and shallow golden things that bend and dip into other things, so you can't tell where one ends and another begins.

"You ever drank?" Earl asks.

"No."

"Good," Earl says. "Don't never start." He takes a long drink and William watches the skin of Earl's neck moving like there is a hand inside of his throat that reaches up to his mouth and pulls the alcohol down, its fingers unwinding against the back of Earl's tongue, the tips of its bitten nails reaching out to catch the scant inch of light that appears as Earl's mouth opens and then closes again.

"Have you seen Misty today?" William asks.

"I ain't seen a soul since that lady from the news this morning. It was the damnedest thing. She said some people up at the college wanted to do some soil tests. Water tests, too. They want to know what's going on," he says, and his voice is hoarse. "I told them to come on down, they can do whatever they want so long as they pay me for it and they don't scratch up any of the growings." He finishes his beer, reaches in the cooler for another. He pops the top on the arm of his chair. He says, "You want to know a secret?"

William shakes his head.

Earl says, "I didn't plant nothing. Not a damn thing."

"I know," William says.

"People keeps asking me how I got it to grow. They think I'm welding them myself, even if it don't make any damn sense."

"Misty thinks they're ugly."

"They don't want to believe nothing I say, but it ain't me. It never was me."

"I thought they was pretty at first, but now I ain't so sure. You think she thinks I'm ugly?" William asks.

The lamps Earl installed over the field start to flicker and buzz. The statues glow under the light, letting it glint off their hard edges and soft edges like sun on water. Even as they watch, something begins to grow. It starts near the back of the field. It twists up slowly, three strong bars of bronze that grow straight and narrow, until some meet in the middle while others keep growing and curving. It's hard to tell what the statue will be before it's finished, but William still guesses: a blue gill, a seashell, a broken back.

"Maybe it's God," Earl says.

"Maybe."

Earl says, "Don't you never start drinking," as he lets another empty bottle fall.

William doesn't move, and Earl doesn't say another word. The bronze braids itself into a bridge with heavy slats and a thick rail, where a hand might hold as its body walked across, staring down at the spaces between the boards, at the earth so far below. The bridge stops halfway, at the very peak of its curve, where it should fall to the other side of the field, but it doesn't. It doesn't.

William takes Misty back to the barn. It's midmorning and her mother is grocery shopping and Penny is with a friend and there is only Misty left, sitting on the front porch with her legs kicking over the edge. This time, William tells her to undo his pants. When she won't, he undoes them himself, and he takes her hand and lays it against him. He does the same thing to her. It is just like the first time, except now he is being touched. Now she is the one who starts. Now they are both the same.

William's mother makes dinner. She puts on a white blouse and dark jeans. She gives him a radio. A present, she says, from Paul.

"Who's Paul?"

"You'll get to meet him soon. He's real nice. It's impossible not to like him. He's just got that way about him, you know?"

She puts more food on William's plate than he has seen in weeks, maybe in his whole life. Green beans and corn-on-the-cob, mashed potatoes, roast beef, and rolls, the kind that you pull apart from the can and fold into little shapes. William eats three before he touches the rest of his plate.

"This is good, Mama. Thank you."

"You're welcome, baby."

She smooths his hair across his forehead and tries to tuck it behind his ear, the way she likes to see it, but it isn't quite long enough. She barely eats, taking from William's plate as she washes dishes and wipes counters and checks the phone.

"I feel like I ain't hardly got to see you with all the extra shifts I've been covering," she says. "It'll pay off come Christmas though, just you wait." She sits on the edge of her seat and smiles. She picks at a thread on the plastic tablecloth and the more she pulls on the thread, the more the plastic comes apart. "Then you're always outside playing with those girls every time I come home. I checked on you in bed the other night and you weren't there." She keeps pulling and pulling at the string. "Where was you?"

"I don't know. Sleepwalking, maybe."

"That don't sound like you."

"Do we have any more beans?"

"I just worry, is all. You're ten now. It might not seem too old to you, but you're getting to be of age and I don't want you making decisions like I did. I don't want you to end up in a place like me, grown before you're ready."

"I know."

"I there anything you want to tell me?" she asks. "Anything at all, baby. You know Mama wouldn't think bad of you for nothing in the world."

The phone rings. William waits as it rings again and again, seeing how long it will take before she gets up. She looks over her shoulder at him as he pushes away from the table, and says, "Remember what I said. You promise me?"

William closes the door to his room. He locks it, too, and later, he doesn't answer when she knocks. He pretends to be asleep. He lies with his head on his pillow and stares at the ceiling as she tells him that she loves him and that she'll never leave him and that everything, everything that she does, is for him.

Misty stops coming outside to play. When William asks Penny where she is, Penny shrugs. "She's sick. She says her head won't quit hurting. I thought she was faking at first, but." Another shrug. "She don't eat much. She cries a lot. She thinks I can't hear her, but we sleep in the same room, you know? I have to hear her."

"Did she say anything about me?"

"No," Penny says. "Why?"

"Have you seen the new statue?"

"God, there's another one?"

They go to the field together. The bridge still hasn't finished itself. It doesn't seem to want to be a bridge at all.

Penny says, "I wish somebody would just burn them all down, you know?"

"No," William says.

He is staring at all the statues together. There are so many now that it hurts his eyes trying to hold them all in one place. Misty hasn't even seen all the things that he's made for her. She hasn't mentioned them, not even once. William's vision blurs and he looks down at his own two feet.

He says, "I still think the green one kind of looks like me. Through the nose."

He turns his head, but Penny is walking back through the yard. There is someone standing in the front door of her trailer, but the sunlight glints on the glass so that William can't see who's looking back at him.

Earl sits in the lawn chair every night. He had the test results from the college framed and hung them from a wooden fence post, the stark white paper and fine print saying things about the field that most of the people couldn't understand. But it means that nothing was found. That the statues are statues and nothing else. Just metal and lead, just grown. There is nothing in the soil or the water or the air to explain where the statues come from and that, the crowd says, makes the field a miracle. Earl doesn't say much at all.

Once, William thinks he sees Misty. Earl has taken to having open house nights on certain days of the week. It draws more people, somehow, the thought of needing permission. The line stretches down the road, out of the holler and out of sight. William likes to stand in the crowd and listen to the things the people have to say about the field and about God, about how beautiful it all is, how perfect. That's when he sees Misty standing at the edge of the woods, near the creek. She's wearing a dark shirt, her hair pulled back in a low ponytail. She's alone and she looks small between the trees, smaller than he's ever seen her.

William yells her name. He pushes through the people, fighting against the bodies, ignoring the complaints. He runs across the yard and between the trees. He wants to tell her that he is sorry. He wants to ask her to help him burn down the barn. He wants to play in the creek with her and hold her hand. He runs through the dark, shouting her name, but there is nothing but trees and leaves and dark, wet earth. He finds the hair tie lying at his feet when he turns around. William buries that, too.

William goes the fallow field one last time. It's been a week since he last saw Misty. A week since anything new has grown. Earl is snoring in his lawn chair, yet William still walks around to the other side of the field to avoid him. He has to get down on his knees and crawl through the fence to reach the field. It is so crowded with statues there is barely room to move. William wedges himself between the unfinished bridge and a heavy hand that reaches toward the sky. He climbs up a series of concentric golden circles and uses the elevation to find one small patch of empty earth, there behind the first statue of green glass.

William is winded now, breathing hard. He is crying, too, but only a little. Only small tears drip from the tip of his nose and fall onto the rich brown earth, and the earth takes that, too, and will use it. William rips his shirt on a barb from a stone statue and there is a scrape on his leg that he doesn't remember getting, but the wound burns now.

William makes his way to the empty spot of earth. This is the only way he can set things right. He has planted bottles and wood and coins and all manner of small things and they have come back. They have been bigger, too, and better than they have been before. They have been something worth looking at. And he will be, too. He will cover himself whole, close his mouth and his eyes, and let the dirt do its work. He will come back changed. Misty won't be afraid of him anymore and his mother won't bring another man home. This will fix the wrong inside of him and everything will be okay.

William starts to dig, and he doesn't stop, not even when his fingernails bend backward and chip away. Even when he hits rocks and has to pry them from the earth and toss them over his shoulder. Even when the rocks become heavy roots tangled together like vines, thick and twisting away in all directions. The sun is bright and hard above him when William finally stops digging. He is standing on a bed of roots, under which a great chasm stretches. The air coming up from the darkness is musty, but warm, and he doesn't know how the ground has been holding itself up all this time.

"Hello?" he says, and a voice answers, but it is not his own. It's his mother walking through the grass, calling his name. William looks into the darkness beneath him, at the place where the dark becomes something else, not light exactly, but close.

William reaches up to the surface. He takes a handful of dirt and pulls it down. He doesn't stop bringing the earth down around him until he can't hear his mother anymore. He doesn't stop until he is planted, whole, in the dark earth.

THE EYES ARE WHITE AND QUIET

⟨⟩

Carole Johnstone

18.02.19 (Clinic: BAR55, 14.02.19)
Consultant: Dr. Barriga
Ophthalmology—Direct Line: 020 5489 9000/ Fax: 020 5487 5291
Minard Surgery Group, Minard Road, SE6 5UX

Dear Dr. Wilson,

Hannah Somerville (06.07.93)
Flat 01, 3 Broadfield Rd, SE6 5UP
NHS No.: 566 455 6123

Thank you for referring this young lady, whose optician suspected optic disc cupping. Her visual acuity is 6/6 in the right eye and 6/4 in the left. Both of the eyes are white and quiet. Intraocular pressure readings are 18mm/Hg in the right and 16mm/Hg in the left. She has open anterior chamber angles in both. The CD ratios are about 0.5. There is no significant visual field defect.

Her eyesight does not appear to be deteriorating. Her chief complaint is that of intermittent visual disturbance, but this was absent in clinic. There is no family history of glaucoma. I have not started her on any medication. Unless she has any further problems, she will be reviewed in the eye clinic in twelve months following a repeat visual fields test and central corneal thickness assessment.

Yours sincerely,
Dr. Rajesh Roshan DRCOphth, FRCS
Staff Specialist in Ophthalmology

((#####))

19.08.19 (Clinic: BAR55, 15.08.19)
Consultant: Dr. Barriga
Ophthalmology—Direct Line: 020 5489 9000/ Fax: 020 5487 5291
Minard Surgery Group, Minard Road, SE6 5UX

Dear Dr. Wilson,

Hannah Somerville (06.07.93)
Flat 01, 3 Broadfield Rd, SE6 5UP
NHS No.: 566 455 6123

This patient was reviewed in the eye clinic today at her own request. Her visual acuity is 6/6 in the right eye and 6/5 in the left. The eyes are white and quiet. The CD ratio remains about 0.5 in both. There is no significant visual field defect and no evidence of glaucoma.

We have seen this young lady at least three times in the last six months, and can ascertain no physical cause for her complaints of intermittent visual disturbance and periods of "complete blindness." These are reported as having lasted up to two hours on occasion, and she believes that their frequency is increasing.

I am of the opinion that we can do no more for her. I have referred her for psychological evaluation and discharged her from the eye clinic, with the advice to see her optician on an annual basis.

Yours sincerely,
Dr. Rajesh Roshan DRCOphth, FRCS
Staff Specialist in Ophthalmology

((#####))

"I mean, all that fuckin' gabbin' and over-sharin' like, everyone thinkin' they're bein' all civilized again, and look how quickly that went the way of everythin' else when they thought one had got in tonight." He rocked back on his heels; the dirt crackled against his boots. The fire warmed her face and she leaned closer to it. She was always so bloody cold.

"Sharin's never a good idea anyways. That posh divvy, he's half mad on that Debbie one, the auld arse don't know half as much as he thinks he does, Jimmy is more fuckin' terrified of wild dogs than anythin' could actually kill us. That's all it is, ain't it? Listenin', findin' out what makes folk tick, what makes 'em shit themselves. Survival instinct—if you're smart like. Say nothin' and let everyone else do the talkin'."

He was from Liverpool and he was on his own. He had terrible teeth; often she could smell his breath before he even spoke. His name was Robbo. That was all she knew about him. That, and he did a whole lot of talking for someone so against it. He liked talking to her; she had no idea why.

"Why don't you leave then?" she asked. It had started to snow: cold, glancing touches against her fire-warmed cheeks. She could hear the growing mutters and cries of dismay on the other side of the parked vans. They always built at least four fires now, one in each corner like a mobile Roman infantry camp.

"Nowhere to go is there? And folk need folk, like. That's just survival instinct too, ain't it? Some folks, they got that more than other folks. And, I mean, it's not like you know which kind you're gonna be till it happens, ay? Soft lads like Jimmy are scared of their own shadow, then you got the likes of Bob fuckin' Marley runnin' straight at everythin' like a proper weapon. Debbie and that other bird—the Scottish one . . . "

"Sarah."

"Right. *Sarah.* I mean, what have they done since we all hooked up, eh?"

"They're just scared."

"*I'm* fuckin' scared. Don't stop me helpin' out, goin' on patrol. I mean, explain that, ay? You look at the animal kingdom, right? It's not like Peter fuckin' Rabbit wakes up one night and thinks, fuck it, what's the point? I can't be arsed runnin' away from anythin' that wants to 'ave me for brekkie. Might as well give up and die like. Or just cry meself to sleep in me nice comfy VW."

She smiled. "It's not the same." He was rattled. He was always wired, always opinionated, but the events of the day and then the wild dog that had snuck past the fires had got to him. His sweat was fresh, but it smelled bad; it reminded her of the days when no one had understood what was going on. When everyone had been trying so desperately to get away from a thing that they hadn't yet realized was everywhere.

"I mean, fuck, look at you, 'ann. You don't just go out on reccies, you fuckin' lead a few. And you can't see your arse from your fuckin' elbow."

She didn't answer.

"Arr ey, you can't, come on like. I'm not bein a fuckin' dick. It's a valid fuckin' point."

She liked the way his *fucks* and *likes* and *dicks* always sounded like the hissing hot water siphons of the coffee shops that she used to hide in when her sight started getting really bad. It was comforting somehow. She liked the way that he admired her too. Even before she'd proved her worth to everyone else, he'd always been the first to volunteer to sit watch with her. Back when she'd just been the blind girl.

There had been many convoys in those first few months, but none had stopped for her—or if they had, they'd moved on swiftly again without her. This one had initially said yes, she suspected, only because of Robbo. And as convoys went, it only just qualified. One of the vans was his beat-up Ford, still smelling of methylated spirits and paint and hash. The other—the VW—had belonged to a Brethren couple whose names she had already forgotten.

Robbo swore when they both heard sudden movement behind him.

"Grub's up, ladies."

"Nice one," Robbo said, pretending that he hadn't cursed, that he couldn't hear Marley's low chuckle. "Want some scran, 'annah?"

She put out her hands and relished the sudden warmth of the foil tray. "Thanks."

Marley was big, she could tell. Sometimes—often—she could sense something other than scorn or tightly wound caution in him, especially when they were alone. Once, he had followed her to the shallow pit that they always dug on the periphery of their camp, and as she'd squatted and peed, she'd felt him watching; she'd breathed in the sea smells of him. If it wasn't for Robbo, she knew that she'd have a lot more to fear from Marley than she already did.

After Marley left them alone again, Robbo attacked his stew with gusto. She suspected that he always ate with his mouth wide open; she found the sound of that oddly comforting too. She ate quietly, mechanically, tasting nothing at all.

"Why won't this snow fuckin' stop?" he eventually muttered. "Last thing we fuckin' need is another fuckin' whiteout."

"I'll be able to hear them," she said, and he heaved a great sigh, even though it was a lie. It never failed to amaze her how easily that lie had been believed from the very start, as though the immediate consequence of her blindness should be a nearly preternatural sharpening of all her other senses. They did believe it though—all of them—and it was just as well. It made her useful, maybe indispensable. She knew that even Robbo's surrendered Peter Rabbits remembered the night that the Whites had ambushed them while they'd all been sleeping. She knew that they remembered her warning scream, the dead White at her feet next to the opened VW door, the bloodied crowbar in her hands. When the Brethren couple had staggered out of the van, they'd pulled their coats tight around their bellies, crying and sobbing that God had saved them.

"Oh, aye?" Robbo had said, after discovering the body of a Pakistani man, whose name Hannah had also forgotten, lying by the makeshift entrance to their camp. "What he do to piss Him off then, ay?" The Pakistani had died badly. Even though Robbo had never told her exactly how, she'd been able to smell it; she'd been able to see it through the horrified witness of everyone else.

They'd burned both bodies on the periphery of their camp, and then buried the smoking bonfire under heavy, wet clods of grass.

"They almost look like us," Robbo had whispered to her later. "When they're dead at least, like. When they're not runnin'."

After that, they stopped sleeping in the vans. After that, not one member of the convoy voiced an objection when she started taking point, same as everyone else. There was always someone ready to hold onto her elbow and take the weight of her pack. A few weeks after the dead White, the Brethren couple didn't return from an easy supply run. No one volunteered to go looking for them.

"So, what kind of folk are you, Robbo?" It wasn't what she wanted to ask, not even close, but she needed to start somewhere. They never talked about anything that was worth something. They never talked about where they'd come from, because none of them believed they'd ever be going back. And they never talked about where they were going, because they weren't going anywhere. They were just moving. And progress was slow. It was safer to scout routes and camps on foot before bringing up the vans behind. The vans weren't for travel any more; they were for escape. She'd been on point today, and the two days before that, and Robbo had held her elbow for all of them. That was why tonight of all nights, she needed somewhere to start.

"I'm still here, ay? What's that tell you?"

She swallowed. For a brief moment, fear swallowed her up, doubt pinched fingers against her windpipe. "Tell me something from home. Tell me something about before, about *you* before."

He sighed. It still rattled a bit inside his chest, even though he'd run out of the last of his *bifters* weeks ago. "Aright, 'annah. Don't see the fuckin' point like, but aright."

She heard him change position, move a little closer. "Anythin's better than bein' on your own, ain't it? That's just how it is. It's why we're all still here, ain't it? I had this mate, right. We'd been mates since school—not bezzies like cause he was a bit nuts, and you know what kids are, you're not about to hang out with the soft lad. Anyways, we stayed in touch cause we lived on the same estate, we both worked in the Asda, and went to the same pubs on the weekend. And this guy, 'ann, he was somethin else, man. He was like them abandoned puppies they used to show on ad breaks. He was built like a brick shithouse like, but soft as shite on account of his ma beatin' him up every time she took a drink when he was a kid, and his da tryin' to shag him every time she wasn't lookin'. All he wanted, right, was someone, anyone. You could fuckin' smell it off him."

When Robbo coughed, she nearly told him that it was okay, that he could stop if he wanted to. But she didn't. She shook the snow free of her blanket before pulling it tighter around her shoulders. She blinked her eyes, brushed icy fingers between her eyelashes, offering Robbo at least the illusion that she could see him. "Did he find someone?"

Robbo's laugh sounded angry, but she knew it wasn't. "Yer, he did. She likely didn't know her luck till she didn't. Folk never know what to do with unconditional love like, d'you know that, 'annah? They think it's all they want till they get it. It wrecks with your head cause it makes no sense at all. It's like them pop-up targets at the shows. After a while you just need 'em to stay down, you know?"

She nodded, even though she had no idea at all.

"By the time they'd been seein' each other six months, she'd shagged half the estate behind his back."

"Did he find out?"

That angry laugh again. "Yer he did."

"What happened?"

When he didn't answer, she stabbed at the fire with a stick, sending up sparks of heat between them. Her heart was still beating far too fast. "Robbo?"

"He walked in on them," he muttered, and then suddenly he was talking too fast and too hard again; she struggled to keep up. "He whacked her over the 'ead with an 'ammer, and then he took a carvin' knife to the fella. And then he fronts up to my house, covered in their blood, and asks if he can come in like, if he can borrow a fuckin' towel. And I say go'ed, lad, no worries, have a shower while you're at it. And I phone the bizzies the minute he does."

He was breathing too heavily. She could nearly feel the hot, choppy distress of it. "You did the right thing, Robbo. He'd killed people. What else could you have done?"

"Are you for real with this shit or is it just an act? I didn't call the bizzies cause he'd killed people and it was the right fuckin' thing to do, 'annah. I called 'em cause I thought he was gonna kill me. And he came to my house cause he knew I'd do it, he knew I'd grass 'im up."

She opened her mouth to speak, maybe to say sorry, but he hadn't finished. She could hear his boots scraping against the ground, and she could still hear the agitated puff of his breath.

"And as they're cartin 'im off, still fuckin' wet from me fuckin' shower, he says to me, *it's okay, Robbo*, like he fuckin' means it, and I stay standin' there on the doorstep in me skivvies and slippers, worryin' about the fuckin' neighbors."

"I used to be a troll."

He coughed again. "What?"

She gestured at the snow. "Before all this. When I still had my sight and the world still had the internet. I worked nightshift in a petrol station as a cashier, and dayshift in online chat rooms as a troll."

She could nearly hear him blinking. It made her suddenly want to laugh.

"You mean, like, you were one of them blerts gets people to off 'emselves for shits and giggles?"

"No," she said quickly, though not for exoneration. "I just did what you said before. I watched and I listened. I worked out people's weaknesses and used them."

"You're pretty fuckin' good at it like," he said, with a low, sheepish chuckle, because he was a lot cleverer than everyone else thought he was.

For a while, he said nothing else. She couldn't hear even the sound of his breathing any more, only the cracks of the firewood, the muffled conversations on the other side of camp, the closing, echoless shroud of settling snow. In her mind's eye, she could see the clustered pine trees that she'd been able to smell just before they made camp. She imagined them padded with new white shoulders, their cones sparkled with frost, dark trunks in shadow. She imagined the abandoned towns and villages and cities made new, smothered under all that breathless white and quiet. And she imagined all the camps doubtless just like this one: small bastions of fiery resistance, like coastal dun beacons passing along messages of doom.

She started when Robbo made a sudden movement, cleared his throat.

"What the fuck d'you do it for?" He sounded angry, and she could understand that at least. Robbo hadn't only thought that her blindness meant she could hear and smell better, he'd thought that it meant she *was* better. Better than anyone else.

And she'd thought about the why a lot too. Most often, she'd posed as a man, a predator, whose misogyny had hidden behind feigned interest and casually cruel charm. "I don't know. I just did."

She heard a sound: the cracking of a snow-heavy branch maybe, or a starving wild dog trying to hunt. In an instant she was afraid again, uncertain again. She reached out her numb hands toward the fire. "Do you ever get tired, Robbo?"

"Sure." That self-conscious chuckle again. "Do I wish I'd just stayed in the house and drunk meself to death instead? Deffo sure."

Some snow crept between her blanket and skin, cricking her neck. "Do you think we're both better people now?"

"No. Do you?"

"No." She smiled, and it hurt her chapped lips. "Is there any more of that nasty rum?"

"There ain't much left, but you're welcome to it."

"We can share it." She heard the screw of the hipflask, and then the tinny slosh of its contents. When Robbo got up to walk around the fire, she could hear his boots sinking into the snow, and the creak-like sound of them shifting inside it before lifting free. The snow had got deep fast. When he squatted down next to her, she could instantly smell the rum, his breath, his sweat. Goosebumps prickled her skin. Perhaps her other senses were getting better after all.

"You okay, 'annah?"

"Yeah," she said, feeling the cool smoothness of the hip flask against her open palms, putting her numb fingers around its opening before guiding it to her lips. She coughed as soon as she swallowed, and then put it to her lips again before pausing.

"It's okay, you finish it," Robbo said.

When he started getting up, she reached out for him, tugging on his coat. And when he squatted back down, she released a breath that she hadn't realized she'd been holding. She didn't take another drink, but she swallowed anyway.

"I can see them, Robbo. The Whites. I've always been able to see them. Right from the start."

He lost his balance. She heard his legs going out from under him, boot heels scraping against buried dirt, his arse hitting the snow with a nearly funny *whump.*

"They're all I can see." She felt a need to explain that was pretty much redundant now—but the omission had been too heavy. All those weeks of people trusting her, holding her elbow, thinking she was benignly special, their good luck charm. She'd helped them, but not enough. Not in the ways that she could have. And now there was this.

"That's boss, 'annah." But his voice was careful, guarded. Maybe even a little disappointed in her. "And I can understand like, why you never let on. You'd be the same as them folk who didn't go blind in that Triffid thing, ay? Every cunt'd want a piece of you."

She tried to smile when he immediately cursed—when he realized what he'd said and tried to take it back. It made her like him more. It made the choppy beating of her heart choppier.

"You're right, Robbo. You're right, it's the same." But it wasn't. She hadn't kept quiet about being able to see those fast and silent white horrors, like nets of bloated muslin twisted by the wind, because she'd been afraid of being exploited. She'd done it because she'd wanted to feel wanted, needed to be needed. Just like all of those yellow days spent hunched over her laptop in the grimy, freezing kitchenette of her bedsit. She'd needed to feel powerful.

She took another swallow of rum and it went down better than the first. This time she didn't cough. When she shook the flask, it gave a tinny, almost empty slosh. "You finish it," she said, pushing it against his coat.

"Why d'you make us stop here tonight, 'annah?"

She could hear the quiet neutrality in his voice, the cleverer, fearful certainty. She pictured those fiery dun beacons again.

"Do you know what I think, Robbo?" she said, feeling self-consciously histrionic despite herself, despite the circumstances. "I think the world would be better off without us. I think the land and the sea and everything living in both would be better off without us. And I think that God—if there is one—would be better off without us too." She stopped, wiped tears as well as fat flakes of snow from under her eyes before turning back towards Robbo, the heat and sweat and fearful certainty of him. "But I need to know what *you* think, Robbo. I need you to tell me what you think."

He shifted, got back onto his haunches. When he spoke, she could hear the smile in his words as well as all that fear. "I think we'd be the ones better off without fuckin' God, 'annah." He immediately tutted, as if his answer had annoyed him, and then sighed a long, low sigh. "I reckon love's just another excuse for hate."

"Good," she said. Her own breath left her in a shuddery exhale that she imagined as a silvery plume of smoke. "Me too."

৩

The world will be white and quiet, she thought. *Nothing but white and quiet.*

"Aren't you going to finish the rum?" she said instead, and her teeth were suddenly chattering too much; she bit her tongue.

"It's okay, 'annah," Robbo said, taking hold of both of her hands and pulling them into the warmth of his chest. She could feel his frantic heartbeat against her knuckles.

She thought of his mate being led out to the police car, still wet from his shower, looking back at Robbo in his skivvies and slippers. She squeezed closed her eyes. *The world will be white and quiet*, she thought, *the world will be white and quiet, like a mantra that she'd once believed in but now no longer trusted at all.*

"I'm sorry," she whispered.

She kept hold of Robbo's hands as she lifted up her head, as she opened her eyes. She gripped them harder as she let herself see all those bloated fists of white wind around them. All those casually cruel eyes, hungry dark mouths. The hundreds—maybe now even thousands—of them crouched inside the expectant silent hush. They weren't waiting for her; they weren't waiting for anything. They were simply taking their pleasure, stretching it as far as they could.

She remembered how it had felt to know that she had someone caught and trapped by her smiling lies; how the anticipation of destroying all she had built up had so often loomed larger than the final act itself. And how that need to purge—to pass along all her fear and furious loneliness, like a contagion of fire along headland and cliff—had never waned, never ever lost its power. She was sorry for it now—sorry for all of it—but she'd never lied to herself. She'd never pretended that if the Whites hadn't come she would ever have stopped.

The world will be white and quiet.

"It's okay, 'annah," Robbo said again, pressing the wet prickle of his face against her own as those eyes, those mouths, all that eager, twisted white rushed over the camp in a suffocating fog that would soon not be quiet at all. "It's okay."

And she believed him, she trusted him, she clung onto him. Even though he was blind.

⊷

SECRET KEEPER

—◆—

Bonnie Jo Stufflebeam

1

You know how this story goes: the girl was kissed in the womb by the devil. When she emerged into the too-bright world, she was missing half her face where his teeth tore it off. The doctors did their best; they grafted skin over the left side, added collagen in her cheeks. "Smile," they said, tickling her feet. But she could not smile, and so no one smiled at her.

A girl is supposed to be beautiful. A girl is supposed to have rosy red cheeks and a laugh that makes men wilt to think of her bright future. A beautiful girl will have a beautiful life. An ugly girl slips unseen through secret doors.

The girl was always good at finding secrets. She was better at keeping them.

2

An ugly girl does what she can to get by. She is thrown into the world of zits and water bras and miniskirts, but none of that matters when she wears a face like flattened roadkill. When she is caught staring at the other faces in the locker rooms—eager to linger long on that which she doesn't have—her interest is misnamed in a world obsessed with naming things. But this girl already has many names: Erica, at first, then ghost, a name given her for the ghastly pallor of her grafted skin.

A ghost girl cries for her first year of middle school, listening to an old Patti Smith song—"Pissing in a River"—and hoping someone might wrap their arms around her and carry her to a home where she is wanted, where there are hundreds of ghost girls like her. When she realizes that no one is coming, she stares into the mirror so long her face distorts into a thing of beauty. She is changed. She tears her eyes away. She must change.

She seeks out secrets like shadows seek their objects, until she finds the shadows' secrets, until she knows how to be shadow when she needs to be.

3

The world of first cars and first fucks and first drinks is different than the awkward world of first kisses. All anyone wants is to be seen. But to be seen is to give away your power. To be hidden is to be known. Her first day of school, the ghost girl disappears, a shadow fleeing from the light. Everyone talks about her for a week, until she becomes a secret. Until she becomes so infamous, she is given credit for secrets she doesn't spill, for wrongs she doesn't commit. The football player's jockey cup is filled with ketchup, and her name is signed to the note: *Ghost Girl*. The capital letters their own new rank. The English teacher's book is shredded in her chair. *Ghost Girl*. Every tire in the parking lot is slashed. *Ghost Girl*.

Though that one *was* her. It hurts to laugh, so she moans as she watches her classmates fail to flee the school in the rain.

They say she creeps through the ceiling. They say she gets a report card, the same as anyone, and that the teachers are too scared to give her anything but A's. They say she and the gym coach are having an affair; they meet beneath the bleachers every morning. Sometimes, late at night, they hear a voice belting a song only one girl recognizes from her parents' record collection: "Pissing in a River."

But the ghost girl is all alone, for one, two, three years of school. The ghost girl won't earn a high school degree. The ghost girl doesn't creep through the rafters. She prefers the home she has built beneath the theater stage, in the drained pool where the swim team used to practice, before the school's swim budget was slashed. Her favorite season: the spring musical, when she falls asleep in the daylight dark to the struggling pitches of budding singers, most of whom will never sing after their high school tenure. The teacher favors the girl with the highest voice, the one who leaves your ears ringing: Aimee. The ghost girl plugs her ears when Aimee sings. Her world beneath the stage is too dark for such shrillness. The ghost girl knows the limit of her own talent. Though she could out-sing every one of these girls, she cannot stand in front of an audience, cannot let that much of her outside her body. She waits and listens, but does not hear anything that makes her shiver the way that Patti Smith record does.

Then, a new girl sings. Her name, she speaks softly into the mic, is Chrissie. When Chrissie sings, the ghost girl's chest throbs with a particular empty ache. From the rafters, the ghost girl watches her: Chrissie with her short dark curls, her beautiful face bereft of makeup, her bright yellow smiley-face shirt and torn jeans. She is kind, the ghost girl notices, to everyone.

The ghost girl follows Chrissie to class, moving in shadows the other students don't see. She has become good at seeing shadows, at inhabiting them. The ghost girl doesn't slash Chrissie's tires when she pulls the prank a second time. When Chrissie is called into the principal, blamed, the ghost girl slips an alibi into Chrissie's files: a psychiatrist's appointment in another city, for a condition Chrissie doesn't like to talk about. The ghost girl has done her homework; the condition is the same one that Chrissie was treated for as a little girl. Though she was pronounced healed, the school buys the excuse.

The ghost girl tracks Chrissie's every move.

A new girl finds it hard to make friends. A new girl eats lunch alone in a bathroom stall. It is there that the ghost girl comes to her, hiding in the walls and speaking in her ghostly secret keeper voice.

"Chrissie," calls the ghost girl, singing her own song. She has had years with little to do but practice. "I am your angel of music."

The ghost girl has been thorough. From Chrissie's files, she found two facts that will make it easier to be a friend. 1. Chrissie's mother died when Chrissie was a little girl. 2. After her death, Chrissie heard voices. These voices? Chrissie called them her angel of music. A ghost girl can be an angel of music; the name seems to fit her better than all the names she has ever clutched in her palms. The Devil, after all, was an angel fallen.

At first Chrissie says nothing in response. Then: "No," she says. "Please, not again."

"I'm not in your head. I am here, with you."

The ghost girl presses her hand against the wall until the wall turns cold beneath her skin.

"Do you feel me, Chrissie?"

Chrissie shivers and runs her hands up and down her arms. "You're really here?" she says. "Has it been you all along?"

"I'm here, your angel of music."

"My AoM. Your voice is beautiful," Chrissie says. "Where did you learn to sing?"

The ghost girl has never heard a compliment as sweet as this. "I have listened," she says. Her belly warms with pride. "I can teach you."

"Would you?"

"I would love nothing more," the ghost girl says.

4

Their lessons begin. Every lunch hour, Chrissie hides in her bathroom stall while the ghost girl gives her lessons in strengthening her voice. Chrissie is a good singer. With the ghost girl's help, she is great. When Chrissie sings, the ghost girl hears her own inflections, her own tones. When Chrissie surpasses the ghost girl, it's time for Chrissie to play the lead.

The theater auditions *The Secret Lives of Fairytale Princesses*, a play written by the theater teacher. Chrissie auditions for the lead of Sleeping Beauty, but is given the supporting role of Snow White. The ghost girl fumes in her underground lair, where she paces back and forth until her feet bleed. She misses the next day's lessons with Chrissie. Chrissie cries in the bathroom, thinking she has disappointed her AoM. The ghost girl hears her tears, but cannot go to her, so badly injured are her feet, her ego.

She hears, instead, a young boy enter the bathroom, crying for himself.

"What are you doing in here?" Chrissie asks.

"Oh please," says the boy. "Look at me. I can't use the men's. If anyone has the right to cry in the girl's bathroom, it's me."

The boy's voice is familiar: the theater teacher's second favorite, Trevor.

"What happened to you?" Chrissie asks.

"That role was supposed to be mine," the boy says. "I'm the best. But I don't 'look the part.' You know what she means by that? She means I'm too gay for it. Stupid fucking hick town." The boy kicks the trash can; the ring of boot on meal reverberates into the ghost girl's walls. It is a dissonant sound, not altogether unappealing. The ghost girl scribbles some notes on her sheet music.

"And you know the only reason you didn't get Sleeping Beauty is because you have short hair. Mrs. Logan isn't very imaginative. If she can't see the exact look she had in mind, then forget it. I've been sucking up to her for, what, two years now? That part should've been mine."

"It was just because of my hair?" Chrissie asks.

"You better believe it." Trevor laughs. "If you think for a second you're not the most talented in the class, you're in extreme need of a wake-up call."

"I'm taking lessons," Chrissie says. "From a great teacher."

"Well, you must give me her number."

"It's complicated," Chrissie says. "She doesn't take new clients? She's a friend of the family."

"Shit," Trevor says. "Well, drop a good word for me? Now let's clean ourselves up and get back out there and make the most of this utmost shitty situation."

Chrissie laughs. The ghost girl's stomach roils; no one is supposed to make Chrissie laugh but her.

5

If the ghost girl can't make Chrissie laugh, she will make her smile. The ghost girl gathers her secrets. She snatches Aimee's phone from her locker. She snaps photos of her out by the tennis courts sneaking cigarettes. She sends the photo to her family, her friends, to Mrs. Logan.

Aimee is grounded, forbidden from the play, given a talking-to by a certain disappointed theater instructor.

"Don't you know what those things do to your voice?" Mrs. Logan says. "I thought you were a serious student. I see now I made a mistake."

Mrs. Logan pulls Chrissie aside. "I had the wrong idea about the lead," she says. "I found the picture you put on my desk. What confidence, to do such a thing! With your nice wig, you could easily be my Sleeping Beauty."

"My wig?" Chrissie says.

Mrs. Logan waves the picture at her; it's a picture of Chrissie sleeping, blond hair spread across her pillow. Chrissie shivers but thanks her teacher. She and Trevor celebrate with cappuccinos at the local Holy Coffee! shop.

6

"You're late," says the ghost girl at their next lunch.

"Sorry," Chrissie says, pulling her sandwich out of her bag. "I was talking with Trevor."

"You haven't eaten yet?"

"I didn't have time."

The ghost girl huffs behind her wall.

"What about you? You didn't even show up last time! I said I was sorry." Chrissie takes little bites.

The ghost girl waits, then waits no longer. "Enough," she booms. "You know who gave you that role? I can take it back. This is it, Chrissie, your shot at being something here, your chance to show them that you're not one of them. Do you want me to go?"

"No, please," Chrissie shoves her sandwich back into her bag. "I can't do it without you."

"Then you must do as I say. To be great takes great focus. That's what you have over all the other girls. Over Trevor with his boyfriend, his endless distractions. You can do this. But you need to make some changes."

"What changes?"

"We're going to have to set some rules."

"Anything." Chrissie presses her hand against the wall; it warms the ghost girl's skin. "Anything as long as you don't leave me."

The ghost girl lays out five rules: Chrissie will practice every day for two hours outside of their lesson. Chrissie will not go out after school or on weekends. Chrissie will not speak to anyone but her. Chrissie will not tell anyone about her Angel of Music. "These are the rules you need to follow if you want to be something. If you want to be the best."

"I do want to be the best," Chrissie says. "I want to make you proud of me."

That evening the ghost girl stares at herself in the mirror. She eats snack cakes from the dumpster. She fingers the scars of her face beneath her mask and pulls at the skin around her belly. She sings to a crowd of no one.

7

Chrissie follows the ghost girl's rules until opening night, when Trevor pulls her into his car and takes her out for a pre-show dinner at the burger place down the street. The ghost girl follows them, moving as shadow through sewers and gas lines and an old buried military complex the town keeps secret. She presses her shadow body against the ceiling tiles and watches through a crack as the two scarf meat and laugh nervously like madmen.

"So what's going on with you?" Trevor asks, dabbing his greasy fingers on his napkin. "Oh my god, are you pregnant?"

"No," Chrissie says. She doesn't smile.

"Honey, I was just kidding. That's not it, is it?" He clamps his hand upon hers. The ghost girl's stomach heaves. "You can tell me."

"It's her," Chrissie whispers. "It's my teacher. My Angel of Music? She's very strict. I have to do what she says, or else I won't be good enough."

"But you're good enough already. There's no one as good as you."

"But I can be better. I mean, I totally fucked up the second chorus in "Bring on the Sleep.""

Trevor rolls his eyes. "The music you're singing sucks, first thing. Second thing, you're seventeen. You don't need to be a pro right now. You need to be a teenager. Chrissie, have you even kissed a boy? Have you even had a friend before?"

"I've had friends." Chrissie shrugs. "I had to leave them all back where I came from. And my AoM. She talked to me when no one else would. She's been there for me, from the beginning."

Trevor sighs and leans across the table, tucks a strand of her hair behind her ear. "I'm your friend. Don't you forget that. If you want me, I'm here."

Chrissie untucks the strand. "You shouldn't touch me," she says. She presses her palm to the wall, checking for the chill. "It's not entirely safe."

8

The performance is everything the ghost girl ever hoped it would be. Chrissie hits the high notes as though her voice were breaking out of its shell: revelation over shrill insistence. The ghost girl watches from the back row, the shadow of a seat. The theater is half-empty. The male lead, Chrissie's Prince Charming, is unworthy but beautiful with his beach boy hair and thick lips.

"It's nearly a shame to wake such a sleeping beauty," he sings, "but if her brains are as big as her bonnet, I'll have made the right decision."

The ghost girl ignores the words. She makes up her own: lonely girls rule the lonely world. Bossy girls rule the bossy world. A ghost girl writes the story she wants to read across the blank slate of her burnt skin.

Everyone claps. Chrissie bows. Prince Charming holds her hand a little too tightly. The ghost girl disappears back underground, where she belongs.

9

Chrissie goes home that first night, and the second, and the third. On their penultimate night, when Trevor demands she join them at the after-party, Chrissie glances around the room as though checking for the AoM she knows will not be there. She smiles. "Why the hell not?" she says. "If my teacher's mad about it, I'll just quit!"

"That's the rebel I want to know." Trevor links his arm in hers. "Your Prince Charming will be there. Let's see which one of us he likes more."

The ghost girl races along the walls to follow them out, but they go too far from the school, out past where she can follow them underground, along long country roads with no shadows to seep into. She seethes in the abandoned theater, stomping her feet until they ache all the way up to her knees. She wanders the halls, ripping the BOOZE IS BAD posters from the walls. DEATH TO THEATER, she scrawls over the front doors. Downstairs, she sets her traps. Chrissie won't go again where she can't follow. She is so lost in her fury, her planning, that she doesn't hear Chrissie and her friends sneak back in through the loading door to the theater. Finally, their drunken giggling breaks through.

The ghost girl makes her way to the theater. They are so busy laughing on the stage in the dark—Chrissie, Trevor, and the Prince Charming—that they don't hear her enter, though, in her anger, she keeps only a tenuous hold on staying shadow, moving in and out of skin, of bone. She watches them as she would watch a show—and what a performance! The ghost girl studies each mess of hormones. They hold wine coolers in their hands; the ghost girl can smell the cheap sugary stuff from the front row. Neither Trevor nor Chrissie is the obvious winner of Prince Charming's affections. They sit on either side of him and talk about their families: hard lives for soft children. They weren't granted the power of invisibility. Their scars are hidden beneath more than masks.

"I don't think my father loves me," Chrissie says.

"My parents love me two inches in," Trevor says. "They don't care that I'm gay, but if I don't end up married with babies, I'm useless to them."

"Mine love me too much," Prince Charming says. "If I'm a step out of line—"

Who can say who is hurt the deepest? It's a game to compare horror. The stories the ghost girl could tell, if she had people with which to share stories.

"Enough pity party," Trevor says, pulling out his iPhone. He plays music with no lyrics, incomprehensibly simple beats. They dance and laugh and finish their wine coolers, leaving the empty bottles in the wings. The ghost girl picks them up and smells them, careful not to make a sound. The smell makes her stomach ache with want: fake fruit and the kind of sugar that leaves your teeth grainy. Calmed by their useless bickering, the ghost girl allows herself entrance into their shadows. She moves around their feet, around their mouths. The human body is full of dark spaces, shadows in their own right. She slips, soundlessly, into Prince Charming's warm mouth. She gleans all his secrets. When Chrissie kisses him, the ghost girl is a shadow that passes from his lips to hers.

From inside Chrissie, the ghost girl speaks. "You disobeyed your Angel of Music," she says. Chrissie shrinks back into the dark, a headache taking hold.

"Leave me the fuck alone," Chrissie says. If pressed, she might chalk her newfound courage up to 3% ABV, but the ghost girl scans her chemistry, her biology. Though she'd never tasted it for herself, she has read of the effect weak booze might have on a girl like Chrissie. It isn't enough to change her kindness into cruelty. There is only one explanation, then: Chrissie was never who she pretended to be. She is an actress to her core.

"Chrissie, who are you talking to?" Trevor kneels beside her and places his hand on her knee.

"Can't you hear her?"

"I don't hear anything," Trevor says. "Chrissie, have you been taking your pills?"

"What pills?" Chrissie says. "I haven't taken those since I was little."

Trevor blushes. "That's not what everyone else says. Chrissie, you can tell me anything."

Prince Charming stands back behind them. "What's going on?" he asks. "What's wrong with her?"

"Not now," Trevor says.

"Don't listen to them," the ghost girl says. "I'm real as you are. Realer, in fact, because I'm not a liar like you. I'm not a pretender."

"What's she saying to you?" Trevor says.

"Tell him to stop interfering," the ghost girl says. She spreads her arms through Chrissie's arms and stretches the shadow inside her until the skin hurts like it's burning, like it's soon-to-break.

"Stop," Chrissie screams. Her voice echoes the way only a performer's can. "Both of you, stop."

"I'm not doing anything," Prince Charming says.

Chrissie stands, knocking a wine cooler over. The blue spreads across the stage like a burst vein bruise. "I'll go with you, I will," she says to the ghost girl. She pushes past Trevor, past Prince Charming. The ghost girl leads her only friend into the darkness underground.

10

Underground, the ghost girl has faked two prescription bottles full of the pills Chrissie took when she was a little girl, dated for the present. The clothes scattered throughout the ghost girl's lair are inscribed with Chrissie's name, black ink on every tag. The ghost girl has been thorough. She's been cunning. She is an actress too. If she can convince Chrissie that they're one, then they'll be one. She whispers untrue secrets: Chrissie never moved to a new town, never met a new friend. The ghost girl has been here, inside Chrissie, all along. A ghost girl is part of you always. She stretches to fit the new body. She sings through the new voice. Her mouth moves in a face that she will never have to hide again.

Girls without friends make ghosts all the time, the ghost girl says. *It's not the worst you could have done.*

A ghost girl keeps her own secrets best of all.

MAPPING THE INTERIOR

—✦—

Stephen Graham Jones

I was twelve the first time I saw my dead father cross from the kitchen door-way to the hall that led back to the utility room.

It was 2:49 in the morning, as near as I could reconstruct.

I was standing alongside the dusty curtain pulled across the front window of the living room. I wasn't standing there on purpose. I was in only my underwear. No lights were on.

My best guess is that, moments before, I'd been looking out the front window, into all the scrub and nothing spread out in front of our house. The reason for thinking that was I had the taste of dust in the back of my throat, and the window had a fine coat of that dust on it. Probably. I'd breathed it in through my nose, because sleepwalkers are goal oriented, not concerned with details or consequences.

If sleepwalkers cared about that kind of stuff, I'd have at least had my gym shorts on, and, if I was in fact trying to see something outside, then my glasses, too.

To sleepwalk is to be inhabited, yes, but not by something else, so much. What you're inhabited by, what's kicking one foot in front of the other, it's yourself. It doesn't make sense, but I don't think it's under any real compulsion to, finally. If anything, being inhabited by yourself like that, what it tells you is that there's a real you squirming down inside you, trying all through the day to pull up to the surface, look out. But it can only get that done when your defenses are down. When you're sleeping.

The following morning—this was my usual procedure, after a night of shuffling around dead to the world—would find me out in the sun, poring over the stunted grass and packed dirt for eighty or a hundred feet past the front window. Mom would be at work, and my little brother, Dino, would be glued to one of his cartoons, so there would be nobody there to call out from the porch, ask me what was I doing.

If I'd had to answer, I'd have said I was looking for whatever it was I'd been looking for last night. My hope was that my waking self had cued on some regularity to the packed dirt's contour, or registered a dull old pull tab that was actually the lifting ring for a dry old plywood door that opened onto . . . what? I didn't care. Just something. Anything. An old stash of fireworks, a buried body, a capped-off well; it didn't matter.

The day I found something, that would mean that my nighttime ramblings, they had purpose.

Otherwise, I was just broken, right? Otherwise, I was just a toy waking up in the night, bumping into walls.

That next morning, though, my probing fingers turned up nothing of any consequence. Just the usual trash—little glass bottles, a few bolts with nuts and washers rusted to the thread, part of a dog collar, either the half-buried wheel of a car long gone or the still-attached wheel of a car now buried upside down.

I wanted the latter, of course, but, to allow that possibility, I had to resist digging around the edges of that wheel.

When I looked back to the front window of our modular house, I half-expected to see the shape of my dead father again, standing in the window. Watching me.

The window was just the window, the curtain drawn like Mom said, to keep the heat out.

Still, I watched it.

How I'd know it was him from a house length out, it wasn't that I would recognize his face or his build. He'd died when I was four and nearly dying from pneumonia myself, when Dino was one and staying with an aunt so he couldn't catch pneumonia, when Mom was still working just one shift. All I had to go on as far as how he looked, it was pretty much just snapshots and a blurry memory or two.

No, the way I'd recognized him the night before, when he was walking from the kitchen doorway back to the utility room, it was his silhouette. There were spikes coming out from his lower back, and the tops of his calves bulged out in an unnatural way, and his head was top-heavy and kind of undulating, so he was going to have to duck to make it into the utility room.

But—for all he was wearing, he was absolutely silent. Zero rustling, like you can usually hear with a fancydancer, when they're all set to go, or have just finished.

Thing was? My father never danced. He didn't go to the pow-wows to compete for cash. One of the few things I remember about him, it's that he didn't call the traditionals down at the town pump or the IGA "throwbacks," like I'd heard. His words always got scrambled in his mouth—Dino's got that too—so that what he came out with, it was "fallback."

My father was neither a throwback nor a fallback. He didn't speak the language, didn't know the stories, and didn't care that he didn't. Once or twice a year, he'd sign on to fight whatever fire was happening, but it wasn't to protect any ancestral land. It was because when you signed on, they issued you these green wool pants. He'd sell those to the hunters, come fall. Once a year, Mom told me, he'd usually walk home in his boxers, with a twenty folded small in his hand so none of the reservation dogs would nose it away.

That's my dad, as I know him.

But in the year or two after he either drowned or was drowned—there's stories both ways, and they each make sense—when we were still on the reservation, when his sisters would still watch us some days, they'd tell us about Dad when he was our age and his eyes were still big with dreams.

He'd been really into bows and arrows and headbands, they said, the toy ones from the trading post. I imagine that when you grow up in a cowboy place, then you're all into saddles and boots and ropes. When you grow up in Indian country, the TV tells you how to be Indian. And it starts with bows and arrows and headbands. They're the exciting part of your heritage. They're also the thing you can always find at the gift shop.

Back then, Dad would always be in the stands at the pow-wows, his sisters told me—well, me and Dino, but Dino was one and two, so I think the stories just skidded right past him, pretty much.

As for me, I really keyed on that, on my dad watching those dancers with every last bit of his attention, his headband strapped tight over his hair. Like he was trying to soak all this in, so it could fill him up. So he could *be* that.

Who wouldn't want to step into a fancydancer outfit? It would be the obvious next step.

The bustles, the armbands, the beadwork, the cool knee-high moccasins—and the facepaint. It makes you look like the assassin-aliens in space movies. With your face black and white like that, you automatically slit your eyes like a gunfighter, like you're staring America down across the centuries.

I can see my dad slitting his eyes in the bleachers like that all those years ago. What he's doing, it's pretending. What he's doing, it's waiting.

"He was going to be the best dancer of us all, once he straightened back up again," one of his sisters had told me. She wasn't a dancer herself, but, playing it again in my head, I think she was talking about all the Indians on the whole reservation, maybe even on the whole pow-wow circuit. I think she was saying that if my dad would have just applied the same energy and forethought to his regalia and his routine as he did to what trouble there was to get in once the sun came down, there would have been no stopping him.

That's how you talk about dead people, though, especially dead Indians. It's all about squandered potential, not actual accomplishments.

My father, my dad, he *could* have been the best fancydancer of us all.

And that's how I recognized him that first night, crossing from the living room through the kitchen.

His boots, his bustle. His fancydancer outline.

In death, he had become what he never could in life.

And now he was back.

Or, he had been for a few steps.

My heart pounded in my chest with what I wanted to call fear but what I know now was actually hope.

Our house, like I said, it was modular.

You can leave the reservation, but your income level will still land you in a reservation house, won't it? I'd heard my mom say this on the phone once, and it had stuck to the inside of my head in a way I knew I was going to be looking over at that part of the inside of my skull for the rest of my life, probably.

I read once that a baby elephant doesn't have the digestive enzymes it needs to live, but it can get them—and does—by eating its mother's dung.

That's an old Indian story, right there.

Anyway, the house we were renting, it was 1140 square feet. I knew that from a sticker on the backside of the cabinet under the sink.

Square feet don't tell you anything, though.

For delivery purposes, our house was almost twenty feet wide and nearly three times as long, about. My tape-measuring involved Dino holding it steady for me every twelve feet, though, a red popsicle melting down his left fist, so there could have been some missing inches.

Twenty feet wide sounds like a trailer house, I know, which we'd also lived in, but the difference in a trailer house and modular one, it's that a modular house, it gets delivered and it stays there, more or less, while a trailer house keeps its wheels and the tongue it gets pulled with, so it can still roam if need be. They've both got skirts that never last the winter, though, and the sidings are pretty much the same, and if you end up with one of each, you can kind of rub them together like puffy Cheetos and make a bigger, more complicated house.

I say all this because, the week after I saw my dad in the house, I scoured every single inch of those 1140 square feet for evidence of his having walked through.

What I wanted was a single lost bead, just one stray, bright-blue feather. Even a waxy smear on a doorjamb, that could be where he'd touched after he'd wiped an itch on his cheek.

He was back watching us, I knew.

It made me sterner with Dino, to prove the good big brother I was being in Dad's absence. How I was picking up the slack.

It also made me ask Mom questions about Dad, on as much of the sly as I could manage. What was the first car he had? What was the last? Where did she meet him? What was he doing? Did he name me, or did she? What was the best fight he was ever in? How much could he lift if he had to?

They're questions a nine-year-old would ask, I know, not a sixth-grader, but I think when you're talking about your dad, you kind of go back in years—the more you become a kid, the more he gets to be the dad, right?

So, we ate crunchy fish sticks over the game shows of dinner, and Mom shrugged and chewed and told me some stories. Not the ones I was ever asking for but ones she remembered from when he was a senior and she was a sophomore. How Dad had come to school with his whole head shaved once, to prove something to a teacher. Or how one time she saw him standing by the lake and throwing a trash bag of shoes into the water, shoe by shoe.

He hadn't made it through to graduation—who ever does?—but he'd been there all the same, and he'd clapped louder than anybody, and hooted for every person who crossed the stage, and Mom thought that was probably either the first or the second weekend he ever had to spend in jail.

When he died, they didn't find him right off. The tribal cops, I mean. But everybody knew where he was. Probably some kids from my own class had even snuck out to see him, dragged by their older brothers and sisters, meaning they knew my dad was dead before I did.

Was it because a truck he was driving had thrown a rod he couldn't afford to pay for, or was it because he was drinking and stumbled, and couldn't get back up?

There were stories both ways, and Mom told us that either being true wouldn't make him alive again, and that—she only said this when she was down—we were maybe better off anyway. We never would have left otherwise.

Now I was going to a school with a higher graduation rate, and there weren't as many fights.

Also, there weren't dogs smiling at us around every corner, or faces we knew in cars driving by, or the snow coming off the mountains the same way, but it was supposed to all be worth it in the end.

And, as near as I could tell, there were no beads or feathers or facepaint anywhere in the house. No proof of Dad having walked through. I even checked the vacuum cleaner bag, even though we hardly ever used the vacuum because the smell from the belts always made us have to eat our fish sticks outside.

That didn't mean I was done looking, though.

If I couldn't find any trace of him, then maybe I could reconstruct what he'd been *doing*.

Over and over, and slower and slower, I walked what I'd seen of his path from the kitchen to the utility room. Maybe fourteen feet—a little longer than the tape measure would go. I looked at every chair back and coffee-table edge and wall he could have brushed by, that he could have touched with his fingertips the way I imagine the dead touch solid things: with wonder.

Then I backtracked, figured he must have crossed the living room before crossing the kitchen, right? Which meant he'd walked right behind me when I was standing there asleep, looking out into the driveway—*meaning* that, maybe, my sleeping self had heard his ghost truck pull up out there. That truck with the thrown rod, the truck he'd killed, that had maybe killed him. I'd heard it and risen to watch him walk up, but, asleep, I'd been too slow. He'd probably been coming through the front door right as I was parting the curtain, and then had been walking behind me when my sleeping eyes were trying to see out into the dark. It was pure luck that I'd sensed motion in my peripheral vision, and that flurry of movement had shaken me awake, pulled my head around to barely catch him slipping out the kitchen.

To the utility room.

Mom caught me in there when she got home from work.

I had her roll of duct tape, was tearing some out, then pressing it to every surface in there, trying to lift something that would prove I'd seen what I'd seen.

"Junior?" she said, standing in the doorway.

I didn't try to explain. What I asked her instead was were there any secret compartments in here, or any old photo albums, or maybe a box of old leftover clothes, something like that?

She didn't answer, just watched me some more.

"What have you been reading?" she asked.

Our questions were going right past each other, as usual.

Another effect Dad being back was having was that I was less patient with Mom now. Quicker to dismiss her. I mean, sure, that could be part of being twelve. But I think it was my way of siding with my dad, too.

I don't claim to be smart or good or right or any of that.

My name's "Junior," after all. I'm my father's son.

When two-thirty rolled around that morning, I was rooted to the exact same spot by the front window. I was even still wearing the exact same underwear. The only difference was that I had my glasses on now. I hoped they wouldn't mess everything up.

What I'd also done, just on the chance this was key, was deadfoot it into the living room. It was something I'd learned at my new school, listening in: if both your feet fell asleep and you walked around anyway, you could accidentally step into some other world. I figured that's maybe what had happened to me the night before—my feet had been asleep but I'd walked on them anyway, into some other . . . not plane, I don't think, but like a shade over, or deeper, or shallower, where I could see more than I could otherwise.

The difference, it was that I wasn't asleep. To try to make up for it, I'd snaked one of Dino's jump ropes—they were supposed to teach him to count, if anything ever would—and pythoned it tight around my thighs until the beds of my toenails had started to darken.

My concern now was that, by being early so as to be sure not to miss anything, I was also insuring that my feet would be awake by 2:49, and I'd be standing in the same waking level or depth I was standing in every other day.

At 2:43, the skin on the outside of each of my feet started to tingle and pinprick. I hotfooted it back and forth without thinking, then just stood there looking down at what was happening. Circulation. It was ruining everything.

I could gamble that it didn't matter what my blood was doing, and whether that blood was somehow connected to my brain in a way that nudged my vision over just enough, or . . . I did it, I sat down right there and tied my legs off one more time, tighter than before, and pulled the rope between my teeth instead of knotting it like last time.

This time, it hurt. I think it was because all the blood that had just got to go back where it was supposed to have been, it had only been starting to make the turn, suck back up to my heart, but now I was shutting it off again. It felt like my feet were balloons. When they weren't supposed to feel like anything.

I pulled tighter, closing my eyes, leaning back to do it, and then jerked forward when our dog Chuckhead brushed my bare back with his mangy, matted coat.

An instant after that, I remembered that Chuckhead hadn't come with us down here. He was living on the streets now, was trying to put on fat for winter, or else becoming fat for one of the bigger dogs.

Meaning?

I twisted around, letting the jump rope sling past my mouth, the handle taking a chunk of lipmeat with it, but I was alone. It wasn't the air conditioner or the fan, either. Mom kept the fan in her room mostly, and the air conditioner parasited onto the back window behind the TV was rusted shut.

I stood, forgetting I was supposed to be watching for some wavery version of headlights in front of the house.

Had it been a feather that brushed the skin of my back? The ermine cuff of a fancy moccasin? The lightest brush of a porcupine quill from a bustle?

Had my dad reached down with his fingertips to touch the back of his oldest son, because that was the most he could do?

I reached my hand as far around as I could.

Another thing I'd learned at school, it was "canteen kiss." It's when you drink after a girl you like, or she drinks after you.

This was like that, I guess.

If my dad had touched me, then there was some kind of countdown where I could touch where he'd touched, and it would matter.

It was two-fifty. Then it was three. I had school the next morning.

I policed my area, being sure there was no evidence of my nocturnal activities—no explanation would cover me out here, mostly naked with a jump rope and a prayer—and walked the uncreaky parts of the floor back to my room, stopping to check on Dino for good measure.

He was spasming in his bed.

It wasn't the first time.

Mom swore she'd not had a drop of anything while carrying him, but still, and lately more and worse, he was kind of . . . It was like there was something in his head not quite making a complete connection. Like the way he wasn't learning his numbers or his letters when, by the third grade, he definitely should have. The school had him on some special learning plan already, but there was talk of special classes now, and special teachers that talk so soft and nice it's terrifying, like they're about to eat you.

At the bus stop, if I didn't stop it, the other kids would push him back and forth between them like playing pinball. And Dino didn't mind. He liked being part of the game, I think.

The last month or two, though, he'd started zoning out in the middle of meals, or while watching a game show, or just while standing looking out a window.

And now this.

"Mom," I called out, just loud enough to wake her, not loud enough that she'd hurt herself trying to crash down the hall, "Dino's having another seizure."

This would be his fifth or sixth. That we knew about.

By the time Mom got there with the warm rag she was sure helped, I had the leg of one of Dino's superhero action figures between his teeth. In the Western movies, they always use a belt or a wallet in the mouth. It's never for a seizure, it's usually for a bullet, but the principle's the same, I figured.

After a few minutes of it, Dino settled down.

I stood to go to bed.

"What were you doing up with that?" Mom said.

I looked down to the jump rope evidently still hanging around my neck.

"Water," I lied, like that was any kind of explanation, and then made good on that lie, felt my way to the sink.

On the way back across the linoleum of the kitchen, my bare foot kicked something that rocketed away. Something light and plastic and round.

My heart registered it the moment it hit the wall under the table, and then my hands reacted just about the exact instant it tapped against the roulette wheel of the heater vent in the floor.

My mouth named it while it was still falling down that ductwork: "Bead."

One single bead.

It was as big as the whole rest of the world.

After school, I held Dino's hand as soon as the bus pulled far enough away. If anybody saw, it wouldn't help his cause any, I didn't think. Probably not mine either, but I at least had the idea—mostly from action movies—that I could go wolverine, fight my way out of any dogpile of bodies.

This is something all Indians think, I think: that, yeah, we got colonized, yeah, we got all our lands stolen, yeah yeah yeah, all that usual stuff. But still, inside us, hiding—no, hibernating, waiting, curled up, is some Crazy Horse kind of fighter. Some killer who's smart and wily and wears a secret medicine shirt that actually works.

Just, if you say this to anybody, you kill that Crazy Horse you're hiding inside.

So, you walk around with this knowledge that he's there if you ever need him.

But, also, you try not to need him. You wait till the bus is a plume of dust before taking your little brother's hand in yours while you both walk past the neighbor's house. It's a ramshackle affair that might have been a tack shed originally, or maybe a camper with the wheels buried. There's chainlink all around the property, and that's usually high enough to keep his four dogs in. Dino walking in his jerky way, though, that activates whatever predator instincts those dogs still have, and they come at the chainlink hard, sometimes even bloody their face on it.

Me holding his hand, it was keeping his jerkiness under wraps, so the dogs just barked, didn't gear down into killer-snarl mode.

Again, we made it, and, to prove to Dino that we're not complete wimps, right at the end of the chainlink, I started making a hurt-rabbit sound in my throat, so that my mouth didn't move—so that anybody in that ramshackle tar-paper house with the three galvanized chimneys wouldn't see that I'm doing anything.

But the dogs knew.

They exploded against the fence but it was taller at the corner, from the remains of what had probably been a chicken coop back in 1910, and that was all they could do: bark. If they knew to double back, they could have cleared the fence, hamstrung us halfway to our porch, have a midafternoon kidmeat feast. But dogs are stupid.

Anyway, it was Mom who hamstrung us.

She was waiting, wasn't at work.

She ran out to scoop us up, was enough of a surprise in the middle of the day that I had to swallow that hurt-rabbit sound and kind of go limp, let her pack us into the back seat of our big heavy car.

What happened, she explained, driving and smoking, it was that in the breakroom at her work, one of the other mom's kids had turned up sick at school, so he was at work with her, was wrapped in a blanket watching cartoons. The first thing this meant was Mom couldn't catch the last fifteen minutes of the soap opera she claimed not to care about, really. The second thing this meant was that, tapping ashes into the big brass ashtray of the breakroom, she was now watching a whole new set of commercials. Ones targeted at an audience into robots and dinosaurs and fighter planes, not vitamins and hygiene and vacations.

What *this* meant was that she ended up tracking the movements of an action figure on screen, and that cued up last night for her, Dino's seizure in his bed, and then she was leaving her cigarette curling up smoke from the ashtray. She didn't even clock out, just raced straight home to wait on the porch for us.

Because she knew.

I'm not saying she was the perfect mom, but she would always pick us over whatever else there was. When we left the reservation, it was for me and Dino. Not for her. Unlike Dad, she wasn't still living her high school years five years after high school. But she did have her own sisters, and one brother still alive, and aunts and uncles and cousins and the rest, kind of like a net she could fall back into, if she ever needed them all.

But she cashed all that in. Because, she said, she didn't want either one of us drowning in water we didn't have to drown in, someday.

Only, now, one of us, he was malfunctioning. And she was the only one who could run him to the doctor in the middle of the day.

We had to sit in the waiting room nearly until dinner, but the emergency room finally took Dino back to X-ray his third-grade body. Not for whatever misfire was making him zone out and seize up—that had to be in his head—but for the superhero foot Mom knew would be there. In the breakroom at work, she'd flashed on the action figure I'd had him bite down on. It was lying beside him in bed once he calmed down. And it had been missing one red boot.

In the breakroom, I spent all three of the dollars Mom had left, ate two honey buns and one hot chocolate from the coffee machine. I sprinkled grainy sugar from the coffee table onto the second honey bun, then, hours later, walking across the parking lot holding Mom's hand, I threw up right in front of a parked ambulance and couldn't understand what was going on.

Mom tried to pull me away from the vomit—puley honey-bun paste, runneled through with dark chocolate veins—but I pulled back, studied it, trying to make a deal: *I* would throw up that superhero boot for Dino. Please. It was my fault, anyway.

That's not how the world works.

Dino was supposed to just keep eating like normal and wait to find that piece of plastic in the toilet. We didn't have to watch for it, though. We could, the doctor had said, but really, the sign that it had hung up somewhere, it would be Dino's appetite fading.

Except—what if his appetite started to go away because of whatever was happening in his head, to keep him from learning his numbers?

Mom was out of cigarettes, so she held on to the steering wheel with both hands and didn't look into the back seat, even with the mirror.

After lights out, still trying to make deals, I snuck Dino's one-footed superhero from his dresser, walked it into the kitchen and pried the vent up, dropped it down into that darkness, and then I tried to wait up for Dad, crossing the kitchen again, but fell asleep in the corner under the table and didn't wake until Mom draped a blanket over me in the morning.

The whole next week was nothing. Dino kept eating as much as ever, Mom got another carton of cigarettes, and I started digging up what I told myself wasn't a car from the front pasture, but a truck. *The* truck. Because ghosts need anchors in the physical, living world, don't they? What might have happened was that, up on the reservation, Dad runs a truck too hard, throws a rod, so that truck gets left behind. But someone else picks it up, drags it down here with plans of using it for a parts truck, or maybe they have an engine from a car that'll mate with the transmission.

What happens instead is that the truck gets left behind, and a landlord wants the place to look clean, so he scoops a hole in the ground with a tractor, then nudges that truck over in the hole, such that only one tire is sticking up, like the last hand of a drowning person. Give the sun and snow a couple years at that tire, though, and it's down to steel belts, then nothing. Just a rusted old rim some stupid kid can bark his shin against one day and then remember later, once the dead start walking.

I dug for the whole afternoon, and what I had convinced myself was an axle housing spearing out from that rusted wheel, it turned out to be a pipe welded to it, with a single chainlink tacked to the top of the pipe buried twelve feet behind me. I'd seen a link of chain tacked to a pipe like that before, at my old school. This was someone's old tetherball pole.

I stood it up. It rocked back and forth, settled, like waiting for what was next.

I had no idea what was next.

I looked to the house, to make sure Dino wasn't sneaking off the porch, and the curtain in the window was just falling back into place.

I went cold inside.

Mom was at work.

I took a single step backward, just instinct, and then I was running for the porch and then up the front of the porch, not the steps, and through the door, into the darkness inside.

Dino was seizing in front of his favorite cartoon, and—I remember this as clear as anything in my life—getting across the living room to him, even though it was only ten feet, it was all slow motion, it was like the carpet was tall or I was small, and I was having to wade through, fight my way over, reach ahead because this was all taking so long.

There was spittle frothed all on Dino's lips and his eyes were mostly back to the whites, and his fingers were going past double-jointed, his elbows pulling in, his pants hot with pee.

I forced my finger between his teeth, gave him that to bite on, and held him until the shaking stopped.

He came back in stages, like usual. By the end of it he was watching the next cartoon, hadn't even realized yet that his pants were wet, I don't think.

"Hey, man," I said. "You see what I found out there?"

He looked over to me like just realizing I was there.

"Out where?" he said.

I tilted my head out front.

He looked back to his cartoon, like being sure this was a moment in the story he could walk away from, and then he stood with his bag of chips, and—this was what I was testing—he didn't go to the window to look out front. He went to the front door, hauled it open, studied the pasture through the storm door.

"It's a flagpole," I told him.

By the time Mom made it home, we had a home-drawn pirate flag up there in the wind, more or less. Because we didn't have enough black marker to make the pale yellow towel from the bathroom look scary, we'd used one of Mom's last two black dish towels. The face and bones were masking tape.

I thought we were going to get swatted, but instead, we ate sloppy joes on the porch and watched the pirate flag whip in the wind and finally break free of its knot, lift into the sky, come down on the wrong side of the neighbor's chainlink.

The dogs were on it right when it touched down. It probably tasted like a hundred and fifty dinners all at once.

"Hated that towel anyways," Mom said, and leaned back in her chair, blew smoke up into the dusk for a long time, and for the first time, I think, I was happy to be living right where we were.

The feeling didn't last.

That night—I want to say it was a dream, but I've never remembered my dreams. Or maybe I walk through them.

Nothing happened. That I knew of.

I just slept even though I hadn't meant to, and woke in my bed, my feet not dirty or anything.

If Dino seizured in the night, he didn't bite his tongue or hurt himself.

Everything was so good, really, that I figured it kind of compelled me to keep my end of a deal I was only just now suspecting.

"Dad's back," I said over cereal, through the hustle and bustle and cussing of a weekday before school.

Mom was walking through the kitchen, on the way to the utility room, for Dino's other pair of pants. She took maybe three more steps and then she stopped, like re-listening in her head, and then she looked back to me.

"Say what?" she said.

"Dad," I said over my next, intentionally big, slurping bite. No eye contact.

Mom looked into the living room, like to be sure Dino had cartoons tuned in, not us.

"I don't know what you're talking about, Juney," she said.

I hated her calling me that.

I plunged my spoon into the bowl again.

"I saw him the other night," I said, shrugging like this was no big. "He's different now. Better."

"You saw him where?" Mom said, giving me her full attention now.

What she was thinking, I know, was the neighbors just had someone get processed out of lockup, and now they were standing out at the fence, watching the little boys who had moved in next door.

"Right here," I said, nodding to the kitchen. "He was going back to the utility room."

Mom just stared at me some more.

"Your father never did laundry," she finally said. "I don't think he would come back from the afterlife to run a load of whites."

In the living room the cartoon swelled and crashed, and we both listened underneath it for the heel of a foot spasming into the carpet.

Dino was okay, though. Sucking on a yogurt.

"He's a fancydancer now," I said. "You should see him."

Mom, even though there was never time for this in the morning, sat down across from me, skated both her hands across to hold the one of mine that was there.

"That's why you were asking about him," she said.

"He's my dad," I told her.

"You look like him," she said back. "I never tell you because I don't want to make you sad. But I remember him from elementary. If we were back home, everybody would be saying it."

This made my eyes hot. I looked away, took my hand back.

"He's coming back to help make Dino better," I said.

Mom wouldn't look away from my face.

"How would he find us, all the way down here?" she said, her voice like she was letting me down soft, here.

"We're his family," I said.

Mom nodded, looked past me, into the living room, and I realized then that she didn't miss him like I did.

It was why he'd shown himself to me, not her. It was why that bead had hidden itself in the ducts under the house, not stuck around for her to—

And then, all at once, like crashing over me, it hit me: I'd scoured every inch of every room of the *house*, sure. I'd even drawn our floor plan out, reducing the inches to millimeters on my ruler as best I could, to make sure there weren't any hidden rooms, any closets that had been boarded over by some past renter.

It was all there in my science notebook.

And, while I'd looked out in the pasture for evidence—only finding a ceremonially buried tetherball pole and the other usual trash of people having lived here once—I hadn't taken into account the most likely place a person who was dead might want to live, to be close to his family: *under* the house.

We were up on cinderblock pylon things, not settled onto a concrete foundation. It was why the landlord had come over our first winter: to crawl down there, rewrap the pipes that had no other insulation. He said the varmints would chew it off again in a year or two, but we'd be good for the cold. And we had been, mostly.

"What?" Mom said, seeing some version of all this wash over my face, I guess.

"The bus," I said, rising with my bowl.

She took it from me, studied me for a moment too long, then flicked her head to the outside world, meaning *go, school already,* and like that, me and Dino were hand in hand down the rut-road to the bus stop, the dogs pacing us on the other side of the chainlink.

This time, when the kid from my PE nudged Dino over into a kid I didn't know, trying to get the game started, instead of my usual repositioning, my usual guiding Dino over to my other side, I lit into this kid without even saying anything first.

The bus driver had to pull me off. The kid was going to need a note for PE today. Maybe all week.

I hadn't even heard the air brakes hiss to a stop behind us.

Dino was just watching me, standing there with my chest heaving, tears coming all down my face.

"I've got him," the bus driver said, his hand to Dino's shoulder, and I nodded thank-you, was already running back along the chainlink, scraping my fingers over the rough wire the whole way, the dogs rising to the top of the fence again and again, snapping and snarling.

I ran faster, more headlong, and was just to the side of the house when the front door opened.

Our car started on the third try for Mom, and she didn't know she should have been looking behind the house for me. I was at school. It was just another day.

You look like him, she'd told me.

I could see him back home, too, just like this. My dad, at my age. Hiding behind my grandma's house, his face wet, the mountains opening up behind him.

But I could also see him standing from that, taller and taller, his shadow feathered and already moving like a dance.

The reason he was only showing up now to help Dino, it was that it had taken him a long time to walk all the way down here.

"I won't let them hurt Dino," I said into the side of the house, but really, I was trying to make sure he could hear me through the windblown cracks in the skirt.

Inside, the cartoon in the living room was still playing.

I sat down on the propane tank and ate my lunch three hours early and watched the skirt of the house for a response. For a finger reaching through. For an eye, watching out. For an older version of me, here to save us.

You could pull the skirt of the house out easy, I found. It was just tin or aluminum or something, corrugated like cardboard, but it would flap back into place as soon as you let go. So, I went out to the tetherball pole, leaned it over like pulling a flag down, and rolled it in about a thousand switchback arcs to the house.

Then it was just a matter of guiding the top of the pole in through a crack and working the wheel so the pole could hold the flap open.

That it worked so perfect told me I was on the right path.

But I still couldn't go in.

He was my dad, yeah. But he was also dead.

I walked back and forth in front of the house. I looked as deep into the dark as I could without crossing the threshold.

I squatted there and said, quiet because ghosts hear everything anyway, "Dad?"

I bet every Indian kid who's lost a dad, he does this at some point. I don't know why it's special to Indians. But I think it is.

He didn't say anything back at first, but when he did, I wasn't sure if it was in my ear or in my head. Either way, it was like he was using my own voice to do it.

It wasn't my name he said, or Mom's, or Dino's, or even hello.

What he said, what I heard, it was *Look*.

It made an instant lump in my throat. I fell back, sat in the dirt, the muscles close to all my bones grabbing tighter on to the bone.

Look.

I leaned forward, thought that was what he meant, but then a rustle behind me pulled my head around.

The rustle wasn't the top cuffs of boots brushing into each other, and it wasn't a rattle being held deep in a hand, to hush it.

It was a dog, standing there, big strings of saliva coming down from its mouth.

It was halfway between me and where the tetherball pole had been buried. The reason it was just standing there, it was that it was probably questioning what it had done to deserve a gift like this. It was waiting for me to just be a mirage, a dream.

One that was making it slobber all the way down to the ground.

It had gone to that dug-up hole first, I think. For the new smells. Maybe that was part of the route it took into the pasture every day, when it jumped the fence, went on patrol, or hunting, or whatever it did.

But now here was me. I didn't even make sense. At first.

When I did, the dog's haunches bunched and dirt shot up behind it and its mouth opened to tell me what all it was going to do to me.

I squeaked a sound of pure fear, twisted around, and kicked through the skirt, into the darkness under the house, and only just managed to guide the tetherball pole out at the last instant, so the flap could shut the dog out.

It clawed at the base of the skirt and barked and snarled enough that the rest of the dogs finally came over the fence for whatever this was.

It was me.

I was crying and snuffling and hugging myself, having to keep my head low so it wouldn't collect all the webs spun under the floor of the living room—which, if this was the underside of the *living* room, then what did that make it, right?

I wouldn't say it out loud, even in my head.

I'd seen coyotes go after a rabbit, when they didn't have anything better to kill. They don't just dig a bit and give up, they excavate until they find a beating heart.

I was that rabbit, now.

The neighbor dogs, they'd been waiting for this ever since we moved in. The only thing that was saving me was that dogs only know to push, not to pull, and the one flap of the skirt that was loose, it overlapped a solid flap, so it would only push in for a car bumper someday.

Not that the dogs weren't trying.

That just scraped my nerves raw, though, which isn't permanent damage. What would be more permanent was when the other three caught onto what the yellowy-white one was already doing: reaching down with one big paddle of a paw, to dig under.

As big as these dogs were, and as sharp as the bottom of the skirt would be, they were going to have to really tunnel. But I trusted that they hated me enough to do just that. The prize would be worth the work.

I swallowed and the sound was loud in my ears.

My eyes had adjusted some now. Enough that the sunlight edging in through the cracks and seams in the skirt showed shapes, anyway.

I'd imagined it would smell like an animal den in here, that it would be moist and sticky.

It was just dry and dead.

I beat the side of my fist on the bottom of the living room, even though I'd seen my mom leave already. Moms are capable of a lot, I knew. I didn't put it past her to hear me needing help somehow and shrike across the thirteen miles from her work, tear into this pack with her bare hands.

What I got back, instead of an answering knock or a footstep, was a faceful of fine dust I was too slow to close my eyes against.

And then something was on my hand, something with feet. I panicked back into a strut or a pipe, shaking my whole arm like it was on fire, and a moth batted into my face. I registered what it was right away but still flinched back all the same, into that same strut or pipe or whatever, nearly knocking myself senseless.

This reinvigorated the dogs.

I didn't have to act like a hurt rabbit for them anymore. It wasn't an act anymore, I mean.

Now each time the yellowy-white paw stabbed down under the skirt for more dirt, it was like it was reaching down out of the sun.

Every few scoops, the paw would be replaced by a nose, breathing my fear in.

I pushed as far away as possible. I wasn't exactly thinking rationally. All I knew, I guess, it's that the more distance between me and them, the longer it might take them to find me.

If you can delay pain, you delay it, don't you? Even when it's inevitable. Especially when there's teeth involved.

The farthest I could get was right under Mom's bedroom.

The whole way there, it was just dirt and the old dead weeds and grass that must have been live weeds and grass when this house got delivered here. They'd turned into mummies of themselves, mummies that crumbled into less than dust when I touched them. Twice I hit my head on something sharp under the house, and when I started ducking, then I hit my shoulder and back on it three more times, something up there tearing my shirt and cutting me, it felt like.

I beat on the floor again, just to say I had, I guess, that I'd tried everything I could, and I pushed back into the farthest corner of the skirt. My idea was that I could push my way out—from this side, the overlap would help me—make some kind of suicidal dash for the pump house roof, which I would magically fly up onto. Fear would give me wings, I don't know.

I didn't get all the way to the crack of light in the skirt, though.

Instead, I planted my hand into . . . a nest?

It was tacky and scratchy both at once, like whatever was living there had pulled all the broken things under the trailer under it, and then slobbered all over them until the trash went soft, could get shaped.

Only—not a nest, no. I looked with hands, traced out the contours.

A nest is open at the top.

This was more like a burst-open chrysalis.

One with a pocket deep down big enough for three of me.

My first thought was bobcats, since that was supposedly why the neighbor had all these dogs—bobcats had used to steal his grandfather's chickens, so now it was a forever war—except this didn't smell remotely feline. It didn't smell like anything, really. And animals always have a scent, don't they? Even the hunter animals, the reason they face into the wind, it's that they don't want their scent to get ahead of them, give them away.

Not this hunter.

It could come from any direction.

"Even the front door," I heard myself say.

Dad?

I didn't say it this time, didn't know if I wanted it to be real, didn't know if what started there could gestate or incubate or pupate into the kind of silhouette I'd felt crossing behind me in the living room. That I'd seen crossing the kitchen.

But you have to come from something, don't you?

I told myself yes, you had to.

Because—because a ghost, it's basically useless, it's just a vision, a phantasm. It doesn't even make sense that it could interact with light, much less a floor or a person or clothes. Meaning it had to have some kind of *organic* beginning, right?

I was still nodding, figuring this out.

When you come back from the dead, you're a spirit, you're nothing, just some leftover intention, some unassociated memory. But then, then what if a cat's sneaked into a dark space like this, right? What if that cat comes here to die, because it got slapped out on the road or hit by an owl or something, so it lays back in the corner to pant it out alone. Except, in that state, when it's hurt like that, when this cat isn't watching the way it usually does, something else can creep in. Something dead.

It's the injury that opens the door, I knew. The corruption.

But a cat isn't a person.

Now that cat that's not dying, is just panting, it has to wait for something else to crawl in, and then something else, and a third and fourth and finally some fiftieth thing. Just one worm at a time. You can build a self like that, if you compact it all together. If you remember how you used to be.

And if someone up in the living part of the house, if they remembered you too.

Dad was back because he loved us, yes. But it was also because I believed in him.

"*Dad!*" I said then, beating again on the floor of the house with the flat of my hands.

My face was muddy, I know, from the dust sifting down onto my tears and snot.

There was more daylight where the dogs were digging now. Almost enough daylight.

I pushed back into the nest, into where Dad had been rebirthed, and my left hand felt out something more regular than the rest.

I brought it up, couldn't see it.

Three pushes over was the crack at the top of two panels. Just enough light.

I held my find up.

It was Dino's superhero action figure.

It was whole now, like it had never been bitten through.

I smiled, understood: this was what I'd been telling Mom. Exactly. Dad was here to fix Dino. To help him. I was holding the proof right here in my hands.

I stuffed it into my pocket.

It was all about timing, now.

Just—the problem was there were *four* dogs, not one. With one, I could wait until it slithered under the skirt, then push through on this side, race for the pump house. With four dogs, though, they'd have to one-at-a-time it. Meaning that if I pushed through right when one crawled under, that would give the three waiting their turn a chance to hear me, come barreling around the side of the house.

And if I waited until all four crawled under, then the first would be to me by the time the fourth was crawling under, and I'd never get to push out.

There was no way to win.

I told my mom I was sorry. I told Dino his numbers up through twelve, and told him not to laugh about "8" like he always did. It could be funny, his funny snowman, but let it be secret-funny, and just keep going, on to nine and ten and eleven and twelve.

I told my dad it wasn't his fault. That he never would have left us. That that truck had probably been going to blow a rod any day now anyway.

I was crying hard by then. From fear, from feeling sorry for myself. I was even already picturing ahead to what Dino would find when he got home from the bus stop alone. The dogs probably would have dragged me out front. Would I even still be a body? Would he play with it like it was just a squirrel or a cat they'd torn into? And would he then have to grow up knowing that it had been my thigh meat he'd flipped over three times, to see how much dirt would stick to it?

Mom would know right off, of course.

I hoped she wouldn't blame herself for moving us here. I hoped all kinds of things, except what finally happened, right at the last moment, when there was a yellowy-white head under the skirt, snapping and snarling, in a frenzy.

What happened was footsteps crossed the floor of our house with authority. With impatience. Heavy footsteps.

And then the door opened, shut, and the first dog squealed.

Then the next, and the next, and then that yellowy-white head that was pushed under the skirt, it stayed there. But blood was coming from the mouth now.

My breath hitched twice—I was about to scream, I couldn't help it, it was welling up from a place deeper than I could tamp down—and I stood all at once, to just leave this place, this scene, this everything, and what I stood into was a strut or a pipe or I didn't know what, just that it was one thousand times more solid than me.

My face washed cold, my fingers tingled like they were going to sleep all at once, and all I knew with the world tunneling down from black to blacker, it was to claw for that one line of light I could see.

‿

I woke with my mom hugging me to her. It was still daytime. She was hold-ing me to her and she was screaming to someone, at someone.

It was the neighbor. He was on his knees with his hands behind his back. There was a shotgun on the ground before him, broken over. That's how I knew it was a shotgun.

When I could see around my mom better, there was a sheriff's deputy there. He was tall. His hat was on the ground. I kept looking from his hat to his head, like I didn't understand they could separate.

The sirens in the air were the ambulance, coming for the way my head was bleeding.

When the paramedics reached down for me, I shrunk away from their monstrous silhouettes, my breath going deep again, so my mom went with me. It was sixteen stitches. I didn't even feel them. The reason I didn't, it was that I think I finally went into shock, being led past our porch, where the dogs had been digging. Where the tetherball pole and wheel still were, the pole standing up now.

The whole front of our house was splashed with blood that had dried while I was knocked out.

And—this was the theory—evidently I'd sleepwalked again, once my conscious mind lost its grip.

Laid over the eyes of each destroyed dog were pieces of black fabric. Even the yellowy-white dog-head that had been left behind under the skirt, it had been pulled out, got the blinder treatment. On that dog the blindfold was more like a mask. Its tongue lolled out, was swelling.

The whole time I was getting stitched, the neighbor was yelling that I was a menace, that I wasn't natural, that I wasn't right. That a human couldn't do this to four dogs, and any human that did needed to be put down, and that it was his God-given duty to do just that, he didn't care how many deputies the county sent.

Even when the sheriff's deputy guided him into the back of the cop car, the guy was still going off.

He'd come over with a gun, after his dogs. He wasn't coming home for a few days at least, my mom told me. And when he did, he'd be under strict orders from the sheriff himself, probably. She smoothed my hair down on the uncut side of my head and told me that if I even stubbed my toe in the future, that neighbor would probably go to jail.

Dino was just standing by Mom's leg, watching me.

I was now the brother who had taken on the dogs next door, and won.

Except it hadn't been me.

The sheriff's deputy kind of knew it too, I think. In his job, you see what a human body can and can't do, I imagine. You assess a scene right when you walk onto it, so you can apportion blame out appropriately. And some of it comes down to simple laws of nature.

Can a slight twelve-year-old tear into a pack of dogs like that, when each one of those dogs outweighs him?

Never mind that they said I was groggy when Mom got there, called in by Dino, who couldn't count to twelve but was able to read her number off the wall well enough, dial it into the phone.

That was the real miracle of the day, as far as I was concerned.

Mom just pulled me to her again, when the ambulance and the sheriff's deputy were pulling away. When it was quiet at last.

Where I'd been when she found me, she said, it was halfway crawled through the house skirt over at the corner, under her bedroom. It wasn't a question, exactly. But I could have answered it, I think.

I didn't.

She didn't ask after her last black dish towel. The one I would have had to get inside the house to unfold from its drawer. I had a key, but why would I have relocked the door behind me? Why would I have come outside at all, with the dogs there? Why was I even *home* at all?

The way I would have torn the dish towel into even strips, though, I imagined I would have done that with my teeth, starting the tear at the edge, then pulling steady down in a straight line, three times. My hands bloody from not holding my own head, and not from hammering them into the ground with the wheel-base of the tetherball pole, but from grabbing the four dogs at both ends and, one by one, tearing them in two.

About dusk, the sheriff's deputy came back in his personal truck and shone his lights onto the front of our house, the light coming through our window bright enough, it threw Dino and my shadow onto the back wall by the television. We were standing in the window, watching him shovel up what was left of the dogs.

He lifted the remains into the back of the truck, and then the deputy stepped onto the porch and we shrunk back.

Mom talked to him at the door in muttery tones we couldn't get any words from, and they didn't hug at the end of it or anything. But I think they could have.

For Dad, I pretended not to see.

༄

After stew from the can—mine and Dino's favorite, because stew came with
unlimited club crackers we could lick the salt off first—Mom screwed a different lightbulb into the porch and dragged a rake back and forth across the
dirt in front of the porch.

The reason she got a different lightbulb, it was that when she'd turned
it on for the sheriff's deputy, it had shone red, had been misted or splashed
or clumped with gore—I never saw the actual bulb, just the bloody light
it smeared onto the porch. The sheriff's deputy had unscrewed it, tossed
it into the back of his truck like nothing. Just more trash to be dumped at
some dead-end pit out in the pasture.

He had taken the big parts, and now Mom was working the smaller bits
into the dirt.

I guessed about anything might grow up from there, now.

When Mom came back in, I could tell she wanted to ask me a thousand-
and-one questions, but instead we just watched a detective show where the
detective had a cool car, and then she made sure to tuck us each into our
beds tight, and kiss us into place like she used to.

I woke hours later, thought I was finally dreaming at last, because I
couldn't feel myself standing. That meant I was floating, right? Wrong. It
meant my feet were asleep again. I'd deadfooted it out of bed. And I had the
distinct feeling in my throat that I'd just been saying something.

That left me two questions at once: what had I been saying, and who
had I been saying it to?

I was alone in the kitchen, the refrigerator open behind me, cold on the
back of my thighs.

"Thank you," I said to the darkness, to the night. Because it seemed like
what I should be saying, for that afternoon. For the dogs.

Instead of going back to bed like usual, like makes sense if you don't
have a blanket, I dodged the creaky parts of the floor across to the couch,
and laid there with my head cocked up on the arm. There was a line of glare
in the dead television screen from the lamp and I watched it, blinking as
little possible, because as soon as that line of light broke, that was going to
mean something had passed between me and it. And, if it came from the
right, that meant Dad was done with fixing Dino. And if it came from the
left, that meant he was just getting started.

What I wanted was to see him again, for real. Not just thinking about
how he must have been at my age. Not just building him up in my mind

from the stories Mom told. Not just seeing him through his sisters' words, where they only remembered the best parts. I wanted to see him as the dogs had, in full regalia and facepaint.

Hell yes, they'd squealed. Not that it mattered.

Death hadn't even been able to stop him. Four big dogs didn't stand much of a chance, had they?

When the interstate lights finally blotted out, it wasn't because I was drifting off, it was because a body was there.

Dino.

He was saying my name, looking for me.

All over his back and stomach were cusswords and pictures that Mom hadn't seen, because he'd fallen asleep in his school clothes, watching the detective-and-his-car show. He'd got hot in the night, though, peeled out of his shirt.

"Deener," I said without sitting up.

He looked over to the sound of my voice, his face blank, not expecting anything. I led him back to our bathroom and used a washcloth with warm water to rub off all the words that had got written on him on the bus. All the pictures that had been drawn onto him because I wasn't there to stop it from happening.

In my head I told my dad I was sorry. That I would be there next time, and all the times after that, too.

Up under Dino's ear on the left side, there was a hickey, even. Which no way could be from lips. I'd seen the kids at school doing them other ways. The best way was to get someone to Uncle-Sam their chin—to squeeze their chin-skin tight, into a prune, until somebody came down from the top, slammed that hand off, bruising the skin—but there was some way that was kind of like frogging an arm muscle. I hadn't seen it close up. As near as I could tell, you pinched somebody's skin between your first two knuckles, then spit down onto it and twisted hard.

That was the image I had to have, of Dino's bus ride home.

I guided him by the shoulders back into bed. I'd been able to get all the ink off, but not the hickey under his ear. You can't rub a bruise off, no matter how hot the water is.

The hickey was big, had to have been a high schooler, to have hands like that.

And how many people had trailed their lines of spit down?

I hated them all. I hated them so much, it made my eyes hot.

I tucked Dino in, kissed him in place just like Mom—he was groggy by then, probably didn't know who I was, exactly—and when I was standing back up, my eyes dragged across the reflection in his window.

There was a man standing in the doorway of Dino's room.

There were feathers coming off him at all angles.

He was just a shape, a shadow in the glass, but I knew him.

I closed my eyes, let him leave.

Two mornings later, at the bus stop, Dino counted to nineteen all by himself. And then he fell right into a seizure, the worst one yet.

One of the girls who carried her books with a strap, not a bag, she ran back to flag Mom down.

It was the second time the ambulance had come out. At three hundred dollars per trip.

The sheriff's deputy showed up too and just watched, but afterward he said something to the medic who was the driver, and that medic shut his metal clipboard in a way that Mom had to look away from to cry about.

When the sheriff's deputy came to talk to her, she picked Dino up and ran inside, pulling me behind her.

I didn't know what was happening.

The sheriff's deputy sat out there for a while—I watched him from my bedroom window—and then he backed up, eased away, his left arm patting the outside of the door of his truck in a way that kind of made me know him.

Because Mom couldn't miss any more shifts—she also wasn't supposed to be late even one more time, but it was a little late for that, she said—I got to stay home from school with Dino. She explained to me that when your brother's sick, then you can count as sick too.

We weren't sick, though.

After she was gone, I used some kite string and a football to rig us some tetherball action, to make up for what had happened on the bus.

We batted the football back and forth, but the point hurt when it caught you in the head or the side, so we ended up playing a game where we would throw the ball like a football, like it probably wanted to be thrown. Who won was who got it to go around the most times before it touched the pole. I was the one who had to count the revolutions, but I did it out loud so Dino could chime in, help me complete the word of each number.

What I found was that if you threw downwards, sort of, you could get more times around. I explained it to Dino until he got it, had the idea he was going to have friends over at some point and would need to know how to win one game.

When he picked it up, that you throw down to make it go longer, I let him beat me three times with the trick. In between throws, I found myself always watching the dark cracks between the house skirts. It was funny: from inside, they were cracks of light, but out here, they were cracks of darkness.

I imagined Dad watching us from that crack.

His boys, his sons.

We were going to make it, I told him.

We were all right.

That night, after cornbread with beans cooked into it like Grandma used to make, I got my science notebook out. The one with the map I'd drawn of the interior of our house. I turned the page, made a chart now. It was Dino's seizures on the vertical arm. The only thing I could think to put on the horizontal arm, it was the idiots at the bus stop.

Was there a correlation? Was this a nerves thing to him? Did pressure or getting pushed around activate something in him that was already going wrong?

I drilled inky dots into the corner of the page, trying to think it all through, and finally decided I needed more data.

I was just getting started on the next page—on the scary silhouette of a fancydancer I was going to tell Mom was just anybody, just something I was making up—when Dino was standing in my doorway.

"The show," he said.

I sighed my best big-brother sigh, made a production of setting my notebook aside, and pulled my way across the room, down to the living room.

His show, he was right: there was a fuzz of static over it now.

"Tell me when it's better," I said to him, and went out the back door, sat down on the ground to twist the base of the tall antenna, try to find the signal, the door open behind me so Dino could call out when I found the sweet spot.

Mom came out and sat on the back steps and smoked a cigarette, watched the horizon, and, I think, me.

"You were talking about your father," she said.

"*Better yet?*" I called out to Dino, because I'd nearly worked the antenna all the way around in its base, and the wire was going to wrap soon.

"He's playing with his heroes," Mom said, shrugging like what could you do.

I gave up on the antenna.

"It's only natural," Mom said then, narrowing her eyes at a pair of headlights out on the interstate, maybe. Or just to get her words in order. "You're—the age you are, this is when you start really needing to have a dad around."

I pried a clod of dirt up, lobbed it at the propane tank just to watch it explode against all that silver paint.

"I'm all right," I told her.

This is the lie, when you're twelve. And all the other years, too.

You never tell your mom anything that might worry her. Moms have enough to worry about already.

"You do need a man around," she said anyway, then smushed her cigarette out on the second step from the top and deposited the butt in the coffee can she kept under the stairs, like hiding it.

Minutes after she'd gone back inside to get Dino started in his bed process, it hit me, what she was saying—no, what she was asking: What if that sheriff's deputy came over for dinner one night? Or to drag a harrows across all the packed dirt, so maybe something could grow up from it?

I lobbed another dirt clod at the propane tank, missed altogether, and then came down to my knees fast, scrabbling all the dirt clods and rocks to me that I could, to sling right into the heart of that propane tank.

Hit, hit, miss, hit.

I was breathing hard.

The skirt of the house, it was right behind me.

I turned, regarded it up and down its whole fourteen inches of long triangular darkness, and finally, like a trade, picked all Mom's old butts from the coffee can and pushed them through one at a time. It was an offering.

Then I put the can back but tipped it over like the wind might have blown it over, so it could get a last drag on all those cigarettes.

In my head I was walking the floor plan in my science notebook. I was a stick figure pacing the halls, looking in every room. On patrol.

The television wasn't working, you say?

Could it be because there was somebody under the floor right exactly there? Not because he wanted to hear that show better but because his youngest son was sitting right in front of that screen.

Indians, we don't have guardian angels—if we did, they'd have been whispering to us pretty hard when some certain ships bobbed up on the horizon—but we do have helpers. I think usually it's supposed to be an animal.

Maybe when you need more, though, maybe then you get a person.

Maybe then your father gets special permission to come back, so long as he stays hidden.

So long as nobody tries to rat him out.

Meaning, yes, it was me who'd killed those four dogs. It was me who laid that torn-in-four black dishcloth over their eyes.

And it was my fault the cartoon wouldn't play without static.

Just for luck, I dug up one more dirt clod, a big flat one, and aimed hard, slung it as hard as I could into the side of the propane tank.

It exploded exactly as I'd wanted it to: a big dusty cloud, billowing out and thinning.

Then that plume took on a dim glow.

I stepped one step up the back stairs, my hand to the knob of the door, and then I saw the glow for what it was.

The neighbor's back porch light.

He was home from jail.

Instead of asking the deputy sheriff over for dinner right away, like all the cop shows said would happen, the deputy sheriff drove me and Dino to school the next three days. He'd heard what happened at the bus stop.

I just stared out the window on my side. I was playing the prisoner. I was being transported to my next holding facility. An armed guard was transporting me. He was under orders not to talk to me. Not that I was going to try.

On the way back from school, in the big empty space before you got to our clump of houses, he let Dino flip the switch that fired the sirens up. Later, while Mom was warming spaghetti and then forgetting she was warming spaghetti, I told Dino to shut up so I could hear the television. He was playing with his trucks in front of the couch and making siren sounds with his mouth.

Dino did stop, and then I had to watch the show I hadn't even been watching.

I just picked at my burned spaghetti.

That night when I was standing at the window, I was in my pants, not just my underwear. I was watching for the deputy sheriff's truck, now. To do what? I had no idea. Just to prove it to myself, I guess.

I tried not to blame Mom. She didn't know Dad was back, and she wouldn't believe me if I told her, and if I told her, it would make him leave, anyway. So, all I could do was watch.

I fell asleep with my head leaning against the glass and the wall, and when I woke, I jerked around, to try to see a shape just stepping past.

The living room was empty.

But you're supposed to be getting more *solid,* I said inside.

Not more invisible.

Nothing invisible could have done that to the four dogs.

And—and Dino. He hadn't had a seizure for days now.

I pushed away from the window to go to bed, because nothing was working, because everything was stupid, and I nearly had my eyes pulled all the way away when I saw motion out front.

I'd thought the wheel at the base of the tetherball pole was going to be a truck with a thrown rod.

What I saw now told me maybe it was—that maybe the truck hadn't been dragged down here, but parts of it had come down all the same.

The wheel, maybe.

The football was going around the tall pole.

I smiled.

Because the front door squeaked and squealed—Mom said it was the best alarm—I went out the back door, by Dino's room. He could sleep through anything.

The football was just tapping into the pole by the time I came around the side of the house, having to test each step for sharpness before giving it my weight.

I let the football hang there for a few breaths, and then I picked it up, handed it around and around the pole until I had to walk it around.

It was my turn.

"Watch this," I said, and flung the ball at a spot in the dirt maybe six feet in front of me. The string grabbed it in a perfect parabola, flung it high and around, so I had to fall away from getting hit. I kept on falling, too, caught myself on my elbows.

That was why the headlights didn't spear me in place.

I stayed down, turned over onto my stomach.

The truck was just coasting, not turned on.

When the headlights turned to wash across the front of our house, they cut off just in time. Just the brake lights flaring in the barely there dust the tires had coughed up.

The sheriff's deputy.

Mom stepped out onto the porch, didn't turn the light on.

The sheriff's deputy guided his door shut, just one click deep, and followed her back inside.

I told my dad not to look, not to listen.

No lights glowed on in the house.

I rolled onto my back, stared straight up.

The football just hung there on its string.

I understood. Lying there then, I patted my pocket for the superhero I was just remembering, from the day all the dogs died. It wasn't there, had been too long, and these were the wrong pants anyway.

What I'd wanted to do, it was hold it up against the backdrop of all the stars so its silhouette could fly back and forth.

Except I wasn't a kid anymore.

I was the man of the house, at least until Dad got solid enough for Mom and Dino to see him too.

I stood, my hands balled into fists by my thighs.

I walked back to the house, my line taking me to the front door so I could open it, let it squeak and squeal, but then I stopped at the sheriff's deputy's truck.

The driver's side door opened easy, with no sound at all.

I sat there behind the wheel, my hand cupped over the dome light.

There was the siren switch right there.

I smiled, was slow-motion reaching for it and all the excitement it would bring to this night when I remembered how the sheriff's deputy had guided Dino's hand *there*, instead of to the glove compartment Dino had been going for, because, in our car, that's where Mom let him keep his road toys.

After checking the front door and all the windows again—nothing—I opened that glove compartment myself.

Tucked way back there was a short little revolver.

I held it in wonder, careful of where the barrel pointed, and then I looked to the front door again. And then I went in through the back of the house, testing each step again, because I was one pistol heavier now, plus however many shells it held.

This time I didn't have to be asleep, or just waking from it, to see Dad.

I'd had the pistol held low, pointed at the ground, and had only looked in Dino's room to be sure he was there, and not shaking under the covers.

What I saw nearly made me pull the trigger, shoot my foot off.

Dad—my years-dead father—he was leaned over Dino, had maybe been listening to his heart or whispering into his mouth. His fingertips were to either side of Dino's sleeping shape, and he had one knee on the bed, one foot on the ground. And he was looking across the room like an animal, right into my soul. His eyes shone, not with light but with a kind of wet darkness. The mouth too—no, the lips. And curling up from them was smoke. From the cigarettes and ashes I'd funneled behind the skirt.

My breath choked in my throat thinking about that, that taste, and I wavered in place there in the hall, caught between a scream and a fall, and when I sensed a body behind me, in the back door that was just a doorway because I'd left it open, I knew it was because I'd looked away from Dad in Dino's bedroom. That I'd broken eye contact just long enough for him to step around the rules of the physical world come out here with me for a little father-son discussion.

And—just because he couldn't get whatever he needed from my neck, that didn't mean he didn't still have hands.

The big pistol jerked up almost on its own, my arm straight behind it, and my finger was already pulling the trigger over and over into the middle of that darkness, that body.

What I was saying inside, if anything, it was to stay away from my little brother. That you're not helping anymore. That I'm sorry, I'm sorry, but—the shots cracked the world in half, then quarters, then slivers of itself.

The flashes from the end of the barrel were starbursts of orange shot through with black streaks, and they strobed the inside of the hall bright white. And my shots, because of the recoil, because of the way the barrel jumped up each time I pulled the trigger, they were climbing from the midsection, higher and higher.

Five.

I shot five times.

And the sound—I heard the first one deep in my head, and felt the other four in my shoulder, in my jaw, in the base of my spine.

I know it's too fast for tears to have come, but the way I remember it, I was crying and screaming while I shot.

It was the worst thing ever.

It was my dad.

I was killing him again, wasn't I?

He'd clawed and fought his way back to us, and he'd come back better, he'd come back in the regalia he'd been supposed to wear, before everything else found him.

And he danced. He was dancing now, with each shot.

First his right side flung out, his arm following, and then his left, from the next bullet, and then, for just an instant, there was a clean hole right through the middle of the front of his head. Through his face.

Just ten minutes ago, we'd been playing catch with the football.

When you grow up with a dead father, this isn't something you ever expect to get to do. It had felt like cheating. It had been the best thing ever.

But now it was over.

Because—I had to say it, just to myself—because he'd been feeding on Dino, I was pretty sure.

The wet lips. The empty eyes.

Dino's seizures had started before I'd seen Dad walking across the living room, but that didn't mean he hadn't been making that trip for three or four weeks already, then, did it?

Dino was never going to set any math records, but his counting, it had been going all right, anyway. He was last in his class, was on special watch, was a grade or two behind. But whatever Dad was drinking from him, whatever Dad needed from him in order to get whole again, to come back, it was something Dino needed.

It made me hate him.

That fifth time I pulled the trigger, the last shot?

It was the most on-purpose of any of them.

I was holding that revolver with both hands by then, a stance I knew from TV. I was trying to get the front of the barrel to stop hopping up.

The fifth shot, it went center mass. That was a term I knew from the cop shows, too.

Dino, he knew all about dinosaurs and fairies and talking cars, from what he watched.

Me, I knew about justice.

And, thinking back on it now, we're lucky not to have all blown up that night, from one of my shots hitting the propane tank.

I was shooting at someone taller than me, though. That was the thing. It meant my shots were more or less pointing upwards, and climbing, once they splashed through.

All that was behind us was empty pasture.

One with a few more ounces of lead in it now. A few shards sprinkled down, coated in blood for the bugs to crawl over and lick, if bugs even have tongues.

All this in maybe three seconds.

A lifetime, sure. But an instant, too.

The world was so quiet, after all that sound. And because I was deaf.

I let the pistol thunk to the floor.

It hit on the barrel, tumped over into my bare ankle. I flinched away, took a step forward to see what I'd done.

Lying on his back just past the back stairs was the neighbor, who'd come for me just like he'd said he was going to. A different shotgun was clamped in his hands like if he just held on to it, he couldn't fall back through whatever he was falling through, because its length would snag, would hold him up.

It didn't.

He had no face, had a mass of bubbling red for a body.

My chest sucked in, my whole body kind of undulating, and when I looked up, it was because the sheriff's deputy was standing beside me, naked.

A lot of grown men would have simply backhanded the upstart twelve-year-old punk who had taken a gun, unloaded it out the back door like that, just for attention.

Not this sheriff's deputy.

His name was Larsen.

Years later he would run for sheriff.

His campaign speech probably didn't include driving his knee into my side, so that I ragdolled over into the paneled wall. He probably didn't put on any of his posters the way he didn't let me fall but held me up with his left hand, for his right fist to drive into my teeth.

I was a murderer, though.

Killers, they deserve what they get, don't they? You cash in your rights when you start blowing people away like I just had.

By the sheriff's deputy's third punch, my mom was riding his arm.

Me, I was on the carpet by then, my head turned to Dino's open doorway.

He was standing in it, his face slack, a thin line of clear water seeping down from behind his ear.

I took a picture of him in my head to save for later—for all the jail and cameras and whatever was coming.

It's a picture I've still got.

૭

None of us left the house the next day. Not me or Dino for school—it's not like we had grades to wreck, really—and not Mom, for work. It would mean she'd have to get another job, probably something at night instead of day, but that was all for later.

We sat on the couch and watched whatever the television gave us.

There was so much static we could hardly tell who was who.

When Mom finally turned it off with the bulky old controller, the curvy green screen reflected the three of us back at ourselves.

The sheriff's deputy—I didn't bother knowing his name until high school—wasn't there.

Mom hadn't just scratched him. She'd grown up on the reservation, I mean. She'd started fighting on the playground, had moved on to parking-lot scraps, and had even crashed a vase into someone's face at a wake once. When the sheriff's deputy had finally left, he'd left limping, and had to crank the window on his door down with the wrong hand.

And no more deputies showed up. Not the sheriff either.

I stared at my shape in the television screen, sure that next time we turned it on, that outline would stay but it would get filled in with my face. NATIVE AMERICAN ALMOST-TEEN SHOOTS NEIGHBOR OVER PETS, or something like that.

But. Except.

Where was everybody?

Why was I still here?

Did it have to do with the fact that I'd used the sheriff's deputy's drop-piece—I knew the term—and not his department-issued service revolver? Would turning me in mean he was turning himself in?

It didn't track.

For most of the night I'd been in a daze, Mom trying to get my lips and nose and ear to stop bleeding. It wasn't shock, but it wasn't being completely awake, either.

Now I was awake. All the way awake, my heart pounding.

When the sheriff's deputy had left, he'd left alone.

He'd left once before with the dead—evidence—shoveled into the back of his truck.

This time he'd just left it for us to deal with.

For me to deal with.

I wormed away from Mom and the blanket, guided Dino's arm onto her leg instead of mine, and went to the sink first, for the coffee cup of water I didn't want. But I needed an excuse to untangle from the living room.

Next was the bathroom I didn't need, at the end of the hall.

On the way there, I stopped to whisper the back door open.

There was no body. No blood.

I swallowed a lump, stepped out to be sure. Then down the three wooden steps, the soles of my feet ready for the splinters I knew I deserved.

Maybe ten feet to my right, one section of the skirt was . . . it wasn't *flapping* shut, exactly. This was slower. This was that piece of corrugated tin or aluminum or whatever being *held*, and guided back to its careful overlap.

I was breathing too deep now. I missed a step, my foot going through to the coffee can ashtray, the lip of the can scraping the back of my ankle, the sole of my foot whumping into the ash, sighing that smoky smell up into the air all around me.

But I could still see. I had to see.

There were drag marks in the dirt.

Not from just now, but from—I guessed from when I was getting punched into the carpet in the hall. When I was staring into Dino's room.

Dad.

If a cat and bugs and drinks from Dino could bring him far enough back to drag a full-grown, shot-dead man under the house, then what could a full-grown, shot-dead corpse do for him?

I pulled back inside the house, shut the door, twisted the deadbolt, and hated that I had to call it that in my head.

After the weekend, which mostly involved me standing in Dino's doorway all night, then falling asleep on the couch to cartoons, we were at the bus stop again. The sixth-graders and even the seventh-graders either gave us room, or they didn't see what worse they could do to my face that wasn't already done. Mom said that if the school tried to call Child Services on her, to tell them to call the sheriff's department, too.

Walking past the neighbor's chainlink, there'd been no dogs to harass us. And no neighbor to harass us, either.

How long until he was missed? Was he on probation now? Was he going to skip a check-in soon, and then the next check-in as well?

I hadn't been under the house again.

There had to be a matted nest of hair and grass and saliva pulsating down there, though. Not pushed into the corner anymore but probably dug into the ground, in case I pulled all the skirts off at once, let the light in. I wasn't sure whether what I was seeing in the secret parts of my head were my dad trying to crawl inside a corpse, wear it like more regalia, or if he was drinking it in somehow. All I *did* know was that if I uncovered him down there, then there would be a corpse riddled with bullet holes under our house, and that corpse would belong to a neighbor we already had bad history with.

Everything was screwed.

Soon Dad was going to be solid enough, he could just knock on the door. Except he wouldn't knock, I knew.

I always thought—I think anybody would think this—that when you come back from the dead like he had, that you're either out to get whoever made you dead, or you're there because you miss your people, are there to help them somehow.

The way it was turning out, it was that you could maybe come back, be what you'd always meant to be, but to do that, you had to latch on to your people and drink them dry, leave them husks. After that, you could walk off into your new life, your second chance. With no family to hold you back.

It wasn't fair.

He was going to be out there on the pow-wow circuit, taking every purse, walking out into the campers and lodges and back seats with whatever new girl, and nobody would ever know what he'd had to do to us in order to dance like that. After a few years, he'd probably even stay on one of those other reservations, have two more sons. Ones who weren't broken. Ones he could teach things to, ones he could tell stories to.

It made me want to throw our tethered football so hard into the ground that the whole pole fell down.

Game over.

School was school, like always.

Teachers reading to us from lesson plans, hands going up, trays of food getting doled out. In the bathroom, with a dollar I'd stolen from my mom's purse, I bought a tube of cinnamon toothpicks. They were the hot thing at this school—everybody trying to outburn the last batch. I threaded one between my teeth, but the liquid cinnamon the tube was swimming with found the cuts in my lip and gums, and made my eyes water.

"Perfect," the guy who'd sold me it said, and patted me on the shoulder, left me there by the paper-towel dispenser.

After school, I made Dino watch cop shows with me. Which meant he did what he always did: melted off the couch like I wouldn't notice, dug his toys out from under the coffee table, and walked and flew and drove them across the carpet between me and the television.

The way I knew Dad could smell him, that he was right under that part of the floor now, it was that the show went all static.

He was up, then. Out of the ground, cracked out of his chrysalis, however it worked. It didn't even matter anymore. Figuring it all out wouldn't change how any of it had to go.

What could we do against him?

Nothing.

Even if he wasn't dead or a ghost, he would still be our dad, wouldn't he? What could a sixth-grader and a third-grader and a mom do against a dad? When they're drinking, you can slip away, hide. But the only thing Dad was going to be drunk on, it was us.

Dino, at least.

Was that what I was supposed to do, to save me and Mom? Leave Dino like an offering? Trade him for both of us?

None of the cops on my shows would ever do that. Even for the worst criminal.

Because of justice. Because of what's right.

Dino flew a superhero action figure up into the air to swoop back down against some convoy of dinosaurs—dinosaurs on the trailers of trucks, all lined up—and I recognized it as the one I'd rescued from under the house. Meaning I'd left it in my pocket, Mom had found it in the laundry, and she'd returned it back to Dino's room. It's the natural life cycle of toys. Even ones that had been bitten through, partially digested, then somehow been born again, whole.

The reason I could see that superhero action figure so crisp, it was all the snow behind it on screen.

When it swooped down, though, the cop show cleared up.

Instead of telling Dino to do that again—fat chance—I waited for it to happen on its own.

A T. rex batted the superhero back, and he tumbled up into the crackly white snow background then gathered himself, angled himself down, leading with his left fist, and when he came at that open-mouthed, ready-for-battle heavy metal T. rex, my detective on-screen cuffed another perp. The picture was clear enough I could see the tiny key he was holding between his teeth, that he spit down into the drain in the curb just to show this bad guy how soon he was getting out of these particular handcuffs.

I didn't care about the show anymore, though.

That night, after Mom had lingered too long in each of our rooms like she wanted to say she was sorry—for what?—and after she'd stopped with the dishes in the kitchen, I crept into Dino's room with my sloshing tube of toothpicks. What gave them their extra kick, I'd heard, it was a single drop of mace stolen from a mother's purse.

"Turn your head," I said down to Dino, and he did it without questioning, in a way that made me hate myself, and the whole world.

The hickey hidden behind his ear, I should have known it for a spigot the moment I saw it. You couldn't grab any skin there, where it's pulled so tight to the bone. Where there's no meat, no muscle.

Was that what made it good for Dad? Was he drawing something from the inside of Dino's bones? Would Dino's kneecaps also be raw in the same way? The knobby parts of his wrist?

He wasn't getting clumsy, though.

He was getting slow. Numbers were slipping out of his head. Into my dead father's mouth.

The hickey was worse now too. Deeper, darker, rougher in a way that made me think of a cat's tongue.

I uncorked the tube, wet my index finger, and painted that red with heat.

Dino tensed up, every muscle in his little body tensing, but he didn't turn his head around.

This wasn't new to him.

"It's to make you better," I whispered to him.

His eyes were squinched shut. He nodded yes, okay, do it, but I was done already.

I nudged him with the back of my fingers.

He looked up to me and breathed out, clear drool stringing down into his pillow in a way that made me think of lake water. The kind people drown in.

Standing there, I promised myself that if I ever had kids, I was going to be different.

It's a promise every Indian kid makes at some point.

You mean it when you say it, though. You mean it so hard.

The second time I saw my dead father cross from the kitchen doorway to the hall that led back to the utility room, and to my little brother's room, it was technically my thirteenth birthday. With everything that had happened that week, the only one who remembered was my PE teacher. It was because we'd all had to put our birth dates on a fitness form, and he'd ordered them on the wall by those dates for some reason known only to PE teachers.

Without him telling me, I might have forgotten too.

My feet were cold, the beds of my toenails blue.

This time I'd used shoelaces to crimp the circulation off. Because they make better knots. And I'd done each leg by itself so I wouldn't fall over first thing.

I couldn't fake sleep, and couldn't risk it since there was no trigger for sleepwalking that I knew, but I *was* tired from standing guard the last few nights. And from my face trying to knit itself back into some semblance of myself. I'd nodded off a time or two, I mean. At least I know I'd woken with my top lip dried to the window glass—the reason it was my top lip was that when a face eases forward to a window, and when the neck muscles abandon it in sleep, it slides down until the top lip rolls back to wet, stops that slow fall.

When I licked my tongue back into my mouth, it tasted like metal. It didn't make sense, but maybe glass doesn't have its own taste. Maybe that's why drinks come in it.

What I wanted to do, it was dream. Or, no, I wanted more. I wanted to dream and to remember it.

The next time I woke, it was because something had woke me, I knew.

It's a different kind of waking up when there's still the ghost of a sound in the small bones of your ear.

It was the floor in the living room, creaking.

It meant Dad was solid now. That he had weight to give, and be careful of.

Maybe he was just now realizing it too.

At least, there hadn't been a second creak yet.

I could see his reflection in the glass, dim and close.

Full regalia. The fancydancer he'd always meant to be.

My dad.

My throat was shaking. My heart would be his drumbeat.

"When you died," I told him, like I'd been saving up since I was four, "I was all crying. You probably know. But it wasn't for you. I was crying because Mom was crying. I was crying because of your sisters. I couldn't even remember what you looked like, until the wake."

No response.

But—I was listening with every part of my body—there was a breath, finally.

He was learning that again too, then.

"And Deener, he doesn't even remember you at all," I said.

My plan was for this to core him out somehow. But my plan, it hinged on him still caring about us.

Really, he only needed us to convert into a future he'd already assumed was going to be real.

Not if I could help it.

I turned around all at once, the superhero action figure held tight in my fist like a weapon—I had no idea what it could do to him, just that it was connected, that because part of it had passed through Dino, it mattered, was some sort of tether—but he was gone, had kept on walking. Maybe seconds and seconds ago.

If he was solid enough to creak, to breathe, then maybe this was the last night, then. Maybe this was the night he drank Dino dry, left him open-eyed and dead in his bed, another tragedy at the poverty line.

And because Dino had already been slowing down, or, really, topping out, he was the only one Dad could take from, finally. It made Dino have something inside him that I didn't have, that Mom didn't have.

Still, Dino having to die like that, us trying to deal with it, to keep living—it wouldn't happen.

Mom would collapse into herself a hundred times a day, wouldn't be able to work any shifts for a year, for two, and I would walk down to the bus stop with a two-by-four, and I wouldn't stop until there was nothing left of any of them down there. And then the sheriff's deputy would come for me like he'd always known he'd have to someday, and Mom would take off with me in the Buick, just driving straight across the pasture, for the mountains, for the memory of mountains, both her hands on the steering wheel, and this is already the way Indians have been dying for forever.

And it would be Dad killing us.

I shook my head no against all of that and ran for the hall, made it just in time to see Dad come reeling out of Dino's room, his mouth open wide, so I could see that it wasn't teeth in there at all but wrinkly black muscle, like a worm.

What he was recoiling from, what he was trying to brush away from his mouth, it was the heat I'd left there. The cinnamon, the mace.

In order to make a connection as deep as he was making with Dino, he had to touch the most raw part of himself to that tight skin behind Dino's ear.

I hadn't even planned on him getting that far, though.

We were supposed to still be having a big standoff in the living room.

What was supposed to happen, it was me striding right past him into the kitchen, and dunking that superhero into the dishwater Mom had left for the pans to soak in.

He'd drowned once, my father. I was going to drown him again.

He was going to stand there in the living room and spit up white, bubbly water, and he was going to fall to his knees, reach out for me to stop. But I wouldn't.

I didn't even have a real plan for what to do with his body, with the corpse that was not going to make any sense at all to Mom, but first was killing him. After that, I would figure the rest out.

Only, now, he was banging back in the hall. Into the back door.

It flapped open and he held on to both sides for a moment, long enough for me to see that his eyes weren't shiny black anymore. The pupils or irises or whatever were still too big, bigger than human, what you'd probably need for living in the dead space under a house, but there was some white at the edges now too.

It was how I could tell he was looking at me.

It was how I could see everything he wanted to do to me.

I ran ahead, my arms already straightened, and pushed him the rest of the way out, then stood there, my chest heaving.

He didn't fall up into the sky. There wasn't any rule about that, evidently. He could be outside or he could be inside.

Because he was solid now, though, that meant gravity could pull on him.

He'd fallen backwards down the steps, had landed hard on the packed dirt. Meaning there was still time for me to rush and fall back to the kitchen, dunk the superhero in the dishwater and hold it there. But, it would take two, three minutes to work, wouldn't it?

Those would be two or three minutes I wouldn't have a line of sight on him. Two or three minutes he could have with Dino.

It might be all he needed.

I slammed the superhero into the weather-strip edge of the doorframe face first, but nothing happened.

No choice, then. The kitchen. I had to try.

When Dad took his first step toward me, I was already falling back, one hand to the paneling in the hall, to guide me to the glow of the range light Mom always left on, the only part of the stove that always worked when you hit the button.

I swayed my back away from the thick fingertips reaching for me, and it threw me enough off balance that I slipped on the linoleum of the kitchen, hit a chair, sent it tumbling into the living room, my right hand already clawing for the handle of the refrigerator door. I caught it as barely as I'd ever caught anything, but then the door opened and I slung out farther with it, Dad's knee or shoulder or head slamming the door, stopping it dead in its arc.

It shut back hard, taking its light with it, and the fingerprints of my middle and ring finger, it felt like, and then Dad was standing there, his regalia making him so much taller than the refrigerator, the darkness making him still a silhouette.

I'd fallen with my back to the cabinet, a sharp metal handle digging into my shoulder.

"Not—not Deener," I said, and pushed one hand up behind me, like to use that hand to pull myself up.

But what that hand was holding was the superhero action figure.

It slipped into the cold water, and then—

—and then the water, it was lapping all around us. Around both of us.

It was night. Outside. And the air was crisper somehow. No: thinner.

We were on the reservation.

It was trees all around, except under us right now. Under us right now, there was water.

We were in the shallows of the lake, and—and I was taller, I was grown. I couldn't see my face, but my hands, my arms, my boots, I didn't know them. I'd never known them.

And then it hit me: the same way that, when sleepwalking, I was kind of inhabiting *myself,* that's what I was doing here. Just, now I was inhabiting someone *else.* Someone before. Someone who had sneaked up on a dying campfire by walking around the whole edge of the lake, numbing his feet, leaving him open for me to inhabit. Someone who had been looking for my dad ever since my dad had left a certain truck in the ditch, a rod thrown through the block.

I had access to this truck owner's memories, too, and remembered them like they'd *happened* to me: two days ago, Dad—"Park" in this memory— had come over because he knew where a moose was. He'd seen it twice over the last week. *Twice.*

This wasn't some big dumb cow, either, my dad had said. *Park* had said. This was a proper bull.

Forget the meat. That kind of rack, Park knew a guy down in the city who would go fifteen hundred for it, in velvet like that. He already had the rifle borrowed, and already had a chainsaw himself. All he needed now was a truck, so he could stake out that curve by the little pond, then pop them a high-dollar moose, saw the head off, carry it direct to that guy he knew, the rack wrapped in plastic bags so all the velvet wouldn't dry up, blow away before he could get there.

Fifteen hundred, split two ways.

And he'd said he'd return the truck with a full tank of gas, even.

It was easy money. The easiest money.

Just like that, even though I knew better, I'd worked the square-headed key off my ring, passed it across, and didn't see the truck again until four days later. Until yesterday.

It had been on the side of the road, abandoned, walked away from.

There wasn't an actual rod thrown through the hood, but I'd figured that part out soon enough.

I hadn't gone back to work that afternoon, or all day today.

Park had been hunting a moose. Now I was hunting Park.

Where I found him was sitting by a dying fire, beer cans lined in a circle all around it. Just, on the way to finding him, he became Dad. Not because he'd changed. Because I had.

I stood there in the water, watching him like a spirit come up from the deep.

When he looked up, he even said my name: "Junior." Then he said it three more times, softer and softer: "Junior Junior Junior."

Every fourth person on our reservation, that's their name, like the same stupid person is trying life after life until he gets it right at last.

Still, *this* Junior was me, now, not the one he'd loaned the truck to. Maybe it was because we had the same name that I was able to go back, inhabit him, *be* him, or maybe that action figure, this was his heroic power—to grant the one thing that can save a little brother.

Dad offered me his beer and I swatted it away, liked this new strength, this new, adult reach.

Right now, the four-year-old me was twenty miles south, dying from pneumonia—maybe from how cold it was where this me was standing right now.

There are rules, I know.

Not knowing them doesn't mean they don't apply to you.

I couldn't stop looking at him either, my dad. Not just from this other Junior's height, but at *all*.

This was the Dad that Mom had known. That she had loved. That she had thought was going to last forever.

He was still young. Stupid too, you could tell just from the way his eyes were, you could tell from his loopy grin, but he would get better. He would figure this all out. He would come home, wouldn't he? All his sisters told my mom he would. She just had to wait.

"It wasn't there, man," he said, shrugging.

"The moose or the truck?" I must have said, since I heard myself saying it, even though it wasn't my voice.

"Third gear," my dad said back, snuffling a laugh out, and like that, I had crossed to him right through the dead fire, was kneeing him in the face. He rolled backwards out of his trashed-out lawn chair and I went with him, my arm a piston, my fist the hammer at the end of it.

Dad, though, he wasn't even fighting back. That was the thing. He just kept holding his hands out to the side, saying this was okay, he deserved this, do my worst. It was like—it was like he knew who was inside this Junior. Like he couldn't fight back, since it was his son. Like he knew he deserved this for what he hadn't even done yet. Like he knew I'd dove into a sink miles and years away, come up in the shallows of this lake.

I don't know what he thought, finally. I don't know what he knew.

Just that I had to save Dino. No matter how much it hurt.

I pushed Dad back as hard as I could, and he sat down in the shallows of the lake, was still kind of laughing.

"What are you . . . What are we *doing*, Junior, man?" he said, shaking the wet from his fingertips, his mouth running blood down onto his chest.

I stood there in front of him, the cold water lapping over my feet, and knew this could end now. That it *should* end here. It was just a truck.

But—maybe this is the way it had always been, every time this happened. For the truck, Junior was just going to deal out a beating, a shaming.

To keep Dino safe, I was going to have to wade farther out.

That's why nobody ever got sent up for it. This is why Junior never told anybody about this—even whoever his girlfriend had been eight years ago.

Because he didn't know about it.

He didn't know the why of it.

He was sleepwalking.

There were just two people here in the shallows. Not three. Me and Dad.

Me finally getting to see him as he was, as I'd always wanted to see him, as I'd always dreamed of seeing him. And then having to step forward, knee him hard enough in the face that a line of blood slings up behind and above him.

He falls into the water, and the blood goes out farther.

And then I'm on him, my knee to his chest, my hands to his face, to push it back, to push it under the surface.

It's for leaving us. It's for coming back.

I'm screaming right into the top of the water, and his eyes are open inches away, his hair floating all around, and then, right at the end, he opens his mouth, breathes in what he can't.

I hold him there for longer, to be sure. And then for longer after that, hugging him to me, which is probably a blurry image the other Junior still remembers in jagged bits. And then I push him out like a raft, and I slam my hand into the top of the water over and over, the splashing droplets stinging my face harder each time, but never hard enough.

What floats in around me, from behind me, are porcupine quills, and feathers, and plastic beads.

I stand away from all that, and when I look back—

—it's to an empty kitchen, miles and years away from then.

But there's water on the floor where Dad was standing.

I edge closer to it, then rush past it, sure that where he's retreated, it's to Dino's room, because he can fix all this, because it's not too late.

Where he is, it's through the back door, the wooden steps wet with his staggering footprints. Where he is, it's facedown against the packed dirt, his hand reaching ahead of him.

This is what it's like to kill your father.

This is what it's like to kill everything your father could have been, if only the world hadn't found him, done its thing to him.

"Don't come back again," I said down to him, my throat filling with tears like I was drowning too, and then Dino was standing beside me in his nightshirt, his expression emptier than it should have been. Even if he didn't recognize Dad, still, there was a dead man in full fancydance regalia lying dead in the dirt four feet from us.

It was all the same to Dino.

"One, two, three, four," he said, one side of his mouth smiling.

He said it again—"*Four*"—and I tracked where he was wanting me to look.

Standing just past where Dad was dead, there were the shapes of four dogs.

The yellowy-white one padded forward, pushed its nose into Dad's neck, and I breathed in fast, let go of Dino's hand so I could put my palm to his chest, to keep him from trying to pet the pretty dogs.

They were anything but.

Not only had they died weeks ago, but when they'd come back together, it had been in a pile, in whatever pit the deputy sheriff had dumped them in.

The yellowy-one had the front leg of the black-and-tan one and the body of the brindle.

They were all like that, their legs just enough different lengths to make their movements awkward.

But they got where they were going. And they remembered who had done this to them.

Like all animals, they went for the soft pieces first—the gut, the tongue—and when Dad's porcupine-quill bustle was in the way, one of them grabbed it in its jaws, pulled it away. Instead of coming untied, it peeled from the muscle.

The regalia wasn't ornament, it was part of him. It was what he'd been growing.

Maybe when he just started out, when he was just an impulse, coming back, all he'd had to go on was that dim shape of what he'd meant to be. No clear lines between what he was wearing and what he was.

He really could have been anything.

What he was, though, it was dead. Again.

When the dogs started dragging this feast deeper into the night to take some time with it, pull muscle from bone and tilt their heads back to help it down their throats, I stepped Dino and me back, closed the door as quietly as I could, pushing with my left hand up high, my right hand pulling on the knob, slowing this down.

It didn't matter.

Mom was already there, sitting at the kitchen, her head ducked down to light a cigarette, her hair a shroud over that process.

"What is it?" she said.

I looked out the door again, at the impossible thing happening out there, and then back to Mom, waiting to mete out punishment for whatever was going on here.

"A moose," I told her, and this stopped her second roll on the lighter's wheel.

She stared at me through her hair.

Had Jannie—we used to call her "Jauntie"—told her the truth of what happened to Dad? Had she been carrying this alone for all these years, promising herself to move us away from the stories, so we would be sure never to hear that one?

I should maybe say that we were down in the flats, here. Not that moose are only on the reservation, but they're for sure not all the way down here where they'd be taller than everything.

It was then that I cued in that I was soaking wet.

Mom had noticed too, was about to say something about it, it looked like, when Dino cut in.

"One two three *four!*" he said.

Mom redirected her attention over to him, then back to me.

"You two are the most amazing things I've ever seen," she said, her cigarette still not lit. "I'm—I'm not sorry, I would do it all over again . . . your dad. Everybody told me to stay away from him, that he'd break my heart. But it was worth it, wasn't it? It was all worth it?"

At which point she was sweeping forward to gather us in her arms, in her robe, in her hair, and I think this is where a lot of Indian stories usually end, with the moon or a deer or a star coming down, making everything whole again.

Those stories were all a long time ago, though.

That was before we all grew up.

What finally killed Mom, it wasn't her lungs. It was just being sixty-three years old, and nearly a whole state away from all the girls she was in first and second grade with. If she'd had someone to talk with about the old days, I think she'd have maybe made it a few more years.

If she's sixty-three, that would mean I'm thirty-nine now, yeah. Except she died two years ago already. I'm in my forties, Dino his late thirties.

Mom's not why Dad coming back matters now, though. Why I'm feeling through it all again.

Why it matters—well.

It's hard to know where to start, exactly. Each thing has one thing before it, so I can go all the way back to when I was twelve again, easy.

So, after that night, we just kept growing up. High school was high school. The reservation wasn't the only place with parking lots to fight in. Mom got a desk job, Dino got checked into the first of his facilities and institutions on the tribe's dime. At some point in there, a girlfriend took me to her uncle's house while he was enlisted overseas. He had all the regalia, and when he didn't come back, she smuggled it out to me.

It's backwards, I know—you're supposed to start dancing, then accumulate your gear item by item, piece by ceremonial piece—but this is how I did it. The first time I looked at myself in a full-length hotel mirror, I felt lake water was rising in my throat.

You can dance that away, though.

You can lower your head, raise your knees, close your eyes, and the world just goes away.

I'm not a champion, can't make a living off what I win, but I get around enough, and there's always odd jobs.

News of Mom passing caught up with me two weeks after the funeral. Evidently, Dino had been taken there. He'd fidgeted in the front row, I imagine, not sure what was going on.

In movies, after you beat the bad guy, the monster, then all the injuries it inflicted, they heal right up.

That's not how it works in the real world.

Here's one way it can work in the real world: the son you accidentally father at a pow-wow in South Dakota grows into the spitting image of a man you remember sitting in the shallows of a lake that goes forever. Like to remind me what I did, what I'd had to do.

You don't see him constant, this son, this reminder, but you see him a few times every year. At least until word finds you—this time, the day after—of a car rolling out into the tall yellow grass. Rolling faster and faster, slopping burger bags and beer cans up into the sky. My son was dead by the time they all landed.

I showed up at the funeral, most of the family and friends strangers to me, and that night, instead of getting in a fight, I walked out into land I didn't know and smoked a whole pack of cigarettes down to the butts. Just staring at the sky. Interrogating it, I guess.

I'd never smoked—you need your lungs if you dance—but after that night, I kind of understood why Mom always had. It makes you feel like you have some control. You know it's bad for you, but you're doing it on purpose, too. You're breathing that in of your own volition, because you want to.

When you don't have control of anything else, when a car can just go cartwheeling off into the horizon, then to even have just a little bit of control, it can feel good. Especially if you hold that smoke in for a long time, only let it out bit by bit.

But eventually I stood from that first pack, and made my way back to my camper, back to the circuit.

Until I got to thinking about what happened when I was twelve.

Which is why I pulled my truck into Dino's parking lot this morning.

Because I'm family, I can check him out with a signature and proof of ID.

He remembers me, too. After his third grade, nothing really changed for him. Just, it's the rest of us who kept changing. But he still sees me as the twelve-year-old I was, I think. The one who fought the monster for him. For all of us.

On the drive out, I tell him about my son. How, if he'd been able to make it through that wreck, how he was going to have taken over the world, Indian-style. Maybe he'd have been a male model, maybe he'd have played basketball, or maybe he'd have been an architect.

Just—that was all gone now.

Unless, right?

When we pull up to the old rent-house, there's nothing there, of course. Instead of dogs in the neighbor's long yard, there's goats behind the chainlink now. They stare at us, never stop chewing.

The house burned down years ago—again, not from cigarettes— but what's still standing, what I wasn't expecting even a little bit, it's the tetherball pole.

There's no ball, no string. But even that it's just still there, it means this can work.

Once, years ago, in the old-time Indian days, a father died, but then he came back. He was different when he came back, he was hungry, he was selfish, but that's just because he already had all that inside him when he died, I know. It's because he carried it with him into the lake that night.

My son—I won't say his name out loud yet—all he would have taken with him, it's his smile, and everything he could have been.

So what we do, it's wait until dark, and walk into the burned pad where the house used to be. The cinderblock pylons are still there, holding up my memory of the floor plan.

I settle us down under what was Mom's bedroom.

Something happened here once, see.

A cat or a possum or a rabbit, it crawled into this darkness to die. But because it was hurt, that gave something else access to it.

Under the tarp in the bed of my truck is all the roadkill I could scrape up, to be turned into body mass, and in raccoon traps at the front of the bed are four hissing cats.

They're not hurt, yet.

There's four because four's the Indian number.

But that's all later.

Right now, I'm just sitting across from Dino. Waiting for him to remember. Is there the least amount of blood seeping down from behind his ear, from where a razorblade might have traced a delicate X?

There is.

He turned his head to the side for me to do it, like he knew this part already, and I almost couldn't press that metal into his skin.

Almost.

Before him in the dead grass I've set four action figures.

One of them—one of them, I know its life cycle. That morning after, it showed back up on Dino's dresser in his bedroom. Because Mom had found it floating in the dishwater.

It was the only artifact from then. Except for Dino himself.

And now, if he picks that one up instead of the other three, now they'll be together again, and it can all start all over.

Except—like I say, I know the life cycle, here.

What's going to happen, I know, is that Dino's going to pick up the superhero, not any of the other action figures, and then, because this is part of it, I'll force the left leg into his mouth as gently as I can, as gently as any big brother's ever done a thing like this, and then I'll come up under his chin with the heel of my hand once, fast, so he can bite that foot off.

Maybe he'll swallow it on his own, maybe he'll need help, I don't know.

We've got all night, I mean. He can sit there trying to figure this out and I can dance softly around him in my regalia for as long as it takes, chanting the numbers up to twelve, to prime him, to remind him, the balls of my moccasin feet padding into the dirt over and over in the old way, to wake anything sleeping down there. Anything that can help us get through this ceremony.

And, for my son—*Collin,* Collin Collin Collin—for him to get as solid as he needs to go out into the world like he was supposed to, he's going to need the same thing Dad needed, the same thing Dad got with the neighbor's corpse, the same thing seeping down the side of Dino's neck already.

When will the facility miss him?

It doesn't matter.

They'll never find us way out here, at an address that doesn't exist anymore.

It's kind of like we never even left, really.

I can see the old walls rising around us. I can see the shadow of the roof, the way it was.

When I was twelve years old, I mapped the interior of our home.

Now, sitting across from my little brother, I'm sketching out a map of the human heart, I guess.

There's more dark hallways than I knew.

Rooms I thought I'd never have to enter.

But I will.

For him, for Collin, I'll walk in and pull the door shut behind me, never come back out.

—◆—

THE DINOSAUR TOURIST

―◆―

Caitlín R. Kiernan

The South Dakota summer sky is a broken china teacup, and I have the distinct impression that when I finally stop the car and step outside and dare to let go of the handle on the door, I will fall straight up into that broken china sky. And I will not stop falling until the world below me is so small that I can make a circle of my thumb and forefinger and catch it all inside. And hanging there, I will freeze like a rose dripped in liquid nitrogen or my blood will boil, but I'll have captured the world's disc in one hand. There's country music on the radio, George Jones and Tammy Wynette singing "Golden Ring," and I turn the volume up just a little louder, to help take my mind off the smell. On either side of this seemingly eternal highway, there's shortgrass prairie and patches of bare earth pressed flat beneath that brutal, hungry blue broken cup, and I rush past a comical sort of billboard, an old prospector and his cartoon mule, and the mule is luxuriating in a horse trough, and the billboard promises *Refreshing! Free Ice Water!* at the Wall Drug Store if I just keep going straight ahead twenty more miles. The kid in the passenger seat is still sleeping. I picked him up last night just outside Sioux Falls, just after I'd traded 1-29 North for I-90 West and the kid said he'd blow me for a ride to Rapid City. And I said shit get it and I have an empty seat don't I? You don't have to blow me, if you don't mind that I smoke, and if you don't mind the music. The kid said he'd blow me, anyway, because he didn't like taking anything for free. Yeah, okay, I said, and so we found a truck stop, and he did it in the stall, and I tangled my fingers in his blond hair while he sucked my cock and fondled my balls and, for no extra charge, slipped a pinkie finger up my asshole. I bought him a burger and fries and told him don't worry, it wasn't for free, he could blow me again later on, so we'd be even. But I had to feed the kid. He looked like a stray dog hadn't been fed in a month. And then I drove, and for a while the kid talked about his boyfriend in Rapid City, and I played the radio, and he finally fell asleep. In his sleep, he looked more like a girl than a boy. I pulled over near Murdo, just before four a.m., and I slept a little myself. I dreamed of the White Sundays. "You ever been to Rapid City?" I ask him, and he says no. I ask how it is his boyfriend is in Rapid City when he's never been there himself, and he tells me they met on the internet. "You've never met him face to face?" I ask, and the kid wants to know what difference that makes. "Does he know you're coming?" I ask him, and the kid just shrugs. "That means he doesn't, right?" I ask. "He'll be glad to see me," says the kid, and I let it go at that. "What kind of drugs?" he asks me, and I've already forgotten the lie. It takes me a second to figure out what he's talking about. "What kind of drugs got you fired from the college?" he prompts, and now he stops watching the prairie and stares at me, instead. "Heroin," I tell him. "Heroin and pills. And a little coke, just to sweeten the deal." And he says, "So you're a junkie. I gave a junkie professor a blow job. What if you gave me AIDS back there? I didn't know you were a junkie." I tell him I don't have AIDS, and he frowns and sighs and wants to know if he's just supposed to take my word for that? Don't I have some sort of papers to prove that I'm clean, and when I say no, I don't have any fucking papers saying I don't have AIDS, he turns off the radio and goes back to staring out the window. "Your car smells like road kill," he says, and I say yeah, I hit a dead skunk back at the state line, just as I was leaving Nebraska. "I pulled over at a truck stop and washed off the tires and underneath the car with one of those high-pressure jet nozzles, but I guess I didn't get it all. "It doesn't smell like skunk," he says. "It just smells like road kill. It just smells like rot." So I ask him if he wants me to pull over and let him walk, and he doesn't answer. I turn the radio back on. Hank Williams is crooning "You'll Never Get Out of This World Alive." "You catch shit from your parents?" I ask him, and he says, "I caught shit from everyone, okay? I caught shit from the whole fucking town," and I say fair enough and that I wasn't trying to pry. "It would be just my luck you gave me AIDS back there," he mutters. "People back home would say I got what I deserve." I ask him if he's got any open sores inside his mouth or any bad teeth or anything like that, and he says no (and looks sort of offended at the suggestion), and I tell him fine, then he can stop worrying about catching AIDS from giving someone a blow job. We pass a rusting red Ford pickup truck stranded in the black-eyed Susans at the side of the highway. The front windshield is busted in and all four tires are flat. "Lucas has a red pickup truck," says the kid, and when I ask if Lucas is his boyfriend in Rapid City, the kid nods and reaches for his pack on the floorboard between his feet. I told him he could toss it in the backseat, but he said no, he'd rather keep it with him. He'd rather keep it close. I didn't argue. The kid lifts it onto his lap, black polyester bulging at the seams with whatever the kid holds sacred enough that he's brought it along on his sojourn west. He unzips the pack, digs about for a moment, then takes out a little snub-nosed .38-caliber Smith & Wesson revolver. The sun through the windshield glints dully off stainless steel. My heart does a little dance in my chest, a surprise tarantella, and my mouth goes dry. "That thing loaded?" I ask, trying to sound cool, trying to keep my voice steady, like it's nothing to me if the kid's carrying] a gun. I tell myself, shit, if I were hitching in this day and in this age, I'd be carrying a gun, too. "Wouldn't be much point in my having it if it weren't loaded, now would there?" And I say no, no I guess there wouldn't be much point in that at all. He opens up the cylinder to show me there's a round in all five chambers, and then he snaps it shut again. He aims the pistol out his open window. "You any good with it?" I ask, and the kid shrugs. "I'm good enough," he replies. "My brother, he was in the Army, over in Iraq or someplace like that. He came back and taught me how to shoot. And then he killed himself." I glance at myself in the rearview mirror, and then I glance at the kid again, and then I keep my eyes on the road. "Sorry to hear that," I say, and the kid says, "No, you're not. You don't have to pretend you are. I'm sick to death of people pretending shit they don't really feel." We pass another billboard for Wall Drug Store, and the kid pantomimes taking a shot at it. Bang, bang, bang, like he's seven years old, playing cowboys and Indians, cops and robbers, with the neighborhood brats. "Baghdad," says the kid. "That's in Iraq, ain't it?" I nod, and I tell him, yeah, that Baghdad is the capital of Iraq. "Then Iraq is where they sent my brother," the kid tells me. "He saw a buddy of his get blown up by a landmine. He saw another buddy of his kill a woman because just maybe she was carrying a bomb. Something like that. He said everyone was afraid all the time, no matter how many guns they carried, and he came back still scared. He had to take pills to sleep. I guess he just eventually got tired of being fucking scared all the time. I know I would. He couldn't get into college, so he got into the Army, instead." I repress that reflexive urge to say *I'm sorry* again. Instead, I say, "We're gonna be stopping just a couple of miles up ahead, so you better put that thing away until we're back on the road again. You never know when there's gonna be a state trooper or something." The kid fires off another imaginary shot or three, and then he says, "Dude, South Dakota's open carry. What the fuck is it to me whether there's police around." And I say fine, whatever, suit yourself, kid. He asks, "Does it make you nervous?" And I admit that it does. "Just a little," I say. "I've never much cared for guns. I didn't grow up around them, that's all." And now I'm thinking about three nights ago at a motel outside Lincoln, sitting on the hood of the car in a motel parking lot, and I'm thinking about the oddly comforting smell of cooling asphalt and about staring up at an ivory-white moon only one night past full. I crane my neck and look up through the dirty, bug-specked windshield and wish there were a few clouds this morning to break the tyranny of that broken china blue sky pressing down on me. Or if not to break it—because that would be asking an awful lot of a few clouds—at least to pose a challenge, at least to stand as a counterpoint. The kid opens his backpack again, and he puts the .38 away. I allow myself to relax a little, quietly sighing the proverbial sigh of relief. "This is the farthest west I've ever been," says the kid, and then he asks, "What's in Wall?" and he sets the backpack down on the floor between his feet. "Not much at all," I reply. "Less than a thousand people. There's a deactivated Minuteman missile launch control facility, just outside town.

In fact, just a few miles north of where we are right now." I take my right hand off the steering wheel and point north. "You mean nuclear bombs?" he wants to know, and I say, yeah, I mean nuclear bombs. "But the site was deactivated in 1991, after Bush and Gorbachev signed the START treaty. So, there aren't any bombs there anymore." The kid, he just sorta gazes off into the distance, off the way I've pointed, out across the prairie. "Jesus," he says, and then he laughs a nervous, hard laugh, a brittle laugh that would seem more natural coming from someone much older than however old he is, and the kid runs his fingers through his dirty blond hair. "I wasn't even born yet. There could'a been a war, and those missiles could'a been fired, and I never would have been born. Jesus." And then, to take his mind off an apocalypse that never happened, I say, "There's also a dinosaur in Wall." He stops staring at the prairie and stares at me, instead. "What do you mean? Like a dinosaur skeleton?" he asks, and I say no, not a skeleton. "You'll see," I tell him and I manage a smile, just to spite that sky. There's only an hour left until noon and the day's getting hot, so I tell him to roll up the window and I'll turn on the air conditioning. He does, and I do. We pass a billboard that proclaims in crimson letters ten feet tall that abortion is murder. We pass another broken down truck, this one missing all four of its tires. We pass the turnoff for Philip. A few hundred yards to the north, there's a deeply gullied ridge now, running parallel with the interstate, weathered beds claystone and silt-stone and mudstone laid down thirty million years ago, beds of volcanic ash and layers of sandstone from ancient Oligocene streambeds, a preview of the vast badlands farther south. I recall my dream from the night before, of titanotheres and lumbering tortoises. In the bright sunlight, the rocks are a dazzling shade of gray that's very nearly white. The kid says he needs to piss. I point at the windshield, and I say, "There it is." He asks, 'What? There's what?' But then he sees it, the queerly majestic silhouette of the Wall Drug Dinosaur stark against the sky. The kid says, "Wow," like he really means it, like he's someone who can still be amazed by an eighty-foot-long concrete dinosaur, even after all he's been through. That catches me off my guard almost as much as the sight of the Smith & Wesson did. The sun glistens wetly off the brontosaur's painted Kelly green hide, off its sinuous neck and tiny head. I tell the kid how at night the eyes light up, how at night the eyes glow red, and he says he wishes he could see that. I take Exit 110 off the interstate, rushing past the dinosaur, turning right onto Glenn Street. "Last time I was here," I say, "I was still in college. That was back in 1985, when there were still missiles in those silos, aimed at China and the Soviet Union." The kid doesn't take his eyes off the dinosaur, but he asks me what's the Soviet Union. "Russia," I say. "It's what we used to call Russia." The kid frowns and says, "I swear to fuck, dude, sometimes I think people change the names of shit just to make the next generation feel stupid." And I tell him, yeah, that's exactly why we do it. "I'll tell you something else that's changed," I say. "Last time I was here, all this crap hadn't been built yet." And I mean the Day's Inn and the Exxon station, the Conoco and all the convenience stores and a Motel 6, a Subway and a Dairy Queen, something called the Cactus Cafe and Lounge that promises home cooking and "western hospitality." I'd meant to head straight for the venerable Wall Drug Store, the time-honored crown jewel of this exit, a gaudy oasis to mark the dead center of nowhere, but suddenly I'm no longer in the mood for tourist traps. Suddenly, I feel ill and lightheaded, and I pull into the Conoco's parking lot, instead. The kid says, "Hey, ain't we going to see the dinosaur?" I wipe perspiration off my forehead, because now I'm sweating despite the AC vents blowing in my face, and I reply, "I thought you had to piss." And he says, "I can piss after," and I tell him, "You can piss first. That dinosaur's been there since 1967. It weighs eighty tons, and it isn't going to run off anytime soon." There's an enormous convenience store attached to the Conoco station, the Wall Auto Livery, and isn't that smart, isn't that clever. I pull into an empty space between two other cars, one with Oregon plates, the other from Kansas, and I shift into park and cut the engine. I know now that I'm going to be sick, and I know that I'm going to be sick very soon. I taste hot bile in the back of my throat "You get whatever you want," I say to the kid. "Go on and get whatever you need." Then I'm out of the car, and Jesus it's hot beneath that heavy, heavy sky, and for just a second or two I think maybe I'm gonna wind up on my knees, mired in the soft asphalt like a La Brea mastodon, praying for the mercy of vultures and slow suffocation. But then the door jingles and I'm swallowed by a blast of icy, impossibly cold air, and I realize that I'm inside the store. There are people moving and talking all around me, but I don't make the mistake of looking anyone in the eye. I don't care if maybe they're staring. I just keep walking, past long aisles of snack food and coolers filled with row after row of soft drinks and energy drinks, bottled water and fruit juice. I'm lucky, and there's no one in the restroom. I lock the door behind me and vomit into the toilet, revisiting my breakfast. I sit down with my back pressed against cool ceramic tiles and try not to think how dirty the floor must be. I can smell urine even over the pungent, antiseptic stink of pink deodorant cakes, even over the stink of my own puke. I shut my eyes for a moment, fighting another wave of nausea. I've always hated vomiting, and I don't want to do it again. *What the fuck is happening?* I ask myself. *What the fuck is wrong with you? Get it together, man. Get up off this filthy fucking floor and get it together before some nosy SOB starts asking questions.* I'm trying hard not to think about the weight of the sky endeavoring even now to flatten me, even though I can no longer see it I'm trying harder still not to think about the way the car smells. But you know how that goes, the white bear problem, ironic process theory, fucking Dostoevsky. "Try to pose for yourself this task: not to think of a polar bear, and you will see that the cursed thing will come to mind every minute." So, I puke again. And then someone knocks at the door. I look at my watch and wonder how long I've been in the restroom, and then I get up and straighten my clothes. I brush off the seat of my jeans, and I go to the sink and wash my hands with mint-green powdered soap from a dispenser. I wash my hands three times. I rinse my mouth with water from the faucet. Again, the knock at the door, and I say, "Yeah, okay. Just give me a second." I splash water on my face, then realize that I didn't flush the toilet, so I walk back over to the stall and flush. I jiggle the handle a few times, out of force of habit, because my toilet at home runs if you don't jiggle the handle. I unlock the bathroom door, only to find there's no one waiting. I spot the kid perusing at a display of beef

jerky, and then I go over to one of the coolers and take out four cans of
Coca-Cola. I get a bag of ice for the Coleman chest wedged into the
floorboard behind the driver's seat. The kid walks over to me, and he asks if
I'm okay. "I'm fine," I tell him, because what's one more lie when all is said
and done. "You don't look fine," he says. "You got what you need?" I ask
him, and I wipe at my lips; my face is rough against the back of my hand.
How long has it been since I last shaved? The kid says yeah, he's got what he
needs, but he tells me again how he doesn't like taking charity. I tell him to
shut up, and we walk together to the cashier and wait in line until it's our
turn at the register. The kid has a pack of Starburst fruit chews, a bag of
Skittles, some teriyaki-flavored beef jerky, a can of Red Bull. I ask the cashier
for a pack of Marlboro Reds, and the girl behind the counter asks to see my
license. She's wearing a tiny gold cross around her neck. "You don't look so
fine," the kid says to me again, while the cashier stares at my driver's license
like she's never actually seen one before. "I might have gotten a bad sausage
or something at breakfast," I tell him. "How about you? You feeling all
right?" He says, "Yeah, sure. I'm feeling fine," and I can tell he's not buying
the food poisoning story. "You don't get car sick, do you?" the kid asks, and
the question strikes me as so absurd that I almost laugh. Somehow, I manage
only to smile, instead. Finally, the cashier figures out that I'm forty-eight
years old, so it's legal to sell me cigarettes, and she rings us up. I tell her to
add a bag of ice. I pay for everything with my Visa card, because that one's
still good, and I tell her I don't need the receipt. She bags the candy and beef
jerky, the drinks and my smokes, and I ask the kid, wait, didn't he need to
take a leak. "I used the women's room," he tells me. The cashier sort of
glares at him. He glares back at her twice as hard. The name printed on her
name tag is Brooklyn, and I wonder who the fuck in Wall, South Dakota
goes and names her daughter Brooklyn? I tell the kid to grab the ice, and
then I go back outside into the broiling day and stand by the dented left
front fender of my car, staring westward, back towards the highway. Towards
Rapid City and the Black Hills and the Rocky Mountains, towards the
goddamn Pacific Ocean, and I wonder how I've gotten this far. The kid
comes back with ten pounds of ice, and I see that there's a polar bear wearing
a toboggan cap printed on the plastic bag. I think again about Dostoevsky.
I contemplate synchronicity and meaningful coincidence. "I was thinking,
maybe I'll get a room," I say to the kid, and he sets the bag of ice down on
the hood of the car. "I haven't had a good night's sleep in a couple of days
now. It would do me good to sleep in an actual bed. You're welcome to join

me, if you want" The kid stares at the bag of ice, and he shrugs. "You still going all the way to Rapid City, or should I start looking for another ride?" I ask myself how far I'm gonna go this time, if I'm in for a penny, in for a pound, or if I should let this one walk. "Sure," I say. "I just need to catch a few hours shuteye, that's all. If you want to hang around, we can get dinner tonight, and then you can see the eyes of the dinosaur." I fish out my keys and open the back door on the driver's side. The cooler is a third full with chilly water, and I pour that out onto the hot asphalt. It pools beneath the car with Oregon plates. "Yeah," he says, "I don't know. Maybe I should keep moving. I'm late, as it is." He hands me the bag of ice, and I slam it on the blacktop a couple of times to break it up, and then I rip open the plastic bag and fill the cooler halfway. I dump the rest out on the pavement, and it begins to melt instantly. I put the cans of Coke into the cooler, and I tell the kid, "Whichever. No pressure. I just thought I'd offer. I don't want you to feel like I'm going back on my word. I just gotta get some sleep." He asks if I really think I have food poisoning, and I tell him maybe, I don't either," I say. "Two beds?" he wants to know. "Sure," reply. "Of course. Two beds." The kid sighs and gets back in the car, so it's decided. Just like that. I drive back across Glenn Street to the Day's Inn and get a room with twin beds. The clerk looks at me, and then she looks past me out the sheets of dusty plate-glass fronting the lobby. The kid is waiting in the car, sipping a Red Bull. "Is he your son?" she wants to know, and I can hear the suspicion in her voice, coiled like a rattlesnake, waiting to strike if I give the wrong answer, waiting to say, sorry Mister, but turns out there's no room at the inn, but maybe next door at the Motel 6 they have a vacancy. It's just down the way, and they don't ask so many questions. "No," I say, too tired and hot and queasy to lie. "I picked him up yesterday, hitchhiking. We're both headed the same way, and, you know, there are bad people on the road. Homos and perverts looking to take advantage of unsuspecting innocents. You know how it is." I'm wondering if maybe I laid it on too thick with the bit about perverts and homos, but apparently not, because then she asks, "How old is he?" I reply, "I honestly haven't asked. But he said something about graduating high school back in May, so I'm guessing he's not a minor. Look, I really don't want to cause you any grief. If you're not comfortable with this, that's okay. That's totally understandable. I just couldn't keep driving when I saw him. It's not safe out on the road, hitching." The clerk stares out at the kid just a little while longer, and then she says, "Nah, it's fine." She apologizes for being a snoop. That's the way she put it; her words, not mine. I tell her no problem. These days, the way things are, it pays to be on the alert. See something, say something, right? She gives me a keycard for a room on the first floor. She asks if I mind that it faces the interstate, and I say no, not at all. The sound of traffic helps me sleep. "Almost as good as train tracks," I say, and I smile, and she smiles back at me. She's missing a front tooth, a lower incisor. She asks me for the kid's name, and I tell her his first name's Lucas, but I don't know his last name. She tells me when she was a kid she had an uncle named Lucas, died in the Gulf War, and I say how that's a shame. Then I walk back out into the heat and find a place to park, and me and the kid retire to Room 107. It's dingy and smells of pine-scented disinfectant and stale tobacco smoke. But the beds are clean and the bathroom's clean. The kid brings in the cooler, puts his remaining Red Bull in with my four cans of Coke, and then he switches on the television set. He waits until after it's already on and tuned to ESPN to ask if I mind, if the noise is going to annoy me. I say no, just keep the volume down, please. There's a baseball game, the Yankees against the Detroit Tigers in Yankee Stadium. I pull the drapes closed, drink one of the Cokes, and watch the game for a few minutes. I unbutton my shirt and lay down on the bed nearest to the door, not bothering to turn down the comforter or the sheets. I'd like to brush my teeth, maybe even have a shower, but it can wait. I don't feel like going back out to the car for my suitcase, and speaking of luggage, the kid's backpack is sitting across from me on the other bed. I think about the loaded .38 revolver, about the kid aiming out the car window, firing pretend bullets at invisible targets. I wonder if he's ever killed anything, and I wonder if he has the nerve. I ask myself, if I got up and opened the bag and took the gun, would he try to stop me. Would he dare? Then I tell him, "I'm just gonna nod off, okay?" The kid says, yeah, okay, fine, and he tears open the bag of beef jerky. The salty-sweet odor of teriyaki seasoning immediately fills the room, and my stomach rolls. "So, you know all about dinosaurs and stuff?" the kid asks around a mouthful of dehydrated meat. "Yeah," I answer, and I close my eyes. On TV, there's the sharp crack of a baseball bat making contact, and the crowd cheers. "Is that what you do, dig up dinosaur bones?" he asks. "Not exactly," I say, then open my eyes again and stare at the cottage cheese ceiling. There's a dark stain above the bed, and I figure that's where the mildew smell's coming from. "I study animals that lived at the same time as dinosaurs." He wants to know what sorts of animals, and I sit up again. I reach for my cigarettes, open the fresh pack, light a Marlboro, and belatedly wonder about smoke detectors. I stare at the

TV and explain about plesiosaurs and mosasaurs and extinct species of sea turtles, about marine reptiles and secondarily aquatic tetrapods, animals that have given up on land and gone back to the sea. I tell him about my work in the Niobrara Chalk of Kansas, the Pierre Shale of Wyoming, and the Mooreville Chalk of Alabama. "Were you telling the truth about getting fired over drugs?" he asks, and I say yeah, but I'm clean now. Well, mostly clean. He asks where it is I'm headed, and I tell him I'm headed nowhere in particular, that after a stint in rehab I just needed to get out on the road and clear my head, figure out my next move. "I thought I'd take a road trip, visit some places out West that I've never actually seen or haven't seen since I was in college." The sort of places that are of interest to geologists and paleontologists, the South Dakota Badlands, Dinosaur National Monument, the Florrisant Fossil Beds in Colorado and Como Bluff in Wyoming, a bunch of quarries and museums, and so on and so forth. I tap ash into the palm of my hand. No smoke alarms have gone off, so I guess I'm in the clear. The kid asks, "What's there in Rapid City you want to see," and I tell him about the museum at the School of Mines. "You're gay?" he asks. "Yeah," I reply, and he sort of grins and says how he could tell right off, how he wouldn't have offered me the blowjob if he hadn't been sure. He tells me he'll be nineteen the week before Christmas. I didn't ask. He volunteered as though it were the next most natural thing to say. "Lucas," says the kid, "he's a lot older than me, too. Maybe I just have a thing for older men." And I reply, "Maybe so, but you should be careful about that. There are people who will take advantage of that predilection in a young man. Out in the big wide world, out on the road, there are men whose appetites get the better of the better angels of their nature." He says I talk like a college professor, like someone who's read a lot of books, and then he goes back to watching the ballgame. I return to staring at the water stain on the cottage cheese ceiling. I lie there thinking about wolves and Red Riding Hood, the road of needles and the road of pins, about foolhardy children straying from the paths set out before them, about Lincoln, Nebraska, and before that, the inky shadows beneath a highway overpass just outside Sioux City, Iowa. And then I drift off to sleep, and I dream of a sky above the prairie that isn't any sort of sky at all, a sky that is, in fact, the waters of an inland sea, and I drive and I drive and I drive. Gigantic white worms have plowed the winding, switchback trails that I follow, and I anxiously check the rearview mirror, again and again, to be sure that I haven't been followed. I roll along between cathedrals that once were the skeletons of leviathans, bare ribs for flying buttresses, an arching line of vertebrae to support the vaulted dome of Heaven. Monstrous reptiles and fish and sharks the size of whales swim and fly and sail the mesopelagic liquid sky laid out above my car, and their shadows move silent across the land, sirens leading me on. Behind the wheel, I recite a protective zoological mantra, Greek and Latin binomena for an infidel's blasphemous benediction, an atheist's string of prehistoric saints and petrified rosary beads—*Tylosaurus, Archelon, Dolichorhynchops, Xiphactinus, Thalassomedon, Cretoxyrhina mantelli,* Good Lord deliver us. I take a wrong turn and stop at a deserted gas station, but all the pumps are out of order. The flyblown windows of the gas station are filled with jackalopes and pyramids made of empty oil cans. A sign nailed to the door reads "We're Open!" but all the doors have been locked against me. I peer inside, and there's an antique Bell & Howell 8 mm. home projector throwing images on a sheetrock wall. Angry men on horseback riding the hills of a rough and wooded country, hunting a wolf, a ruthless murderer of lambs and babes in cribs and travelers caught unawares. The flanks of the horses are encrusted with barnacles. The wolf turns out to be something else altogether, not a proper wolf at all. And then, on the way back to my car, passing the useless, broken down pumps, I watch a solar eclipse that is really only the circumference of an enormous ammonite's shell passing between me and the sun shining down on the ocean. *Placenticeras, Hoploscaphites, Oxybeloceras, Sphenodiscus pleurisepta,* Our Father who art forsaken, hossannah, amen, amen. I get back in the car, wishing that I could stop smelling that terrible, terrible stench, wishing it were only from having hit a dead skunk, wishing it were only the funk of road—though, in a sense, is it not? I drive, wandering out to where the deeps get deeper, and the sky grows darker, and the roof of the car begins to groan and buckle from the weight of all that water pushing down on me. And then the kid is shaking me awake, and he says that I was talking in my sleep. "Sounded like you were having one hell of a nightmare," he says. I say it wasn't as bad as all that, but sure, I have bad dreams. He's opened the drapes, and I see that the sun is down. The kid sits down on his bed, which doesn't look as if it's been slept in. I glance at the clock on the table between the beds and see it's almost midnight. The TV's been switched off, and the only light is coming from the open bathroom door. I smell soap and shampoo and steam, and I ask the kid if he had a shower. He says yeah, he took a shower, and then, he says, he found my keys and went outside and looked in the trunk. His hair's still wet I sit up and rub my eyes, and now I see that he's holding the revolver from his backpack. Quel courage. I see that it's aimed at me. "What I want to know," he says, "I mean, what I most wanna know, is whether or not you're afraid of dying, whether you're afraid of going to Hell for what you've done?" And I reply, "Or maybe just for being a faggot? That would be transgression enough, right?" And I ask him if I can get one of the Cokes from the cooler, and if he minds if I light a cigarette. Isn't that how it works? The condemned man is at least accorded a final cigarette? He tells me to sit still, and he goes to the Coleman icebox and takes out one of the cans of Coca-Cola and drops it on the bed beside me. He lights one of the Marlboros, and passes it to me, and I sit smoking and trying to wake up. But the dream still feels more real and less improbable than sitting in a motel room in Wall, South Dakota, staring at the muzzle of the kid's dead brother's gun. I take a long drag on the cigarette, and then I answer his question. "Yeah," I say, "I'm scared of dying. I probably would have stopped a long time ago, if I weren't afraid to just lie down and fucking die." He asks, "You were gonna do for me what you done for them?" and he nods towards the door to Room 107 and towards the car outside and towards the broken things he found in the trunk. "I hadn't yet decided," I tell him, and that's the truth, for whatever the truth might be worth. "Did you fuck them?" he wants to know. "Did you fuck them, and if you did, was it before or after they were dead?" I ask, "Are you going to ask me questions all night long? Is that how this is gonna go? You sitting there, holding that gun on me, satisfying your morbid curiosity." And he tells me, "Yeah, Mister, maybe that's how it's gonna go. Or maybe I already called the cops. Or maybe I'll take the gun and the car and be on my way. Maybe I'll even leave you alive." I laugh and smoke my Marlboro. "Well," I say, "that's an awful lot of choices. How are you ever going to decide which it's going to be?" He says, "You don't sound scared." I shake my head or I shrug or something of the sort. "Kid, I've been afraid so long I don't know anything else. I've been afraid so long I got tired, and I got sloppy, and I'm starting to think it was all on purpose. Maybe you've been sent by the gods to hand down my sentence and be my salvation, both at the selfsame time, doom and deliverance wielding a suicide's revolver. " The kid looks a little taken aback, either by so many words or by the sentiment I open the Coke and take a drink, then set the can down beside the clock on the table between the beds. "I'm not afraid of you," he says, and he only almost sounds as if he means it "Fear isn't anything to be ashamed of," I tell the kid. "Fear isn't cowardice. Fear isn't weakness. Maybe you'll figure that out one day, a little farther down the road." And then I ask him if he really has a boyfriend in Rapid City or if Lucas is nothing more than a useful fiction, a convenient lie. "That ain't really none of your business," he replies, and I agree, but he's not the only one with questions. "Why do you do it?" he asks, and I tell him I don't know. "That's a lie," he says, and I suggest that if he'd called the cops, they'd be here by now. And he tells me that he doesn't believe I was ever really a college professor, and I say fair enough, you believe what you want to believe. "But it's getting late," I say. "And you're holding all the cards." I imagine that I can hear the hooves of the horses from my nightmare, the horses bearing Wild West wolf slayers charged with a holy task of vengeance and retribution. "How do I know, if I leave you alive, if I leave you free, how do I know you won't come after me? How do I know you won't follow me?" I taste tinfoil and copper and a dozen poisons hiding in the cigarette smoke. Then I glance past him at the window, at the night waiting out there, at the headlights and taillights of cars and trucks racing by out on the interstate. "Kid, you don't know shit, and however I were to answer that question, you still wouldn't know shit. Whatever course you choose," I say, "it's a gamble. Just do me a favor and don't take all goddamn night about it." And he sits there watching me, and the clock strikes twelve midnight without making a sound. I think about the concrete Wall Drug dinosaur gazing out across the plains with its incandescent scarlet eyes, standing guard just as surely as any gargoyle, a sentinel watching for the evil that sometimes comes rolling along on steel belts, padding up to the off-ramp on four rubber paws, inevitable as rain and taxes and death. Then the kid asks me if next time I'll let him tag along and let him watch, if maybe that's one of the choices laid out before him. "If I don't call the cops," he says. "If I don't pull the trigger. If we could come to some sort of understanding." I have to admit, he catches me entirely off my guard. I don't answer right away. I tell the kid with broken china-blue eyes and dirty blond hair how I have to think on it a little while, that it's no simple proposition he making. And he says that's fine by him, that he figures neither of us is in a hurry, that neither of us has anywhere else to be. Then he lights a cigarette for himself, and he waits for whatever I'm going to decide, and the indifferent, all-powerful, unknowing clock starts counting down another day.

━━◈━━

EXCEEDING BITTER

Kaaron Warren

The first that Mrs. Jacobs knew of the Gray Ladies were the ashen footprints she found on the front step. She blamed the chimney sweep, furious that he had come to her front door dirty like that, or at all. She sent her husband to the Chimney Master, wanting a name, wanting that child to come and clean up his own mess, but her husband returned to say no sweep had come knocking and if he had, two shillings sixpence were owed.

"Awful man," her husband said, and she got him settled by the fire before he bored her with the usual talk. "Should have been drowned at birth, most of them, and I mean that kindly."

"Of course you do, dear," Mrs. Jacobs murmured, but in her mind's eye she pictured the baby rats he'd drowned in a bucket last week. Dropped them in then forgot about them, and she was the one who had to scoop them out and bury them.

He was asleep within minutes and she could settle to her busy work.

In the morning she swept the ashen footprints away.

She had just put the broom away when she saw the chimney sweep through the front window. A tiny, filthy boy and she lifted her broom to shoo him away.

He'd left more footprints, she saw that, but when she raised her broom and saw him shrink away, her heart melted.

"Boy!" she said, "What are you doing here?" Her cheeks were pink from exertion and she had her mum's old patchwork apron on.

"It looks so warm inside. The ladies showed me."

"What ladies, dear? Your aunties?"

He shook his head. "I've got none of those, nor a mother, neither. It was the gray ladies showed me." He tucked his shoulders down, cold in himself. He stared inside. "You're nicer than them, though."

Her husband was at the office and the street was quiet so she took him inside.

"Bath first," she said, but his stomach rumbled loudly and he seemed weak, so instead she sat him in the laundry and fed him porridge.

There was a knock on the door.

"The gray ladies!" he said. He seemed frightened.

"I thought you liked them."

"Only they look at me as if I'm real," he said. "But I don't like them."

Mrs. Jacobs opened the laundry door, wondering as she did so how the door was reached being, as it was, behind their high brick surrounding walls.

"Yes?" Mrs. Jacobs said, then drew a sharp breath.

Three gray ladies stood on her step. She could see the agapanthus through them, and they floated above the ground. They were tall and skeletally thin. Their skin was gray, flaccid, hanging off their cheeks in folds. They didn't look at her, only at the boy.

One lifted her hand and Mrs. Jacobs recoiled at the sight of long, sharp fingernails. They were silent as they turned, glided to the back wall and disappeared through it.

Mrs. Jacobs stood staring, knowing she couldn't tell her husband what she'd seen (*Imagination is the indication of an unsteady mind*, he liked to say). The boy shook.

"You better be off. My husband will be home soon for his lunch. Come back in two hours when he returns to work and I'll make you a plate." She put the hob on to make bubble and squeak and took out the bread knife ready to cut a slab to go with it.

He didn't want to move so she physically picked him up. He weighed as little as one of Mr. Butcher's chickens, no more. The morning had passed too quickly, though, because there was Mr. Jacobs at the front door, staring at her as if she was a beggar on the streets.

"Why are you carrying vermin?"

"Oh, Alfred. He's a poor motherless boy, that's all. Let me just bathe him. He can spend one night here, when he's clean, then he'll go after breakfast. We can't send him out in the night."

"It isn't even close to night, woman."

Mr. Jacobs had no patience for children. Never had done. If they'd been blessed, perhaps he would have changed his mind.

"Just the bath then and I'll send him away." She had the boy help her heat the water in the cellar and carry it to the laundry sink. The boy stared at the water as if mesmerized. The afternoon was gray and they needed what light they could but still Mrs. Jacobs pulled down the shutter. It was surely only shadow, but out there she thought she saw the three gray ladies, watching.

"You have a good scrub. I'm going down to clear up the lunch," she told the boy. He stared at her. His eyes were ash gray and his skin had a gray pallor she hadn't noticed before. His lips were drained of color and she saw streaks of ash in his hair.

"You take your time. Get yourself nice and clean. Go on."

She tugged at his shirt, trying to help, but he shied away, so she called her, asking him to convince the boy he needed to remove his clothes for the bath and she left them to it.

Mr. Jacobs came back down and settled by the fire a few minutes later.

"How is he?" she called out.

"You mean the vermin? He's as he should be."

"He's not vermin, he's unfortunate," but something in her husband's tone made her run down the hall and throw open the laundry door. He spoke like that when he'd bested an opponent and was pleased with himself.

At first she thought the boy must have climbed out, the water was so gray and murky. Then one hand floated to the surface and she plunged both hands in to pull him out.

What she thought was ash was not at all but his own gray color.

She lifted him easily (was he lighter now? It seemed so) and she cradled him in her arms, holding him as if she could bring life back to him. She began dry him tenderly.

She heard a rustle, a hiss behind her and turned, still holding the boy, to see the three gray ladies standing there.

One bent forward and reached out as if to stroke the boy, but instead she worked her fingers between his ribs as if trying to pry something loose. One did stroke his hair gently, but the last knelt down and began lapping at him, as if drinking something spilled.

Mrs. Jacobs held the boy closer, trying to keep their fingers from him, but they reached through her, chilling her to the bone, and all she saw was gray.

"How did you know?" she whispered. "How did you know my husband would be capable of that?"

She rocked back and forth. Their eyes followed her while they kept still, then she saw their faces change as they aped her sorrow. They rubbed their hands together as if cleaning them, then went back to work on the boy, separating soul from body with long, sharp fingernails.

Did they gain color? Glow?

She wasn't sure.

It would be weeks before Mrs. Jacobs could see color again.

The gray ladies were once Julia, Amara, and Magdalena. Pretty names for pretty girls, long since forgotten. *How did you know?* the woman asked, and they watched her, not answering her question. Truthfully, they did not know the answer and besides, they no longer spoke at all. Did they miss not talking to each other? Or had they no recollection of hours spent chattering?

They never knew where they'd knock. It was not their choice. Something moved them. It was death foretold by them, not delivered.

They knew they were doing good. A wise man (Wise. Cruel. Murderous.) told them often that one of the greatest gifts in life is to know when death is coming. It was a chance to say goodbye. To prepare.

If only people would listen. If they were stubborn, like the woman and her chimney sweep, no good was done to anyone.

She was colorful, that grieving woman, her cheeks pink, her eyes red. They were colorful once, these three.

Before.

They'd had a brighter life than many others like them, because their mother, Eliza, loved to travel, gathering friends like other people gathered pebbles or mementos. She'd been to Finishing School in Paris, where she met all manner of girls from all manner of places she'd never heard of before, like Lucia from Romania and Dao from the Principality of Phuan. And she learnt that each of them had a different idea of how things should be. This benefitted her daughters, giving them more freedom of expression and behavior than many others. Julia in particular thrived in this way, and as a girl loved to climb trees and sit in the branches, when the neighbors weren't looking.

There was less travel once Eliza married Phillip and the girls came along, but she had trunks of treasures to enjoy, and to share with her three daughters. "This one is for you, Julia," she said, lifting out a delicate blue scarf. "To match your eyes. For Amara, this green, and for Magdalena, this golden." The tiny girls were swamped in the lush material and they danced around the room with their mother spinning in the center.

"What is this?" their father said. He pretended gruffness, but he wouldn't have married her if he didn't love her ways.

They had a good life until the Romanian came.

Eliza had written letters to her dear school friends, especially Lucia, for ten years, fifteen. They kept in touch, and then there were no more letters. "I miss you!" Eliza wrote. "I wish we could visit with each other monthly and talk about foolish things."

It was not Lucia who visited. It was her brother, Mihai.

The girls would not remember his first visit, although their lives changed because of it. Their mother said he arrived in a large coach, with servants following behind. His voice louder than the most raucous of men in the village and his skin bright, glowing. He arrived on their doorstep with no announcement. He said, "I am the brother of the magnificent girl Lucia."

He was not as handsome as Eliza had imagined (the girls had told stories under the covers when they were at school, squealing at the inventions) but he was charming and vulnerable.

"I bring sad news. My dear wife died in childbirth, and the baby as well. In my sorrow I am traveling the world until now, when I reach my sister's dear friend and this beautiful land."

He looked out, lifting and shaping his hands as if measuring the place.

"Here I will build a castle, with the help of a great man."

Their father Phillip managed the project over the next fifteen years. This was his sole job, to build a mansion for the mysterious Romanian Mihai Adascalitei.

This brought success and financial security to the family, and each night Phillip insisted on raising a glass to Mihai, "Our benefactor."

"Our slave master," Eliza said, because Phillip worked twelve hours a day with little time for family.

Then it was done. Word came that Mihai would arrive to inspect, that he was traveling with a large retinue and that he was anticipating great pleasure on seeing his new home.

"He doesn't mention Lucia but surely she will come," Eliza said. "Perhaps she and I will go to London. She always said she'd love to go."

"They can't come," Phillip said. He couldn't sit down but paced in agitation. "He can't see his home. Can you imagine what he will say? He will be disappointed, to say the least."

"What's the worst that can happen?" Eliza asked. He looked at her. He didn't say anything.

"And what if he wants to visit here? Look at our house!" He was not a wealthy man. "He's going to think us very poor specimens,"

They all looked at their house. The fittings were shabby but solid and clean, well made. "You are the architect. The clever one. Let his financiers show him wealth. We show solid family love."

Mihai was tall, broadly built, his clothes cut well to hide how large he'd grown. His cheeks were red and round, his teeth spaced out and yellowed, his breath like cheddar or, Julia whispered like the Thames in summer. He had long hair brushing his shoulders (Phillip tried to hide his distaste at this), and he topped it with a small gray hat that was almost formless. He had blue lips, like a lizard's and his eyelids hung low, making him look sleepy.

"Aah, your lovely ladies. So tall! So delicate in the limbs and colorful! All three like princesses of an exotic place. You must all come to dinner at my home now it is complete. I'll have them serve beef broth and black pudding. That will get some meat on your bones."

Amara blushed, which made him laugh.

"You know I last saw these two older girls when they were tiny. Just born! All blue in the face and furious," he said. "How well I remember!"

The three girls barely contained themselves. They chattered all at once, drowning him out, until he burst into laughter and bade them hush.

They all heard his stomach rumble, like a crack of thunder, and Amara giggled. "Oh, you must be ravenous," Eliza said, " Let's get you something to eat."

"He's not about to waste away, Mildred," Phillip said.

"Alfred! So rude!" Eliza asked the cook to fix salmon en croute, because she knew they had leftover salmon from her order with the fishmonger. Some of them do it on purpose in the hope of taking the extra home but Eliza wasn't having that.

The girls raced to their rooms, returning screaming with laughter. They wore salmon pink scarves, all three, to match their food. Even in their rush they exuded grace, their fingers long and delicate, their step light.

"Like angels," Mihai said.

At dinner, Eliza couldn't contain herself any longer. "And my dear friend Lucia? It has been so long since we communicated."

Mihai shook his head. "I bring sad news. My dear sister died in childbirth. She did feel envy of your beautiful three, when she could have none. I'm sorry she no longer wrote to you. Perhaps hearing about your girls and their accomplishments became harder and harder as her years passed fruitlessly."

"And yet you said she was with child. What joy that must have brought."

"Ah," he said.

"So sad that she should pass in the same manner as your wife," Phillip said.

"Ah," Mihai said, and Julia wondered at his eyes, how they shifted about, not wanting to focus, and how he smiled nervously, and how his hands shook.

"Your father is a clever man. My house is something to see," he said, as the pudding was served, as if they hadn't seen it five dozen times. As if every meal hadn't been dominated by talk of this house.

"You've certainly changed the way things look," Eliza said.

"My philosophy; take something to its basics and rebuild it. Hair will grow back differently on a shaved head." Eliza thought he was dashing when he first visited, his hair a golden yellow, his shoulders broad.

"But hair grows back easily enough. By its very nature it is meant to fall."

"Your house is certainly sturdy, if not very beautiful," Phillip said. He had made many suggestions of design, all rebuffed.

"You know of the tulip?" Mihai said. "It grows weaker the more beautiful. There is little to be said for beauty, much for strength," Mihai said. "You are the strongest, Amara. That is clear."

Eliza well remembered the two-hundred-year-old house he'd had torn down to build his home.

He had bade her stand there in the rubble. She was flattered, a young wife with babies; you'd think she'd lost all of her allure. But no, Mihai, the brother of her dear friend (and, if she would only admit it, she had made up stories about him at school, when her friend spoke of him and his dashing ways) asking her to grace his home or the foundation of his home. "Stand there," he said, and bade his man mark where her shadow fell. That was where the foundation stone was laid.

"And now you must prepare," he had told her.

"For what, Mihai?"

"For your passing forty days from now."

She had known of this curse but had forgotten. He seemed gleeful about the death.

"It's a blessing to you. Knowing when you'll die gives you every chance to make amends, say goodbye, indulge your desires."

"I have no desires," but she did, of course. Small, sustaining dreams.

"And yet you are not dead," Mihai said in the present as she relayed this story and he roared with laughter. "My blessing failed."

"But look at my daughters. They are the true blessing. Magdala wouldn't be here, and who knows what sort of young women Julia and Amara would have been, raised by their father and hired women."

"What do you know of hired women?" Mihai said, and he gave Phillip such a look. He led him to the drawing room but the girls weren't going to miss out. Julia crept into the room next door, the little-used storage space and heard such things as made her sick to the stomach.

"There is a house of whores," Mihai said, "Whose skin is dyed blue. Glorious. Like the naked bodies taken out of plague houses, a sight I've seen and never anything so beautiful."

Julia wondered, *How old is this man? Unless there was a plague more recently in Romania?*

"These whores hold the same tinge and even more, as the blue fades it begins to look like bruising. Also beautiful."

Julia noticed her mother kept them all close and allowed them no time alone. She was ever so protective, but not it seemed as if she offered a barrier between the girls and this charismatic man, as she saw him. The girls were not so inclined.

"You could do worse than that man," Phillip said afterwards, but what his four ladies said in return burned his ears and made him shrink into his collar.

"Are we going to have to poison you to stop you marrying our girls off to awful men?" Eliza said.

The maid listened in. She always listened.

"He's not so bad," Amara said.

"But look at him! Like a monster!"

It was soon after this they traveled for dinner at Mihai's mansion.

Outside was solid gray brick, with very few windows. "You see how I save money on the window tax? Your father chose his materials well," Mihai had said, though Phillip had little choice in the matter. Inside, all was gray, muted.

He said, "It will be named for you, Phillip. Your name in brass, over the door."

Phillip was embarrassed by this. An honest day's pay for an honest day's work was all he asked for, and a good life for his girls and for his wife to be happy, because her happiness brought joy to his own life.

"No need for that," he said.

"One of your daughters, then. Julia, Amara, Magdalena. Which one?" and he rubbed his great beard, eyeing them off. Only Julia understood he was teasing.

"More wine," Mihai said. "More food." The girls and their mother fell asleep as the two men finished bottle after bottle.

It was after midnight when Mihai arranged a carriage to take them home. Their father groaned and whimpered all the way, filling them all with irritation. Silly drunk man. He wasn't amusing at all, just dull and odorous.

It was the last carriage ride the family would take together.

The next morning Phillip did not rise. He was never a lazy man, always up with the dawn, even on the nights he was up well past midnight. But after the amount he drank it wasn't surprising that he was still not risen by noon.

"Silly fidget," their mother said. "He's poisoned himself with wine."

"Mother!" Julia said. The maid stifled a smile; she was always far too free with ears and eyes, Julia thought and true; it was she who whispered so loud that Mihai came to visit.

"What's this I hear? A house of women left unattended?" he roared.

"He is wine-ill, nothing else," Eliza said. "He deserves a small amount of suffering for the noise he made last night."

The maid heard this as well.

"Real men don't suffer from the drink, and this is a man who can build a magnificent house. Leave me with him."

Not knowing why, they did leave, even the maid.

In there, Mihai roused Phillip. He gave him a draught and when the man bent over double in pain he said, "I think that woman's poisoned you. That wife of yours."

The maid gave evidence at Eliza's trial for attempted murder. "Oh yes," she said, "I heard them talking about poisoning him."

༄

With their father weak and ill, their mother incarcerated, the girls had no one to watch over them.

Mihai made an arrangement with Phillip. If the three girls went into servitude for him, he would ask for mercy for Eliza using his influence. His wealth. He would ask the authorities not to put her to death. "I won't work your girls hard," he said. "Think of it as finishing school."

The father had never physically recovered, nor mentally. He agreed.

It was not what they imagined. Even in their worst nightmares they couldn't imagine what Mihai had in store for them.

Mihai's closest companion was a cruel, weak man called Cyril. He was the mayor of a town far away who never seemed to be at home for his duties.

Cyril and Mihai drank great goblets of wine, but the girls were given crystal glasses of blue water.

"Isn't it a beautiful hue? Indigo water. A rare thing, rare indeed but fitting for these beautiful tulip flowers I have before me."

Later, in the lavatory, Amara would scream in terror and the older girls laugh to see how their water had turned blue.

"Look at your lovely ladies," Cyril said, his eyes glinting. "You'd think they were dolls they are so lovely. Or puppets, perhaps. Dance for us, lovely puppets."

"Go on," Mihai said, "Do as he says."

So the girls drew out their scarves and danced. They brought the only color to the place; there was scant art, much of it dull, and the food served on plain plates. Only the wine goblets shone golden, and the enormous candles brought a warmth and a glow.

"Have them dance on my grave when I'm dead," Cyril said, and the two men laughed until they fell off their chairs.

Looking back, the girls would see that as the best night of their captivity. The last color they saw. As the sun rose, Mihai said, "And now."

As he imprisoned down below, in solid dark rooms, his eyelids lifted so his eyes stared dark and hard and Julia understood that he would not listen to reason.

Each girl had a cell to herself. The cells were bare; no bed, no chair, no window, no light. It took them a while to understand they were there to die.

They wondered; did their father build these rooms? Didn't he wonder what they were for? Or did he imagine coal, or wood, or wheat?

Day by day Mihai told them how long they had to live.

"How good I am to you," he said. "What a gift I give to you. To know the truth." He said this every day.

He allowed them water. He passed tall thin jars to them through small cracks and while they saw nothing in the pitch dark, they knew this water was blue. He told them so, he said, "Your insides will be such a lovely color."

Julia thought, *this is because of the whores.* He wants us blue like them. He couldn't see them in the dark; it was their corpses he wanted to see.

They couldn't hear each other. They could barely hear themselves; the walls were dense, almost absorbent, drawing in all sound and most of the air.

So hungry. So very, very hungry. No moss or mold on the walls, no rodents, so day by day they weakened. Amara was the bitterest; she alone had believed he would marry her and she would live a life of adventure. She felt such fury at what he stole from her. Not just her own moments of joy, love, success, but those of all her future generations. He stole her name, her family's future, he ended her line, and this made her exceeding bitter.

Mihai fattened. Larger and larger so quickly his servants thought he was a devil and ran for their lives. He grew so large he could no longer walk down the stairs, and so he did not know that those three girls died together, within an hour of each other.

They oozed through the gray brick walls, waiting till they are all three dead and spirit.

They found him, fat, repulsive, sunk deep into his bed. He wept. "Oh, glory. O great glory of god, they are beautiful. Ah, great day."

Julia said, "Is this how your wife died? And your sister?"

"Great glory of god they were beautiful too," he said. And they watched, feeling victorious, as he rose and stumbled to the stairs, as he tripped and fell down, as he bled out, alone and foul.

Many years hence, Eliza was old and dead in the tongue from keeping silent. She had not hated living amongst the women and had enjoyed her work as nurse during the war, but she despised the filth, the jailors, the cruelty. She was not expected to see freedom, but during a transfer to a new gaol, where a woman of her years could see out her time, there was an accident.

The horses reared up. The driver called out "Get off the road you stupid girls," but nothing was there. The horses reared sharper, the wagon tipped over into the river, and only Eliza, of the five being transported, the guards, and the driver, survived.

Free at last, wearing prison-made clothing, carrying one small bag of belongings, she had nowhere to go but to her daughters in captivity. Her husband was long since dead of the drink; she'd always known that's where he was headed.

She found herself walking in the shadows of the shallows of the river, her feet so cold she thought perhaps they'd been severed, like the poor soldiers at the hospital who woke to find their feet removed by a surgeon's blade.

But no, her feet were there, she didn't walk on stumps at all.

No one had aided her find her daughters. No one listened.

She saw a gray washerwoman holding up what looked like cloth but, Eliza thought, was the tattered souls of the girls. It filled her mortal despair. It was too late; they were lost. Still she walked on, to pray over their graves at least.

There were times she imagined she was elsewhere, to help the forward steps. At school, when they did walk long miles for punishment (maybe not) or she'd imagine herself doing laps of a beautiful boat, the girls at play, her husband still alive and in love with her

At last she found the mansion. Long abandoned, uglier than ever. No name over the door, so Mihai had not even kept that promise.

She walked around and around, not sure how to get in. There were no windows and the door seemed locked tight.

She thought she heard moans and cries. Her daughters crying. She was suddenly sure they were alive and waiting for her, and she pressed her fingers against the gray brick, seeking entrance. One small door where the servants had entered was ajar, and there she entered, and then she found her girls.

They were bone.

They were long dead and she was old in the bone but she loved them.

She was cold, though, so cold, and she had been since the river, chilled to the bone and when she found an old rug by the hearth, and at the top of the house one small window where the sun crept in, there she lay down and allowed herself to sleep.

༄

As sad as she was, and drained gray by grief, she achieved death at last and her soul passed on to another place. Her daughters, the gray ladies, would never find that peace.

They did feel something. From where they were, a world away, the three stopped as one. For a moment, a wash of red passed through them, the color of love, perhaps, and for a moment they clustered, almost remembering, but then they were drawn away, drawn towards, and they found the next door and they knocked on it, bringing their gift of knowledge to the person within.

⸺◆⸺

(Author Note: The title "Exceeding Bitter" is inspired by *Requiem*, Op. 48, by Gabriel Faure: " . . . ah, that great day, and exceeding bitter, when thou shalt come to judge the world by fire.")

⸺◆⸺

WITCH-HAZEL

—◆—

JEFFREY FORD

Back in the day, in the Pine Barrens of South Jersey, from October 31 to November 2, All Souls' Day, people who lived in the woods or close to them would pin to their coats, their blouses, the lapels of their jackets, a flowering sprig of witch hazel. It's a shrub that grows naturally in the barrens and blossoms right around Halloween. The flower looks like a creature from a deep-sea trench, yellow tentacles instead of petals radiating from a dark brown center that holds a single seed.

The name of the plant could have something to do with real witches and witching but not necessarily. The word "witch" is derived from Middle English *wicche*, and all it means is "pliable" or "bendable." It's a reference to the use of the branches of the witch hazel shrub in the art of dowsing by early homesteaders to the barrens. Dowsing is the practice of locating things underground with and through the vibrations of a Y-shaped tree branch. One thing's for sure, the "hazel" part of the word comes from the fact that in England the branches from the hazel tree supposedly made the best dowsing rods. That tree didn't grow in the barrens, though, and so the settlers found a substitute that was equally pliant—a shrub with crazy flowers that blossoms in the season of Jack-o'-lanterns.

The practice was fairly prevalent until well after World War II, but most of those who still don witch hazel for the holiday don't know its symbolism, and only do so because they remember a parent or grandparent wearing it. In this manner the tradition might limp a little further into the future before completely disappearing. There's a tale, though, that is now rarely repeated save around the kitchen tables and fireplaces of real old-timers. It begins in the year 1853, in the barrens village of Cadalbog, a place that presently exists as only one crumbling chimney and the foundation of a vanished glass factory lost among the pines. The loose-knit community of glassmakers, blueberry harvesters, colliers, and moss rakers, had been there since 1845. By 1857, the village was deserted.

A reminiscence of the place that has survived in the diary of one Fate Shaw, the wife of the factory owner, describes Cadalbog as "an idyllic place of silence and sugar sand as soft and white as a cloud. The local cedar ponds are the color of strong tea, and along lower Sleepy Creek there always seems to be a breeze shifting through the pines, even in the heart of August." Supposedly Mrs. Shaw did everything within her power to provide for her husband's workers and their families. She was well liked and well respected, as was Mr. Shaw. One of the events she put on every year was a Halloween celebration.

Unlike the citizenry of most of the other settlements of the barrens, either Swedish or Puritans from Long Island, Cadalbog was founded by Irish immigrants fleeing the potato famine back home. Their Halloween antics were brought with them from the Old World. There was disguise, not as monsters or ghouls, but people would dress up and pretend to be dead relatives. Turnips were carved instead of pumpkins. There was always a huge bonfire, dancing, fiddle and tin whistle music. Out in the middle of a million and a quarter acres of pine forest, in the spooky autumn night, it didn't seem so outlandish that those who'd passed on might return to beg for prayers to shorten their stays in purgatory. In that setting, even these pragmatic people, who'd survived much, could believe for a few nights that spirits were afoot.

In 1853, Halloween fell on a Monday, and the celebration could not be held on the night of a workday. Likewise, Sunday was out of the question, as it was given over to the lord. So it was Friday, October 29 that the incident occurred. There was a cold breeze out of the north. A roaring bonfire licked the three-quarter moon with a snapping flame, and the music reeled. A strong fermented brew called heignith, concocted from crab apples, wild blueberries, cranberries, and raw honey, among other ingredients (its full recipe is lost), was consumed by the barrelful.

Attending the celebration that night was Miss Mavis Kane and her sister, Gillany. These two women, identical twins, were well-known even though they lived on the outskirts of the village. Gillany had been married at one time, but her husband, Peter, a Quaker collier who'd been born in those woods, succumbed to a rattlesnake bite, leaving the sisters to fend for themselves. By the account of Fate Shaw, they managed quite well. To quote from her diary, "The Kane sisters are a stoic pair—dour and pale and of few words. They move silently like ghosts around their property, chopping wood, repairing the steps to the front door, throwing a stick for that black dog of theirs, Brogan."

As reported by Fate, their sole uniforms were ankle-length black dresses of a sateen weave. Even in summer, out in the forest, hunting the yellow shelf fungus that grows on the sides of trees (they made a good profit drying it, crumbling it up, and curing it with honey to make a kind of sweet brittle), they wore light corsets and high collars. Their long black hair was gathered into one large knot and left to lay upon the spine. To the Halloween celebration they brought a basket of Kane's Crumbs, as the local treat had come to be known. The sisters, though both handsome women, weren't asked to dance. They didn't drink or eat but sat and simply stared at the fire and the goings-on. Their fixed expressions were the only masks they needed.

Sometime after the drunken singing had turned to whispered laughter a small meat cleaver appeared, as if from nowhere, in Gillany's left hand. Its blade glistened in the glow of the dying fire as it sliced the air, struck, and split the backbone of Ray Walton, the foreman at the glass factory. As he screamed, blood immediately issuing from his mouth, Mavis put a knife through the throat of the Ahearn girl, who folded to the ground like a paper doll. They each went on hacking out their own private trails of horror: fingers flying, blood and bowels falling, eyes skewered, ribs cracked, wrists hacked. A storm of screams broke the stillness of the barrens.

It took some time for a group of factory laborers—male and female—to subdue the sisters. The Kanes fought, it seemed, without awareness—as if they were under a spell. By the time the two murderers were tied up and being led away, there were six dead and twenty wounded. That's a lot of people to dispatch in a relatively short time with only sharp kitchen utensils. The Burlington County sheriff in Mount Holly was sent for, and the twins were incarcerated in separate store rooms in the glass factory. Old Dr. Boyle, once of Atsion and since run away to the woods after accusations of malpractice, was already on hand, drunk, pronouncing death and treating the wounded. He agreed with Mr. Shaw's assessment that the attack was too random and mindless to have carried an intention of murder. Most everyone who witnessed it firsthand agreed.

When his duty to those injured at the celebration was finished, Boyle went to the factory to inspect the Kanes. By then the sun was coming up, and the breeze dropped yellow oak leaves in his path. The smoke from the bonfire pervaded the air, bottles lay strewn about the clearing behind the factory and down the path into the deep pines. He entered the brick structure and was greeted by Shaw, who showed him down a back hallway to a small door hidden by shadow. Boyle, a careful man, put his ear to the door and listened. The factory was empty and unusually silent.

"Who can tell the difference, but I think someone who would know said this was Gillany," said Shaw.

"Is she tied up?" asked Boyle.

"Oh, yes, quite securely."

"Did she say anything when you got her in here?"

"Nothing. She foamed at the mouth and spit. Growled some."

"Okay," said Boyle, and nodded.

Shaw moved forward and inserted a long iron key into the door's lock. He turned it, there was a vicious squeal from the hinges, and they entered. The room was small, with a low ceiling and one window at eye level looking out across an expanse of reed grass toward the pond. The only light in the dim room came from that source. Boyle felt claustrophobic. He set down his bag, took off his hat and coat, and hung them on the back of a chair. The only sound was that of the woman's breathing, steady and strong. She was asleep on the floor, her hands bound behind her back, feet tied. Her black hair was unknotted and covered her face. Blood soaked the sleeves and skirt of her dress.

The doctor had Shaw fetch him a lantern, and by that, he examined her. When he rolled her onto her back, he discovered her eyes were wide open as she slept. "Most unusual," he said, bringing the light closer and closer to them, unable to make the dilated pupils constrict. As he wrote in his personal report of the case (held, along with surviving files of his other cases, at the Joseph Truncer Memorial Library at Batsto Village), "There were a number of odd signs upon the first of the Kane women I examined, not the least of which was a high fever. The eyes were like saucers, the skin around the sites of her lymph nodes had gone a vague green, her eyelashes had fallen out, and there was a silvery substance dribbling from her left ear. All of these struck me as potent signs of disease. When I inspected her lower body, I found her legs covered with insect bites, which I knew were chiggers from that feel of sand when I brushed my open palm against her shins."

According to the story, it's then that Shaw, standing by for support along with his wife, who had since joined him and Boyle in the store room, took a small jump backward and gave a grunt, pointing at something white wriggling out from beneath Gillany Kane's undergarments. Boyle swung the lantern to give a better view. There wasn't just one bloodless worm inching down her legs, but it was clear there were a dozen or more. Fate Shaw put her hand to her mouth and gagged. The doctor got to his feet and moved away as fast as a man of seventy-five with a bad liver and bad knees could. He went to his bag, hands shaking, and removed his tools to extract a blood sample. As he leaned over the body again, he called over his shoulder for Shaw and his wife to get out. "No one is to enter this room or the one in which the sister is being kept until I return. Make sure to lock them both as soon as I'm gone."

Back in his home halfway between Cadalbog and Harrisville, Boyle brewed himself a pot of coffee and brought out the brass microscope a wealthy Dutch patient of his had gifted him early in his career for saving a favorite son. Still not having slept from the previous night's festivities and mayhem, he peered bleary eyed into the tube of the mechanism at a slide holding Gillany's blood. What he wrote in response to what he witnessed through the eyepiece was only this—"A strange pathogen, blossoming, from the woman's blood cells—many armed, like the wild witch-hazel flower. I've never seen the like." He stood from his table on which the microscope rested and stumbled to bed. There he slept for a brief interval before heading back to Cadalbog.

He arrived at the factory in late afternoon to find a commotion. It seems that the woman who was hot with fever and in a trance, sleeping with eyes open, somehow revived enough to smash through the small window that looked out upon the cedar pond. As Fate Shaw put it, "We were novices as prison guards. No one ever suspected she'd break out. It was beyond possibility to us. A search party has been sent out after her."

Boyle told the Shaws and a few of the workers not home grieving for murdered loved ones or caring for those wounded, "Gillany's got a disease I've not ever heard of or seen before. Something that has crawled out of the dark heart of the barrens, no doubt centuries old. She's got the telltale signs of a bad chigger infestation on her legs. I believe she spends a good deal of time in the woods? She and her sister are mushroom gatherers, if I'm not mistaken."

Fate Shaw nodded.

"I'm guessing the chiggers carry the bacterium. She's infected. We've got to find her and treat her, or if she's discovered already dead, burn her."

"Not to mention, she's diabolical with a meat cleaver," said Fate.

"Whatever it is, it's like typhus, a parasite that affects the brain."

"What about her sister?" asked Shaw.

"Take me to her," said the doctor.

The factory owner handed Boyle a rusty Colt revolver. "In case she becomes murderous. It's loaded."

"You hold on to that. I'll end up shooting myself in the foot," he said.

On the opposite side of the factory, they came to another door cast in shadow. This one opened into a storeroom with no window, but larger than the first. In the middle of it, surrounded by shelves holding various bottles and tools, was Mavis Kane, bound to a straight-backed chair with her arms joined behind her. Boyle noticed immediately that she was awake and alert. She too had blood on her black dress, but her hair was still in a single knot. He found another chair in the corner of the room and moved it around so he could sit facing her. He found the resemblance to her sister distracting. As he set his bag on the floor, he said, "Miss Kane, how are you feeling?" She was placid, expressionless. She stared straight through him. Her lips moved, though, and she answered.

"I've a fever," she said. "An infernal itching down below."

"Your sister is also ill. When did she begin not feeling well?"

"After we met the woman out by the salt marshes."

"Who would that be?"

"An old woman, Mother Ignod, the color of oak leaves in spring. She wore rags and told us she was a witch who had been put to death by settlers almost a century before because she spoke to the deer and they listened. She found magical power in the lonesome, remote nature of the barrens."

"How did they dispatch her?"

"Drowned her in a bog."

"And now she's back?"

"'For revenge,' she told us."

"Upon whom?"

Mavis remained silent.

"Do you recall your sister being afflicted by a bad case of chiggers?"

"Yes."

"What about you? Did you also have them on your legs?"

"Yes."

Boyle retrieved from his bag at his feet a blue bottle with a cork in the top. "I'm going to give you something to drink. It's going to cure you," he told her.

Mavis didn't say a word, didn't look at him when he stood from his chair and came toward her, pulling the stopper from the blue bottle. "Drink this," he said, and handed it to her. He was a little surprised when she took it, put it to her lips, and did as he commanded without a question, without spilling a drop, without grimacing at the bitter taste. What he'd given her was a tea made from the witch-hazel blossom, toadleaf, and ghost sedge. She drank till her mouth filled and overflowed and dribbled down her bloody dress. He let her finish the entire bottle. She handed it back to him; he put the cork in it and returned it to his bag. As he sat in his chair, he reached back into the bag and took out a different bottle, this one brown. Black Dirt Bourbon, Boyle's self-prescribed cure-all. He sipped and mused while he waited for his elixir to work.

In his notes on the case, the doctor stated that he believed the invading parasite had caused swelling of the women's brains, which caused their psychotic behavior. The witch hazel was an anti-inflammatory, and the other two ingredients had what today would be called antibiotic properties. Although he'd been trained at the University of Pennsylvania's medical school, a few years living in the barrens and he'd combined his formal knowledge with the teachings of folk medicine. He writes, "The two of them must have been under the influence of the disease for weeks as it slowly grew within them. Gillany was further along for some reason, and I had lost hope for her—feverish, catatonic, birthing worms, wandering through a labyrinthine wilderness."

Shaw woke Boyle from a sound sleep. Though there was no window in the room, immediately the doctor could tell it was night. The factory owner held a lantern. Mavis was sleeping peacefully, her eyes closed, her bosom heaving slowly up and down at regular intervals. Boyle got out of his chair and walked across to her. Lightly slapping her face, he spoke her name, rousing her. Before long her eyelids fluttered, and she made a soft moaning noise.

"She looks better," he said to Shaw.

"Remarkable."

"Her sister?"

"The search party just returned without her. They combed the woods, twenty men and Chandra O'Neal, the tracker, and not a trace of her."

"Even if you could find her, and I could administer my cure, she's no doubt too far gone," said Boyle.

Shaw was about to admit defeat as well when Mavis opened her eyes and murmured something. Boyle put his ear down to her lips. "What was that?" he asked. She mumbled some more, and Shaw asked, "Is she speaking?" The doctor nodded.

Boyle went back to his bag and pulled out another blue bottle full of the witch-hazel elixir. He slipped it into the pocket of his coat.

"What did she say?" asked Shaw.

"She said to get the dog, Brogan. The dog will track Gillany if you speak her name to him."

Heading out into the Pine Barrens at night, even with a torch and a gun, was daunting. People who knew how unpredictable the wilderness could be usually stayed close to home at night. Still, the doctor, the factory owner, Fate, and three other workers most loyal to the Shaws headed out with guns loaded. There were two shotguns and two pistols among the party. Fate carried an over-under, double-barreled pistol, and the doctor went armed only with his elixir.

The night was cold as the world moved toward winter. There was a strong breeze, and the leaves from scarlet and blackjack oak to maple and tupelo showered down around them. The moon was a sight brighter than on Halloween, and in the clearings it reflected off the sugar sand, glowing against the dark. They found the black dog, Brogan, a powerful beast with a thick neck and broad chest, chained up next to the outhouse beside the sisters' home. He was happy to see them, having gone unfed since the morning of the day prior. Fate thought to bring a cut of salted venison from her kitchen for the beast. This made her and the dog fast friends. Shaw undid the collar from Brogan's neck while he devoured the meat.

"Find Gillany," said Fate in her most soothing voice. "Find Gillany."

The dog looked from one member of the party gathered around him to another. Mrs. Shaw repeated her order one more time. Brogan barked twice and padded down the path into the pines.

"Stick together," said Boyle, and they were off at a slow jog trying to keep up with the dog. The torches crackled and threw light but also made it difficult to see anything near the intensity of the flame. They passed down a sandy trail all of them were familiar with and then the dog dove into the brush and all followed him winding among the pitch pine and cedar. Luckily, there were no chiggers or mosquitos still active. The doctor heaved for breath as they moved quickly along, wishing he'd brought another bottle of bourbon. An owl called far off to the west. He knew from the direction they were heading that the dog was leading them toward the marsh.

It wasn't long before the doctor found himself alone in a meadow of marsh fern gone red with the season. He'd lost the others a good twenty minutes earlier but could hear the dog barking not too far ahead. The ground was soggy, and he moved slowly, knowing that in a moment he could be in water up to his neck. At first, he intended to call out, but on second thought he realized that Gillany might be somewhere close by with a sharp weapon of some kind. He thought silence a better strategy. It's then that he heard the dog yelp and whimper in a manner that could crack ice. A gun went off. There was a human scream followed hard by a splash.

A brief moment of silence and then more screaming, more shots. The din of the commotion sparked Boyle's adrenaline, and he so wanted to run away. Finally, he called out, "Shaw!" at the top of his voice, and then stood still, listening to the night over the pounding of his heart. He shivered in the breeze for a long while, and then he heard the crack of brittle twigs and the crunch of dry leaves. "Shaw? Is that you?" he called. But it wasn't Shaw. A pale figure staggered through the marsh ferns toward him. He backed up into a clearing of sand, wanting to flee but was unable, as fear robbed his energy.

She came toward him in the moonlight, her hair loose in the wind like the tail of a black comet. She wore nothing but carried a hatchet stained with blood. He swept the torch in front of him as a means of warding her off. As she approached, he could see a gunshot wound to the hip, the bloody hole writhing with white worms. "That's it," said Boyle. He turned and ran as best he could, which wasn't all that good. With no idea which direction he was headed, he stumbled forward through the marsh ferns toward where the moonlight showed him a tree line. Not even a hundred yards, and he'd slowed to a hobble, out of breath and caught in the grip of a coughing fit.

It was work to get control of his breathing, but he finally managed. Behind him he heard or thought he heard, even above the sound of the wind, the tread of Gillany. He turned and saw her only yards away. Her breathing was like a whistle, and she limped stiffly. She lifted the weapon when she saw him looking, and he groaned, knowing there'd be no more running. His heart was pounding. She came for him and he crouched away from her. She lifted the hatchet, and from above his head, he saw an arm descend from behind him. At the end of that arm there was a hand aiming a derringer. The finger pulled the trigger just as Gillany was upon him. The pistol exploded with a dull thud, smoke and sparks, and the two balls of shot ripped off her face. There was blood and flesh, and just below the skin there was a tangled layer of worms. She fell on him and he screamed.

Fate Shaw and the doctor made it back to the village at daybreak. Once there, she turned doctor and prescribed a bottle of bourbon for Boyle. When he was comfortable, she called the village together by ringing the bell outside the factory. She told those who gathered how they'd tracked Gillany Kane into the marshes and how she'd attacked Mr. Shaw and the others. A dozen men volunteered to go and search for survivors in the daylight. Fate decided to accompany them as did two of the wives whose husbands had been part of the posse. They uncovered the remains of Brogan's mangled body, but no sign of any of the men. They searched every day for the better part of a week. Nothing. They followed the creeks and streams in case the bodies had been deposited in the water and swept along with the tranquil current. Nothing.

Finally, the sheriff from Mount Holly arrived and was told the tale just as it happened. Fate and Boyle gave much of the testimony, and the other half was supplied by Mavis, who had made a full recovery from the disease that gripped her sister. She referred to the illness as the suspicions, for the paranoia it engendered with a fury that took over the mind. The sheriff couldn't make heads nor tails of it and eventually slunk back to Mount Holly to file five missing persons reports. Somewhere in the middle of that very harsh winter, Mavis Kane disappeared. No one was sure exactly when it happened, but everyone was certain it was after the snow came and before it left. She could have slipped away from Cadalbog, but there were also many who weren't willing to forgive her part of the Halloween mayhem. Maybe the barrens took her, but after that most forgot, leaving only Fate and Boyle to wonder what actually had happened.

Three years later, in spring, Fate Shaw reported in her diary on the passing of Dr. Boyle. "I'd go to see him out there at his place on the way to Harrisville. He'd drink and talk, and I'd listen. He was the one individual who didn't mind hashing over the enigma of the Kane sisters' disease. He was convinced it was a matter of biology and chemistry, the psychosis of a fevered mind. I, on the other hand, knew better, because I was privy to the end of the story. The helper I'd hired to look after the doctor reported to me that the day the old man died he'd had a visitor, an old woman in tattered clothes with a strange green-tinged complexion. She was accompanied by a black dog. The helper didn't know how long the old woman had been there, but when he returned the next morning to make a fire and cook breakfast for the doctor, he found Boyle in a chair, head flung back and white worms crawling from his nose and ears, squirming out through his tear ducts.

"The last thing he told me on my final visit to him was, as he put it, 'His confession.' It so happened that the reason he'd come to the Pine Barrens in the first place was due to a botched delivery. It was a breech birth, and he was pie-eyed drunk. 'Twin sisters with the cord wrapped round their necks,' he said. 'As they struggled for their freedom, they strangled each other. I was passed out on the floor. Unsettling that the tragedy occurred on All Souls' Day. The parents wanted to put me in jail, and I fled like a thief in the night.' I didn't have the heart to wonder aloud about the twin connection and neither did he. The strangeness we'd been part of was already too complicated.

Before I left him that day, he gave me, written out in a shaky hand, the recipe for his elixir against the suspicion. 'Sooner or later, it'll be back,' he told me. Twenty years have passed since then, and I've long ago misplaced that scrap of paper. But every year at Halloween, I wear a blossom of the witch hazel in honor of Boyle, and oddly enough, it's beginning to catch on."

LITTLE DIGS

Lisa L. Hannett

Three generations are buried on Wheeler land, starting with Great-Grandaddy Winston, the only one to live up to the surname. A far-traveler, he was. Crossed seven county lines to reach Napanee, carting a new wife, her faith in the old gods, and a wagonload of beehives along with him. Winston named his first and only child Queenie, back when he still held high hopes for honey riches, but slipped into the habit of calling her Teenie when she grew no bigger than his bank account.

After planting her Pops in the first mound out back, Teenie took root on the homestead, settling it and the household accounts. Had such a knack for numbers, in fact, she saved up for a pesticide rig that kept the larder well-stocked, the fields bug-free and her son in a job for life. In her seventy-odd years, she never took no man's name, nor his hand in wedlock. But, on one occasion at least, she invited him into her bed—and kicked him back out again long, long before she birthed that plane-loving heir of hers.

Nowadays, Queenie surveys her property upwards from the wormside of mound number two, while her boy most often sees it from the clouds. When Buddy Wheeler brings that Piper Cub of his in for a landing, stinking of diesel and creosote, his own daughter Bets teases him something merciless. Poking and prodding, she checks him for extra limbs, sudden chemical-spawned tentacles, or indiglo skin. If he minds, he sure doesn't show it: Bets' daddy knows how to take a joke. He's open-minded. He gets the bigger picture. Always has.

Winging hither and yon in that biplane of his, Buddy's seen far beyond the confines of this hand-me-down property, this cornbread county. Way farther than Bets or her Mamma ever did.

Once upon a time, before Queenie had wheeled groundwards, Buddy used to haw on the harmonica between harvests. Even gathered a decent following—or so he says—at honkytonks here, there, and everywhere, thanks to the unique style of bluegrass he played. Tunes whined extra soulful against that ugly set of metal teeth he wore, temporary inserts he kept in permanent on account of the sharp glint they gave off, the steel shine they lent his smile.

"These chompers of mine's worth their weight in twenties," Bets' daddy used to say, especially when whiskey-soaked, too numb to fly anywheres much less lift a blues-harp to his lips. Thick-tongued, he'd toy with the bridge, running the blunt tip along silver valleys and peaks. "They's the brightest map outta here, understand? The trustiest, most valuable map . . . "

Mesmerized, baby-girl Bets had watched the thing wiggle in and out of his mouth. She'd read about touch-maps them Artick injuns used, little sculptures that looked every bit like her daddy's teeth, except they were whittled hunks of wood. Those carvings' dips and whorls, Bets later learned, were landscapes shrunk small, coastlines and mountain ranges tucked in pockets or carried inside seal-fur mitts. Portable 3D worlds, in other words, and more reliable than paper or memory. At high noon or moon-dark, travelers could run fingers over them cracks and bumps to get their bearings, certain they'd never be led astray.

Now standing on the back porch her Nanna Teenie built, Bets hefts a shovel and looks out on the hummocked land Great-Grandaddy Winston claimed. Releasing a pent breath, she pats her back pocket for the hundredth time that morning, feels the folded paper's reassuring crinkle. Guts all a-flutter, she sends a silent prayer to the gods. Thanking any and all of them for blurring Daddy's sights with clouds and moonshine, filling his mouth with them precious silver directions. Asking—not begging, she's too reasonable for that—any and all of them to look kindly on her venture, to reward her for putting herself out there, putting on a brave show. *Gods favor the bold*, she tells herself, hoping their invisible eyes have already turned her way. Hoping they'll approve. Hoping they won't leave her stranded.

More than halfway through spring, the ground's still almost hard as it was in mid-January. The last shaded knolls of snow finally sank about a week ago, leaving patches of grit on winter-squashed grass in the backyard. Filth gathers like crumbled shadows under the boundary's split timber fences. Weathered barriers divide dirt for the living from that for the dead, keeping ever-fallow acres separate from budding maples and crabapple trees, and from planting-fields in the back forty beyond.

In the distance, a range of low mountains gently curves across the horizon. Each graystone peak is bare and blunt as a molar. Six or seven of the things are pressed close together, so's the ridge as a whole looks to Bets like a broken set of dentures. Closer to home, between the rusted swing-set she used to ride for hours—failing to muster enough courage to leap off the seat at its highest point, to wind up and let go, to fly—and the ploughed rows waiting for the new season's crop, three soft hillocks push their swollen bellies out of the earth.

Until last autumn there'd only been the two big ones on the left, bulging side by side, reminding Bets of that joke about Dolly Parton lying in the bathtub. "Islands in the Stream." Now that the third's been added, a much smaller mound they barely got covered in burlap before the blizzards set in, she thinks the trio looks more like a giant snowman got drunk and toppled over, his soft noggin slumped to the right. It was a hasty job, building that grave, but Mamma only became *more* pig-headed when upset, *less* inclined to listen to—much less heed—anyone else's advice. She'd wanted that soil piled high while the body was still warm, understand? It wasn't *skimping* if it meant getting her own way. Hell no it wasn't. Just get the burial over and done.

Don't cut no spirit ditch round the site, she'd said to the teamsters Daddy had booked for the job ages ago. *Waste of time. Any soul what can scrape its way free from all this ain't going to trip up on a little ol' channel in the ground. Don't be too precious with the backhoe; the hole ain't got to be perfect, just deep. Y'all know the drill. Speaking of which: don't fetch no auger for this dig, no concrete, none of them posts neither, nor them two-by-fours, nor them planks. Why fuss with tombs or chambers when already we're sinking a case of good steel down there? How many coffins does one corpse need, anyways? This ain't ancient Egypt and sure as hell ain't no pharaohs round here. Waste of good money, that's all this burial business is, a waste of good goddamn cash. Go'on and bulldoze the dirt back where it were scooped from; we'll tamp it ourselves later on. Nope, nope. Don't bother stacking no cairn over the whole shebang. Our goats can't graze on no goddamn heap of stones.*

When it came time, Mamma wanted the mess of death scrubbed clean out her house, swept from the yard, put in its place. Out of sight, out of mind.

Red Lucifer'll trade his pitchfork for a halo, Bets knows, before the old lady ever admits she might or should have done otherwise.

There's a whiff of clay in the breeze this morning, damp leaves and work-able mud. Bets tucks the legs of her baggy overalls into knee-high rubber boots. Zips her acid-wash jacket up to the chin. Sucks in cool air, breathes it out warm. It's too early yet for the sun to offer much in the way of heat, but already it's squint-making, bright as the bell-song luring folk down the lane to church.

"Ain't going to make much progress with *that*," Daddy had said a few minutes ago—words slurring across his bare gums—before answering that bronze-tongued call hisself. Normally, the cinder shovel Bets swipes from the fireplace set goes unnoticed; it's so small, she's carried it outside three times this week alone, used and returned it, without once getting caught. Today, though, she'd misjudged. Thinking he'd already jammed a cap over his balding head, pocketed a few coins for the collection plate, and hustled off to Mass, Bets had snuck into the sitting room and lifted the tool. She'd made it down the hall, through the kitchen, and had *just* slipped her boots on when Daddy had come clomping up the back steps.

"Forgot my Hail Marys," he'd mumbled. Reaching inside the door, he snagged a strand of beads off the key rack. Stopping long enough to deride Bets' choice of shovel. Not to ask why she was digging. Or where. Or what she hoped to find. Not to make a better suggestion.

Only to offer another two cents out of an endless wealth of criticism.

"Reckon Mamma had the right of it," Bets had muttered after him. "Without teeth, you sound just as stupid as you look."

Now she waits for the bells to hush before setting out across the yard. Blue jays razz her from cedar bushes nearby. Further afield, nuthatches and robins chirrup between the stark cornrows, beckoning her with sweet promises of summer. Smiling, she wonders what tunes birds warble in the city, if their notes are smoggy, thick with tar and rust. She tosses the shovel over the low fence, clambers after it, then trudges round to the newest mound's far side. In the field beyond, cheeping their hayseed chorus, a crew of brown-hooded sparrows scolds her for being late. Bold little buggers, they flit and hop and *pip-pip-pip* as Bets unearths a feast of worms.

Despite the harsh ground and harsher opinions, she *has* made decent headway. Kneeling in the groove she made yesterday, Bets digs into a hole already deep and wide as an apple barrel. The shovel's cast iron pan shunts into cold soil, clanging against pebbles. Scoop after scoop of dirt avalanches down the mound beside her, slow but steady. A regular rhythm of progress.

Few more hours should do it, Bets reckons. Not quite so long as it'll take Daddy to cycle through his Thorsday rituals. Reverend's sermon always runs just shy of noon. Wine and bread comes next. Confession and penance after that. Once all tears have been sopped and hankies wrung dry, the congregation drags itself a half-mile north for a palate cleanser of donuts, cherry pie, and sweet tea. As afternoon shadows start reaching for night, folk dust the icing sugar from their laps, brush the crumbs from their whiskers, drain their cups. A short march through the diner's parking lot and they've left the vinyl and Muzak, but not the sugar buzz behind them. After fetching cats and boars and billy-goats from pickup trucks on the way, they assemble in the Lady's glade beyond the streetlights. Knives come out in the gloaming. Bowls.

By the time these gifts have been offered and accepted, the ale-horn passed round, blood and verses spattered upon ancient oaks, Bets is bound to be done digging. She'll have made it through. And down. And *out*.

All by herself.

All with folks none the wiser.

Bets learned *real* young to keep any hopes to herself. Any efforts. To dream the same way she now shovels. Carefully. Quietly. Secretly.

It's the only way to stave off collapse.

Bets must've been ten or eleven when she first recognized that sudden burn in her belly, that hot flutter above her liver, for what it was. Not instinct so much as a flash of true understanding, a gut-deep feeling of rightness, of *knowing* what she has to do, what's to come. Call it a psychic moment. Call it divine intervention. Call it grit. When faced with important decisions— say, whether or not to sing at the Sunday school talent show—Bets felt a blazing hand gripping her innards. Twisting her resolve. Yanking her across the line between *missing out* and *daring to try*.

Silently telling her which path to choose, which future to follow.

Truth be told, the talent show was no big deal. A bunch of local folk and their kids gathered in the church's back room, Reverend on steel guitar and Miss Shayanne on piano. There were no prizes, no ribbons, no certificates. All the same, it was a challenge for a shy gal like Bets. A chance to be seen. To be heard.

To be noticed.

So she'd picked "Song for the Asking," a number she loved, one that ran well short of two minutes. A minute and a half, really. Next to nothing. In the lead-up she'd practically wore new grooves into Daddy's 45 LP, replaying that tune on the spinner in her bedroom, memorizing the words. Singing quietly, ignoring the strain on her throat. Bets had never mastered any instruments—she could get through "Heart and Soul" on her plug-in keyboard, and the first few bars of "Stand by Me"—so she'd decided to sing a capella. She'd wondered what the phrase meant, so went to the bookmobile and looked it up. A capella. *In the manner of the chapel.* Arranged that way, the familiar letters felt foreign on her tongue. Strange and lonely. Fitting, she reckoned. After all, it's just going to be her voice, open and vulnerable. Just her and whatever ears might listen.

Nerves jittered her down the gravel road to the church, then kept her standing in the small square room while most grown-ups sat on cheap plastic chairs, kids cross-legged on the floor. As other acts drew applause— for *what*, Bets can't recall—she leaned against one of many pin-boards, sweater snagging on hymns and construction paper art. Gaze fixed on her boots, she strained to remember the first line of her song. Grasped for the verses dribbling out of her mind. Blanked at the whole melody.

When Reverend finally called her name, so many faces had turned her way, some clearly bored, some smiling. Jesus and all them other wooden gods frowned down at her from painted bricks on high. Breath coming fast and shallow, Bets had pushed herself away from the wall. Heels scuffing between rows of seats, she'd made it to the front of the room. Swayed there a minute. Searching the darkness inside her skull, desperate for the right words.

Thinking it over I've—

What?

So sweetly I'll make you—

What?

Ignoring the burn, the twist, the knowing yank in her guts, she'd lifted her chin. Smiled at her audience. Chickened out.

"I still *sang*," she'd told Mamma later. Her folks hadn't known about the contest; it hadn't been in her plan to tell them at all. Her plan, such as it was, had been to amaze the crowd with her talent. To blow them so far away, it'd take weeks to bring 'em back down to earth. *We heard your gal the other day*, they'd gush to Mamma and Daddy at the Holloway feed store or the Napanee auction house or the gas station at Miller's Point. They'd brag on Bets' behalf. *What a set of pipes she gots! Swear to God, that child's part canary.*

The plan, such as it was, had been to surprise them into being proud.

Once it was over, though, Bets knew she'd missed the mark. *Knew* it but wanted to be told she hadn't done half bad. That she'd come close, which wasn't nothing. That she'd thunk on her feet, even, changing songs at the last minute, choosing a tongue-twisting choir tune folks could tap their feet to, instead of a two minute lullaby. That she'd done *something*, hadn't she just, never mind that she was only a kid.

"I hit all the notes, got all the words," Bets had said. Standing stiff in her bedroom doorway, she'd admitted failure to her mother's back. High up on a barstool, Mamma was hanging wallpaper she'd got on clearance: Christmas green spattered with cream-colored hearts. Bets had wanted navy, plain and dark and classy. Mamma had said it was too boring. Too mature. Too expensive. It was hearts or Holly Hobbie. Her choice.

"Everyone was right kind. Clapping and whistling like that." Bets had paused, grasping. "Still, I wish I'd done the other song."

"Guess you should've practiced more," Mamma had said, without so much as a glance over her shoulder. Cocking her head, she ran her palms over the strip she'd just hung, checking for bubbles. Glue smacked underneath each blister she'd found. The paper bulged, resisting each poke, each prod.

"Hand me a pin," Mamma had said.

The hole's waist-deep when Bets breaks for water and a piece of cold chicken. She swigs out of a dented plastic bottle. Gnaws fried flesh straight from the bone. Sweat's collecting above her lip, trickling down her temples and back, so she unzips her jacket and lets the breeze whisk the salt from her skin. Better that, she thinks, than going underhill like a living salt-lick. Practically begging ghosts to rasp their dry tongues across her damp places when, really, she'd rather they didn't.

Nanna Teenie has only done it the once, drawling a long cow-slurp across the cheek, after Bets had crawled into her grave that long-ago Sunday, determined to sing that goddamn tune from start to finish. Never said nothing, did Nan, but neither did she discourage. As a rule, she nodded way more than ever she shook that veiled head of hers. Like Mamma, she wasn't all that keen on hugging, but showed affection in other ways. She paid attention when Bets read aloud from her library books: atlases, mostly; outdated encyclopedias; dictionaries, so she'll know what's what. While Bets twanged through the entries, Nanna Tee placed a cold hand atop her warm one, squeezing support. And just that once, licking.

"Thanks, Nan," Bets had said, always meaning it, even while inching away. Far as she's concerned, it was a lucky bolt of storm-light that had cracked the middle mound's shell. A garden trowel Bets had wielded *just* so built on that god's work, widening a gap between the metal struts and scaffolding that held the burial chamber up, keeping the space below clear if not always dry. Most times Bets visited Nanna Tee—dropping through dirt, then dank air, then a hole torn in the soft-top of a '57 Buick—she wound up shivering on the car's oversized front seat, wet as clay.

Stuck behind the wheel of her finned casket, the old revenant really listens. Teenie doesn't agree with Bets just for the sake of it, but doesn't patronize. She's there for Bets, body and spirit. She's *present.*

She understands.

Mamma pretended not to know about the tunnel Bets had followed into her grandmother's chamber, nor the tarp she'd taken from the garage to cover it. She and Daddy never did care much what Bets did with her time, so long as she kept to herself, and kept that sameself *here.* After seventeen years under their roof, she's still cheaper than hiring seasonal labor and, in the long run, easier to manage. Though Winston and Queenie once thought it grand indeed, their farm's really too small to support many hands; the annual yield's not worth the price of extra mouths nor fancy machinery to replace 'em. A full pantry come winter relies on Bets helping with the spring planting, the harvest come fall. If she chooses to burrow into the dead lands in between, so be it. No reason the girl shouldn't always be covered in dirt.

Whenever Daddy was away dusting crops, doors were best kept closed at their place. Eyes lowered. Sketchpads held close to the chest. Notebooks scribbled in at night, under cover. Songs breathed, not even hummed. Unseen, unheard, Bets listened while Mamma grumbled on the phone about the sorry state of her house. Her marriage. Her life.

Sure as sunrise, the Aunties would come over next morning, armed with bottles and casks, to float Mamma out of her funk. They'd have Dolly on the turntable, a glass in each hand, smokes burning between chapped lips. The lot of 'em hooting and hollering, having such fun, it never failed to entice Bets into the living room. Soon as she peeped round the jamb, they'd call her in, put her on the spot, ask after her drawings or beg for a ditty, using words like *clever* and *perceptive* and *dark-horse* when she'd finally relent and pass her rough pictures round. Clutching her calico skirt, she'd creep in closer, passing the couch and coffee table, the uncomfortable rocker, and step up on the cold stone hearth to watch the hens peck and cackle. Searching for falsehoods in their flattery. Condescension in their comments. Finding none.

When they put the sketches aside, Bets saw their honesty, generous and plain. They wanted nothing from her but delight, maybe a song. Puffed as a robin, she'd sing 'til her face was pinker than theirs.

"Enough showing off," Mamma always snapped too soon, shooing Bets out.

"Let her stay, Gayle," said the Aunties, but by then Bets was already gone. Back down the hall, back to her books and paints. Back on her lonesome.

The cinder shovel's small but sturdy, the worn handle a good fit for Bets' grip. The blade's got some new notches and the shaft is bending, but it's holding up, keeping pace. *Shunt, spill, shunt, spill, shunt, spill.* Bets grunts as she digs, conserves energy by tipping the dirt gently beside her instead of tossing it like a stupid cartoon character. Folk who don't turn soil for a living have some highfalutin notions about work like this—suburbanites and city slickers pay top dollar to visit hobby farms, to crouch in their chinos and pull weeds for a spell, to shove their manicured hands in manure for a weekend and call it a Zen experience. Being in the moment. Focusing on the *now.*

Horseshit, Bets thinks, shunting, spilling. There's nothing relaxing about the pain in her lower back, the crick in her neck, the afternoon sunlight glaring off the dregs of water left in her bottle. With every spadeful, she's time-traveling. Imagining herself elsewhere. The past. The future. Anywhere but the present.

Anywhere but here.

There had to be someplace to start, she'd thought. Some first step she could take. Some way to catch a break.

"Maybe I could get a gig at the Sugar Spoon," Bets had suggested after dinner one night, when Mamma was mellowing on the couch with a cigarette and a bit of cross-stitch. There'd been an ad in the paper the day before, a local ragtime band looking for backup vocalists. Black and white, no pictures, the opportunity had been crammed in a few lines of text, printed between a psalm and a call for pageant judges.

She'd run the idea past Nanna Teenie that morning; the old ghost had nodded, squeezed, flapped her mouth enthusiastically. *No harm in trying,* Bets believed Nan'd said. So she'd dusted off the grave-dirt, gussied herself up, gone down to the saloon and auditioned before she could overthink herself out of doing it.

This time Bets performed the song she'd intended. Start to finish. And she'd done all right, maybe more than all right, her voice trembling only when she wanted. They said they'd call her tonight or tomorrow.

They'd smiled and said she was good.

Every time the phone rang, her belly squirmed.

"I hear they might be looking for singers," Bets had said, aiming for aloof, managing something more like half-contained fidget. Now that she'd already gone and done it, it was safer to broach the topic. Mamma couldn't ruin it after the fact. "Maybe I could try out," she said.

Mamma had tied off a thread, then reached for her smoke, balanced it between her needle-fingers. She took such a long drag, her chest rattled.

"Be reasonable," she'd said, squinting, exhaling clouds. "This ain't but another whim. Ain't it. When's the last time you picked up a pencil? Or played that keyboard of yours? This ain't no different. You ain't no *singer*, Bets. It's just a phase."

"But," Bets had begun. Stopping as the phone rang.

"Get that," Mamma had said, getting up. Heading off to the john. "I've had so much tea tonight my back teeth are floating."

"Got it," Bets had replied. Reaching over to the side table, she'd laid her hand on the receiver. Didn't pick up.

She isn't asking much. Not some round-the-world cruise on a ship bigger than Napanee County. Not a million dollar lotto win. Not to be fawned over in fancy-girl dress shops like those snobby ladies did Julia Roberts in *Pretty Woman*—a film Bets had adored, immediately and profoundly, and was foolish enough to say so. While the credits rolled on their TV, she'd sighed happily, hand fluttering up to her heart. "That was so *good.*"

"Bets is found herself a new calling," Daddy had said from the recliner, loud so's Mamma could hear it from the kitchen. "Fancies she's gonna be a *hoor.*"

She can still feel the heat of that flush. The lump jagging in her throat. The teary anger at being so misunderstood.

"It's just a movie," Daddy had said, laughing, clicking those damn silver teeth of his. "And you ain't got the figure to make that kind of money."

All Bets wants is to live a while in the city. *Downtown.* In an apartment. A sleek one with granite countertops and stainless steel fittings, picture windows without curtains, and halogen bulbs inset in white ceilings, beaming down like alien spotlights. She wants a place with no yard.

She thinks about the type of someone she'd have to become to match those upmarket joints. A catalogue model. A regular guest at the Grand Ole Opry. A rich man's wife.

Nope, Bets thinks, digging, digging. Scratch that last one.

If she can't find her own shine, she might as well stay home.

Shunt, spill. One little dig after another, accumulating, really gets her pulse going. She braces herself against the mound as the ground shifts beneath her feet. The crest is rising up fast in front of her; if anyone looked out the kitchen window right about now, they'd glimpse her blond bangs over the ridge, her hair teased up in a wave that's beginning to droop. They'd see the cool arcs of brows she's spent hours upon hours plucking. Pale green eyes that blink too much, fluttering to shut out a world that doesn't yet match the one hidden behind her lids.

Although this third grave's much smaller than the one Nanna Tee's in, it's still big enough to swallow a heavy duty Silverado whole. From chassis to skylight, quadruple headlights to a tray that can haul over three thousand pounds, the pickup's well and truly covered. *No sense burying nothing useful, nothing valuable*, Mamma insisted. *Sink rustbuckets instead of good timber.*

Always was so practical, her Mamma. Never did nothing without a solid reason. Never acted on a whim.

Bets straightens up, cuffs the sweat from her brow. Pauses to take in the familiar view one last time. The flag jutting out from the house's back gable, parachute fabric snapping in the breeze. All those red and white lines pointing nowheres, those jagged stars fading to nothing. At the end of the driveway, the rickety toolshed. She won't miss its oil stink, its spiders, its stubborn door. By the stoop, there's the swan-shaped planters Mamma bought at a flea market, cracked from too many cold snaps. The bleeding-heart bushes have grown wild around them, weird flowers bobbing in grass that was overgrown long before winter, and has now sickened into a yard of pukey yellow-green. *Phlegmatic.* That's another word Bets once looked up: means apathetic, unflappable. Literally, she thinks, looking at that useless lawn. So heavy and dull, even the wind can't budge it.

Nothing shiny round here, Bets knows, but what's underground.

Singing low, she keeps digging until she hits some.

Soon as Bets strikes metal, she tosses the shovel and starts using her hands instead. She's not worried about damaging the truck—the thing was a piece of shit long before it was buried—only, she wants to reach the cab without having the whole damn thing cave in. Between each scoop, she packs the dirt walls around and above her, suddenly grateful for the ground-freeze keeping the mound's earthen lid stiffly in place. The sloping tunnel is now twice her width and half again as tall. Cursing Mamma's stubbornness—it'd be so much easier if the pickup had been parked inside a cavern, the way Winston's jalopy and Nanna Tee's Buick were—Bets crouch-claws down to the bottom. Does her best terrier impression. Sprays soil up and out the hole behind her.

Luckily, her aim isn't too far off target. A window's topmost edge is poking up from the ground in front of her: not the windshield she'd expected, but the driver's side door. Scraping her fingers raw, she cleans the glass bit by bit, wiping away grime and the fog of her breath, until the pane is mostly clear. A ragged circle of light filters in over Bets' shoulder, reflecting grey on the panel's upper right corner. In blue shadows inside the truck's cab, a slight figure is buckled behind the wheel, dressed in her Thorsday best. Lace-gloved hands folded in her lap. Permed head bowed as though praying. Refusing to look up.

"Open up, Mamma," Bets says, knuckles rapping on the glass. "Don't make me break in."

Mamma's gaze flicks to the door, then back to her knees. Slowly, she bunches the lengths of her black skirt up onto her thighs, twisting the fabric around a glint of silver. Patting it in place, she straightens her shoulders. Rearranges her tarnished necklace, nestling the cross between ruffles on her blouse. Tilts the rearview mirror and fusses a minute with her hair. Acts like she's alone. As ever.

"Come on," Bets snipes, knocking harder. "*Mamma.*"

The ghost rolls her eyes, unrolls the window. Soon as it's cracked an inch, a dank gust of air whooshes out, reeking of smoke and tar and hospital-grade antiseptic. All the stinks of life that led her into death, clinging for eternity. It wasn't dramatic, Mamma's end. It was efficient. Expected. Not trusting anyone else to get the details right, she'd made all the arrangements herself. Hedging bets, she'd asked Reverend to send her off, *ashes to ashes and all that jazz*, then invited the Lady's diner sect to drive her into the ground.

That's my girl, Daddy had said proudly, before Mamma went and stole his smile for good. Keeping it for herself.

"Got my license," Bets says, talking fast so Mamma won't interrupt. "And a spot on the bookmobile's roster. From next week, I'll be driving the Napanee—Athabaska route. It's not much, but . . . "

Bets stops, swallows. Keeping her gaze down—if the gods are watching, they're watching, whether she's under wide skies or close earth—she wriggles onto one elbow, reaches back with her free hand. Paper crackles as she drags the map from her pocket, then smooths it between filthy palms.

Scrawled on a scrap torn from an old sketchbook, the road-lines are messes of crayon, the landmarks smudges of multicolored chalk, the street names and compass arrows scribbled in illegible marker. No matter which way it's held, the thing's damn near impossible to read. A kindergarten kid could've done better, no doubt about that.

Good thing you're set on broadening your horizons, girl, Daddy'd said when Bets showed it to him yesterday. *Most Wheelers know these roads inside out, but this* . . . He'd shaken his head, turning the map this way and that. *If you ain't inherited my sense of direction, well, you'd better ask yer Mamma for the next best thing. Reckon she'll give it to you easier'n she will me.*

But Bets knows Mamma never gave anything so easily as she did criticism, followed by her own—*the only*—opinion. Death won't have changed her mother that much.

She's counting on it.

Steeling her resolve, Bets holds out the drawing, keeping her hand flat and low, close enough for Mamma to lick. It really *is* the worst piece of art she's ever crafted, as appalling in the gloom as it is in full bright, but Bets yammers like she has so many times before when showing off what she's made. Too quick, too eager for approval.

"The bookmobile stops in the city twice a month to restock," she says, pointing. "*Here* and *here* and *there*. Don't know exactly where else I'm headed, but probably we'll follow the river," she wags her finger at a splotch and a purple squiggle, "then motor alongside the canyon a whiles." Brown penciled nonsense cuts across the page, so ugly Bets can hardly bear looking at it. "Reckon this map's going to lead me on some grand adventures, don't you?"

Chin lifted, Mamma rolls her eyes at the thing.

Don't hold back now, Bets thinks, suppressing a grin when Mamma uncrosses her arms, snatches and crumples the page.

How will you ever get by, the ghost's blue sneer seems to say. Magnanimous, Mamma fumbles at her skirt, freeing Daddy's silver-toothed map from the wool's dark folds. With a huff, she tosses it up into the dirt tunnel. *Don't let me stop you.*

"Oh," Bets says, smiling at last, running a thumb over the mouth-piece's worn ridges. A new song tickling her lips. A coal of certainty burning hot in her belly. "I won't."

———◆———

THE BRIDE IN SEA-GREEN VELVET

Robin Furth

"Have you brought her?" Sir Henry eyed the heavy burlap sack that Kane held in his right hand and impatiently tapped the steel tip of his ebony gentleman's cane against the polished marble tiles of his summer house floor. It was dusk—the time he always preferred to meet with Kane—and the sun was setting over his vast estate and over the crashing, ever-encroaching sea. But neither the beauty of the sunset nor the sound of the waves against the ragged cliffs were what made his pulse quicken. His heart was set upon much more sublime treasures.

"Yes, sir. Of course, sir." Kane half-bowed as he removed his cap, exposing thick, unkempt black hair threaded with gray. Sir Henry grimaced with distaste. He despised Kane's overt show of obsequiousness. It was a sham, and they both knew it. Yet it was as much a part of their twenty-year business interactions as the fat velvet purses which Sir Henry regularly handed over and which Kane inevitably stashed into his seemingly bottomless pockets. Sir Henry pointed at Kane's boots with the spiked tip of his cane. Graveyard mud still clung to his soles and heels in heavy clumps. In fact, he'd left a trail of dirt across the polished floor.

"Come now, man. You could have at least wiped your feet. Especially in the presence of a lady."

"Yes, sir. Sorry, sir." Kane walked dutifully to the doormat and wiped his shoes. There was something comical in his earnestness as he scuffed his soles back and forth, back and forth across the coarse fibers. "She was ever so hard to dig up," he said. "Buried in clay, she was. And ever so deep. No coffin, neither. Had to dig the clay out of her eyes."

With characteristic impatience, Sir Henry motioned for Kane to hand over the sack. But Kane tutted. "She cleaned up ever so well," he said. "But I had to do the work myself. Bought special detergent and all."

"You'll be remunerated, as you always are." Sir Henry held out his hand again, but Kane still did not budge. Instead, he stared at Sir Henry placidly.

"The field gate-guard, he had a gun. I risked my life, sir, to get this one for you. Though I must say, she's a beauty."

It was torture now, and Kane knew it. Sir Henry thought he would burst if he did not feel the sensuous weight of the sack in his hands. "Come, man. There will be an extra guinea for your trouble."

"Six."

"Excuse me?"

"Six guineas, sir. With regret."

Sir Henry rolled his eyes. The man was a pickpocket as well as a grave robber, but Sir Henry raised his hand and clicked his fingers. The manservant who had been standing by the door, quiet as a shadow, slipped out of the room. He returned a few moments later with a velvet purse, even fatter than usual.

"Your money," Sir Henry said as he held out the purse with one hand and held out his other for the sack.

"I would appreciate it if you counted it for me, sir, so that I can see it. It's not that I don't trust you, sir, but it's the guild's rules, as you know."

Sir Henry gave an exasperated sigh. That damnable guild. Thieves, pickpockets, drug dealers, grave robbers. Sir Henry felt demeaned by the need to work with them, but how else would he procure his darlings? He would have had an assassin kill Kane long ago if he could have found a more amenable lackey to cater to his needs, but none was available. In the sordid graveyard circles he trod, Kane was the best. Besides, do in Kane and one of his brethren would come in the night and slit the throats of everyone in the household. Or perhaps they would choose exposure or blackmail. He was certain the guild had a file on him heavier than this velvet purse.

"Forty-eight, forty-nine, fifty. That's fifty pounds, man." Kane did not reply, but waited patiently as Sir Henry counted out the final six shillings of his bonus. " . . . Five-and-ten, five-and-eleven, six shillings." Scowling, Sir Henry held out the purse. "For some men, Kane, that's a year's wages."

"And for some," Kane retorted, "it's less than pocket money." Covered in graveyard dirt as he was, Kane flashed a grin as false as a three-bob bit, then took the purse and stashed it in his coat's deep inner pocket. As he did so, the light caught the skull-and-crossbones insignia of his damnable guild, tattooed on the web between left thumb and forefinger. Sir Henry grimaced in distaste.

"Kane," Sir Henry said as the man turned to go. "Aren't you forgetting something?"

Grin wider than ever, Kane placed the voluptuously rounded sack in Sir Henry's hand—a hand that trembled with barely contained excitement.

"Thank you," Sir Henry said. "You are dismissed."

Kane bowed. "You know how to reach me should you need me," he said, and then stepped out of the French doors and into the shadows of the night.

Listening to the crashing of the sea against the cliffs' sheer drop only yards from the summer house's large glass doors, Sir Henry waited until Kane disappeared. Then, his hands shaking, he reached into the rough burlap sack and withdrew his prize.

His heart skipped a beat. Even in the jaundiced light of the gas lamp, she was exquisite. The very foundation of beauty lay in his hands. No flesh or sinew or muscle to mar the gorgeous symmetry, the perfection of the skull. Large, round eye sockets, gently curved orbital bones, delicate nasal cavity, slightly pointed chin, brow ridge both smooth and understated. She was the very essence of feminine charm. Scoundrel that he was, Kane had outdone himself. Hands still shaking, Sir Henry returned his prize to the grubby burlap sack. Blowing out the lamp, he exited the summer house, carefully locking it behind him.

As he walked toward the château's west wing, Sir Henry inhaled the scent of flowering gorse. To his left was the steep drop of the black cliffs, and beyond them the whispering sea where so many ancient sailors had drowned, mourned now only by the cries of gulls. The waters here were notoriously dangerous, as were the old gods who haunted them. Mara, queen of the hungry deep, keeper of the waters' secrets and of fishermen's nightmares. Sir Henry smiled grimly. She, too, loved to collect bones.

The studio sat at the end of a long, winding corridor, one of the many maze-like passages in this, the oldest part of the château. Once this great sprawl of buildings and subterranean tunnels had been part of a monastery, but the order had been dissolved in the late Middle Ages when the abbot was accused of sorcery. After that, the lands and buildings were taken over by Sir Henry's ancestors—an aristocratic but bastard line that some said the abbot had seeded himself.

As he listened to the echo of his footsteps and the distant rumble of the sea, Sir Henry contemplated the abbot's sad fate. He supposed that the Church just didn't understand what it meant to live this close to the salt, where life was precarious. But then again, any who had been stationed here long enough began to comprehend the risk. Even a hundred years ago, when the local church's façade had been restored, they left the mermaid there with her comb and her mirror, and the barnacle-encrusted skulls that encircled the front door. But then again, the workmen had been locals, and forcing them to obliterate such protective charms would have ended in mutiny.

Lifting the ancient iron keyring from his pocket and selecting an unusually ornate key embellished with gold filigree, Sir Henry unlocked the cast-iron gate that separated the studio from the rest of the building. The only other copy of the key belonged to DeMains.

Traversing the short corridor in a few swift steps, Sir Henry knocked on the studio door. A deep baritone voice called, "Enter!" and Sir Henry opened the door. As the hinges squeaked and the ancient oak portal swung inward, the smell of linseed oil and wet clay filled Sir Henry's nostrils. DeMains was there, as he almost always was. But today he sat at his desk, ink pen in hand, his face bathed in the mellow glow of an oil lamp. No doubt he was expounding on his latest theory about the benefits of flesh-depth measurement.

Glancing up from his work, DeMains smiled. "Sir Henry!" He stood and held out his hand. His fingers were surprisingly long and tapered for such a squarely built fellow. "To what do I owe the honor? I wasn't expecting you until tomorrow."

Sir Henry glanced at the nearby table covered with DeMains's sculpting tools: micrometer, several levels, piping, and bits of leather and sandpaper. On the far side of it sat a guillotine, a drill, and a bowl full of depth pins. They always made Sir Henry think of miniature golf tees.

"Something special today, DeMains," Sir Henry said, and then he passed the sack to his resident sculptor. DeMains withdrew the skull.

"My, but she's a beauty!" With a connoisseur's touch, he rubbed his fingers along the wide brow and the delicate eye sockets, finally fingering the sutures of the skull. "Not a day over twenty. Where did you get her? The palace cemetery?"

"No. The hangman's yard."

DeMains's eyes widened. "Her crime?"

"Murdering a faithless lover."

DeMains's smile spread into a grin as he stroked the girl's bare cheekbone. "Then we shall give her red hair."

"According to the police records, it was black."

"Red for passion," DeMains replied, and Sir Henry nodded.

"DeMains, you are a consummate artist, capturing the soul as well as the face of beauty."

"That's what you pay me for," DeMains replied, and then quieted for a moment. "On the subject of payment, it's your forty-ninth birthday next month. On the night of the Summer Solstice."

Sir Henry tucked his cane into the crook of his arm and sank his hands deep in his suit pockets. "Yes. I've been trying not to think about it."

"Seven times seven," DeMains said. "It's an important one." He tilted his head and stared sympathetically into Sir Henry's eyes. "You will need a special gift. One that entails a sacrifice." He glanced at the skull cradled in his hands. "She would do nicely."

Sir Henry pursed his lips. "It's not fair," he said, "for my birthday to interrupt what could be a lovely relationship."

"Life isn't fair," DeMains replied. "Regardless, the people expect it. With great tracts of land comes great responsibility. Remember what happened to your father."

"That occurred before I was born," Sir Henry stated as he frowned. "And I believe a good part of the tale was fabricated by fishwives eager for scandal."

But DeMains shook his head. "Belief does not change your responsibility, especially in the eyes of the villagers. We don't want outsiders involved, or the police, and local girls won't do. Times have changed. It's an elegant solution."

"Quite." Sir Henry took his hands out of his pockets and tapped his cane on the floor, his lips pouting. "It's still not fair," he said, "but I suppose you're right." He turned to go, then paused at the door. "Spare no expense," he said. "And call me when you give her eyes."

One week later, Sir Henry stood on the cliff edge and stared down at the moaning, ever-hungry sea. In his hand was an unopened bottle of cognac. Sea-fret blew into his face as the incoming tide boomed and crashed, eating away at the rock beneath his feet. It was only a matter of time before the cliff face tumbled into the depths, and with it, a little more of Sir Henry's heritage. But that was what it meant to be an aristocrat in these parts. To hold on to what you could, however you could, sacrificing whatever was necessary. It was rarely a pretty business.

Turning his back to the wind, which was redolent with brine and seaweed, Sir Henry strode to the most ancient part of the old abbey. Tucking the cognac under his arm, he removed a rusted iron key from the vast ring he'd hooked to his belt and unlocked the stout oak door that led to the catacombs. Once inside, he lifted the waiting torch from its iron sconce and reached into his coat for his silver pocket lamp. With the ease of long practice, he pressed the side button to pop the lid, and a second time to ignite the cap. The fluid-drenched wick caught with a crack and a hiss. Sir Henry stared at the yellow flame as it engulfed the torch's pitch-soaked head. It stank, but his nose no longer crinkled with distaste. After so many decades of traveling these lightless tunnels, he was used to it.

Shadows lurked around each corner and the dark spill behind every pebble and stone stretched long and ominous, like poisonous little secrets. Here in this underground place every sound was distorted. His footsteps echoed like the pounding of the sea in the caves below, and the very blood in his veins pulsed like a tide.

Soon he came to the shelves which housed his father's collection. He paused for a moment, letting the firelight play across a delicate crown of bone, the elegant arch of a brow, or plumb the lovely mystery of an eye socket. These were his first darlings, his earliest fantasies. As a boy, he had come down and played with them. In his imagination, he'd dressed them in exquisite flesh, though secretly he'd thought, even then, that bone was best—the very foundation of feminine splendor. In fact, he never found a woman so truly beautiful as one he had seen fully disrobed, one whose face he had been able to rebuild at his pleasure.

Placing his torch in a nearby sconce and setting the bottle at his feet, he reached to the highest shelf and grasped a bony visage by its hollows. He cradled it in his hands, as if it were the most precious jewel. His father had etched a name on every head in his harem, but this one had always been Henry's favorite. Lady Godiva—the woman who had ridden naked through a town, dressed only in her long, luxuriant hair. To her, bareness would be second nature. He kissed her serene, bony brow and tucked her under his arm. Picking up the bottle at his feet, he began to walk deeper into the catacombs. Despite his vows, the abbot always appreciated female company.

By flickering torchlight, Sir Henry journeyed deeper into the catacombs' twisting intestines. Veins of sea-green malachite and foam-colored quartz caught the light like phosphorescent algae. Long ago, before Christianity had been dreamed of, these tunnels were hollowed out by Stone Age miners who used the crystals in the strange rites they performed in honor of their sea gods, and later by men hungry for copper ore. Sir Henry paused near an ancient stone altar scattered with votive offerings of bone. Not even those Bronze Age innovators—mining for copper and trading for tin—could forget about the Old Ones of the sea. Clutching the skull more tightly, Sir Henry hurried on, suddenly eager for company.

Compared to the narrow, twisting tunnels used to reach it, the abbot's cell was palatial. A natural cavern, it had been painstakingly carved into fan arches, though instead of columns, the walls were adorned with glistening stalagmites and stalactites that made Sir Henry think of cascades of glittering seafoam.

After lighting the cell's seven torches, Sir Henry set his own torch in an eighth ornate sconce. The light flickered eerily across wall frescoes depicting the abbot's martyrdom. Images of the man being hanged, drawn, quartered, and burned shimmered in the torchlight. His scorched bones now lay in an oak chest bound with gold, which rested in a niche cut into the granite wall.

Sir Henry placed the skull on the stone slab that served as a table and then sat on a nearby boulder. "I've brought company," he said as he poured cognac into three waiting glasses.

A shadow unfolded itself from the oaken box and drifted toward the table. It had the rough dimensions of a man. Sir Henry knew from experience that the longer he stayed and the more he drank, the more manlike the shadow would become. Whether that was due to the abbot's memory returning or merely to the effect of the alcohol, he had no idea. But he supposed that, either way, the abbot's lack of distinct form was hardly surprising. He doubted he'd remember his own face after five hundred years of dust.

"To Beauty," Sir Henry cried as he stood and raised his glass to Lady Godiva's pale, bony visage. The Shadow raised the shadow of its glass in an equally enthusiastic toast, and the two—man and shadow—drank. Sir Henry swished the cognac around his mouth and felt the dull heat course through his body. It helped to disperse the chill of these ancient sea caves. He took a deep breath, since he wasn't certain how to phrase his next question. In the end, he decided that bluntness was best.

"My dear Abbot," he said finally, "may I borrow your treatise on the transmutation of base clay into flesh?" He could feel his companion's surprise. After all, that treatise had sealed the abbot's unhappy fate. "You see," Sir Henry continued, "it's my forty-ninth birthday soon. Seven times seven, on Midsummer Night."

Sir Henry thought he saw the shadow give a quick nod of understanding, and perhaps of sympathy. Slowly, it rose and drifted to a far corner of the room, directly below the section of the fresco that depicted his hanged body being pulled in four directions by galloping horses. Only in this image, the horses were sea horses, like mad kelpies charging through seafoam.

The abbot pointed to a foundation stone which, at some point in the past, had been loosened. Sir Henry's knees cracked as he knelt down and dragged the heavy stone out of the wall. Just as he'd thought: a hiding place. Slowly and carefully, he inserted his hand and then his forearm. Sifting through dirt and dust, he combed his fingers through every inch of the enclosed space. He soon realized that the hole was much deeper than he'd expected and had to thrust the rest of his upper arm into the hollow before his fingers brushed against what felt like a roll of parchment. Grunting, he pressed his shoulder against the wall and reached in as deep as he could. With a husky cry of triumph, he grasped the manuscript and withdrew it from its centuries-old hiding place.

Knees complaining, Sir Henry stood up with another grunt. Ignoring the dirt on his clothes, he broke the seal and unrolled the furled vellum. Just as he'd hoped: the last surviving copy of the abbot's blasphemous treatise. Brushing dust from his jacket-sleeve, Sir Henry decided to leave Lady Godiva for the night, despite the fact that she was one of his favorites. He only hoped that one day, when he was no more than a shadow, someone would be as kind to him.

The next morning dawned gray and stormy. Sea rain clattered against the windowpane as the wind swirled and howled. Sir Henry awoke with an aching head. His only solace was that the abbot probably didn't feel any better despite—or perhaps because of—a night spent discussing the miracle of transmutation.

At breakfast, his housekeeper informed him that DeMains had sent a message boy. The project was ready to view. Swallowing some peppermint water, Sir Henry wiped his lips and set out for the west wing, his heart beating in his chest.

At the doorway to DeMains's inner sanctum, Sir Henry paused. In an unusual moment of self-reflection, he wondered about the wisdom of the path he was about to tread. Why go through the trouble of winning a girl back from the dead only to then sacrifice her to the demons of the sea?

DeMains was right, times had changed, and sacrificing a living girl would be too dangerous. Yet the thought of abandoning such beauty to the demons of this place troubled and angered him. When it came to magic, he was competent enough, but he knew he could never best that vast power that crashed against stone and beach and cliff face, eating away at the land with its omnivorous hunger. Had it not consumed his father when he'd defied it? It was like time itself—eternal, intractable, beyond the power of any mortal to control.

"But occasionally it can be shaped to one's will," Sir Henry whispered to himself. "That, a mere mortal can do." He opened the door.

The first thing Henry saw when he entered was a sculptor's stand and on top of it, his newest darling veiled in sea-green velvet. DeMains came out of the back room, assiduously wiping his hands on a towel. He was smiling.

"I worked all night," he said. "She's far from finished, but I think you'll like what you see."

Sir Henry unveiled his prize. The pins were still visible and DeMains had only roughed in the fundamental musculature, but her eyes were in place, green as malachite.

"She has a soul, now," Sir Henry said.

"Or will soon," DeMains replied. "Have you thought of a name for her yet?"

"Lady Galatea," Sir Henry replied.

DeMains nodded his approval. "After Pygmalion's ivory lady?"

"In part," Sir Henry said. "But also after the pale nereid. *She who is milk-white*, the name means in Greek. The most beautiful of all."

In his mind's eye, Sir Henry saw the tenuous, invisible thread that still connected this skull to the spirit of a beautiful murderess, sent to the underworld well before her time. Closing his lids, he imagined that thread thickening, and then visualized himself—like the fishermen on that vast stretch of coastline over which he had dominion—hauling her back to the world of the living. It would not be easy. But then again, nothing worth doing ever was.

For three weeks, Sir Henry pored over the abbot's manuscript, puzzling out arcane symbols, referencing and re-referencing dusty books in his vast library. Sometimes he went out and stared at the sea, cursing it. The sea laughed at him. And then DeMains called him. She was ready.

In DeMains's studio, surrounded by the scents of turpentine and wet clay, Sir Henry removed the green velvet veil of his sea bride and gasped. She was

exquisite—from the malachite of her eyes to the ivory of her skin and the
arterial cascade of her hair, she fulfilled every promise of her beauty. "De-
Mains," he whispered, "you are a true artist."

With a small proud smile playing over his lips, DeMains bowed. "And
I finished her just in time," he replied.

"Yes," Sir Henry said. "Tomorrow is Solstice Eve, and the eve of my
birthday."

"Seven times seven," DeMains added.

Sir Henry sighed.

"Is everything else in order?" DeMains asked.

Sir Henry nodded. "The seamstresses have been working for a fortnight."

"Ah. It bodes well." DeMains cleared his throat. "Would you like . . .
um . . . someone to accompany you?"

Sir Henry shook his head. "No. A man's birthdays, like his marriages,
are a private affair."

DeMains bowed again. "As you wish."

"I wish nothing of the sort," Sir Henry added querulously. He was
staring at his sea bride and felt his heart ache at the sight of her long red
hair and green eyes. "But the law is the law."

"So it is," DeMains added philosophically. "So it is."

At half-past nine on Solstice Eve, Sir Henry set out from his château, eager
to finish the night's sordid business. As the sun sank toward the horizon and
the full moon rose in the sky, the pink clouds of sunset deepened to violet,
and then to indigo. The seven-hour twilight had begun.

Though the air was warm, the sea breeze was chill, and Sir Henry
shivered as he carried his shrouded beloved in his arms. Over one shoulder
he'd slung a sack filled with everything he would need to welcome the
dawning of his birthday, as he had every year since he'd come of age.
Tomorrow was his birthday as it had been his father's, and his grandfather's,
and his great-grandfather's. He'd never questioned the oddness of this
reoccurrence any more than he'd questioned the existence of the sea cliffs,
or the gulls, or the hunger of the briny deep. It was as much a part of his
inheritance as the château or the deference of the sailors, the fishermen,
and their fishwives.

Climbing carefully down the steps cut into the sea cliffs, he focused on
the worn stone beneath his feet. How long had this staircase been here? No
one knew, but he suspected it was as ancient as the Stone Age settlements

dotting the coastline, as old as the standing stones and barrows lining the grand processional that led here from the great stone circles of the east and north.

The staircase ended and Sir Henry carefully tucked his beloved into his shoulder sack before beginning the final stage of his journey. With an agility that belied his years, he scrambled down the steep scree-face, holding tightly to the old knotted rope his father had secured to the rock overhead. He knew from childhood outings that the scree, fallen from the cliffside, was full of fossilized sea creatures—oysters, trilobites, and the twisting palaces of conch shells.

Landing on the sand with a thump, Sir Henry turned his back to the cliff and let his gaze drift over the moonlit beach. The tide was out, but this was no natural tide, as this was no natural night. Though at its zenith the sea usually crashed against the black cliffs and at its nadir was reduced to a gentle lapping at the sand just a few yards away, tonight the mellow gold beach was exposed for more than half a mile, and the sea had been forced to lay bare her hidden treasures of kelp and bladder wrack, starfish and coral, wrecked ships and rotting sea serpents. Even those secret creatures usually hidden in the ocean's depths were stranded in tide pools. Now those strange, phosphorescent monsters stared up at the moon and pale stars with huge lidless eyes, or gasped, their razor-sharp gills open, dying on the sand. The bones of a long-dead sailor and those of a mermaid, entangled in a final, passionate embrace, shimmered in Diana's light. But it was on the horizon that Henry's eyes focused as he stood with his back to the cliff.

Halfway between himself and the water's edge rose a stone circle, enormous and ancient, exposed by the withdrawing tide. Like this expanse of beach, it was only visible one night each year. Sir Henry couldn't help but wonder whether it existed in some liminal realm between worlds, a place that came into being during this night's strange twilight.

Behind him, a low croak sounded. Glancing over his shoulder, Sir Henry spied a frog crouching on the scree between two clumps of rough seagrass. Swiftly, he reached down and snatched it. The frog struggled, but Sir Henry held it fast and then secured it in his sack. It kicked and bounced for a moment before lying still. Sir Henry smiled. Finding it was lucky. Carefully balancing his shoulder sack again, he began to walk, bending now and then to gather the strange treasures that would help him accomplish his task.

By the time he reached the seahenge, Sir Henry's arms were piled high with magical finds and he was sweating. But still, as he approached the circle of monoliths, he felt his skin grow cold. Carefully he placed his treasures on the ground, and then his sack. He was so close now. The moon was bright and the tall stones jutted like the ragged teeth from the gaping maw of some enormous buried beast. And at the circle's center, rising like a many-headed hydra or the tentacles of some colossal, fossilized kraken, were the roots of an ancient oak. It had been buried in a time before remembering, its branches and bole within the earth and its lower trunk and thick roots rising and writhing toward the sky. Like the stones, it was only visible one night each year, and belonged to this twilight world which itself belonged to both sea and land, below and above, sleeping and waking.

With a courtly bow, Sir Henry took a step forward and entered the circle. His skin tingled as the shadows of the stones fell upon him. "I have come," he said, "as was promised long ago. I have come as my father came, and his father, and his father before him, back to the time before time when we emerged from your branches and bark; back before we wrested this land from the sea. I have brought you my bride, who is also my gift to you, as she is to the Ancient Ones of the Salt. But first, as you gave us life, I give you light."

Sir Henry approached the tree deferentially. When he was close enough to touch the roots, he reached for his silver pocket lamp and pressed the side button. The cap ignited with a hiss and a whoosh, lighting the wick already drenched with fluid.

Delicately, Sir Henry reached forward and touched the flame to each rootling tip. The old sea-soaked oak caught and sparked and spat and finally burned with the aqua flame of salt-infused driftwood. Around and around the tree he walked, lighting the lowest rootlings like the many wicks of a giant candelabrum. And as each thin finger of wood ignited, the aqua flames spread upward from root to root, until the whole underworld canopy was ablaze and Sir Henry had returned to where he had started.

Stepping back, he shaded his face from the heat of the weirdling fire that flared up without devouring the wood, and which left the bole untouched. Beneath the flaming underworld oak, he loosened the drawstring of his sack. Ignoring the croak and hop of the struggling frog, he reached inside. As the sea slapped its watery hands against the beach, drawing a murmur of pebbles toward the deep before tossing them back with a hiss of seafoam, Henry withdrew a silver knife engraved with runes, a small sack of grave clay taken from his lady's first resting place, a purse of herbs, a vial of elixir, a goblet whose cup had been cut from his great-grandfather's skull, a bottle of his best champagne, a shimmering folded dress, and a huge conch shell inlaid with silver. Finally, he withdrew his veiled prize.

Slowly, like a man undressing his bride on their wedding night, Sir Henry unwound her caul of sea-green velvet. As her long red hair caught in the salt breeze and blew about his arm like freshets of blood, he let her wrappings fall to the sand. Then, in triumph, he held her up to the night sky.

In the aqua light of the flaming tree, her hair burned with all the colors of hell and her glass eyes sparkled, green as sea urchins. The most gorgeous mother-of-pearl could not compare with the luster of her pale skin, nor oysters with the succulence of her lips.

With the deference of a courting suitor, Sir Henry laid the head of his lady upon the sand. Then he set about building her a body.

Her spine—from neck to curved pelvis—he took from the remains of the amorous mermaid. The bones of legs and feet, arms and hands, lovely fingers and precious toes he built from driftwood and coral. Her lungs were sea sponges and her tendons long strands of kelp wrapped around the muscular innards scooped from great scallop shells. Womb and bladder were sea cucumbers, her ovaries starfish, and her liver a giant sea leach. Her gallbladder was a yellow snail and her innards a writhing sea worm pulled from below the sand, its circular mouthful of teeth snapping. For breasts, two more lovely rounded sea sponges, and for nipples, tiny pearls.

Almost finished, he sat back on his heels and gazed upon the body of his beloved, and at her head, which rested several feet away. She looked like a beautiful saint—beheaded and flayed—though the gods this lady served were no Christian ones. Sir Henry sighed. The only missing organ was a heart.

He reached into his sack. With a frightened ribbit the frog leaped, but Sir Henry caught it deftly in one hand. Lifting it high, he felt the strength of its struggles and the rhythmic swelling and pulsing of its throat as it breathed. Oh, it would do nicely! He plunged it into his beloved's chest where it snuggled between the sea sponges and hid.

Now all he needed was skin.

At the tide line, Henry filled his sack with wet sand rich with sea lice and tiny, translucent crabs, then lugged it back to the circle of stones surrounding the flaming tree. Once inside its circumference, he rested the heavy sack on the ground beside his lady's body and knelt down.

One by one, he added grave clay, herbs, and elixir. When the last of these was added, the mixture frothed and bubbled. Tiny lice and crabs rose on the foam and scuttled madly over the sides of the sack, trying to escape. Unbuttoning his fly, Sir Henry withdrew his stiff member and began to stroke it, focusing his mind on the beautiful face of his lady and the lovely skull beneath. He came to climax swiftly, directing his pearly glitter into the mixture. As he buttoned his fly, he thought it was time to add the final ingredient necessary to bring this flesh to life.

Raising the ritual knife, he uttered a guttural prayer and then sliced into the flesh of his right forearm. As blood poured into the sand mixture, he whispered another spell. Arm still bleeding, he reached both hands into the bubbling, frothing mix and began to knead.

He could feel its texture change. The grains of sand—both shell fragments and pebbles—began to dissolve. The smoothness of what resulted reminded him, oddly, that sand was the main substance in glass. But what he kneaded and stretched was neither sand nor glass but something between clay and flesh. Its color, softly ruddy from the red of his blood, was the hue of a lady's blushing cheek.

With the finesse of a skilled sculptor, Sir Henry attached head to body with muscles and tendons formed of stout kelp, and then he began to layer skin upon his beloved. As each delicate membrane was stretched over her muscles and bones and organs, it set for a moment and then softened. Sir Henry could see the little capillaries sprout and grow and spread through the dermal strata as he prepared and stretched each one, thin and delicate as a frond of seaweed, over her sleeping form. As the seventh layer set and softened, her chest rose in a gentle sigh. But though the body had begun to respond he knew that her form was, on the whole, still lifeless, since it was not yet animated by a spirit. And though the form he had given her was beautifully feminine, its nether regions were, externally at least, still sexless. But before he performed that particular surgery, his lady deserved to be dressed.

From the sand where he had laid it with such care, Sir Henry lifted her shimmering folded dress. In the light of the blazing underworld oak, he shook it out.

Ah! His seamstresses had not disappointed him! Blue-green as velvet seahorn and trimmed with sand-gold braid, the gossamer-fine gown glistened in the light of the fire. Turning his back to the flame, he held it up to the sky and saw the Pearl of Diana shining through it. Such translucent delicacy! The great fan sleeves were like the wings of a butterfly and the dainty bodice like a sheath sewn from the overlapping petals of fragrant flowers.

With the care of a lady's maid, Sir Henry dressed his doll. Over her head went the gown, and into the great fan sleeves he slid her arms. The bodice he loosened, since the color of her nipples was not yet complete, and though he pulled the gown to her hips, he left the join between her legs—as yet virginally unbroken—bared.

For this bit of work, Sir Henry would need more of his own fluids.

Uncorking the champagne, he poured some bubbly liquid into the chalice cut from his great-grandfather's skull and drained it. Thinking of God, and of the creation of Eve from Adam's rib, Sir Henry cupped the swell of his Galatea's breasts, traced his fingers over her colorless nipples, then ran his hands along the base of her ribs and clasped the taper of her waist.

He was ready. Once more he brought himself to climax, spraying his jism into what remained of the flesh-clay mixture contained in his sack. Then he squeezed the cut on his arm, breaking the scabby clot so that it could bleed some more.

In his excitement, he'd been reckless with the initial incision, and the reopened wound was deeper than the original. The spray of blood that flooded the sand both fascinated and horrified him. As a wave of weak dizziness swept over him, he quickly bound his wound, fearing he would faint and bleed to death if he did not do so with alacrity. Blinking, he began to knead again. Blood spread through the mix, dyeing it the crimson of a newly opened rose. The mixture, already smooth, was now as soft and silky as petals.

First, Sir Henry gave color to her nipples, and the addition of this ruddy clay made him swollen and erect again. Her legs were—by necessity— already splayed, and so he formed the delicate folds of her labia, fine and slick and smooth. Her full skirt was still rucked high, and so he inserted his middle finger between those nether folds, creating her vagina. Though most of his jism had gone into the making of this, the smoothest and most delicate of flesh, a single pearl-like drop of his own fluid remained, and so he balanced it on the tip of his finger and reached into the recesses of her, where that tight tunnel met the neck of her womb, and deposited it there. After all, it was their wedding night. When this was accomplished and their marriage consummated, Sir Henry stepped back so that he could examine his creation.

Oh! His hands must have been guided by the gods, since not even DeMains at his most inspired could have created a lovelier or more perfect form. With her skirt pooled around her hips and her bodice undone, she looked like a ravished bride, though the porcelain calm of her expression bespoke a serenity rarely experienced by mere mortals.

Slopping more champagne into the bone chalice, Henry drank deeply. Drunk on bubbly and beauty and moonlight and fire, and giddy from loss of blood, he began to dance around his lady, singing and chanting in the guttural language of the dead which he'd memorized from the abbot's treatise.

As the sea wind—until now unnaturally calm—picked up force, Sir Henry danced, reckless as a teenage boy drunk on his own lustiness. With a final rasp of spells, he picked up the silver conch shell and raised it to his lips. Then he blew.

The blast—clear as a silver horn—bounced off the cliffs and echoed over the beach. For a moment the wind calmed, and then, as if in answer to his call, it gusted in his face, carrying with it the smell of salt and the echo of some great droning instrument of the deep. The sound sent a chill down his spine and raised gooseflesh on his body.

The unearthly echoes died back, and for a moment there was silence. Sir Henry could feel the quickening of his pulse and the pounding of blood in his ears. Something was coming. A wave crashed upon the beach with a frill of white seafoam and then drew back again.

From the far end of the beach, where the sand curved and disappeared and the cliffs met the sea, came a woman's high-pitched scream of terror. Almost immediately, it was followed by the angry howl of a pack of dogs.

Holding his breath, Sir Henry waited. His right arm was bloody and bandaged, his trousers sand-caked and rolled to the knee, his shirt unbuttoned, and both cravat and jacket had been abandoned. But for the first time in his life, he had forgotten about himself—so focused was he on the fate of another.

Straining his ears until he thought his head would burst with the tension that stretched from temple to temple, he tried to listen for any new sounds on the beach. At first there were none. But finally, he thought he discerned something other than the throbbing of his blood and the blowing of the wind and the crashing of the wavelets upon the sand.

Yes! Coming toward him now from the far end of the beach was the rapid, crunching sound of someone running. He squinted. In the light of the full moon he thought he saw movement, but the bright blaze of the tree behind his back obscured his vision. He waited, heart hammering in his chest.

Yes! Yes! There it was! Someone or something was most definitely running toward him. Though he could not see what it was, churning sand flew upward, as if sprayed by invisible toes and heels as they hit the beach, flying forward in a panicked fury. Sir Henry squinted again, trying to discern the exact form of the thing. But as it came closer, he realized with a terrible chill that what arrowed toward him was not a thing at all. It was a shadow.

From the far end of the beach, those unearthly dogs howled again. Henry thought of his own hounds at the chase, mad for the scent of blood, jaws lathering, eyes wild. But the beasts that barreled toward him sounded gargantuan. They howled with deep, brutish, unearthly yowls that echoed off the cliffs and rolled out to sea. The air was full of it!

The shadow-girl whimpered in terror. Henry felt the breeze of her movement as she swept past him, saw her footprints impress upon the sand, delicate as a deer's tracks, toes splayed, balanced on the balls of her feet. And for a moment, he saw a wavering silhouette standing between himself and the light of the blazing tree. It was a darkness—a shadow cast by nothing— and then it dove into the vacant body he had made, as if for solace and for shelter. And Henry noticed for the first time that until now his sculpture had cast no shadow of its own.

But there was no more time for thought. The hounds were pounding along the beach, their howls thick with saliva and excitement. They, too, were shadows—great looming blots of muscular darkness. Henry could feel the vibration of their weightiness as their invisible paws struck the sand, sending sharp grains flying upward. He felt them leap and he ducked and rolled— uncertain of his safety if they fell upon him—but even as they leaped into the light to fall upon the girl, the blazing tree sparked and spat and blazed to twice its size, engulfing the shadow-hounds in its blue-green rage.

Screeches of animal pain—yowling and whimpering and squealing, both as pathetic and as terrible as their fearsome, hungry barking. Rising to his knees, Sir Henry covered his ears. He could not bear it! But even as he squeezed his eyes shut, the squealing dwindled and disappeared. Finally, he felt safe enough to open his eyes again.

His lady was no longer inert clay; she was living flesh. She writhed on the beach, her smooth, bare legs shimmering in the oak's bonfire light, her thighs and sex still gleaming with his spent seed. He could see her beautifully formed breasts with their coral-colored nipples and the cascade of her blood-red hair.

But something was wrong. She clawed up her dress to expose her belly and screeched, back arching in agony. Her belly was swelling, doming, a vertical line darkening the flesh between navel and pubis. Dumbfounded, Sir Henry's own legs weakened. He had brought her back, yes. But he had brought her back with child. His child.

Suddenly he thought about the tales of his father's demise and a chill froze his heart. By the blazing tree, the girl held her swollen belly with one hand and coughed into the other, emptying her newly formed lungs of sand. Tiny crabs scrabbled from between her lips, and Sir Henry saw with dawning horror that one of those tiny, almost translucent crustaceans was crawling across the web of skin stretched between the girl's left thumb and forefinger, its tiny appendages pausing, for less than a moment, upon the skull-and-crossbones insignia of the guild.

NO! Sir Henry thought as he shook his head from side to side. He would not be replaced. Not by some bastard child he had not meant to seed, child born of a murderess, a bitch of the guild. Kane had tricked him!

Lunging forward, Sir Henry grabbed the girl by the hair and dragged her toward the encroaching tide.

"They are coming for you!" he screamed hysterically. "They are coming for you!"

Flailing and screaming, the girl fought him. She grabbed the hand entwined in her hair and hammered the sand with her feet. At the circle's edge, she bit his injured forearm, and with a spasm and a curse he released her tresses. As she scrambled toward the fire on her hands and knees, she swept the sand, searching for a weapon. As if by providence, her fingers brushed against Sir Henry's knife.

Braying like a mad beast, he dove at her and grabbed her by the throat. As he shook her, trying at once to break her neck and throttle her, she raised the knife as high as she could and brought it down with all her strength.

A hiss escaped from Sir Henry's lips, a hiss which quickly rose into a wail. The sharp blade had pierced the intercostal space between his ribs, just to the right of his breastbone, skewering his lung.

With a shocked, gurgling cry, he reeled backward, his lax hands releasing his Galatea's neck. Mouth wide, he slapped the hole in his chest, as if he either couldn't believe the blade's edge had been real, or thought he could stanch the blood that now flowed everywhere. But it was too late. Gasping like a fish hauled onto the beach, he fell onto his side, desperately trying to suck air. His skin turned blue and great gouts of blood poured from between his lips.

Still clutching the knife in her left hand, the girl stumbled to her feet. But as Sir Henry gasped and crawled toward her, she danced back on the pretty toes he had shaped, eluding his grasp.

From somewhere on the cliffs above, a conch shell sounded three times, and the flames of the underworld oak flared up into the night, as if eager to eat the stars. Then, as if the oaken bonfire had seeded distant flames, fifty torches flared into life. A chanting began, carried out to the sea on the swirling winds.

Ave Mara, Salve Regina, Dea sancta . . . thou divine controller of sky and sea and of all things . . . winds, rains, and tempests thou dost detain, and, at thy will, let loose. . . . Deservedly art thou called Mighty Mother of Gods . . . divine one, queen of divinities, we invoke thee . . .

A great glowing wave rose up out of the sea and crashed on the beach in a glitter of phosphorescence, bringing with it a spill of bones and shells and long-lost jewels dredged from the deep. And then, as if rising from the seafoam itself, came the Ancient Ones.

They wore the bones of long-drowned lords and ladies, and of sailors washed overboard and lost at sea. Their robes were sea-green and sewn with pearls. Their crowns were of shells, woven with the purple blisters of sea wrack.

In the unsteady light of the burning tree, their faces flickered, now with the delicate beauty of mermaids and the hulking girth of mermen, then with skin like mother-of-pearl, and finally with the faces of sea-eaten skulls. They drifted forward with each incoming wave that crashed upon the beach, their silent robes sweeping the sand and stones and litter of broken shells which murmured softly as they were caressed by the foam.

A woman stepped forward, taller than the rest and both regal and terrible. Her hair was of kelp, her nails sharks' teeth, and her lips pink coral. The jewels she wore must have belonged to a long-dead queen and her crown was a circlet of gold. Her eyes were two snails whose antennae moved back and forth restlessly as they surveyed the scene. From the cliffside, the prayer swelled again: *Te, diva, adoro tuumque ego numen invoco, facilisque praestes hoc mihi quod te rogo. . . .*

The queen smiled a small, mocking smile. Her teeth were white barnacles, finely made but razor-sharp. She gave an almost imperceptible nod and two drowned sailors, still partially fleshed, walked forward. Brandishing her knife, the heavily pregnant girl danced backward. But it was not for her they came.

Sir Henry's head lolled to one side. He wanted desperately to beg for mercy but could barely drag a single rasping breath into his lungs, which felt like they were being crushed by his own thudding heart. His lips were as blue as those of the long-dead sailors who hauled him up. In some fast-fading recess of his mind, he recognized the weave of their pullovers, the particular pattern of stitches and knots that identified this shoreline. These were the ghosts of men who owed him their allegiance, but allegiance, it seemed, shifted with the tide.

Bowing to the pregnant girl, they dragged Sir Henry back into the water. From between his lips burbled one final belch of blood before his skin and muscle and integument—formed from the stuff of this beach and mixed with the blood of his father almost fifty years before—began to re-turn to that from which they were made. Even as he struggled weakly, Sir Henry's flesh fell from his bones in great chunks of sand, like a child's castle built upon the shore and then demolished by the waves.

Though her pulse beat in her throat, the pregnant girl stood tall, as was right for one of such noble blood. The queen regarded her coolly, the snails of her eyes stretching forth. The tide had now drawn in enough to lap at the girl's bare feet, and to occasionally splash at the underworld oak's lower branches, making the flames hiss in that ancient animosity of fire and water even older than the world.

"What will you do with him?" the girl asked quietly.

"'Tis the night of the tithe," the queen responded in a voice as raspy as the cries of seagulls but resonant as whale-song. "We shall suck his bones, as is our right."

"And what of me?"

The queen gave another thin smile. "Serve us well, daughter mine. And remember, this land is ours." As she turned to go, her mermen lifted her high, and her mermaids strewed her watery path with pearls.

"In seven years, then," the queen said without turning, and her mermen transformed into kelpies, great water horses which bore her upon their backs. Then queen and retinue dissolved into a receding wave and were gone.

Alone on the beach, Lady Galatea fainted.

∽

When she awoke, the Solstice was dawning. She lay upon the scree at the base of the cliffs, surrounded by seed pearls. The underworld oak was invisible beneath the waves, as it was on each day of the year, save one.

Wiping her salt-stiff hair out of her eyes, Lady Galatea sat up. Staring at the skull-and-crossbones insignia on the webbing of her left hand, she listened to the hiss of the waves upon the scree and drew in a ragged breath. She could remember nothing before this moment.

The baby kicked and she pressed her hand against her swollen belly. An image of Sir Henry rose before her eyes. Him, she remembered. A shadow fell between her and the dawning light. She looked up.

A man stood before her, his cap in his hand. He had a mop of unkempt black hair, threaded with gray. Between his left thumb and forefinger was a skull-and-crossbones tattoo exactly like her own. She shaded her eyes with her hand.

"Do I know you, sir?"

The man nodded gravely.

She stared at that tattoo again, so black against his pale skin. "I do believe we are related."

The man knelt before her. "That we are, Lady. By blood as well as by calling." He offered his hand and she took it, standing with difficulty.

"I murdered my husband," she said, though she held her head high, both proud and defiant. Kane did not reply, but continued to clasp her hand in his. "He betrayed me and so I killed him. I believe I shall hang for it."

Kane squeezed her hand gently. "Your husband was taken by the tide. All the village was witness. He was given back to the sea as was just and right, like every man of his line as far back as any can remember. It was the tithe they swore to keep these lands."

"Will it happen to me?"

"No, Lady."

"And to my son?"

Kane did not answer at first, but then replied, "He will have many fine years before such a fate befalls him." He offered his arm, and she took it.

"Where are we going?"

"To the Great House on the cliff."

"The château?"

Kane nodded.

"Do I live there?"

"Aye, Lady."

At the base of the cliff, DeMains waited, a brocade shawl in his hands. When she approached, he placed it around her shoulders. "You are even lovelier than I thought possible," he said.

"Your words are kind, good sir," she answered graciously. "And your name is?"

"DeMains, Lady," he said with a sweeping bow. "Ever your servant." Then he took her hand and kissed it.

But even as the sculptor lifted his lips from her pale hand, Lady Galatea gave a little cry and clutched her belly.

"The child," she said. "I think it is time."

The two men exchanged a glance.

"Yes," Kane said. "Today is the Solstice. Come. We must get you to safety."

With the two men holding her arms and gently guiding her, Lady Galatea made her way up the cliff to the château, where the morning fires were already being lit.

—◆—

SUCCULENTS

Conrad Williams

They went on a long bike ride under a punishing midday sun. Much of it was along well-trodden pathways through scrubby brush. Large swathes of deep sand meant there was little traction; you had to get off and push. Graham was sweating hard by the time they reached Cabo Sardao. He was grateful for the rest; glad too that he'd had to bring up the rear because Felix, his six-year-old son, was struggling more than most. The rest of the group stood around watching their arrival. One of them started a slow handclap that was taken up by the others. He gritted his teeth against the urge to offer a rebuke. Watch your temper, he warned himself. It was something Cherry was often remarking upon.

You 're getting worse as you grow older . . . you need to just kick back and not let things irritate you so much . . . there's a heart attack up ahead, you know, just waiting for you. Remember that time . . .

Ricardo, their guide, was talking now in his halting but charming English, about the spits of rock reaching out over the bay. Steep cliffs fell away on either side. Earlier they had watched as intrepid bathers carrying towels inched down the sheer drop, aided only by old ropes left behind by thoughtful climbers. It seemed a big risk to take, no matter that the rewards were your own private beach.

"You walk slowly and carefully if you want to see stork's nest," said Ricardo. "If he trips and falls he has wings. You don't, I think."

"Do you want to see the nest, Felix?" Graham asked.

"Yeah! Is it storks with the big legs? Or is that herods?"

"Herons. They both have big legs. And so does Sheila over there."

No need for that, Graham. You're on holiday. Be friendly.

He thought of Cherry back at the apartment, gorging herself on *pastéis de nata* and drinking Super Bock by the pool. She had booked them the mountain bike activity as a surprise. *Bonding time for you and the ankle-*

biter, she'd called it. When he asked her why she couldn't come along too, she grew defensive. *You know I can't deal with heights. I'd hold everybody up.*

The other members of the group began moving forward along the narrowing path. Graham took Felix's hand and followed. He watched Sheila's backside as she picked her way through the thigh-high grasses. Keep that in your sights and you can't go wrong, he told himself, then had to stifle laughter. He was thinking of Star Wars for some reason, and of Luke Skywalker guiding his X-wing down to do battle against the Death Star. *That's no moon.*

"What are you laughing at, Dad?" Felix asked.

"Nothing. Just mind your step, okay? And keep hold of my hand."

Graham was envious of those who paid little heed to the precipice. Heat haze smeared the sea-chewed promontories further south. If he squinted he could just make out the car park where they had begun their tour. His boy's hand loosened in his grip; he reinforced it, and told Felix not to mess around.

Once he could see the nest—an arrestingly large aggregation of criss-crossed sticks that lipped over the edge of the cliff, as if the stork was cocking a snook at its precarious

situation—Graham felt no compunction to get any closer. He didn't want a photograph; there were no chicks, the stork was not in residence . . . it resembled little more than an abandoned game of Jack Straws.

"Come on, Felix," he said. "Let's get back to our bikes." He felt his relief grow with every step nearer the trail. So far, this holiday had involved too many of the things he preferred to avoid in everyday life: heights, blistering heat, exertion. He wished he was back at the hotel with Cherry. Felix loved the pool; they could bond themselves silly in there without the worry of punctures, or falling to their deaths, or storks attacking.

Or Sheila's backside.

Our cruisers can't repel firepower of that magnitude.

"Are you being okay?" Ricardo asked.

"Fine," Graham choked, turning around to see the rest of the group queuing up behind them as they inched back along the path. "I must have just breathed in some pollen or something. I'll be okay in a minute."

"Take a five," Ricardo said. "There's something anyway I want you to look at."

The group stared at Graham: bovine, sweaty, ill-dressed for the weather and the activity. He could already feel the rough canvas hems of his shorts abrading his skin; there'd be blisters later, or at the very least an ugly red chafing. What happens when middle-aged people get off their arses for a week. Short-sleeved shirts striped with back sweat. Red temples. A sluggishness; a lethargy. He remembered being Felix's age: football and tag in the back garden for as long as it was light enough to see. Drinks and snacks on the lam. When did you lose that playfulness, that drive? When did you go from let's play out to let's lie in?

Ricardo was on his knees in shrubbery that looked as if it had come from a science-fiction film set. The ground was carpeted with stunted plants with thick leaves and fat clustered flowers the color of mustard.

"See this?" he said, pulling one of the flowers clear of its receptacle. An aperture in the ovule wept clear fluid over Ricardo's fingers. He licked it clear.

"Hideous," spat Sheila, her voice cracking with amused disgust.

"Not at all," Ricardo insisted. He took hold of the ovule with both hands and teased it open. There was a clearly audible suck. "This plant she is known as 'Mothers Tears'," he said. "Because, look, she is so crying all the time."

He pulled up a few more of the plump hearts and passed them around. Everyone regarded each other blankly. Graham was reminded of the kids in his class when he handed out musical instruments for the first time.

"Now, you are watching," Ricardo continued. He lifted the parted ovule and sank his mouth into it. Sheila dropped the plant she was holding and turned her back on their guide. Her face was pale and pinched.

Ricardo wiped his mouth with the back of his hand. "Like all tears of the mother, she is sweet." He looked straight at Graham. "Now you must try."

It wasn't a request. Graham had to persuade himself that he would have looked directly at whoever was standing the closest to him. He realized now that Ricardo, though young and lean, was in fact taller and broader than him. He felt a prickle of nervousness—the same loathsome fear that came calling when he had been a child—at the idiotic thought of what the Portuguese man might do if he did not partake of the plant, which now, he recognized, possessed a musky, earthy odor. An animal smell. A human smell, even.

"I don't—" he began, but Ricardo only smiled—revealing white teeth interleaved with pale grey fragments from the ovule—and pressed Graham's hand towards his mouth. He saw the others turning away, surreptitiously ditching the plants they had been given, wiping their hands on their shorts and heading back to the bikes.

He took a bite of the flesh and felt his stomach rise to meet it.

"It's good, yes?"

Graham said nothing, but swallowed the mouthful. It was sweet, but there was a disagreeable taste too, of earth, of rust. But that was nothing next to the texture, which reminded him of the slither of tripe, eaten when he was a child, with onions. Never again.

"If you are in the hot place, and no potable water, this is saving lives."

They went back to their bikes and Graham concentrated on keeping his breakfast where he'd put it. He was irked that Felix had not watched him swallow the plant. At least Ricardo seemed to hold him in higher regard. He told Graham to hold back, that the three of them would bring up the rear.

"Your wife," Ricardo said, once they'd struggled through the remaining sandpits and found a more agreeable rhythm. "She no like the bike?"

Graham balked, convinced the man had just likened his wife to a bicycle. But then he factored in Ricardo's struggle with the language, and saw how the ambiguity had snared him. "She's not much of a cyclist, no," he said.

"You like her ass? It's nice and round, no? Perhaps too much heft."

"My wife . . ."

But Ricardo was staring at Sheila's backside as she struggled with the incline. Graham looked around at Felix, who was concentrating on his pedaling, and watching the butterflies flirt in the hedgerows.

"It's a little inappropriate, don't you—"

"Me, I like a big ass. I like the curvy. I'm skinny as rakes but my girlfriend? She's built like the fucking tank. Your wife. She is the nice shape. Plenty to grab on to when she take you for a big ride."

Ricardo was close enough now for Graham to be able to see his teeth again. They were small and gray, packed tightly into a mouth that seemed far too capacious for them. His lips sagged, the color of the strawberry daiquiris Cherry ordered before dinner. Juice from the plant had dried to a glaze on his chin. Shock had shrunk Graham's windpipe straw narrow; he could produce no noise from it.

"You watch your child," Ricardo said.

Graham hauled on the brakes and slid to a stop; Felix almost collided with his back wheel. He pulled up a few feet ahead, and stared back at his dad, concern pulling all of his features into the center of his face.

Ricardo seemed genuinely nonplussed. "What is it that went wrong? Your bike, it is old and unresponsive?"

Now he read a very definite slight in their guide's words. Ricardo knew the language better than he was letting on. Graham's arms and legs were shaking with anger. He felt weak and febrile, as if he were suffering from low blood sugar. "What do you mean, 'watch my child'?"

"It is in all the news in the Alentejo region. You have heard of O Sedento?"

"No." Graham shook his head. His breath was as empty as the dry, pallid drift of seedpods collected at the side of the path. "What is it?"

"Not it. A him. A person. O Sedento. Meaning the English, it is *the thirsty*."

"The thirsty?"

"This is the correct."

"Thirsty for what?"

Ricardo licked his lips and his tongue was like an undercooked steak, far too big for his mouth. He winked. "O Sedento de Sangue. The thirsty of—"

"The bloodthirsty," Graham corrected him.

"It is like the Draculas coming out of Pennsylvania shadows, no?"

Any other time, Graham would have found Ricardo's abject malapropisms funny; endearing even. Now they gave him the creeps. He pressed on against the pedals, trying to put some distance between him and the guide. His stomach churned.

They completed their bicycle ride at a car park where a minibus was waiting to take them back to their hotel. While the others stood around admiring the view, Graham told Felix to stand with Sheila while he paid a visit to the toilet. Once there, he urinated lustily, but was appalled to see his stream of urine was the color of rust. Hadn't he drunk a good liter of water that morning, in preparation for this arduous task? Then it must be the plant's fault. Yes, there was the same mealy smell; it had gone through him like the odor of asparagus. No more bush tucker. He was looking forward to the evening. Steak all the way. And a carafe of wine.

He left the cubicle and washed his hands; he felt his heart perform a little tumble in his chest.

Remember that time . . .

Stop it. The one thing he hated about Cherry was the way she was constantly harking back. She never seemed to look forward. Forget that he had lost forty pounds over the last six months. Forget that his cholesterol levels were the lowest they'd ever been, or that he treated his body to a mainly Mediterranean diet these days. No. He imagined her at the table tonight casting disgusted looks at his red meat and chips. *You'll not be needing the dessert menu after all that?*

Remember that time . . .

He didn't need the reminders. It hadn't even been a proper cardiac arrest. If anything, it was a shot across the bows. He'd been at school, patrolling the playground with his usual cup of tea (milk, two sugars) when the first signs arrived. He'd been annoyed because he'd been asked by the Head to attend a meeting that evening in his stead, and there was also a problem with Felix who was either being bullied or bullying others depending on the rumors knocking around. Also, that morning he and Cherry had somehow got into an argument during sex, and she had pushed him away. There was an ache in his jaw and a pressure growing—like indigestion—around his breastbone. Later he felt breathless climbing the stairs to the gym after work. He'd decided then, feeling mild palpitations, that exercise was not something he should be doing. A visit to the doctor the following morning led to his GP calling for an ambulance.

A cardiologist conducted an ECG and gave him the all-clear, but there were lifestyle choices to make. He made them. Now his mid-morning tea was sugarless and, invariably, green. He cut down on calories and stepped up the exercise. Butter became olive oil. Battered cod became grilled salmon. He ate salad and brown rice. The pints turned into occasional glasses of red wine. The weight fled from him. But Cherry was unimpressed. Maybe it was jealousy; as they both approached middle age, it was she slowly being overcome by avoirdupois.

Remember that time . . .

He wondered now, as they filed back into the minibus, whether the juice of the plant had carried some kind of poison that was deleterious to the heart. Felix sat next to him, his head against his shoulder, as he thought of his parents (long dead, both heart attacks) and their love of gardening. His father had only ever referred to a plant using its Latin name, just one of the many ways he had tried to trump his only son's greater academic achievements.

Now he thought of monkshood and belladonna, of sweetshrub and Christmas rose. Oleander and foxglove. As a child he had loved apricots and rhubarb, but his father had wagged a finger, telling him that he was a step away from a horrible death. Rhubarb leaves contained oxalates that could cause kidneys to fail; cyanide lurked within apricot stones, and would put you in a coma from which you would not revive. He often wondered if his weight gain had come from such nightmare threats: bread and cake, as far as he was aware, could be consumed without any danger of toxicity.

He was nudged awake by Ricardo. They had arrived back at the hotel. The sun was low in the sky, but its heat seemed undimmed. It struck Graham that the juice on the guide's chin was the color of the vernix that had coated Felix's body at birth. Stiffly he climbed out of the back of the minibus, trying to combat the beats of nausea. Felix was ahead of him, already trotting down the path to the apartments. He could hear splashing and gales of infant laughter from the pool area. Beyond that was a tennis court, and the soft *thwock* of volleys. There was no sign of Cherry in their rooms, and no note to explain where she might be. Graham chased Felix into a hot shower and they dressed for dinner. He brushed his teeth but the taste of the plant remained, an oily film on the back of his incisors.

"Let's find Mummy," he said.

Cherry wasn't at the poolside, though a lounger was adorned with proof of her occupancy: a novel by her beloved Patricia Cornwell; a drained glass carrying her plum-colored lip imprint; the silk scarf with which she tied back her hair. He found her at the bar, another strawberry daiquiri before her, laughing too loudly at the things a much younger bartender was saying.

"We made it," he said, and sat alongside her. One split second. But he noticed it: the expression falling; her flirting over.

Cherry fussed over Felix for a while, telling him what a big boy he was for cycling so far, and for looking after Daddy. They agreed that he could have twenty minutes in the pool before dinner. Cherry took her drink to the poolside table and Graham joined her after ordering a martini for himself. "Productive afternoon?" he asked, as he sat down.

"No need to be snippy."

"I'm not being snippy," he said. He shifted in his seat and felt the efforts of the day leap in his muscles. His thighs sang, but it was an agreeable pain, a righteous pain. Tomorrow morning might be a different matter though.

"Did you overdo it today?" Cherry asked.

"Define 'overdo.' You booked the exertion . . . sorry, excursion. Maybe you were hoping it would be too much for me and I wouldn't make it back. Then you could laugh at shit bartender jokes to your heart's content."

"I do worry about you, no matter what you might think." Graham took a deep swallow of his drink. Ice cold. And what was it they used to say back during his student days, he and the others in the cocktail club? *Drier than the dust from a druid's drill-stick.* The guy might have been trying it on with his wife, but he was an excellent barman. The martini suffused him with good will, not least because it helped to mask the flavor of the plant. He gazed at his wife, at the expression on her face, that *will we, won't we* look. She seemed ready for a scrap. Was there ever a dinner eaten that benefited from a fug of bad domestic air?

"I'm sorry," he said. "It was a good day. I had fun. Felix had fun. We missed you, that's all."

"It sounds like it," she said, but it was mock admonishment, tinged with triumph at having eked out the first apology. She smiled and touched the back of his hand. "Ten minutes more, though, and I'd have been in with that bartender."

They finished their drinks and lured Felix from the pool with promises of chocolate ice cream. Dinner was good, and Cherry did not comment on the amount of wine he pointedly consumed.

Graham carried Felix—who had been nodding off into his dessert—back to their apartment. His mood was souring again; he could still taste the mother's tears plant, despite the slick of pepper sauce that had accompanied his steak.

Cherry was already in her sleeping attire, and it was the kind she wore to signal to him that she was not receptive to any kind of night maneuvers. Plain Jane knickers in beige. An unflattering sleep bra underneath one of her skintight yoga tops that was accessible only if you had access to a variety of chisels and pliers. He left her to her nocturnal rituals of cleansers, toners, and moisturizers and returned to the bar.

He was pleased to see that Cherry's barman was off duty and had been replaced by a woman. He thought of turning on the old charm, but realized he was too tired and agitated. And he just did not feel like flirting. Pain lanced his sides, like the colic he had suffered from greatly as a child. He should have just gone to bed and tried to sleep it off, but the churning of his insides had made him jittery. Some late night fresh air—and fresh it was; cliffs of cloud were rising out to sea, signaling a storm's approach—might do his efforts to relax later the world of good.

He ordered a glass of tonic water in the hope that the quinine's analgesic effects would counter his symptoms. He took the drink into a far corner of the dining room where a TV was showing grainy repeats of the evening's football match. He couldn't tell who was playing, or what the venue was, let alone what they were playing for. But it was something to focus on while his guts seethed and the wind tested the strength of the building with growing muscle.

"Tastes good."

Graham jerked in his seat; he was not alone. What he thought was a nest of shadow turned out to be a man leaning against the wall, arms folded. He too was watching the game and Graham had sat directly in his line of sight.

"I'm sorry," Graham said, meaning it as an apology for blocking his view, but the man took it as a request to clarify his statement.

"The taste. It is good."

"I'd prefer there was some gin to go with it, but yes, it's a refreshing drink."

"Not your glass. The juice in the body. The meal of it."

Now Graham saw that the man held a newspaper in one fist. He brandished it. Graham couldn't translate the headline, but he recognized some of the words he had already heard today.

O Sedento.

"Ricardo ?"

The guide offered a loose salute in return.

"You sound as if you admire him," Graham said.

"Who said it was him?"

"A woman then. Whoever it is."

"Who said woman?"

"Then what? A witch? A curse? A bad dream?" Graham wished he'd go away. He wanted to watch grainy football on a shit TV, drink his tonic water and go to bed.

"I don't know," Ricardo said. "Maybe all of those things. Maybe none. Maybe O Sedento is the appetite we all carry. The best of us keep it hidden, no?" He folded his newspaper and slotted it into his back pocket. He touched a finger to his forehead. "I sorry. I don't mean to annoy. Have a good night. Do not go to bed thirsty, yes?"

Any other day and Graham—who hated confrontation, hated the feeling he might have slighted someone in some vague, infuriatingly British way—would have offered some sop in reply, bought the guide a drink, invited him to stay.

But he was glad to see the back of him. The door banged shut and through the window he saw Ricardo's hair leap in the wind before the shadows consumed him.

Graham finished his drink and headed back to the apartment. Rain was in the air now, a fine mist that the wind seemingly would not allow to settle anywhere. It seethed around him. He was soaked by the time he reached the door.

He toweled himself dry and sat in the chair. Sleep came on like a rehearsal of death. He had not felt like climbing the stairs to bed; the meat from his dinner sat heavily in his stomach as if his teeth had not macerated it first. His hands gripping the arms of the chair, looking too much like the bleached white carapaces of dead crabs they'd seen in the harbor earlier that week. His sweat was dry glue on his skin. His gut rumbled; it was as if the plant had spoiled him for any sort of nourishment.

For some reason he was thinking of the first time he had seen Cherry, on a quadrangle in the university where they had both studied. He was coming to the end of his first year of some Mickey Mouse degree that would prepare him for no job at all; she was cramming for her finals, with a placement at a City bank already secured . . . but that was knowledge for the future. All that he knew at that moment was the back of her neck and that she was curled on the grass and the pile of textbooks by her side. The sweep of her neck, unusually long, the way her hair was up, stray strands teased by the breeze, the dimples either side of her spine . . .

He stared at those dimples until he was sure she could feel the weight of his scrutiny; she sat up, her head twitching. She planted a hand in the grass and pivoted on it. Insane dream logic showed him Felix within the circle of her arms, though he was seven years away from being born.

Everything around them shivered, as if he was watching it on a TV screen with a bad reception. And then the mown grass was gone, and he was alone with his family, on the nearby beach where an ancient ship was rusting into the shingle. She dragged Felix away, the both of them casting fearful glances back over their shoulders. They disappeared inside a giant rent on the ship's port side. He followed, but every time he called their names, the juices in his throat caused him to gag.

He pressed his hands to his eyes and pushed until he saw shoals of color sweeping across that inner dark and when he opened his eyes again he was alone in the room and it was full night, and the storm had matured, was battering the coast and their door was flapping open in the wind.

Alien flavors rose in his craw.

"Cherry?" he called out.

There was no answer. He thought she might have drunk a little too much and decided to reignite the flame he'd seen hopping between her eyes and those of the young bartender. Or maybe she'd decided to go for a midnight dip in the pool. Or maybe she'd just conked out after her long day of leisure.

He closed the door and clattered up to the bedrooms. Empty. Felix's bed was a mess of blankets, as if he'd suffered restless dreams. Or, his mind mauled itself, he'd struggled with an assailant as he was snatched from his bed.

He checked the bathroom in the insane hope that they'd decided to have a late shower together, but every room was empty. He returned to the lower level, almost tripping on the spiral staircase, and flew into the rain. He called out but his voice was spirited away by the thrashing wind. Shutters all across the complex were rattling in their frames, or, where they had not been secured properly, were crashing rhythmically like stoked metal hearts. The trees seemed aghast. The pool area was empty. All the loungers had been tied down but some of the large cushions had been blown free and floated in the water.

Steel blades flashed behind gray cloaks lifting on the horizon. He heard the police helicopter moments after it blatted overhead and watched it, momentarily distracted, amazed that the pilot had braved the violent winds tonight. A spotlight on the choppers belly created a beam busy with rain. It picked out the fevered tops of trees, the roofs, the edges of the cliffs. Had someone been found out there? A body on the crags? His gorge rose again and he tried to let it come: he wanted his stomach to rid itself of the textures and tastes of the plant. But its coagulated syrup was not ready to leave him just yet.

He ran through the hotel grounds to the tennis courts at the rear. In one corner was a gate, which led on to a sandy path to the beach. He was there in minutes, and could see the foam-topped combers on the sea as if they were lit from within. The helicopter was hovering as best it could above the hillside that sloped down to the cliff edge. Figures were arranged upon it, like toy soldiers on a blanket. There were half a dozen black shadows and a single figure in an acid white T-shirt. Even at this distance, Graham could see that it was Ricardo: the wavy hair, the limp posture. He held something in his hands. The uncertain spotlight flashed around and over it, but would not settle. Was it . . . no, Christ, no. Was it Felix's jumper?

Ricardo turned to look at him. And then raised his hand as if to wave. And then he dropped, as if he had been instantly deboned. A moment later and the sound of gunfire reached him. The light shifted on the hill; he could no longer see what was happening. The police helicopter was returning along the coast. It passed directly overhead and its light picked out the rusting remains of the ship from his dream.

Was that a figure, slipping back into one of the fissures in the hull? He was torn between going to the hill to confirm what he thought he had seen, and continuing his search for his family. If it was Felix's jumper, then so what? Maybe Felix had taken it off that morning because he was too hot. Perhaps Ricardo had simply been trying to return it. His mind could not cope with the narratives he was forcing upon everything; he had to cling to the positives. The alternative was too hideous to contemplate.

Graham stumbled back along the rocky outcrop, conscious that the ground fell away from him to needles of rock some thirty feet below. The rain slashed almost horizontally across the path, stinging his face. Here was the channel leading down to the beach where the rusted ship was incrementally disintegrating into the shingle. He passed into a zone of relative calm. Now the wind was negated he could hear the rattle of rain on the decaying hull, the crisp attack of the waves upon the stones.

Lightning jagged around the inlet. The aperture in the bulkhead where the figure had sought shelter was ink black. Iron ribs edged it, splayed inward: presumably this had been where the ship was fatally breached. He approached, conscious that the flowers Ricardo had entreated him to suck were arranged around the failing metal hull as if they were somehow taking nourishment from the oil sweating from the sumps, the soot in the stack, the endless, psoriatic rust.

At the hole he paused. Another level of quiet accumulated. There was a high stench of iron and diesel and rotting marine life. He could hear his breath, ragged in his throat, echoing in the cavernous chamber, unless it was that of another he could not yet see. He bit that thought off at the root and spat it away. He called his wife's name and it fell dead at his feet, as if poisoned by this air.

He was about to move into the ship and beggar the dangers when lightning arced once more across the night. It lit up the inside of the hull for a millisecond, but that was enough for him to be able to see what looked like the limp remains of a body hanging from a metal spar thrusting down from the ceiling. He was put in mind of filled coat hooks in winter bars.

Though darkness had rushed back into the space, it remained imprinted on his retina. Emptied . . . drained . . . Or maybe just a coat after all, he hoped. But no: there were crimson-tipped knuckles, where something had been chewing. He imagined the grind of tiny metacarpals in pistoning jaws. A sound like bar snacks being munched.

He staggered backwards and slipped on one of the plant leaves. He fell into a nest of swollen stems. The smell of mother's tears rose like a terrible seduction. His mouth flooded with juices, all red and raw. To deny them, he tore up a fistful of flowers and sank his teeth into their centers. That sweet, brackish slime burst across his tongue and he drank it down. Now his stomach railed against the stew of textures mingling in his gut and he felt his back arch violently as he regurgitated his meal. Before darkness became absolute, he was able to gaze upon his mess and discern, within the half-digested lumps and granules, the wet gleam of a wedding band upon what was left of a finger.

MOON BLOOD-RED, TIDE TURNING

Mark Samuels

Of course what took place back then wouldn't have seemed so disturbing had I not encountered her again just over two decades later. At that earlier time, you must realize, there was more of the farcical than the horrible in what transpired, or so I supposed.

I was only twenty-four, and when I think of myself as I was then, I realize how much of a stranger that younger man appears to me now. The memory of his hopes, his dreams, his view of life, all fill me with contempt. He would hate this future self, and regard me as a usurper.

But there are worse fates than regret.

And I believe I discovered one of them.

After a handful of jobs, none of which I particularly enjoyed and each lasting less than a year, I found myself employed at a small publishing house in Fitzrovia, close to its local landmark, the British Telecom Tower. The business specialized in what are termed "acting editions," which are stage plays that are designed for the use of actors rather than the general reader. The only real difference is that these editions usually contain the likes of a furniture and property list, a lighting plot, and an effects plot, all printed after the play text itself and which are there to assist the director and the stage crew. My activities at this firm were in the department that licensed performance rights to companies who wished to mount productions of our titles, and for some reason (the job had little interest for me), I stayed on.

Perhaps I remained because the other staff were invariably interesting, coming from a theatrical background, and there was a high turnover of them. Aside from the board of directors, who had been there for decades, almost everyone else came and went within a few months. As you might imagine, a large proportion were "resting" actors, and as soon as a new role came up they handed in their notice and disappeared. Some returned and then left again, some didn't, though I have to confess that only one or two out of the multitude ever achieved anything close to prominence in the theatrical world.

One of these "resting" actors employed by the publishers was a young woman whom I shall call "Celia Waters." It is not her real name, naturally, but that detail is of no consequence.

We struck up an acquaintance of sorts. It was easy to do so, since the business was quite generous in subsidizing its staff to see performances of new plays that might be suitable for its publishing list. Often too, of course, free tickets were provided to the firm by the playwright's agents. It was regarded as a staff perk I suppose, since their wages weren't exactly generous. I accompanied Celia Waters on two or three occasions to shows playing in London, sometimes just the two of us, sometimes with other staff members.

One time, after a long evening (a play I have forgotten and post-performance drinks at a pub I can't recall) I even ended up spending the night back at her flat in Shepherd's Bush. We didn't sleep together. I am not sure that either found the other sexually desirable. She was attractive in her own way, slim, petite, with long black hair and by no means without personal charm, but there was no chemistry between us.

And over breakfast at a nearby cafe the next morning she told me she was going to be leaving the publishing firm in a month to take up a part in a brief run of a new play being staged down in Cornwall.

She said it was being put on by a new repertory company rim by a wealthy theatrical *auteur*.

I can't say that any of this was of great interest to me, and I asked in the spirit of polite enquiry, though I was genuinely curious, as to where it was going to be staged. There aren't exactly a large number of playhouses in Cornwall and the most likely venue had already suggested itself to me. I had a Cornish cousin with a cottage down in Sennen Cove whom I visited once or twice a year, located only a mile or so from Porthcumo, the site of the Minack Theatre. Moreover, I was due to visit him when Celia Waters would also be in the area.

"Is it the Minack Theatre?" I asked her.

"Why, yes it I," she replied. "Do you know it?"

This coincidence of our being in more or less exactly the same place at the same time gave an outside impetus to our continued association. Frankly, when she first told me she was leaving the publishing company I assumed our brief, unconsummated relationship would dissipate of its own accord, as they often tend to do with two people in their early to mid-twenties, neither of whom wants commitment.

I promised that I would come and see her in the play while I was down there, and she was keen for me to do so, presumably with a view to the idea of its being reported on favorably and published by the firm. I didn't think there was much chance of that, since the business only really took on plays that benefited from a higher profile, but I didn't voice the thought.

Still, I asked her to tell me about it.

"Well," she said, "it's all rather a mystery really at this point. We have had some formulaic rehearsals for the last couple of weeks here in a space above a pub. It's all very ritualistic. But definitely cutting-edge and experimental."

It sounded awful. Like something a group of students obsessed by Berkoff would try and put on.

Over the next few weeks I saw next to nothing of Celia Waters. We didn't work in the same department; she was in the showroom on the ground floor and I was up on the second floor in the licensing department anyway, but we exchanged pleasantries whenever our paths crossed. I felt as if we had already disengaged from one another.

One day she wasn't there at all. A director told me she had quit a week earlier than planned and had already gone down to Cornwall.

"Actresses, eh?" he said.

Back then even female actors themselves used the term.

I will admit that I didn't really feel anything much about her having left early and without telling me. My only worry was whether or not I was still obliged to keep my promise to go and see her in that play at the Minack. I knew she was primarily interested in my being there for her own reasons, to the benefit of the play itself, but I decided to delay the decision until I was down in Cornwall myself.

Perhaps the most grueling thing about deepest Cornwall, if you are traveling from London, is the train journey itself. For some reason—and I had never shaken it off, despite several trips there—I had the feeling that it always took longer than one might reasonably expect from looking at a map. After four hours one gets to Exeter in Devon and from there one soon crosses the Tamar into Cornwall and imagines it can only be another ten or twenty minutes more to Penzance. It's not, it's another hour. And it's this last hour that's the most trying, because it seems so unexpected, as if the region itself extends time to fox outsiders. Of course one recognizes it's an illusion, but it's no less disconcerting even when one admits the fact. My cousin had an apposite phrase he would often use in jest and whose use he solemnly advised me marked out a true Cornishman. It was, when asked to do a thing, that a Cornishman would reply that it would be attended to "dreckly" which means not attended to directly at all, but rather in one's own good time. I suppose, too, that this warping of time was brought to mind most noticeably when one returned to London from Cornwall, because it then seemed that everyone and everything in the metropolis rushed around insanely to no useful purpose.

After two days spent at the cottage in Sennen Cove, occupying my time with walks along the beach, cycling along sunken lanes to little villages like Sancreed and drinking in coastal pubs where Cornish fishermen still grumbled darkly into their cider about "English settlers," my thoughts were turned again by an outside agency to Celia Waters.

It was while drinking in the local pub, The Old Success Inn, I noticed someone had posted up a flyer on its noticeboard which advertised a play and its performance dates at the Minack. The thing was shoddily produced, being a black-and-white photocopied sheet of A5 paper with what looked like a still from one of those 1920s silent German Expressionist films at its center. It was bordered with Celtic latticework. The cast were listed, amongst whom, was, of course, Celia Waters. And I now learnt the title of the play for the first time: *New Quests for Nothing*. The writer, director and producer was listed as one "Doctor Prozess."

The first night was this evening at 7:30 p.m.

I looked at my watch. It was just after five.

I ordered another scotch and soda, trying to make my mind up whether or not to honor my promise.

By 7:25 p.m. I was seated at the Minack Theatre, rather the worse for drink. I had stuck to scotch and soda, with only one beer in between, so as not to fill my bladder during the play and perhaps suffer the awkwardness of having to wander out mid-performance in search of the public conveniences. But I wasn't really used to drinking spirits and, one packet of crisps aside, the booze had worked on an empty stomach.

I had been to the Minack for the first time last year but the unique nature of it as the setting for a theatrical show impressed me just as much on this subsequent occasion. The venue is an amphitheatre carved into the side of a cliff with incredible views of the Atlantic stretching to the horizon.

Huge gulls whirl and twist in the air currents, their cries echoing against the boom of the waves crashing on the rocks far below. And as the sun goes down one is hard pressed to keep one's attention on events on the platform stage right at the bottom of the tiered open seating.

I had plenty of room to myself, with only one other person on the same row, and he was some fifteen yards away. I counted around thirty people inside, dotted here and there, which made for an atmosphere very much like the venue being empty given its large capacity. There was no buzz of conversation from the patrons before the show began, no rustle of programmes being consulted, and no real sense of anticipation whatsoever.

The effects of the bracing sea air and the half hour walk to get from Sennen Cove to the Minack had finally begun to sober me up when the four actors entered the arena and began their performance.

They were all in formal black tie and tails, as if at a dinner party, both the two men and two women. It was very difficult to tell them apart. They were also all caked in white face-paint with dark circles marked around their eyes and with their scalps closely shaven. I only barely recognized Celia Waters.

When she had described the play to me as an experimental piece I realized it had been an understatement. After some fifteen minutes of watching and listening to the actors I was still at a loss to know what was going on. Their dialogue was risible and incoherent, wandering from one subject to another with no definite purpose, and full of allusions and references that were never explained. They acted the piece in the stylized, melodramatic manner of the silent films of the 1920s with grand gestures and overwrought expressions. I wondered whether, quite deliberately, as with Brecht, the intention was to alienate the audience.

In my case, all I felt was a sense of profound depression and boredom. Eventually the dialogue even began to repeat itself, with one refrain in particular cropping up time and time again:

> *the fear of masks removed*
> *as black lightning illumines*
> *new quests for nothing*
> *the amnesiac thoughts*
> *of dying brains*
> *repeated but forgotten . . .*

Well, this same farrago went on for another hour and a half, without any interval and by now the sun had set and the moon had risen. Most of the audience had simply got up and left by this point, and were probably demanding refunds at the box office.

I would have left too, but for the natural, outside event that accompanied the play. I imagine that this performance had been carefully scheduled by the *auteur* behind *New Quests for Nothing* to coincide with the phenomenon. I hadn't known of it in advance, and indeed, I cannot say I saw the event reported in the press thereafter, but it certainly occurred. I am convinced I did not imagine it.

A lunar eclipse was taking place and gradually the moon turned blood-red as it passed through the Earth's shadow.

During this event the actors fell to their knees, arms raised aloft, and started chanting gibberish.

I watched for another five minutes and then left just as the eclipse began to finish. I had no idea whether or not the play continued, but I didn't want to see it through until the end. Nor did I want to have to run the risk, afterwards, of having to speak to Celia Waters about it. As I have said, there was scarcely anyone now left in the audience, and there was a chance she may have noticed me sitting there, having kept my promise to attend.

I returned to London the next day, having cut short my trip. My cousin in Sennen Cove advised me, some weeks later, that the play had been pulled after that one performance and had caused something of a rumpus locally as an obvious attempt at a publicity stunt. Eventually, the actors had to be physically removed from the stage by the management, for they carried on with the thing even when the theatre was completely empty.

Another play was hastily scheduled at short notice by the Minack to fill the gap; something by Alan Ayckbourn I believe.

I never heard anything further about *New Quests for Nothing* or "Doctor Prozess" over the years. Though for some reason I half-expected it to turn up again at the Edinburgh Fringe Festival.

But I did encounter Celia Waters again, twenty years after the events I've already described.

By now I had long since left the play publishing business and taken up employment in another field altogether, working for a small property development agency situated in north London. One of our clients, who owned a number of derelict properties in Cornwall, but who lived in London, contacted us for a feasibility study on the erection of three new houses on a place about a mile or so from Sennen that had been, during the 1970s and 1980s, a "surf village" called "Skewjack." People would bus over from it to the sandy beach at Sennen Cove. The place had been closed for decades, although a cottage on the site was still occupied and was rented out to a tenant who also acted as nominal caretaker for the grounds. No maintenance duties were required, but simply an on-site presence to keep the chalets and other buildings free from the likes of squatters or arsonists.

I hadn't been down to that part of Cornwall since that last trip, twenty years earlier. My cousin had emigrated to Australia six months after my visit, having met, fallen in love with, and hastily married a young woman from Sydney who had been on holiday in this country.

After arriving in Penzance (the last leg of the journey as interminable as I remembered it to be), I took a cab from the station in order to reach the remains of Skewjack surf village. We were almost at Land's End before it turned left off the A30 into a lane. One more left turn, then ahead for a few hundred yards and the vehicle parked at my destination. I told the driver to wait for me. I didn't think my business there would take more than twenty minutes at most to conclude. This was simply a preliminary evaluation.

I had telephoned ahead and the occupant of the cottage came out to meet me as soon as he heard the taxi pull up outside.

He was a man in his early thirties, quite tall, very thin, with long blond hair and a goatee. Back in the doorway of the cottage I could see his partner, a woman around a decade younger than he was. She was red-headed and looked like something out of a Rossetti painting. From the way they dressed, the two of them struck me as arts and crafts types, and I wouldn't have been surprised to learn they made a living selling pottery or jewelry to tourists at Penzance market.

"Brian Kelsey," he said. "Pleased to meet you."

He stuck out a hand and I shook it.

"I won't keep you long," I said. "I just need a quick look around."

"Redeveloping the old place are they? Been like this for ages now I reckon," he said.

"Possibly. I imagine it wouldn't happen for another year, if ever," I said.

"Don't bother me and my girlfriend if they do," he said. "We're off to St Ives in a few months. Make more money up that way we will, I daresay."

"What do you do?"

"Sculptures, small ones. Heads mostly. Hand crafted. Want to see? Have a cup of tea beforehand?"

I shook my head.

"Wish I had the time, I really do. But as you can see I've got the taxi waiting and this is all a bit of a rush. Can you just show me around the grounds quickly?"

He looked at me steadily. It wasn't an unfriendly stare, but I could tell he didn't really like what I'd just said.

"Oh yes, I see, you're a busy man. Well, let's get on with it then."

He set off and I followed.

What was left of Skewjack surf village only covered a few acres.

Its series of holiday cabins, shop, reception, and bar/discotheque were all half-derelict and the pathways and grounds overgrown with weeds and brambles. Some of the roofs had collapsed into the cabins and mold had taken over the interiors. The drained, kidney-shaped swimming pool was choked with rubbish.

It seemed to me that the first thing would be to get a quote as to the cost of demolishing the buildings and clearing the whole area. I was making mental calculations when Brian Kelsey said: "Got some tenants here, you know. In the cabin right just over there, behind the old reception building."

"Tenants? What tenants?" I said.

He grinned sheepishly.

"Four old tramps. I warned them off at first, but they kept corning back."

"You mean squatters?"

"Call them what you want. Anyway, they never did anyone any harm. They mind their own business so I ended up leaving them alone. Live and let live. Turns out all my predecessors did likewise the same as I did in the end," he said.

I didn't reply.

"Let's go and take a peek. It's quite a show, believe me. Why not see if they're at home?" he said.

I followed him as he rounded the reception area building and onto a path beaten through the brambles.

After several yards we stood outside a lone cabin. Its exterior paintwork depicting multi-colored sun-rays was peeling away. The entrance door hung off its hinges. There was a single dusty window, half-covered with a filthy curtain that was little more than a rag.

"Keep your voice down," he whispered, putting a finger to his lips.

He crept up to the window, peered through it, turned and beckoned me after him.

When I got close enough, I could hear indistinct voices muttering to one another from inside the cabin. And then I looked through the window myself.

There were four people in there, huddled together in the semidarkness. They were dressed in crumpled, torn dark suits. Their scalps were either bald or shaven, the dead-pale skin pockmarked by craters and sores.

Three of them had their backs to me but I could just make out the face of the fourth, a woman, much older now than when last I'd seen her. She was facing me but staring vacantly into the distance with black-rimmed eyes.

Celia Waters.

I heard a snatch of dialogue: "The fear of masks removed . . . "

And then I turned away, and hurried back along the path, making straight for the taxi.

Kelsey was at my elbow.

"It's the same old thing all the time with them," he said. "Over and over again. Like the tide coming in and out."

⟞◆⟝

SKINS SMOOTH AS PLANTAIN, HEARTS SOFT AS MANGO

Ian Muneshwar

The beast in the folds of Harry's gut had no heart and it did not need one for his was strong enough to keep them both alive. It had neither heart nor mind nor eyes to see; it was only lips and teeth and fingers like needles that slipped inside his tongue and his bowels and even those places he did not know he had. Those unfilled hollows made its gums throb with an emptiness that might have been desire.

That night a man came to the house whose face Harry remembered from the dimness of a childhood memory. His thinning hair was combed forward over the shining dome of his skull, and the line of a moustache traced the contours of his upper lip. He sweated with an unnatural persistence from the pock-like pores on his cheeks.

"You remember your Uncle Amir," Father said, a statement.

Harry's eyes flickered over to Mother, who stood just behind Father, her arms crossed over her stomach. The way she sucked her tongue over her front teeth told Harry all he needed to know: this man was no brother of hers.

Uncle Amir smiled. His teeth were too large for his mouth; when the smile faded, his lips still didn't cover the thick, yellowed ends.

"It's good to see you again, Harry. It's been a while."

His English was excellent, almost unmarked. He reached a hand out, and Harry took it.

"Dinner must nearly be ready," Mother said, pulling away. "Come, Amir. Majid's been cooking all afternoon."

The dining room was at the end of the hallway, behind a heavy hardwood door. The table was set for four. White candles stood in pewter holders; Mother's best plates—white and blue chinoiserie shipped all the way from London—sat perfectly centered before each empty chair. The tablecloth had begun to yellow—because of the humidity of Guyana's summers, Father would always say, jovially cursing the tropics.

Father sat at the head of the table, striking up a conversation with Uncle Amir, and Amir immediately took the chair to his right. Harry cursed inwardly; this meant he would need to sit next to Mother.

Father took the white linen from under the fork and knife, shook it open, and placed it neatly on his lap. Everyone else did the same.

The cook, Majid, burst in from the kitchen, shouldering the door open, dinner balanced on the trays in his upturned palms. Harry had been listening to Father talk about work—a tedious monologue about the rising price of equipment for the mill, which had Uncle Amir nodding in vigorous assent at the end of every sentence—but his attention drained away as soon as Majid laid the plates on the jaundiced tablecloth.

It was a richer meal than what they had most weekdays: two large tilapia, one leaned against the other, their meaty sides slit open and stuffed with lemon wedges and sorrel; plantain baked until its edges had crisped, caramel-brown; a steaming bowl of channa spiced with cumin and ginger and topped with rings of sautéed onion—

—and back he came with still more plates: a pie of beef and goat (Majid's poor facsimile of Father's favorite: steak and kidney pie); okra roughly chopped and fried in ghee—oh, he could smell the fat!—and mango, sliced thin, spread like an orchid in bloom.

Harry reached a fork out to the tilapia, and Mother swatted his hand away.

"We have to say grace," she scolded. Then, raising her eyes to Uncle Amir: "Would you mind?"

Uncle Amir recited a short, elegant grace, thanking Father for giving him and the others at the mill such fulfilling work. Father nodded thoughtfully, and the meal began.

Harry went at once for the fish, taking a whole tilapia for himself. He cut it open just down the middle, pulling away that sweet, flaky meat with his fork before lifting out the spine and troublesome ribs—he'd come back for those later. He scarfed down the fish skin and all, gratefully swallowing and immediately returning for more. The beast rumbled pleasantly in his stomach, its jaws receiving the food Harry chewed for it, its snakelike throat slicked by Harry's saliva. He returned to the tilapia's charred head and used the point of his knife to carve out its fleshy cheeks. He especially loved the salt, the sweetness, and the softness of the cheeks—next, the eyes.

He only slowed when he noticed, after a few more throatfuls of fish, that Mother was pinching him under the table. She had dug her fingers into the skin just below where his shorts cut off, twisting the fat on his thigh.

"Harold," she hissed, mouth drawn. "You're eating like an animal again."

Harry put his fork down, pulled his leg away, and wiped his mouth with the napkin. He ignored the heat of her stare, the nettle of her prying, meddling eyes, and focused on his plate.

"That's settled then!" Father broke away from a conversation with Uncle Amir that Harry hadn't been listening to. "Harry, my boy, you're coming to see the mill tomorrow. How about that?"

Harry lifted a slice of the pie off of the serving dish.

"Sure."

He ate a heaping forkful. It was wonderful: the goat was soft, savory, fatty; the salt and animal juices and hot water crust all came together on his tongue. The beast pushed up, stretching open the base of his esophagus, unfurling its own eager tongue.

Mother put her fork down as she watched, then pushed her full plate away.

"You'll be lucky to have your father's job one day," Uncle Amir said, wiping his moustache with the crisp edge of his napkin. "You have a few years yet, but it's never too early to get started at the family business." He gave an ostentatious wink.

Mother excused herself, saying she was beginning to feel nauseous, and Majid came to clear the plates. As he did, heaping dirty silverware on top of plates balanced expertly up his arms, Uncle Amir came and sat next to Harry.

"I have something for you," he said. "Something you might like too, Reginald."

Father leaned in, his curiosity piqued. Harry swallowed a mouthful of plantain.

Uncle Amir removed a thin magazine from his briefcase and placed it on the table in front of Harry. It was an old copy of *The Cricketer*. A player posed heroically on the cover, his bat pitched at a perfect angle, his eyes on an unseen ball spinning into the distance. Beneath the picture it said: FRANK DE CAIRES DOES IT AGAIN!

"Good lord." Father reached for the magazine. "This was your mother's, Harry. She had a dozen of these, back when we were together. She loved this man. Worshipped him. What was his name?"—he spoke it slowly, savoring the syllables—"I never thought I'd see this again. Do you know, Amir, did Bibi ever get to see him play?"

"Oh, sure! Mommy went to Bourda whenever they could." For the first time since he'd come, Amir's accent slipped through. He corrected himself: "I remember it fondly."

Father passed the magazine back, and Harry took it gently. He didn't care much for cricket—sacrilege, if you were to ask the other boys at school—but he knew his mother had, and that was enough.

"Thank you," he said, glancing up to Uncle Amir.

"My pleasure."

"Well," Father said, pushing himself up from the table and giving a mighty stretch, "your Uncle and I have some things to talk through. You should get to bed, my boy. We'll have a long day tomorrow."

Harry was in no way looking forward to a long day at the sugar mill, but he gave Father a quick smile, thanked Uncle Amir again, and closed the dining room door behind himself.

The beast flexed its long fingers, pushing a little deeper into the warmth of Harry's groin, and settled its tongue against the lining of his stomach. There were whole hours when Harry would forget the beast was there at all, hours when he could let his mind wonder at a life that was not consumed by its needs. But it would pop another vein, gorge itself on his blood, his bile, his mucus—and then heal his broken body. He suffered it all without so much as a bruise.

Instead of getting to bed, he eased open the kitchen's side door. Majid was still there. He had his apron on while he washed grease out of dishes, his face buried in a cloud of steam rising from the sink.

"Oh!" He started when he heard the door close behind Harry. The dishes clattered back into the sink. "You scare me, boy!"

"I'm sorry, Majid. I'm just looking for a little food, if you have any left," Harry said, playing at coyness as best he could. "Sometimes I'll just get a little peckish at night."

"You not eat?" the cook replied testily, cracking open the icebox. "Look how skinny you are, boy."

"I ate. I'm just still hungry."

Majid wrapped yesterday's roti and a hunk of leftover tilapia in paper towels, then put it all on a small plate. Harry took the plate, and the cook returned to the dishes in the sink.

Food in hand, he headed upstairs. Father and Uncle Amir had retreated to the drawing room. He watched for a moment as their shadows moved behind the door's frosted glass inlay; their voices were pleasant, muffled baritones.

He padded along the hallway at the top of the stairs as softly as he could. The door to Mother and Father's room was just ajar and the lights were off. The hallway grew darker the further he went along, until he came to his room at the very end. He pulled the door just shut behind himself, slow, then switched the lamp on.

The room had been his for the twelve years he'd lived in this house, but it had been Mother's collecting room before then. She had a fascination with the tropic wildlife, a real naturalist's eye, as Father said. She trapped insects—damselflies, dragonflies, orange-spotted butterflies, blister beetles, darkling beetles, velvet ants, boring weevils—and pinned them to huge sheets of Styrofoam leaned against the walls. She'd refused to relocate the collection when Harry moved in, so he'd grown up with them here. Year after year, the bugs' hollow carcasses would be eaten away by mites, but there was an infinite number of insects in the jungle and Mother never tired of finding more.

Harry was allowed the two bottom drawers of the dresser in his room; all the others were filled with longhorn beetles and boxes of pins. In the very bottom drawer, tucked in a corner behind his always freshly starched school uniforms, he kept the few things he had that reminded him of his birthmother: a fishing hook, a photo of her in front of her old house, and now, *The Cricketer*. On his knees, he took out the photo. She wasn't especially beautiful. Her skin was dark—at least, because of Father, Harry was light enough to pass as British—and, like Uncle Amir's, her front teeth stuck out when she smiled. But his only memories of life with her were golden, sweet things—memories that didn't include the beast.

"This is disgusting, you know."

Mother stood in the doorway. Harry shoved the picture back into the drawer, slid it shut. She stepped into the room, blocking the lamplight, and reached a finger down to the plate of food. She flicked the corners of the paper towel apart, revealing the heaping roti and half-eaten fish.

"What're you going to *do* with all this?" She adjusted the bow at the neck of her powder-blue nightgown, pulling it breathlessly tight.

"I get hungry at night."

"You should be eating downstairs. With a fork and knife. At a table."

She crinkled her nose at the lukewarm tilapia, covered it again. "I'll tell Majid not to let you upstairs with food anymore."

She left, and Harry closed the door tightly this time. Even cold, the roti smelled of garlic and mustard oil—he had to stop himself from reaching out. He was hungry now, but the beast would be much hungrier before the night was over.

He turned the light out and lay on top of his sheets. He listened until Majid finished in the kitchen, Uncle Amir said goodbye, and Father had come upstairs and eased the bedroom door shut behind himself and the house was entirely silent, entirely still.

Harry packed the food into his schoolbag, slung it over his shoulder, and made his way downstairs. He knew just which floorboards would groan under his weight, just which stairs would squeal in the early morning's dusty quiet. He never left through the front door—the clunk of the deadbolt as it slid open would wake Mother from her shallow sleep—so he padded down the hall, to the kitchen. Majid was long gone by now, back in his home with wife at the far end of town. The kitchen had a door that opened onto the backyard so Majid could take garbage out unseen by Harry's parents. Harry gently opened this door, left it unlocked, and slipped into the warm night.

The waxing moon split the world into pale grays and slanting darkness. No light came from the queer, square houses of the compound, but even in the dark Harry knew his way across the lawns and to the break in the wooden fence that separated British families from the town itself.

The beast lurched as soon as he stepped onto the street and the fence hid the compound from view. Harry expected this, though. He feared, sometimes, that the beast knew his mind as well as his body; he stayed up some nights imaging that if it pressed its long tongue to curve of his brain it could taste his intentions in the sparking of his synapses.

The beast settled, pressing its weight into his bowels, and Harry walked on.

Provenance was a long city, a strand of streets and homes clinging to the hem of the Demerara's silty waters. He walked to the river's edge, turning off of the paved roads and onto smaller, muddy paths, and continued west. The city changed the further out he went. The British Officers' groomed, orderly houses gave way to smaller homes: squat, wooden constructions, balanced on stilts, that overlooked the swollen river and the jungle beyond.

He finally had to stop just before he reached the docks. He could stand a little pain from the beast: a clip of its teeth, a prick of its fingers. But it grew more incensed the further out he went, sinking its fingertips into the knobs of his spine and drawing its teeth over the tendons holding his kneecaps to their muscles. He fell heavily onto his hands and knees, his breathing labored.

He slid the backpack off and took out the tilapia and roti. He ripped off a chunk of the roti and crammed it into his mouth, barely chewing before choking it down and readying another fistful. He felt the beast heave upward out of his stomach and reach its greedy jaws to the base of his esophagus. It downed the food heartily, thoughtlessly. Harry ate and ate until there was only a thin layer of roti remaining and the beast had settled back into his intestines, gorged for a time.

He came to a narrow pier at the end of the street. It rocked gently with the current, the water sloshing beneath. A girl, Alice, stood at the far end. She raised a hand to wave; Harry smiled and waved back.

"Wasn't sure you'd make it," she said when he got to the pier's end. She sat back down, dangling her bare feet over the edge.

"Every Friday." He took a seat beside her and scrounged a lighter out of his backpack. "Wouldn't miss it."

Alice slipped two loose cigarettes out of her jeans pocket. She was an Arawak, one of the people who lived in the jungles before the blacks and coolies were brought by the British, and before the British, too. She lived on the other side of the river with her brothers, who fished the Demerara by night.

She put a cigarette between her lips, and Harry fumbled with his lighter, rubbing his thumb raw against the wheel.

He didn't care much for girls at school—another failing in the eyes of his cricket-obsessed classmates—but Alice was different. He wasn't sure that what he felt for her was sexual: she was older than him, and boyish, too, with her close-cropped hair, square face, and jeans. She smoked with a practiced, world-weary ease, and when he first told her that he'd never even lit a cigarette before she did not laugh or condescend; she simply showed him how.

Harry finally got a steady flame from the lighter and he lit the cig, breathing in deeply. He let the smoke settle in his chest for as long he could stand. The beast was quiet while the tobacco lingered in his throat and pricked his gums; for the time it took for the cigarette to burn itself low, Harry could try to forget that his body was not his own.

"My father's taking me to the mill tomorrow," Harry said after a while. "He wants me to be ready to work with him when I'm done school."

"Is that what you want to do?" she asked.

"I haven't really thought about it."

Swarms of gnats hung low over the river, rising and falling as if touched by the breath of an unseen giant. A fish broke from the water, leaping high in a flash of silver, its sinuous body curved with the effort of flight. When it fell it hit the river with a crack like a gunshot.

"It's not such a raw deal," Alice said, tilting her head to look at him. "You'll have all the money you'd need, and a job lined up. Better than fishing this river for money. Better than cutting cane."

"You know," Harry said, regretting he'd brought up the mill at all, "I've never been on the other side of the river. At least not since my mother died. It's so long ago, I don't remember."

Alice laughed her dry laugh. A cloud covered the moon, and for a moment the only light came from the reddened ends of their cigarettes.

"I'm not sure you'd like it. It's not like Provenance. No shops, no bakeries, no buses to take you to school."

She pulled her feet out of the water and positioned herself closer to Harry, her elbow on the pier and the back of her head cupped in her hand. She looked up at him, and smoke drifted lazily from between her lips. Her eyes flickered upward, made contact with his. The urge to lean down and touch her—to just kiss her—overtook him suddenly, and he slid his hand along the pier's pulpy wood, closer to hers.

The thought must have occurred to the beast, too, for it rumbled awake out of its nicotine-coated sleep. Its fingers pried clumsily at the bottom of his esophagus; its tongue slithered up, soft and wet.

Harry let it rise in his throat. He felt a warmth spread through his chest, a confidence he'd never before possessed; he felt he could lean down now and kiss her on the lips and it wouldn't change their friendship, wouldn't change that at all, it would only—

A motor rumbled downriver. Alice sat up, pulling herself away, and the dream collapsed. The beast slithered back, dragging any confidence Harry might have felt down with it. Alice took a last, long pull, then stubbed out the cigarette on the pier.

"Sounds like my brothers are almost back. You'd better get going."

"Yeah," Harry said, giving a small, false smile. He felt the heat of his face going red; he couldn't let her see the shame that filled hollow where the beast had been. "Time to get home, anyway. Thanks for the smoke."

He put his lighter back in the bag, waved goodbye, and started back down the pier.

The beast had been with him from the time before he was. It found its skin off the stone-cradled coast of Baleswar and took teeth from the mouths of sightless catfish slicked in the muds of the Hooghly; it found fingers in the splintered iron wreck of a sunken steamer—those half-eaten Company men suspended in the deep watched, unseeing—and then pushed onward, upstream, to break the surface off Kolkata's restless, sweat-streaked banks. Its lips—what practiced, deceitful lips—it pinched from a gora in a white cotton shirt and crisp straw boater, bent at the waist over the rail of a ferryboat, his clean-shaven face so close they all but kissed as it rose to meet him.

On the banks it found a Bengali farmer, a devout Muslim and a newlywed, too, and it buried itself deep inside him. It stayed with him for a year, in guileless sleep, until the man and his wife sailed that unbordered ocean to a place they knew nothing of, a world they could hardly imagine but was richly described by their sahibs and Her Majesty's Officers.

One night when the ocean churned and the ship's passengers cowered in darkness, all lanterns gone out, the merchant lay with his wife. The beast slicked itself inside the man's heavy cock and spread itself inside his wife and when, at last, they emerged from the belly of that ship and stepped onto Georgetown's streets, the beast lived inside yet another: a child who would be born to this unknown country, this ancient jungle.

Father had a motorcycle that had been brought by ship from London; a sleek, chrome-buffed Norton Manx painted a royal oxblood and fitted with all the most fashionable accoutrements. Though the sugar mill was only just over a mile from the house, Father still drove the bike there and back every day.

"She's got enough space for the both of us," he assured Harry as they readied themselves the following morning. "Just be certain to hold onto me good and tight—they need to have another go at paving this road."

They puttered down the main road slowly, Father steering around rain-filled potholes but still managing to hit bumps and stones that jarred them both. The other officers' homes spun by, just beyond the wooden fence, and when they had passed the compound he took a turn that put them on a dirt road that traced the edge of the river. Indian and Arawak fishermen worked the banks, hauling crab pots out of the water, throwing nets, dragging buckets out of their mud-streaked boats that writhed with the morning's catches: eel, chiclid, bushymouth catfish, snook, croakers, and lungfish as long as Harry's arm.

This flew by them, too, and soon they were past all the houses, past the docks. Harry knew they were close when they came to the prison: a building as uncannily tall as it was narrow, set back from the road, with rows and rows of blacked-out windows. A hundred years past, maybe more, it had been one of the colony's first sugar refineries; its thick walls and iron-barred doors made it a prime candidate when the British decided the city needed holding cells.

Father's mill was just back from the prison, over the railroad tracks. It was, from what Harry could see beyond the stepped fence running the perimeter, like a small city itself. Several small, shack-like buildings encircled a three-story, whitewashed structure with a slanted roof. They crossed the fence, and Father slowed the motorcycle.

The mill was already busy. Sweating men—Indian and black alike—heaved six- and eight-foot bundles of sugarcane out of the backs of trucks parked in the lot. They pressed the cane along what looked like a low gate that was banded together by a long iron bar along its top. The bottom of the gate swung inward, and the loose cane fell onto a conveyor that rolled it into the mill. Men stood on the other side of the low gate, huge bamboo rakes in hand, pulling the cane down onto the conveyor belt.

"Come," Father said after he'd parked in front of the mill. The motorbike's polished, red chassis seemed alien amidst the white-and-brown tedium of the cane workers. "Let's find Uncle Amir."

The interior of the mill was darker and noisier than Harry had expected. The conveyor belt carried the sugarcane into a central chamber filled with machines whose purposes he could hardly guess at: steel-sided shredders with rows of spinning teeth, thick pipes that ran the walls and hissed with steam, and vats filled with dark, boiling liquids. Men with heavy gloves moved like ants in an underground colony: each knowing exactly where he was going, but none saying a word to the others.

"He should be up here," Father said, shouldering open a door labeled *Management Only*. They climbed a steep flight of stairs that doubled back on itself and opened into a small room with a glass wall. The whole mill was visible beyond the glass, much as fish could be watched in a child's aquarium.

"Harry! So glad you came today." Uncle Amir stood from behind a small oak desk, came over to shake his hands. "I haven't seen you in so long, and now we get to see each other twice in one week! What grand luck. Would you like milk tea?"

Harry shook his head, but Father insisted on tea for the three of them.

While Amir boiled water, Father enumerated the job's various daily tasks—invoices, vendor inquiries, customer relations, and management. "It's tough keeping the coolies on track and making sure production is where the bosses need it to be. So much slips through the cracks. Right?" he asked, looking to Uncle Amir.

"Right," he said with a nod as he poured tea from a steaming pot.

Father sat Harry down at a chair with a stack of invoices—"clerical work keeps the mind organized, son"—and retreated to his own desk to answer the ringing rotary phone.

Harry's concentration left him after alphabetizing the first six. He sat beside the only window in the room that looked outside. The view was bleak—mostly men hauling cane from the trucks, staggering with the weight—but the window had a small, wooden ledge and on the ledge was a dead caterpillar. It was an enormous, bloated creature that had only recently died. He peered closer: he recognized the markings. Mother had several moths in her collection with the same rows of dots on the wings, the same shallow—

—Harry blinked. The caterpillar was dead, clearly dead, yet could have sworn he'd seen its skin ripple. Just a slight protuberance, as if some small heart, deep inside, beat once.

His stomach turned at the thought, though the beast inside him didn't move. In fact, despite being so far from the compound, the beast had hardly protested at all. It purred complacently—contentedly, even—from the thin lining of his intestines; he could barely tell it was there.

Somewhere inside the mill, men started yelling. This was followed by the sound of metal shrieking against metal and a long hiss of steam.

"Amir?" Father said.

Uncle Amir looked up from his paperwork, keeping his gaze away from the window onto the workers.

"Amir," Father repeated, hanging up the phone. "Would you go look into that?"

Uncle Amir feigned surprise. "Oh yes! Yes, of course. I'll—I'll just be back." He nearly tripped over himself getting down the stairs.

Father gave a pained sigh and, when Harry didn't inquire as to the reason for the sigh, he elaborated: "He's been having trouble with the men.

He's usually so good with them, but this blasted People's Progressive Party is driving them apart. Amir's a reasonable man—he understands the benefits of us being here, running things. All coolies are not as reasonable as your Uncle, Harry. That's a good first lesson."

The caterpillar's skin had started moving again. First, one pulse—a single, small heartbeat—but then it came again, more strongly, pushing up against the necrotic flesh, distending it. The caterpillar's skin tore with the pressure, and a small mouth emerged from inside: two black mandibles, sharp as sickles. A pin-waisted wasp pulled itself free, its wings slicked with the caterpillar's viscera.

Another wasp crawled up through the hole, and the caterpillar's body began to boil: ten more heads pushed up into the dead skin, biting hole after hole until the caterpillar was nothing more than a heap of dislocated parts, a first meal for a host of sickly-orange wasps with legs sharp as needles.

"Reginald!" Uncle Amir called from the bottom of the stairwell. "Might you—might you come down, please?"

"What's the trouble?" Father asked from his desk. The shouting from the men downstairs grew louder as Uncle Amir kept the door propped open.

"You should bring the boy with you!" Amir yelled, and then they heard the door slam shut.

Harry pulled himself away from the caterpillar—there were just two wasps left, now; the others had taken off into the midday heat—and he followed Father downstairs.

The mill's workfloor was chaotic: workers ran back and forth, some with pails of water from spigots outside, others with burlap tarps. The far end of the chamber was starting to fill with black smoke, and the room reeked of burning timber. One of the workers, a tall, broad black man, was yelling at Uncle Amir. His accent was too heavy for Harry to understand much of what he was saying.

Father stood paralyzed at Harry's side. He gripped the back of Harry's neck in his hand, squeezing just too tight.

"Should you see what's wrong?" Harry asked.

"I—I think we should just—"

Uncle Amir jogged over. "It's one of the processors, Reginald," he said, his voice hoarse with inhaled smoke. "It's lit the cane chips somehow. You should get him out of here."

"Are you sure? I could stay if there's anything—"

"It's under control," Amir retorted. He turned to go back to his men.

Father took Harry by the hand and they started out of the facility. Harry turned just before they got out, though, to see the workfloor one last time. His gaze slid from the billowing smoke to the black worker, who was standing there, watching them go. His face dripped with sweat and was streaked darkly with ash and his eyes went wide and wild with such fear, such rage, that Harry had to turn his face away.

The fires were put out, and the mill and all the cane workers survived. The mill would need some time for repairs, Father explained, but it would be back in no time at all. The fire started due to faulty machinery. All of the processors were years too old, but that wasn't *his* fault, he was careful to say, that was something Amir should have told him about long before it had gotten *this* far.

He spoke with the bluff of bravery, but he was clearly shaken by the incident. He kept to the drawing room, fingertips stained from the endless chain of cigarettes passing through them. He came out for short, silent meals with Harry and Mother, then excused himself.

The image of the mill worker had stayed with Harry, too: he had never seen such terror carved into one man's face. Father's immediate retreat from the mill filled him with embarrassment, but he couldn't bring himself to talk to Father about it, or to be there when Mother found out what had happened.

So he stayed away from the compound. Later in the week, after a day spent in too-hot classrooms thinking about his mother and her love of Frank de Caires, he found himself wandering back toward the Demerara, picking his way along a road he'd walked many times when he was a child. His mother's house had been down this way, he thought. He had few memories of the place—he'd been so young when Father took him away to live at the compound—but there were still feelings that stayed: the croaking calls of toucans with beaks the color of ripened papaya; the static joy of hearing cricket games in countries across an ocean, broadcast over transistor radio; his mother coming home from work, her apron curry-stained, her smile wider than the river.

As it always did, the beast grew restless. It smelled the river's sucking mud and the jackfruit trees in bloom; it tasted the brick-red dirt he kicked up from the road and the winds that brought clouds from the west blue with rain. But Harry had pilfered the kitchen before he left for school, taking what little Majid had left after breakfast: a pine tart and a tennis roll. He took a starchy bite out of a tart, and the beast quieted itself.

He came upon a house he thought he remembered. It was a split-level with wide, screenless windows, a green-tiled roof, and small yard full of mango trees. Two boys, one his age and one much younger, played with a ball and cricket bat in the front yard. Harry thought he recognized the older boy. He watched them play for a while, and, when the younger boy went to fetch the ball after a particularly enthusiastic hit, the older boy came over.

"I remember you," he said, to Harry's surprise. "You're Harold, right?"

"Yeah. I'm sorry, I don't remember . . . "

"We grew up down the street. You're Auntie Bibi's kid, yeah?"

"That's right," Harry said. He flushed with the embarrassment of not remembering anything about this boy.

"Yeah, I remember. You always looked white. You know, like your father."

Harry, opened his mouth, unsure of what to say.

"Well, I'm Bobby," the boy continued, rapid fire. "Want a turn with the bat?"

He offered it over. Harry paused, startled. He wasn't any good at cricket, and he had very little food left for the beast. It had started its rumblings again; slipping itself around the pit of his stomach, prodding those tender walls with its tongue.

"It's gonna rain soon," Bobby said, gesturing with his full eyebrows to the changing sky. "Might as well get a few hits in while you can."

Harry took the bat, and walked to meet Bobby's little brother.

He played for fifteen awkward minutes, missing more throws than he should have and failing to catch any of the balls that came his way. The other boys were good sports, though, and Harry found himself laughing more than he had in a long while.

Then, while he stood between the mango trees, watching the younger brother, Abed, pitch to his brother, Harry saw a man coming down the road. He came from the direction of the prison and the mill, dressed in a fine suit and a starched shirt. He walked haltingly, swinging long arms and drunkenly swaying.

The boys stopped their game; the ball went rolling through the grass, into the thickets beyond.

"Do you know who it is?" Harry asked.

"No, I can't quite—"

The man staggered closer, and Harry saw that there was something wrong with his face. Half was swollen, his left eye nearly shut, and his lips were distended and purpled. Blood had run down his forehead and dried over his eyebrows, caking them.

He came near enough that all three boys could make out the rest of his face: his thin moustache, his teeth so thick his lips could hardly cover them.

They all went running.

"Uncle Amir!" Bobby called as they neared.

He looked at them but there was no recognition in his eyes, no light behind them at all. He half-fell into Bobby's arms, and the boy couldn't hold his weight so they collapsed together into the dirt.

"Run and get Bhauji," Bobby said to his brother. "Run!"

The boy took bolted for the houses far down the road.

"And you, go and get the ferryman's wife. She's a nurse," Bobby said.

Harry balked; his heart stuttered in his throat.

"I don't know who that is."

Bobby looked up. He had taken the corner of his shirt, wet it with his tongue, and was wiping blood off of Uncle Amir's face. Uncle Amir's one open eye closed.

"Down this road. Left at the fish market, left at the baker—"

Harry was nodding but he was hardly listening. The beast had grown hungrier still; it pulled at the inside of his guts with its practiced fingers; it licked at the base of his throat so he had to swallow, and swallow, and swallow—

"Shit, man," Bobby said. "I'll go. You stay here with him!"

Bobby ran in the opposite direction, puffs of dust rising behind him.

Harry got to his knees beside Uncle Amir. He had never felt a hunger like this before; it opened his mouth for him, wet his tongue. A long line of spit trailed from the corner of Uncle Amir's mouth; as it moved down his cheek it crossed a line of dry blood. The beast hummed inside Harry, it pressed lips to the back of his frantic mind.

Harry leaned down. His nose brushed Uncle Amir's cheek and his lips touched the line of spit and the flaking blood. Oh, what sweetness, what sugar! His tongue lapped out of his mouth and he soaked in the rest of Uncle Amir's spittle and blood. He licked the face clean of dirt and sweat and the beast rejoiced with the flavors: the salt, the tang, the sticky sweet!

Harry pulled back. He was filled with the desire to take a bite—Amir's cheek was so full, so fatty. The beast asked, then begged. Then it didn't beg, it demanded. Pain ripped through his bowels like the sting of spider-killing wasp boring through his intestines. He leaned forward at once, opening his mouth—

—and pulled back. He couldn't feed the beast, if this was what it needed. He couldn't, and yet no tennis roll had ever look as soft and as perfectly firm as Amir's licked-clean cheek. It was plump as a quail's breast, and it smelled like ghee. He leaned in once more and fitted his teeth into the thin, soft flesh just above Amir's jaw. He pressed in, his crushed nose breathing in the savory warmth of his Uncle's skin: the scent of freshly fried pholourie. Amir's blood seeped into his mouth, washed in along his gums.

"Amir!"

Harry pulled away from his Uncle's face and wiped the blood off his lips. Abed came hurtling back down the road with Bhauji. She was a small woman who wore a purple-flowered headscarf that flapped at the nape of her neck as she hurried to keep pace. She was out of breath from running, and her words came through in spit-racked sobs:

"He done vex those mill men now!"

She dropped to the ground. Amir seemed to be coming to himself again; his right eye blinked open when he heard her say his name.

"Come here, boy," Bhauji said to Harry.

"Come on!" Abed implored. He pulled at his uncle's hand, trying to get him to sit up. "Help us get him up!"

But Harry could go no nearer. It was not the pain that stopped him, not the beast's razor-toothed insistence that he return to the man's broken body. It was the shame. It was the taste of Amir's sweat and blood and spit still lingering in his mouth and the pleasure that came of tasting it. He couldn't tell if it was the beast's pleasure or his own.

"I'm sorry," Harry said, backing away. "I'm so sorry."

He started running in the direction Bobby had gone to look for the nurse. The storm was all above them now; the rain started with slow but heavy drops that cratered the dirt road. It started coming faster, harder, and he turned and was running along the river, back to the piers. He didn't think about where he was going; the beast kept him from that. It had started growing inside him, swelling his small stomach, pushing into the surrounding blood vessels and yellow fat. It crowded his lungs and his breaths brought less and less relief with each step but he still kept running until he came to a pier where some fishermen were untying their boat, readying to set off.

"Hey!" Harry called, but his voice was lost as the rain crescendoed. He knew one of those fishermen—they were Arawak, and one was Alice's eldest brother. He ran to the end of the pier. "Hey!"

But the men were already pushing off, their boat's small motor kicking into life.

Harry looked back. Provenance was behind him: the nurse and the ferryman he didn't know; Abed and Bobby and Bhauji, who he hardly even recognized; Amir, broken, bleeding. Beyond them was the compound, where Father and Mother were probably starting to worry, if they'd even noticed he was gone.

Harry heeled his shoes off, took off his pants, and jumped into the Demerara.

The beast howled. It ripped at soft, pink tissue; it sunk its teeth into flexing muscle; it wrapped its long tongue around his spongy lungs and squeezed. It did not stop to heal him.

Harry swam with the current. He tasted the blood that was coming up from his throat, but he could not see it as it mixed with the murk-brown water that filled his mouth. He couldn't see where he was going for all the rain—it was driving now, cutting—but he knew the Arawak were somewhere downriver.

He swam until he couldn't anymore, until the pain shuttered his vision blue and black. His muscles burned and his knotted stomach cramped and distended in ways he had never felt before. The water was starting to come over his head now; the silt stung his eyes and he felt himself begin to go under. So he turned onto his back and simply floated. The rain filled his mouth, and washed his dark blood out toward the sea.

A light broke the beat of the rain. The curved bottom of a boat came into view, and an Arawak man bent over the edge and reached a hand down. Harry took it; the boat tipped and righted as he scrambled on board and the hands of six and eight men pulled at his sodden clothes, his chilled skin.

The men spoke amongst themselves in their native tongue, and then—

"Where you from, boy? Where is your home?"

Here, in the middle of the river, Harry approached a place beyond pain. He wiped the blood and snot off his lips, and swallowed his senseless, ocean-deep craving.

"Please," he said, "please let me come with you." Then, louder, so the rain would not silence him: "I don't have a home."

The rainy season will come to an end, as it must: the rivers recede, the land dries, and the lungfish bury themselves. They open their gasping mouths and tunnel into the cool mud where the sun will not touch their earthbrown skin. They sleep these long months curled tight, swaddled in a film of their own dried mucus, their bodies slowly decaying as their muscles and fat are consumed to nourish what little is left to nourish.

Some will die like this.

But the rains will come again—with a brutal crack like the sky cleft open—and the land returns to itself: the rivers swell, the swamps fill, and the dirt is gorged, sated. The lungfish wake as their cauls dissolve, and they thrash themselves free of the clay. As they writhe their slick bodies across the storm-soaked land they are so consumed by hunger, by the nerve-deep need to return to the water, they will not remember that they had ever lived before.

CHILDREN OF THORNS, CHILDREN OF WATER

Aliette de Bodard

It was a large, magnificent room with intricate patterns of ivy branches on the tiles, and a large mirror above a marble fireplace, the mantlepiece crammed with curios from delicate silver bowls to Chinese blue-and-white porcelain figures: a clear statement of casual power, to leave so many riches where everyone could grab them.

Or rather, it would have been, if the porcelain hadn't been cut-rate—the same bad quality the Chinese had foisted on the Indochinese court in Annam—the mirror tarnished, with mold growing in one corner, spread down far enough that it blurred features, and the tiling cracked and chipped in numerous places—repaired, but not well enough that Thuan couldn't feel the imperfections under his feet, each one of them a little spike in the khi currents of magic around the room.

Not that Thuan was likely to be much impressed by the mansions of Fallen angels, no matter how much of Paris they might claim to rule. He snorted disdainfully, an expression cut short when Kim Cuc elbowed him in the ribs. "Behave," she said.

"You're not my mother." She was his ex-lover, as a matter of fact; and older than him, and never let him forget that.

"Next best thing," Kim Cuc said, cheerfully. "I can always elbow further down, if you insist."

Thuan bit down the angry retort. The third person in the room—a dusky-skinned, young girl of Maghrebi descent, who'd introduced herself as Leila—was looking at them with fear in her eyes. "We're serious," he said, composing his face again. "We're not going to ruin your chances to enter House Hawthorn, promise."

They were a team: that was what they'd been told, as the House dependents separated the crowd before the House in small groups; that their performance would be viewed as a whole, and their chance to enter the House weighed accordingly. Though no rules had been given, and nothing more said, either, as dependents led them to this room and locked them in. At least he was still with Kim Cuc, or he'd have been hopelessly lost.

For people like Leila—for the Houseless, the desperate—it was their one chance to escape the streets, to receive food and shelter and the other tangible benefits of a House's protection.

For Thuan and Kim Cuc, though . . . the problem was rather different. Their fate, too, would be rather different, if anyone found out who they really were. No House in Paris liked spies, and Hawthorn was not known for its leniency.

"You're relatives?" Leila asked.

"In a manner of speaking." Kim Cuc was cheerful again, which meant she was about to reproach him once more. "He's the disagreeable one. We work in the factories." They'd agreed on this as the most plausible cover story: they had altered their human shapes, slightly, to make their hands thinner and more scarred. They didn't need to fake the gaunt faces and brittle hair: in the days after the war that had devastated the city, magical pollution affected everyone.

"The factories. The ones behind the stations?"

Kim Cuc nodded. She looked at her lap, thoughtfully. "Yes. Only decent jobs there are, for Annamites in this city."

"That's—" Leila started. The House factories by the ruined train stations employed a host of seamstresses and embroiderers, turning them blind and crooked-handed in a short span. "People don't last long in there."

Kim Cuc looked at her lap as if embarrassed. "It sucks the life out of you, but it pays well. Well, decent considering it's not for House dependents." She fingered her bracelet. It and its matching twin on the other side looked like cheap, gilded stuff, the kind of wedding gifts the Annamite community gave each other, but they were infused with a wealth of Fallen magic. If found out and pressed, she'd say they were savings for an upcoming operation—not an uncommon thing in devastated Paris, where the air corroded lungs and caused strange fungi to bloom within bones and muscle. "What about you?"

Leila's face froze as she exhaled. "Gang," she said, shortly. "The Deep Underground Dreamers, before they got beaten by the Red Mambas."

"Ah," Kim Cuc said. "And the Red Mambas didn't want you?"

Leila's gaze was answer enough: haunted and taut, and more adult than it should have been. Beneath her hemp shirt and patched-up skirt, her body was thin, and no doubt bruised. Thuan felt obscurely ashamed. He and Kim Cuc were only playing at being Houseless. The dragon kingdom under the waters of the Seine might be weakened, its harvests twisted out of shape by Fallen magic, but they still had enough to eat and drink, and beds to sleep in they didn't need to fight or trade favors for. "Sorry," he said.

"Don't be," Leila said. And, when the silence got too awkward, "So what are we supposed to do?"

"Damned if I know." Thuan got up, and picked up one of the figurines from the mantlepiece. It was a shepherdess with a rather improbable waistline, carrying a small and perfectly fashioned lamb in her arms. One of her eyes was slightly larger than the other, an odd effect that most mortals wouldn't have picked up on.

There is one day of the year when House Hawthorn takes in the Houseless, and trains them as servants or potential dependents. One of you needs to get in.

Hawthorn was the kingdom's closest and most uncomfortable neighbor, and they were getting more and more pressing. Till recently, they had shown no interest in the Seine or its underwater cities. But now they were encroaching on dragon territory, and no one at the imperial court had any idea of why or what the stakes were.

We need an agent in the House.

Kim Cuc was fascinated by Fallen magic and by the Houses. Thuan—a dragon, but a minor son of a minor branch of the imperial family—just happened to be the definition of convenient and expendable.

He'd have cursed, if he hadn't been absolutely sure that Kim Cuc would elbow him again. Or worse, continue the small talk with Leila, picking up on all of Thuan's imperfections as if he weren't there. Trust her to share secrets with someone who wasn't even a dragon, or a relative.

The door opened. Thuan, startled, put the shepherdess back on the mantlepiece, and straightened up, feeling for all the world as though he'd been caught stealing dumplings from the kitchens by one of his aunts.

The newcomer was a Fallen, with a round, plump face, and the same slight radiance to her skin as all former angels, a reminder of the magic swirling through them. She turned to look at all of them in turn, her brown eyes lingering longer on Thuan, as if she knew exactly what he'd been doing when he entered the room. "My name is Sare," she said. "I'm the alchemist of the House, and in charge of these tests."

The one in charge of making all their magical artifacts, and turning Fallen corpses into magic for dependents. She *definitely* reminded Thuan of Third or Fourth Aunt, except that his aunts wouldn't kill him for stealing or snooping where he wasn't meant to—no, they'd come up with something far worse.

Sare waited for them to introduce themselves, which they did, awkwardly and in a growing silence. Leila's eyes were wide. Kim Cuc, by the looks of her, was unimpressed and trying not to show it.

"So you want to enter Hawthorn," Sare said. She didn't wait, this time. "Let me tell you a little about how it works. I'll pick a few people from everyone who showed up today: the ones who show the most resourcefulness. The House will take you in, feed you, clothe you and teach you. If not . . . " She shrugged. "The streets are full of the Houseless. Any questions?"

"Dividing us into teams . . . " Thuan said, slowly.

"Because a House stands together," Sare said. The look she gave him could have frozen lava. "Intrigues are allowed, but nothing that threatens our unity. Am I clear?"

She wasn't, but Thuan nodded all the same.

"What are we supposed to do?" Kim Cuc asked.

"To start with?" Sare gestured, gracefully, towards the large table in the center of the room. "You'll find supplies in the cupboard on the right, and other materials in the room on the left. You have an hour to come up with something that impresses me."

"Something—?" Thuan asked.

Sare shook her head. "Resourcefulness. I look forward to seeing what you make."

He shouldn't have, but he raised his gaze to meet hers. Brown eyes, with light roiling throughout the irises, flecks of luminescence that looked like scattered stars. "I'm sure you won't be disappointed," he said.

Something creaked in the corridor outside the room, and Sare looked away for a moment, startled. When she came back to Thuan, something had changed in her gaze, a barely perceptible thing, but Thuan was observant.

"Cocky," Sare said. "I'm not too sure I like that, Thuan. But we'll see, won't we?"

And then she was gone, and it was just the three of them, staring at each other.

Kim Cuc was the first to move, towards the cupboard Sare had shown them. She opened it, and stared at its contents. Thuan heard her suck in a deep breath. "Well, that should be interesting."

Thuan wasn't sure what he'd expected—some kind of dark and twisted secrets, weapons or knives or something, but of course that was nothing more than fancies born of nightmares. Inside the cupboard were metal bowls and plates, and a series of little packets of powder.

"Is that—" Leila asked.

"Yes," Kim Cuc said. "Flour, sugar and salt." Her face was carefully composed again, mostly so she didn't laugh. She looked, again, at the table in the center of the room, a fragile contraption with the curved legs characteristic of the Louis XV style, except that they'd been broken once already, and that the white marble surface was soot-encrusted. "I'm assuming we should make our best effort not to break that."

Servants. Kitchen hands. Of course.

Leila pushed open the door of the other room, came back. "There's a sink and a small stove in there." Her face was closed again, pinched and colorless. "I can't cook. We never saw all of this, outside—" On the streets of Paris, flour was grit-filled and grey, butter thin and watered-down, and sugar never seen. As tests went, it was actually quite a good one: how would you handle cooking with so much more wealth than you'd ever seen in your life?

Clever, Thuan thought, and then he remembered that he wasn't supposed to admire the House that was his enemy.

Kim Cuc was gazing at him, levelly. "You're in luck," she said to Leila. "Because I can't cook either. But Thuan was paying way too much attention to old recipes, back when he was trying to seduce the family cook."

"It did work," Thuan said, stung. Not for long, true. It had soured when Thuan was called to the innermost chambers of the court, and last he'd heard, the cook had found himself another lover. He'd have been bitter if he could have afforded to, but that wasn't the way to survive in the intrigues of the imperial court.

"It always works," Kim Cuc said. "Until it doesn't." She stopped, then, as if aware she was on the cusp of going too far.

"You said you weren't keeping score," Thuan said.

Kim Cuc shrugged. "Do you want me to?"

"No." They'd parted on good terms and she wasn't jealous or regretful, but she did have way too much fun teasing him.

"Fine," Kim Cuc said. "What can we do in one hour?"

Thuan knelt, to stare at the contents of the cupboard. "An hour is short. Most recipes will want more than that. And . . . " The supplies were haphazard, bits and scraps scavenged from the kitchens, he assumed. He had to come up with something that wasn't missing an ingredient, and that could be significantly sped up by three people working on it at the same time. And that was a little more impressive than buttered toast.

"Chocolate éclairs," he said, finally. "Leila and I on the dough, Kim Cuc on the cream. We'll sort out the chocolate icing while the dough cools down." Time was going to be tight and the recipe wasn't exactly the easiest one he had, but the cake—pâte à choux filled with melted pastry cream and iced with chocolate—was an impressive sight, and probably a better thing than the other teams would come up with. Assuming, of course, that everyone had been assigned a cooking challenge, which might not be the case.

The downside was that, unless they were very fast, they'd leave the place a mess. One hour definitely didn't include time for clean-up. Better, however, to be ambitious and fail, rather than come back with a pristine room and nothing achieved.

But, all the while, as he directed Leila to beat eggs and sugar together—as he attempted to prevent Kim Cuc from commenting on his strings of previous lovers and their performances as she boiled butter and water together—he remembered Sare's eyes, the way she'd moved when the floor in the corridor creaked.

It had been fear and worry in her gaze, something far beyond the annoyance of having to deal with the Houseless in the course of a routine exam she must have been used to supervising every year. And, for a moment, as she'd turned, the magic within her had surged, layer after layer of protective spells coming to life in Thuan's second sight, spells far too complex and sturdy to be wasted on the likes of them.

"Something is wrong," he said, to Kim Cuc, in Viet. They couldn't keep that conversation up for long, or Leila would get suspicious.

Kim Cuc's eyes narrowed. "I know. The khi currents in the wing are weird. I've noticed it when we stepped in."

"Weird how?"

"They should be almost spent," Kim Cuc said. "Devastated like the rest of Paris. But they're like a nest of hornets. Something's got them stirred up."

"Something?"

"Someone. Someone is casting a spell, and it's a large one." Her voice was thoughtful. "Keep an eye out, will you?" Fortunately, questions in Viet sounded like any other sentence to foreigners, marked only by a keyword that was no different from the usual singsong rhythm.

"Of course." Whatever it was, they were locked in a room somewhere near the epicenter of it.

Great. What ancestor had he offended lately, to get such a string of bad luck?

Thuan was down to making an improvised piping bag with baking parchment when Kim Cuc said, sharply, "Younger uncle."

"Is anything wrong—" he started, and then stopped, because the khi currents had shifted. Water had given way to an odd mixture of water and wood, something with sharp undertones Thuan had never felt before.

The key turned in the lock again: it was Sare, her smooth, perfect face expressionless, but with the light of magic roiling beneath her skin, so strongly it deepened the shadows around the room. "Out," she said. Her voice was terse and unfriendly.

Leila, startled, looked up with her hands full of congealed chocolate. Kim Cuc merely flowed into a defensive stance, gathering the rare strands of khi water in the room to herself. Thuan just waited, not sure of what was happening. Except that the ground beneath his feet felt . . . prickly, as if a thousand spikes had erupted from it and he was walking on a carpet of broken glass. "What's wrong?" he asked.

"Enough," Sare said. She looked at Thuan and Kim Cuc for a moment, her gaze suspicious—surely she couldn't have found out what they were, surely dragon magic was as alien to Fallen as the sky was to fish? But then she shook her head, as if a bothersome thought had intruded. "We're evacuating the wing, and you're coming with us."

"Caring about the Houseless?" Kim Cuc's voice was mildly sarcastic, the remark Thuan had clamped down on as being too provocative.

"Corpses are a mess to clean." Sare's gaze was still hard. "I see both of you are equally cocky. Don't give me a hard time, please."

Kim Cuc grabbed him, as they came out. "It's over the entire wing," she said, in Viet.

"Not the House?"

She shook her head. "Don't think so." Her hands moved, smoothly, teasing out a pattern of khi water out of the troubled atmosphere. "This smooths out the khi currents. Got it?"

Thuan's talent for magic was indifferent, but his memory for details was excellent. "Yes."

"Good. Now hold on tight. This could get messy."

In the corridor, a crowd of other Houseless mingled, waiting in a hubbub of whispers, until Sare clapped her hands together and silence spread like a thrown cloth. "We're going into the gardens. Follow the dependents—the grey-and-silver uniforms. And don't dawdle."

And still no mention of whatever was causing the evacuation—no one who'd dared ask, either. Thuan fell in line behind two gaunt men in white bourgeons and blue aprons, Leila and Kim Cuc following a little behind. His neighbor was one of the House's dependents, a middle-aged woman with a lean, harsh face who didn't seem inclined to make conversation. She held a magical artefact in her clenched hand, but by the faint translucency of her skin she'd already inhaled its contents. Bad enough for everyone to be prepared for magic, then.

He still felt, under him, the spikes. They were moving, slowly weaving a pattern like snakes as he stepped over them, pushing upwards to trap his ankles. Their hold easily snapped as he stepped away, but it kept getting stronger and stronger. How far away were the gardens, how much time did they have? And what would happen, if he faltered and stopped? Something was trying to invade this part of the House, was trying to find a weakness, but he couldn't see anything or anyone.

He glanced behind him. A small, skeleton-thin girl in a torn hempen dress had stumbled, and one of the dependents, cursing under her breath, was trying to help the girl up. Magic surged through her chest and arms, a light that threw the girl's cheekbones into sharp relief. "Get up," the dependent said, and the girl stumbled on.

So he wasn't the only one, then. And it wasn't only people with magic, Fallen or dragon who were feeling this.

Something moved, at the back. For a moment Thuan thought it was a child who'd gotten left behind, but it was too small and agile, and its joints didn't seem to flex in the right way. Its eyes glittered in the growing shadows. And then, as swiftly as it had appeared, it vanished.

A child. The shape of a child. And—Thuan's memory was unfortunately excellent on details like this—not something made of flesh and muscles and bones, but a construct of parquet wood, prickling with the thorns of brambles.

Of hawthorns, he thought, suddenly chilled.

When he turned to look again, the shadows had lengthened, and there were more of them, trailing the group, here one moment and gone the next, flickering in and out of existence like lights wavering in the wind. He scanned the crowd. Most Houseless appeared oblivious; but, here and there, people stared with growing fear. The House dependents didn't appear to see the children of thorns at all.

That wasn't good.

But, as they moved forward—always driven, always following the elusive light of Sare's magic, following a corridor that twisted and turned and seemed to have no end—Thuan couldn't help looking back again. Every time he looked, the children of thorns were more solid, more sharply defined. And not flickering in and out of existence, but more and more there.

The shadows at their back lengthened, until the light of the dependents' magic seemed the only safety in the entire world. And the spikes—the branches, weren't they?—grabbed his ankles and slowed him down, and more and more people stumbled, and they weren't making good enough time, they were going to slow down and fall . . .

Someone grabbed Thuan's hand. And it was definitely not human, or Fallen, or dragon—a dry, prickling touch like kindling wood. Thuan fought the urge to grab his hand away. "What are you?" he asked, and—where its breath should have been coming from—there was only the loud creak of floorboards.

It whispered something that might have been a name, that might have been a curse, but didn't let go. "Stay," it whispered. "Or the House will fail you as it failed its children."

Thuan's feet felt as though he was stuck to the parquet floor. With his free hand he called up khi water—it came slowly, agonizingly slowly—and wove it into the pattern Kim Cuc had shown him, throwing it over the spikes like a blanket. The currents smoothed themselves out. He lifted his feet, trying to stamp some circulation back into them, but he couldn't get rid of the hand in his.

"Enough," Sare said. She turned, ahead of them, to face the group. Light streamed from her face, from her arms beneath the grey and silver dress she wore—a radiance that grew steadily blinding, a faint suggestion of wings at her back, a halo around her fair hair.

By Thuan's side, there was a sharp, wounded sound like wood snapping, and the hand withdrew from his as if scalded. He didn't wait to see if it would come back, and neither did his companions. They ran, slowly at first and then picking up speed—not looking back, one should never look back—leaving the darkness behind and heading for the end of the corridor, door after door passing them, dust-encrusted rooms, rotten paneling, broken sofas and torn carpets and burnt wallpaper—and finally emerged, gasping and struggling to breathe, in the grey light of the gardens.

They stared at each other. Leila was disheveled and pale, breathing heavily. Thuan was still trying to shake the weird feeling from his hand. When he raised it to the light he saw a dozen pinpricks, already closing. He'd never been so happy for dragons' healing powers.

Sare stood on the steps of the wing, eyes shaded to look at the rest of the House. "Just this wing," she said, half to herself. She gestured to one of the dependents. "Get a message to Lord Asmodeus."

"He said—" the dependent started, with fear in her voice.

"I know what he said," Sare said. She sounded annoyed. "He's grieving and doesn't want to be disturbed. But this is an emergency." She breathed in, a little more calmly. "No, you're right. Iaris. Get Iaris. She'll sort this mess out."

Thuan showed no sign he'd understood what was going on. From his briefings he knew that Iaris was the House's chief doctor, and Asmodeus's right hand, seconding him in his work of ruling the House.

Sare turned back to Thuan and the others, huddled on the steps, struggling to catch their breath. "We'll find you some food until this gets sorted out."

Of course. They weren't going to be allowed to leave, were they? Just in case one of them turned out to be responsible for whatever had happened.

Leila withdrew something from her pocket: it was soggy and broken in half, and left trails of chocolate in her hand. "They'd have tasted great," she said, forlornly.

"We can always do them later," Thuan said. And then he stopped, as his brain finally caught up with him. "Where's Kim Cuc?"

She. She wasn't there. He hadn't seen her since the hand had grabbed him in the corridor. A fist of ice was squeezing his innards into mush. Where. Where was she?

He moved, half-running across the steps, gently shoving people out of his way—a gaunt girl with the round belly of starvation, an older man from the factories, his clothes slick and stained from machine oil—no Kim Cuc, no other Annamite, not anywhere. "Older aunt!"

She wasn't there. She wasn't anywhere. She . . . he stopped at last, staring at the Houseless on the steps, at the grey, overcast sky, so unlike the rippling blue one of the dragon kingdom under the Seine. Gone. Stuck inside. With the children of thorns and the floorboards and whatever else was going on inside.

Stay.

No.

"What do you think you're doing?" Sare, towering over him, with the remnants of the magic she'd used to extricate them from the wing, a dark, suffocating presence far too close for comfort. Within him, the khi water rose, itching for a fight, for anything to take his mind off the reality. But he couldn't. Even if he'd been the most powerful among the dragon kingdom, he couldn't take on a Fallen within her House.

"My friend," Thuan said.

Sare was quick on the uptake. Her gaze moved, scanned the crowd. "Not here. All right. Is anyone else missing?" she called out.

It should have been chaos, but fear of what Sare would do kept them all in check. At length, after some hurried, whispered talks among themselves, the other Houseless established that, if anyone had gone missing, it was someone who'd come alone, and whom they hadn't noticed.

Great.

Thuan looked at the wing they'd just come out of. The doors were a classic: a lower half of faded wooden panels, once a shade of purple but now just flaking off to reveal pale, moldy wood underneath, and broken window panes on the top half.

But, around the handles . . . faint and translucent, and barely visible in the autumn light, was the imprint of thorn branches. Thuan sucked in a deep, burning breath. "What's going on?" he asked Sare.

Her face was hard. He thought she'd brush him off, put him in his place with the other Houseless, but he must have caught her at an unguarded moment. "I don't know. This wing has been odd since Lord Asmodeus came home from House Silverspires. Since . . . " she stopped herself, then.

Grieving. Thuan thought back to his mission briefing. Asmodeus's long-time lover, Samariel, had died in House Silverspires. He wouldn't have thought the head of House Hawthorn was the type to mourn, but clearly he'd been wrong. He opened his mouth, closed it, and then chose his words a little more carefully. "They say he lost his lover, in House Silverspires."

"Yes." Sare was still in that oddly contemplative mood.

"Does this have anything to do with it?"

Sare's face closed. "Perhaps. Perhaps not." She looked at him; seeing him, not as a Houseless, not as a candidate to join the House, but as a person—a scrutiny he might not be able to afford, no matter how good his disguise was. "Cocky and curious. Who are you, Thuan?"

The only thing that came out of him was the truth. "I'm the one whose friend is stuck inside the wing. Assuming she's even there anymore." Assuming she was even alive anymore. Assuming . . .

"Don't do anything you'll regret later." Sare gestured to the other Houseless, who'd fanned out on the steps. Someone had found a deck of cards, and a raucous game of tarot had started, cheered on by half the crowd, though the atmosphere was still subdued. "Now go wait, will you? Iaris has got a lot of experience at cleaning messes." She looked as though she'd roll her eyes upwards, but stopped just short of actual disrespect. "You'll be just fine."

It was gently phrased, but it was an order. Thuan walked back to the group, and found Leila a little way from the doors, leaning on the railing. The éclair had vanished. He guessed she'd eaten it. Good on her, this wasn't a time to waste food.

"Thuan. Did she—"

Thuan shook his head. "They don't know what's happening." And neither did he. He eased, cautiously, into his second sight, trying to see what was happening with the khi currents. Wood and water, curling around the door; but weakened, just an after-effect of what was happening within the wing. And those same little spikes everywhere, like a field of thistles underfoot, but nothing that made sense.

"I'm sorry," Leila said.

"It's all right," Thuan said. It wasn't. He should have paid more attention to Kim Cuc, but of course he'd assumed she'd take care of herself, because it was what Kim Cuc always did. He squeezed her hand, briefly. "Why don't you watch the tarot game?"

Leila made a face. "Not interested." She slid down the railing, her eyes on Sare. "I'd rather know what they will do."

"The House?" Thuan shrugged. He didn't expect much from the House. They weren't its dependents, and Sare had hardly seemed heartbroken to lose someone.

A tall, auburn-haired magician with an elegant dress in the House's colors had arrived. She was huddled in conversation with Sare, a frown on her wrinkled face, fingering a filigreed pendant around her neck as if debating whether she should inhale the magic contained within. Leila watched them, fascinated.

Thuan turned his gaze, instead, on the wing they'd just come out of.

Kim Cuc would have joked about his inability to see further. She'd have teased him, infuriating as always, and told him to keep his head down, to not make waves. Better to remain hidden and safe, as the kingdom was hidden from Fallen.

Except, of course, that the kingdom wasn't safe anymore, and that Houses Silverspires and Hawthorn had both encroached on its territory. Except that, like the Houses, they were ruined and decaying, and so desperate they had no choice but to send Thuan and Kim Cuc on a dangerous mission to infiltrate a House.

Stay safe. Stay hidden. As if that'd ever worked.

He crept closer to the handles. Sare was still in conversation with the magician, who was tracing a circle in the dust-choked earth of the gardens, while Sare was interjecting suggestions that the magician didn't appear to approve of. Leila had crept closer to them, her gaze still full of that enraptured fascination.

Thuan's hand closed, gently, on the left handle. The spikes of khi wood shifted, lay parallel to his fingers. His palm prickled, where the hand had held him, but nothing bled again, more like the memory of a wound than a real one.

He looked, again, at the steps. The Houseless were engrossed in the tarot game or in their own private thoughts, and Sare was still arguing with the magician. He could imagine what Kim Cuc would have said if she'd seen him. She'd have known exactly what he was thinking, and would have told him, in so many words, exactly how foolish it all was.

But, then again, if their situations were reversed, she'd still charge in.

Thuan turned the handle, slowly. Greased, it barely creaked as he pushed the door open and slipped, invisible and forgotten, into the wing they'd just evacuated.

Inside, it was dark. Not merely the gloom of dust-encrusted rooms, but shadows, lengthening as he walked, and his own footsteps, echoing in the silence. Doors opened, on either side, on splendid and desolate rooms, with fungus spreading on chairs upholstered with red velvet, and a pervading smell of humidity, as if everything hadn't been aired properly after a rainy day.

And, as he walked, he became aware he wasn't alone.

It was only one presence at first, but soon there were dozens of them, easily keeping pace with him: the same lanky, dislocated shapes of children made of thorns, their eyes glittering like gems in the darkness. They didn't speak. They didn't need to. It was creepy enough. Thuan could feel the spikes beneath his feet, dormant. Of course, he wasn't trying to escape the wing. He was headed back into it.

He didn't even want to think of all the sarcastic words Kim Cuc was going to come up with, after this one.

"Where is she?" he asked, aloud.

They seemed . . . made of khi wood and khi water, of old things and memories, cobbled together by someone with only a rudimentary idea of what was human. The khi currents didn't pool around their feet, but went straight through them, as if they were extensions of the floor, and the only noise they made as they walked was the creaking of wood. "You're not human," he said, slowly, carefully, and again, there was no answer. It was a stupid thing to say, in any case. Sare wasn't human, and neither was Thuan, and they were vastly different beings.

What there was, instead, was a bright, blinding light, coming from behind him. And loud footsteps, from someone brash enough to think discretion didn't matter. The children scattered—no, not quite, they merely stepped back into the shadows, flowing back into them like smaller pools of ink rejoining a bigger one. Thuan mentally added that to his growing list of worries. Though so far, they didn't seem aggressive. It was going to be rather different when they tried to leave.

"I told you not to do anything you'd regret," a familiar voice said, behind Thuan.

Sare was alone, but, with so much magic flowing through her, she didn't need to be accompanied. A pendant swung over the collar of her dress, shining in Thuan's vision: an alchemical container she'd emptied for its preserved power. As she moved, the faint outline of wings followed her—an inverted afterimage, all that would remain after staring too long at blinding radiance.

He was in the middle of a wing invaded by magic, unsure of whether he'd ever be able to escape it, looking for Kim Cuc and with no leads whatsoever. He no longer had any room for fear of Sare. He didn't even have room to worry about whether she'd choose him for Hawthorn. "Regret. You mean rescuing my friend? I think I won't regret that on my deathbed."

"That's assuming you get a deathbed and not a violent death." Sare shook her head, as if amused by the antics of a child. The sort of thing that might be borne by mortals, who were younger than she was and in awe of her. But Thuan was immortal and over three hundred years old, and running out of patience, fast.

"I thought you were waiting for Iaris," Thuan said.

"I was," Sare shrugged. "She might be a while, though. She's currently entertaining the envoys of another House, and she needs to extricate herself gracefully."

"Why are you here?"

"Curiosity. Also . . . " she shook her head. "We take turns administering the tests, every year. And because this year I'm the one in charge, I am responsible for whatever you get up to."

"You don't care about the Houseless." Thuan *was* annoyed. Normally he wouldn't have let the words get past his lips.

"No, but I do take my responsibilities seriously. And Iaris wouldn't see it kindly if I were to lose two of you, not to mention an entire wing of the House."

"The magician—"

"Albane? She's preparing a spell, don't worry. Now, you seemed to know where you were going."

"No," Thuan said. "*They* knew."

"Who?" Sare turned, to look at the corridor. There was nothing but motes of dust in the dim light.

So she still couldn't see them. And Thuan could. Which wasn't good. A heartbeat, perhaps less, passed, and then Sare said, with a frown, "You're not a magician."

"No," Thuan said, with perfect honesty. He had no need of angel breath or other adjuncts to perform magic, and he drew on khi water, a power Sare couldn't see and wouldn't be able to make sense of. But it wasn't the khi currents that made him able to see the children, because the Houseless had also seen them.

But the House dependents hadn't. Because of their magic?

Sare's gaze held him, for a while. She couldn't see through him. She couldn't even begin to guess what he was. He was in human shape, with not a hint of scales showing on his dark skin, not a hint of antlers on his head or pearl beneath his chin.

At last, after what felt like an eternity, Sare asked, "What did you see?"

"Thorns," Thuan said. "Beings of thorns."

"Thorns don't—" Sare started, then stopped. "You mean trees that moved."

"No," Thuan said. "Children. They were children. They said . . . they said the House would fail me as it had failed its children."

Sare said nothing. Thuan considered asking her whether it meant anything to her, decided against it. He would gain nothing, and only make her suspicious. "Let's have a look," she said, carefully.

Room after room, deserted reception rooms with conversation chairs draped in moldy coverings, closed pianos that looked as though they wouldn't even play a note, and harps with strings as fragile as spun silk, rooms with moth-eaten four-poster beds, bathrooms with cracked tiles and yellowed tubs . . .

As they turned into the servants' part of the wing—narrower rooms with shabbier sloped ceilings, all with that air of decayed grandeur—Thuan spoke up. "What's this wing?" he asked.

Sare's eyes narrowed. "You mean why here?"

"Yes."

Her gaze held him, for a while. Beneath him, he could feel the spikes, quiescent. Waiting. Like the children, in the shadows, the ones he couldn't see.

"I don't know," Sare said. "It's the water wing—the one with the spring and the pump room—but it's not the only one."

The spring. He could feel it, distantly—khi water, far, far underground, all reserved for the House's use, a trove of power that would never be his. But Sare was right: there were other springs, too, that he could feel on the edges of his thoughts, other currents of khi water being funneled into the House.

"Then that can't be it."

Sare's gaze was hard. "You want everything to make sense, don't you."

Thuan fingered dust on a marble table, followed it down the curve of verdigried legs. "I want to understand."

"Then this is what I want to understand," Sare said, closing the door behind her. "How come only your friend vanished, Thuan? What made her so special?"

She was clever. But then, he'd expected nothing less of her. She hadn't gotten where she was—head of the alchemy laboratory, in charge of Hawthorn's vast troves of stored magic—by being a fool.

"I don't know," he said, thoughtfully. It couldn't be that she was a dragon, or Thuan would have vanished, too. He wasn't stronger than she was. "They tried to hold us all."

"Yes," Sare said. "But they gave up when we proved no easy prey. Except they did snatch your friend, who presumably fought back, same as everyone. Why?"

"I don't know."

"You're the only Annamites."

"Yes," Thuan said, startled. This wasn't where he'd wanted the conversation to go. The immediate threat of the thorn children had receded, but Sare's grilling almost made him regret the creepy escort. "But not the only colonials. And I didn't vanish."

"No," Sare said. "But perhaps you're stronger than her."

Thuan snorted. "No. If anything, I'm weaker than she is." He hesitated, then said, "She's been the one always looking out for me."

"Like a mother?" Sare's gaze was sharp.

Children of thorns. No. Thuan shook his head. "She wasn't the only motherly figure in that crowd, was she? That's a rather facile explanation."

"That children want mothers? It seems to me rather natural," Sare said, with the ease of someone who'd never actually have any children. All Fallen were sterile.

Mothers, perhaps not. He thought, again, of the bracelets on Kim Cuc's arms, of the wealth of Fallen magic stored there, something most Houseless would never see. In Paris, the Houses had hoarded nearly all the magic, and the rare artefacts went on the black market for a fortune. But no, that couldn't be it. Otherwise Sare and the other dependents would have been the first to vanish. "Why children? They can't possibly be the only dependents the House has failed."

He thought Sare was going to berate him, but instead she walked a little further down the corridor, and stared at the darkness in front of her. "You're here, aren't you?" she called, magic streaming out of her like light. "I can feel you."

Again, that odd feeling in his feet, as if the floor itself were twisting and disgorging something; and two children, stepping out of the darkness to gaze levelly back at her. Their arms were branches woven together, their hands three-fingered, and their bodies merely frames on which hung flowers the color of rot. And, in the gauntness of their faces, they had no eyes, just pinpoints of light.

"Stay," the one on the left said.

"Where is she?" Sare asked. The light that came out of her was subdued, but Thuan could still feel the power; could still feel it pushing against the children, compelling them to answer.

She might as well have been pushing on thin air.

"Where we all go," the rightmost one said. "Into darkness, into earth."

Thuan opened his mouth to ask why they'd taken her, and then closed it, because it wasn't what mattered.

"Show me," Sare said.

A slow ponderous nod from both of them, perfectly synchronized, and two hands extending towards her.

"Sare, wait—"

But she was already moving—before Thuan could grab her away, or even finish his warning—extending both arms to clasp them.

There was a sound like cloth ripping, and then only shadows, extending to cover the corridor where Sare had been.

Thuan gave up, and used all the colorful curses Second Aunt forbade him to utter in her presence. It seemed more than appropriate.

He didn't know how long he remained there, staring at the darkness, which stubbornly refused to coalesce again into anything meaningful. But, gradually, some order swam out of the morass of his thoughts, a sense that he had to do something rather than succumb to despair. He was—no matter how utterly laughably inappropriate this might seem—their best chance at a rescue.

Where we all go.

Into darkness, into earth.

Sare was right: there were other wings with a spring, and a water room. But this was also the wing where the House received the Houseless. Which meant the expendable one. And—if he was to hazard a guess—the one least protected by the wards.

And Asmodeus, the head of the House and its major protector, was shut in his rooms, grieving and not paying attention to what was going on within the House. An opening, for something that had lain in wait for years? An attempt to seize a weak and unprotected part of the House, or to weaken Hawthorn?

Demons take them all. He didn't want to help the House, didn't want to involve himself in its politics. But, if he didn't, Kim Cuc wouldn't come back.

Thuan closed his eyes, and sought out the spring again. It was muzzled, bound by layer after layer of Fallen magic—wards that would singe him, if he so much as thought of touching them. It flowed, steadily, into the House, giving it everything it had, the diseased, polluted waters of the Parisian underground, sewage no one would have thought of drinking before the war and its devastation.

The House will fail you as it failed its children.

The only thing Thuan wanted the House to do for him was to forget he existed, and not look too closely. He hardly expected any protection, or wanted to pledge it any allegiance. Not that Second Aunt would let him, mind you. She'd carve out chunks of his hide before she allowed this to happen.

A comforting thought: there were things scarier than unknown children of thorns with shadowy agendas.

Thuan walked downwards, towards the spring.

There were two children waiting for him outside the corrugated doors of the water room. They didn't appear, or fade: they were just there, like guards standing at attention. By their size, the human children they were mimicking couldn't have been more than five or six.

"What are you?" he asked, again.

He hadn't expected an answer, but they both bowed to him, perfectly synchronized. "The Court," they said.

"The Court." Thuan's voice was flat.

"The Court of Birth."

Thuan was abysmal at a number of things, but his memory for details was excellent, and he'd been briefed on the history of the House before being sent there. Before he became head of the House, Asmodeus had been leader of the Court of Birth.

Children. The Court of Birth was in charge of the education of children and young Fallen. In charge of their protection. "There is a Court of Birth," he said, slowly. "In the House." Not here, in this deserted wing filled with thorns and shadows.

There was no answer. Thuan grabbed the doors, and pushed.

He didn't know what he'd expected. It was a low room with several rusted pumps, their steady hum a background to his own breath. The air was saturated with humidity, the tiles on the walls broken in numerous places—repaired so many times they looked like jigsaws, with yellowed grouting running at odd angles through the painted windmills and horse-drawn carts.

In a corner of the room, Sare was fighting children of thorns—small, agile shapes who dodged, effortlessly, the spells she threw at them. The pipes lit up with magic, showing, at intervals, the flow of water going upwards through the pumps.

And, in the center of the room . . .

Thuan walked faster, his heart in his throat.

It was an empty octagonal basin of water, the khi currents within it all but extinguished, except where Kim Cuc was. She wasn't looking at him, but kneeling, her hands flat on old, cracked mosaics. The khi water within her, the currents running in her veins and major organs, was slowly spreading to cover the entire surface of the mosaics. Her green bracelets were fused to the floor, the light from them spreading across the mosaics. She—

She was taking root in the basin.

This wasn't good.

"Big sis—" Thuan started. He didn't get to finish his sentence, because someone else spoke up first.

"So you're her friend."

Thuan turned around, sharply, hands full of khi water—or rather, they would have been, if all the water within the room hadn't been either extinguished or claimed. There was nothing in his palms but a faint, pathetic tug, as if he held a dog on a distant leash.

The being of thorn who stood in front of him was tall; taller than Thuan, and rake-thin. When it bowed, the gesture wasn't like that of the others, smooth and synchronized and in no way human. This was elegant and slow, with a hint of mockery, as if the being couldn't quite disguise amusement. It reminded Thuan of . . .

In fact, it reminded Thuan of nothing so much as Sare's demeanor. "You don't have wings," he said—a stab in the dark, but given where he was it could hardly get worse.

"No." The being straightened from its bow, stared at Thuan. The face wasn't just branches arranged to have eyes and nose. This was someone's face, carefully sculpted in wood and thorns: plump cheeks, and a round shape, someone who must have been pleasantly baby-faced and young, except that now not a single muscle moved as it spoke, and the eyes were nothing but pits of darkness, like the orbits of a skull. "We don't keep them, when we Fall. As you well know."

"I don't know," Thuan said. He pulled on khi water, and found barely anything that would answer him. Not good at all. "You were alive once, weren't you?"

The being cocked his head, watching him like a curiosity. "You ask the wrong questions," it said, at last.

"Fine," Thuan said, exhaling. "Then why are we here? Because the House failed you?"

He thought the other was going to make him some mocking answer about following his friend in harm's way, but it merely shook its head. "The House didn't fail me."

"You make no sense." Thuan said.

The being was still watching him. It made no move to seize or stop him. "She was willing."

Thuan took in a deep, burning breath. Willing to do what, and what questions had it asked, before binding Kim Cuc to the basin's floor? Words had power here, which was good, because they seemed to be all he had to bargain with.

He hesitated—every instinct he had telling him not to do such a stupid thing—but then turned his back on the being, to look at the basin. Kim Cuc's eyes were closed, her breathing slow, even. "Big sis. Big sis."

He wanted to shake her, but he wasn't a complete idiot. She'd put her hands in the basin, on the mosaics, and it had seized her. She didn't need Thuan caught in the spell, either.

She shouldn't have needed Thuan at all, demons take her. She should have been in charge; fighting, like Sare, trying to figure out the riddle that had Thuan stumped.

"We asked her to help," the being said, behind him. He'd still made no move to take Thuan. And though Sare was fighting, she wasn't harmed, either.

Magic. Fallen magic. That was why they seemed summarily uninterested in Thuan, or in any of the other Houseless: Thuan's magic was invisible to them. But they hadn't taken Sare, or the other House dependents. He'd thought it was something dark, something the House couldn't keep at bay, but . . .

But when Sare had pushed against the children of thorns, Thuan had seen nothing, in the khi currents.

And none of the House dependents had seen them, or been threatened by them.

He breathed in, slowly. It was as if they were part of the House, weren't they. Ghosts or spirits or constructs that hadn't been made by any magicians. And they hadn't taken Sare or the other House dependents, because theirs was a power already bound to the House. As Kim Cuc wasn't.

"You're the House," he said.

"A small part of it." Its smile would have been dazzling, if it hadn't been made of branches and twigs.

"Willing. You asked her if she wanted to be part of the House," Thuan said, slowly. "That's why she's here."

The voice that answered him was mocking. "Was there any need to ask? She was there, taking the tests."

In order to enter the House, not to become subsumed within its foundations. But he doubted the being would know, or care about the difference. "She's not House," he said, carefully. A glance upwards: Sare had dispatched one of the two children, but it was already reforming.

What did he have, to bargain with? Not the kingdom: even if he'd been willing to expose and sell it, it'd have no value to a House of Fallen and magicians. Not his magic, for the same reasons. Sare, possibly, but how did you bargain with something the other already owned? "You don't need her," he said, slowly.

"In ordinary circumstances, no."

"Because Asmodeus is grieving for Samariel? All grief passes, in time."

"The grief of Fallen?" The being's voice was mocking again. "That could last an eternity." Thuan found a word—a name—on the tip of his tongue, forced himself not to utter it. The being wasn't Samariel any more than any of the children of thorns had been flesh and bones, or real children. They were all just masks the House wore as a convenience. "And meanwhile, our protections weaken."

"He's head of the House," Thuan said. "He won't leave you undefended."

It was going nowhere. He couldn't negotiate from a position of weakness, and he couldn't share his only strengths for fear of being caught out. "If you start taking people, they'll tear the wing apart stone by stone."

"Would they? They're Houseless," the being said. "Not likely to be much missed, in the scheme of things."

Spoken as only a House-bound could.

"What you take, they could give freely."

A low, rumbling noise mingling with that from the pumps. Thuan realized it was laughter. "No one ever gives freely. There's always an expectation of being paid, in one currency or another."

"You're . . . " Thuan fought a rising sense of frustration. "You're the House. All you do is take!" He pointed to Sare, flowing in and out of combat with unearthly grace, her pale skin lit up with the radiance of magic, the white shape of bones delineated under her taut skin. "Do you think she'd be as useful, if you shut her in the foundations of the wing?"

A silence, then, "One day, when she's spent almost all the magic she was given when she Fell, that might be her only use." A low, amused chuckle. "But this isn't how dependents are rewarded."

He'd had lessons of diplomacy in the dragon kingdom. He should have paid more attention to them, instead of trying to come up with plans to impress his cousins. He . . . he'd always thought Kim Cuc would be there, and of course she was the one in need of rescue, and he couldn't come up with a single idea that would make sense. He couldn't fight off a House, or even a part of a House, all by himself—and especially not with both hands tied down, and no access to his magic lest he reveal himself.

No.

He was looking at it from the wrong way around. Because fighting or threatening wasn't what he needed to do, if he wanted to use his magic. He needed . . . a distraction.

Which meant Sare.

He didn't trust Sare. He couldn't even be sure she was going to follow his lead: for all he knew, she'd be happy to leave Kim Cuc there forever, if it was for the good of the House.

But.

But she'd come back for both of them, and it was the only chance he'd get. "You don't want Kim Cuc," Thuan said, slowly. There wasn't much khi water in the room, but he could gather it to him, slowly and methodically. He could fashion it into razor-thin blades, held within his palms. "You want Asmodeus."

A silence. "You're Houseless. You can't possibly promise me anything that involves him."

No, and neither would Thuan ever consider getting involved with the head of House Hawthorn. The last thing he needed was attention from that quarter. But it didn't matter, because all he needed to do was lie smoothly enough.

"I'm not House. But she is." He pointed to Sare but finished his gesture with a wide flourish, which enabled him to throw the blades of khi water in his hands towards Kim Cuc's wrists. They connected with an audible crunch.

Water was stillness and decay and death. Thuan breathed in, slowly, moving his fingers as though he were playing the zither, weaving the pattern Kim Cuc had shown him earlier. The blades slowly moved in response, digging into the green stone, their edges turning it to dust, a thin, spreading line across its surface—so agonizingly slowly it was all he could do to breathe. "Ask her," he said.

A silence, broken only by the slurping sound of the pumps. Then the being moving as gracefully as water flowing down, and the two children facing Sare vanished. She turned to Thuan, snarling, her face no longer in the semblance of anything human; and then saw the being of thorns, and sucked in a deep, audible breath.

Her mouth opened, closed. "It's a bit of the House," Thuan said, quickly. "Not . . ."

Sare's face was unreadable again. "Is it?" She bowed, very low. "Tell me," she said to Thuan.

Thuan gathered thoughts from where they'd fled, and put as many of them as he dared into words. "It wants Lord Asmodeus."

Sare's gaze moved to the basin, and then back to Thuan. "And, failing that, it will take the Houseless?" She showed no emotion. But then why would she have cared about Kim Cuc? Thuan waited for her to speak, to tell the being it was welcome to Kim Cuc and whatever else it saw fit to take. But Sare didn't say anything.

"We need to be strong," the being said. Thuan watched Kim Cuc's bracelets; watched the thin line that was spreading across the stone, a widening crack. He would only get one chance to seize her and run, and he couldn't even be sure that Sare would follow them. "Not distracted."

"Distracted." Sare's face was hard again. "Grief is *allowed*."

The being said nothing. Of course it wouldn't understand.

Thuan shifted, moving closer to Kim Cuc, both arms outstretched to grab her.

"Lord Asmodeus isn't available," Sare said. "And we work on the principle that people are safe inside the House, regardless of whether they're dependents or not."

A hiss, from the being.

"Sare," Thuan said.

She looked at him, startled, as if she'd forgotten he was there, or that he would speak.

"Be ready."

The bracelets split with an audible crunch. Thuan reached out, lightning fast; grabbed Kim Cuc and pulled—she came light and unbearably fragile, a doll he could have snapped with a careless gesture—threw her over his shoulder, and ran.

He didn't look back.

The spikes under his feet tensed, but didn't surge—behind him, a blinding light, that filled the pump room until he could hardly see. He ran for the open doors, and the maze of corridors leading back to safety.

He'd expected to have to fight the children at the entrance, but they'd vanished in the wash of light. He could still see their silhouettes in the midst of the radiance, shock-still. Stunned, but recovering. He didn't have much time.

Which way had he come? The corridors all looked alike, all with that same faded flower wallpaper, and the stains of blackened mold spreading from the carvings on the ceiling. The light behind him was dying down, the spikes at his feet quiescent. Waiting.

"You're fast," Sare commented, as she caught up to him.

"You—" Thuan was breathing hard. He'd slowed down to see where he was going. He expected, at any time, to see the spikes reforming, children of thorns waiting for them in the darkness.

"I hit him hard." Sare sounded cheerful. "It was easier, knowing what I was dealing with."

"You—" Thuan found a breath, finally. "You didn't have to do this." It was the House. It was the wards that kept all their dependents safe. She only had to look the other way.

Sare raised an eyebrow. "As I said, I'm responsible for the safety of the Houseless during those tests. And there are some choices that I won't make. We're not monsters, Thuan."

Thuan clamped his mouth on the obvious response. "The Court of Birth," he said, instead.

"This way," Sare said, pointing to a corridor that seemed like the others, cracked parquet and faded wallpaper with an alignment of the same doors, all painted with stylized flowers. And, in the growing silence, "Children died, because Lord Uphir wouldn't protect them. Before Lord Asmodeus took the House from him. It remembers."

And Asmodeus protected children? Thuan didn't voice this question, either, but Sare answered it regardless.

"The House keeps faith with its own. Lord Asmodeus understands this," Sare said.

"Fine," Thuan said. He wasn't about to argue with her. "Any plans?"

"Yes." For someone who'd been through Hell and back, Sare was still inordinately cheerful. "My turn. Be ready to run. It's straight ahead, and left at the first intersection, the one with the two chairs and the pedestal table with the Chinese vase."

"I don't understand—" Thuan started, but she was looking past him, at what was coming up.

He turned, slightly—Kim Cuc a growing dead weight on his shoulder—and saw the maw of darkness, rising from the bottom of the wing—flowing like ink, like polluted oil, glittering with the shadows of thorns.

They couldn't possibly outrun this.

By his side, Sare was leaning against a wall—the light coming out of her pale and weakened, the artefact around her neck open, with no hint of magic left within. The shadows flowed around her, not touching her—House, she was still House, and it didn't care for her, didn't want to hurt her, just in case she turned out to be useful one day. Under Thuan, the floor seemed to have become broken glass. And, as the shadows came forward and extinguished the light, they pooled—becoming the shape of children, the shape of a Fallen.

They didn't speak, anymore: just a thin thread of sound that might have been the creaks of floorboards, the trickle of water. *Stay. Stay.*

Thuan backed away, until he stood in the center of the corridor, with threads of magic stretching, trying to bind him to the floor, to make him part of the House as they'd tried to do with Kim Cuc. He could barely hold on to his human shape. Any moment now, he was going to lose it, and Sare was going to see antlers sprouting from his temples, scales scattered across his cheeks.

Stay. Stay.

Never.

"I told you." Sare's voice was conversational, her face utterly emotionless, as if she was merely shepherding Houseless through tests. "We guaranteed their safety. It's not an idle promise."

The being that looked like Samariel was stretching past her already, making for Thuan. Sare was leaning against the wall, winded and exhausted; but her gaze found Thuan's, held it.

Be ready to run.

There was no blinding light, no rising magic. Instead, the floor under Thuan changed—as if someone had smoothed out the broken glass, stroked raised spines until they lay flat again. The threads under his feet snapped.

He ran.

The darkness would follow him, but he couldn't do anything about that. His lungs were burning, his legs trembling. Kim Cuc wasn't heavy, but he couldn't keep carrying her forever. She kept sliding off his shoulder, head lolling against his chest.

Turn left at the next intersection. Two chairs, a pedestal table with one of those horrible Chinese porcelain vases on it. He almost tripped over one of the chairs, had to force himself to change course, calves burning.

On either side of him, the wallpapers were turning black again, the painted flowers and birds merging with the growing shadows, and he could see the shape of children, pooling from the paneling like ink, thorns and branches and a House he couldn't fight, a power that was slowly choking the dragon kingdom.

Demons take them. Demons take them. He couldn't possibly—

At the end of the corridor was the door to the garden, so close, so impossibly far. Whatever Sare had done was nothing more than a sop, a few moments' safety gained. He was never going to make it. He was going to freeze there, within sight of the exit . . .

He'd started to shoulder off Kim Cuc's weight, ready to stand over her and defend her—when the magic hit.

It came, not from behind him, but from the door. And it wasn't harsh, blinding light, but something smoother and softer; the voices of children, laughing and teasing each other; an echo of a lullaby, sung over and over; a smell of fried onions and warm bread, and a hint of unfamiliar spices.

In front of Thuan, the being of thorns formed, stared at the light, empty eye-sockets shining in the darkness. Khi water pooled around its feet, circled its shape on the parquet. It didn't move. It stood, entranced, as if listening, its head cocked.

Thuan would have run, but he had no energy left. Instead, he straightened out Kim Cuc on his shoulder, and hobbled towards the light.

An eternity of walking, with Kim Cuc growing heavier; and the spell—whatever it was—spreading around him, a warm embrace, a promise of small, ordinary things; of fire in the hearth, water and wine in crystal glasses, the smoothness of cotton sheets at the end of the day—never mind that the bed was moldy and broken, the wine sour, the hearth cracked, it was still home.

But not his home. Never.

When Thuan stepped outside, the light blinded him for a moment. Then he saw the magician—Albane?—kneeling in the middle of a circle traced in the mud. Light streamed, highlighted the words she'd written, as fluid and as deliberate as a master's calligraphy. Leila was kneeling by the side of the circle, both hands plunged deep into the earth, the light coming up to her wrists, making her swarthy skin seem pale and colorless.

Thuan kept walking—he wasn't sure he could stop. His feet carried him down the stairs, by the side of the circle: Albane looked up at him and nodded once, grimly. Leila withdrew her hands from it and grabbed him. "Thuan!"

Thuan stopped, at a loss for words. He laid Kim Cuc on the grass, blinking once, twice, as he knelt by her side, looking for a pulse—feeling it, slow and strong. "Come on, come on," he muttered.

"She's alive," Sare said.

She must have come out of the wing straight in his wake, but he hadn't heard her. Everything felt . . . unbearably real, unbearably distant, and he couldn't seem to process thoughts. Magic flowed from Sare into Kim Cuc.

She convulsed, the bruises on her wrists becoming darker. "You—" Thuan said, struggling to speak.

Kim Cuc's eyes opened. "Thuan? What—what happened?"

"It's all right. You're safe." He could have wept.

"I would advise you not to bring Fallen magic into the House," Sare said. Her face was smooth once again, emotionless. "Not unless you're strong enough to use it."

Thuan looked up. The wing was quiescent once again, the thorns a fading smear of darkness against the door handles. "Sare—"

She wasn't listening to him: she'd moved, coming to meet an older woman with the same kind of smooth face, wearing a doctor's white gown over the colors of the House. "Iaris."

Iaris nodded. "Apologies for the delay. I needed to figure out how to keep this contained."

"And—?"

"A slip-up," Iaris said. "My mistake. We hadn't checked the wards on this wing for a while. It won't happen again. I've set magicians to reinforcing them. We can't have the House seeking out magic to maintain itself."

As if they'd care.

"I saw." Sare closed her eyes. "I saw him. Samariel."

Iaris's face tightened. "Samariel is dead. You'd do well to remember this. And whatever you saw is dormant now. Contained, and it will remain so for centuries, God willing."

"Let's hope so," Sare said.

"You all right?" Leila asked Thuan.

Thuan still held Kim Cuc's hand. She'd fallen back into unconsciousness, looking older than she should, weak and vulnerable and *fragile*. Any time now, she was going to open her eyes, and make some flippant, sarcastic remark. Any time.

But she didn't.

"I'm not sure," he said, finally, to Leila. "I didn't know you could use magic."

"You learn things, in the gangs." Leila squeezed his hand, briefly. "Besides . . . we're a team."

Thuan stifled a bitter laugh. "For the tests? I don't think these turned out very well."

"Oh, I don't know. The éclairs tasted nice, even though they were a bit wet in the middle. I gave mine to Sare, before she entered the wing."

"You—" Sare hadn't mentioned this, but why would she? "What did she say?" He didn't even know what it'd have tasted like, half-made and with the pastry filling falling out of it.

"Nothing," Leila said. She shrugged. "I know it looked horrible, but we might as well not waste our work." Her face grew serious again. "This isn't about tests."

He stared at her, for a while; thinking of the streets and how lonely they could be. "We are a team," he said. "Thank you." He couldn't give her everything that he wanted, but friendship? The dragon kingdom would surely let him spare that.

Except, of course, that he wouldn't be able to tell her the truth about who he was, or Kim Cuc would box his ears out. Some friend.

One problem at a time.

Beside them, Iaris and Sare were still talking. "The Court of Birth." Iaris snorted. "As if that'd have impressed Lord Asmodeus."

Sare didn't answer. She was opening and closing the clasp of her pendant. "It might have. Dredging up the past."

"We're looking to the future," Iaris said. "He has plans, believe me." Her gaze rested, for a moment, on Thuan, moved away. "The mourning period is over."

"I see." Sare closed the pendant with an audible click. "Plans. That will be good."

Plans. Thuan's ears prickled. But neither Iaris nor Sare appeared ready to discuss further. Of course. Not in front of outsiders.

"Do you want to debrief them, or shall I?" Sare said.

"You can do it," Iaris said. "Report to me afterwards, will you?"

"Yes," Sare said. "I will." Thuan held Kim Cuc's hand, and said nothing. Sare hadn't seen anything. He'd barely used any magic, and he'd smooth it over. He'd have been worried in other circumstances: but if she wanted him dead, he'd already be.

"And once the wing is shored up, we'll have to reschedule the tests." Iaris sounded annoyed.

"Oh, I don't think so." Sare turned, briefly, to look at them. "I know exactly who passed."

Iaris raised an eyebrow. "That's . . . unusual."

"You have objections?"

"None. It's your own business, Sare."

"My responsibility. Yes, I know."

"So these three?"

Sare shook her head. "Two."

Two. Leila and him. Thuan looked at Kim Cuc. "Sare—" he said.

"I told you," Sare said. "Resourcefulness. And strength. I appreciate your loyalty to your friend, but—"

But, from Sare's point of view, she'd been nothing but trouble.

He needed Kim Cuc. He couldn't possibly take on the House by himself, couldn't make it far without her support. He needed her jokes at his expense, her reminders of his failures in bed and elsewhere—and, more importantly, he needed to not be alone in Hawthorn. Leila, for all that he liked her, wasn't from the kingdom, and could never fill that role.

He . . .

He'd gone through this all, without her help—and now he'd have to do much, much more. The breath in his lungs burnt, as bitter as ashes and smoke. "I see," he said. "Thank you."

"Good," Sare said, briskly. "Welcome to the House, Thuan." She smiled mirthlessly. "I'm assigning you to the kitchens to start with. Your pastries were too soggy, but not that bad, considering. Never fear, you'll have plenty of classes to learn better cooking skills."

Thuan forced a smile he didn't feel. He remembered darkness flowing to fill his entire world, that feeling he would never escape the corridors.

"I'm glad I passed," he said, smoothly, slowly. He stared, in silence, at the looming shape of the House before him, at the fading imprint of thorns on the handles, and wondered how many secrets it still held—how many things waiting to bite and grasp, and never let go.

⋖◆⋗

THE THULE STOWAWAY

Maria Dahvana Headley

I have reached these lands but newly
From an ultimate dim Thule—
From a wild weird clime that lieth, sublime
Out of SPACE—out of TIME.
Edgar Allan Poe, "Dream-Land"

The Poet's Tale

The dreamer, born bleak, invents an existence elsewhere. He tosses in his sleep, his hair tangled. His hands grasp at nothing, and his nightclothes oppress him. He roams a land of chill seas and stony cliffs, and when at last he arrives at a kingdom, he passes through its gate cautiously, seeking a fire, but finding only silvery surfaces surrounded by cliffs. It is a frozen place, no metal, no wood. It is a place where even the knives are made of ice.

There is a tower before him. The dreamer enters the tower and climbs the staircase.

In the tower there is a creature, and in the creature there is a heart made of lost love. The heart takes flight from the creature's breast, and a raven rises against the frozen gray sky, over a coastline bordered in coffins, a world of women with bound hands and blindfolded eyes.

As the heart departs, the dreamer wakes a poet.

He stumbles to his desk and opens a pot of ink. He dips the raven's feather in it and begins to write, sleep still half upon him, his mind full of creatures that fade as he commits them to paper, caging them line by line, his pen drawing their prison.

He wrings the night into dawn. He covers pages with calligraphed serpents, a poem twisting into a story filled with another story, a novel pushing against the edges of the paper. As he writes, his kingdom comes into being, and he breathes life into it, his fingers leaving prints on the pages, his companion beginning to take shape, an appetite made of points of light, a creature made of the hours of an insomniac.

If a man makes a monster, he wonders, is he responsible for it? If one is the master of the monster, what happens when the monster is left alone? Does it wander in wrath? Does it rage? The poet does not consider his monster's future. He makes it and sets it free in his kingdom.

The poet is a young man when he begins to build the kingdom called Thule, and he builds for years.

He dreams alongside his dreamers, and in the waking world, he wanders, writing roads alongside his own, sometimes crossing them. A dream within a dream, he thinks. Thule and its king with his dark heart and longing for love, Thule and its ruler, its forests, its floods of ghosts. Dream-land, he thinks, embroidering the edges of a realm stitched in silver.

Into the drawer of the desk the poet puts his Thule, locked and keyed, while he goes into his own life, a marriage, a misery, years of scrimping and sickness, a beach, a bride, a breaking.

Thule continues about its business without its god, and when the poet returns to it and publishes a map of its boundaries, the companion he invented as a young man has been roaming the earth for years.

There has been a dead wife washed up on the shores of Thule, her name Annabel or Lenore, or . . .

Call this body Virginia. Call this, that was a girl, a ghost with violet eyes and black hair, dead at the age of twenty-four, consumed.

The poet opens his drawer, and finds his kingdom of grim comforts. He looks into the distance, seeking the raven-shaped heart, the starry skin, the sharp teeth, but the creature is nowhere to be found.

The poet remembers a ship left sailing into the line of the horizon, but he can't recall the direction, not with a compass, not with the sun. Dim, the land he made as a boy, and darkness abutting the edges. But out of that land, in the brightness of the world, there is something he made, and he must capture it.

He writes a trap for the monster, a story filled with dreamers. A woman, a demon, a journey, a town by the water and something floating out in the harbor. He writes a tale for himself to inhabit, a dream within a dream.

This tale.

〜

The Thule Tale

There are certain stories, any reader knows, that recur in towns boundaried by water. A captain's wife stares into a gale, and suddenly her husband's face appears in that green-gray miasma, a vision of his wrack and ruin. Ghostly sailors struggle from the waves, only to fall back again. Ships are found adrift, crews missing. Messages in bottles are discovered ten years after their sender's drowning, inscribed with predictions of futures unlived.

I need not remind the reader, gentle or no, that these tales are fictions made of desire, that the act of missing a beloved may conjure miracles. For myself, I never held with such. I held with hope, and so I came to Providence for a worldly version of Salvation, in the year eighteen hundred and forty-eight, carrying an umbrella and wearing a long dress, my hem draggling in the mud.

No one turned head to look at me when I emerged from my carriage. I was no longer a girl, but a woman of nearly thirty-five. I'd had money, and then I had none, or at least none in hand. A cutpurse I never saw, and that was gone, though in the hem of my skirt I'd sewn enough to carry me. I was no innocent. By all accounts I was a lost cause and a fallen woman.

The mistress of the inn was slender, with bones that ridged through her skin in distinct knobs.

"I am Mrs. MacFarlane," I informed her, with as much dignity as I could. "My husband is delayed on the road."

She looked into my eyes and offered a tight smile. I felt certain that my ruse had not been accepted.

"And every husband is delayed on the road," she said. "And every road leads to hell."

It was not as though I had better options. The accommodations were homely but the linens were of a fine hand. The food was good and plain.

I'd come to Providence to make a portrait, a particular rendition of my own visage, and the man I meant to meet had no notion I was coming. It was a wild afternoon in November, and my arrival was veiled by weather. I had no wish to be recognized, and so the rain bothered me not at all, though when I ascended to my room, I hung my dress to dry and returned to the dining room in another gown, this one charcoal hatched with violet stripes, a changeable taffeta petticoat in rose and canary.

In the daguerreotype I planned, I'd look like a woman dressed in dark, but in truth, I was as a nightbird's wing, flashing my colors. There was a whimsy in that, and though I had suffered, I still had enough humor to see the wit of a woman garbed in silk peacockery, appearing, when drained of color, to be a widow in mourning. I wanted levity in the daguerreotype, if indeed I would be carrying it with me for the rest of my life.

I sat at a small table with a plate of boiled meat, and the innkeeper kept my tea hot. There were curtains hanging all about me, toile printed with scenes of exploration in some unknown country, a legacy of a former life. They were of French manufacture, I believed, though this town was on the eastern coast of America. I ate quietly, contemplating my mission, considering the streets with their cobblestones, the daguerreotypist's parlor, the items in my valise upstairs.

Eventually the innkeeper emerged again. She'd taken down her hair and drawn a muted paisley shawl about her shoulders. Her hair was an unlikely platinum, near enough to white that I'd thought her older than she was, and it was loose now, in waves down from her pins. It was beautiful, though she was not. It seemed to me that this mattered, though I'd known beautiful women dead in the same circumstances as those whose faces had less grace. Beauty, it seemed to me, was a lie told to girls, a fairytale of prospects and princes, and as my own face had aged, I'd come to wonder whether anything of it was truth at all. Whatever beauty I possessed had only brought me trouble.

"A sip for a storm," the innkeeper said. I looked at her, feeling weary, though the fire blazed up, and it was warm enough in the room. I'd left New York scarcely recovered from the last fever, and from the ghastliness thereafter. This portrait and photographer were my only hope.

She sat opposite me. I could smell her perfume, a mixture of salts and camphor.

She poured sherry, her hand steady, and I could see her smile, though her head was bowed. It was a smile that said she knew my history. Some jilting, some man turned marauder, or perhaps wed to another lovelier than I. Perhaps she thought I'd promised myself to a sailor, and now waited in vain for his bones to walk out from the bay.

I saw her glance at my waistline, but there was nothing there to betray me. No, what inhabited me hid more efficiently than that.

Beneath my dress, I wore a strand of beads made of amber, the better to absorb the energy of the thing I carried. Sometimes at night I woke, chilled and sweating, gasping, unable to swallow, but I was here, was I not? I'd managed the journey. It had been a question, my body racked with spasms, curled against the hard leather seat.

I'd twisted my wedding ring seven times around my finger, and then taken it off and put it on a chain about my neck for fear of losing it. My father was certain I'd acquired it of a tinker, roadside shine bought as an additive to my delusions of a paramour. He understood nothing.

I'd reduced in weight during in the sixmonth I'd spent an invalid, plagued by visions and panics, surrounded by delicate pieces of dark. This in spite of the midnight meals I'd consumed—no, nothing to speak on, nothing to think on. They had not fed me.

Now I was here. This was a cure, or so a medium in New York had told me.

"Go to this daguerreotypist," said the woman met in a district otherwise filled with stables and snorting animals, passing me a card with an address. She was in the upper quarters, a gown of dark pink embroidery, a face like a crystallized fig, all folds and sugary creases, poisonously edible. "Hire him to take your portrait."

A photographer of ghosts. There was a fashion toward such things at that time, but this studio, that of Masury & Hartshorn, was particular. Both of the main photographers there were of unusual lineage, she told me. Messr. Hartshorn was a stag turned man by a jealous god two thousand years before, and Messr. Masury was the son of a ghoul, but, by all accounts, tremendously polite. They ran a specialist studio. There was a photographer there, this medium swore, who might use the camera to save my soul, if anything remained of it. His name was whispered in these circles, though it was not one the studio advertised.

That was why I had come here, at considerable peril, and this was my aim. A session that would save me. A portrait that would free me from the burden I carried.

The man I was to meet was called Edwin Manchester, an apprentice who had come to photography from the spiritual movement. He was well known in the circles I'd come to rely upon, and had, according to the medium, purged one Miss Valpareille of a demon that had taken up residence inside the chambers of her heart. His method of photography extracted whatever creature had nestled within the person being photographed.

If there was a stowaway inside my body, this portrait would snatch it out. The portrait, then, would depart with me, and though it was necessary I keep it under lock and key, the stowaway would be trapped inside it for as long as the portrait existed. So I hoped and so I prayed. I could not spend my nights the way I'd spent them of late.

The mistress leaned back in her chair. I noticed a woven bracelet around her wrist, the same platinum as her own tresses, twisted into a complicated pattern, a mourning bracelet, but for the large gemstone at the center, wreathed in hair. A star sapphire. The star gleamed in the same way her eyes did. It was not from here. A sailor for her too, it seemed, someone who'd raided a faraway treasure, or traded with a woman for her jewels.

"Best to close the curtains," the innkeeper said, calmly as though she were telling me she'd prepared hot milk to better my sleep. "Men may come out from the water at night, and you would rather they not see you, though if you desire you may look out from behind the drape."

"Men?" I asked. "What men? The men from the town? From a ship?"

She spoke as though what she said was nothing strange, nothing the least unusual, and in truth, my recent history had convinced me there was nothing impossible in the world, that anything might happen, and to anyone.

"There is a ship anchored in the bay. Out of it come explorers, drenched and walking inland toward the light of the town. They carry lanterns, and come bearing maps, but the maps do not depict any place the barmen have heard tell of, nor do they reveal any mark in their topographical lines to remind one of anything near here. Drear, the men are, dressed in creamy silk waistcoats, and long black tails. With the dawn they walk back into the water."

"I had not realized I was to hear of ghosts," I commented, mildly enough, but the story, I worried at like a knot. I'd heard stories before, and some of them were true. I lived in the center of a narrative that no reasonable person would perceive as plausible. This one, that of a ship of the dead, chilled me. I had known other stories about ships.

I peered out into the street and saw all sorts of men with all sorts of countenances, all in their dark and drear, all with their eager eyes and long mustaches, but none of them came out of the bay.

"One always hears of ghosts at this time of the year," she said, and shrugged. "The season is turning dark and the storms are upon us. The living walk beside things that would be stricken by sunlight. Now it is time for your tale, Mrs. MacFarlane, for it is clear you have one."

I flinched, my sherry sloshing in my glass. The bones of my corset oppressed me and I felt as though I'd been caged inside a skeleton not mine own. Perhaps it was that of a whale, and I was a Jonah, adrift and punished by God. I put the glass to my lips and drank the balance.

"Tell me why you've come here, to this town on the water. The wind is cold, and the streets full of trouble, and no one comes without a reason. Will you sell your soul as a stowaway? Will you go to Thule?"

"Thule?" I asked, my heart racing with that word. "What do you know of Thule?"

She tilted her head, appraising me with the attention of a jeweler looking through a loupe.

"Tell me your tale, and I shall tell you."

I had never spoken of Thule, nor had I heard tell of it from anyone but the notorious one who haunted me, the minder of my misery.

The innkeeper tilted the decanter, and sherry filled my glass again. I looked at her slender figure, her strangely ageless countenance, and though I had kept mine own counsel for twenty years, her mention of Thule persuaded me. I found myself confessing my sorrow to her.

"I will not sell my soul, no, for it is not mine to sell at present. To Thule, though, I may be bound."

I had never told this tale to anyone, or no one beside the medium, and she only in the utmost desperation, my skin heaving and quivering, my burden boiling my blood. I would begin.

The Lady's Tale, First Part

"This is my soul, then, and this the history of my trouble, the history of the Thule I know too well. My second cousin was twenty-five years my senior, and his announcement at my birth that I was to be his wife, and that he would devote himself to the welfare of the family, stirred my parents. On my fourteenth birthday, a carriage arrived at our house, and my mother stood on the roof of our building looking down as my cousin's manservant settled me into the cushions, my small trousseau, my books and belongings.

I went to my bedchamber in his house uptown, dined with him twice, and then he was gone to his business, traveling by ship to the far North for the next year."

Thus far, my story was nothing strange to the innkeeper, a trouble known to women, perhaps not terribly different from her own.

"He was lost at sea?" she prompted.

"Not in the usual fashion. My husband returned to me a hard shadow of his former self, mustache white, though it had been black when he left New York. He came into the house, and I came down the front stairs to meet him. I was there when he opened his trunk. Something unfolded out of it, stood in the center of our foyer, and looked at me with burning eyes.

"I am dreadfully sorry, dear Cousin Annabel," said my husband to me, and there was no emotion in his voice. "But on my voyage, I have made the acquaintance of a new master."

I looked at my husband, and at the thing standing beside him. It was tall and slender, with an excess of fingers, dressed in a long black coat, which I remembered as having belonged to my husband. There was the pale blue monogram I had embroidered, on the collar. Beneath the hem of the coat I could see hooves, and a lashing tail, somewhat feline, somewhat . . . else.

Had my husband met the devil at sea? I did not love my husband. I scarcely knew him. He was an old man and I was only a girl. This, though, was nothing I desired for him, nor for myself.

"What, praytell, is the name of your companion?" I managed to ask. "Will your friend be staying here long? Shall I tell the servants to prepare a room?"

"My companion's name is Night," my husband said, as though I ought to know already.

The thing looked at me, and it glittered like a sky full of stars, but it was a lacunae in the center of the darkness, a place where a star had died, and beyond the edge of the dark there was something much worse, a roiling red planet, hidden behind a thin black veil.

"And where did you meet?" I asked, my voice that of a polite hostess. I had in my hands a tray of cordial, and I could hear the glasses rattling, but I held myself as steady as I could.

"Thule," said the thing, its voice a hiss containing an unlikely mellifluence. I felt myself sway at its sweetness. "Thule was my kingdom, but I am banished by a mortal dreamer. I was the ruler of Thule, and now I shall bide a time with you while I seek for the dreamer who dares injure me."

"I found my friend on the ship," said my husband seemingly oblivious to the creature's foulness. "A stowaway, fled from the land of dreams. And oh, that such a one could be hidden amongst coiled ropes." He turned to look at the creature, and on his face there was nothing but worship.

I turned and walked back up the stair, feeling eyes on my spine. I went directly to my own chamber, and locked the door behind me, pressing my back to the wood, gasping.

I was the ruler of Thule. The creature said again in my mind, and the words resonated terribly inside me, over and over."

I looked at the innkeeper, and her eyes were on mine, steady. She nodded.

"Thule," she repeated. "I thought as much."

I continued.

"From that night forward, I listened to the sound of whispers, but I never knew what they discussed. My husband took to drink, and the stowaway took to meat. The butcher brought us wrapped packets, tied tightly with red string, and in these late days, whenever I saw any red fabric, I thought of this, the way that string had unspooled down our front staircase, twisting like intestines on the white marble of the floor.

It was not long before my husband was dead. I looked into his open grave on a snowy day in February and saw something at the bottom of it, dozens of long and tangled arms embracing the coffin. Inside it, his frozen body bore the marks of hooves. In the official version, he died of drink.

My woe continued with my husband's death, for though he left me his fortune, he also left me the stowaway. I spent my evenings sitting in the dark, opposite a pair of glowing eyes. And so went my misery, nearly twenty years of it.

The creature was neither husband nor companion. We shared the house, but that was all. The stowaway did not visit my bed, nor did it seem eager to woo me to any unsavory realm. It went about its own business, sometimes leaving a trail of blood or of thick, black fluid. In the night, I'd wake to sounds I couldn't parse, shrills and moans, a music like a piano being dragged down a flight of metal stairs, the scuttlings of animals both small and large, but the stowaway did not speak to me with its honeyed voice, nor did it touch me with its burning fingertips.

It did not, that is, until one fateful night six months prior to this evening. That night is the reason I am here now."

I looked to my audience. She had leaned forward in her chair, drawing her shawl more tightly about her shoulders.

"Go on," she said eagerly, but I could not. The knowledge of the thing I carried had overwhelmed me, and it was necessary I retreat to my chamber. It was too dark. Night had fallen, and I no longer trusted myself to remain among humans.

"I have heard many tales," the innkeeper said. "It may be that I can assist you, whatever it is."

"Tomorrow," I told her. "I will tell you the rest of my woe, and you will counsel me, if indeed you can. For tomorrow, I may be liberated from the misery that has haunted me."

"A sleeping draught," she said, offering me a hot cup, though sleep was beyond me. I could not allow myself true unconsciousness, not with my burden.

In my bedchamber, a brick at my feet, I sat up in my wrapper, a feeling of possibility in my chest. I was feverish, yes, and my skin was damp with it, but tomorrow there would be a portrait, and the portrait would save me. The portrait would free me.

At last, fearing dreams and the consequences of same, I removed certain items from my case: chains, locks, a key. I twined the chains about the posts of the bed, and around my ankles, and locked myself into place. The key, I threw to the cushion across the room, out of my reach, and thus secured, I allowed my eyes to close. There could be no more dawns like the ones of the past sixmonth, waking to find myself alongside the river, the pale gray light, my hands clutching at small mementoes, but nothing more to tell what I had done. I could not allow that to happen here. There would be no wandering along the bay, no waking choking in an alleyway, my mouth wet and my clothing torn, not from the outside, but from within, the seams stretched and the bones bent.

In dreams I walked, and in dreams I stalked, and in dreams I did things I would never do in the waking world.

Inside my heart, the stowaway whispered endlessly in verse, a sad lament and a hunger for words. Inside my skin, the monster languished, longing and lonely, but nothing of its loneliness was kind. It sent me dreams of ghosts and of ladies walking into the ocean. It sent me dreams of death.

The Stowaway's Tale

The monster is invented on a whim, a ruler for a kingdom of woe. Night, sitting enthroned in a dark city, looking out over stones and water, decreeing all those who wake to wander blind within Thule.

Now, Night walks with ice inside it, seeking heat. Night moves between dreams and not, through the corners of gazes, out the edges of windows. There is no place a shadow can't bide, and it hides in lockets and scent bottles, in barrels full of salted fish. The monster is resourceful. It flattens itself between folds of an overcoat, and when the coat is donned, the monster latches on, its mouth full of teeth, enough to consume a man in moments. A long night can make an explorer lost, and this night is long. This is an Arctic evening, twenty hours of darkness, and with each hour, the night devours ships, crews, husbands, captains.

Night is disappointed, consuming wishes and letters, consuming last words, but none of them the words of its maker. It hungers for even a faint lantern lit on deck during a storm. Night was king in Thule, and then its maker fell in love, only to wreck on a shoal far from the northern clouds.

Look at that beach made of broken bones, look at that sea made of ink, look at the way Thule can expand and shrink again, the unknown country vaster than any other. Look at this country of ghosts. They are all ghosts here, all but Night, who lives on fire and blood. Night is the loneliest ruler, on a black throne, and up the throne's sides rise dark water.

At last, Night flees, killing ghosts and leaving them in their white shrouds, seeking another ending to the story. There is no joy in Thule, not written, not lived, and in Thule the monster is in misery.

The monster slips into a ship leaving Thule for the world. Dream trade and export, slaves imported in again. There are those in the waking world who never wake, shanghaied onto ships of sleepers, corpses crimped.

Night stows itself in a crow's nest and pretends to be a raven, perched on the basket to look out over the sea, and when the crew ascends, they see only a bird. Night hides in black feathers. The Thule ruler revises itself, a secret hid amongst coils of rope.

It finds a man who looks like its maker, and wraps around him, hidden in the lining of his coat, and when it discovers the man is no poet but only an invention of a poet, it presses the man down in the darkness of the drive and drinks his dreams.

Night inhabits a house, hidden in closets and beneath beds, and when the world is in shadow, it wanders the streets, seeking its god and his pen. It finds only the young wife, an invention herself, her skin pale and her hair black, her eyes violet. It binds itself to her body.

Annabel, Night hisses, or *Lenore*, or *Virginia*. It calls her every version of the names its creator has called his loves. It hides in her hair, plaited among flowers, and in her skin it anchors, a ship full of the lost souls of Thule. It makes its way into the world with Annabel, this creature, and to a city it finds familiar. It feeds on poets, amputating sentences, lyrics, love letters, but none of them are the right ones.

And then.

The Dreamer's Journey

The poet writes in a frenzy, in an attic room in a city by the sea. There is sun, but he denies it. The world he belongs in is a world of rain, and the only climate is one of mist and dim. He writes a ship in a harbor, and on the ship a crew of sleepers. He writes a sail made of paper, and written on it is a poem about a kingdom burning. He writes himself, swimming in water made of something that can catch fire. He closes his eyes, dreaming the dream within the dream, and in it, he dives, the water filled with nothing but hunger, the sea below him ice and skeletons. He swims to shore in evening dress, shivering, shuddering, chasing the raven that fled his companion, chilling and killing the poet by the sea, dreaming and drafting a story of a stowaway captured.

He thinks of years spent following love, and of years spent losing it. Shaking at the desk in the dark now, the dreamer watches snow falling into the world he's made. He spins a net of words and weaves sentences into rope.

Now he is in a hotel in Providence. His mind has moved him from city to city, along the rails and to this place. He has built and sold imaginary kingdoms and now, at the end of his life, he is responsible for monsters.

All this he writes over the head of the innkeeper, a woman living between worlds, her hair pale and about her neck a gemstone mined in a pretender's place.

Poe is broken with drink and disaster, and something has bitten him in a street, a rangy dog with blood in its eyes and foam at its jaw. He doesn't mind it. Things have bitten him all his life. He is a man born of dreams, and in dreams he remains, the child of actors, and all his life a play.

He wanders as he writes, pacing the room in Providence, here to no end but his own. The world of his dream and the world of his story are entwined now, and he walks real streets in imaginary places.

Somewhere out there is his companion, invented as a cure for pain. Somewhere is a beast made of morphia, a soothing icy hand on the forehead, something that will cure his pangs and fevers, something that will walk with him when he walks toward the land of the dead. Though it is a monster, it is his monster.

He writes it into this hotel, and places it in hiding in a woman he's made of words. He writes himself into the sea, and feels it rising in his rooms, the water green and salty, the cuffs of his trousers drenched, his belt sopping, his shirt transparent and floating, his white ascot tightly tied about his throat.

Edgar Allan Poe swims in a sea of ink.

〜

The Lady's Tale, Second Part

Sometime in that night at the inn, I saw movement outside my window.

Phosphorescence, I thought at first, a ripple cresting a hidden shoal, but then it was more, a man in a cream-colored waistcoat and black string tie, emerging from the water, drenched and heaving. He crawled up, and I sat up in bed, drawing my wrapper more tightly about myself. A long black mustache and long black hair, his eyes desolate and his face forlorn. I dared not move. He looked rather like my former husband, and he shared with that man a visible despair. I wondered how long it would be before he was dead, if he were not already.

He stood beneath my window looking up at me, and his gaze did the opposite of burn. I did not open the window, but I found my fingers stretching toward the sash. Only the chains kept me from reaching it.

Wake, he whispered, but I did not know how.

I must have fallen into sleep, for an insistent bell woke me at dawn, and the innkeeper entered with a tray. There were no burning eyes in my memory, nor was my body tender. I did not feel pains in my body that might suggest a night walk, nor did my mouth taste of metal. Within my body though, I felt the telltale motions of the stowaway, swimming in a tight circle.

"What is this?" asked the innkeeper, looking at my chains.

I looked at her with as much dignity as I could muster, and I said, "Might you release me? The key is on the pillow, just there."

She placed the tray on the bed and fetched the key.

"How am I to know if freedom suits you?" she asked.

"My agonies occur only at night," I told her, for the stowaway took no notice of the innkeeper. It did not wish for women, nor did it care for daylight. It slept within me when the sun was high.

"Will you continue your tale?" the innkeeper asked, unlocking my chains with less caution than I might have imagined she'd use. She poured a cup of coffee and delivered it into my shaking hands.

I indicated that I would, and the innkeeper withdrew long enough that I might tidy myself. Back then, to that sitting room downstairs, with its view of the silvery bay, a pot of coffee rather than tea, to increase my strength for the day ahead.

The innkeeper sat opposite me. "The night six months past," she said, prompting me back to my tale.

I ate a spoonful of porridge and sipped my coffee, feeling the heat in my body, a healthy heat, not that of the stowaway. For a moment I felt hopeful.

"Though the stowaway's presence prohibited guests to my house, I was at liberty to leave it. The stowaway seemed to see me as a gentle pet, a cat who might play about in the garden while its owner remained in the house. Thus were my days spent, with concerts and the usual occupations of a lady. It was not, despite the trouble in my house, a terrible life.

On the evening in question, I sat at the piano, picking out a song, and as I did, I noticed a stirring in the wall. I withdrew my fingers from the keys, fearing a mouse or moths, never imagining—"

I looked around the sitting room, fearing eyes and ears in the walls, but there was nothing visible here.

"A man emerged from the wallpaper, hair silken as fur, eyes like seaglass. Out of the floral pattern he came, his suit patterned with falling leaves, and I knew I could not trust a man who arrived that way, but there was no help for it. He stepped into the room, hung his coat on the tree, and walked across the carpet making no sound at all. I looked down at his feet, and they did not touch the ground.

He nodded at me, implying that I continue to play. I did, though my playing was nothing to be proud of, neglected in my duties as the keeper of a dead man's house. When, at last, I stopped, the man looked steadily at me.

"Who are you?" I whispered. "Have you come to deliver me from my stowaway?"

He looked at me, and said "I am a dreamer come to save you from darkness, Annabel MacFarlane, if you will be saved."

Why should I not allow the haunting, I thought. Why should I not give myself over to a dream? I had been alone for a very long time, and it seemed no harm to invite air into the house.

The dream gave me a ring, bent of a length of gold wire. He ran icy fingers over my skin—"

I hesitated.

"—and my nights became other than they'd been for nearly twenty years. For weeks, the stowaway stayed to its own side of the house. I heard the usual sounds of animals, of wind, of whispers, but nothing came through my chamber door. I thought the man in my house was, if not my secret, a guest the stowaway had no objection to. Indeed, I sometimes believed that he was an illusion, and that my joy was only something manufactured by waking dreams. I did not ask the dream who had sent him, and indeed, I did not dare to, for what if he came from the same realm as the stowaway? I did not wish to know.

The white marble of our staircase was sometimes marred with red footprints, and the rail as well, the marks of hands attempting to cling to the bannister. I had known of the stowaway's habits these long years, but though I read the papers, I saw no sign that the stowaway preyed upon the unlucky of our region. It may seem cold, my failure to investigate the nature of the victims, but I was as frightened of the stowaway as any prisoner of a jailor, and I did not. I wished only that the beast be fed, and not by myself.

One night, though, there was a thunderous sound and down the hall outside my rooms ran a thousand hooves. Boar? Horses? I could not say. There was a wrenching creak, and a roar from no animal I'd ever imagined.

"Go!" I whispered to the man beside me, but he did not. The stowaway stood in my doorway, eyes flicking over the chamber. I stayed still in the bed, coverlet drawn close about my throat. The stowaway inhaled deeply, and then dropped to the floor, undulating until it reached the wall through which my husband had arrived.

Up the wall the stowaway seeped, leaving an ichorous ooze, and the leaves and flowers on the paper, previously verdant, began to wither. Night began to fall over the green kingdom from which my dream had entered, and slowly I saw stars beginning to reveal themselves, cruel points of light in a sky that had been day.

The stowaway looked at me briefly, eyes glowing red, and the printed plants withered and blackened.

"Come," the stowaway said, and took a step toward me.

It was only then that my dream revealed himself, emerging from beneath the bedsheets. In his hand he held a pistol, and he aimed it at the stowaway, shouting.

"I am a hunter of Thule, and you will return to your prison!"

The stowaway's eyes glowed brighter, and it growled the growl of a lion over an antelope. Its entire flesh was stars now, and its tail whipped as it leapt at the man who had been my own true love, and covered him as though the skin of the sky had slid down and over the land.

"I am stronger than I was," the stowaway hissed. "You will not take me."

The man I'd chosen as a husband was gone, hidden by pulsating dark.

The stowaway flowed over the carpet toward me, bringing cold, but also bringing fire. I felt my edges crackle.

"Annabel," said the stowaway, its voice still the honey it had always been. "You have betrayed me. You might have spent your life dreaming, but you've made yourself hostess of a nightmare. Now you are mine, and I am yours. You will hide me in your skin, and together, we shall seek for my creator."

It took my hand and pressed its lips to my flesh. I felt the points of its teeth like lightning striking, and the stars of its skin glowed brighter. With a rush, the entirety of the creature was absorbed into me.

The stowaway is no longer visible to the world, but I can feel it. The physician I visited in the city told me I carried nothing at all, but I know him to be wrong.

"Hysteria," my father insisted, and the diagnosis was that. There was a movement from the men in my family to send me to a sanatorium, and though I resisted, I knew it was only a matter of time before they overpowered me. Hence my flight.

"This story explains my presence here, in your inn," I concluded at last. "To no one's satisfaction, not my own, nor yours. Yet am I here, and here I will remain until the stowaway is gone."

The innkeeper looked steadily at me, seemingly aware that I'd omitted certain terrible facts, certain shameful aspects of the possession. I could not speak them. I would not. My mouth watered, even still, and my ribs ached. One morning I'd awakened with claw marks rending my garments, and traveling up and down my torso, and another I'd woken in the river itself, drenched and half-frozen, clutching a bloody fingerbone. In the papers, I began to see notices of disappearances, men of letters, men with dark dreams. Their bodies were not found.

I knew where they were.

"Guests come here to die, some of them. Perhaps you are one of them?" she asked.

"I mean to be saved," I said. "I mean to save myself from this creature. I will not offer it harbor. It is a criminal fled from the land of dreamers, and it is a nightmare."

"Thule," she said. "That is the origin of the ship in the bay, in and out of our waters these twenty years," she said. "There have been men from aboard it here. Those curtains came from a Thule trader, once, long ago, and this sapphire as well. There are beautiful things to be had in the land of dreams, as well as horrid ones. The ship is a ship of explorers, hunting something fled here years ago. I believe you may know all too well what it is they seek."

I looked at her. Her skin glowed pale and her eyes shone, and I wondered when she had lost her own ghosts, or whether she boarded them here in hope of being transported one day to their realm.

I glanced at the curtains. I'd not examined the toile the night before, and today I saw the pattern was quite other than I'd imagined. Explorers, yes, their spears raised and pressing into the flesh of something without edges, a blot in the fabric speckled with stars. Another scene of the darkness taking them, dead men in the snow. Another of ships filled with vague forms, their faces stricken, and beneath them, the water itself made of night.

I shivered. What was it I contained? Would I be free of it?

"What shall I do?" I asked her.

"If it emerges," she said, "you must wrest it back into the land of dreams. Only then will you be free."

I went out into the city, trying to calm myself for the portrait. It was a silly thing, to attempt beauty in a portrait such as this one. It did not matter, or so the medium said. All that mattered was the method.

Half to the studio, worrying that perhaps my fever had returned—the stowaway heated my body to an uncomfortable degree—I felt a presence behind me.

I spun on my boot heel, but saw no one. It was full daylight, and there was no reason to suspect another thief, but I walked on, shifting toward a busier street, listening for steps behind me. I knew better than to rove alone, even at this time of morning, a time not unreasonable for any lady to be unaccompanied. I wouldn't be mistaken for any of those nightingales who'd be swaying toward their rooming houses at this hour, rather than away from them, but something possessed me to keep on my own path, to pass quickly by any carriages for hire. I had a horror that if I looked to the drivers I'd see a series of monsters leaning forward over the reins.

How many could there be of the creature that plagued me? Where had my first husband found the stowaway? I'd scanned map after map, but on none of them could I find the country called Thule. No, all that was on those maps was a vague area of nothingness with that label. Had it come aboard as cargo, hidden in a barrel of sugar, a secret folded in the silk? Had it pretended to be rope? My husband had been an importer of trade goods, but what had he gone to dreamland to acquire? He had filled his hold with a devil, and now the devil held me.

There were no steps in the street behind me, but only the sound of a cane, tapping, tapping, each cobblestone scratching beneath it, and the sound of splashing as well, as whatever wraith it was moved over the stones. I readied myself to scream, to run, but there was no need.

"Lady," a weak voice whispered. "Lady, will you hear me? I am a broken man, and not long for this world. The mistress of the inn sent me after you."

I turned and saw him for the second time: the man who'd walked out of the bay, still drenched, his waistcoat dripping, his black suit hanging on him as though he was a cadaver. He was correct in his assertion. Blue shadows bruised his eyes, and his cheeks were gaunt. He looked as though he'd climbed from out of a tomb.

"Where have you come from, Sir?" I asked him. The Sir was an afterthought. He was not demon, not ghost, but not whole either.

"A ship," he said, and I knew him to be deranged, but who was to say that I was not? He was a kindred spirit in that fashion, and so I let him speak. "I swam from a ship that floats there still—on the border of Dreamland—"

He extended a trembling finger toward the horizon, as though I would see his ship. There was nothing to be seen. "—and up again into the light."

"And what is your name?"

"Edgar," he said, and swayed, leaning heavily on his cane.

I felt the stowaway twist inside me, and I flinched, bending at the waist. My corset was laced particularly tight, some vain hope of caging the creature and keeping it still. It did not wish to be still.

"Are you well?" he asked.

"I am not," I said.

"Nor I," he said, and gave me a look of profound sympathy. "Not since the death of my wife."

I was reminded of my ghost husband. There were no men made of anything more than trouble in my history, and this one was no different.

"My name is Mrs. MacFarlane," I said.

"What is your Christian name?" he asked. He was no threat, his body wizened like that of an ancient, though he could not be much older than I.

"Annabel," I told him. Recognition flickered on his face for a moment.

"Ah, then it is true," he murmured. "Annabel. I have heard your name in passing, yes, in passing through the night. I have heard it whispered in a dream I had."

"Are we acquainted?" I asked. He was oddly familiar to me, it was true, more so than just the vision of him staggering up from the sea.

"No, no. We have never met in the waking world," he said, and the alert look he'd had was gone again. I smelt the alcohol on him, and more than that. He smelled of the sea, of salt, of blood. "I am a dreamer destined only for sorrow, Annabel, and there is one more thing I must do before I end my days."

Was I entranced by his suffering, so akin to my own? Or his handsome face, his history of loss. Some part of my heart, one I had not noticed in some time, felt enticed to compassion for one so miserable.

"I thought that I was destined for death as well," I told him recklessly, "but I refuse to accept it. I am to the portraitist. Will you accompany me, sir? I dislike undertaking the journey alone."

Quite unexpectedly, he smiled.

"You would take *me* to a photographer?" he asked. "This broken poet? Four days ago, I attempted suicide on a train. When I woke, it was on a ship in this bay, and I knew the crew of tattered men, and I knew the captain. He hunts the night for a beast he cannot find, a thing from his own sleeping kingdom which has fled to this one. He has sent me into the town to seek on his behalf, Annabel, to seek the beast. Have you seen it?"

He stood, his hands hanging, a pleading expression on his face. And here was I, containing the beast he sought. Here was I, an unwilling case for a spirit I'd never invited in.

"I have not," I told him. I could not trust him yet. I'd met handsome men before. I'd met a handsome ghost, a betrayer of my body. "I do not even know your full name," I said.

The man before me winced.

"Edgar Poe," he said. "I am a writer of horrors. It is only reasonable that I should end in horror myself. I have spent my life a dreamer, and now my dreams haunt me in daylight." He lifted his shoulders and his expression was that of profound regret. "It was a dream I made, long ago, and I worked at it, night after night, inventing its appetites. The dream made itself flesh and escaped the boundary of the land I'd made for it. After that, I know not where it went, though I am told there have been tales of its takings. I did not imagine I would be held here to reckon with my imagination, unable to die unless I captured it."

I felt faint, but still more resolved. The lacings of my corset bowed behind my back, and I gasped, pulling my own flesh in as the stowaway pressed against it. I felt the bones bend, and the silk threads, in the claws of something horrid.

"A dreamer," I said, thinking of my own miserable, missing nights.

"That does not matter. What one does in the dark is not a thing one must own in the light."

"If that were the truth of things, then murders might be done at midnight and never a murderer jailed for them," Poe said.

I thought of fingerbones, of a ribcage, of a man's wedding ring I'd found in the bosom of my dress. I thought of pocket watches and ink pens, of men I'd never met, of a black silk tie undone and knotted again about my wrist. I thought of a carved ivory cane I'd found beside my bed, the knob carved into the shape of a skull. All these things could have belonged to a man like the man before me, and too, he resembled a man I'd known once, long ago, a man who had been my husband.

I thought of the true reason I'd fled, a sudden waking in the darkest hours, finding myself far from home. I thought of the man I'd found before me, on his back, a man who looked enough like this one to be a twin to him. This one was not dead, no, but moaning on the platform of a train, swearing up and down that he was not waking but dreaming, insisting that he was doomed. It was too early in the morning for a crowd, and I leaned over his face and heard my own hiss, my own voice honeyed and covetous. I felt my body hum at proximity to the man and to his mind, but he was drugged and nearly insensible, and the lights in the station were beginning to be lit. I fled. My body was nothing human at all. I had torn his papers from his case, and rifled through them, hunting I know not what. What did the stowaway want? A maker? A parent? The man who had created it? What did it want with me, but a vessel? I'd been too long a vessel for this monster. I'd been too long hungry for meals I did not wish to consume.

"Take it away from me," I said to the poet. "Can you do that?"

"Perhaps," the poet said. "That is my aim."

I felt the stowaway longing for something, but what I knew not. It did not want me, though it accompanied me. It had never wanted me. It wanted a man, or a friend, or a companion other than I. Where had it come from? The country beyond the wall? The ship anchored in the bay? The place where night slept when the sun was in the sky?

If I could not be rid of my monster, I would go to Thule myself. If it was death I courted, so be it. I glanced up at the angle of the sun. Still enough time in the day for safety. The stowaway slept.

"Accompany me," I said, and the poet looked at me. The stowaway clasped and unclasped my fingers, stretched itself inside the borders of my body. It had been days since I'd fed on the meal the stowaway wished for, and I knew I had only hours before it would overcome me.

Poe took my arm and I felt him trembling. Together, we walked to Winchester Street, three beings, each breathing and longing, each desirous of its own story.

The Poet's Annotation

And now the story of the poet and the story of the lady and the story of the stowaway converge into one line, fiction and fact pressed too closely together to tell one from the other. The waking world and the sleeping one are the same, each engineered by dreamers of one kind or another. The poet writes an obituary for himself. The poet writes a tale of grief, his wife lost, his love dead. The poet is in a pit, and above him a pendulum. He will not marry again. He will be denied, and with that denial will come the rest of his life, the last year on earth. He writes on, the monster beside him, and the lady he's made of all the ladies he's lost. He writes himself down Winchester street, walking with a companion who may or may not be visible to anyone else in Providence. There will be no record of anyone named MacFarlane, nor of anyone met at a hotel. There will be nothing but this poet walking through the streets and to a portraitist, in the worst week of his life.

Is he raving? He is raving. Is he drunk and damaged? He is. Has he been bitten by a dog and does he wish to drink the ocean itself? Does he wish to transport himself to Thule by sipping the boundary between the imagined and the real, drinking it down until all that lies between his words and his life is a tender desert?

He does.

Annabel Lee is a child and he is a child (he is not a child) and Lenore is nevermore. Virginia is coughing and singing at a piano, blood spattering the keys, and then she is drunk on charity wine, and then she is dead, her cheeks flushed a color that cannot appear in Thule. Made of ice and gray is the heart of the poet, and in his kingdom, on his dark throne, he sits, as all of it melts into a bath of silver nitrate and acid ink.

He wishes himself extinguished.

The Portrait

The studio of Masury & Hartshorn was on the second floor, and we made our way up the stairs, my companion half-collapsing as he climbed. Inside my body, I felt the sleeping stowaway dreaming of meat. I would not feed it. I would resist. The stairwell smelled of chlorine and chemicals, a bracing scent that revived me to the task at hand. I had a body that was my own still, despite its inhabitant, nostrils that could burn and a throat that could close. I glanced at the man beside me, and wondered. Could I deliver him? Could I deliver us both?

We entered through glass doors into a room suffused in blue light, a sort of greenhouse with an intricate mechanism of shades and shadows. The walls were papered in cobalt, and the ceiling was a skylight with reflecting mirrors set at an angle beneath it. There, we found a young man polishing a silver plate with a soft cloth. He looked up at us through thick glasses, and raised his eyebrows at the spectacle before him. It was little wonder. A woman in a gaudy dress accompanied by a man on the brink of death. I could see the photographer considering us as subject.

"Messr. Masury?" I asked. I brought out the card the medium had given me in New York.

"No. I am Edwin Manchester," he said. I could not believe my luck.

"You, then, are the man I am seeking," I said, and passed the card to him. He read its contents, and looked more closely at me. He took my hand and weighed it in his own, and then pinched my wrist between two fingers. My flesh was denser than it ought to be, I well knew. I felt as though I contained sand, and indeed, I did. The night was made of sand and stars, and all of it was too heavy for a human body to bear.

"I see," he said. "And your companion?"

"This is Mr. Poe," I said.

The photographer's eyebrow raised higher. "It is an honor," he said. "A man of your stature in the spirit world."

"He suffers a similar malady," I said. "I believe it is related to the kingdom from whence my trouble came."

The photographer looked closely at Poe.

"He has suffered a loss rather than a weight," he said. "You have more than you require, and he has less."

"I have enough in my purse to pay for both portraits, if you might assist him as well as I."

"I will need no payment for his image," Manchester said. "It will be displayed in this shop as advertisement of our services."

"I am not possessed," Poe said. "I am in debt. I have left something aboard a ship as collateral."

"I see as much," said Manchester. "You are missing your soul rather than carrying another within your body. I can assist in this as well."

The daguerreotypist took off his apron, placing the silver plate on a table. I looked into it and was startled by the mirror it presented, my hair in disarray, and for a moment, my eyes glowing the way the stowaway's eyes glowed, my skin a sea of stars.

I glanced at the portraits on display in the studio, the way their subjects seemed to float, each in their own transparent darkness, their faces made of gilded dust. Did some of those portraits contain demons and ghosts? Were some of them exorcisms, or were they only portraits of the wealthy? I could not say.

"You will be first," Manchester said. "Mr. Poe after. The sun is bright enough today."

Poe nodded. I felt his fingers clench my arm more tightly, but he did not waver. Inside my skin, the stowaway extended sleeping fingers to touch those of Poe, but I did not acknowledge it.

Manchester gestured me onto a staircase, a platform with a small chair at its center, and I ascended, feeling my skirts draping down the stairs. Was I climbing to heaven?

"Stare into the sun," Manchester told me, positioning me in a brace, my head supported by a stand, my skirts spread so that I seemed to be airborne. "I will remove this burden from you, but you must stay perfectly still for sixty seconds."

I looked down at the poet, whose face was hopeful, though the evidence of years of despair was written on it, a cloth pleated by pain.

My spine convulsed where the stowaway wrapped about it, and I saw Poe glance at me, his face concerned, as Manchester aimed the camera at the tableau vivant he'd arranged.

A dark cloud passed over the sun, and a raindrop splattered on the glass panes above me. The monster moved.

Ten seconds. Twenty. My heart quivered in my breast and the stowaway stretched. Thunder outside, and the building rattled. Darker still.

Thirty seconds, and something began to shift inside my skin. I began to feel night falling over my body, stars appearing on the tips of my fingers, coming into light all over my flesh, beneath my dress and up and down my arms, brilliant points of pain and fire, and myself an indigo woman curtained in silk and satin. I heard my own voice cry out as the stowaway began to emerge.

"Stay still!" Manchester shouted. "Do not let it move you!"

I resisted the urge to let my body fall down the stairs and upon him.

Not only upon him, but upon the innocent Poe. Their blood and bones, their organs like bright ink on a page made of snow. I would write the story of Thule with their flesh, I would—

Darkness slithered over my eyes, and I held them wide, trying to keep from doing what Night wanted me to do. I tasted metal where I'd bitten my tongue, and I heard myself hiss. A sound a dreamer might make whilst wandering a long passage, the way a scream might transform, in the voice of that sleeper, into a song. All these nights of invisibility, a wandering swath of stars falling upon the unlucky, all these nights, a woman made of nothingness.

There was a crashing sound, and there, before me, was Poe, his face pale as the moon, his eyes no longer anguished, but purposeful.

"TO ME," he roared, and lurched up the staircase, his hands reaching for mine. He spun to face the camera as the shutter closed, his ungloved hand still clasping my own.

I felt the stowaway leave my body and rush out, into the air, into the camera, away.

The thunderclouds fled the sun, and the sky brightened. Night receded. I drew in a ragged breath.

The daguerreotypist withdrew the plate from the camera and darted to the developing room, donning a set of India rubber gauntlets as he went, but I could only look at Poe. He would not meet my gaze. What had he done?

Manchester emerged from the developing room.

"View it," he said, and gestured us into the room. "It is not as you imagined it would be, and yet."

A gleaming tray of mercury, held over a spirit lamp, and fumes that felt golden upon inhaling. The plate rested above the heated mercury, an image emerging in salt on its face, delicate as dust on a butterfly's wing.

I watched it, praying that I'd see what ought to be in the daguerreotype and not something else. Hoping to see my image containing the stowaway, and all of it trapped within this plate of glass.

But as it emerged, I did not see the creature, nor did I see my own face. It was dark shadows appearing and then shifting through red and blue to black again, the eyes first and then the rest.

I saw Edgar Allan Poe, and within him, all around him, Night. The image was of the poet, suspended in the darkness of the background, and I could see myself in ghostly silhouette behind him, my face covered in stars, my eyes glittering, my fingers laced in his own.

The poet looked at me, and reached into his jacket. He removed a pot of ink, looked at me tenderly, and opened it. I watched him, uncertain, and then, suddenly, he flung it over me.

"Thank you," he said.

Darkness. A blotting out, a removal from view.

The Thule Daguerreotype

The original Poe portrait, taken in desolate circumstances in the year eighteen forty-eight, the year before the poet's death, is, over the years, lost and found, discovered in the possession of a traveling hypnotist, fallen from a drawing room wall, set on fire. It lives in legend, copied and etched, discussed, tattooed, made the subject of academic texts.

After the image was taken, the subject wandered the streets, visiting the home of a woman he had proposed to, and raving that he was doomed, that he was done for good. He screamed for his soul.

The daguerreotype depicts a man in a half-buttoned black dinner jacket, a rumpled white shirt, an ascot tied and wrapped tightly enough to suggest that it is keeping his head from tumbling off. He has a high white forehead, a dark mustache, tousled hair, and eyes sunk deep in a face lined with grief. He is a year from dying, but in the Ultima Thule portrait, he appears to have emerged from his tomb, and indeed, the image depicts the poet four days after his failed suicide by laudanum.

If one looks closely, with the proper knowledge, it is possible to see the figure behind him, a spectral form, a radiance draping over one of the man's shoulders, an image of the missing, left in dust on a silver plate. Perhaps it is a woman, or perhaps it is something else entirely.

The business of portraiture is one of silver and gold by the ton, and the miserable face of the poet is immortalized in precious metal. The presence behind him is a stain rendered in darkness, silver nitrate, an abyss that reflects light.

This is a saint's icon, Edgar Allan Poe's image pressed like a kiss to a ground glass windowpane, and the form holding him is a glittering ghost, mutable as frost over a view of a city at night. Does it hold him as a lover or as a captive?

What is left inside this portrait?

That is one way to look at a photo of a ghost. Another way is to look at both figures, this portrait, this imaginary kingdom and its creator flickering in and out of the light, and see it as a record of more than one event, the moment when a poet's soul was removed, the moment when a man counted down the seconds remaining in his life.

He counts them in syllables. He counts them in sentences. He counts them in stories. *All that we see or seem*, he writes. *Is but a dream, within a dream.*

Open the glass panes that house the portrait and blow, a single breath, and the image is only imagined again. Press a finger to the face of this ghost and watch him become thin air.

The Lady's Last Tale

I felt myself disappearing, but I remained scored into the world, my skin a page with lines on it, my hair streaked with silver, my dress still as bright as it had been, but now obliterated.

The photographer faded as I faded, and the studio as well, whether they had been there or no. An imaginary Providence or a true one, I could not say. The blue wallpaper was night, and I was part of it now, and the mercury bath was stars, and I was part of that as well.

Thule was before me then, a white landscape of cliffs and women shrouded, a body—was it my body?—washing up on a coastline made of bones. I was the sea and I was a ship, and I was a city of ghosts.

I did not disappear from the world, though it seemed I might. I stayed, and this kingdom by the sea stayed. I climbed the stairs in a tower, I in my black dress, its lining like the inside of a redbird's wing, my magpie-feathered stripes, my bosom spattered in ink. There was a throne there, and then there was myself seated in it, reigning over the great and frozen unknown.

I ruled over a kingdom I had not made, but would not surrender, and out there, in the mist, there was no ship and there was no sinner. There was no poet with his quill, writing my world.

Here in Dream-land would I love and live forever. Here would I contain the soul of the poet, transferred to me in silver and in ink, even as I traded to him the creature I'd harbored.

I was Annabel Lenore Virginia MacFarlane, and no one would ever find me again.

DON'T TURN ON THE LIGHTS

Cassandra Khaw

Stories are mongrels. It don't matter whether they were lightning-cut into stone or whispered over the crackle of a dying flame; no story in the world has pedigree. They've all been told and retold so many times that not God himself could tell you which one came first. Yes, every story in creation.

Including this one.

Especially this one.

You might have heard it before. There was a girl once. Her name was Sally. It could have been any other name, really. But let's go with Sally. It's solid. Round-hipped and stout, the kind of Midwestern name that can walk for hours and don't mind it much when the sun burns its skin red.

Anyway.

Sally was, maybe, about eighteen or nineteen, some freshman at a local college. And like every teenager, she sometimes got behind on her school work.

So one night, she took all her books and went down to her dormitory's basement, telling herself she'd study till the dawn brindled the sky in gold and claret.

Halfway through, she realized she'd forgotten a book. And back up she went, feet making no sound at all on the old carpet. (Was it thick? Yes. Lush like nothing else. It had to be, or what happened next would make no sense.) Silent, she padded along until she reached her room and opened the door.

Click.

It was black inside. No lights at all. The curtains were drawn. You couldn't see the glow of the distant town. But that was okay. Sally knew the room like the map of her palms. Slowly, she felt her way along the walls to her bed. Slowly, she realized—

There was a smell in the air: pennies and salt.

There was a sound in the air too: breathing, rasped and ragged, heavier than anything she's heard. Sally knew the beat of her roommate's breath. This wasn't it.

And maybe, she might have said something if it wasn't for the itching under her skin, something that whispered, "This isn't all right."

So, Sally didn't. It was late and she was tired and it was probably just her imagination. Thus decided, she got what she needed and clicked the door shut behind her as she left, just as something began to drip, drip, drip.

"Damn faucet," she mumbled as she swayed back down to the basement.

The next day, Sally went for her exams. How did she do? Truthfully, it didn't plain matter. She took her examinations and then she went home, feet crunching across dried autumn leaves and cobbled stones.

Into the dormitory, she went up the spiral staircase, unease laving its way down her spine. There were far too many people out and about, their faces bright and afraid, but that wasn't Sally's problem, no sir. Someone else could go worry about that. All she wanted was to sleep.

Sleep wasn't in the cards, though. Hell, I don't know if she ever slept again. I know I wouldn't be able to. Because when Sally finally walked all the way to her room, pushing past co-eds in their flower-printed pajamas, she found police tape and policemen.

And a smell in the air: pennies, salt, a stink of dried urine and shit.

And a sound in the air: a *drip drip dripping*, oozing between the noise of the walkie-talkies.

And a sight like nothing anyone should see: her roommate, cut up like beef, words scrawled on the wall above her head:

"Aren't you glad you didn't turn on the lights?"

That's the *popular* version.

The socially acceptable one, as they like to say in polite company. After all, it's one where no one really is at fault. Not Sally, not the roommate, not even the butcher who sliced up that poor girl. (You can't pin a sin on a thing with no face, can you?)

But there are other retellings, crueler ones. Or truer ones, I guess, depending on who you're asking.

And since you asked, one of them goes something like this:

Sally was eighteen, maybe nineteen, but she might as well have been seventy-two. Hers had not been an easy life, although it isn't for me to explain how. That's another story, and also not mine to tell.

But she survived it, or at least some of her did; the girl that shambled into college was one part Sally, three parts grit, and nine-tenths rage. The world hadn't been fair to the poor child.

It could have been worse.

It could have been Sally who'd taken a murderer to her bed, Sally who'd been pushed down onto the covers with a palm over her mouth, Sally who'd laid there twitching as someone carved a smile under her chin.

Now, I bet you're wondering: how'd Sally know about all that?

Because she was there, of course.

As with every variant of this story, Sally was out too late for one reason or another. Realizing she'd forgotten something, she stumbled upstairs to her room. In the popular version, all she heard was breathing, a drip drip dripping to tell her that something was wrong.

In this one, her roommate whispered:

"Sally, help."

And she froze.

There was a smell in the air: pennies, salt, an ammonia reek. There was a sound in the air too: a gurgling noise, a *shlick* of steel peeling through skin, someone kicking against a bulk too big to move.

I don't know why she walked away, why she didn't flick on the lights, and scream for the police. Maybe, she was scared. Maybe, it was late and she was tired and certain that it was all her imagination. Maybe, Sally thought to herself, ""I ain't dying for someone I barely know."

Whatever the case, she left.

And well, you know how the rest of this tale goes, so I won't bore us both with its end.

Was that one of the meaner tellings?

Hell no.

See, no one likes much talking about it, but everyone's got a little blood on their hands. Most of the time, it's metaphorical. That little lie that gets our siblings in trouble. The broken heart we blame on someone else's lacks. Everyone is guilty of a few small sins.

What Sally might have done? It wasn't *evil*, per se. A little selfish, maybe. But can you blame her for being frightened? Imagine being on the cusp of freedom, full of hope for the first time in your life. Would you give that up for a stranger? Would you lay down and die for them?

Yeah, I thought as much.

I digress, though.

Stories are defined by a beginning, a middle, and an end. In more literary circles, people talk about denouements and layers, textures, the way a word can transcend to a synesthetic experience. But at the end of day, it all comes back down to those three things. A beginning, a middle, an end.

You'd be amazed as to how much detail gets lost in between, how a good storyteller can make you forget the bits that don't make sense.

What happened that night?

What drove Sally down to a drafty basement when she could have found sanctuary in the library? If you think about it, none of that makes sense. Every college has its reading rooms, its communal spaces. So why a basement, exactly?

Did she *really* go there of her own accord?

It's possible.

It's possible too, that someone decided that it'd be a mighty fine way to terrify the freshman. No better method for earning respect than kidnapping someone from their beds and throwing them into the waiting dark, a hood over their heads, the concrete cold against their legs.

Maybe, that someone was Sally's roommate.

It's possible.

Maybe, this incident wasn't the first of its kind.

It's possible.

Maybe, as Sally sat crying in the basement, too afraid to call out, something wormed out of shadows. Something old, hungry, smelling of salt and pennies, like the taste of blood in the back of your mouth.

Maybe the thing said to Sally, "What's your heart's desire?"

And Sally, too full of grief to think straight, replied with something that she would regret.

That's possible too.

Is that what *really* happened?

Don't ask me.

There are only two people who really know, and one of them might not even be called Sally. Truth is, I don't think anyone gives a shit either. With stories like this, all people want are their bones. People like putting their own spin on things.

It could have gone any number of ways, this tale. A lot can happen between the main events. Did Sally run straight out of the room? Did she listen for a while? Did she tell her roommate to be wary, to lock the doors and watch out for strange faces? Did she know the assailant?

Was there an assailant?

Who knows.

Still, before you go, let me tell me the version I like best. It's one that few know and fewer care for, but it makes the most sense to me.

Or maybe, I just like my stories bloody.

Sally was eighteen, maybe nineteen, a freshman like any other, full of hopes and newborn dreams. The future had never seemed so bright.

There was just one problem.

Because of circumstances, she had to share a room with someone she knew, someone she didn't rightly like. It might have been her sister. The records aren't clear on that. A cousin, possibly, or her mother's best friend's favorite daughter. Who the hell knows? One way or another, it was someone with whom Sally just had to play nice.

And she tried.

Oh, she tried.

In the beginning, Sally did her absolute damnedest to be civil with that other girl, but you'd only drown that poor horse if you forced it to drink. Their relationship took no time at all to ripen to hate, soured by the need to suffer each other's proximity, both of them jostling for space neither could afford.

Still, it was almost bearable for a while.

Then, Sally's property started to disappear. Her food, her clothes, research texts, little odds and ends. Then, Sally's father died, and her roommate used the news of his suicide against her, ransoming Sally's reputation.

It got worse from there.

Sally stayed quiet, but you know what they say about people like that. And this wouldn't be so bad if Sally was ordinary, but she wasn't, no sir. She had a bit of witch in her blood, which is to say that she had a little too much. Sally had just enough power to talk to things the wise leave well alone.

So she did.

One day, Sally decided she had enough and went down into the dark, carrying the hairs from her roommate's brush. True enough, there was something there waiting.

She fed it those long black strands, one a time, saying nothing throughout. Only smiled when the thing politely asked for more.

The next day, she came back with nail clippings.

This went on for a time.

One night, the thing, taught to hunger for one specific taste, asked Sally, "Where'd you get all that fine food?"

"Upstairs," she said.

"Upstairs in the light?"

"Yeah," Sally replied, licking her dry lips. "I could show you where."

"Huh," the thing said. "I'd like that. But I don't like it much when someone watches me eat. It's one thing when it's little nibbles like this, it's another when you're talking about a feast."

(Do such creatures really talk with so much eloquence? Who knows. They do in this story, though.)

"That's fine," Sally said, rising to her feet. "You can keep the lights off."

Thus decided, the two left the basement. Sally followed the thing up the spiral stairwell, her footsteps quiet, its footfalls silent. She followed it into her room and sat down on her bed, quiet as a mouse as the thing began its work. Sally stayed true to her word. She kept it pitch-dark. Not even the glow of the distant town to light their way. Thankfully, her imagination was enough.

When the sound of chewing stopped, when the air was the stink of piss and flayed meat, when there was nothing left to do but leave, Sally got up and walked away.

The thing followed behind.

The next morning, she came back to find her room transformed into a slaughterhouse, the air thick with button-black flies. There was an apology scrawled in her roommate's blood. Sally had to hide her smile.

"Aren't you glad you didn't turn on the lights?"

No, she thought. It would have been fun to watch.

⊏◆⊐

EVERYTHING BEAUTIFUL IS TERRIFYING

◆

M. Rickert

"But we, when moved by deep feeling, evaporate."
—*Rainer Maria Rilke*

The Strangos come all year, identifiable by the clothes they wear, the giggling behind open hands, the wide-eyed pretense of innocence; like belled cats they give their trespass away. I ignore them—for the most part—though recently the baristas have begun giving directions to Laurels tree. They think this is funny, apparently, even if they never witness the punch line. Strangos standing in the middle of Wenkel's cornfield clutching their little purses. Strangos in the Piggly Wiggly parking lot next to the dumpsters, noses squinched against the stench. Strangos in front of my house—not funny at all—so close to each other the heels of their black shoes touch. I found them early on Christmas morning, standing beneath the streetlamp, upturned faces dotted with flakes of snow, matching pea coats frosted with ice, knees trembling above soggy ankle socks and black shoes.

They arrive all year, undeterred by the season. July and August bring a few carrying guidebooks and taking selfies (which no legitimate Strango would ever do) things get more serious in September, but October is Strango high season. In October the scent of wood smoke mingles with the beeswax candles perfuming my home with honey. Give me that and a blood moon casting everything in a mortal glow. Give me that and the ghost the Strangos seek, though I am not one of them, but an original.

She was buried, they say, in an unmarked grave at her mother's request. It was generally understood this was done in the usual manner, but after that movie came out with its silly premise that Laurel's weary ghost haunts the mysterious location of her body's interment, the Strangos arrived with their earnest obsession. I, myself, seeking answers, once stood on Laurels porch until her mother threatened me with a kettle of boiled water.

"Forgive me?" the Strangos murmur as they pass. It's just coincidence. The Strangos murmur their forgiveness request because in the movie that's how it's done. I stand in white ankle socks and black shoes, clutching the little purse with the clasp that clicks open and shut. Laurel stands beside me, dressed to match; though it's not really us, of course, but actresses portraying me and her ghost. When I whisper, "forgive me?" she doesn't say anything. The camera pulls back until we are in a circle of light surrounded by black; then a dot, then nothing at all.

I resisted watching for quite some time until one dreary night, while clicking mindlessly through cooking shows, women-buying-wedding-dresses shows, and fertile-family shows I stopped, stunned, as though experiencing a sudden change in altitude. There she was—Laurel—in her black shoes and white socks, wearing a dress I'd never seen; spinning beneath a bright arc of autumn leaves.

That particular scene comes quite close to the end—as you may know—but it was one of those stations that plays the same movie repeatedly. I can truthfully say that by the third viewing I was eating popcorn again; less enchanted by the Laurel look-alike and more annoyed by what they got wrong, which was almost everything.

Though accused and found not guilty, my innocence was never restored. The Strangos (and the screenplay writer) are convinced I am a murderer but the truth is so much more benign. Ask the Strangos and they will whisper, in sibilant tones, "forgive me?" over and over again until the reporter, either irritated by their petulance, or thrilled to have gotten a good clip for the weird news story gives up trying for more while the photographer waits for that moment when the Strangos open and close their purses making a sound like click beetles.

I am disinclined towards empathy with Strangos, but must confess I understand. Reporters are so annoyingly persistent in asking the wrong questions (as are parents, detectives, attorneys, and everyone) that some-times a person can find no response more perfect than the defiant sound of purse latch. I did not do it to be annoying or frightening though the movie portrays me as both. I was a child then, accused of murder. I was terrified, not terrifying.

The tree isn't hard to find, if one knows where to look as, of course, I do. And, while I hate to attribute anything of value to that movie, I must admit after watching it several times I, too, became obsessed with the old oak as a potential location for Laurels ghost. I did not, to be clear, think her mother would have her buried there. I believe she was cremated; her ashes now in Florida.

But her ghost? It seemed possible the tree would make a perfect host. (Like the Caribbean Lagarou tree where people have reported seeing, from a distance, flickering orbs of lights in its branches which, I know, is meant to sound ominous but I find reassuring.) Thus began my October quest through the backyards of my youth to that small hidden field we discovered all those years ago.

When the seasons turned to Halloween we, best friends forever, chose to be twins. The movie would have you believe we dressed alike for years, but in truth it was only a single month, and not even all of that.

When October comes I close the windows, happy to sever any tie with murmuring Strangos. I take out the old photographs: Laurel and me in our bathing suits (not matching) eating popsicles (and in the left corner, beneath the azalea bush the toes of my father's shoes. He used to like to play that game of spying on us.) Laurel and me on her swing set (there was a time when I was a welcomed guest). Laurel and me in sleeping bags, wide awake, Laurel giving the finger, and me frozen in shock by her bold gesture. I remember how my brother ran to report what she had done and how my mother (still innocent in her own way then) laughed. The last photograph has been widely duplicated—I'm sure you've seen it in some fashion or other—Laurel and me in the matching cotton dresses that Mrs. Sheer made in a single weekend. She had extra time on her hands, my mother said, since Laurel was an only child. We are standing in front of my house in those dresses, ankle socks, and white Keds spray-painted black. I can't remember why we did that. Sometimes too much is made of the casual choices of the young.

My mother found the purses at the dime store and splurged, buying both. I think she felt a little competitive with Mrs. Sheer, though this is pure speculation on my part and, as one who has suffered by what people assume, I try not to guess the motivation of others. My mother bought the purses. They were red. Matching white hairbands completed the look.

I suspect that arranging photographs of Laurel on the mantel might seem macabre to others. I can't be sure about what "normal" people think; they got everything so wrong with me that I have never adjusted to their ways. Halloween has, by necessity, evolved over the years into my own manner of celebration. Not for me the freedom of cheap costumes and pillowcases full of candy. That was lost with Laurel's death; first to my grief, then to my shame, and finally to my compromised life. While others were content with false ghosts, I hoped for the real thing. To be forgiven. Not for a murder I never committed, but for leaving her where she was later found with dirt and skin beneath her fingernails.

It is true that, as they said, the skin was mine. So much was made of this! We had a fight. About what, I can't remember. There was dirt on my dress and shoes and socks. We ran through backyards and fields to get to our tree. Dirt is not blood, or criminal in any way, but try telling that to folks set on vengeance, or any of the Strangos who think they know so much.

When October comes I decorate with photographs of the dead: Laurel and me as already mentioned, my parents, and my bother whose suicide is not a part of this story. Also my cats, Batman and Robin, each found with strings around their necks and, I believe, victims of my notoriety. I arrange the photographs in a display of fake autumn leaves ever since trying to use real ones which brought bugs into the house, an infestation I do not want to repeat, appropriate as it may be to the occasion.

Sadly, no one begs treats from me; a pattern I ignored for years, stocking up on candy bars, popcorn balls, and fairly expensive caramel apples which I ate throughout winter, solidifying the caramel flavor of loneliness, the apple bite of regret. While others dress as someone else, I dress as myself (or the girl I once was) in yellow gingham, white socks, black shoes, headband; waiting until dark before I sneak through the backyards, everyone so distracted I make an easy passage to the tree where I wait. The first time I did this I panicked when I realized how, without awareness, I had so thoroughly become Laurels last moments, or what we know of them, before she was murdered, but no one came to reenact the crime. I just sat shivering, in the dark.

We had gone trick or treating with strict instructions to return home by ten but, if you haven't picked up on this by now, Laurel was cheeky and I, her happy co-conspirator.

"Heyo," she said, (using our twin language) "Let's go-o to our-o tree-o."

Why? Oh, I don't remember though I suspect it seemed just enough of a transgression to deliver a delicious thrill, running through moonlight on that night inhabited by the occult. It was meant to be fun! We giggled and whispered, lugging pillowcases heavy with loot.

The paper reported candy wrappers littered amongst the leaves. I suppose this is right. We probably delighted in our feast, drunk on sugar. We fought. About what, I don't remember. She scratched me and I ran home, though to this day I can hear her cries. "Come-o back-o," she called.

"Im-o afraid-o of the Strangos." A false laugh, and then, "Don't go-o-o."

Later, the policeman handed me a cider doughnut and said, "I often think what I would say if I had one more day with my friend who died. Heck, I bet you know what that's like, don't you?"

Click-click.

"Go ahead. Close your eyes. Picture Laurel."

Click.

"Say it."

"Forgive me."

"Who but the guilty ask forgiveness?" The prosecutor intoned over and over again. In my youth I thought this was compelling, but as a grownup I am shocked that adults fell for this false equivalency. Though I was guilty to be sure, it was not of the crime I was charged with. In the end, I was just a bad friend. No danger of repeating that mortal error again. Who would want to be friends with me? I can tell you the answer is no one. Not even a ghost.

Yet, I persist. In spite of the solemnity of the season I have come to enjoy my celebration which begins, as I have said, with the altar of dead and so forth until the great night arrives when I turn off all my lights and— dressed as myself all those years ago—sneak away from streets teeming with Strangos of all shapes and sizes; generations of Strangos with no connection to Laurel or her life to stand beneath our tree where I beg her to forgive me, jump when a leaf falls (briefly seeing too much meaning in it) and look at my hands. So large, though once they were so small. I shiver in the cold. Walk home alone, shoes and socks dampened by frost.

The next morning I pack photographs, dress, headband, purse and the rest. I toss out the caramel apple sticks and pumpkin tea wrappers. I stand at the closed window noting how the tree limbs scratch the gray sky, the fallen leaves decomposed of color. November is the worst month, that brutal time after they found her body and my own mother began the wandering which defined her final years. She paced at all hours; locking doors, sprinkling sugar on the floor ("It will mark his footprints," she said) and cut up tablecloths which she insisted made perfect fabric for new dresses, though I never saw any sewn. Perhaps I outgrew them in that time between the charge and my acquittal. My father found solace in fantasies of revenge, which he described in our new ritual of bedtime stories. "First, I'll tear off his fingernails," he said and so forth, seeding my sleep with nightmares from which I often woke to find my brother weeping in a dark corner.

I was arrested in December so it would not be unreasonable to assume the month ruined for me but I have recovered the season; enlivened by the tradition of Christmas ghosts. Laurel loved the holiday; it made sense she would use the occasion to make a grand entrance. In spite of what that movie inferred she never would have become zombified with an appetite for blood; even dead she would remain a life force. I know she wasn't always sweet, or even good but she could make me laugh when no one else did. She told Petal Mearlot and Tina Schubert to stop throwing stones at me, and the day after Christmas—that last year—she pretended to be impressed by my meager haul then brought me to her house (it smelled of peppermint and evergreen) where she dumped the contents of a giant stocking on her bed, dividing it between us because, she said, Santa meant for me to have an equal share. "Were just so alike. Sometimes he gets us confused."

So it came to be that I made the error of inviting the Strangos I found standing beneath the streetlamp into my house. They looked cold and forlorn and, I admit, I was curious. Why would they choose to be Strangos when they could be daughters; loved and loving on early Christmas morn?

"Why are you here?" I asked, as I hung their wet coats in the downstairs shower where they dropped chips of ice on the linoleum.

"We came to see Laurel's tree. Did you cut it down?" they asked. "Did you save the wood? 'Cause it's haunted."

"Here." I offered the blue willow cup and saucer my mother once loved, trembling with excitement at my first Christmas guests, ever. "Do you take lemon, cream, or sugar?"

"Oh, I don't drink tea," said the first Strango, frowning into the cup.

"Me neither," said the other. "What else you got?"

They reminded me of Laurel. She would have sounded bossy, just like them. It put a smile on my face, it really did.

"I have Coke and milk. There might be juice."

"What about eggnog?"

I shook my head, no. "My mother said it is dangerous because of the eggs."

"There are no eggs in eggnog," said Strango One, frowning into her cup.

"What about cocoa?" asked Strango Two. "But it must have whipped cream. I hate marshmallows."

"Laurel hates marshmallows too," I blurted.

"We know," the Strangos said in unison.

An uncomfortable silence settled over us. I wondered how they knew this about her. Was it buried somewhere in the movie; in the early scene when we met in kindergarten, perhaps? Or maybe noted in the companion volume, which I never purchased though I did page through it once, in the library, hunkered between shelves like a voyeur, my worn copy of Rilke temporarily abandoned?

"What's it like?" Strango One asked. "To live in her house?"

"Whose house?"

"The murderer."

I knew how Christmas was supposed to be and, while I had never entertained visitors, I had an idea how they were supposed to behave. I decided to rise above my guest's poor manners. "Would you like toast? I can cut it in the shape of a star, or a boot.

The Strangos, sitting side-by-side on the couch in their matching dresses with knocked knees and wet socks, looked at each other, wide-eyed then clapped their hands; three quick claps.

"Goody," said one.

"Yes, please," said the other. "With cinnamon."

Laurel liked cinnamon too. It made me sad to remember, though it did make the toast glitter pleasantly. I wished I had cocoa, but the Strangos didn't seem to mind the Coke and one of them even commented favorably on the combination, saying she planned to make it a tradition. I'm not sure if she was serious. It is very difficult for me to differentiate between mockery and affection.

After the Strangos finished their snack we sat and stared at each other. I studied them closely for clues on how to proceed but when Strango One began picking her dress with long fingernails as though harvesting fleas, I began to fear my little party was in trouble. "Would you like to play charades?"

"How about hide-and-seek?" Strango One replied.

Personally, I never liked the game and didn't see what it had to do with the holiday but in the spirit of being a good hostess, I agreed.

"You hide," Strango One said.

I thought it unkind, to send me off alone while they counted to a thousand and five, yet they were guests and, as such, should be graciously accommodated. How strange it was, then, to be alone again in this new fashion; knowing there were those nearby who shared companionship while I had none. Even though they were Strangos, it made me lonely in a way I hadn't been for a long time. Hearing their voices count together brought to mind the sound of Laurel and me reciting "The Night Before Christmas," which we learned in its entirety in second grade. The memory only made me want to create more distance between me and the Strangos. I crept up the stairs; careful to skip the third from the top. The sound of their counting became a murmur that reminded me of waking in my bedroom when I was young, listening to the sounds my parents made.

What had I been thinking? Why had I invited Strangos into my house?

Before then it had never occurred to me to enter the forbidden attic, but it offered a perfect hiding place; its narrow door blended neatly with the paneled wood and the small hole that once housed a doorknob appeared to be a whorl. It was off limits when I was a child, the occasional source of strange noises my father attributed to ghosts, though I had seen him take my brother up there and knew the moans belonged to him. I stood at the bottom of the jagged staircase, looking up the dark portal with the odd feeling of assessing a giant jigsaw piece, memorizing it before pulling the door shut and slowly walking up the stairs, imagining all sorts of frightening things like mice and bats, spiders, and the like.

The attic was surprisingly small and, once I adjusted, cozy in a way. As a child I often "played mole," rolling up in a blanket and hiding in my bedroom closet; it made sense that I enjoyed the confined space with its low slanted ceiling jutted at odd angles over inviting corners. There wasn't much up there—an old bed, broken lamps, boxes filled with tools—but it was surprisingly warm. I sat, leaning against the wall and felt something like happiness, or what I remembered of it. "See Dad," I whispered. "I always knew it was you," which led to tears that surprised me with their sudden, inexplicable arrival.

The single, old window offered a patch of bruised sky I stared at; finally hypnotized into a slumber until revived by a luminescence that filled the room with a holy glow. "Laurel?" I whispered, but did not wait for a flicker of acknowledgment; instead, I turned away, curled into the reassuring crook of my elbow. For some, hope is an annihilation; a greater loss than the loss from which it is born.

I don't know how long I slept, but when I awoke the attic was consumed by darkness, there was an uncomfortable crick in my neck and my knees ached as I carefully unwound myself. I bumped my shin on my way across the room, maneuvered carefully down the stairs, suspecting the Strangos were long gone; if I fell and hit my head I would likely die and be decomposed before anyone even noticed I was missing.

What a mess the Strangos made! The house was in chaos; furniture moved, lamps unplugged, cupboards left open. What, I wondered, did the Strangos think I had shrunk myself small as a pin—the refrigerator drawers drawn full to reveal a pale head of lettuce, carrots and eggs thrown to the floor—before I accepted they had not been guests, but invaders. I closed the drawers, tidied up as one does, returned each thing that could be returned to its rightful place and tossed what was ruined; when my eyes fell to an errant orange, an orb of brilliance I plucked from its shadowed corner and peeled, getting skin beneath my nails as the bright spiral fell against the white porcelain. I wiped my tears with orange scented fingertips, finally understanding the answer I had been given: the sweet taste, the holy glow, the great loss and widening absence; to be robbed day-after-day, month-after- month, year-after-year; left to fall deeper into the void, find an orange there, and destroy it.

—⟨◆⟩—

SWIFT TO CHASE

⚒

Laird Barron

In medias res part II:

After a hard chase and all-too brief struggle, the Bird Woman of the Adirondacks loomed over me; demonic silhouette, blackest outspread wings tipped in iron; gore-crested and flint-beaked. Her thumbnail-talon poised to spike me through the left eye.

"To know itself, the universe must drink the blood of its children." Her voice cracked like an ice shelf collapsing; it roared across an improbable expanse of inches.

The talon pressed against my iris. It went in and in.

Rewind and power dive from the clouds. Join the story, *in medias res,* part I:

Where in the world is Jessica Mace? That scene when the superlative secret agent gets captured inside the master villain's lair is where. Instead of a secret agent, here's little old me doing my best impression. Rather than a rocket station beneath a dormant volcano, I'd gotten trapped on an estate (1960s Philip K. Dick-esque) nestled among the peaks of the Adirondacks. Cue jazzy intro music; cue rhinestone heels and a dress slit to *here*. My nemesis, billionaire avian enthusiast and casual murderer of humans, Averna Spencer, wasn't playing. Except she *was* playing.

First clue of my imminent demise (more like the fifth or sixth clue, but just go with it): a leather-bound copy of *The Most Dangerous Game* parked on the nightstand of my quarters. Second clue? The woman herself said over the intercom, "Fly, my swift, my sweet. When I catch you, I'm giving you a blood eagle."

Viking history isn't my specialty, but I know enough to not want one.

There I sat, dressed to kill or be killed. The loaner evening gown was a trap. Spencer had set it when she laid the fancy box across the sheets of the poster bed, and I sprang it as I slipped the dress on. Bird-of-paradise-crimson, gilded with streaks of gold and blue, a bronze torc to cover the scar on my neck (so thoughtful of my hostess), and four-inch rhinestone heels amounted to a costume worth more than I'd make in a lifetime unless that lifetime included a winning lotto ticket or sucking millionaire cock on the daily.

The ensemble transcended mere decoration; it reorganized my cells and worked outward like magma rushing through igneous channels. I'd stared at myself in the mirror and come face to face with a starlet. A tad hard-bitten. Close, though. Action heroine on the precipice of unfuckability by Hollywood's standard. Regardless, the illusion of fabulous me radiated heat—live-wire alive.

Yep, slipping into the dress had been to stick my head right through a dangling snare. Call it the price of admission. Too late to change a damned thing that was coming. I grinned like a prizefighter to keep my gorge down. I'd been here before and survived. Double-edged blade, the notion of past as prologue, and so forth. Resilience in prey excited Averna and made her want me that much more.

A girl on the run in a dress and high heels wouldn't run far is what Spencer bet, and why not? She owned the house. The house always wins.

The isolated mountain house of a high-toned serial killer isn't the kind of joint you accidentally wander into. I'd been recruited, seduced, and deployed. Dr. Ryoko and Dr. Campbell (more on my patrons—and their sexy, sexy bodyguard, Beasley—in due course), possessed a special interest in Averna Spencer's activities. My mission was to infiltrate her estate and conduct hostile actions on their behalf.

A few words about our mutual foe:

Averna craved the chase. She wasn't a slasher of (hapless) womenfolk or a sniper of unsuspecting coyotes. She didn't howl at the moon; hadn't been born under a bad sign or suffered childhood trauma. A hunter, nonetheless. Pure predator evolved to the job at hand. Sixty-three kills, if the cobbled-together records told it true. Sixty-three on U.S. soil; only INTERPOL could speak for the body count in Europe where she frequently traveled.

The manifest of persons missing and presumed dead since 1988, included loggers, hikers, ex-military, a baker's dozen hardened criminals, and a former Olympic decathlete. These folks vanished across the U.S.; law enforcement records established the deeds, but the authorities hadn't officially put it together. Unofficially, there were rumors. A retired FBI agent in Houston, a discredited private investigator in Wisconsin, and other assorted kooks, rocked the boat now and again. It came to nothing, as these situations usually do.

The track and field star haunted me. Strapping lad. Last known photograph taken at sunset, ice cream cone in hand (an athlete's notion of decadence), a tall, dark-haired chick hanging on his arm. Track and field dude—let's call him Rocky since he looked a hell of a lot like a Rocky I knew in high school—dressed nicely, smiled nicely. Only missed snagging the bronze medal by hundredths of a second. I imagined how he must've been later, after the kidnapping—alone, lost in a trackless forest. Pressed flat against the trunk of a pine, head cocked, every cord in his neck straining. Then, *slice*.

Rocky the Olympian's tragic story ended the same as the rest. Worm food.

Fast, strong, tough. Hadn't mattered, had it? Can't fight what you don't see coming, can't fight if you're prey. Dharma 101, friends and neighbors. The rabbit runs and the hawk dives.

Where do I fit into the grand scheme? I muck around in the rising tide of cosmic night. I'm hell on wheels. My totem animal is the coyote, the mongoose, my blazon a bloodied Ka-Bar in a clenched fist against a field of black.

Lest I join the dearly departed in their unmarked graves, the moment had come to make myself scarce. The original extraction plan struck me as sketchy at best—on the bright side of the equation, Spencer's houseguests normally returned to the world unharmed. The data led Campbell and Ryoko to theorize that those whom she kidnapped (and I qualified) were subsequently hunted across her estate grounds. Should the operation go pear-shaped, I was to flee Averna Spencer's home and rendezvous at a hunting cabin a mile past the estate's southeast boundary. My patrons had assured me they'd done the math forward and back--it wouldn't come to such an extreme. Bastards.

A grand staircase spiraled down into gothic gloom. Marble raptors guarded the way. I ripped the dress to upper thigh, removed my heels, and transformed into a new creature; slippery and dangerous.

I hustled through the door and past a phalanx of artificial eggs arranged on the front lawn. Almost did a doubletake. The eggs were outsized and exaggerated, Andy Warhol style; waist-tall, maybe three feet in circumference, cast from milky-lucent porcelain that glowed in the porchlight. The one nearest my left was bisected at its apex, like a hollow rocket missing its conical nose. An egg and a coffin are antipodes of a closed circuit. Made it halfway across the yard before Averna's evil sidekick, Manson, shot me in the ass with a dart from a rifle. She waved when I glanced back. I flipped her the bird (ironic to the bitter end). Strength drained from me like blood from a tapped artery. Five more steps and I sprawled.

Averna rolled me onto my side. She moved her lips against mine in a not-quite kiss. Would've punched her in the throat except whatever Manson had loaded the dart with froze every muscle in my body. I tabled the impulse. She licked the salt of my tears and leaned back to regard me from the shadows. Eyes without a face. Yellow eyes with strange-as-shit pupils. Hawk pupils. I wanted to ask how she'd *known*. Maybe she didn't; and if she didn't, despite her rhetoric, I might escape with my skin.

This feeble hope persisted for less than five seconds.

"The doctors asked you to acquire a certain document, yes? They promised some grand reward for your service; appealed to your sense of honor. Couldn't you detect the evil in their black little hearts? Did you not whiff the deception?"

Had I been capable of speech, I'd have said nobody's perfect, and spat a gob in her eye.

She smiled. "I delivered the formula to them months ago. Payment for your sweet self. I got the best of Campbell and Ryoko, as usual. The formula is worthless, lacking a specific strain of Jurassic protozoa, which, let us pray, no one ever resurrects. Blink if you can hear me."

I'm stubborn, so I glared, bug-eyed defiant. Impossible to tell if she was lying, and if so, how much. My "power" to behold the evil in the human heart doesn't work on women half as well as it does on men, and if she was telling the truth, it didn't work half so well on men as I'd thought.

A sociopath will say anything to make her victims squirm, which meant I dared not believe a word from her lips. Yet, and yet . . . I tried to speak; to scream, actually. Had my preparation and training been a ruse? Had those kindly eggheads really double-crossed me? Had their man-at-arms (and my lover) Beasley, participated in the con? *Et tu*, Beasley? *Et tu*, you handsome sonofabitch?

Averna said, "None of this is an accident. The doctors do not trade in coincidence and neither do I. We've observed you for many years. Something happened to your mother as a young woman. She met a friend of mine, a foreigner, you might say, who contracted with the CIA to enhance various programs. Lucius was part of an experiment, alongside many of her friends. She and the other surviving test subjects have been remotely monitored since the latter 1970s, as are their offspring. The . . . conditions that altered Lucius skipped her firstborn, Elwood, and bloomed within you. Curses can be finicky.

"Did those old goats suggest they knew Lucius's fate? Spoiler alert: mother dearest isn't living in a trailer in Tennessee with a failed country singer. She didn't drink herself to death or get eaten by a bear. I am not privy to the machinations of Campbell and Ryoko. I *do* have my own brand of intuition. My intuition says they murdered Lucius Lochinvar Mace. Did her in in the name of science." She rose and gestured to Manson who lurked nearby.

Manson hoisted me with her arms extended as if I were a crash test dummy. My field of view revolved off its y axis. I went bye-bye into the hollow belly of night.

Backtrack, backtrack. Maybe you're wondering how a nice girl like me ended up in a place like this . . .

A pair of infamous scientists figured I might be game to solve a mystery and save the world. Unlikely, yet no less so than the rest of the improbable bullshit that increasingly defines my existence. My current boyfriend, the aforementioned Beasley, happened to serve as bodyguard, valet, and moral compass to the renegade doctors. He introduced us. This set the ball rolling. Happy (unhappy) coincidence? As I've come to mutter on a routine basis, there are no accidents.

Most people born prior to 1980 have at least heard of the inseparable duo, Toshi Ryoko and Howard Campbell (erstwhile academic favorites of every male-oriented pop magazine in existence). Renowned for death-defying expeditions, gauche stunts, and outré theories in their heyday; less celebrated of late. The naturalists retired (voluntarily mothballed, as Beasley put it) to a quaintly decrepit New England farm. Ryoko in his wheelchair, Campbell stooped to push. The inseparable duo as drawn by some virtuoso graphic artist; say Mike Mignola or Patch Zircher.

Prior to our first meeting, I did my homework and read the news stories (which traced back into the early '80s), watched myriad videos, and listened to radio programs devoted to their exploits (the *public* exploits; turns out the pair really and truly deserved the "mad scientist" appellation). Iconoclasts and apostates to the hilt. Neither man would go quietly to a nursing home. These two were fated for an exotic demise: they'd vanish in the Bermuda Triangle, or into the Amazon rainforest and leave behind a ravaged campsite, cryptic research notes scattered, a cursed Neolithic medallion dangling from a bush; or, an unmarked government van would whisk them to a black site for a final debriefing.

We got along swimmingly. Didn't mean I'd be a cheerful pawn in their schemes.

"The Shadow of Death slides across the floor," Dr. Campbell said, and nodded at his shoe in a sliver of sunlight.

"The Shadow of Death!" Dr. Ryoko struggled to light a cigarette. His palsy tremors came and went.

"Soon it will crawl onto us and dig in the spurs. Time yet . . . "

" . . . a few years yet. We can do some good."

"*You* can do some good, Jessica. Help us hold back the darkness."

What they wanted wasn't difficult. Hazardous to my health, yes, but not difficult. Some rich lady possessed a formula; a cure for a deadly strain of avian flu, or a recipe to weaponize the virus, nobody could be sure which. Campbell handed me an envelope full of notes and photographs and that's how I came to acquaint myself with the legend of Averna Spencer—AKA the Bird Lady of the Adirondacks, AKA (my addition) the Cuckoo Killer. She'd briefly made a public splash on nightly news programs when they profiled her participation in the emergent wingsuit craze during the late 1990s. As one of the few women rich enough and ballsy enough to leap off cliffs and sail like a flying squirrel, she'd represented a curiosity.

Averna kicked it old school, pre-Information Age—nothing left to chance in a computer database, otherwise Ryoko and Campbell would've enlisted a hacker and done the job by remote. She kept the formula locked in a safe at her residence; a cliff-side mansion-slash-fortified stronghold amid thousands of acres of wilderness. The aforementioned master villain's lair. Called it the Aerie.

The broad owned more land than Ted Turner in his Montana heyday with Jane Fonda and the Atlanta Braves. Closest road lay twenty miles southeast. Traffic came and went via a helicopter pad. Power derived from generators, turbines, and solar panels. Security? Ex-military goons provided by Black Dog; armed drones; bloodhounds and German shepherds. Land mines. The wilderness and its many teeth waited for scraps.

How did the doctors score this information? Dr. Ryoko claimed a contact on the inside. A spy in the house of love. While this shadowy individual didn't possess direct access to the formula, the person had provided a detailed description of the item and the combination to the safe where it currently resided.

My natural skepticism asserted itself. Setting aside reservations regarding the veracity of the alleged spy, why in the hell would Averna Spencer, noted recluse, grant me an audience?

"Never fear, we'll arrange it," Dr. Ryoko said. "You are the mistress of inevitability. The opener of the way. Occult forces magnetize to you."

"Spencer delights in taking things apart. Unbreakable individuals are her weakness." Dr. Campbell actually rubbed his hands when he said this.

"Oh, goodie," I said.

"If she isn't familiar with your résumé as a survivor of massacres and slayer of maniacs, we'll enlighten her. She won't be able to resist. You're a blue-ribbon prize."

"Nice as that sounds, I'd prefer to live a while yet."

Ryoko said, "The universe built you to destroy human predators as it built the mongoose to destroy serpents."

"Dang, as a little girl I adored Kipling's tales to the max."

I inquired at length as to what they meant by occult forces and got nowhere fast. Slick as politicians dodging press questions, they relentlessly pivoted to the matter of Averna Spencer and her formula.

Charisma, resourcefulness, and grit notwithstanding, *Mission Impossible* wasn't my bag. The doctors hung in there with the hard sell. Dr. Campbell said I owed it to the missing persons and their distraught families. Dr. Ryoko insisted I bore a patriotic duty to obtain the formula from Spencer. Heaven help us if the avian flu developed into a more lethal strain.

This dragged on.

"What's your decision?" Dr. Campbell tried on a hopeful, earnest smile. "Will you help us avert a global catastrophe?"

"Pass."

"You're a born meddler," Dr. Ryoko said. "Consider the stakes—mass extinction of multiple species . . . "

"Not for all the chickens in the world." I actually meant, sweeten the pot, you cheap sonsofbitches. They sweetened the pot.

Dr. Campbell said, "Twenty-thousand. Cash. Our entire rainy-day fund."

"Tempting, but no thanks."

The doctors exchanged a glance I'll take to my grave.

"We'll tell you what really happened to your mother," Dr. Ryoko said. Ding-ding-ding. Winner.

The Aughts exacted a hell of a toll on the Mace family. It felt personal between us and the universe.

Mom took a permanent vacation to parts unknown.

My brother, Elwood, stepped on a landmine. Elwood was "technically" the eldest of my fellow brood—he'd plopped onto the hospital sheets about forty-five minutes before me back in 1980. We didn't share the Corsican Twins psychic bond as romanticized by pop lit. Elwood and I had barely acknowledged, much less dwelled on, the fact we were twins. I was shocked as anyone to get the bad news from Afghanistan.

Jackson Bane, love of my life, went down with his fishing boat.

Dad followed suit in a separate accident on the Bering.

A bunch of friends and colleagues got murdered by the Eagle Talon Ripper. The Ripper almost did me in as well, hence the scar on my neck. Melodrama galore.

Hindsight: Mom's final disappearance began the unholy countdown sequence. Unlike the many other instances where Lucius slapped Dad and hit the road for a week or a month, she didn't return. Didn't call, didn't write, didn't leave a hint where she'd gone and after a couple of years, her fate gradually became the stuff of legends.

Flash forward the better part of a decade. When the mad doctors offered to solve the nagging mystery of Mom's vanishing act, my instincts were to skip the whole middle part where I went off on a fool's errand into the den of a sadistic murderer. Quicker and more reliable to extract their information with a sharp stick.

Beasley presented a major obstacle. He watched over Campbell and Ryoko with zeal. The adorable brute exhibited a ruthless streak when it came to protecting the codgers. His bulging biceps and handiness with gun, knife, and hobnail boot, gave me pause.

It's seldom wise to tackle an irresistible force of nature head-on. I played it coy.

He implored me to forget the mission and slip away into the night. No amount of money was worth the risk, he adored me, et cetera. I informed him the old bastards had made me an offer I couldn't refuse—and then refused to tell him what the offer entailed. I asked if he'd ever met a woman named Lucius, real slick like. He shrugged and said yeah, she'd blown into camp a few years back, consulted with the doctors, then departed on an evening breeze.

Innocent, and I'm a decent judge of a man's soul if I gaze into his eyes long enough after a good hard screw. On the subject of screwing: I didn't have the heart to ask if he'd banged my mom.

"Spencer is a monster," he said as we smoked cigarettes in bed and slugged from a bottle of vodka. "She's protected by the powers of darkness. I've seen the file. I've seen all their files . . . "

"Who else are your bosses spying on?"

"Don't ask questions you'll come to regret. You're not a professional. The docs aren't either. Meanwhile, Spencer is queen of her little mountain fiefdom. Absolutely untouchable. The FBI knows. The Department of Defense knows. Everybody."

"The government is aware that she's a serial killer?" I feigned shock. Experience had taught me that we primates were capable of anything, everything. There ain't no good guys.

"Always room for one more creep on the payroll. Uncle Sam wouldn't give a shit if Spencer had Joseph Mengele's brain implanted. As long as she keeps her activities on the property and doesn't kill anyone important, she's golden."

"Golden," I said. "Reminds me of something . . . "

I loved Beasley, after a fashion. It isn't unusual, as Tom Jones might say. Big, sorta-handsome (he looked like a soap star who got smashed in the face with a shovel), mean guys rev my motor, and the Bease had it going on in spades. He loved me back, far as I could tell. Our mutual affection complicated matters; made what I had to do to get close to Averna a dilemma of scruples versus pragmatism. My scruples aren't what they used to be.

"Since I can't change your mind, I can show you what you've signed on for." He plugged in a laptop and ran three video clips. Surveillance or home footage as shot by an anonymous someone with Ingmar Bergman's ice-cold aesthetic.

Clip one, black and white: *a man sprints along a seaside cliff toward the camera. The fuzzy shape of an enormous bird sweeps through the frame and plucks him in its claws. The man struggles as the bird cruises toward the horizon. They shrink to a distant blot—the smaller blot separates and plummets into the ocean.*

Clip two: *an actress clad in an elaborate costume (skintight suit pricked with gemstones; a demented mask with a red and yellow feather plume, a vicious iron beak, underarm webbing, and steely talons) glides the length of a vast solarium. She rebounds from the walls to alter course with horrible grace. Naked men and women scatter beneath her. Every pass, the performer decapitates a victim with the swipe of a talon or the slash of a spur. Viscera streams in her wake.*

I know from Wire-Fu. I can't find the wires.

Clip three: *Averna Spencer stands near a bonfire with her arms spread. An assistant (the woman in the photo with Rocky the Olympian) fits her into a wingsuit designed by Satan. Spencer's arms are harnessed to actual wings designed after some gigantic specimen—twenty feet, tip to tip. The feathers ripple, hinting at a spectrum dulled by the black and white film. The fire illuminates queerly-hooked calf-high boots, steel (titanium?) talons strapped to her wrists, metallic panels across her breast, and a bronze helm crafted in the likeness of the god or devil of all avian-kind. Beneath the cruel beak, she grins.*

I stared overlong, evidently.

Beasley apologized, mistaking silence for dismay. Truthfully? The images had stolen my breath. A close race between disgust and awe. That's how much I'd evolved since Alaska. He figured I would react as any normal, rational person and tell the doctors to stuff their espionage mission. Quite the contrary.

Averna Spencer seldom emerged from her mountain fortress. She traveled in rarified company under various aliases and in disguise. Tracking her movements abroad proved a no-go. Campbell and Ryoko approached the finest detective agencies and were rebuffed without explanation. Beasley wasn't kidding when he said Spencer enjoyed protection from on high. Somebody ran major interference on her behalf, and I suspect that baloney had a first name, spelled CIA, and a second name spelled NSA, and a last name starting with Homeland Security. Spread enough money around and the baddest intelligence agency will act as your very own private concierge.

Since flushing out our quarry didn't seem a viable option, we needed to attract her interest. Birds appreciate shiny objects. The doctors devised a plan that involved getting me onto the guest list for an exclusive seminar featuring a famed ornithologist rumored to be an on and off again flame of Ms. Spencer. The doctors pulled strings and away I went to make the magic happen.

The lecture occurred in Kingston, New York at the home of a wealthy naturalist who reveled in this kind of groovy shit. Real nice place, if a tad stuffy. Kind of a museum, although the owner rarely opened for tours; he collected documents, weapons (a veritable shit-ton of knives), landscape paintings, and animal artifacts for his sole viewing pleasure. I've met a few guys with that particular pathology; the type who stored priceless art in bank vaults. Creepy bastards, the lot of them.

The ornithologist (Henry-something or other), on the other hand, seemed normal enough for a whack-a-doodle birdwatcher. We hit it off after I revealed my secret identity as a retired biologist. Dude gave his talk to a parlor-load of eminently bored stuffed shirts, then took my elbow and introduced me around. Scotch started flowing and I made tons of new friends.

One of these friends shook my hand and said to call her Manson. Manson stood tall and Amazonian in combat boots. She wore a bomber jacket (unzipped to flash DETROIT in block type across a stretched-tight T-shirt) and makeup fit to front The Cure. Cropped hair, heavy eyeliner, cherry-black lipstick, cherry-black nails. Yeah, I'd read her file too—born and raised in the Motor City, ex-con, worked as muscle for hire until Averna Spencer rescued her from the mean streets. I recognized Manson as the mystery girl in the last photo of Rocky, Mr. Decathlete, and in the video of her girding Spencer for mayhem. Guess that made her Oddjob to Spencer's Goldfinger, or Renfield to Dracula.

We adjourned to the veranda, admiring an autumnal blaze in the eye of the sunset. Manson reminded me of a female iteration of Beasley—big, tough, ruggedly attractive, and not overly gifted in chitchat. Manson came right to the point. She explained that her mega-rich, mega-private employer desired my presence at her estate for dinner and light conversation. The mysterious employer approved of my various exploits (especially the way I'd dispatched the Eagle Talon Ripper in Alaska). Should I be so gracious as to accept the invitation, my forbearance would be well-compensated. A helicopter waited nearby. No need to pack; my every need would be fulfilled.

Damn, the forces of darkness moved in fast. Manson's Plan B probably involved a rag and chloroform, so rather than play hard to get, I acted tipsy and said, hell yeah, take me to your leader. What girl turns down a ride in a private helicopter? Not this girl! Manson ran a wand over my body from stem to stern and patted me down with more intimacy than a zealous airport security agent. Smart call, leaving my knives at home.

The helicopter carried us north for the better part of an hour.

Our pilot wore a snow-white uniform. His (or her) visor concealed his (or her) identity. I thought of Jonathan Harker's carriage-ride, Dracula at the reins, hell-bent for leather on the way to the castle. Dracula possessed a cold grip and the strength of twenty men. How strong was Averna Spencer's grip?

The answer—firm. That old saying about a velvet glove and an iron fist applies here. A few minutes after we touched down (and nope, I never saw her and the pilot together), the lady herself greeted me near the front lawn and its koi pond and assorted Greco-Roman statuary. Red dress and sensible shoes; she didn't wear any jewelry or makeup. She gently closed her hand around my throat and planted a lingering kiss on my cheek. Felt as if she could've torn my head off with a twitch. We locked gazes—her pupil flickered yellow and back to black again, foreshadowing troubles galore. I gave not a shit. My legs trembled. Anxiety evaporated, replaced by thrill. Pheromones, mad pheromones.

The plan, such as it was, was to play hard to get, work the charm offensive, gain access to the Bird Woman's home and acquire the formula. Babies, those best-laid stratagems went out the window the instant I got a whiff of her scent.

No, man. Averna didn't have "sharp features," or a "cruel nose," or "talon-like" hands (usually), or any such shit. Dark hair, brown eyes (usually), athletic. The record put her on the backside of fifty. Up close and personal, she felt a hell of a lot younger; ripped as a gymnast (a decathlete?), and nary a wrinkle or crow's foot. Averna understood how to walk, how to hold herself motionless the way politicians and models do, how to project her personality with kinetic force. Cool to the touch. Worth forty billion and enamored of esoteric scientific research. Spencer's corporations funded an assortment of crazy projects. Despite this massive wealth, her name seldom surfaced outside of highly insulated circles. A bizarre, protean vibe emanated from her and her retinue. Is evil (capital E evil) protean? That would explain much.

Invited me to freshen up (my quarters contained every amenity including evening wear in my size) and take a stroll with her resident PR man. Dinner at seven on the dot.

I toured the house. Bizarre and immense (immense even before factoring in a network of shops, garages, and the sector of hexagonal cottages where she stashed her off duty workforce and security personnel).

Envision a three-wing mansion of redwood logs and slate, mated to a giant bisected Bucky Ball on loan from the Martians—soaring, crystal-domed atriums with copses of full-sized pine trees and willows and a river falling over glass-smooth rocks; cozy parlors where fake flames danced inside hearths; steel bulkhead hatches concealed by cherry wood paneling and illustrated hangings that were sufficiently moth-eaten to indicate pricelessness; and an array of security cameras, some obvious and others less so. Most of the art was of the abstract genre. I didn't recognize anything.

Averna Spencer's PR lackey (a chipper guy named James who smiled like a hostage in fear of his life) took me in tow. According to my guide, the floorplan included a sauna, gymnasium, theater, bowling alley, discotheque, shooting range, and a spa. When his back was turned, I peeked inside vases and cabinets—no corpses, no skeletons. The circuit ended with a glimpse inside a museum gallery that would've made a nice addition to the Smithsonian. Dinosaur bones, suspended biplanes, and a two-story spire of glossy, radiant yellow crystal. The usual weird stuff one might expected to find in the trophy den of a megalomaniacal billionaire murderess.

When I craned my neck to get a better look, James became nervous.

"Ms. Spencer would prefer to show you these special exhibits herself. Someone accidentally left this open . . . "

"That's a huge chunk of crystal, Jimmy," I said. "Last I saw something like that was on the cover of a 1970s science fiction novel. And the bird skeleton . . . What's the wingspan? Twenty feet? Is it a pterodactyl?"

"No, ma'am, it is not a pterodactyl." James pulled a pair of brass-plated doors shut. "*Argentavis magnificens.* An extinct predator. Among the largest of her kind. She devoured prey whole. Shall we move toward the dining room?" He wiped his brow and checked his watch.

"The crystal. You simply have to give me the scoop, Jimbo."

"Ms. Spencer awaits." He led the way, and briskly.

"Does Manson handle the executions around here?"

He glanced over his shoulder, eyes glassy-bright. "Mainly, yes."

A woman spends her early adult years at hatcheries and aboard fishing trawlers doing the honest labor of tracking and cataloguing salmon (that great Alaskan export), and nobody cares. Americans want their food marginally harmless in a marginally attractive package; the fewer details, the better. A woman gets attacked by a mass murderer and lives to tell, everybody wants a piece of the action.

Type *Jessica M* into any search engine and the auto-form will suggest *Jessica Mace & Eagle Talon Ripper; Jessica Mace US Magazine; Jessica Mace Nude Photos; Jessica Mace Final Girl.* Averna Spencer hadn't merely followed my career as portrayed in the media, she knew my whole origin story—how a while back, I'd barely survived an apartment complex massacre and fire; how I'd risen from near-death and killed the killer; how I'd bailed on my fifteen minutes and vanished (like mother, like daughter). She'd also obtained facts regarding my unpublicized excursions on the road. Averna confessed her fascination regarding people who had confronted the vicissitudes of existence in an intimate manner. I took it to mean she'd burned ants with a magnifying glass as a kid.

We finished supper and wandered through her hanging gardens and lesser aviaries. Flocks of tropical birds dwelled inside a dome of sparkly mesh that protected a lush jungle biome. It would take the gross national product of a small country to stock and maintain such a preserve.

Our path wound through an imported jungle. Paper lanterns (grotesque busts of birds of prey) cast our primeval surroundings in the light of an animated Kipling adaptation. Climate control simulated the tropics. Humidity soaked my clothes and I almost believed the sliver of moonlight peeping through leaves was other than a subtly masked klieg.

She said, "You're rather trusting for a woman who's had her throat slashed. Do you jump into a helicopter with any total stranger?"

"Manson isn't the kind of person you argue with." I raised my voice to compete with raucous chatter of birds and mating frogs.

"Manson is an extension of my will. I made her."

"Made her? As in Pygmalion?"

"Isn't that the idiom the cool kids are using?"

"Yes. Do me next, pretty please."

"I projected my life essence into her puny mortal frame and voila, a million-year evolutionary leap. It's a messy process. Not for weak stomachs."

Seemed an appropriate point to change the subject. "I read in an article that you employ a team of geneticists and zoologists. You want to protect endangered bird species." Campbell and Ryoko's dossier alleged that Averna Spencer hired mercenaries to shoot nest robbers and sabotage the infrastructure of land developers who operated in environmentally-sensitive regions such as South America.

"The science team pursues much grander designs," she said. "We work to resurrect a spectrum of extinct species. Avian, reptile, amphibian. I'm worried for honeybees. As our apian friends go, so go we."

"The research is conducted here, in house?"

"Yes, and in twenty-three other countries."

"Good thing you're loaded. Woman could burn through a fortune on fringe research."

"She could. Or she could manipulate a host of international political actors to foot the bill. Drug lords, warlords, bored industrialists . . . It isn't as difficult to separate them from their spare millions as you might think."

"Any luck raising the dodo from the dead?"

"Sixty-eight percent of this aviary system is populated by animals that no longer exist in the outside world."

I flashed to the giant bird skeleton in the private museum, and how the tall, crystal had seethed with a weird yellow fire. Decided to zip my lips. Averna's stride, long and graceful, reminded me of her unnatural strength. Her friendly smile hinted at savagery.

"My most prized work isn't specific to avian research," she said. "I hope to create a trigger of human evolution. A radically accelerated process."

"Mutation."

"After a fashion."

"Toward what end?"

"The ability to survive dramatic climate change. To withstand nuclear radiation and acid rain. To think faster. To dispense with antiquated paradigms of morality and ethics. To soar with the eagles and swim with the fishes."

"Things mad scientists say for five hundred, Alex," I said. "Any notable successes, a la *The Island of Doctor Moreau?*"

"Me, a scientist? Hardly. Certainly, I'm slightly bonkers and quite ancient. Old people acquire knowledge. We spread it around, for weal or woe. As to the matter of success, I'm banking on getting lucky tonight, at least. Let's swing by your room for a nightcap."

"Mine? Surely yours is more luxurious."

She took my arm rather possessively. "I sleep hanging upside down from a trapeze bar in Aviary 4. It's not a cozy rendezvous."

All I could see was the mask of the devil bird in the video clip, the feather plume; her victim's corpse tumbling toward the water; men and women screaming in a solarium, its walls splattered in gore. Averna, radiant and exultant as a blood god from the bad history books.

Half a magnum of 1928 Krug later:

"Final girls are a necessarily rare breed." Averna studied my calloused palms, the yellow bruises along my shoulder. Her nails were trimmed close to the quick and unpolished. Dark specks of blood had gotten under some of them. "Your training regimen is fierce. No enhanced strength or ESP? No telekinetic powers?"

"I skate along on woman's intuition."

"No secret weaponry of any kind?"

"Apparently, I'm a mongoose. Natural weaponry. Rawr!"

"She kissed my (also bruised) belly. "I am curious what combination of pathology and trauma drives you to seek danger."

"This from Miss I-jump-off-cliffs-in a-wingsuit?"

"Pretend a normal person you'd like to fuck asked the question. The event in Alaska opened the world for you."

"Opened the world? Like I should be grateful? I never volunteered to get brutalized. I didn't tip that domino. The attack fucked me up royal." I resisted the urge to touch the scar on my neck.

"Or it awakened dormant DNA. Your latent adrenaline junkie gene."

"You know how it is—at first, it's about the rush, then the rush becomes a habit. After a while, you're basically screwed."

"Give it an eon. Who's your favorite superhero?"

"Let me think . . . "

"Don't think, tell me."

"Like tic-tac-toe?" I stalled.

"Cheating already."

"Okay. The Batman."

"Not Batgirl?"

"Defending my answer wasn't part of the game. I want every bit of power. You?"

"Captain Midnight."

"Who's Captain Midnight?"

"Seriously?" Averna cupped her chin and regarded me. "I'm reevaluating this whole relationship."

"All six hours of it."

"My time is precious, Mace. Bouquets of thousand dollar bills could rain from the sky and it wouldn't be cost effective to stoop for the ones that didn't fall into my pocket."

"Okay, don't be rethinking anything. Give me a mulligan. Who the hell is Captain Midnight?"

"Ace World War One pilot. Could fly anything. Total badass."

"You're busting my balls over a cartoon from World War One?"

She undid my bra and tossed it over the side. "Radio show."

"Seems like an odd choice for a hero," I said.

"Not if you knew me for more than six hours."

Ultimately, I told her my darkest secrets: Mom and Dad fought over the heavyweight title and it brought the Mace kids together; my first real love rescued me from the galley of a fishing boat right before it went to the bottom of the sea and a few happy years went by and nobody was around to rescue him; Mom ran out on us a hundred times, and finally, she stayed gone for good, either dead or reborn; when the Eagle Talon Ripper sliced my throat, I thought I'd died. Such a relief! The real reason I emptied the gun into the sonofabitch was because he'd done a half-assed job putting me out of my misery.

"At last I understand your motivation," Averna said. "It isn't thrill-seeking behavior. You experience suicidal ideation, probably stemming from survivor's guilt."

"I'm not suicidal anymore. Guilt? Not so much of that ether."

"Dying isn't easy for most people. Instinct is a real bitch and she wants to live. Sadly, those with a true death wish, suffer terribly. O cruel universe. It imbued you with unbearable misery and a rational mind. Care to guess what the mind says?"

"Let's fuck? Let's drink? Let's forget?"

"The mind says, no more, let's stop. The universe also imbued you with the genetics of a survivor. *Your* subconscious resists annihilation; it says, okay, you can die, but only after jumping through fiery hoops, only after completing an obstacle course in hell. Some people with your particular affliction drink themselves to death or go hunting for Mr. Goodbar. They take on risky jobs. You, my dear, follow this hard road. It led to my doorstep."

"The other shoe droppeth," I said.

"Just your panties, at the moment."

What's *your* motivation?"

Her long, cruel fingers dug into my hips. "I like it when my prey runs screaming through the forest. I like the idea that animals will inherit the earth. I like the idea that with a little push we could be apes again."

"Oh," I said.

On day two we buzzed the estate in the helicopter. Trees, tree-covered mountains, tree-covered valleys, and more trees. Averna piloted. She wore a shiny black flight suit that exaggerated her figure into comic book proportions. Manson sat in the rear, loose-limbed and heavy-lidded. Her suit and mine were dull gray.

My secret of the day: I'd seen this before. In the course of training for the mission, Dr. Campbell had put me into a hypnotic trance and shown dozens of satellite images of the territory. Military grade imagery that dialed right down to the individual acorn. He explained that a photographic memory wasn't necessary to retain this information—if I got lost in these woods, a certain phrase would trigger the implanted memories and I'd have access to a 3D "mind map" of the surroundings.

I keyed the mike in my headset. "Averna, I read somewhere that you almost died testing a wingsuit in Finland."

"Norway. Bad landings happen. Fortunately, the crash appeared nastier than the reality."

Witnesses said she'd hit the turf at an estimated one-hundred and thirty-miles per hour. The article also claimed it required a team of surgeons four operations and a roll of duct tape to put Humpty-Dumpty together again.

"Tycoons evidently score the world's greatest docs. I know women with C-section scars that could've been done with a boar spear."

"Flawless skin was a gift from my mother. Hold on." She banked hard right and put the helicopter into a shallow dive toward the foothills. We shot through a notch in the tree line and she leaned back on the yoke into a near vertical climb to hop over the rocky crown of a hill, then pushed hard and dropped hard to skim several feet above a lake, and steeply up again at the last second as a wall of evergreens closed in. My heart remained where it had leapt from my chest, a couple miles back.

Upon our return to the house, I retreated to my room and pondered the implications. Eighteen hours with Averna Spencer convinced me she didn't possess a scintilla of spontaneity. Her brain functioned on a beautiful, cold algorithm that perfectly mimicked human thought, human desire, yet possessed the nascent spark of neither. Rich folks often exhibit outsized egos and a narcissistic compulsion to impress the peasants. Averna didn't give a damn. She'd taken me on the flyover to demonstrate the geography and parameters of her estate for a practical purpose. In retrospect, the message was no less subtle than if she'd leaned over and whispered that I should get my track shoes laced. It's on like Donkey Kong, girlfriend.

The second message was delivered much later in the evening as I prowled through the house, casually testing locks and poking my nose where it didn't belong. Happened to peek into an antechamber and Lo! Averna (naked and gleaming) straddled Manson (naked and gleaming) atop a couch. Averna swallowed grapes from a prodigious clump. She regurgitated into Manson's wide-open mouth and sealed it with a kiss. She winked at me. Her yellow eye reflected the epoch when scales and dagger-length talons were king (queen).

I backed away slowly, as one does when menaced by a large and partially satiated predator. Propelled by unreasonable jealousy, I strode to Averna's quarters, temporarily dismantled the security feed with an electromagnetic device disguised as an earring (in addition to zoology, exobiology, physical anthropology, and several other disciplines, including hypnotism, obviously, Doc Campbell dabbled in experimental engineering), and went straight for the safe. I'd memorized the combo and the doctors assured me that all I needed to do was glance at the documents; vital contents would be retrieved via hypnosis during my debriefing. Campbell assured me the mind operated like a camera and everything it experienced was undeveloped film.

The safe lay empty but for a piece of paper that read, *Bluebeard is a cautionary tale, lover*, and signed with a lipstick kiss.

I decided to hoof it, mission be damned, and take my chances in the mountains with the bears and the wolves and the inevitable pursuit. Two guards were posted on either side of my bedroom door. Stony-faced guys in military uniforms, assault rifles at port arms. So much for sneaking off, stage left.

Day three, several guests emerged to join the fun. Averna behaved as the convivial lady of the manor. We played games of the mundane variety. Mini golf and horseshoes in a horseshoe pit worthy of the Roman Coliseum. Manson caught my attention and casually straightened an iron horseshoe with her bare hands.

Then supper.

While gnawing on a pheasant wing and swilling fancy imported lager, I rubbed elbows with the new folks. Three of them had arrived at the estate a week prior; two others had gotten flown in that morning. Young men, down at the heels, but strong and athletic. Army guys who hadn't readjusted to life stateside; a boozy ex-cop; a kid maybe six months clear of high school where he'd wrestled varsity; and a couple cop/soldier wannabes. Each of them hoped to score a permanent security gig or at least a free ride as long as it lasted. I chatted the boys up—no close family; they were at loose ends. Nobody back home would notice, much less care, when they went missing.

I won't bother with names; simpler to think of them as Hapless Victims #1 through #5.

Manson stood next to me at the bar. She wore a dark gown and a star pattern of heavy purple eyeshadow. "We don't usually entertain more than a couple of guests. This is special."

"What's the occasion?"

"It's Tuesday. Go back to your quarters. Ms. Spencer left you a gift."

"Because it's Tuesday?"

"Because there will be entertainment later this evening and you may wish to dress appropriately."

This is where you came in . . .

Averna kept me stewing (quite literally) for forty-eight hours, plus or minus; a fact I estimated by the phase of the moon and an above average internal clock.

Why giant synthetic eggs? The design of the incubators was strictly symbolic. The contents--a contemporary primordial soup chock full of vitamins, proteins, and assorted mystery elements intended to cleanse her chosen, to heighten our reflexes and provide sufficient high-test nourishment for a proper hunt--could've done its work in a tank. She preferred elaborate theatrics; a consequence of eternal life. Have to wonder which came first: murderous rage or immortality. Since I could only hazard a guess, I guessed the eggs were deposited at various predetermined sites on the estate. We prisoners "hatched" and were subsequently hunted by our hostess and her majordomo.

During incubation, my dreams were psychedelic and fantastically, Lucio-Fulci-strength, macabre. Visions, perhaps. I beheld the male guests pelting through a night forest roiling with phosphorescent mist. Averna glided down on stiff, black wings. Her wingsuit defied physics. She tilted vertically and her toes dug into the soil every third or fourth gigantic stride and beheaded each of the fleeing men with a casual swipe of her metallic talons. She accelerated in dizzying curlicues through gaps in the trees.

Averna crooned to me through an intravenous drip. She spoke of evolutionary slippage, of natural mutation and genetic manipulation.

I die and live again and again. My soul regenerates into new flesh.

I have broken the hearts of countless men. I have eaten the beating hearts of countless men. I have devoured so many beating hearts, I shit and piss black heartblood.

I am a fountainhead of raped vitality.

I am a supplicant of the gods of eternal return.

I mean to devour you as I've devoured the rest in their multitudes.

You'll regenerate as I have done since the dawn of hominids. We'll meet again in a hundred million years at the dawn of the hominids. We'll meet again between one scream and the next.

Wake up, wake up, wake up . . .

I love and hate *The Vanishing*. The Dutch version by Sluizer; don't bother with the American remake, hunky Jeff Bridges notwithstanding. In a previous life, I made my bread as a marine biologist. I survived many a tedious night aboard fishing tenders on the Bering Sea with a stack of paperbacks and VHS tapes while the rest of the crew was drunk or unconscious. Somewhere in the middle of *The Vanishing* a character describes a nightmare of being trapped in the darkness of a golden egg. Love it because the image got to me on a primal level and stuck. Hate it for the same reason.

These many years later, waking to fluid blackness three thousand miles east of Alaska, tubes up my nose and down my throat, body coiled like an embryo inside a golden egg of my very own? Must be the abyss everybody talks about.

I kicked, one-two, and dove deep into a sea of blood. Crimson light churned. The shell cracked and broke and the universe spilled me onto a carpet of pine needles. Out came the rubber tubes with a yank; then a bout of projectile vomiting--pheasant, sorbet, and copious amounts of whiskey and synthetic amniotic fluid. The blood in my eyes seeped down and dried into scales. Tears dug diamond furrows through caked-on grime. My convulsions subsided. I stood and leaned like a drunk against the bole of a hemlock and assessed the fucked-uppedness of my situation.

A mild evening in early October. Mosquitos whined; could have been worse. Clouds rolled over a crescent moon. Had to think fast, had to move. Standing still would get me dead. *Moving* would get me dead. Where was Rikki-tikki-tavi in my hour of need? An owl screeched. The bird glided past; the very shadow of death itself.

I'd trained for the direst scenarios—spent the previous several months jogging barefoot to toughen my feet; I also worked on traveling in New England forests at night to sharpen my lowlight vison. An affinity for rough and tumble notwithstanding, no way, no how am I a martial artist. I sparred with Beasley, who agreed (after I walked into his right hand three or four times) keeping it simple would be for the best. He honed my bag of dirty tricks and taught me a couple new ones.

Should've done more. Should've stayed in bed.

For all the roadwork and psychological preparation, and despite my alleged "purpose" and indomitable resolve, it was a psychological body blow to wash up on the proverbial lee shore: naked in the middle of the woods in the dead of night, pumped to the gills with experimental juice and on the run from Elizabeth Bathory II and her army of mercs. I intoned Dr. Campbell's mnemonic phrase (*the mind is a camera*) that would supposedly trigger a pseudo-holographic image of the surroundings. It worked, too.

I waded down a stream to confuse tracking dogs, then dug a hole near the roots of a tree and covered myself in clay, pine needles, and sap. I hadn't worn hair products or used scented soap or perfume in months. The docs put me on a regimen of an experimental, military grade antiperspirant.

Smeared head to toe in muck, I ran like hell through the dark, dark woods like the doomed heroine of a slasher flick. I angled southeast for the extraction point (would Beasley await my arrival?); kept right on trucking until daylight and then burrowed into a deadfall and slept. Night came around. I slurped brackish water from a puddle and set forth again, skulking from tree to tree with a wild animal's determination to survive. For a while, I believed I'd successfully evade and escape. Hope makes fools of us all.

Contrary to the cliché, I didn't trip and sprain an ankle, didn't sob or shriek to give away my position, and didn't glance over my shoulder every ten feet. Perversely, that last detail proved my downfall.

She hit me the way a hawk or an owl does an unsuspecting squirrel. Instead of severing my spine on impact, Averna merely snagged my long, luxurious mane and ascended vertically, yanking me off my feet. Similar to those rides at the State Fair—the ones where a scabrous, hungover carny straps you into a harness that dangles from a big metal wheel and up your sorry ass goes, with nothing between your sneakers and sod but a sheer drop.

The radiant sickle moon gashed the clouds; first above, then below. Averna clutched my hair in her left fist and skimmed treetops at a precipitous velocity, dragging me several feet lower like the tail of a kite. We dipped and swooned; accelerating, decelerating. If she had a jet pack strapped on her back, I didn't hear it. The only sounds I heard were the hissing breeze, and the clatter of branches when she swung me viciously against the canopy. Each blow knocked the breath from me and tore my flesh.

God knows where the bitch's flight plan would've taken us. I didn't stick around for the surprise. It required a metric fuck-ton of grit to recover from the initial whiplash and saw through my hair with a shard of the designer egg I'd carried (and managed not to drop) this entire time. Sliced my fingers and palm, but it got the job done—half a dozen convulsive hacks later, the last strand parted and I bailed. She cried my name.

Momentum hurled me in a broad arc. I caromed from leafy boughs and they snapped beneath my cannonball passage. Five seconds? Five thousand years? Those few heartbeats stretched across multiple lifetimes. Don't remember hitting the earth. Black stars cleared and I lay in a pile of dead, slimy leaves, oxygen smashed from my lungs, gaping at the moon.

A circling shadow blotted the light. I caught a glimpse of Averna in her radiant glory and realized the mysteries of the universe dwarfed my comprehension. She didn't need a wingsuit. She didn't need wings. She didn't need anything.

Manson strode from the depths of the forest. She didn't put a bullet through my skull as I might've logically assumed. She scooped my battered self (broken ribs, lacerated hand, and a world class concussion) into her arms and lugged me half a mile to the cabin. I don't recall a hell of a lot about the next couple of days except that the place was empty. No phone, no Beasley. Pretty clear my fate had been sealed from the beginning.

Manson played nursemaid by firelight from a decrepit hearth. Stuffed me into a sleeping bag and got an I.V. drip pumping fluids into my veins. Everything went blurry after the adrenalin wore off.

I dreamed that Averna, garbed in her horror show suit, shattered the cabin door and loomed over me as I lay helpless. Her wingtips scraped furrows in the walls. *Behold. I am the apex. I stand where humanity begins and where it will end.* She lovingly popped my eyeballs with her claws.

Woke screaming to beat the band.

Averna, dressed in a natty jacket, tenderly stroked my brow with a damp cloth. She revealed I was merely the second person to ever make it across the finish line. For me to plummet from the treetops and bounce instead of splat, represented a bona fide miracle. I didn't argue the point. Fell unconscious for however long it took for my injuries to mend.

Jessica, you must understand we're all meat and blood for the slaughterhouse. Regardless, we should learn until the very end. Sapient beings exist to acquire experience. The beasts of the wilderness kill and eat us. The wilderness itself kills and eats us. Every scrap down to our quintessence reduces and divides among maggots and dirt and adds to the sum.

Go in peace, dear girl. You and the world have unfinished business. Far be it from me to stand in the way.

Could've been a fever dream, could've been legit; either way, Averna and Manson let me live. Eventually I roused from blind sleep, aching, traumatized, and swaddled in gauze. The girls left clean clothes, pain pills, and an envelope with a few bucks inside a knapsack. Also, a loaded pistol and keys to a Jeep parked by the front porch.

Time passed. I bided it with grim patience.

Beasley the vigilant had to sleep sometime. I waited until he embarked upon one of his not infrequent drunks to make my move. Walked into the New England farmhouse around dawn. The doctors were seated at a table in the den, bickering over a pile of research papers. They registered surprise at my appearance, although less than one might expect. Fuckers had seen everything at least once, I suppose. Dr. Ryoko reached for a drawer, then noticed the pistol in my hand, and sat back with a resigned sigh.

"Hello, boys," I said. "Tell me about my mother."

THE LAMENTATION OF THEIR WOMEN

—◆—

Kai Ashante Wilson

pre.

"Hello," answered some whiteman. "Good morning! Could I speak with—?" He mispronounced her last name and didn't abbreviate her first, as nobody who knew her would do.

"Who dis?" she repeated. "And what you calling about?"

"Young lady," he said. "Can you please tell me whether Miss Jean-Louis is there or not. Will you just do that for me?" His tone all floured with whitepeople siddity, pan-fried in condescension.

But she could sit here and act dumb too. "Mmm . . . it's hard to say. She be in and out, you know? Tell me who calling and what for and I'll go check."

Apparently, the man was Mr Blah D. Blah from the city agency that cleaned out Section 8 apartments when the leaseholder dropped dead. Guess whose evil Aunt Esther had died of a heart attack last Thursday on the B15 bus? And guess who was the last living Jean-Louis anywhere?

"But how you calling me—it's almost noon—to say I got 'til *five*, before your dudes come throw all her stuff in the dumpster?"

"Oh good," exclaimed Blah D. "I was worried we weren't communicating clearly."

"She live out by Jamaica Bay! It'd take me two hours just to *get there*."

"Miss Jean-Louis," he said. (Public servants nearing retirement, who never got promoted high enough not to deal with poor people anymore, black people anymore, have this tone of voice, you ever notice? A certain tone.) "There's no requirement for you to go. This is merely a courtesy our office extends to the next of kin. The keys will be available to you until five." Blah hung up.

"*Fuck* you!" She was dressed for the house, a tank top and leggings, and so went to her room for some sneakers and a hoodie.

Mama was scared of Esther, said she was a witch. Both times they had went out there, Mama left her downstairs, waiting in the streets, rather than bring her baby up to that apartment. Now, *she* didn't believe in that black magic bullshit, of course, but she also wasn't trying to go way the hell out there by herself. Mama, though, wouldn't want no parts of Esther, dead sister of the dead man who'd walked out on her some fifteen years ago. Naw, better leave Mama alone at work and call her later.

She'd get Anhell to go. They were suppose to had been broke up with each other at least till this weekend coming, but whatever. She could switch him back to "man" from "ex" a couple days early. Wouldn't be the first time. *I'm a be over there in twenty*, she texted.

She put a scarf on her head and leff out.

1
how can I word this?
you ain't been perfect

Damnit. Forgot the keys to his place back in her other purse! She texted again from the street, and then hit the buzzer downstairs for his apartment. That nigga was *definitely* up there parked on the couch, blazed out and playing videogames. She knew it, and leaned on the button, steady.

"Yo! *What*?! Who is this?"

"I leff Mama's without the keys. Lemme up."

" 'Nisha?"

"Yeah! Ain't you get my texts? Buzz me in, nigga."

"I was, uh . . . I been busy. Could you, like, uh, wait down there real fast for me, baby? Just *one* minute."

With her thoughts on buried treasure in the far east of Brooklyn, not on boyfriends who step out the minute you turn your back, she wasn't ready for the panicked fluttering that seized her heart and bowels, the icy flashes that turned sweaty hot—the anger, pure and simple.

Chick or dude. What would it be this time?

Dude. Not too long, and Anhell's piece got off the elevator and crossed the vestibule toward the outer doors. Dude looked regular black, but was obviously Dominican from the loafers and tourniquet-tight clothes. He lived, you could tell, at the gym. Titties bigger than hers, a nasty V-neck putting his whole tattooed chest out on front street. **Mas Líbranos Del Mal**. Heading out, he politely held the door so she could go in. No words, they kept it moving.

The problem was, if you liked pretty boys, and she did like pretty boys, then Anhell was it. You couldn't do no better. She looked okay—*damn good*, when she got all dressed up, her hair and makeup tight. But Anhell was pure Spanish butterscotch. Lightskin, gray eyes, cornrow hangtime to the middle of his back. He answered the door in a towel, naked and wet from a quick shower. Hickies on him she ain't put there.

There's rules to whooping your man's ass. He tries to catch and hold your fists, dodge your knees and elbows and kicks, but accepts in his heart that every lick you land he deserves. You don't go grabbing a knife, or yanking at his hair, either, as the electric fear or pain those inspire will make him lash out with blind total force, turning this rough game real in a way nobody wants. Stay in bounds, babygirl, and you can whale on him till you're so tired you ain't mad no more, and his cheating bitch ass is all bruised up and crying. But fuckit. She wasn't really feeling it today. After getting in a few solid hits, she let Anhell catch her wrists. They were on the floor by then and he hugged her in close and tight, starting up with them same old tears and kisses, same old promises and lies.

" 'Nisha, what can I do? Whatever you need, just tell me what I can do. I'll do it."

Stop laying with them hoes! With them faggots! But this was just the little sin, the one convenient to throw back in his face. She might not even give a shit anymore, if she ever bothered to check. What couldn't be fixed was his big sin. The one they'd cried about, fucked and fought about *all the time* with fists and screams, but not once ever just said the words out loud, plain and clear. Now that a couple years had slipped by it was obvious they were never going to say the words at all.

You know what you did, she said. *You* know *what you did.* And Anhell did know, and so for once shut up with all the bullshit. They lay for a while just breathing, just embraced, their exhausted resignation like a mysterious disease presenting the exact same way as tenderness. "My aunt died and left me all her shit."

"¿La bruja?"

"Yeah. I need you to come out to Brooklyn with me, see if there's anything worth something."

"My case worker coming by tomorrow." Anhell felt good, smelled good, left arm holding her, right hand stroking her shoulder, back and ass in a loop that made everywhere he touched gain value, feel loved. "You know I gotta be here."

"We just going out there," she said, "look around, and then come straight back. It ain't no all-night kinda thing."

"Well, lemme get dressed and we'll head out." He let her go and sat up.

"Wait," she said. "Hol' up." She hooked her thumbs under her panties and leggings. "Eat me out a little fowego?" She rolled em to her knees.

It's gotta be hard, right, when they keep asking for what you can't give, but so *good*, when they want exactly the thing you do best? Anhell grinned. "I got you, mami." He pulled her leggings down further, rolled her knees out wide. "Lemme get in there right . . . "

Somebody suicide-jumped at Grand Central, so the 5 train was all fucked up. They were more than *three* hours getting out there.

Block after block of projects like brick canyons, a little city in the City, home to thousands and thousands and not one whiteface, except for cops from Long Island or Staten Island doubled up in cruisers or walking in posses. It was warm as late summer, the October rain falling hard enough to where you'd open your umbrella, but so soft you felt silly doing it. Anhell walked just behind, holding it over her, the four-dollar wingspan too paltry to share. Drop by drop his tight braids roughened.

Aunt Esther's building was over a few blocks from the subway. Not one of the citysized ones, but big enough. The kind, you know, with the liquor store-style security booth at the entrance, somebody watching who comes and goes.

"*Excuse me*," called the man behind the plastic. "Hey, yo, Braids—and you, Miss? Visitors gotta sign in." Behind the partition, he held up the clipboard.

They went over to the window and scribbled their names. Though basketball-player-tall, up close you could see he wasn't grown. Just some teenage dropout on his hood brand cell, Youtubing bootleg rappers.

She tapped the plastic. "It should be some keys in there, waiting for me," she said. "So I can get into my aunt's apartment."

"Nobody tole me nuffen about that."

"What's that right there?" she said, pointing to the desk beside the boy's elbow, where an envelope lay with her name written across it.

He gave this revelation several blinks and turned back. "Well, you gotta show some ID, then."

She got out her EBT and pressed it to the partition. Squinting, the boy leaned forward and mouthed the name off the card, *Tanisha Marie Jean-Louis*, and then, slower than your slow cousin, compared this to what was written on the envelope, *Tanisha M. Jean-Louis*.

Although allowing, at last, that these two variations fell within tolerance, the boy still shook his head. "Naw, though . . . I on't think I can give you this. You suppose to show a driver's license."

His stupidity flung her forward bodily against the partition. She smacked her palms on the plastic to lend the necessary words their due emphasis. "Nigga, this *New York*. Ain't nobody out here got no fucking driver's license. You better hand me that envelope!"

2

ain't nobody gon' sleep
here tonight!

To the left of the elevator the hall continued around the corner, but 6L, Aunt Esther's apartment, was in the cul-de-sac to the right.

Stink rushed out as the front door swung in. Week-old kitchen trash. Years of cigarettes. Old ladies who piss theyself. Ole Esther had caught her heart attack on the bus, so at least there wasn't that, not the funk of some bloated mice-nibbled corpse leaking slime.

On a corner table inside the door was a huge, nasty religious mess. Ugly dolls, rat bones, weird trash. If all Satan's blue-black devils had wifed all God's blue-blond saints, then a gaudy likeness of their brats was painted on the clutter of seven-day glass candles. She went over to take a look. Breathing through some open window the moment after Anhell followed her in, a breeze slammed the front door shut. The sudden breathless dark had him slapping at the walls desperately until he found the lights. She sneered. "Come peep this. She was on some real hoodoo shit."

"No, mami." He came over reluctantly. "This ain't Voodoo or Santería, ni nada parecido. Your Auntie ain't bought nunna this at no botánica. Look at that."

"Yeah? A cross—so what?"

"You don't see nothing weird about it?"

Though fancy and heavy-looking as real silver, it was just cheap ass plastic junk when she thumped a finger against it. Rather than about-to-die, the face of Jesus looked more like a man nutting, but apart from the crucifix being upside down she couldn't see what had Anhell all freaked out. She shrugged.

Anhell was superstitious. His grandma had wanted him to go to Miami for some expensive Catholic thing, accepting his saint or some shit like that. But his trifling ass had just bought tracksuits, Jordans, and smoked up all the money she'd left him. Now, he touched the bare skin of his neck as if there should've been beads hanging there, some guardian angel to call on today of all days. Her pretty babyboy, so full of regret! She saw how she could fuck with him.

There was a Poland Spring, label ripped off, in the middle of all that voodoo mess. She picked it up.

"You can't drink that, 'Nisha!"

"It ain't even been open yet." She cracked the seal, untwisting the cap to show him. To fuck with him. "It's clean."

"It's blessed water," Anhell said. "*Cursed*—blessed, I don't *know* what! But I swear to God, don't drink it, 'Nisha."

"Mmm," she sighed, after gulping down half the bottle. "I was sooo thirsty, though . . . !"

He got quiet, but she could read these signs from being hugged up with him on the couch so many nights. Forcing him to watch the kind of movies she laughed at, but turned *him* into a motherless six-year-old, afraid of the dark. While she rummaged the apartment, pulling out drawers and dumping worthless old lady trash onto the floor, Anhell followed close, brushing up against her as if onna'ccident. He was scared as shit and wishing she'd change the channel. But, no, nigga. *This* is the show. This is what we're watching.

Not under the mattress, not in the dresser, she didn't find a fat stash of benjis anywhere. Ratty old bras, holey socks, musty dresses. She sorted highspeed through a folder labeled "important papers," dropping a blizzard to the ground as her audit turned up nothing but Social Security and Con Ed stubs, obituaries clipped from newspapers, yellowing funeral programs. Her father's. But the treasure had to be buried in here *somewhere*. Anhell came to sit by her on the edge of the coffee table. He jumped to his feet when it teetered up like a seesaw. There!

"Get that end," she said.

They dumped over the coffee table top, its old school *Ebony*s and dish of peppermints scattering. Underneath was a trunk, a real pirate ass looking trunk. *Now we're talking!*

No hinges or latches were visible on it, but when Anhell tried to pry up the lid, he fell back on his butt, saying, "Shit's locked up *tight*."

She said, "No, it ain't," and effortlessly lifted the lid herself. Folded up inside was a tall, tall man or woman, long-dead and withered black and dry as stale raisins, their longest bones broken to fit fetus-style in the confines of the chest. Anhell screamed all girly and jumped back onto the couch. She rolled her eyes at him. "*Dead.* And how many times I told you what *dead* means?" she said. "Can't *do* nothing to you, Anhell. Nothing to worry about!" He started whining but she ignored him.

There were two things in there with the body (its skin cheap-feeling, just leather*ish*, like a hundred-dollar sofa from the ghetto furniture store, and the body weightless and unresisting as piled laundry). One was a shotgun that could have come from the Civil War, half made of wood. She set it aside. The other was *her* baby, a knife equal in length and width to her own arm, its handle protruding from a rawhide sheath.

You-know-who sidles up and offers . . . what? *Change.* Not for the better, not for the worse, just a *change.* But one so huge that you can't even dream it from the miserable little spot, miserable little moment you're at now. And don't go expecting wishes granted, or that kind of boring shit, because transformation belongs to a whole 'nother category. But, oh, babygirl, this could be a wild hot ride. *Are you down?*

Anhell had slipped off the couch and knelt beside her. He was reaching toward the shotgun, but hesitating too . . . up until *she* did it. Until *she* pulled out the long knife, no, *machète*, from the leather sheath that flaked apart in her hands like ancient pages from an ancient book. Anhell picked up the gun.

Oh, fuck yeah!

It felt like being at the club, three, fo' drinks in, every chick in the place hating, every nigga tryna holler—and then your song come on. The beat drop. She felt loose as a motherfucker. "Ooo, Anhell." Groaning, she wedged the heel of a hand down between her thighs. "You feel that, too?"

Yeah, the nigga was feeling it! She oughta know that look on his face by now, about to bust a *really* good one.

She tested the machète's edge with a fingertip and found it all the way dull, however sharp it looked. Even pressing down hard against the edge hardly dented the pad of her thumb.

Anhell, too, reached out wanting to test the edge of that weird machète. But then he sort of thought twice, stopped short, and shied his hand right on back again. Just like that, she got it. Understood all the possibilities for black magic murder. "Come on, papi," she purred, cat-malicious. "Don't you wanna see what kinda edge it got?" She nudged the machète out toward him—*very* recklessly. Woulda cut his ass, too, if he hadna jumped back so quick. "You ain't skurt, is you?"

She was getting her hands all wet in *somebody's* blood today. That was for *damn* sure.

"Whoa, 'Nisha! Why you playing, though? Back up with that!"

Keys rattled in the lock and the front door swung open.

Two dudes in Dickies and T-shirts came in talking whatever they do over there in Czechoslovakia or Ukraine. The workers were the right color to come to New York and get fat business loans or good union jobs right off the boat, buying a house on a tree-lined street, and all set up for the good life, before their kids even graduated high school. Perhaps for supernatural reasons they didn't notice the shotgun and machète. For natural ones, she and Anhell weren't invisible exactly, but seemed to the workers' eyes only two vague black and brown shapes where they didn't belong.

"You, Miss Jean-Louis? Boss said you gotta be outta here by five o'clock." The law on his side, one of the Serbians held up some important piece of paper, typed, with signatures, etc. "Or we call the cops."

It was instinct. It was *thirst*. Pivoting, she swung like a Cuban phenom at bat who'd better hit that fucking ball or take his damn ass back to the island. Best *believe* she hit. A red-hot knife would've had more trouble with butter, the Polack's astonished trunk separated from his bottom two-thirds so easily. Blood and viscera went splashing by the bucketful but none, impossibly, hit the ground.

A thousand frog-tongues lashing out to snatch as many bugs from the air, every glob of gore vanished in the twinkling of an eye, slurped up by the thirsty machète. How long had this poor baby lain in that awful, *awful* chest?

Though drinking to the last drop was neither delicious nor easy as that first perfect pull, she kept going and swallowed the man down.

The Russian in two pieces desiccated, turning to a spoonful's worth of blown dust between one breath and the next. What, maybe twenty seconds had passed since the door opened? Russkie number two, quick on the uptake and fast on his feet, had spun around and was booking up the hall.

She looked at Anhell and jerked her chin toward the runaway. "Pop 'im."

"I ain't never even shot a gun before."

"Just pull the trigger, dumb ass."

Hoisting it up to his shoulder, he aimed. "But what if it ain't loaded?"

It was, though. The discharge, noiseless on earth, made no flash, either, resounding instead throughout hell. All the souls screaming in their lakes were startled into a moment of silence, so loud was that report, so bright. A burst watermelon of gore blew out the white back of the running man's t-shirt. He was snatched forward—off his feet and several yards through the air—by the impact of the demonbullet, which smashed him facedown into the checkered tiles with such goofy, slapstick violence, she and Anhell turned open-mouthed to each other, dead. They died laughing, grabbing at one another and collapsing to the floor, it was that funny how dude had thought he was getting away, but *psych*!

"Okay, okay," she said finally. "Let's get serious." She pointed to the problematic scene in the hallway. "Get out there and clean that shit up, fore somebody come out they apartment."

Unlike firing a gun for the first time, she didn't need to break it down for Anhell how the devil got his due. He walked up the hall, she with him, and put the thirsty muzzle of the gun down into that sucking wet wound.

In no time the juicy corpse was all bled out, the borschty color of a freshly dead whiteman depinking into gray. Anhell lifted the gun from the dry pit of torn lavender flesh, shattered pale bone. "I don't want no more," he whined, screwing up his face. "The sweet part's gone."

"Shut the fuck up," she said, in zero mood for his finicky complaints. "*Finish it.*"

Anhell pooched his bottom lip like a four-year-old with just the broccoli left on his plate, but he put the muzzle back down in.

Soon he was gagging, and not faking, either. "All right, all right," she conceded. "Carry the rest back to the apartment." There was no splatter on the floor or walls, no more mess, only a shrunken dry thing like the historical Christ, if those skinny bones were pulled from a tomb in Sinai today. She stomped the old body down into the chest and it burst and crumpled like papier mâché, till there was room for Anhell to roll the new one on top. Fingerprints, wipe shit down, tidy up? Nah, fuck that. The devil got you. He looks after his own.

They bounced, Anhell following her out to the elevator.

"So we just kinda slide into the fires sideways, *not* far, and from there nobody can really see . . . "

"I *get it*," Anhell said. "You always think I'm so stupid, 'Nisha, but I got it all same time you did!"

"Well, don't fuck it up, nigga. Cause we carrying this machète and shotgun right through the streets, onto the MT fucking A."

Just newly knighted to this darkest order, they hardly dared more than a step into hell, and so their half-assed little cantrip that first night wouldn't have worked at all, except in a place like New York, where everybody was already trying so hard not to notice strangers.

Night had come to Brooklyn, but you could still see a half inch of daylight glowing behind Manhattan's fallen constellations. They didn't slink from the building like street dogs after grubbing through some alley trash, their heads down, eyes slewing nervously left and right—oh no! They loped like winter wolves, thin yet, but bellies hanging full of fresh kill, and future tooth and scenting nose toward all these little lambs gamboling on every side. Nay, *sweeter* than lambs! For creatures even so gentle can yet scent the beast that would eat them, while men and women and children walking home under soft rain don't know to fear the slavering jaws, the click of claws on concrete.

Shadow and flame licking in the corners of their eyes, machète and gun in hand, they strutted through the evening rush. When they descended to the subway, nine-to-fivers were trudging up and teenagers, just out of basketball practice, leaping stairs two at a time. Down in the station, patrolmen to bust fare-jumpers and dudes selling swipes, and more patrolmen posted at the terrorist table, didn't even blink when two murderers fresh off the deed, weapons naked in hand, rolled past. Busker on the sax, "You've Changed." Nobody tried to bogart, nobody jostled them on the crowded way back uptown. Where you woulda *swore* there was none, space opened up on the packed train. Coupla seats came free.

You can pray all day, babygirl, but God won't answer. He ain't *thinking* bout you. Now that other guy, though? Will treat you like a fucking rockstar. VIP. Perks.

3
when I say people
that's what I mean

Anhell crawled across the bed, over her, flipped on the lights, crashed around the studio. He gathered up and threw out all the bottles, flushed the roaches and ashes, hid the tray, opened the windows and turned the fan on high. He came to the bed whispering. "You don't wanna put on some clothes, mami?" Sleepy and cold from the fan, she just groaned and pulled the covers over her, his pillow over her head. His caseworker buzzed at 8:45, as always, as bimonthly, this middle-aged African bitch who hated her and thought she was the biggest slut on earth, but *loved* Anhell, no doubt to the point of hand-on-the-Bible swearing his shit smelled like patchouli and roses. Um, *hello* . . . ? That nigga gave it to *me*.

Mrs. Okorie asked Anhell the same stupid social worker questions that had you like *duh* . . . ! the answers to which not only hadn't changed since last time but couldn't. Spotting in the heaped up blankets on the bed signs pointing to the presence of a certain fast ass American black girl, Mrs. Okorie reminded Anhell that it was against the rules for "company to cohabitate." There was, in fact, this scholarship program which Mrs. Okorie thought Anhell (who *wasn't* no fucking college material, not unless y'all got a PhD in PS4) could apply to, even earn his associate's degree, if not for the influence of a certain fast ass American black girl.

Special for people who controlled his benefits, Anhell had this soft sweet voice, this lightskin innocent voice. Saying things like "just visiting" and "a couple days," he almost had Mrs. Okorie calmed down when she got up booty-nekkid from bed, crossed to the bathroom and, just half-closing the door, pissed *loud* for a mad ass long time, like some loose bitch who'd been up till four in the morning drinking with her man. Anhell had to work them gray eyes, that good hair, *hard* to get Mrs. Okorie calmed down again.

They napped and woke up at noon. They fucked but that wasn't it. Neither was a puff or two off Anhell's first blunt of the day, nor coffee light and sweet, bagel egg and cheese from the corner. And, no, TV wasn't it, and not a nap, and not fooling around again later in bed. Nor staring out the window while Anhell played his videogames. He that giveth thee all shall too expect somewhat in return.

O gluttons of murder, wherefore do ye fast? Bring down the red rain, for in hell we are greatly thirsting . . . !

Below, crossing the courtyard, were a Spanish girl, her nigga, and their little baby in a stroller. Smiling church ladies, fat and overdressed, stood by the intersection passing out tracts. On the benches, every cell phone out, a girl clique was holding conference. Boys on bikes, on scooters, on skateboards. She didn't want the blood of these people, her people, but somebody had to die and pretty fucking soon. A whole *lot* of somebodies, and day in and day out. How to be evil without doing bad? There's a problem for you, huh?

Around seven they ate take-out tins of chicken, yellow rice and beans from the joint around the corner, sharing a Corona 24 oz. between them— plenty of food and drink, you would've thought, except this fare only made them hungrier, thirstier, for another repast richer by far than this shit. She kept having to move the machète from here to there. Whether propped against the wall, or laid on the floor, table, or bed, its metal seemed to pick up some vibration and whine slightly, a rattle and hum that was setting her teeth on edge. Anhell said he couldn't hear it, but then *she* couldn't hear the weird crackling noise he said the old wood of the shotgun kept making. He stuffed it in the back of the closet, under laundry, but said that didn't really help. He was on his cell a lot, restless. In and out the bathroom, texting hoes. In and out that closet.

"And where you call yourself going?"

"Nowhere," Anhell said, giving his lips a little lick. "Just about to grab a couple phillies at the deli."

"I see you got that gun."

"It's mine, ain't it."

"What, you just gon' head up the block, pop whoever you see first. That's ya plan?"

"Naw! I just, uh . . . "

"Leave it here, Anhell. Tomorrow, me and you will go fuck shit up real good, okay?" She knew what he was feeling, because she was fiending just as bad. But first she needed to figure this thing out, the how and who and all that. Cause the way you start is how you go on. "Us, *together.* At least one sweet kill each, I promise."

"Look, I just need to step out real fast, baby." Nigga wasn't even trying to run game! Where was the smoothness at, the slick lies? "Just for a minute. I be *right* back."

He turned his back on her like he was gonna just walk out that door still holding the shotgun. Right now she could care less about him fucking around, but *she* was the boss of murder up in this bitch, and it wasn't gon' be no extracurriculars on that front.

She threw a Timb at his head with intent to kill. Anhell's ducking and dodging was some next level shit, so it missed. "You heard? I said, *leave it here* gotdamnit! Or I will chop yo ass up fast as I did that whitenigga yesterday. *Try me.*" She thought she'd left it across the room, under the bed, but no, the machète was right here in her hand, eager to make good the lady's word.

There was a moment where you could see him wondering whether females with just a knife should really be coming out the side of they neck at niggas holding guns. She laughed and flicked beckoning fingers. "Play yourself, then. *Come on.* I wish to fuck you would."

They fought a lot and they were both tired, both sick of it. Anhell's litebrite eyes took on a glint far more sharp and steel-like than diamond-pretty.

"Oh yeah, daddy," she moaned, as if muvver were wet from all the foreplay and good to go now. "You only gotta *act* like you wanna raise that gun at me, and I will pay you back *every motherfucking thing*. Let's do this." The gun trembled in his hand, his eyes hard, and the odds that his arm would come up went up—thirty, forty, fifty percent. Satan had her hype as fuck. "*Do it*, you bitch ass faggot ass PUNK!"

Mumbling under his breath, making faces with his eyes down, Anhell propped it with the umbrellas beside the door and leff out. She went and got the gun, laid it on the table in front of her.

Madison, Tiphanie, Arelys, and nem sent a group text right then, tryna get the crew together to go to this new Harlem club, and at first . . . but then she thought of the narcotic bass, the tight-packed bodies writhing together to the music, and her just swinging the machète through all the niggas and her girls like some reaper in the corn . . .

Nah, she texted back. *I'm in for the night. Sorry.* One of em called. "Yo, put ya nigga on, girl. I'm bout to tell Anhell we just going out dancing. Ladies' night. Fuckit, he can come too. Ain't nobody seen you in a minute—'*Nisha*! What *is* it . . . .?"

She was sobbing and she never cried. "He said, he said . . . " Anhell had muttered *I hate you* when going out the door, and it had hurt her feelings bad. You just don't *say* shit like that!

"Oh my God, *Anhell* said that? Well, what led up to it?" Madison said. "Tell me everything that happen, *exactly*."

She sketched a version of events that, mmm, *skimmed* the details of the Brooklyn adventure and double homicide, swearing fealty to infernal powers, and the carnivorous griping of demonic weapons. Perhaps not every fact concerning her own foul-mouthed instigation made it into the story, either.

They talked a long time, until the girls were all in the taxi together on their way to the club. And because Madison was that ride-or-die friend, always one hundred percent team 'Nisha, she felt a lot better when they hung up.

It was very late, but Mama would still be winding down from the hospital, nodding on the couch in front of some documentary. She called.

"Oh, hey, baby." Soft voice, sleepy. TV muttering in the background. "I guess you went back over there, huh?"

"Yeah."

"You know you ain't gotta stay with him, right? You could definitely get into nursing school. Girl, you *smart*, and that boy—"

"Let's not do this tonight, Mommy, please. Okay?" Mama talked a tough game when Anhell wasn't up in her face, but them gray eyes worked on her, too, getting her all *oh-you-want-a-plate-baby?* and *tee-hee-hee* in person. "I don't feel like talking bout him. And is that gunshots I hear on your TV? I thought you hated them cop shows. What you watching?"

"Turn on channel thirteen," Mama murmured. "Just for today, PBS is showing that new film DuVernay won Sundance with, *BLM.*"

"Oh, word?" She reached for the remote, but kept the TV muted, her eyes on her Sudoku book. "What's it about?" She penciled in numbers while Mama sleepily ran on and on and on.

. . . of us gunned down six days out of every week by the police. Hoping that cell phone camera and video technology . . . to disrupt the historical impunity of police brutality and extrajudicial murder . . .

"Yeah?" she said, paying attention only to the cadences. Mama's voice soothing, lovely, there since the beginning. 6. "Huh."

. . . reinstituting Jim Crow and slavery through the carceral state and prison labor . . . felons, afterwards, barred from the franchise, employment, or even basic welfare benefits.

"That's awful, dang." 6.

. . . electing Trump . . . a direct consequence of Pence, for example, sending state police troopers to close down African-American voter registration in Indiana.

"Wow, I ain't even know that." 6.

Mama fell asleep, so she hung up.

Anhell came in, eyes all droopy and red from smoking in the street. Mostly she just felt, as usual, glad to see his fine yellow ass home again, though she fronted like whatever, *who cares?* Smelling very clean, of coconut lime bodywash that wasn't in the bathroom here, Anhell leaned in to kiss her. *Ew!*

Nice of him to take a shower, but his breath was giving funky receipts for all his recent activities.

She caught his face in the palm of a hand and pushed him off. "The way yo bref kicking, you just been down on some bad pussy for *real*, for real."

He ran for the Listerine and then crept back, looking at her with dog's eyes—a very bad dog. So handsome, though, so hot, he blessed the room just by being in it. And girl you know this dopey bloodshot gaze is full of the purest love you'll ever get. She sighed, reached out a hand, ran fingers down his scalp between frizzy cornrows. "Ya head's looking pretty rough. Hand me that comb and sit here. I'ma take these out." Anhell sat on the floor between her knees. She turned up the volume a little, just to a friendly mutter. He pulled the table closer to pinch open a phillie and roll up his late-night .5 grams.

Ready for Iraq in combat armor, whitepolice in Missouri and Louisiana held machine guns, rode tanks. Natural hair sisters holding poster board signs. Baltimore niggas wilding like the cops won't shoot. Close-up of a brother, his face fades out. Baby mama crying. Close-up of another brother, that face fades out. *His* muvver crying. Another face, another wife. Face, mother. Wife, mother. Faces. Crying.

"Know what I wanna see?" Anhell, with each word, scrawled cursives of smoke on the air. "Some crying *white*bitches on this TV."

Normally she had better things to do than ponder the reefer ramblings of a nigga fly as hell, yes, but oh so simple. Now, for whatever reason, her hands paused in the springtime flood of his hair. Fascinated, she said, "Yeah?"

"*Yeah!*" Anhell said, throwing out a preacherly hand at the TV. "Why's it always *us* gotta have the sad story? Let me see some bad ass niggas who get away with nothing but stone cold murder. Then let me see *white*mamas, *white*wives, cameras all up in they face, weeping and wailing outside the church. Now *that* would be some funny shit!" His laughter caught on hooks of smoke, broke into helpless phlegmy barking.

The hair stood up on her neck, goosebumps chilling her arms. She slapped on his back, inspired to her soul. It came to her with a bright ten-story-high clarity, like the LED billboards at Times Square. True vocation. God's work and the devil's!

4

#killers4lyfe

4.1 *police massacre, October*
4.2 state funeral, November
The sky at one a.m. hung low above the city, orange clouds damn near bright as day. Gypsies bumped the horn when slowing and sped back up. Draped in colored Christmas lights, almost, the curbside mountains of

garbage bags, all beaded by spitting rain, winked under headlights, brake lights, sodium and neon. The piped corridors of all the scaffolding over the sidewalks, all the doorways, and all the stairwells going down breathed back at them *parfum de piss*. It was unseasonably warm in the Bronx, and a lovely night for an atrocity. There was the precinct house just ahead. Time to make the bacon, Mr, Pig.

A sextet of cops were smoking on the precinct stairs. Three cigarette cherries flaring with the draw, three redder and dim hanging hipside. Who knows but that qualms might not have stirred the hearts of dark gods, who then might have brought down the storm elsewhere, on some other night, if all those cops out front *hadn't* been white? But police have their own little clicks, too. Spanish tight with Spanish, black with black, whitecops keeping to their own kind.

Anhell laid down an enfilade that had him doing numbers before half a minute was out. The devil, if it ain't been said, saw to questions of ammo and aim, chambering embers *di l'Inferno* just faster than Anhell could squeeze the trigger. Hellfire tracers went streaking through the dark and one, two, three, four, five whitecops turned explosively to redmeat. Number six, before losing the lungs to do so, gave a shout. She and Anhell ran—not away, *toward* the trouble. Just vibing on the slaughter at first, thrilled how babyboy had put em down like that, now she felt eager for a taste of her own. A bitch gotta post up, right—get her hands dirty, too?

Some cavalry came pouring out the precinct front doors to see about that shout, and *chop, chop, chop* were three who had been whole made all in twain. The machète went in and through without effort, but still she felt, somehow, a slow buttery drag across the blade, as if demonic steel were stiff meat belonging to her own body and sinking deep into a lover all wet, hot and open for her. No need, as it turned out, to drink down whole gallons from any one body when this much blood was flowing. The first cupful's sweetest, anyway. Naw, a spoonful will do, given this abundance.

Stepping over the bestrewment, they went in.

4.1 police massacre, October

4.2 state funeral, November

4.3 police massacre, October

Lastly, twelve widows filed on camera. Whitewidows, all white, though their eyes sought reflexively for any who weren't. Only one widow would be allowed to speak, and not an ugly one. They knew which one it would be the very instant she, blond, stepped into view. The black lace she wore overlaid a silk sheath that, iridescing under the lights between deep purple, reddish black, and . . . *indigo?* lent her gown the dark complexities of a raven's wing seen in direct sun. Not the dress your granny would wear to the funeral, this number, and "gorgeous" only got you about halfway there. The camera lingered a bit over the distinctive red soles of her glossy black pumps.

"Eight outta them sixty-three we kilt weren't even white," Anhell complained. "How come they ain't let nunna *them* widows on TV?"

"Optics, baby," she said and swallowed deeply, in wisdom and resignation, from her tumbler. "They gotta keep shit looking a certain way for the message."

45 hadn't won the presidency for no damn reason: He quit reading off the 'prompter all wooden and halting and started ad-libbing for his base.

"Studies show, there's a *yuge* amount of science, so many studies showing that our African Americans, the blacks, actually kill *each other* 99.9% of the time. Facts!"

Anhell sucked his teeth. "Ain't nobody wanna hear this cheeto ass looking fool! When they putting the widows on?"

"President first," she said, "then the mayor. Widows go last." One more watery sip drained the ice in her glass, and she looked around with increasing consternation for the bottle. "*Yo*, my nigga—how you drank up all the Henny that quick?"

"Ain't even that serious, ma." Anhell leaned over the couch's far side. "Got the bottle right here . . . " After pulling it up from where it sat (still one-third full) on the floor, he poured over her ice until, clinking, the cubes floated up.

"*Oh*," she exclaimed. "Cause I was getting ready to *say* . . . !" She took a good, long swallow.

4.2 state funeral, November
4.3 police massacre, October
4.4 state funeral, November

With a step backward into the brimstone sirocco, they couldn't be seen well from here, earth. And so from there, hell, the screams of the damned and heat blasting at their backs, they juked around wildly shooting cops and took the whiteones *bang!* to the head, *swap!* through the neck. It was less a trick of witchcraft than basic physics, time in hell running at a faster clip than our earthly clock, and so much so that, when they stood on the smoldering threshold, all these police, by contrast, were moving in slo-mo and clumsy as fuck.

Anhell dropped them as if this were some damn videogame. Kevlar, steel desks, security doors, ducking around the corner of cinder-block walls. All this could've just as well been cardboard, a wish and a prayer, because none of it was saving cover. Satan whispered a name to each bullet, and if that one which the boy shot had heard yours, well, baby game up. You was done. Every shot traveled on a rigorous and unbroken line to its target no matter what intervened.

Anhell had a do-not-kill option, the gun making in that case a strange bark and blowing no two-pound red mass off that brown or woman's body. Indeed no wound at all appeared, though these lucky ones allowed to live, these few shown this presumptive mercy, all fell down writhing to the ground, their screams matching the damned for raw-throated abandon. Here in the police station, there was a little noise like that in hell.

Semiautomatic muzzle-flash all about her, a ricocheting glitter she batted away, the incoming slow as water balloons lobbed by a three-year-old. She hacked would-be heroes in half. Funny, how you think the first shift at the slaughterhouse will be so hard, really seeing how the sausage gets made, where pork chops come from. But it turns out, you're about that life. You were *made* for this, babygirl! Don't shit faze you. Flinging swatches of crimson over every surface surrounding her, she felt almost bad. It was *too* easy. ("At places, the blood in there so deep, your shoes stepped in, your socks got wet . . . ") Best of all she liked it when they tried to hide. Chopping in after them through the barricades, the doors, the little under-desk shelters. Then one pretty moment, when most cowered and begged, some rallied to squeeze off a last shot, and she finished that piggy and went for the next. You ever just start *laughing*, can't stop? The party's so good, you're having such a nice time?

4.3 police massacre, October
4.4 state funeral, November
4.5 police massacre, October
Mrs. Liam Conor O'Donnell, *dec.*, stood and approached the pulpit. You could see she ate salads, worked out, no bread. A face for TV, makeup on point, and that gown fitting very well—but everything tasteful.

Addressing St. Patrick's navy-clad pews: "I know that all of you join with me and the rest of America in grieving the loss of so many of—and truly they were—New York's Finest."

"Bitch won't cry."

"That hoe will *definitely* cry. Now, shh."

"But look at her makeup," Anhell said. "How she tryna mess that up? Nope. Watch, not one tear."

"Bet you some bomb ass head we getting tears from her." And you know she had to be sure, because she *hated* giving head! "Now, shush, so I can hear."

" . . . our respects to the slain and honoring their sacrifice. Ladies, when our men fall, we must take up arms and the battle cry. To contribute to the cause and the future I've borne two beautiful daughters. I've been a good wife." She smiled sadly and the camera flashed on two blond cherubs in white blouses, black jumpers. "I still remember those last moments when Liam—Lieutenant O'Donnell—when he was going out to work . . . I *wanted* to tell him." She lay a palm over the flatness of her immaculate belly. A murmur and stir convulsed the pews. "Yes. A new baby. This one, I know, will be the son Liam always wanted, a boy who will now never—"

"Lemme get a puff of that, yo."

"Thought you wasn't fucking with the weed like that? Damn, girl! Keep smoking like this, you bout to turn into a 'head like *me*."

"Nigga, just pass the blunt."

"All of us gathered here today know that a darkness is falling over this nation and over the earth itself. As demographics shift, the struggle for the continuance of Western Civilization has become existential. Diverse elements would see the blood and soil of this nation washed away in a dismal tide. But it is incumbent upon the Herrenvolk to secure the future for our children and for *theirs*. No, there can be no parley with evil; strength must be our answer. Before the Almighty, I swear to you that we *will* prevail over our enemies, and the perpetrators of this tragedy shall soon know our vengeance . . . "

4.4 state funeral, November
4.5 police massacre, October
4.6 state funeral, November
Knocking motherfuckers out really don't work the way it do in movies. Sad to say, but not all the black cops she smashed upside the head with the flat or blunt of her demonic machète lived to tell the tale. And, to be honest, Satan was from jump like *You can miss me with all this conscious killing, organic*

murder crap. Whenever she tried to spare the lives of too many women, black, Asian, Spanish in a row, buddy got fed up and made the machète spin in her grip from play side to business end. *Oop!* A couple of the wrong heads went flying too. Oh, shit, sorry! Bees that way sometime, though. The third or fourth time Satan decided enough with this woke ass bullshit, and caused the machète to spin from "knockout" position to "decap," the unbreakable barrel of Anhell's shotgun intervened, clangingly, before her always-fatal edge could claim *this* victim.

"I thought we was only killing the whitepeople, the men?" Anhell said, and jerked his chin at the policewoman kneeling between them. "*She* ain't neither one."

Brownskin. Not short, not tall. All right looking, although the uniform's shapeless navy slacks and boxy polyester shirt were doing her thickness *no favors.* The policewoman was definitely a stranger, but seemed incredibly familiar at first glance . . . and then she realized why. "Get yo ass outta here," she snarled, gesturing up with the machète. Go!

Commuted from slaughter, a fawn clambering to her feet between the lioness and leopard, the policewoman stood up warily.

"Go on," Anhell said, smiling warmly. "We gotta finish up here."

About to run, the policewoman did a double take. "Oh, you got some *pretty* eyes, though!"

"Well, *thank* you," Anhell exclaimed, giving light skin, delighted surprise, a charming smile. "It's so nice a you to say that!"

Oh see? We can't have this. He got the broad ready to put the pussy on him right *here!*

"Bissh," she slushed, hefting the machète in a manner that said *I'm not the one.* "You can run or you can die. How you playing it?"

Anhell peeped her face real quick for resolve, and said, "Yeah, sorry," to the policewoman regretfully. "But you better run now, for real."

Brownskin sister heard and took her leave in such haste, the peaked hat of her uniform was knocked off her head, the hair underneath all short, every which way, and toe up.

He liked exactly the kind of dudes you'd expect, elevens on the ten-point scale, this jet-black Senegalese model, that Colombian semipro futbolista, another "big dick country ass redbone nigga from down south," quote unquote, overheard. Anhell only wanted the brown girls, though, and they had to look just like her.

〜

4.5 police massacre, October

4.6 state funeral, November

4.7 police massacre, October

Eulogy done, the apostle widows came to surround, weeping, the beautiful one at the podium. They clutched one another's fingers, their red-blotched wet faces becoming downright ugly with sobs. The cameras knew where and on whom to linger, blond Jesus widow who, blinking her tear-jeweled black lashes, smiled bravely and freed up two or three telegenic drops for St. Patrick's Cathedral, for New York City, and for the United States of America. Did her mascara smudge or run? *Fuck* no! And, God, did the bitch look good!

"*Aww* . . . !" said Anhell, every gambler's exclamation, when his bet goes bad.

Cracking up, she fell back on the couch. "*Didn't* I say, nigga?" She rolled around on the pillows. "*Told* your ass!"

Anhell pointed at the recession of president, mayor, widows. "Shit came out just like you said, though. And we ain't even *done* yet." Tumbler in hand, he took the bottle in his other, liquoring up his meltwater and ice. "Copkillers? *God*killers! And we don't stop." As if, sitting down, he just couldn't get the feeling out right, Anhell jumped to his feet shouting at the blue televised ranks filing from the church. "*Fuck* the poe lease! It's on for life. We gunning for *alla* you motherfuckers!" His eyes came alight, red as the EXIT sign far down a dark hallway. In his wild hand, the bottle sloshing. "Fiddy shots shot, fiddy cops dropped!" His pretty lips sputtering, like a lighter that won't catch, *sparks*, not spit. And though it was commercials by now, this nigga steady yelling. " . . . end up dying, staring at the roof the church, ya ladies crying . . . !"

She knelt up on the couch and smacked him in the face with a throw pillow.

Anhell woke up. "Oh, fuck, though, baby," he said, shaking his head. "You seent that? Devil had me like *tweaking*!"

"Yeah, I saw," she said. "Now gimme that fucking bottle. You spilling shit everywhere . . . "

4.6 state funeral, November

4.7 police massacre, October

She'd once seen his long curly hair blown out bone-straight, a black curtain hanging to his ass. Now, auburn, it sat heavily upon his shoulders—huge and soaking wet. She reached into his hair and wrung a handful like some sponge that had sopped deep spill off the slaughterhouse floor. The squishing mass gushed police blood. She pulled his salty mouth down to hers and they kissed.

Spots lit the night out front to anachronous noon, splashing blue 'n' red emergency lights, a cordon of NYPD ESU with machine guns at every surrounding intersection, snipers on every overlooking rooftop. From "three" a SWAT team was counting down to storm the place. They made fools of the whole kingdom arrayed against them, and walked out through deep hell, across the burning floor of Gehenna.

tag

To avoid the curfew they took the subway downtown at rush hour every third or fourth days. They'd walk in some other borough until happening upon today's luckless whiteboys in blue. Afterwards, they'd come on back uptown. Once, they went all the way out to Staten Island on the ferry, and it was like a date, the sunlight on the water, Statue of Liberty, a whale breaching in the harbor. Incredibly romantic—though probably not for that pair of transit cops at the terminal, whose last vision of this world was of two shadows swaggering up through heat shimmer, a teenage lankiness and the width and curves and thickness of a woman, barely glimpsed against a whole continent of fire. But the City under martial law was boring as fuck, and so she called Mama and got her talking again on that *BLM* tip. Kind of slipped the question to her sideways. *Hey, what's the worst police department in America?*

"Chicago," Mama answered. "Or maybe the LAPD. Why you asking?"

"No reason," she said. "Oh, by the way, me and Anhell been talking about getting outta town for a while. Maybe just taking the bus somewhere, a road trip."

"Cali?" he said, getting excited when she'd made up her mind. Nobody likes wintertime in New York. The same day their cash allowance came through, they packed some underwear, machète and gun, their pills. A backpack each, just the necessary.

"What we gonna do, though," he asked, "when the prescriptions run out?"

"Walk up in any pharmacy," she said, "and be like, I want another month's worf, or *every motherfucker up in here* getting they head chopped off."

"Oh, yup yup," said Anhell, seeing the sense, nodding. "That'd work!"

And so down to Port Authority, and on a Greyhound going west.

ABOUT THE AUTHORS

Simon Avery's fiction has been published in a variety of magazines and anthologies including *Black Static, Crimewave, The Third Alternative, The Best British Mysteries IV, Beneath the Ground, The Black Room Manuscripts: Volume 4, Birmingham Noir, Terror Tales of Yorkshire, Something Remains*, and *Occult Detective Quarterly*. A novella, *The Teardrop Method*, was published in 2017. He lives and works in Birmingham, UK.

Laird Barron, an expat Alaskan, is the author of several books—including *The Imago Sequence and Other Stories, Swift to Chase*, and *Blood Standard*—and many short stories some of which have been reprinted in numerous year's best anthologies and nominated for multiple awards. He is a three-time winner of the Shirley Jackson Award. Currently, Barron lives in the Rondout Valley of New York State and is at work on tales about the evil that men do.

Ashley Blooms was born and raised in Cutshin, Kentucky. She received her MFA as a John and Renee Grisham Fellow at the University of Mississippi. She's been awarded scholarships from the Clarion Writer's Workshop and Appalachian Writer's Workshop, served as fiction editor for the *Yalobusha Review*, and worked as an editorial intern and first reader for *Tor.com*. Her stories have appeared in *The Magazine of Fantasy & Science Fiction, Strange Horizons*, and *Shimmer*, among others. Her nonfiction has appeared in the *Oxford American*. She currently lives in Oxford, Mississippi, with her husband and their dog, Alfie.

Aliette de Bodard lives (with her husband and children) and works (as a System Engineer) in Paris. She is the author of the critically acclaimed Obsidian and Blood trilogy of Aztec noir fantasies, as well as numerous short stories, which garnered her two Nebula Awards, a Locus Award, and two British Science Fiction Association Awards. Her space opera books include *The Tea Master and the Detective*. Recent works include the Dominion of the Fallen series, set in a turn-of-the-century Paris devastated by a magical war, which comprises the British Science Fiction Association Award-winning *The House of Shattered Wings* and its standalone sequel, *The House of Binding Thorns*.

Rebecca Campbell is a Canadian writer and an academic with a PhD in English (specifically Canadian literature) from the University of Western Ontario. Her speculative fiction has been published in *Shimmer*, *Beneath Ceasless Skies*, *The Magazine of Fantasy & Science Fiction*, *Tor.com*, and other venues. Her story "The Glad Hosts," published by *Lackington's*, was nominated for a Sunburst Award. *The Paradise Engine*, her first novel, was published in 2013.

Jeffrey Ford lives in central Ohio and teaches at Ohio Wesleyan University. He has contributed over 130 short stories to numerous magazines and anthologies including *The Oxford Book of American Short Stories*, *Conjunctions*, *Puerto Del Sol*, *Hayden's Ferry Review*, *The Magazine of Fantasy & Science Fiction*, *MAD Magazine*, *Weird Tales*, *Clarkesworld*, *Tor.com*, *Lightspeed*, *Subterranean*, *Fantasy*, *New Jersey Noir*, *Stories*, *The Living Dead*, *The Faery Reel*, *After*, *The Dark*, *The Doll Collection*, many "year's best" venues, and more. He is the recipient of four World Fantasy Awards and two Shirley Jackson Awards as well as the Nebula, Grand Prix de l'Imaginaire, and Edgar Allan Poe Awards.

Robin Furth's fiction, nonfiction, and poetry have appeared in numerous magazines and journals including *The Magazine of Fantasy & Science Fiction*, *Cemetery Dance*, *Gramarye*, *Orbis*, *The Beloit Poetry Journal*, and *Interpreter's House*. Her book, *Stephen King's The Dark Tower: The Complete Concordance* (originally created for King's personal use), has been translated into five languages. Furth is the co-author of Marvel's bestselling Dark Tower comic book series and has contributed to numerous other Marvel publications.

Lisa L. Hannett has had over seventy short stories appear in venues including *Clarkesworld*, *Fantasy*, *Weird Tales*, *Apex*, *The Dark*, and "year's best" anthologies in Australia, Canada, and the U.S. She has won four Aurealis Awards, including Best Collection for her first book, *Bluegrass Symphony*, which was also nominated for a World Fantasy Award. Her first novel, *Lament for the Afterlife*, won the Australian National Science Fiction ("Ditmar") Award for Best Novel. A new collection of short stories, *Little Digs*, is coming out in 2019.

Maria Dahvana Headley is the *New York Times*-bestselling author of the novels *Aerie*, *Magonia* (one of *PW*'s Best Books of 2015), *Queen of Kings*, and the memoir *The Year of Yes*. With Kat Howard she is the author of *The End of the Sentence*, one of NPR's Best Books of 2014, and with Neil Gaiman, she is co-editor of *Unnatural Creatures*. Her short stories have been included in many "year's best anthologies" and have been finalists for the Nebula and Shirley Jackson Awards. Her highly acclaimed novel *The Mere Wife*, which adapts *Beowulf* to modern-day New York, was published earlier this year.

Carole Johnstone is a British Fantasy Award-winning Scottish writer, currently living in Essex, England. Her fiction has appeared in numerous venues including *Black Static, New Fears, Horror Library, Interzone, Terror Tales of the Scottish Highlands, Dark Minds*, and *Sherlock Holmes and the School of Detection*. Her work has been reprinted in "best of" anthologies in the U.S. and UK. Her novella, *Cold Turkey*, and debut short story collection, *The Bright Day is Done* were both shortlisted for a British Fantasy Award.

Stephen Graham Jones is the author of sixteen novels, six story collections, more than two hundred and fifty stories, and has some comic books in the works. His latest novel is *Mongrels*. He's been the recipient of an NEA Fellowship in Fiction, the Texas Institute of Letters Jesse H. Jones Award for Best Work of Fiction, the Independent Publishers Award for Multicultural Fiction, the Bram Stoker Award, and three This Is Horror Awards. Jones teaches in the MFA programs at University of Colorado at Boulder and University of California Riverside-Palm Desert. He lives in Boulder, Colorado.

Hailed by the *New York Times* as "One of our essential writers of dark fiction," **Caitlín R. Kiernan** has published twelve novels, including *The Red Tree* and *The Drowning*. She is the recipient of the Barnes and Noble Maiden Voyage, Bram Stoker, IHG, James Tiptree, Jr., *Locus*, and World Fantasy Awards. Kiernan studied geology and paleontology at the University of Alabama and the University of Colorado and has published in several scientific journals, including the *Journal of Vertebrate Paleontology*. A prolific short fiction writer, her most recent collection is *Houses Under the Sea: Mythos Tales*. Two more, one from Subterranean Press and *The Very Best of Caitlín R. Kiernan* from Tachyon Publications, are forthcoming.

After receiving a PhD from Centre for Medieval Studies at the University of Toronto, **Helen Marshall** completed a postdoctoral fellowship at the University of Oxford. She was recently appointed Senior Lecturer of

Creative Writing and Publishing at Anglia Ruskin University in Cambridge, England and is the general director of the Centre for Science Fiction and Fantasy. Her first collection of fiction, *Hair Side, Flesh Side*, won the Sydney J Bounds Award. Her second collection, *Gifts for the One Who Comes After*, won the World Fantasy Award and the Shirley Jackson Award, and was shortlisted for the British Fantasy Award, Bram Stoker Award, and the Aurora Award from the Canadian Science Fiction and Fantasy Association.

Kate Marshall is the author of the Young Adult novel *I Am Still Alive*. Her science fiction and fantasy fiction has appeared in *Beneath Ceaseless Skies*, *Crossed Genres*, and elsewhere. She writes historical romance as Kathleen Kimmel and works in the video game industry as a writer and occasional designer. Her love of books runs through every aspect of her career; she serves as both a developmental editor and a cover designer for fellow authors. She lives outside of Seattle with her husband, a dog, a cat, and a baby.

Ian Muneshwar is a writer and teacher currently based in Raleigh, North Carolina. His short fiction appears in venues such as *Clarkesworld, Gamut, Liminal Stories*, and *The Dark*. In both his writing and course design, he is concerned with queer subjectivities, cultural memory, and the ways in which queerbrown identities are shaped by diaspora. Muneshwar holds a BA from Vassar College and is a graduate of both the Clarion West and Odyssey workshops. He is currently pursuing an MFA in fiction at North Carolina State University.

Before earning her MFA from Vermont College of Fine Arts, **M. Rickert** worked as kindergarten teacher, coffee shop barista, balloon vendor at Disneyland, and in the personnel department of Sequoia National Park where she spent her time off hiking the wilderness. She now lives in Cedarburg, Wisconsin, a small city of candy shops and beautiful gardens. She has published numerous short stories and two collections: *Map of Dreams* and *Holiday*. Her first novel, *The Memory Garden*, was published in 2014, and won the Locus Award for Best First Novel. Her first collection, *Map of Dreams*, was honored with both the World Fantasy and Crawford Awards. Her latest collection, *You Have Never Been Here*, was published in 2015.

Rebecca Roanhorse is an Ohkay Owingeh Pueblo/African-American writer and a VONA workshop alum. She is also a lawyer and Yale grad. She lives in northern New Mexico with her daughter, husband, and pug. Her debut novel, *Trail of Lightning,* was published earlier this year. Her children's book *Race to the Sun* is coming in 2019 from Rick Riordan Presents. Her recent nonfiction can be found in *Invisible 3: Essays and Poems on Representation in SF/F, Strange Horizons, Uncanny,* and *How I Resist: Activism and Hope for a New Generation.*

Eden Royce describes herself as "Freshwater Geechee. Charleston girl living in the Garden of England" who grew up around rootworkers and hoodoo practitioners. A Speculative Literature Foundation's Diverse Worlds grant recipient, her short stories appear in over a dozen anthologies and magazines. She's voiced podcasts, been a reptile handler, bridal consultant, and stockbroker, but is now a full-time writer. She enjoys roller-skating, reading, cooking, traveling, and listening to thunderstorms.

Mark Samuels is a British writer of weird and fantastic fiction in the tradition of Arthur Machen and H. P. Lovecraft (although his story here was published with a nod to Reggie Oliver). Born in deepest Clapham, South London, his short stories often focus on detailing a shadowy world in which his protagonists gradually discover terrifying and rapturous vistas lurking behind modernity. Samuels work has been highly praised by the likes of Thomas Ligotti and Ramsey Campbell and has appeared in prestigious anthologies of horror and weird fiction on both sides of the Atlantic.

Priya Sharma is a medical doctor who lives in the UK. Her fiction has appeared in periodicals such as *Albedo One, Interzone, Black Static,* and *Tor.com* and anthologies including *Once Upon a Time, Black Feathers, Mad Hatters and March Hairs.* She's been anthologized in several "year's best" anthologies in the U.S. and UK. Her work has appeared on the Locus Recommended Reading List. Sharma's story, "Fabulous Beasts" was a Shirley Jackson Award finalist and won a British Fantasy Award for Short Fiction. Her first collection, *All the Fabulous Beasts,* was published earlier this year.

Robert Shearman has worked as writer for television, radio, and the stage. He is probably best known for being one of the writers for the BAFTA Award-winning revived Doctor Who series starring Christopher Eccleston. (His episode "Dalek," was nominated for a Hugo Award.) Shearman's first collection of short stories, *Tiny Deaths,* won the World Fantasy Award, and was shortlisted for the Edge Hill Short Story Prize and nominated for the Frank O'Connor International Short Story Prize. His second collection, *Love Songs for the Shy and Cynical* won the Shirley Jackson Award, the British Fantasy Award, and the Edge Hill Short Story Reader's Prize. His third collection, *Everyone's Just So So Special,* won the British Fantasy Award Shearman's first collection published in North America, *Remember Why You Fear Me*, was shortlisted for the Shirley Jackson and British Fantasy Awards.

Angela Slatter is the author of the urban fantasy novels *Vigil, Corpselight*, and *Restoration* as well as eight short story collections, including *The Girl with No Hands and Other Tales, Sourdough and Other Stories, The Bitterwood Bible and Other Recountings*, and *A Feast of Sorrows: Stories.* She has won a World Fantasy Award, a British Fantasy Award, a Ditmar, an Australian Shadows Award, and six Aurealis Awards. She has an MA and a PhD in Creative Writing, is a graduate of Clarion South and the Tin House Summer Writers Workshop, and was awarded one of the inaugural Queensland Writers Fellowships. Slatter served as the Established Writer-in-Residence at the Katharine Susannah Prichard Writers Centre in Perth. She has been awarded career development funding by Arts Queensland, the Copyright Agency and, in 2017/18, an Australia Council for the Arts grant.

Bonnie Jo Stufflebeam's fiction and poetry has appeared in over forty magazines and anthologies such as *Black Static, The Toast, Clarkesworld, Lightspeed, Hobart, Interzone, Beneath Ceaseless Skies*, and *Fairy Tale Review.* She and her partner collaborated on the recently released audio fiction-jazz collaborative album *Strange Monsters.* She holds an MFA in Creative Writing from the University of Southern Maine's Stonecoast program and created and coordinates the annual Art & Words Collaborative Show in Fort Worth, Texas.

Steve Rasnic Tem's collaborative novella with his late wife Melanie Tem, *The Man On The Ceiling,* won the World Fantasy, Bram Stoker, and International Horror Guild Awards. He has also won the Bram Stoker, International Horror Guild, and British Fantasy Awards for his solo work. His recent novel *UBO* won the Bram Stoker Award. His previous novels are *Deadfall Hotel, The Man On The Ceiling* (written with Melanie Tem as an expansion of their novella), *The Book of Days, Daughters* (also written with Melanie Tem), and *Excavation.* Tem has published over four hundred short stories. His ten story collections include *City Fishing, Celestial Inventories, Twember, Here With The Shadows,* and the giant seventy-two-story treasury, *Out of the Dark: A Storybook of Horrors.* A transplanted Southerner Virginia, Steve is a long-time resident of Colorado. He has a BA in English Education from VPI and a MA in Creative Writing from Colorado State.

Katherine Vaz is the author of two novels, *Saudade* and *Mariana,* as well as two short story collections, *Fado & Other Stories* and *Our Lady of the Artichokes & Other Portuguese-American Stories.* Her work has appeared in six languages and has received numerous accolades, including the Library of Congress' Top Thirty International Books of 1998, the Drue Heinz Literature Prize, and the Prairie Schooner Book Award. The recipient of fellowships at Harvard University, the Radcliffe Institute for Advanced Study, and the National Endowment for the Arts, as well as the Harman Fellowship, Vaz has lectured internationally about Portuguese and Luso-American literature and is the first Portuguese-American to have her work recorded for the archives of the Library of Congress (Hispanic Division). A native Californian, she lives in New York City and East Hampton with her husband.

Kaaron Warren has published over seventy short stories, some of which are collected in *The Gate Theory, Through Splintered Walls, The Grinding House,* and *Dead Sea Fruit.* Her short fiction has won Australian Shadows, Ditmar, and Aurealis Awards. Her four novels are *Slights, Walking the Tree, Mistification,* and *The Grief Hole.* An Australian, she's lived in Melbourne, Sydney, and Canberra, with a three year stint in Fiji. She currently lives in Canberra with her family, two cats and, possibly, rats in the roof.

Conrad Williams is the author of nine novels (*Head Injuries, London Revenant, The Unblemished, One, Decay Inevitable, Loss of Separation, Dust and Desire, Sonata of the Dead,* and *Hell is Empty*), four novellas (*Nearly People, Game, The Scalding Rooms,* and *Rain*) and three collections of short stories (*Use Once Then Destroy, Born with Teeth,* and *I Will Surround You*). *One* was the winner of the August Derleth Award for Best Novel, while *The Unblemished* won the International Horror Guild Award for Best Novel. He also received a British Fantasy Award for his novella *The Scalding Rooms.* He is an associate lecturer at Manchester Metropolitan University and lives in Manchester, UK, with his wife and three sons.

Acknowledgements

"Sunflower Junction" © 2017 Simon Avery. First Publication: *Black Static #57*.

"Swift to Chase" © 2017 Laird Barron. First Publication: *Adam's Ladder*, eds. Michael Bailey & Darren Speegle.

"Fallow" © 2017 Ashley Blooms. First Publication: *Shimmer #37*.

"Children of Thorns, Children of Water" © 2017 Aliette de Bodard. Exclusive for *The House of Binding Thorns* preorders/*Uncanny #17*.

"On Highway 18" © 2017 Rebecca Campbell. First Publication: *The Magazine of Fantasy & Science Fiction*, September-October 2017.

"Witch Hazel" © 2017 Jeffrey Ford. First Publication: *Haunted Nights*, eds. Ellen Datlow & Lisa Morton.

"The Bride in Sea-Green Velvet" © 2017 Robin Furth. First Publication: *The Magazine of Fantasy & Science Fiction*, July/August 2017).

"Little Digs" © 2017 Lisa L. Hannett. First Publication: *The Dark #20*.

"The Thule Stowaway" © 2017 Maria Dahvana Headley. First Publication: *Uncanny #14*.

"The Eyes Are White and Quiet" © 2017 Carole Johnstone. First Publication: *New Fears*, ed. Mark Morris.

"Mapping the Interior" © 2017 Stephen Graham Jones. First Publication: *Mapping the Interior* (Tor.com Books/Tom Doherty Associates).

"Don't Turn on The Lights" © 2017 Cassandra Khaw. First Publication: *Nightmare #61*.

"The Dinosaur Tourist" © 2017 Caitlín R. Kiernan. First Publication: *Sirenia Digest #139*.

"Survival Strategies" © 2017 Helen Marshall. First Publication: *Black Static #60*.

"Red Bark and Ambergris" © 2017 Kate Marshalk. First Publication: *Beneath Ceaseless Skies #232*.

"Skins Smooth as Plantain, Hearts Soft as Mango" © Ian Muneshwar. First Publication: *The Dark #27*.

"Everything Beautiful is Terrifying" © 2017 M. Rickert. First Publication: *Shadows and Tall Trees 7*, ed. Michael Kelly.

"Welcome to Your Authentic Indian Experience™" © 2017 Rebecca Roanhorse. First Publication: *Apex #99*.

"Graverobbing Negress Seeks Employment" © Eden Royce. First Publication: The "Spilling Tea" issue (#2) of *Fiyah Magazine of Black Speculative Fiction.*

"Moon Blood-Red, Tide Turning" © 2017 Mark Samuels. First Publication: *Terror Tales of Cornwall*, ed. Paul Finch.

"The Crow Palace" © 2017 Priya Sharma. First Publication: *Black Feathers: Dark Avian Tales*, ed. Ellen Datlow.

"The Swimming Pool Party" © 2017 Robert Shearman. First Publication: *Shadows & Tall Trees 7*, ed. Michael Kelly.

"The Little Mermaid, in Passing" © 2017 Angela Slatter. First Publication: *Review of Australian Fiction*, Volume 22 Issue 1.

"Secret Keeper" © 2017 Bonnie Jo Stufflebeam. First Publication: *Nightmare #57.*

"The Long Fade into Evening" © 2017 Steve Rasnic Tem. First Publication: *Darker Companions*, eds. Scott David Aniolowski & Joseph S. Pulver, Sr.

"Moon, and Memory, and Muchness" © 2017 Katherine Vaz. First Publication: *Mad Hatters and March Hares: All-New Stories from the World of Lewis Carroll's Alice in Wonderland*, ed. Ellen Datlow.

"Exceeding Bitter" © 2017 Kaaron Warren. First Publication: *Evil Is a Matter of Perspective: An Anthology of Antagonists*, eds. Adrian Collins & Mike Myers.

"Succulents" © 2017 Conrad Williams. First Publication: *New Fears*, ed. Mark Morris.

"The Lamentation of Their Women" © 2017 Kai Ashante Wilson. First Publication: *Tor.com*, 24 August 2017.

About the Editor

Paula Guran is an editor, reviewer, and typesetter. In an earlier life she produced weekly email newsletter *DarkEcho* (winning two Stokers, an IHG award, and a World Fantasy Award nomination), edited magazine *Horror Garage* (earning another IHG and a second World Fantasy nomination), and has contributed reviews, interviews, and articles to numerous professional publications

This is, if she's counted correctly, the forty-fifth anthology Guran has edited. Instead of what had become the usual multiple titles per calendar year, it is the only anthology that will appear from her in 2018. That's probably a refreshing break for most people. She's got mixed feelings about it herself. After more than a decade of full-time editing, she's now freelancing. Guran enjoys the variety but regrets the lack of a monthly paycheck.

She has four fabulous grandchildren she would be happy to tell you about.

Guran still lives in Akron, Ohio, but has moved from the crumbling family manse into a condominium apartment. Even though she got rid of a great many books, she still has far too many.

⸻◆⸻